"*Gluais!*" Aranok threw a Thakhati back into the trees. God knew how he had any energy left. She certainly didn't. Nothing but terror keeping her going.

A thud behind them. One must have dropped from the trees. She heard Mynygogg cry out, more in anger than fear. The familiar sound of metal on stone.

"Is he all right?" she asked, not daring take her eyes off the path. Barely a path, really. Wide enough.

"Aye," Aranok answered breathlessly. "Keep going!"

The ground was uneven. Roots everywhere. She had to be careful. That was the only reason the Thakhati could keep up. She'd seen at least eight of them. But there must be more.

The light of Traverlyn beckoned ahead. It was safety and home. Salvation.

God, please let us reach it. Let us reach the light.

A scream from behind. Not human.

Fuck.

PRAISE FOR

JUSTIN LEE ANDERSON AND *THE LOST WAR*

"An eclectic cast of characters traverse a war-ravaged kingdom as Anderson's cleverly constructed plot winds its way toward a truly unexpected denouement. Rich in action and intrigue, this fantasy adventure with a Scottish flavor is sure to please fans of David Gemmell."

—Anthony Ryan, *New York Times* bestselling author

"Excellent—full of great characters, tense action scenes, and truly surprising twists. A highly recommended read."

—James Islington, author of *The Shadow of What Was Lost*

"Justin's book reads like you've been dropped in the middle of a classic fantasy adventure, full of familiar elements twisted to be terrifying again—and then ramps up the tension to distract you from the sucker punch he's been planning all along. Exquisite."

—Gareth Hanrahan, author of *The Sword Defiant*

"A fantastic read. A twist that is just magnificent. It's an exceptional book, and I can't recommend it enough."

—Steve McHugh, author of *The Last Raven*

"Strikingly intense.... Immersive and thoroughly compelling." —*SFX*

By Justin Lee Anderson

THE EIDYN SAGA

The Lost War
The Bitter Crown

THE BITTER CROWN

The Eidyn Saga: Book Two

JUSTIN LEE ANDERSON

orbitbooks.net

Cover design by Lauren Panepinto
Cover illustration by Jeremy Wilson

Map by Tim Paul
Author photograph by Melody Joy Co.

Orbit
Hachette Book Group
1290 Avenue of the Americas
New York, NY 10104
orbitbooks.net

First Edition: December 2023
Simultaneously published in Great Britain by Orbit.

Orbit is an imprint of Hachette Book Group.
The Orbit name and logo are trademarks of Little, Brown Book Group Limited.

Library of Congress Cataloging-in-Publication Data
Names: Anderson, Justin Lee, author.
Title: The bitter crown / Justin Lee Anderson.
Description: First edition. | New York, NY : Orbit, 2023. | Series: The Eidyn Saga ; book 2
Identifiers: LCCN 2023013527 | ISBN 9780316454308 (trade paperback) |
ISBN 9780316454414 (ebook)
Subjects: LCGFT: Fantasy fiction. | Epic fiction. | Novels.
Classification: LCC PR6101.A53 B58 2023 | DDC 823/.92—dc23/eng/20230324
LC record available at https://lccn.loc.gov/2023013527

ISBNs: 9780316454308 (trade paperback), 9780316454414 (ebook)

Printed in the United States of America

LSC-C

Printing 1, 2023

For truth, and everyone who fights for it.

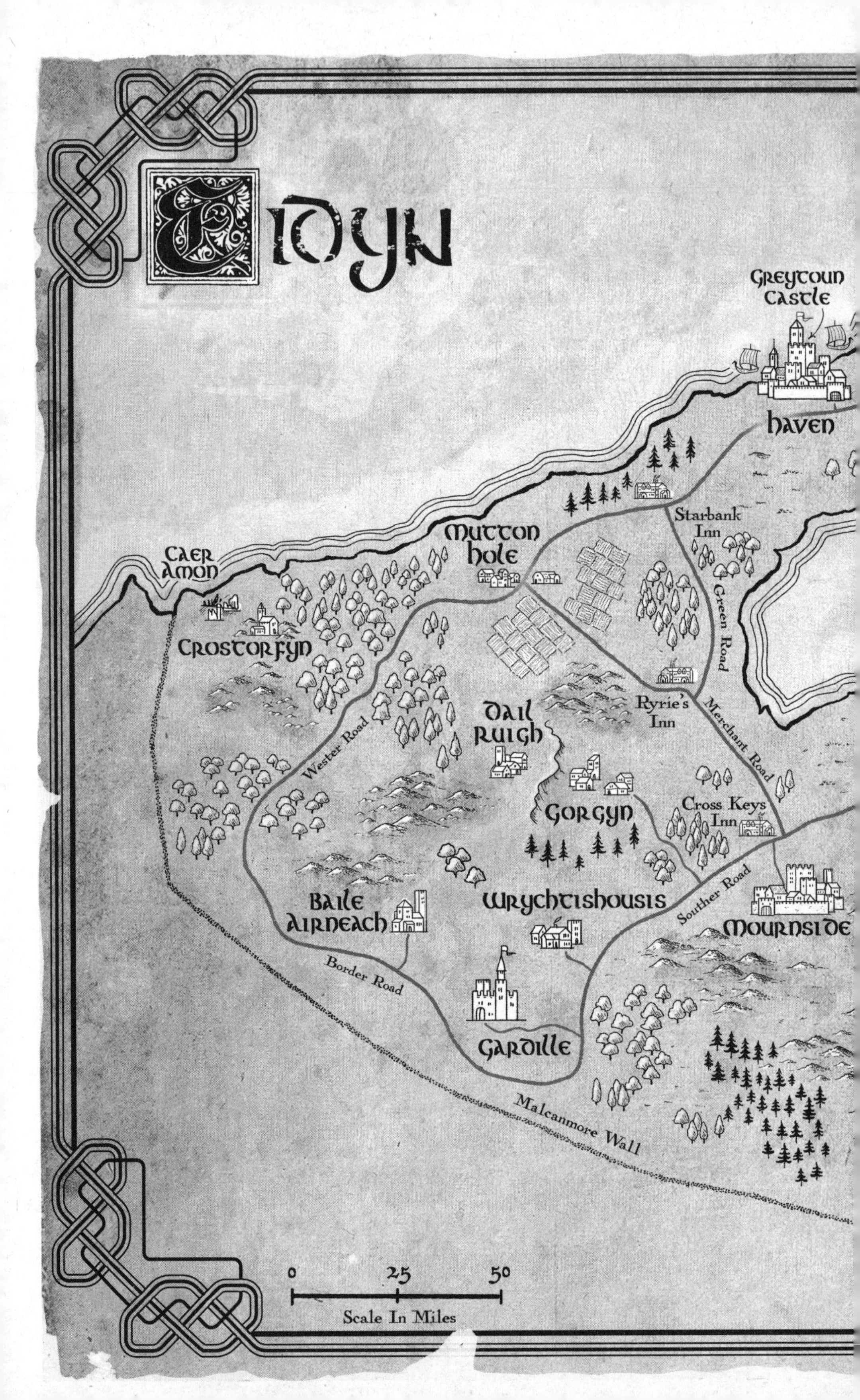
Tidyn
Greytoun Castle
Haven
Starbank Inn
Mutton Hole
Caer Amon
Crostorfyn
Green Road
Ryrie's Inn
Merchant Road
Dail Ruigh
Wester Road
Gorgyn
Cross Keys Inn
Baile Airneach
Wrychtishousis
Souther Road
Mournside
Border Road
Gardille
Malcanmore Wall
0
25
50
Scale In Miles

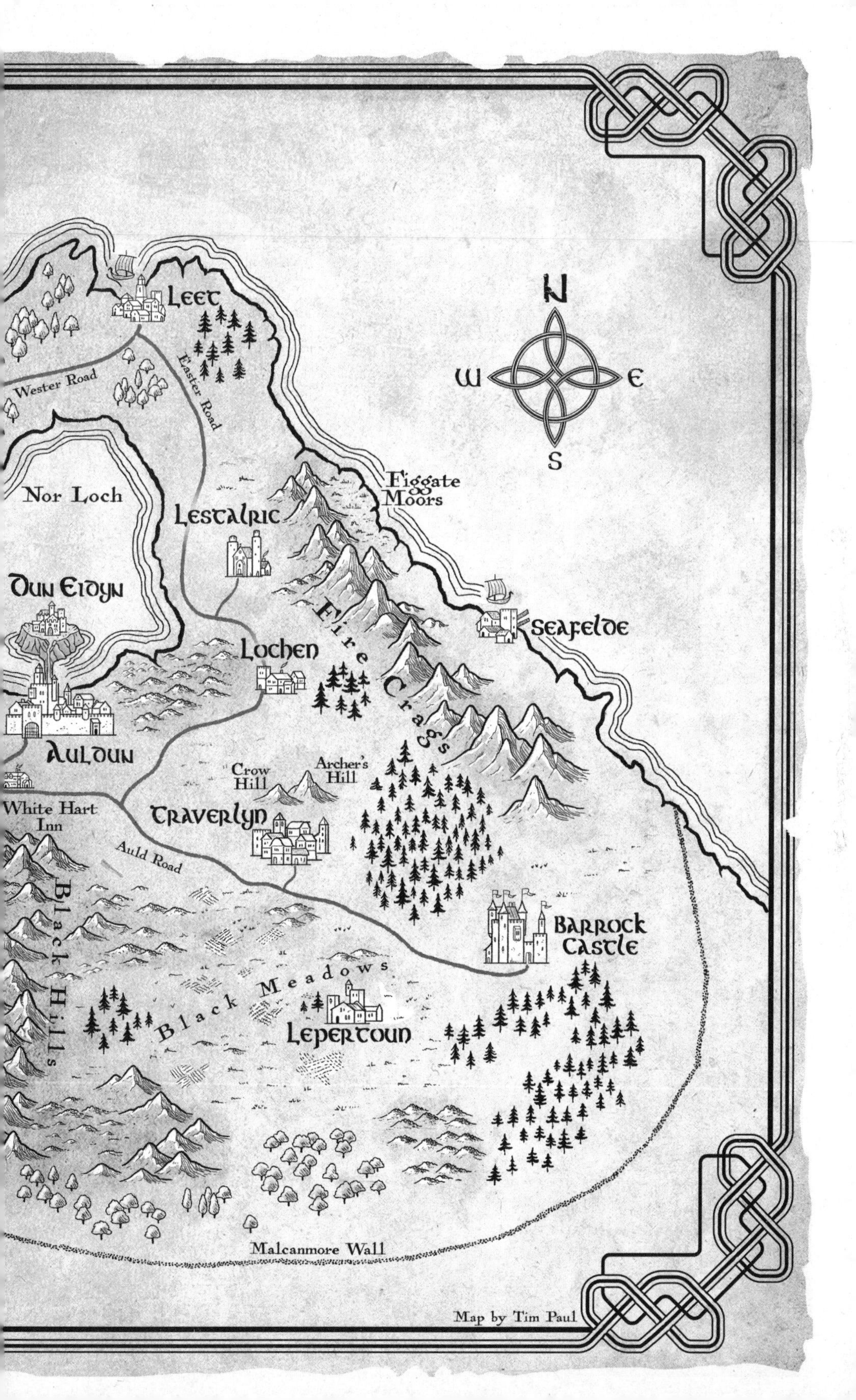

Leet
Wester Road
Easter Road
N
W
E
S
Nor Loch
Figgate Moors
Lestalric
Dun Eidyn
Fire Crags
Seafelde
Lochen
Auldun
Crow Hill
Archer's Hill
White Hart Inn
Traverlyn
Auld Road
Black Hills
Barrock Castle
Black Meadows
Lepertoun
Malcanmore Wall
Map by Tim Paul

A STORY OF A LOST WAR...

The old boy scans the busy bar with a mischievous grin and settles back on me with a sparkle in his eyes brighter than the meagre candle lighting our table. He ducks his head as if the dark, low-hanging beams might eavesdrop. A sup of his ale; a conspiratorial glance under bushy eyebrows. When he speaks, his deep voice hums with the excitement of a child bursting to tell a secret.

"Aye, you think you ken the story, don't ye? We all think we know what happened. But the truth of it? I've met people. Heard stories. See if they're true? Nothing we've been told is real. None of it."

He twitches with anticipation, running a hand over his head, searching the room again for eyes that linger too long, ears that hear too much, hands that reach for weapons, or irons. After a moment, he licks his teeth and, inevitably, the tale spills from him.

"So after a year of fighting off his demons and Dead, Mynygogg was trapped in Dun Eidyn, right? That's where we start. Aye. So after that's all done, King Janaeus puts together a new king's council: Laird Aranok; a soldier by the name of Glorbad; a sailor called Nirea; and Brother Meristan, the head of the White Thorns."

I nod. I know this. Everyone knows this.

"First thing he does is send them on a secret mission, though. See, apparently, auld Queen Taneitheia of Gaulle was secretly still biding in Barrock Castle and Janaeus reckoned they could help get her back on the throne, and make an ally of Gaulle. Except Meristan hadnae turned up. So it was just the three of them, plus Allandria, Aranok's bodyguard, and a wee blacksmith Aranok had sort of adopted. Boy called Vastin.

"Now, first they went to Mutton Farm. Killed a demon there. Well, *they* didn't. By mad coincidence, Meristan turns up *there* with a White Thorn—girl called Samily. They'd been on their way to Haven—to Greytoun—but heard about the demon and...anyway, they showed up; Samily killed the demon.

"And she turns out, because Glorbad was hurt in the fight, to be"—he leans forward and waves a performative finger at me—"a *healer*."

My mouth puckers involuntarily. There's no such thing as healers.

"Aye, aye, I ken," he says, waving away my scepticism. "Just wait.

"So they all head off for Barrock—except Aranok's got other plans. 'Cause y'see, back at Greytoun, Janaeus told him Mournside, where his family's from, had been breached wi' the Blackened. And Aranok wanted to go, but Janaeus said no. And Aranok's intent on going anyway. But Glorbad's no having it, so there's a massive argument and it ends up with Aranok and Allandria going off on their own to Mournside.

"Well, they get there and find out Mournside's fine, right? No Blackened, nothing. But while they're there, a king's messenger who's been reporting stuff that doesnae chime wi' what Janaeus knows is murdered in the same pub where they're meeting wi' Aranok's pa, just before Aranok can speak to her. Suspicious, right? But they've no got time to hang about, so Aranok leaves the town guard to look into it.

"Oh, also, while they're there, they find out Aranok's niece is *draoidh*. That's important later."

He pauses to take a long slug from his ale, then wipes the suds from his grey beard. "With me so far?"

I nod, smiling indulgently. He takes the pause to re-evaluate the room—lingers a while on a woman standing by the door, until she turns and stalks out into the dreich night. With a quiet "hmmph" he turns back to me.

"So, next morning, the other lot are heading along the Auld Road, and *they* run into the Blackened. And they are in deep, deep shite, until

Laird Aranok and Allandria show up and bail them out. They make it to an inn—d'you know the White Hart?"

I nod again.

"So with the Auld Road blocked, they reckon the Black Meadows must be clear, right? So they go over the Black Hills and end up at Lepertoun. The place is abandoned. Or so they think."

Again with the waving hand.

"Because what they miss is a Blackened baby at the river, and both Vastin and Meristan end up Blackened!"

He sits back, eyes wide, waiting for my reaction. I smile and try to give him the mix of surprise and wonder he craves. It seems to be enough.

"But then there's this woman, see, Morienne, and *she's* immune to the Blackening. And she's got this curse, going back through her family—and because of her, Laird Aranok works out that the Blackening isnae a plague at all... it's a curse!

"So this leads to another fight, 'cause now he wants to go to Traverlyn and work out how to lift the curse but Glorbad's still all, 'We've got orders fae the king.' Anyway, they end up going to Traverlyn.

"Oh, but on the way there—I forgot to say before, when they were going to Mutton Hole, they met these demon things that came out of cocoons, like people, but with four arms and stone skin, but sort of with slatted armour? Anyway, they died in sunlight. *Thakhati*. So they run into a bunch of these on the road into Traverlyn and damn near get killed, but Aranok's got this stone that's been storing sunlight and he blasts them with it, so they get away. But Vastin's hurt. *Bad*.

"When they get to Traverlyn, Aranok's old teachers, Conifax and Balaban, they find a spell to lift the curse. It works on Meristan and they've got a plan to do the same to Vastin and then have Samily use her healing powers on Vastin to save him, right? But it doesn't work out like they thought."

Again he leans in, and his voice falls to barely more than a whisper.

"Because it turns out, she's no a healer at all, but a *time draoidh*. And so both her and the boy end up Blackened! They sort her, but they can't lift the boy's curse without him dying from his wounds. So they have to leave him at the hospital.

"So they can cure the Blackening, right, but how do they cure everyone? Well, Conifax finds mention of a relic called the heart of devastation in Caer Amon which is supposed to massively boost a *draoidh*'s powers and they reckon that might be the very thing. But of course"—he spreads his hands wide—"massive argument. Aranok says they have to go to Caer Amon, Glorbad says they finally have to go to Barrock. In the end, they split up. Aranok, Allandria and Samily go to Caer Amon. Glorbad, Nirea and Meristan go to Barrock.

"Oh, another thing. While they're there, Aranok hires a tutor for his niece—a metamorph *draoidh* called Rasa. That's important later too.

"Right, so, they head off in opposite directions. Aranok's lot stop off at Mournside and find out they've caught a boy who says he's the dead messenger's husband and that he killed her. But his story doesnae add up, and he ends up cracking his own skull open, supposedly. All a bit off, ken?

"Then they stop off to stay with Anhel Weyr, at Wrychtishousis, right? And this is where it gets proper mad."

This time, he spends an age looking around the room, carefully examining every drinker, deciding that they're not a threat and moving on. There's some genuine fear in his eyes now. Maybe regret that he began this story. But he can't stop now that he's started.

"So they stop for dinner at Weyr's," he whispers, "and he tries to poison them. Because *he's* a demon summoner. And in fighting off him and his demons, it's them that burn down Wrychtishousis."

Silence and raised eyebrows. He leaves me to take that in. I give him a considered frown; take a drink of my own. When I say nothing, he continues.

"Meanwhile, the other lot make it to Barrock—except there's naebody there. It's empty. Has been for months. But what there is, is a demon, and it's waiting for them. Kills Glorbad. Nearly kills Nirea. Meristan and her barely make it out alive and run back to Traverlyn.

"Aranok and the others get to Crostorfyn kirk and from there down to Caer Amon to look for the relic. Some weird shite happens—time's sort of broken. But there's no relic. But then back at the kirk, the priest tells them that *he's* got the relic. Except when he goes to get it—it's no there! Been locked in a keepsafe in a crypt for years, and it's gone! Just like that."

A wave of the hand tells me more drama is coming.

"That's when Rasa arrives—the metamorph. And she tells them the news. Glorbad's dead. And so is Conifax." A raise of the eyebrows. "He's been murdered in the university library! So Aranok's now convinced Mynygogg must have the relic and he's behind everything, so he goes off on his own to face him in Dun Eidyn.

"And he gets a fair way through Auldun before the Dead are too many for him, and Rasa has to save him. Then Allandria and Samily catch him up and Allandria is proper pissed off at him for running off. Anyway, they send Rasa back to Traverlyn—because she can fly there, as a bird, aye? She goes off to Traverlyn to tell the others what they know, and the other three go on to Dun Eidyn.

"First they kill a massive lizard demon on the Crosscauseway and Samily has to use her time powers, so she ends up knackered, and then there's a weird magic barrier that prevents Allandria from getting through the gate, so Aranok ends up having to go in alone.

"Now..."

He sits back again. We're getting to the *interesting* bit. He rubs his hands in anticipation. Takes another long sup of ale. The mug is almost empty.

"Here's where it gets interesting. Because, see, Mynygogg's no interested in fighting Aranok. He just wants to talk. And the more they talk, the more Aranok starts to feel sick, right? Like his head's no right. Like something's really, properly wrong. And finally, eventually, Mynygogg gets him to hold this charm and say a spell and..."

He leans in, grabs my hands and pulls me toward him. I feel the heat of the candle sharp against my lips.

"...Aranok remembers.

"Ye see, the *truth* is that *Mynygogg* was the king. Janaeus was a memory *draoidh* who was in a group with Aranok when they were kids—the Hellfire Club—with Anhel Weyr, an illusionist called Korvin who was Aranok's best mate and his niece's real dad, and a necromancer called Shayella. The *real draoidh* war was against Anhel Weyr and Shayella, and Janaeus won it by using the heart of devastation to change the whole country's memories."

He empties the dregs of his ale, sits back triumphantly, crosses his arms like a laird and waits. Does he believe it? Or does he just want to believe it? It's a seductive conspiracy.

"All right," I say, smiling, "so then what?"

"Well, then they gathered Allandria and Samily, restored their memories too, and set out to take back the country. If you're interested to hear, there's plenty more..." He waggles the empty mug between us suggestively.

I laugh. "All right. Two more." As I go to stand, he grasps my arm.

"A wee teaser for ye. There was a messenger, back at the beginning, old boy called Darginn Argyll. Got sent to take an urgent message to Baroness de Lestalric. Thought he was lucky she'd offered him sanctuary for the night.

"Lucky, until he woke up strapped to a board wi' his legs missing..."

CHAPTER 1

Fetid air whipped across the chasm. Only yesterday, Aranok had torn fifteen feet of the majestic, white stone Crosscauseway from its place and remade it as a wall, protecting them from the Dead during their battle with Anhel's great lizard demon. Then it had been protection. Now it was a barrier.

Once they got to Auldun's roofs, getting out would be straightforward. But the path to the rooftops was now across a fatal drop to the Nor Loch and through an agitated horde of Dead.

So he was going to try something he'd never done: use his wall spell to make a second bridge, connecting them directly from the north Crosscauseway to the nearest buildings on land, bypassing the Dead completely.

With his mind clear, Aranok was remembering things lost. If he focused completely on the earth, pictured what he wanted, it should run the path they needed. But if he tore too much from the depths of the loch, he'd unsettle the foundations of the Crosscauseway and dump them all in the freezing water.

A hand on his shoulder.

"Aranok, I've seen you do a hundred miraculous things. This is just another one."

Mynygogg was almost unrecognisable. The king had shaved his striking black hair and beard and wore a simple set of black leathers.

In contrast, Samily appeared hewn from marble—the rock upon

which Eidyn could rely. Maybe the greatest warrior he'd ever seen, but for the man who'd raised her or the woman beside her.

Allandria. His own rock. It had been awkward since they discovered Janaeus's trick—convincing them they were lovers. Instinct said she was angry with him. But they had no time for the kind of discussion she might want—might need. Hopefully that storm would blow itself out, given time.

This was their army. The four of them carried the truth that would restore Eidyn.

Having Mynygogg with him again was comforting. He felt his friend's confidence in him like air, buttressing his belief. Aranok looked down at the water, up to the rooftops, breathed deep and closed his eyes.

"Balla na talamh."

Focus.

The loch roiled as sodden earth broke the surface. It rose like a beast from the deep, and Aranok was reminded they'd left a demon's carcass down there just the night before. In moments, the mound reached the edge of the causeway. Now it had to stop going *up*, and go *out*.

Another deep breath and he watched as it extended, mud and rock surfacing in a rough line toward the shore. His mind was barely clinging to the magic. At any moment, it felt as though he'd lose his fragile focus and the bridge would collapse back into the water.

The ground shifted beneath Aranok and a shock of pain stabbed as he dropped to a knee. Someone caught his arm. He couldn't look up, couldn't look away. The bridge crashed through the sea wall and he was no longer pulling up loch bed, but stone and cobbles of Auldun street. Almost there.

"Aranok!"

He was yanked back as his makeshift barrier against the Dead came crashing back through its old position, taking several feet of the causeway's edge with it.

He landed against someone, confused.

Unfocused.

Out of control.

Another rumble.

A festering avalanche of Dead poured into the loch as the other side of the Crosscauseway crumbled.

"Fuck! Move!" Allandria pulled Aranok to his feet as their side of the causeway shifted and lurched to the east, away from the new bridge.

"Go! Go!" Aranok gestured urgently to the others. The new bridge was only about eight feet wide, and they slowed as they reached it. The earth was slick with seaweed—move too quickly and they could fall, too slow and the bridge might collapse before they reached safety.

Allandria reached the edge just before him. She slipped, recognising what he already knew, but her balance was sound. Aranok followed, stepping off the Crosscauseway as it finally lurched away.

He was on. With a sigh of relief he turned to see the north half of the Crosscauseway groan and stretch away.

Then, horrifyingly, it slowed, stopped and swung back.

"Run!" Aranok scrambled to keep his feet. What was left of the northern Crosscauseway battered through the earth bridge, sending debris plummeting back to the depths.

Twenty feet ahead Allandria danced along the ridge, each step finding solid ground. Aranok forced himself only to look forward. If he looked back... He had to keep running, keep moving, keep—

A sickening lurch as the dirt sank beneath his foot.

Aranok fell.

A second of panic, of terror, was all he had. In moments he would hit the freezing water and, if he survived that, be crushed by falling debris. Instinctively he pulled his hands tight into his sides and tensed his arms.

"Gaoth."

The burst of air threw him upwards, back toward the makeshift bridge. He could see the others, looking down at him hurtling toward them. It just had to be enough to reach them. He stretched out as their faces came closer and... went rushing past.

He'd overshot.

Aranok reached the zenith of his rise, slowed and fell again. They were maybe ten feet below him. But he was going to miss the bridge. *Gaoth* was a blunt instrument. Another uncontrolled burst could overshoot him so far he'd never make it back. Using it to cushion his landing would blow the others off.

Aranok stretched again, willing his arms to reach the edge, hoping he might catch just enough purchase to...

He screamed as his shoulder wrenched out of its socket. Ribs crunched, battering air from his chest, and something in his back popped as he slammed against wet stone.

It took him a moment to realise he was half on the bridge, his legs dangling useless over the edge.

A second pair of hands grasped his free arm and yanked him, agonisingly, the rest of the way on.

"Are you all right?" Allandria asked.

Was he? Half of him screamed in pain, the other was numb. He coughed up a glob of bloody phlegm.

Aranok tried to move, but his back seized, forcing him still.

"No," he wheezed.

"Where?" Samily's voice was urgent.

Aranok tried to point with his good arm. An awful, rasping sound and a nauseating sensation in his chest suggested his lung was torn.

"Never mind." He felt hands on him. *"Air ais."* The shoulder clicked back into place, ribs snapped into shape and his back popped in a way that was somehow more painful than the injury. Aranok sucked in a deep breath of damp air.

"Can you move?" the knight asked.

He could. He had to. With a grunt and support from Allandria, Aranok forced himself to his feet. It was another five hundred yards to the edge of the water. The bridge wasn't perfect. The lurch at the end had cost him, and the wall of earth had carried on too far, carving a great gash into the stone tenements.

"Who caught me?" Aranok moved carefully along the slick surface now that it wasn't actively collapsing.

"Samily," Mynygogg shouted. "She's everything you said."

"Thank you!" Aranok called to the knight.

Samily did not turn to shout her answer.

"I am sorry I missed you the first time."

"Bloody Hell." Aranok stifled a gag as a dank fug of horse effluent seeped from the White Hart's doorway.

"Good country air." Mynygogg grinned. He thought he was funny. He wasn't funny.

Aranok pushed a small *solas* ball into the dark. Whinnies told him the horses were alive.

"Hey!" Mynygogg slapped his shoulder. He was being bloody annoying about Aranok using magic "unnecessarily."

"What? It's a tiny spell—hardly any energy. We need to see."

"People always need to see." The king strode into the tavern. "They invented candles. Stop wasting energy."

"I already have a mother." Aranok followed him in.

"She'd be on my side," he answered without turning.

"He's right. She would," Allandria agreed. "You need to stop relying on it for everything."

Now there were two of them. Though it felt as if there was more in her words than the face of them.

After a short search, Samily sparked life into a candle behind the bar. Another few were enough to give them a view of the whole room, and Aranok dropped the *solas* spell. All three horses were there, disgruntled, but alive.

The hay Aranok had brought in for Bear had been sorely depleted, but not exhausted. Several large empty bowls told him the women had left more water out.

So despite their own fatigue after travelling across Auldun's rooftops, and the five miles to the inn, they had three well-rested horses. Good. They needed to keep going.

Mynygogg took a seat, pulled out rations and gestured for the rest to join him. Aranok itched to keep moving, but he was not in charge—not in the way he was used to. Nobody there would take his word as an order if it contradicted the king. Hell, nobody there would take his word as an order if they disagreed with him.

Maybe a quick rest and some food was wise. They had a long way to go.

Allandria took a share of the bread and cheese, and leaned on the bar, just across from Mynygogg's table. She was being evasive, and he could do without it. It was well into the night and for all Mynygogg's coddling was annoying, he wasn't entirely wrong. Aranok had used a lot of energy creating that bridge, and worse, Samily had used her time skill twice—once to catch him and once to heal him. Add fighting their way through the Dead at Auldun's gates and they'd already burned too much.

But nothing was ever ideal. If they didn't stop Rasa from going to Janaeus, they'd lose before they began. Besides which, she'd saved his life just, what, yesterday? A great bear dropping from the sky. How could he do less than anything to save her?

"Three horses, four riders," said Allandria. "Bear will take two."

"Bear's the big one?" Mynygogg spoke through a mouthful of cheese.

"Aye." She pointed to the others. "That's Dancer and Midnight."

Samily walked to the big horse and stroked his huge face. Bear snuffled amiably and nudged her hand. Aranok doubted he'd get the same reaction, considering how hard he'd ridden the great beast. It was good Bear had had the chance to recover. He was going to work hard again tonight.

Seventy miles, minimal sleep. They could arrive late tomorrow night, at a push. Hopefully.

"Huh," said Samily. "Bear. I have just realised. That is why it felt familiar."

Of course. One of Meristan's nicknames was "the Great Bear." While she didn't remember that, the name Bear must have sparked a reaction. Fascinating how memory was entangled with emotion.

"Right." Mynygogg stood, packing away the remaining rations. "Let's get moving, then. Samily and I will take the smaller two. Aranok, you ride with Allandria. We could do with your hands free without us having to slow down."

Allandria's eyes flickered. She didn't like it. But she wasn't going to argue with the king.

"Of course, sire. Makes sense." She didn't even look at him as she brushed past to the horses.

Oh good. This won't be awkward at all.

It was painfully awkward.

Allandria tried to focus on the horse. The ride. The rhythm of the hoofbeats.

But what she felt were Aranok's hands on her waist and his chest against her back. It was familiar and nice and awful and wrong.

There was no conversation. No banter. No playful nudges. Just nothing. A door had closed that neither of them knew how to open. The awful truth was she'd been happy. It had been good. Right. All of it. Despite hating that little prick Janaeus for lying to them, she missed it.

But was it real? Did she like it because she remembered liking it, or because she actually did? She couldn't trust her own mind.

Had she had feelings for Aranok before? It was all a muddle. Maybe? Maybe she'd been attracted to him. Maybe she just remembered being attracted to him.

There had been moments, she thought, where it seemed like something might happen. Like there was a spark between them that was... more.

Her memories of the war—the real war—were returned. Instead of fighting Reivers, she remembered the waves of Dead. Running from the Blackened. The Thakhati—the bastard Thakhati and that cocoon. And the demons. Mostly smaller ones. The big ones were usually taken by the Thorns, with help from what *draoidhs* they could muster. So many chose to stay neutral, stay out of the fight. And who could really blame them in a country where they were despised?

The skilled masters had stayed at the university to protect their students—and the skilled students were children. Allandria had come across three *draoidhs* other than Aranok that she remembered. What was the physic's name? Gast? Gost? Gart? Poor bastard had been torn in half by a demon north of Gardille. Held it for a long time, protecting a farm. Allandria and Aranok had arrived with a battalion of soldiers too late to save him. Just in time to hear his spine crack and rip as his strength finally gave out against that huge, red, four-armed thing. They'd forced it back. Aranok threw everything he had at it. He'd seemed to find energy from nowhere. From rage. The soldiers too—flaming arrows had stuck like pins from the thing's hide, and they'd done their best to hurt it up close, but reaching it was challenging, past all those damned arms. There had been Reivers too. Men and women she'd thought her enemies until yesterday. Hells, she'd hated them; thought them the worst traitors imaginable. But they'd died just like Eidyn's soldiers, protecting strangers from nightmares.

It was Thorns who saved them. A pair of them. To this day she didn't know their names. They were gone almost as quickly as they arrived. Green blades cut through the demon's skin in a way no other weapon did. They worked together so perfectly, their movements coordinated, fluid, like water—two bodies acting with one mind.

They took the backs of its knees, bringing it down. One attacked head-on, taking the demon's attention, while the other came around behind and, somehow, leapt high enough to reach the base of its skull, where they buried the blade that ended the fight.

When it was over, the knights didn't even remove their helms. Allandria couldn't have told if they were men or women, never mind what they looked like. They slit the thing open, reminded them to burn it, and were mounted and gone again, as if they'd just returned a lost sheep.

They lit the remains next to a pyre for the *draoidh* (Gort?) and the four soldiers they'd lost. Burning was the best they could do for their fallen. So many were left to carrion and rot—no chance to return and offer them dignity. Precious little dignity in war.

They'd limped back to Gardille to recover, and Allandria remembered that night, lying on a bedroll beside his, looking into his sad, exhausted eyes, she'd felt something. Something *more.* It had come and gone, but it was there, and it had shifted the world beneath her. In the middle of all the slaughter and death and exhaustion, she'd felt something real. But was it? Was it just a moment of shared emotional extremes between two souls who'd been through a new Hell together every day for months? Of hope for an end? For tomorrow? Was any of it real?

God damn it!

Whatever the truth of it, they'd spent weeks as lovers. They couldn't put that arrow back in the quiver.

They were going to have to talk about it. Eventually. Not yet. Not until she figured out what was real and what that fucker had put in her head. Not until she could work out what she actually wanted from the conversation. From him.

Aranok's hands lifted off her waist and she sat upright.

"Gluais." To her right, a Blackened boy, no more than eight, disappeared back into the darkness. He was the third they'd seen.

Aranok sighed heavily as he replaced his hands. Gooseflesh raised on her neck, the tingle running down her spine. He'd be thinking about how he could have saved the boy, and whether he should have. And then how the time they spent doing that might make them miss Rasa and cost them everything. And how the boy might not survive without a medic anyway. And how he should have found a way to do both.

He was a good man. And an idiot.

Mynygogg slowed ahead and raised an arm. Samily slowed Dancer to match Midnight's pace, allowing them to ride alongside.

"What?" Aranok asked sharply.

Mynygogg pointed ahead. Just visible from the *solas* orb was the edge of what looked like a clearing.

"We should stop here. Camp for a few hours and the sun'll be up. Then we have less to worry about in daylight, right?"

"All right." Aranok didn't argue. He must have been exhausted.

A few hours' rest here would be good for everyone, including the horses. They'd made good ground, but they weren't even halfway, and it had been a long night. Thank God they'd had no sign of Thakhati. The monsters had probably been on the road into Traverlyn to keep them away from the university. So it was more likely they'd come across them when they got closer. Sometime tomorrow night—or tonight, as it would be. Or tomorrow morning? God, she'd lost all notion of time.

Sleep now.

CHAPTER 2

"Just show us the evidence."

Nirea winced, not so much at Master Opiassa's booming exhortation as the fact that there was no particularly good response.

It had seemed like such a simple idea.

Tell the masters they had evidence that implicated Conifax's murderer and would make an arrest once the envoy returned. Then wait and see who came looking for the evidence. But sitting there in her wheeled chair watching Meristan explain to the hastily convened masters' council why he didn't just present the evidence was almost as painful as her aching wounds.

The high-roofed chamber was square on three sides and semicircular on the fourth. A stage rose at the square end, where speakers presented themselves in front of the raked rows of seats opposite. Each row held thirteen places, with the senior masters at the front and two rows of junior masters behind. The senior masters' chairs were high-backed, intricately carved wooden affairs, the juniors' plain and functional. Up the side walls, previous masters' names were chiselled into stone.

The thing Nirea could barely look away from, though, was the black velvet sheet draped ceremoniously over a front-row chair. A soft, empty shroud begging justice for its absent master.

Conifax would be sitting there now had he not gone looking in the *caibineat puinnsean*.

There was a second vacant chair in the back row. Calavas's, she assumed. If there was a splinter of guilt over Conifax's death, Calavas's was an open wound. Nirea approaching the record keeper, accusing him, likely instigated his death. He might yet prove to have been involved in Conifax's murder, though. She hoped he was. It would be better if he was.

"I am the university's head of security. I have jurisdiction here. I do not require the presence of the envoy." Opiassa stood, jabbing an indignant finger. Only distance prevented her from looming over Meristan, a fair beast himself. The master had used her physic ability to enhance her size. Nirea wondered whether it was deliberate, or if, perhaps, it had happened unconsciously as the *draoidh* grew into her anger.

"I understand, Master Opiassa, of course. And nobody is questioning your authority. Far from it." Meristan's voice was even, but she could hear uncertainty beneath it. "I am sorry to have to ask you to trust me—and Lady Nirea." The monk swept an arm toward her. They reckoned it would be hard for the council to refuse the head of the Order of the White Thorns, but with the addition of the wounded king's councillor in a wheeled chair, flanked by her personal "medic," Morienne...

Nirea tried to look pathetic. It was not a role to which she was suited, and she did not enjoy it.

Opiassa raised an eyebrow, sighed expressively toward Principal Keft and threw herself back into her seat.

Keft had a shock of pure white hair countered by a full red beard, which made him very difficult to age. He could have been anywhere between forty and sixty, to Nirea's mind. His energy *draoidh* skill was apparently one of the most powerful. Nirea wondered what had kept him from the war, if that was the case.

The principal shifted in his seat as if Opiassa's disquiet were a thorn in his rear. "Brother Meristan, you must understand our reticence. If there is a reason for withholding the evidence from us and, further, allowing a suspected murderer of two masters to remain amongst us, it is both reasonable and imperative that we should understand what it is."

"Of course, Principal, I understand your position." Meristan remained smooth but strained. "I would have similar questions in your place. However, the very act of giving reason for the delay would reveal more than is prudent, and thus, I regret we must insist on awaiting the return of the envoy. In the absence of the king, only Laird Aranok is in a position to deal with the... complications which arise."

The monk was blundering in the dark, spewing words without saying anything. They needed the killer to believe they knew something. They had to tease everything and reveal nothing. The murderer might know they had the book. That was the real bait. This was theatre.

She scanned the row of senior masters. One of them could be the killer. One probably was. They had access to the *caibineat puinnsean*, and some of them had the skills to take Conifax—particularly if he didn't see them coming. And trusted them.

Master Opiassa seemed keen to find the murderer, but wouldn't investigating the crime be an excellent way to avoid being caught?

Their other early suspect, Master Macwin, gave very little away. He was a round, pleasant-looking man. She didn't recall him speaking at all. But their reasons for suspecting him and Opiassa were moot. The murder wasn't personal. Conifax did not die for a vendetta—he'd died to keep him away from the book.

They still hadn't fathomed its purpose. Why rewrite history with Mynygogg in Janaeus's place? Whatever the *draoidh*'s allies had planned, it was worth killing for. And maybe that was good. Maybe it was fragile and could be shattered in the light of truth.

Only the senior masters were permitted to speak unbidden, so when none of them did, there was a long, oppressive silence. A few juniors had raised hands and been recognised by the principal. This seemed to be the purpose of the huge decorative mirror on the wall behind them—allowing Keft to see without turning in his seat.

Master Balaban sat to the right of the principal. The owlish man had also been quiet, but he flashed Nirea a tired, sympathetic smile in the awkward quiet.

A hand raised in the second row.

"Master Rotan." Keft waved a permissive hand.

A familiar young red-haired man stood. Nirea couldn't place him.

"Brother Meristan, Lady Nirea." He made the barest of bows to each as he spoke their names. "While of course we recognise and accept your authority, you must also see the position in which you place us. Two of our colleagues have been murdered." He gestured to the empty seat behind him, and Nirea suddenly recognised him. The young master who'd come looking for Calavas. For tea? A friend, anyway. The sting of guilt bit again. "You are asking us not only to accept that you know who the murderer is, but also to accept that we are unable to arrest them immediately. How are we to know they will not kill again? Or that they will not escape while we delay? Indeed, with this very announcement, you are surely giving them every motivation to do so, are you not? Would it not be more prudent to at least give Master Opiassa the name of the suspect so that they can be detained until Laird Aranok's return?"

Damn.

Those were all good points. Rotan sat with a final, more respectful bow to the principal.

"These are valid questions, Brother Meristan," said Keft. "Are we not in danger, even now, of losing the killer, or worse, another colleague?"

Nirea hoped the monk had a good answer. Her dulled brain had nothing.

"Thank you for your question, Master Rotan. Indeed, it is valid and I understand your concern. The answer is this: We are confident the suspect has accomplished their aim. We believe they have motive to remain in the university and that they have no reason to suspect they are discovered. They have neither reason to kill nor flee unless word of our discovery leaves this chamber. This is why, Principal, we must ask that you make an order of silence upon the masters. Only those within this room can be trusted with this information. I can, if I must, tell you that it is a matter of import to the entire country."

Oh, very good.

Should a monk be such a good liar?

Not only had Meristan shut down the questions, he'd led the killer to believe they did not suspect a master, while also suggesting again that they knew more than they did. If anything, now the killer was going to want to find out what they did know, safe in the knowledge they were not suspect. It was a deft playing of a poor hand.

Keft raised an eyebrow, captain of the unquiet sea at his back. It occurred to Nirea this must be a crippling experience for students. Mostly she found herself irritated. She did not enjoy being questioned to this extent. The pirate in her burned to tell them all to fuck themselves and do as they were told.

Best Meristan was handling it.

"Fine." Keft sighed. "If this is how it must be, it must be. But I remind you, Brother, that the university holds independent status. When this is resolved—sooner rather than later—I trust the explanation will be satisfactory to justify your actions."

There was a clear threat implied in the principal's tone. Nirea wondered what power he perceived he had over the head of the Order or the king's council. Perhaps he was asserting his authority for the benefit of his staff. It was an empty threat, but she had never been one to be concerned by words. Nirea acted when a sword was drawn against her, not when it rattled in its sheath.

Keft stood, stepped toward them and turned to face the masters.

"I instruct you all to remain silent on this matter. It is not to be discussed outwith this room. Anyone breaking this silence will have their tenure revoked and will be ejected from the university without trial or appeal. Is that understood?"

There was a general nodding of heads and a few surly faces. A woman with short dark hair in the back row seemed to scowl at Nirea as if it was her fault. Another friend of Calavas's, perhaps?

Fine. She'd lived with plenty of animosity. This was small coin.

"In that case, thank you all for coming together so late in the evening. This extraordinary meeting is adjourned," said Keft.

The silence erupted into chatter as every person in the room turned to their neighbour. Keft approached them, his face stern. "Brother. Lady." He gave the same curt bows Rotan had performed, turned and left.

"That could have gone worse," Morienne said quietly.

"It could have gone better." Meristan rubbed his hands absentmindedly.

"Fine." Nirea winced as the pain pierced her opium cloud when she spoke. "Done wha' nee'ed."

"Well, that was interesting." Balaban had quietly sidled up beside them. Nirea smiled, such as she could.

"Master." Morienne smiled warmly. Balaban had provided her with the totem that kept her curse in check—allowing her to be in close human contact for the first time in her life. Of course she viewed him fondly.

Actually, this was opportune.

"Bahbah," Nirea said slowly, "who 'at?" She pointed as subtly as she could.

He looked up and leaned in conspiratorially. "Master Rotan, you mean? Who spoke earlier?"

"No. Ness. Womah."

"Ah, that is Master Dialla. Why do you ask?"

"Sees annoy." Nirea frowned, and winced again. *Damn it.*

"Ah, no, you see, Masters Dialla and Rotan were close to Conifax. He was a mentor to them. She will feel his loss greatly."

"Hmph," Nirea grunted. That only made her more suspicious.

"I wanted to ask, may I see you back to your accommodation?" Balaban sounded as if he were proposing a pleasant evening stroll.

"That won't be necessary, Master," Meristan interjected. "Morienne and I will see Nirea safely back to the hospital."

Balaban gave an enigmatic smile. "Oh, I have no doubt," he said, and lowered his voice, "but I'd welcome an opportunity to discuss your trap."

Fuck.

The wheels of Nirea's chair rattled over the Traverlyn cobblestones. It would have been less jarring to walk, but after her farrago with Calavas, Egretta had insisted she was only to leave the building if she remained seated. Morienne was under orders to keep her there by force if necessary.

Despite the hour, the light was as good as late afternoon. The glow from the bulbous onion dome atop Traverlyn's kirk illuminated the path, making the torches that would normally have lit it redundant. Conifax had arranged the "sunspire" after Aranok had used the same magic to kill the Thakhati on the road. The plan was to keep Traverlyn safe by having the highest point in town absorb sun all day and slowly release it through the night. Of course, there were streets lost to the shadows, but enough were lit to make the town as safe as it could be under the circumstances. Creatures averse to light would not be attracted here.

Conifax had only survived to work the spell himself for a few days.

Nirea pointed toward the spire and looked up at Balaban. "Who now?"

"Ah," he said, somewhat mournfully. "We have had to recruit one of our students. A fine young lady named Girette."

"A student?" Meristan asked. "How old?"

"Fourteen," Balaban answered. "She is being supported by staff. Principal Keft visits her regularly."

The energy *draoidh*. That made sense. Aranok had said the spell drained him while it charged. Hell, a child, younger even than Vastin, responsible for protecting the town from the Thakhati. And they could only hope the Blackened didn't wander up this way. One or two they could handle, but if a horde came, they'd have to make some difficult choices.

She wondered whether the town elders now regretted the historic decision against walling Traverlyn in. As a place of learning, art and culture, it was traditionally open to all and generally respected for that. Even Reivers tended to leave it alone. But there were buildings around the edges under repair. The war had not spared them completely.

Nirea thought she felt a tiny splash on her cheek, held out her hand and confirmed it was beginning to spit with rain. They hastened their walk back to the hospital, but the heavens fully opened just as they turned the final corner off Kirk Wynd. By the time they got inside they were soaked.

Nirea left the chair and walked back to her room with Morienne's assistance. A medical student they passed in the hall was sent scurrying for towels. As soon as they reached their room and the door was closed, Nirea turned to Balaban.

"How you know?"

Balaban smiled benevolently. "There is nothing sinister to reveal. It was simply…obvious."

"Ohvus?" Nirea was appalled. She'd thought it at least a competent plan.

"My dear, you have just addressed the sharpest minds in Eidyn. For all Brother Meristan's fine words—and they were fine—the only logical explanation for your actions is that you intend to flush out the murderer."

Damn it.

She thought she'd been clever, but her great secret plan was as transparent as water.

"Well, I..." Meristan started, but Nirea put up a hand to stop him. Morienne burst into laughter. What the fuck was *funny*?

"I'm sorry, it's just...we were so worried about anyone finding out what we were really doing and...Well, it's funny, isn't it?" Morienne's open hands asked for Balaban's agreement.

"That is not to say everyone will have worked out your plan," said the master, in a tone Nirea found uncomfortably patronising. "I certainly have not said anything to anyone, and nor did anyone else say such to me. Perhaps I simply have a suspicious mind."

Meristan sighed deeply and sat on his own bed. "No. If you worked it out, we have to assume others did."

He was right. They hadn't thought it through enough. They should have had a more plausible reason for waiting—for not arresting the suspect. Damn her for being in such a rush. Her shoulder stabbed with pain as she realised her taut knuckles were white.

She must have winced, because Meristan stood abruptly. "Are you all right?"

She waved him off with her good hand.

"Does it matter, though? I mean, in the end—does it matter?" Morienne asked.

"Wha?" What the Hell was she talking about? Of course it mattered.

"Well, I mean, either the killer knows it's a trap, and they stay away, so we're no worse off, or they don't know and come looking for it—which we want. Right? And we still have the book, which they didn't want Conifax to have, so we must be onto something..."

"Book?" Balaban perked up. "The evidence is a book?"

Nirea's mouth was open before her brain stopped her voice. She glanced to Meristan, whose raised eyebrows reflected her question back at her.

Could they absolutely trust Balaban?

The master cocked his head and made the decision for her. "Ah, of course. If you suspect the killer is a master, which makes sense, you must also suspect me."

"Uh, well..." Meristan fumbled.

"No, no, I understand." Balaban raised a hand. "You need not tell me anything. In fact, perhaps the less I know, the better, on reflection. My intent was merely to let you know that I suspected your real plan, and I have served that purpose. Proceed with caution, my friends. And good luck."

Nirea felt even worse. The man was handling being suspected of murder, without any grounds, with utter class.

Wait.

If the killer was in the meeting, and saw them all leave together...

"Bahbah. Noh safe."

"Pardon?" the master asked.

"You. Noh safe." She turned to Meristan and stabbed a finger at the old man. "Noh. Safe."

She watched her meaning dawn on the monk.

"Ah, Master Balaban, you were seen leaving with us—perhaps even watched escorting us back here. If the killer suspects we have laid them a trap, instead of coming for us, they may think it prudent to come for you. Two masters are already dead—I fear they would have no hesitation in making it three."

Colour drained from Morienne's face. "I'll escort you home, Master."

"No." Nirea shook her head. They needed her here. She was their element of surprise. She was the reason the trap could work.

Damn it all!

Nirea pulled the book out from under her mattress and slapped it on the bed. Balaban touched the cover lightly, as if it may burn.

"This is the book?"

Nirea nodded. If her judgement was wrong, she might be about to get them all killed. But if not—and hellfire, she hoped not—she might be preventing another murder.

"A history book? I don't understand."

Meristan explained what Conifax had told Egretta, how they'd come to suspect a master, and all of the odd fiction of the book itself, including its missing counterpart. The master stood quietly throughout the story, arms crossed with one hand over his mouth.

When it ended, Balaban sat on the end of the bed and lifted the book. "No. It doesn't make sense."

"We know," Meristan answered. "It's confusing."

"Oh, I'm sorry, I mean the book. Specifically, the book doesn't make sense."

"In what way?" the monk asked.

"What possible reason is there for writing it now? If there is some plan to have a time *draoidh* go back and change history—and I have no idea if that is possible—then this book will be written when that happens in a—what would we call it—an alternate time? Thus, writing this book now serves no purpose.

"If this book represents an original time which has already been changed, again, why would this book exist?"

Balaban looked around the room. None of them had answers, and their blank expressions made that clear. He closed the book and placed it on his lap.

"Let us say that someone wished to change history, but was unable to do so. How else could one effectively do such a thing?"

"By making everyone *believe* a different history," said Meristan.

"Exactly," said Balaban. "Now, how would one do that? The propagation of such a lie would require a huge amount of power and influence. To simply decree it to be true and rewrite history books would take generations for the people who remember the truth to die out. Of course, dictators have achieved this through brutality, but there are always those who keep the truth alive. However, with the right kind of magic, and a way to amplify that power..."

"Master, are you saying Mynygogg has the ability to control people's minds? That he may use that ability to make us all believe this fiction to be true?" Meristan gestured dismissively at the book.

"Wha?" Nirea's head swam with a familiar dizziness.

Damn it! Not now!

"What I am suggesting is this—Mynygogg is the first *draoidh* we have ever known to have more than one skill. If he has two, it is not beyond imagining he may have more. There are many theorised *draoidh* skills that we have only heard about in oral tradition. If mind control were one of them, and if Mynygogg were in a position to exercise that power over the entire country—say, using the relic that the envoy has gone in search of—it would then make sense for this book to be written in preparation for that spell being cast.

"When it is, this book is placed on the library shelf, taking the place of the original book, which, I would guess, has already been destroyed, if Mynygogg's agent has any sense."

Nirea gently pressed her hands to her temples.

"Dear lord," said Meristan, "that's... that's inhuman. It's incredible!"

"Incredible as it may seem, it fits the facts as we have them, does it not?" Balaban asked.

There was a long silence. Nirea's head was reeling—her eyes refusing to focus. The wall opposite danced to and fro.

"Nirea?" Morienne put a hand on her arm.

"I fie, juss..." But she was slurring like a tavern drunk.

"Morienne, would you fetch a medic, please?" Meristan asked. The woman's footsteps disappeared down the corridor.

Why was she feeling like this again? She hadn't overdone anything.

"I will get out of your way," said Balaban. "I feel, perhaps, some research into theorised skills may be to our advantage now."

"No!" Nirea garbled. "No. Danjuss."

Balaban stood. "I shall take a few students with me, Lady Nirea. Skilled students. I will be in safe hands. I will tell them they are earning extra credit. Worry not. I assure you that I am on your side, for what comfort that gives you. I will take every precaution."

She tried to reach for him, but the room spun, and she felt Meristan's hand under her neck, guiding her back to her pillow.

Damn this bloody infirmity!

Balaban pulled the door behind him.

Nirea closed her eyes. Something wet on her forehead. A cloth. She focused on the sharp cold and the world began to harden again.

"Just relax," said Meristan. "Help is coming."

It needed to. If the murderer showed up right then, they were in trouble.

By the time Morienne returned with the medic, Nirea was just lightheaded and mildly nauseated.

"Can you sit up?" he asked. Nirea thought she recognised him, but she'd seen a number of medics in the days she'd been here. This one stuck out, though. Maybe the man who'd helped with Vastin?

"I'll need to check your wound, Lady," he said. "And we should change your dressing."

"Ah, I will, uh, step out," said Meristan. She'd have insisted on him staying, except that Morienne was back. The sooner they sorted this out, the sooner they could get back to the plan. Well, that's if the plan was worth the name anymore.

The medic got her out of her shirt and unwrapped the dressing on her shoulder. He gently poked and prodded around it, frowning as if it refused to answer a simple question.

Finally, he shrugged. "It's fine. No tearing, no sign of infection. In fact, it's looking as well as I would expect."

"Theh wy?" Nirea waved at her head.

"I'm sorry?" the medic answered, unwinding a clean dressing.

"Why did she feel strange?" Morienne translated.

"I honestly can't say. Have you eaten? Drunk plenty of water?"

She'd had soup, as usual, for dinner. And she'd drunk plenty. She nodded.

"Then perhaps it's simply fatigue. Your body has been through a great trauma. From what Egretta has told me, you haven't been kind to it." He smiled gently, in the way one does at a child who insists they are not tired despite their half-closed eyes. Her shoulder complained as she lifted her arm, allowing him to replace the bandage.

Once she was settled again, the medic placed a glass of opium on her table.

"Drink this and get a solid night's sleep. From now on, you stay in that bed. No more excitement until you're healed. All right?" His smile was gentle and genuine.

Nirea shrugged.

Unfortunately, that was not up to her.

The night passed uneventfully, which felt like both a blessing and a curse. Nirea had needed the rest, and Meristan had eventually convinced her to take the opium, while he and Morienne took shifts on guard. The fact that nobody came looking for the book reinforced Nirea's belief that her plan had been as obvious as Balaban thought.

She was finishing her porridge when a knock at the door set all three alert. Meristan lifted his axe and stepped behind the door.

Morienne carefully opened it with one hand, a dagger in the other. "Oh, hello!"

Nirea relaxed as Morienne stepped aside to reveal Rasa. But the metamorph's face was darkly serious. She looked exhausted, and she flinched when Meristan stepped out from his hiding place.

"I'm sorry, I didn't mean to startle you." The monk placed a huge hand on her shoulder.

"It's all right, I just...I have a lot to tell you." The metamorph all but stumbled to a chair and slumped into it.

"Did you find the envoy?" Meristan asked eagerly. "Is he on his way back?"

"Yes, and no...That's what I need to tell you."

Rasa relayed a story Nirea would have assumed was the ramblings of a diseased mind a week before. She'd lived through some madness in her time, seen some things she'd never told the story of for fear of sounding insane, but this put it all to shame. Anhel Weyr working for Mynygogg; Caer Amon engulfed in some sort of broken time "bubble"; and Aranok, Samily and Allandria going to face Mynygogg alone.

Idiots.

"No, no, it cannot be!" Meristan stood and paced the room. "I know Anhel Weyr! He's a good and righteous man. The man they encountered cannot have been Weyr."

His voice was on the verge of angry. Rasa visibly shrank from him. Morienne poured her a glass of water.

"Mehsan, cahm." He snapped his head toward her and she waved him back to his bed. He sat, but picked at his fingernails. He must be terrified, knowing Samily was going to face Mynygogg.

"Maes sess. Bahbah. Plahn," Nirea said, hoping he'd see just how well it all fit without her having to lay it out. Her cheek was already beginning to ache again.

"I'm sorry, what?" Rasa asked.

"S'grace, you're right." Meristan glanced at the door. "Morienne, would you?"

She pulled the door closed.

"Rasa," the monk said, "it's a long story, but we have evidence that Mynygogg is preparing some sort of spell to change history as we know it. To put himself in Janaeus's place. If he has the heart of devastation, as the envoy suspects, then we are potentially in great danger."

Nirea looked back at the metamorph to see tears rolling down her face. She sat forward and grunted when the pain reminded her to be still. Instead, Morienne knelt before her. "What's wrong?" she asked, taking the other woman's hands in her own.

"I'm sorry," said Rasa. "It's... I promised Laird Aranok I'd get this information to the king, and now it seems even more important and... I'm sorry, I'm just so tired." She slumped forward and sobbed. Morienne rose into a crouch to meet her and took her head onto her shoulder.

"It's all right, it's all right," she said softly.

"Oh, child." Meristan rose and put a hand on her shoulder. "You have been heroic, truly heroic. But for all your miraculous abilities, you are still human. You need rest. Something I have to keep telling people these days."

He looked pointedly at Nirea. She did her best to smile back at him.

Aranok was right, the king needed to know what was happening. But she was in no fit state to travel. And they still had a killer to catch.

All right. Someone needed to get to the king. Someone he would trust. Rasa turning up alone would be useless. Janaeus had no idea who she was and no reason to believe her. They needed a full assault on Dun Eidyn as soon as possible. If Aranok failed and they'd lost three of their greatest assets, they were going to need numbers. Every soldier they could get—every *draoidh* too. Which meant the university.

They had to assume the worst. Assume Aranok, Allandria and Samily were lost. And they still had a spy in the ranks here.

Damn it all to Hell!

Right. First priority, get to Janaeus. Meristan would have to go. Janaeus would listen to him. But he'd need a guard. Morienne was needed here to keep Vastin alive, which left Rasa. She was perfect—except she was exhausted. They could have asked Principal Keft for help, if only they knew he wasn't the very person they were hunting. No reason the principal was immune from suspicion. Far from it.

Well, that was their limitation. Rasa needed to rest. One day. One day for her to recover, and maybe time for Balaban to find something that could help explain what Mynygogg was planning—some evidence of the kind of magic he might be preparing to use. Maybe a way to fight it. Tomorrow, then. Meristan and Rasa couldn't take the Auld Road, because of the Blackened and Thakhati. So they would go north, skirt Crow Hill and stay in Lochen overnight, then take the Easter Road for the ferry to cross the Nor Loch. From the other side it was a day's ride to Haven. That was the quickest route. Still three days, but it was the best they were going to manage. They had to hope that whatever had prevented Mynygogg from performing his magic until now would stay his hand a little longer.

Right. Now how the Hell was she going to communicate all of that?

"Mehsan?" The monk turned toward her and she spoke as clearly as possible. "Get paper."

CHAPTER 3

Ride.

Ride.

Ride.

Breathe.

Allandria daren't glance back. She kept her chin up so Aranok's sunstone hanging round her neck would light the way without blinding her. Twisted shapes darted into shadow before her. Screeches of anger from the dark. Bear was doing all he could, but the horse's legs must be exhausted.

"Gluais!" Aranok threw a Thakhati back into the trees. God knew how he had any energy left. She certainly didn't. Nothing but terror keeping her going.

A thud behind them. One must have dropped from the trees. She heard Mynygogg cry out, more in anger than fear. The familiar sound of metal on stone.

"Is he all right?" she asked, not daring take her eyes off the path. Barely a path, really. Wide enough.

"Aye," Aranok answered breathlessly. "Keep going!"

The ground was uneven. Roots everywhere. She had to be careful. That was the only reason the Thakhati could keep up. She'd seen at least eight of them. But there must be more.

The light of Traverlyn beckoned ahead. It was safety and home. Salvation.

God, please let us reach it. Let us reach the light.

A scream from behind. Not human.

Fuck.

"Do we stop?" she asked.

She began to ease up on the reins, just in case.

"No," Aranok growled. "Keep going!"

Allandria could barely catch her breath. Kept her head up. Forward, only forward.

A screech from her left. A Thakhati shrank back from the light. Out of the trees, and the first buildings of Traverlyn were visible. And the light.

The light of a giant sunstone.

Only another two hundred yards. They were going to make it.

The familiar sound of an arrow whipped over her head. She ducked. Another whipped past. She noticed the light this time. Flaming arrows?

"Truce!" she called as loud as she could manage. "Allies!"

"They're not firing at us," said Aranok.

Of course. They were firing on the Thakhati. Might not help, but it wouldn't hurt.

Several more whipped overhead, and she pushed Bear forward the last few strides.

A deafening crack, a lurch and Allandria was flying.

She tucked her shoulder and rolled into the landing, but not quickly enough. Pain sheared through her shoulder as it crunched on impact and she tumbled out of control, landing face down in the mud.

A moment of stillness, as her squealing ears denied the chaos and joints throbbed in a union of complaint.

Every inch of her wanted to lie there, to just stop and rest. The pain, the exhaustion...but then, the skittering, clacking sound of the Thakhati and—*Hells*—she was lying on the sunstone!

With a grunt, Allandria pushed up, only to throw herself back down as a Thakhati lunged at her. She rolled back the way it had come, drawing her sword as she rose to her feet. The monster came back at her again and she parried its two-armed swipe. A quick glance to see what was happening with the others, but it was difficult to see because...

It was dark. The only light came from the dotted arrows of flame.

Another lunge and Allandria deflected the blow, but she could only defend. She needed some space to figure out why the light had gone out.

But again it came, crouched and then, rising onto two legs, launching up at her from below. Again she parried and rolled away, but this time, the thing anticipated her dodge and followed. She wasn't going to have time to...

A crunch of hooves as Midnight rode roughshod over the Thakhati, Mynygogg bellowing a war cry. A tangle of limbs then, as king, horse and demon fell together.

That was the moment she needed.

Allandria grasped the sunstone and pulled it out before her. Its cage was filled with mud, drowning the stone's light.

Fuck!

To her left, the Thakhati was moving again, climbing over the fallen Midnight, gouging chunks from the animal's hide as it crawled toward Mynygogg—trapped beneath the stricken horse. He'd be dead in moments.

Allandria surged across the sodden grass and did probably the one thing the Thakahti would never have expected—leapt on it. A solid grasp between its upper and lower arms was enough to roll it off the horse and away from the king.

They landed together only yards away, but Allandria had put herself between the hunter and its prey.

Behind her, she could hear the sounds of struggle. Aranok and Samily would have to take care of themselves.

She needed the light.

The Thakhati shrieked that awful, grating squeal and came at her again. Swiping first left and then right. With some distance, with more light, she could take this thing out with her bow. But at such close quarters, she struggled to do more than avoid its flailing attacks.

But she had the answer. She just had to free it.

"Allandria! Light!" Aranok bellowed.

"I know!"

As she parried again and again with her right arm, her left hand fumbled with the cage. But her glove made her fingers too clumsy for the delicate catch. Allandria jammed her middle fingers in her teeth and yanked the glove free, spitting it onto the ground as she dodged another lunge from the beast.

The attacks grew more urgent. More reckless? Did it understand what she was trying to do?

Swipe.

Parry.

Swipe.

Parry.

"Will..."

Swipe.

"You..."

Parry.

Swipe.

Parry.

"Please..."

Lunge.

Dodge.

"Fuck..."

Swipe.

Dodge.

The latch finally clicked open and the sunstone fell into Allandria's hand. She sidestepped the next attack and lunged forward herself, slamming her palm against the Thakhati's head.

"Off!"

A shriek like the gates of Hell and the monster burned to ash, searing the mud and Allandria's hand in the process. The pain was excruciating. Did she scream? Maybe.

But she had the light now, and the light was all.

"Samily! Aranok! To me!" Allandria raised her arm high, letting the stone's light create a bubble of shelter over her, the king and his horse.

Now she could see what was happening with the others.

Aranok was back on Bear, throwing Thakhati back like leaves in a storm. Either the horse had been lucky not to be hurt in the fall or Samily had healed him. The Thorn was no longer on Dancer, though, and stood facing two Thakhati attempting to flank her.

Thank God only one of them had come for Allandria, or both the king and she would be dead.

Samily skewered the creature before her, leapt into the air and landed behind Aranok on Bear. The great horse quickly made the ground between them and reached the safety of the light.

Aranok thrust a hand toward her. "The stone!"

Allandria tossed it to him, allowing him to hold it higher still, giving them more safety.

Samily launched herself from the horse. "Majesty! Where are you injured?"

"Midnight," the king wheezed.

Samily hesitated a moment before placing her hands on the animal.

"Air ais." The horse made a half scream Allandria had never heard from an animal as a leg clicked back into place and the crimson gashes on its side reknit themselves. Midnight scrambled back to her feet and Mynygogg gave a sucking cry of pain.

God, now she could see him. His legs were crushed along with half his abdomen. It was a miracle he was still alive. And it would take a miracle to save him.

"Samily!" She gestured urgently at Mynygogg.

The knight knelt beside him. *"Air ais."*

God knew how much energy the girl had left, but she showed no sign of flagging. Incredible how much she'd mastered her skill in a short time under Aranok's tutelage. A week ago this one act would have rendered her senseless.

Mynygogg groaned as the magic took effect, resetting shattered bones, rebuilding crushed organs.

"All right." The king pulled himself to his feet. "Two horses. Two pillions. We stick side by side in the light. No rush. Yes?"

"Agreed." Aranok watched the shadows crawling just out of sight. As long as they had the light, they would be safe.

Samily retook her place behind Aranok; Allandria and Mynygogg mounted Midnight.

"What happened to Dancer?" Allandria asked.

"She bolted toward town," said Samily.

"Walk," Mynygogg commanded. They did. The Thakhati were staying back but, even so, made an occasional feint. Their intermittent shrieks were a mewling complaint—like agitated cats threatening to pounce.

The walk lasted an age, and Allandria's hand began to throb in urgent agony, but, finally, they made it. Back into the light. Allandria breathed.

"All right." The relief in Mynygogg's voice was palpable. Horrors danced in the light of scattered flames, but the shadows would come no further. Traverlyn's giant sunstone had them now.

Allandria slid off the horse and all but fell into the arms of a waiting archer.

"You all right?" he asked.

None of them were all right. But they were alive.

"Let me help you, Lady." The boy looked barely out of his teens. But for his fresh face, he was strongly built. Good. She could lean on him.

Others arrived to help. Only Samily seemed at all steady on her feet, but her face was pale as the Dead.

"We need to get to the hospital," said Aranok. "Now."

"Laird Aranok, we've been watching for you," said an ebony-skinned woman with sharp cheekbones. "But unless you need urgent medical care, sire, the hospital's closed up. You should rest."

Allandria's hand at least needed attention. Possibly her shoulder too. But they had Samily for that. Rasa was why they had to get to the hospital.

"No time," said Mynygogg. "This is a matter of national importance."

The woman, who wore the mark of a captain, looked at him curiously, as if sizing him up, before turning to Aranok. "Is that so, Laird Envoy?"

Of course, she knew Aranok but not the king. Mynygogg gave a wry, tired smile.

"It is," Aranok said. "This is Laird Gogg. You should regard anything he says as carrying my authority."

Gogg? That was a bit close to the truth. Aranok must be tired to pick such a lazy alias.

"As you say, sire." The captain turned to her retinue. "Ganard, Darcia, stay here. Make sure those things don't find a dark alleyway. The rest of you, with us."

The boy was all but holding Allandria upright. "What's your name?"

"Killarn."

"Killarn, I'm going to lean very heavily on you now. Carry me if I pass out, will you?"

Nirea whittled absentmindedly at the wood. She'd forgotten about it until she'd needed something to keep her awake through the night. Her eyes stung despite her opium-induced nap that afternoon and Morienne's deep, restful breathing was irrationally aggravating.

The hospital was eerily quiet at night. Occasional footsteps put her on edge, but the only person who'd come to the door was Egretta. The matriarch had tutted disapprovingly at Nirea being awake, but left with a kind smile and a nod. It was only fair Nirea took a watch.

She turned the wood over in her hand. Only a wee while ago had she realised what it was. And it hurt.

A shield. She'd been glad to be the only one awake so her tears were her own.

The shape was done, and now she carefully carved the crossed hammers. It would have been a comfort to Glorbad that the boy should recover. But she dreaded having to tell Vastin what had happened to the soldier. She might leave out that the demon's spiked tail went through his shield. He'd only feel guilty, and truth was that if it went through the shield and Glorbad's armour, nothing was going to stop it—not without magic. Glorbad was dead the minute he went up those steps.

And for all he was an irascible old bastard, if he'd known what was waiting, he'd still have gone first. Been more adamant. Nirea had no faith, but she hoped maybe there was something next—somewhere that Glorbad could have the peace he deserved. Maybe see his family again. She missed his laugh. God, she missed it. Like a bleak hole at her side.

Footsteps. Many, moving quickly. Voices—their words urgent.

"Moyen," she whispered. The woman didn't stir. "Moyen!" Louder. With the voices ever closer, she carefully nudged the woman in the side with her sheathed sword.

Morienne jerked awake. "What?"

"Lithen." Nirea nodded at the door.

Morienne took Nirea's sword and moved beside the door. Nirea snuffed out the candle and they waited in the dark.

They hadn't planned for more than one person showing up. If it was a *draoidh*, they knew what to do. Most needed gestures or incantations—or both—to use their magic. Morienne stood ready to gag them and bind their hands. If she didn't have time, a sword in the back would do the job.

But more than one? A conspiracy with multiple people—multiple *draoidhs*? Until that moment she hadn't even considered it.

Fuck.

Nirea threw off the sheets with her good arm and slipped bare feet onto cold stone. Morienne's jaegerstock was there somewhere. She slid her feet carefully until her toe found the wooden handle. Scooping it up, she held it like a spear. It wasn't ideal, but it would be better than nothing if they faced multiple enemies.

The steps halted outside the door. Hushed voices.

This was it. She steeled herself.

The handle turned slowly and a crack of light spilled into the room. It reached her bed—the bed she should have been in—and stopped.

She grasped the jaegerstock tight, ready to murder whoever came through that door.

"Morienne?"

Wait. What?

"Nirea? Meristan?"

"Wha?" she asked, confused. The voice was so incongruous.

The door opened further, light now illuminating half the room, including Nirea, perched half-dressed, weapon raised.

The man's face went from curious to confused, then he burst out laughing. "Who the Hell are you expecting?"

"Laird Aranok!" The envoy flinched away as Morienne stepped from behind the door.

"What?" he exclaimed. "Who *are* you expecting?"

Nirea relaxed her shoulders and lowered the weapon. "Law sawee."

"What?"

"Long story," Morienne said as she relit the candle. Now they had better light, Nirea could see the envoy's pale, haggard face.

"God, Nirea, I'd heard... but... your cheek."

She shrugged her good shoulder. "Beher an Glohbah."

Aranok ran a hand through his hair. "Fuck, yes." He stepped toward her and, with more familiarity than she expected, gently wrapped his arms around her. "I'm so sorry." After a hesitant moment, she put one arm around him.

"Me ooh." They'd both lost close friends.

After a long time, he released her and they sat on the bed.

"Sorry, Morienne, it's good to see you too." He reached out and took her hand. "Wait. Your curse...?"

Morienne beamed as she held up the charm that negated her curse's effects. "Master Balaban gave me this."

"Wonderful." Aranok gave a weary smile. He looked drained. Exhausted.

"Thank you, sire." Morienne beamed back at him.

"You all ight?" Nirea asked.

He turned to her with a deep sigh. "I don't even know where to start. We didn't want to overwhelm you—not until we saw how you are."

"I fine." She wasn't, but she wanted to know everything.

"All right—but first, this is urgent. Did Rasa get here? Where is she?"

"Ess, buh..." It would be too difficult to explain in her bloody mumble. She gestured to Morienne instead.

"She arrived a few days ago, Laird. She told us everything, about the heart, about you going to face Mynygogg. What happened?"

Aranok raised his hands placatingly. "I'll explain all of that, I promise, but first, where is she?"

"Gone. She and Meristan left for Haven this morning."

Aranok's already pale face turned ashen. "Fuck. Fuck. Fuck!" The envoy punched the bed and stood. "Wait here." He stalked back out into the hall.

Morienne looked as confused as Nirea felt. He'd specifically said someone had to get to Janaeus as soon as possible. Why would he be unhappy about that? Raised voices again in the hall. Agitated. Maybe Allandria? Another male voice that she couldn't place. It felt important, though, and her heart stuttered. Who was that?

Aranok returned with Samily. The knight looked as tired as him.

"Sammy." Nirea half smiled.

"Lady Nirea, I am so sorry for your loss." She made an odd sort of bow. What was going on?

"Nirea, we have a lot to get through and very little time, so we're going to have to do this quickly. Samily is going to heal you, all right?"

Nirea nodded enthusiastically. It would be wonderful to be fit again. She could finally be of some bloody use. But Samily barely looked capable of standing, never mind healing her. "You shua?"

"Yes. It's important." Aranok moved out of the way and Samily sat beside her. The girl placed her hand on Nirea's wounded shoulder.

"Air ais."

The pain spiked briefly and drained away, the swelling reducing. A tingle of pleasure ran up the side of her neck. When had she last not felt that damned pain? Nirea stretched her arm out and balled up her fist. Oh God, it felt so good. The absence of pain is such pleasure.

Samily reached for Nirea's cheek. Without knowing why, she grabbed it defensively. The knight's mouth curled. "I'm sorry, did I hurt you?"

That wasn't it. She needed this. She needed a memento. A permanent one.

"Fowahd? Noh bah. Fowahd."

"Forward?" Samily looked questioningly to Aranok. "I...can try. But you will have a scar. A substantial one."

"Ess." Nirea was vehement. "Scah."

"Nirea, you don't have to do that," said Aranok. "Nobody's going to forget him."

The envoy was oddly adamant for a man who'd all but drawn swords against Glorbad days before he died. It didn't matter. He'd given his life for hers. The least she could do was wear the scar she escaped with. "No. Scah."

Aranok shrugged.

"If that is what you wish, Lady," said Samily. "But I am not as practised with this form of my skill."

"S'fine." Nirea put her hand on Samily's. "I russ ooh." God it would be good to be able to speak properly again.

Samily nodded and raised her hand to Nirea's swollen cheek. She closed her eyes and breathed deeply.

"Air adhart."

Nirea felt the swelling go down, felt the inside of her cheek pull away from her teeth. She felt the tear knit together, tissue hardening and tightening, tugging slightly at her eye, making her blink. And then it was done. Her balance lurched sideways and she was glad to be sitting.

Samily looked awful. Her eyes fluttered as if she might collapse. Nirea caught her under an arm.

"Whoa!" Aranok moved to catch her other arm. "Morienne, can we...?"

Morienne helped them manoeuvre Samily onto the other bed. Her eyes rolled in her head as if she'd drunk a pint of poppy milk.

"Is she all right?" Nirea smiled reflexively when she heard the words out loud.

"She will be," said Aranok. "She's been through a lot. We all have."

"Tell me," said Nirea.

"I don't have time. I need you to trust me."

That was an odd thing to say. "Of course. What do you need?"

"I need you to lie down."

"What? Why?"

"Please, Nirea, if I had time I would explain, but lives are at stake. Hell, the kingdom is at stake. I need to do this. Now."

"All right." She clambered back onto the bed. He'd better have a good reason—she'd been pleased to get out of it.

Aranok took a small yellow pendant from around his neck and held it out toward her.

"Hold this."

She took it, slightly nervously. "What is this?"

"Clìor."

The room tipped on its end as a sea of faces, memories, feelings crashed over her. Nausea hammered her in the gut and she vomited as the floor lurched up toward her. A hand on her shoulder pushed her back into the soft pillow. She grabbed at the sides of the bed, desperate for something solid to hold. To stop the spinning, the lights, the waves of nausea. Nirea closed her eyes and willed the world to balance, but still her head swam and the room rocked until a flash of red and then there was nothing.

Just blessed, quiet black.

CHAPTER 4

Allandria tutted as the lock pick clattered to the floor. Aranok almost went to shush her but caught himself. Samily had healed her burnt hand, but she was still hanging from a frayed rope. They both were. Aranok's eyes itched to close and his muscles complained with every step. They needed to hurry, but they needed to do this first. To find out who they could trust. Meristan and Rasa planned to stay in Lochen that night and ride for the ferry in the morning. They could beat them there if they went straight for the ferry.

Maybe.

A resonant click. Allandria smiled and the door swung open. The masters' residential quarters were off-limits, but this was an emergency. A wooden board on the wall opposite the door listed the masters' names alongside floor and room number. They found the one they needed and crept quietly up the stairs.

Allandria walked awkwardly, wincing with every step. He almost made a playful comment about it but decided against it. She stopped outside door 213.

Aranok had a quick look up and down the empty corridor.

"You sure?" Allandria whispered.

The doors were quite far apart, but not so far that knocking would go unheard. They didn't need a scene. Aranok nodded, hoping he looked more certain than he felt. Allandria knelt and carefully slid in first one brass pick, then the other.

Come on, come on.

Aranok's impatience must have been obvious—Allandria backhanded him across the thigh. "Stand still."

He took a deep breath, straightened and put his shoulders back. Something cracked in his chest. In the silence, it echoed like an axe strike. Allandria looked up at him incredulously.

"I didn't mean it," he whispered. She sighed and returned to the lock. It gave a familiar click and Allandria stepped back.

Slowly, carefully, silently, Aranok turned the handle and pushed the door. The old hinges creaked in complaint and the pair froze, waiting for a response.

Nothing came. The door wasn't quite open enough, though. Slowly, he pushed again, lifting slightly to ease pressure off the hinges. It was a little stiff, but quiet. They slipped inside and carefully closed the door.

Moonlight split the wall beside them, cutting through a sliver in the curtains opposite. Aranok could just make out the door to the bedchamber. Allandria crossed to a table and lit an ornate candle. Now they could see. The chamber was neat, in contrast with the master's office. A bookcase full of arcane texts, books on history, philosophy and religion. An elegant and well-used chair beside the fireplace.

They crossed to the bedchamber door. It was also locked. That seemed excessively careful, all things considered, but then they had just broken in here relatively easily and there was a master killer somewhere in the university.

Allandria raised a questioning eyebrow. There was no need for quiet here. Aranok knocked firmly on the door. Muffled grunts from inside, and then quiet. He knocked again. This time there was movement.

"Who's there? Who is it? I have a weapon!"

Aranok smiled. "Master Balaban, it's Aranok. And Allandria."

"What on earth are you doing in my chambers, boy? What time is it?"

"Sorry, Master, but it's urgent. And you will want to know what we have to tell you."

The door opened to reveal the old man in a long white nightgown. His remaining hair stuck out from his head like wisps of smoke and he fumbled his round glasses onto his face. Balaban put a frail hand on Aranok's shoulder. "It's good to see you alive, boy. Both of you." He smiled at Allandria. "We feared the worst."

"I know," said Aranok. "Master, we're short of time. Can I ask you to take a seat, please?"

Balaban looked confused, absentmindedly smoothing the front of his nightgown. "A seat? I suppose."

The master's bare feet slapped on the stone floor until the fireside rug muffled them as he took the chair. "All right. Now what?"

Aranok took out the memory charm. Balaban would have recognised it had Janaeus not taken his memory of it.

"What's that?"

Allandria took his hand between hers. "This might be difficult, Master. But it will be all right, just try not to fight it. I've been through it."

Even exhausted, she was made of compassion. He really needed to sort things out with her. Just not now. Not tonight.

"Master, this is a memory charm, it's designed to protect..."

"Oh my God!" Balaban crawled back up his chair. "He's done it, hasn't he? He's already done it!"

Aranok wasn't sure how to respond. "I'm sorry, what?"

"Mynygogg. He's cast the spell. Changed history! Damn it, I knew this was coming."

Well, that was something. Aranok knew Balaban was sharp, but apparently he'd got bloody close to figuring it out.

"Wait, no," he continued. "That makes no sense. I still remember Janaeus. I remember history. What has he changed?"

They didn't have time for this. He needed to get it over with.

"I'm sorry, Master, but if you could please just hold this, it will all make sense."

Balaban looked at him suspiciously. "Wait. You two went to take on Mynygogg. Alone. And survived." He sat back in his chair like a startled cat. "No. Both of you get out. Now. I'll scream!"

Fuck.

"Hold him," he said. Allandria frowned, but quickly stood and grabbed the old man's shoulders. Aranok forced the charm into his hand. He'd forgive them when it was done.

"Help!" So much for quiet.

"Clìor."

Balaban opened his mouth to shout again but stopped as his eyes rolled in his head. He slumped back and was quiet.

Allandria released his shoulders. "That could have gone better."

"Lock that door, would you? Just in case."

She did, not taking the chance of checking the hallway. If anyone had heard the cry, they probably wouldn't know where to go looking unless someone stuck their head out and showed them.

"You're absolutely sure we can trust him?" Allandria asked.

"As sure as I can be." Other than Conifax, Balaban was the master he had spent the most time with as a student. Everything he knew about history, morality and politics he learned from the old man. His teachings had laid the groundwork for what he and Mynygogg were trying to achieve. It would make no sense for a man with his belief in a fairer society to be working with Janaeus. And the thought he might betray their personal relationship was... unthinkable. He'd had to pick one master he knew he could trust, and Balaban was it.

After about ten minutes of impatient and slightly awkward silence, Balaban's eyes fluttered and his head turned. He let out a woozy groan and smacked his lips as if he hadn't drunk in an age.

"Water?" He pointed to a sideboard where a half-full jug sat alongside some glasses. Aranok filled one for him and he drank it down greedily.

"My God. My God. It's... it's unbelievable." Balaban looked up at Aranok. "Janaeus did this? Did all of it?"

Aranok nodded.

"How? He was such a quiet, awkward boy. Too much inside his own head. He never had this kind of power."

"The heart of devastation. He's had it all along. We were looking in the wrong place," Aranok explained.

Balaban gasped and his eyes widened. "Of course. Of course, yes, that makes sense. Everything we know makes sense. Blast it all, I was so close to understanding."

"You were," Allandria said appreciatively. "Closer than anyone else got."

Balaban crossed to the jug and poured himself another glass of water. "Well, mainly because of the book."

"Book?" Aranok didn't know about a book. "Actually, tell me later. For now, I need your help."

The master sipped at the newly filled glass and smacked his mouth contentedly. "Of course. What can I do?"

"Can I trust Principal Keft? Is there any chance he could be Janaeus's agent? That *he* killed Conifax?" Saying it out loud hit Aranok like a blindside punch. He'd distanced himself from the idea that his old teacher was gone. Pretended he was still there—in his office, asleep in his chair. But the stark fact of the words coming from his own mouth made it real and the exhaustion was suddenly too much. His legs gave way and Aranok all but stumbled into the empty chair.

Allandria's reassuring hand squeezed his shoulder and he instinctively put his hand over hers. Her touch raised the hairs on the back of his arm.

"I knew his death would hit you hard," said Balaban. "I'm so sorry."

Aranok blinked back the tears welling in his eyes. They didn't have time for emotions.

Balaban looked at the floor as if considering a puzzle or a chess stratagem. Aranok was grateful for the chance to compose himself.

Finally, the master took another long drink of water and looked up. "Not only am I confident you can trust Keft, but I believe I know who killed Conifax."

Aranok sprang to his feet, his legs suddenly stable again. "You do?" He hadn't expected to solve Conifax's murder tonight. He'd been resigned to waiting until he got back. "How?"

Balaban cocked his head. "Because there's a 'master' here who… isn't."

Nirea crawled through thick black mud. Her head pounded, red flashing against her eyelids with each beat of her heart. The acrid taste of vomit on her tongue. Someone was holding her hand. Meristan?

Slowly, she blinked her eyes open. It wasn't the monk beside her bed.

Of course not, he had gone. Instead, a bald man in dark leathers smiled down at her. "Hello, my love."

His eyes. She saw his eyes and everything came back. Nirea gasped as her chest threatened to burst. She wrapped her arms around him hungrily, gripping him tight. She might never let go.

"Oh God, oh God." She didn't know what had happened. She didn't care. She had Mynygogg back and nothing else mattered. She was whole again, the lingering, nagging void finally sated.

"I know." His breath on her ear...

She kissed his cheek, his head, ran her hands over it and held his face before her. "Your hair. Your beautiful hair."

"Um." He half smiled. "We cut it."

She needed to kiss him; more than anything she needed to feel his lips against hers, but she could still taste bile. "Wait." She took a mouthful of water, swished it around and spat it onto the floor. Someone had cleared her vomit. She turned back to her husband, grasped his head with both hands and pulled him down, pressing her lips against his. The spark flew through her, the passion, the excitement, the arousal. All of it a crashing wave. She could stay there forever. Screw the rest of the world, this was all she'd ever need.

Too soon, Mynygogg pulled away. "I've missed you so much and God I'm glad you're alive. But we have a lot to discuss."

"What the Hell happened? How did Janaeus become king? How did he make us forget?" She was still holding on to him, crippled by the fear this was an awful waking dream.

"I'll explain, I promise. But we have another priority first. We have to stop Meristan and Rasa from reaching Janaeus."

Fuck. Of course.

"All right. Let's go." Nirea swung her legs off the bed.

"No. We stay here for now. We need to regroup and plan. And rest."

Only then did she see the dark bags under his pale eyes, the slumped shoulders and pallid cheeks.

"When did you last sleep?"

He smiled weakly. "Too long ago. But it's all right, Aranok has a plan."

"Oh. So there's nothing to do right now?"

Mynygogg raised an eyebrow and nodded to the other bed. Samily lay sound asleep, still in her full armour.

Nirea smiled. "She'll be out for hours. Nothing's waking her before she's rested."

Mynygogg looked to the door. "People will be here any minute."

"Oh, come on." She pulled him toward her. "It's been an age. We won't need long."

Aranok was torn. Their mission was urgent, but the chance to get Conifax's murderer, to see them brought to justice, was too strong. Anger and excitement seethed within him, begging to be free. Still, they couldn't waste time, so Allandria went to rouse Principal Keft.

In Aranok's exhausted state, he and Balaban had made a stop on the way for reinforcement.

He hammered on the door several times before it finally creaked open. Opiassa filled the doorway, making it difficult for Aranok or Balaban to see into the room. But he knew what he'd see.

"Master Opiassa?" There was fear in the small voice. The head of university security did not visit in the middle of the night without reason.

Opiassa glowered down at him. "Rotan, you are under arrest on suspicion of the murders of Master Conifax and Master Calavas, and of treason."

"I don't... I don't..." he stuttered.

Opiassa stood aside and allowed Rotan to see the men behind her. Aranok didn't recognise him, but Balaban had explained how he'd insinuated himself with Conifax. He'd been a troublesome student—one of those insufferable pricks who expected to be forgiven anything due to his wealthy family, charming smile and silver tongue. Aranok knew the type. Thought the rules didn't apply to him. The kind who would offer flattering words and a hand on your shoulder while the other slipped a knife between your ribs.

Of course he wasn't a master. He'd been expelled a year before graduating. The only way he'd ever become one was to cheat. There was no reason Janaeus would have made everyone believe Rotan a master unless he was working for him.

The bastard blinked at the pair of them, his pretence at innocence so compelling Aranok might even have doubted himself. Instead, he lifted his hand and allowed the memory charm to dangle.

Rotan looked over his shoulder nervously, and back to Aranok. "I'm sorry, I don't know what that is."

"It protects against memory magic," Aranok answered. "I got it from the king."

Rotan's face changed. He looked up at Opiassa and back to Aranok as if desperately calculating his options.

"Please run," Aranok growled.

Opiassa shot him a dark look. It was a threat. He wouldn't kill the man here. Not yet.

Rotan lurched for the door handle and tried to pull it closed. Opiassa was so much faster, he barely moved it at all before she broke his arm. He howled and dropped to his knees, cradling the arm across his chest.

"You'll get nothing from me!" he spat, the mask shattered by pain.

Aranok crouched before him, their faces inches apart.

"I don't need anything from you, except to see you suffer, you little cunt." He grabbed the broken arm and yanked the man, screaming, to his feet. "Try to escape. Try to warn Janaeus. Try anything. I'll be back. I'll hunt you with my last breath, you understand? The safest place you'll ever be again is a gaol."

Rotan glowered back, but his eyes wavered.

"He'll likely hang," Opiassa said flatly. The law of the land was generally against hanging since Mynygogg had taken the throne, and Janaeus hadn't changed that. But double murder and treason? She was right.

"I know. But hanging's over quick."

CHAPTER 5

Principal Keft had snapped at Allandria for waking him and complained all the way to the hospital. The grumpiness faded when his restored memory told him he was in the presence of Eidyn's monarchs. Morienne had also fetched Egretta at Nirea's suggestion. They planned to use the hospital as a base. Keeping Mynygogg hidden until they could restore enough memories was crucial. But with Aranok, Allandria, Mynygogg, Nirea, Morienne, Egretta, Balaban and Keft crammed into one room, and Samily still unconscious on the bed, there was little space to move.

When Mynygogg finished bringing everyone up-to-date, he sat beside Nirea. She took his hand without looking. It was nice to see her happy. To see them together again. They deserved each other.

"So what do you need from me?" Keft asked.

"The four of us are exhausted," Aranok said. "We need energy so we can go after Meristan and Rasa tonight."

The energy *draoidh* looked around at them thoughtfully. "When did you last sleep?"

"Last night," said Aranok.

"Properly, two nights ago," Mynygogg corrected him.

Keft frowned. "I can restore your physical energy. I just need a source. A fire. But going too long without sleep has consequences."

"How so?" Allandria knew relatively little about energy *draoidhs*.

"Your brain needs sleep," Egretta answered. "People who go too long without it go mad. Start seeing things that aren't there. Make bad decisions."

"We'll have to risk it," said Aranok. "Allandria and I will go."

"Actually," Allandria interrupted. "I don't think I should."

Aranok looked at her with confusion and surprise. She knew he would, but she'd been thinking about this. She needed some space. But there was another reason—the reason she'd give him.

"The king and queen are here. We can't leave them unprotected. You should go, and take Samily. She can kill Thakhati better than I can. And if you go after Meristan without her, she'll be furious and follow you anyway."

It made perfect sense. He wouldn't be able to argue. Still, his crest-fallen shoulders were a dagger stabbing at her guilt.

"We can look after ourselves, Allandria." The restored queen stood proud and regal.

"No, she's right." Aranok looked away from Allandria. "You shouldn't be unguarded, and Allandria's the best. And she's right about Samily. We'll be fine." His voice was dispassionate. Flat. He was hurt. Tough. He'd get over it. "Principal Keft, if you could just wake Samily, we can get moving."

The principal placed a hand on Samily's forehead, closed his eyes and said something too quiet for Allandria to make out. After a moment, the knight sprang to life. "Oh!" She sat up, taking in the crowd around her. "What is happening?"

"Come on," said Aranok. "I'll tell you on the way."

The king's envoy shepherded the White Thorn out of the room after Principal Keft without a backwards glance.

"Tobin, isn't it?"

The stable boy looked up from rubbing straw across Dancer's hind-quarters. Aranok was pleased to see the horse had found her way home. "Aye, sire."

He stiffened when he saw Principal Keft. That was interesting. Did Keft have a reputation Aranok wasn't aware of?

"Tobin, we need Bear and Midnight. Can you saddle them, please?"

The boy's face turned first to confusion, then horror. "Beg your pardon, sire, but no, I cannae. They're exhausted. I've only just finished rubbing down Bear and he was a mess. They'll die if you try an' ride them the night. They're Calladells, no demons!"

"Mind your tongue, boy. You are addressing the king's envoy." Keft stepped forward and Tobin took a step away, but he kept himself between them and the horse.

Aranok put a hand on Keft's arm. "It's all right, Principal, he's only protecting his animals, as any good stable hand would."

Footsteps behind. Aranok glanced round to confirm Samily had joined them. She looked as refreshed as he felt since Keft had rejuvenated them. His mind seemed clear enough too. Samily had then healed their physical ails, for which Aranok's knee was immensely grateful.

"Tobin, you have my word that the horses will be fine. We have lit a small fire outside and Master Keft will replenish their energy. They'll be fresh as a winter morning." Aranok winked with a positivity he didn't feel.

The straw in Tobin's hands twisted and bent. "That's all well, but their muscles, sire. Their bodies need to recover. It's no just they're tired—they're worn out!"

"Boy, Laird Aranok gave you his word," snapped Keft. "That is the end of it."

Aranok raised an eyebrow at the principal's tone. The man had expressed the same concerns quite ardently, regarding both their health and the horses'. They'd had to explain Samily's power in order to quiet his objections, which had excited him somewhat too much. Keft had been a picture of curiosity and avarice. It was unreasonable for him to chastise Tobin for asking the same questions. Now that he was in on the secret, he was apparently keen to protect it—to the exclusion of others. Of lessers, like a stable boy. No wonder Tobin distrusted him.

The boy lifted a protective hand to Dancer's back. "But…"

"Do you have faith in God?" Samily stepped forward.

Tobin's head lowered. "Aye, Lady."

"And you know who I am?"

Tobin eyed her white armour, lingering momentarily on the holy symbol etched onto her shoulders. "Aye."

"I give you my word that we have a way of protecting the horses from harm and that they will be fine." Samily paused for a moment. "Do you believe me?"

Tobin looked up warily. He glanced at the horses and back to Samily. "I want to."

"You've seen the magic that men like these can do, have you not?" she asked.

"Aye. Some," he answered quietly.

"Please believe me when I say we will do them no harm." After a nervous moment, Tobin finally nodded and Samily smiled. "You are a good man, to care for your charges so well."

The boy's cheeks flushed. "Thank you, Lady." He gave a slight bow before looking up nervously at Aranok. "I'm sorry, Laird, can I ask..."

"Go on."

"It's just...why Midnight and Bear, but no Dancer? Is there something wrong with her?"

Aranok caught the horse's eye and she huffed air through her nose. "Nothing at all. I just don't think she's very happy with me."

"Ah." Tobin smiled. "Aye, she can be like that. Don't worry, she'll get over it."

Aranok sighed. "I hope so."

The bonfire of old straw and broken fence rails crackled in the early murk as light threatened the horizon. Samily loved watching the sun rise. The glorious pinks and yellows bleeding across the sky brought God closer in her heart.

She warmed her hands against the fire, knowing the flames would soon burn low. Principal Keft would replace her energy after she restored the horses. Taking the animals back a few days should also restore some of their own energy, as it had done for Aranok at Dun Eidyn. But the principal had explained that, in theory, his own power was more effective and would provide them a greater well of energy to draw upon. She was just to focus on turning their bodies back, so as to protect them. Samily hadn't been aware of treating Aranok any differently at Dun Eidyn—of focusing on restoring his energy as well as his physical health, but perhaps she had done so simply by it being her intent. There was so much about her ability that she did not yet understand. It had been so little time since she learned the truth of it and she'd barely stopped to think about what it might mean.

Principal Keft's excitement at learning of her abilities and his ravings about her potential had given her pause. She wondered what else might be possible, beyond what she knew. What the girl in Caer Amon had done with the relic was disturbing. That was the first time she'd felt wary of her skill. God would not give Samily more than she could handle, but it was a burden to wield that kind of power. When she'd just been a "healer," there was no negative to her magic, but now she knew she could do much more. "Fixing her mistakes," Rasa had said. She must guard against becoming reckless, seduced by her new possibilities. If her head came off, she would stay dead.

"Here y'are, Laird." Tobin drew the horses reluctantly from the stable. Neither looked happy to be saddled again so soon. They would not understand what was about to happen to them. Samily hoped they would've slept for some time, at least.

The principal and the envoy had been in deep, hushed conversation since they'd come outside. At first, she'd felt an unfamiliar and unwelcome cut of exclusion. However, Aranok had given her a subtle wink and smile over Keft's shoulder while the principal was gesticulating about something. She took it to mean he was keeping the man from barraging her with questions, and for the moment, she was grateful of it. The two walked toward her as Tobin approached with the horses.

"So your plan is to reach the ferry before them and cut them off?" Keft asked.

"Hopefully," Aranok answered. "Meristan and Rasa planned to stay at Lochen tonight and should be heading from there this morning at the earliest. They should keep to the Easter Road. If we ride flat out across country on the Calladells, we should beat them there by tonight. We'll have to cut across the foothills below Crow Hill."

"Careful you don't get bogged down in the gorse," said Keft. "It's thick up there. Worse on Archer's Hill."

Samily swung her pack over Bear and the animal gave a tired snort. Tobin lingered awkwardly, likely still anxious to see something done for his horses, or curious to see what it was.

"Tobin, you can leave us." Aranok tossed him a coin. The stable boy caught it absentmindedly. He made as if to speak, seemed to think better of it and walked away. Aranok gave no sign he had noticed.

Samily followed the boy as the envoy loaded up Midnight. She would prefer to leave him with peace of mind. "Tobin?"

He turned back to her. "Lady?"

"Was there something else you wanted to say?"

Tobin shifted uncomfortably, glancing back at Keft. "It's no my place, Lady."

"I give you leave to speak freely, without repercussion. On my honour." If something else concerned him, she'd rather know now than later. If it was something she could put at rest for him, she'd rather that too.

"It's just...well, I thought I heard you're trying to catch Brother Meristan and Lady Rasa, them that left yesterday—is that right?"

Samily perked up. Tobin must have outfitted their horses, of course. "We are."

He glanced at Keft again. "Well, it's just that Principal Keft sent a message with them—to be taken to the Lestalric estate. Would you no be better catching them there tonight?"

What?

That made no sense. If Keft had sent them on an errand to Lestalric, why not mention it? Perhaps they couldn't trust him after all? Samily's heart sank. They'd revealed her secret to him. If he was a traitor...

She had to know the truth of it. "Tell me exactly what happened."

Tobin's big eyes widened even further as he stepped closer. "As they were setting off, the master arrived with a letter. Said it was urgent, from Keft, and could they take it to Lestalric on their way. Brother Meristan said it was no bother—would be a good place to spend a night."

Tobin opened his hands to show that was all he had.

"So it was not Principal Keft who came with the letter?"

"No, Lady. It was another master."

"Which one? Did you know him?"

"I've seen him," said Tobin. "No sure of his name. Young for a master, though."

S'grace.

"Come with me." Samily led Tobin back to Aranok and Keft.

"Please, tell them all you've told me."

Tobin nervously recounted the tale and was dismissed. Principal Keft stood bemused.

"I take it you know nothing about the letter?" Aranok asked.

"It was not me," said Keft.

"What do you make of it?" Samily asked.

Aranok looked at her with something Samily was not sure she'd ever seen from him.

Fear.

"I have mixed memories of Lestalric, but the barony should be abandoned. However, I also recall Baroness de Lestalric running the estate."

"What does that mean?" Samily asked.

Aranok's face was ashen.

"I think Rotan sent them to Shayella."

Midnight twitched beneath Aranok, one hoof scratching at the dirt. He understood. Their need to leave was even more urgent now. If Rotan had sent Meristan and Rasa into a trap, they were going to have to catch them on the road. Rasa would be able to defend herself, to escape, even, but until Meristan knew who he was... Then again, he'd killed a demon at Barrock without his memory. His instincts remained, maybe.

"They will be safe. God is with them." Samily sat atop Bear beside him in the northern meadow, where the sunstone cast long shadows. There were only homes out here—no shops would set up so far from the town centre.

Aranok realised he was rolling the memory charm between his fingers. Janaeus had made one for each of them. They'd become a symbol of their membership of the Hellfire Club, such that Janaeus had even taken to wearing a decorative one, despite his innate defence against memory magic. Korvin's was buried with him. Seven years ago. How was it already seven years? And yet, so much had changed, it was a different world. He was a different person. Back then, he might have sided with the others. He'd been angry and hurting and guilty and drunk. He remembered very little of Korvin's funeral. Shay and Janaeus had been there. Anhel too, surely? As the oldest, Weyr had been like a leader of sorts. Pushed them to take risks in the name of developing their skills. Dangerous things. Things children shouldn't be doing.

Aranok would never have imagined one day he'd hate the man that boy had become.

And Shayella. He'd wanted her for such a long time. She was mysterious and wilful and strong. Her chestnut hair and lilac eyes were magnetic to a teenage boy. Aranok suspected Janaeus had a thing for her too. Maybe they all had—but those eyes were only ever for Korvin. They were together on and off for years. Korvin was almost thirty before he had a relationship with another woman that lasted longer than six months and didn't see him going back to her eventually. They shared a bond. They all did. But Shay wasn't that girl any more than Aranok was that boy. The world had changed. Now Shayella was a threat to his friends, just as she had been for the past year. She'd killed thousands. She'd probably cursed the Blackened and she'd probably created the Thakhati with Anhel. She was a murderer, and she had to be stopped. There was no way back from this. Whatever he'd once felt for her, shared with her, it was long dead. It had to be.

As soon as the sun rose over the trees they would go. Between them, they could fight off a small number of Thakhati, but they needed energy if they were going to ride hard all day. Again.

Aranok rubbed the reins between his fingers and looked again to the horizon. Light was just beginning to split the canopy. Was it enough?

He looked back at Samily. Through her helm, he could only make out her eyes. They told him to go.

He peered into the trees, shading his own eyes. Was there any movement? The Thakhati had mostly gathered on the southern road into town and then to the western edge, following them in earlier. No major reason to suspect the monsters would also be in the trees to the north. But they didn't know.

Fuck it. They were going.

Aranok snapped the reins and spurred Midnight forward. The horse gladly took the cue and cantered toward the trees. Bear whinnied behind them as Samily did the same. The peak of Crow Hill disappeared behind the canopy of trees.

One day.

One day's ride to save their friends. And the country.

CHAPTER 6

Meristan sat tall in the saddle, stretching his back and pulling back his shoulders. Rasa gave him a sympathetic smile and did similarly. They had been mercifully untroubled so far, passing the time in pleasant conversation. Rasa had been interested in the Order, and Meristan had found hearing of life at the university to be fascinating. It might be in Samily's interest to spend some time there. Her devotion to God was unimpeachable; her martial skill impeccable. She was, however, a little naïve about the world. She'd studied at Baile Airneach, of course, but perhaps she would benefit from spending time with her fellow *draoidhs*, learning how best to use and control her ability. And maybe she could do with socialising outwith the Order's confines. The girl had a pure heart, but she was sometimes awkward in conversation.

Meristan felt some guilt at having kept her from them. Had he been selfish, keeping her power to himself? He'd believed her a healer, a miracle from God. But had he pursued it further, looked deeper, might he have discovered the truth?

"Wait." Rasa raised a hand and pulled up her horse. Meristan intuitively did the same, scanning the overgrown road ahead, the trees at their sides. It was not yet dark, so they should be safe from Thakhati. What had Rasa seen?

He turned to ask but stopped when he saw the finger raised across her lips. She nodded toward the trees.

Meristan listened. A light breeze shushed through the leaves, insect life buzzed and hummed, birds fluttered and sang to the sky. But there was something else. Something low and rustling. Something moving. Something big.

Meristan reached for his axe, but again, Rasa stopped him. She gestured, palm down. But still, silence. With a raised hand telling him to stay, she handed Meristan her reins, and her clothes collapsed on the saddle.

A small bird—a sparrow, Meristan thought—emerged from the heap, danced into the treeline and was gone.

Suddenly he felt terribly exposed. If something happened now—if a predator came for him—he was in trouble. He hadn't realised just how reassuring it had been travelling with a *draoidh* at his side. Without her, he felt naked and vulnerable. Meristan grasped both sets of reins in his left hand and the hilt of his axe in the other. He looked up the road ahead. It was cold, quiet and desolate, stretching on into the grey-green distance. No sanctuary there, nor behind them. The silence was a hole, sucking the air out of the world. But still, that rustling. Coming closer.

Come on, Meristan!

He would not be ruled by fear. He would not.

Clear your mind, trust in God and stand your ground.

A deep breath and courage found him. He gripped the axe hilt firmly. Whatever came, he would be...

"Ride!"

Rasa reappeared beside him and slapped Meristan's horse. It kicked into action, dragging Rasa's mount with them. "What is it?" he called back. First one, then more stumbled from the trees. A dozen. At least.

Oh God, no.

Blackened.

S'grace, this far north? They couldn't hope to subdue that many without being turned—or killing them. A sturdy man was the first to see Rasa. He turned and lurched toward her.

Meristan pulled up on the horses, slowing them. He couldn't leave her alone. She was running toward him. Why wasn't she changing?

"Trust me! Go!" the metamorph cried. "I'll catch you!"

Meristan was caught between reason and instinct. Everything in him said he could not abandon her here. That it would be an act of unforgivable cowardice. But she was a *draoidh.* And a powerful one. Though what if she was sacrificing herself to save him? He couldn't allow that.

Reason prevailed. He had to respect Rasa—and that meant trusting her. If she had a plan that required him to run, he would run. And pray to God to keep her safe.

With a half-hearted wave, he kicked his horse into life and they rode for Lestalric.

Heavens, how long had it been? An hour? More? Too long. Should he turn back for her? What if something had gone wrong? What if she'd stumbled or been caught unaware, and now she was wandering aimlessly in the woods, a victim of the accursed plague? Meristan slowed the horses. He needed time to think. If she had been turned, what could he do? Perhaps, if he could find her alone, he could subdue her the way Morienne had described. Carefully. Cover her eyes and bind her wrists. Don't let her touch his skin. Load her over her horse and... then what? Go back to Traverlyn? There was nobody left there to lift the curse. With Conifax gone and Aranok...

When Aranok came back, he could...

Hells, at least she'd be safe! Balaban would find a way. Another way. But if he got himself Blackened again...

Damn it all!

He couldn't risk it. If they were both Blackened, the message they carried to King Janaeus would never arrive, and nobody at Traverlyn would know. The kingdom could be lost by the time anyone realised they had gone missing.

He had to go on. He hated it, but he had to. Rasa would...

A bird of prey screamed overhead. It dipped, hovered above the vacant horse and transformed into the *draoidh.*

"Oh, thank God!" Meristan's heart raced with relief.

"Slow them!" she called, and Meristan obliged, reining in the animals.

He looked back anxiously. "What happened? What did you do?"

The horses stopped and Rasa dropped to the ground. "I had to stop them following us to Lestalric. So I led them back into the trees once you were out of sight." Rasa pulled her dress back over her head and for the first time it occurred to Meristan she'd been in even more peril than he'd considered, with no clothing to protect her from the Blackened's touch. Another pang of guilt spiked at his gut. But she was safe. She was here.

"How did you escape?"

Rasa pulled a pair of boots from her pack—presumably her previous pair were somewhere back on the road. They hadn't had time to pick them up. The fact she'd brought an extra pair suggested this was a problem she'd had before. "I turned into a mouse once I had them all far enough into the trees, then into a falcon when I had the room to break cover. Once they lost sight of me, they calmed. I left them milling in the woods. For now, the best place for them."

"Miraculous," Meristan whispered, feeling a huge smile spread across his cheeks.

"Pardon?" the *draoidh* asked, lacing a boot.

"I was just saying, brilliant. An excellent strategy. I was right to have faith."

Rasa smiled up at him. "God's plan?"

"Oh, no. I meant I was right to have faith in you, Rasa."

The metamorph finished dressing and pulled herself back up into the saddle, replacing her cloak last. She turned and smiled. "We should still hurry. There may be more Blackened in the trees. We need to get off the road as soon as we can."

Meristan looked ahead. Even in the gathering dusk, the way forward was lighter. They couldn't be far from Lestalric.

"After you."

Something fouled the evening air. The stench of death, perhaps. Or horse flatulence.

Meristan raised his scarf over his nose.

"Is that it?" Rasa asked.

Meristan followed where she pointed. Gates in the distance. The sky was almost fully dark. They would be safe, thank God. They could sleep at Lestalric and cross the Nor Loch in daylight, assuming the baroness was happy to offer them charity for the night. The delay in reaching Haven would be slight, and the urgent message Principal Keft had for the baroness would be delivered.

"I assume so. I haven't been here, but this is where Master Rotan said we'd find it."

"Good." Rasa looked around, a hint of apprehension in her voice. "I will be happy to get off this horse. And I suspect she will be happy to be rid of me too." She reached down and stroked the horse's neck affectionately. The animal cocked its head against her touch and snorted appreciatively. How much more affinity must Rasa have with animals, having taken their form herself? She would know where they ached in a way all but a handful of humans never could. It must give her a completely different perspective on all life, he thought. Having been a deer, how did she feel about killing and eating one? How did she feel about hunting for sport, as the lairds did in Curidell Woods? He might ask at a more opportune moment.

They pulled up at the gates and dismounted. Meristan rocked back and forth on his feet as returning blood stabbed its tiny needles. His hips complained as he rotated them. It had been two long days and difficult final hours.

The gates were surprisingly unkempt for a high house, and there was no obvious way to garner attention. He grabbed one of the gate's bars and felt rust crack beneath his glove. A slight rattle sprinkled flakes of decayed iron.

"How do we get in?" Meristan appraised the gate. It was at least ten feet high. He had no desire to climb it but an urgent need to be on the other side.

A bell clanged to his right. Rasa held a mouldering rope through the bars. "Like this, I hope."

The sound had jolted him, but his first thought was whether it might attract other attention. Unwanted attention. The Blackened might not come for sound, as Morienne had assured him, but was it dark enough for Thakhati yet? Maybe. S'grace, was anywhere in Eidyn truly safe anymore?

"Oh!" Rasa startled when a young man appeared at the gate. He was ragged and thin—a scarecrow given life. Dull eyes stared disconcertingly through the bars.

Meristan recovered his poise and remembered his purpose. "Good evening. Is the baroness at home? Brother Meristan of the Order of the White Thorns. I bring her a message."

The boy gave no acknowledgement, merely turned and hobbled for the house.

"He surprised me!" Rasa whispered, hand against her chest.

"Indeed." The stench Meristan had noticed earlier was stronger. There was a stable to the left of the courtyard. Perhaps it needed clearing out. A mild breeze was rising and falling from different directions, making it difficult to determine where the source lay.

After a while, a woman in a long purple dress crossed the courtyard. Her light brown hair was tied up and she wore a particularly serious look. Almost irritated. There was something familiar about her, though they'd never met, as far as he remembered.

"Can I help you?" she asked firmly.

Meristan was taken aback. "Uh, sorry, m'lady, did your boy not say?"

"Somal is mute," she answered flatly.

"Ah, well, I am Brother Meristan of the Order of the White Thorns. I bear you a message from the university."

"Oh, yes?" The baroness looked him up and down suspiciously, then gave Rasa the same inspection. "You don't look like a monk. And she doesn't look like a Thorn."

Indeed, in the leathers and riding cloak, he did not look himself. "Excuse me being out of my usual robes, Lady. The roads are somewhat hazardous at the moment, and I have found it expedient to travel in more protective clothing. This is Lady Rasa, lately of the university. She is accompanying me."

"The university?" She gave Rasa another look, this time more detailed. "Student or master?"

"Graduate, my lady," Rasa answered. "But I hope to become a master."

"Is that so?" The baroness gave an odd smile. Rasa nodded, slightly hesitant. The lady was less than warm in her welcome. Perhaps she would thaw with time.

"So you have something for me?" she asked.

Meristan reached into his pocket. "We hoped that we might impose on your charity for a pair of beds for the night, if we may?"

"Did you?" Baroness de Lestalric answered dryly. Meristan proffered the letter as evidence of his sincerity. She surely wouldn't leave them out there, would she? He daren't look at Rasa; his worry must be writ large on his face. Perhaps they'd have been better going straight to the ferry after all, and damn Keft's "urgent message." The baroness looked between them several times before speaking. "It is the custom to offer charity to members of the Order." It was somehow neither a statement nor a question.

"It is." Meristan tried his best to give her a genuine smile.

"And I suppose that can extend to their travelling companions. Especially a future master of the university." Her tone was slightly prickly—almost patronising. Just on the edge, where, if challenged, she could wave it off as nonsense. Meristan was not warming to the baroness any more than she apparently had to them. Rasa simply smiled and looked down respectfully.

"Somal!" The boy appeared again from the shadows. Heavens, he moved like the night itself. Meristan hadn't even realised he was there. He looked eagerly at his mistress. "Open the gates and stable the horses."

Somal nodded, shambled over and unlocked the gates. They creaked open, complaining like old men. The boy passed them as if they weren't there, taking the horses' reins.

"Follow me." The baroness turned back toward the house. "We'll arrange rooms and some food."

"Oh, no need to trouble your staff on our account," said Meristan, starting after her. "We travel with provisions."

"Nonsense!" She waved a hand as if swatting an insect. "I will not have it said that you received less than impeccable hospitality at Lestalric!"

She swept into the house without a backwards look. Rasa raised her eyebrows. He returned the gesture and shrugged. They had nowhere else to go. They were only staying here for the night—it wasn't a particularly godly thought, but he had no desire to spend any more time in the company of Baroness de Lestalric than absolutely necessary. Rasa seemed to echo his thoughts, her mouth curling into a resigned frown. But what was the alternative?

The old house loomed before them, only a handful of windows showing any sign of light and life; the rest shadows, lit only in reflection of the courtyard's flickering torches. Hairs rose on Meristan's neck as they stepped through the weather-beaten old oak doorway. It wasn't much warmer inside than out.

And there was still that awful smell.

CHAPTER 7

Meristan lifted a cleaver from the chopping block, its edge caked with gristle. The kitchen was deathly silent, lit only by the moonlight that cut through the glass strips in the door that led out the side of the building. A vast counter for food preparation dominated the room, and a huge dark green oven was set into an arch in the far wall. The room was oddly dilapidated, like the gates. A cupboard door hung ajar, a loose hinge preventing it from marrying with its cabinet. Under the lingering odour of the evening's meal, a hint of mould.

There was something wrong with this house. Something unsettling and dank. The servants were mournful and joyless. They spoke little more than the mute boy and one woman had a tremor down her left arm. When Meristan had noticed it at dinner, she'd shied away.

When at last he'd settled in bed, Meristan had been glad that the next he would see of this place was the back of it.

But a noise had raised him in the pitch black. A scream. And Rasa's room had been empty.

He hadn't known where to begin looking, but he had known he needed a weapon. Vastin's axe should be with the horses, but the servants' stairs had led him to the kitchen first.

Meristan tested the weight of the cleaver, gripping it firmly. If he was to surrender here to some malice, it would not be meekly. Perhaps it was the leathers, or the knowledge of what he'd somehow done in Barrock, but Meristan was overcome with an unfamiliar calm. He would not cower. He would not run.

The kitchen door creaked open onto a path. Crickets scratched a welcome and an owl called from the sky. And that stink again; thick, like smoke, catching the back of his throat. In the near distance, moonlight lit the trees overhanging the estate wall.

Thakhati.

It was trees where the others had found their cocoons. Meristan was suddenly very aware of being outside, alone, at night.

No time for dillydallying.

He strode up the side of the house and through a small, ornate iron gate embedded in the garden wall. Torches threw shadows dancing across the main courtyard.

He crossed quickly to the stables, glancing back at the house. The building had three floors facing this side and not a light in any window. That gave him no more clue as to where to begin searching for Rasa. The bolt on the half door of the decaying stable opened easily and Meristan slipped inside. He quickly located their horses halfway along the left. Were there more? It didn't matter. In a nook to the right of his horse's stall, behind a bench, Meristan found his pack and saddle unceremoniously dumped on the floor.

He put his hand on the bench and leaned over to lift the pack. Underneath it, embedded in straw, was the axe.

Something moved to his right. Meristan ducked away instinctively but was relieved to find only the stable boy gazing back at him.

"Somal, you scared me." Meristan put up a defensive hand and made a show of breathing out heavily.

The stable hand did not respond. In fact, he barely moved. And, actually, what was he doing out there in the middle of the night?

The boy was on him before Meristan realised he'd moved. The right side of his head exploded in pain as he stumbled to the ground under the surprising weight. Was he...biting Meristan's ear? He punched at the boy's head once, twice. The third time he came away, but Meristan felt a chunk of his own flesh tear off. Warm blood streamed down his neck.

Meristan brought himself to his knees and looked up. Somal stared at him hungrily, chewing like a vacant cow, Meristan's blood dripping from his chin.

"What in Heaven, boy?" Meristan bellowed. He raised his right hand—there was little left of his ear but gristle, and his hearing on that side was hollow and wet.

Somal lunged. Meristan swung the cleaver up, catching the boy across the chest. He staggered back, giving Meristan time to stand and get his bearings. He had to focus on the boy, not the screaming pain in his ear. Horses whinnied and snorted.

Meristan braced himself with the cleaver, unwilling to turn his back on the boy in order to retrieve the axe. Somal came at him again, and again Meristan swiped, this time catching him solidly in the right shoulder. The boy grunted but kept coming. Surprised, Meristan leaned sideways and the boy stumbled over his hip, twisting to land on his back.

"What are you doing?" Meristan looked down at the cleaver. There was no blood, only thick black ooze along the edge. The boy scrambled to get back to his feet. Neither wound bled.

It took Meristan a moment to accept the truth of it.

Somal was Dead.

"Dear God." He kicked the boy hard in the face, knocking him back to the floor. That gave him a moment to reach the axe. By the time he did, Somal was on his feet again, bloody mouth open in a silent roar.

Meristan battered him back with the end of the axe, giving him the space to wield it properly. When Somal came again, he brought the axe down, splitting the boy's skull down to his wet red mouth. He dropped like a sack of offal.

Meristan bent double. What in Heaven was happening? He'd never seen the Dead this close before, but he was certain they weren't supposed to look so... alive! Though now that he saw the thick black ooze leaking from the boy's head, that illusion was shattered.

Blood ran through his beard and dripped from his chin. Meristan needed to dress his wound. But first he needed to see if there was more danger. Sticking his head out of the stable door, he confirmed there was nobody else in the courtyard. But he hadn't seen Somal coming. Had the boy been in the stable the whole time?

He returned to his pack and dug through it, looking for something he could use to stem the blood. His spare vest was clean, at least. Using the cleaver as a knife, he quickly carved strips of cloth, bundled some up and secured them to his ear. He would have to ignore the searing, pulsing pain.

He used what was left of his vest to mop up the blood that had gathered in his beard, then shoved it into his belt. He would need it again if the dressing didn't hold.

Meristan slipped the cleaver's handle through a loop on his belt. He lifted the axe and took a moment to centre himself.

Clear your mind, trust in God and stand your ground.

Rasa was in trouble. This wasn't how this had been supposed to go. She was his protection, not the other way round. But she needed him. And whatever cowardice lay in his soul, he would not let her die for lack of trying to save her.

Heart pounding, Meristan crossed the courtyard and walked back into Lestalric.

The house drowned in silence as he moved through it back to the kitchen. To his right, shelves and an opening into what was likely a pantry. Between the shelves and the stairs that led back to his room—a door. He'd walked right past it earlier, but something had called him back here. A nagging, lingering notion that he'd missed something.

And there it was: a flicker of light beneath the door. The house might be dark, but a fire burned somewhere. The door opened with a groan. A burp of dank air revealed worn stone steps descending into flickering half-light.

Fumbling in the shadows, Meristan lit an oil lamp he found in the pantry. Storing the axe on his back, he wielded the light like a shield and drew the cleaver from his belt. The axe was a better weapon, but the cleaver easier to wield one-handed, and if he was going to have to fight, he'd need to see what he was facing.

The cellar was one long stone arch with recesses dotted along each side. Stone reflected flame in wet mirrors, the air thick with the musky tang of mould. To the right, silent gloom, but to the left, the source of the light. Forty yards away, a warm glow from a doorway. Someone was down there.

Meristan steeled himself and walked toward the light. Beyond the reek of damp and decay, something unfamiliar and unpleasant. Something growing stronger.

As he passed a darkened archway, a metallic click drew him up sharply. The lamp cast enough light to see some way into the space, but the back remained in shadow. Meristan glanced nervously to his right—no movement from the end of the tunnel. He moved slowly toward the room, lamp in one hand, cleaver raised defensively in the other.

As the lamplight pushed farther into the gloom, the back wall became apparent. It was an odd shape. Partially collapsed? He reached the arch and stopped, peering into the dark. What was that? It was sort of bulbous. Like…

Oh God.

Like a cocoon.

The shriek came from above him.

Meristan dropped the cleaver to grab the limb that came at him, ducked away and pulled the monster with him, throwing it to the floor. Abandoning the lamp on the cobbles, he drew the axe from his back and stood.

A six-limbed insectoid thing with metallic skin rose before him. Eyes glinted orange against the lamplight, teeth chattering aggressively.

Thakhati.

Heaven, he hoped there was only one.

What did Allandria say?

Slatted armour.

Cut up.

His reaction had made the thing wary. It swayed and bobbed, looking for an opportunity to strike.

Meristan glanced back toward the stairs. He couldn't outrun this thing. As soon as he turned his back it would be on him. His only chance was to face it. Like he'd done with the demon, for Nirea. Rasa was here somewhere. He would not lose her.

Was the monster intelligent enough to see his size as a threat? Fear gripped Meristan's throat, but he held the axe wide, puffed out his chest and punched his fist against it, grunting a challenge.

It banged two upper fists against its chest and gave a guttural growl in return. Not intimidated, then.

The Thakhati crept toward him, cautious this time. It swiped an arm and Meristan parried. Another swipe, another parry.

Whatever element of surprise he might have had was gone. Anyone in that lit room must have heard this. Must know he was here.

The Thakhati lunged again, shrieking like flint on steel. Again, Meristan ducked and brought the axe up in a sweeping move over his own head, catching the thing's stomach and forcing it on, over him.

He could do this. He could do this.

But now he was exactly where he didn't want to be—with his back to the light. The Thakhati stood again. It looked angry. Was that a wound on its stomach? Had he hurt it?

It lunged again—this time low. Meristan swept the axe down and stumbled sideways as a clawed hand caught his foot. He landed hard on his side, shoulder taking the bulk of the blow, axe clattering from his grasp.

The Thakhati came again, and Meristan was gone, rolling back to his knees, then to his feet. But the monster was between him and the axe now.

But just to his right, the cleaver. Meristan lunged to retrieve it. A few steps back and there was the lamp too.

Did he remember Thakhati didn't like fire? Was that right? Or just sunlight?

The beast lunged again.

Meristan danced sideways and smashed the lamp over its head. The reservoir shattered, and burning oil cascaded over the monster.

A vision from Hell—a monstrous frame with a flaming head. Two upper hands batted at the fire, but the oil just transferred, and they burned too.

But it made no sound.

The fire may not harm it, but perhaps that was its armour. Meaning it had to keep its mouth closed.

And its eyes.

Meristan feinted as if to attack.

The beast made no reaction, still wiping at its head, trying to throw off the flaming oil. It would burn out soon. If he was going to take advantage, it had to be now.

Meristan dashed past the monster to grab the axe, praying he was right. If the thing could see, he'd just invited a killing blow.

Nothing came. The flames were low now, not as angry. He had moments.

Meristan got as close as he dared to the beast, choked his hands up the haft of the axe and swung it up. An agonised shriek as the blade wedged between two slats, finding the soft muscle of the thing's abdomen.

But opening its mouth was a mistake. The fire found its way inside, and now the Thakhati was in trouble. It dropped to its knees, shaking its head violently and choking with agony. Meristan freed the axe, paused to gauge his moment and swung with all his strength. The beast's mouth split to its ears.

A squealing gurgle of panic and pain as the monster fell to its back. The fire was catching the soft flesh now—it was only a matter of time. Still, he couldn't wait. The axe's edge curled with flame as Meristan lifted it high and finished the job, splitting skull from jaw.

His blood up, Meristan scanned his surrounds for any other threat. He looked toward the glow—now to his right. A silhouette there, at the end of the tunnel. A woman's figure.

"Rasa?" he gasped hopefully, only now realising how hard he was breathing, and feeling the ache in his shoulder.

"Interesting," the woman replied. "Join me, Brother Meristan."

Baroness de Lestalric turned and swept back through the lit doorway.

Meristan stared directly into the face of Hell.

The old man—what was left of him—was strapped to a board. At his left shoulder and both hips, stumps were blackened and singed. Rope had rubbed the skin raw on his remaining wrist, across his chest and around his neck. Thick black stains spattered the wood. But the room reeked not of death or mould or any other rot that pervaded this hideous underworld but with the faintly sweet aroma of roast meat.

The thing that broke Meristan, though, was the shallow rise and fall of the man's chest. He lived.

A young blonde girl casually observed him from a decorative armchair that seemed ludicrously out of place. The arch here was larger than the others and went farther back, creating a room that belonged upstairs. The front of the arch was filled with newer stone, in which sat the door he'd come through. A roast over the small fireplace sparked fat onto a hearth rug bookended by chairs. Against the far wall was a small bed—the girl's, he assumed. If not for the naked, half-murdered old man hanging from a bloody board, it would resemble a modest family home.

Baroness de Lestalric stood rigidly beside the fireplace as if she'd ushered him into a drawing room. Meristan stumbled over himself, grasping for a place to begin.

"In the name of God, what is this?"

The old man's head bobbed at his voice, drowsy eyes searching the room. His mouth opened with a dry smack, giving an unintelligible moan. Meristan placed a gentle, trembling hand on the man's cheek. His eyes were wide black moons in sickly yellow skies. Likely too addled with poppy milk to know what was happening. Hopefully. The mouth opened again, and Meristan saw why he couldn't make words.

His tongue had been cut out.

Meristan turned, axe raised, blood all but boiling. "What is happening?"

The baroness did not turn to face him. "Brother Meristan, we both know you're not going to hurt me until you know where your companion is. In fact, as a man of God, are you even allowed to make an unprovoked attack?"

"Unprovoked?" Meristan pointed to the wretch. "*That* is provocation."

Still, she was right about Rasa, so Meristan chose mercy, using the cleaver to cut first the rope over the man's wrist, then the ones around his neck and chest. With a pained groan, the man collapsed into Meristan's arms. He was so small. So fragile. Meristan was afraid to break him. Carefully, he carried what was left to the bed and gently propped his head on the pillow.

"Shh, my friend. You're safe now," he whispered. When Meristan turned, neither woman nor girl had moved, except to watch him.

"Who are you?" Meristan was barely restraining his anger. He badly wanted to punish this woman, however ungodly that might be.

Whatever this man might have done was not worth this unholy torture. And she was clearly holding Rasa, which made her an enemy. S'grace, what had they unwittingly fallen into?

"Who are *you*?" Her tone was light. Mischievous. As if they played a game. "Are you a brother of the Order? Or are you a warrior?" She nodded to his axe.

"I am a man of God who will not tolerate God's children being abused," he spat through gritted teeth.

"But that doesn't answer my question." She moved casually past the child, absentmindedly stroking her golden hair. The girl stared blankly at Meristan.

"I am a brother of the Order." Meristan was calming, retaking control of his passion. He needed to think clearly. He needed to know where Rasa was.

Damn it!

The baroness must be a *draoidh*. She had a Thakhati. That meant something. Could she control them? Perhaps she created them? They were near to Lochen. Allandria remembered Thakhati from her childhood—was this why? What *draoidh* skill would give her such control? Were they demons after all? But that didn't explain the Dead stable boy. No, she must be a necromancer. It was all that made sense.

"The boy. Your stable boy. He was Dead."

"He was a good boy. Kind." A cold edge crept into Lestalric's voice. "Fell from his horse. Never recovered."

"You're a necromancer."

She smiled down at the girl and looked back to him. "Do you know how necromancy works, Brother?"

She was playing a game, but what was it? Stalling, perhaps, for more monsters coming?

"Where is Rasa?"

The baroness continued as if he hadn't spoken. "We bond with the Risen. It allows us to command them. From a distance, we can summon them to us. But those we form close bonds with, we can feel. They become part of us."

"Where is Rasa?" He scanned the room for any sign, any clue as to where she might be.

"I felt Somal die." The baroness looked Meristan in the eye with a hatred he'd rarely seen. He mirrored it. For what she'd done to this poor man; for what she may have done to others.

"He was already dead. Where. Is. Rasa?"

Lestalric cocked her head, listening, and smiled. "It doesn't matter."

What was she hearing? Footsteps? Slow, scraping, but yes, footsteps.

She'd summoned Dead. He was trapped.

Meristan stepped toward her and raised his axe. "I assume if I kill you they go too." A searing pain in his thigh sent him reeling backwards. He looked down to see the handle of a blade jutting from a bloody tear in his trousers. Pain darted up into his abdomen.

The girl. The little girl. She leered up at him, hungry. The baroness smiled. "You're not going to do that."

Meristan grabbed for the girl, but she moved too fast, ducking his hand and escaping to hide behind the woman's skirts. The lurch threw him off balance, though. His legs caught the edge of the bed and he tumbled backwards. The pain in his leg radiated out. Heaven, no, was this how it ended? In a cellar, alone? Perhaps it was appropriate.

A solitary death fit for a coward. Maybe this was exactly what he deserved. The old man looked to have passed out again, bless him. Probably for the best.

Wait. Was that what awaited him?

Hanging from that board?

Never.

No.

Meristan pulled the spare cloth from his belt. With a grunt, he jerked the blade free and clamped rags over the wound. A wave of dizziness threatened to overtake him and he leaned back against the wall until his eyesight cleared. He looked up at the woman, daring her to interfere, but both she and the girl simply watched him, like an oddity they'd come across on a stroll in the woods. They weren't worried about him. They didn't fear him. Another strip, tied tight around the wound, holding the others in place. Using the axe as a crutch, he pulled himself back up. If he was going to die, he would do it on his feet.

The baroness, for the first time, looked a little uneasy. Good. He lurched forward and swung for her. Dancing sideways, she moved out of range of his blade. She gestured and the girl moved back behind her, still watching him blankly.

He had to get to her before the Dead arrived. Meristan shoved the chair over and hobbled toward them.

A muffled cry in the distance. *Rasa?*

Ah, Hells. If he killed the woman, would he be able to find her?

"Meristan!" Not Rasa's voice. Male.

Was he hearing things? His mind was playing with him.

"Meristan! Are you down there?"

Thank God.

Oh, thank God.

"Aranok, I'm here!"

The noise turned to battle. Bodies clattered and fell. The baroness was worried now.

"Seems we both have reinforcements," Meristan said, grinning.

The first corpse flew past the doorway and shattered against stone.

"To me!" the baroness shrieked. "Protect me!"

The shuffling of feet intensified; the sounds of battle drew closer. He needed to help. But his head felt light, as if it might float away from his body. He looked down, trying to control the spinning. The wound. Damn it all, blood trailed down his leg. The bandages weren't enough.

"Meristan!"

"Here! At the fire!"

The baroness looked around agitatedly, a trapped rat searching for a drain. She grasped the girl protectively and backed to the wall.

Meristan stepped forward and loomed over the woman, now huddled in the corner. "Stay." The hatred in her eyes remained, but there was fear now too.

Meristan stumbled to the nearest chair and all but fell into it. That helped. That was better. His head cleared a little.

A bang behind him. Meristan turned to see the envoy—thank God!—slam the door shut behind him and drop the bar across it. Aranok's mouth fell open when he scanned the room. After a brief moment, he turned to the baroness.

"What have you done?"

CHAPTER 8

Aranok's lungs heaved, sucking in air. He'd hoped, maybe, for some respite. A chance to catch his breath and free Meristan. He'd expected—what? A dungeon, maybe? Some sort of cell? Not this. Not... what in Hells was he looking at?

Shayella stared defiantly back at him from the corner of the room, her hand protectively across a young girl. Aranok's heart tripped at the sight of the woman. The grief for an old friend; the sting of betrayal; the rage at a murderer. Meristan sat slumped before a fireplace, his head and leg wrapped in bloody bandages. To Aranok's right, a blood-streaked board, hung with ropes. And in the corner, the remains of an old man propped in a child's bed.

Where to even begin?

He didn't have time to think about it. Samily was alone, upstairs. She was incredible, but even she couldn't last forever against that army of Dead.

"Shay. Release them."

She raised her chin and set her jaw. "Or what?"

"Teine." Aranok's fist rolled with flame.

A flicker from Shayella. Fear? Or something else? She pulled the girl behind her.

"No, Aranok." Meristan grabbed his arm weakly. "She has Rasa."

Aranok scanned the room, his eyes landing back on Shayella. A cruel smile curled her lips. He hadn't been about to kill her anyway. Because if he was right, if she'd cursed the Blackened, it was possible that killing her would end it. And if he did that right now, a lot of people would suffer and die. Including Vastin. He just needed her not to know that. But she knew there was another reason he wasn't likely to kill her.

Fuck!

He didn't have time to question her. Aranok marched across to the necromancer and grabbed her by the wrist. "Come here."

"Careful of the girl, she's the one that stabbed me." Meristan's words trembled from pale lips. He needed to stop the bleeding. The girl? She looked entirely sedate. There wasn't a flicker of emotion in her face, barely recognition in her eyes. In fact...

Bloody Hell.

"Shay, is she Dead?"

"Don't touch her!" the woman shrieked, clawing at his face. Aranok stepped back to dodge her lunge and the two almost fell back together. He grabbed her other wrist and held both above her head, pulling their faces awkwardly close.

The girl came at him, hands like claws and mouth wide. Aranok kicked her back against the wall. Her head made a sickening crunch and she slid to a seat, but she was almost back up again before Aranok had time to speak. "Stop her, or I will." The fear returned to her eyes. The girl was her weakness.

"Kiana, stop," she spat, her eyes never leaving his own. The girl paused like a candle snuffed out, melting back into calm repose. They stayed there a moment, faces inches apart, a tempest in Aranok's chest.

He needed to move.

He pulled Shayella to the board and bound her hands there. The girl submitted meekly when he did the same to her.

First things first. Meristan was moon pale.

"This is going to hurt," said Aranok. "But it will stop the bleeding."

Meristan nodded and closed his eyes. Aranok pulled the bandages from his leg and yanked the fabric of his trousers apart where the knife had penetrated them.

"Teine." A quick, controlled burst of flame seared the flesh, cauterising the wound.

Meristan growled like a wounded animal, his body jerking in pain.

When Aranok looked up, the big man's eyes were shut, his head slumped against the chair. All right, if he was unconscious anyway, Aranok might as well see to his head wound. He unwrapped the bloody rags and gasped at the stump of gristle left of the man's ear. What the Hell had done this to him? A glance at Shayella told him nothing. Another burst of flame stopped that bleeding too.

But now he had another problem. He needed Meristan. He needed the Great Bear. Aranok pulled the yellow memory charm from his chest, again glancing at Shayella.

"Hmmph." She raised an eyebrow. Nothing more.

"Clìor." No reaction from Meristan. He was out cold. At least he'd wake with his memories.

Now what? Could he leave the man here to go back for Samily? How was he going to get back through the Dead outside? *Gaoth*, again, was his best option, but he was running low on the energy Keft had given them. And it was becoming hard to concentrate. Everything felt a little...sharp.

No. He could do this. Now they'd found Meristan, they could come back here. Regroup. Had he definitely tied Shayella and the girl tight enough? Yes, yes. It was fine. She wasn't going anywhere.

All right. Time to face the Dead. Again.

S'grace, they just did not stop coming.

Samily danced back as an axe carved a lazy arc before her. The Green blade took the corpse's arm off and she kicked it back down the steps. But still they came. Another and another and another. As each one went down, another clambered over it, reaching, crawling, scraping.

Aranok's theory that Shayella the necromancer was likely Baroness de Lestalric had been all but confirmed when they arrived to find a swarm of Dead in the courtyard. The smell had found them a quarter mile up the road.

Fighting their way into the house had been challenging, but she and the envoy had made short work of it. When Aranok suggested they separate to find their friends quickly, Samily had reservations. Tactically, it made sense to stay together. But time was against them. They had no idea what danger Meristan and Rasa might be in, and despite Principal Keft's efforts, a long day's hard ride had been draining. If they were to be victorious, it had to be quick, sharp and elegant, before their strength failed.

She'd fought her way through the first floor without finding anyone. The steps to the second floor doubled back on themselves, opening onto a wide landing painted with moonlight through large windows.

"Meristan! Rasa! Are you up here?"

Nothing.

Still the Dead came.

She could not keep up this rearguard action forever.

Her blade took the head off one, scythed another at the waist. That gave her a moment. These Dead were already withered. Slower than the living, if relentless. She ran across the landing, giving herself space to think. An ornate grandfather clock ticked impassively beside her, its rhythmic knocking vastly outpaced by her heart.

"Meristan! Rasa!"

Still nothing but the scraping of feet and the clank of iron.

Heavens, where could they be?

A fleeting, awful thought that they were already too late stabbed at Samily. She flicked it away, refusing to countenance the idea. She would scrape every inch of this house first.

Right, which way?

Another beheaded.

To her left, a doorway leading into some kind of antechamber.

She kicked at one, its spine cracking resonantly as it folded in half.

To the right, a long hallway, doors on each side.

Left gave her a chance to put a door between her and the Dead.

"Samily!"

The envoy!

"Here! Top floor!" She had to bellow to be heard over the clattering murmur.

A gust of wind followed by a shattering of metal. "Cellars! Come to me!"

S'grace, either he had found them or he was in trouble. They shouldn't have separated. She was going to have to wade her way back through the tide of Dead like a salmon fighting upstream. And her arms were beginning to tire. Passion would carry her so far, but...

She feinted left, as if to run for the door, ducked below the swing of a broadsword and darted right. As she stepped away, her Green blade removed another head.

A swarm of Dead yet flowed up the stairs. How was she to get through this quickly?

Wait.

Time. She needed more time.

And that was something she could claim.

"Air adhart."

Samily stood at the bottom of the stairs, a trail of Dead in her wake. The envoy stood before her, mouth agape. It must have been interesting to see her manipulate time like that in close quarters without being affected. She'd planned it carefully, keeping the scope of the spell to the stairs. It was a slight risk, of course. If she'd made a mistake fighting her way down...But Samily was not careless. She did not often make mistakes.

What did hit, though, like a wave washing over her, was a bone-deep fatigue. Why had that use of her power hit so hard? Because it had taken her forward instead of back?

The envoy had cleared many of the Dead from the foyer, blocking doors with sideboards and bookcases. A statue of some long-dead Lestalric lay across the front doors, holding them shut against the horde outside. One corpse shambled from her right.

Instinctively, she threw out her arm, her blade clattering against its helm, knocking the thing on its back. She stepped across and snapped its neck with her boot.

Now, a moment to breathe.

"That was risky." Aranok's hand on her shoulder. "I'm not surprised you're shattered. You not only spent the energy on the spell, you also used the energy it took to fight your way back down here. You have to be careful, Samily—you could have ended up completely sparked out."

Ah, of course. Going backwards, she only expended energy on the spell. S'grace, that was a risk, then. She'd be careful of using *air adhart* on herself in future. "The cellars?"

The envoy nodded. "I found Meristan. We'll have to fight our way back to him. You up to it?"

Samily grinned. He'd found Meristan.

Hell itself wouldn't stand between them.

Hells, they were in trouble.

Aranok threw another brief burst of wind, knocking the Dead back. That was going to be the last. He couldn't afford any more energy. Crouching, he pried a rusty sword from skeletal fingers. Samily was at his back, the knight still scything through cadavers like wheat, but her breath also came in bursts. Sheer determination was all that kept them up. But worse—Aranok's *solas* ball lit the swarm of corpses battering the door into the room where Meristan lay unconscious, shadows and light flickering across bones and metal, arms flailing, weapons crunching into old wood.

That door was about to give.

"Samily!" Aranok pointed ahead. The knight glanced back over her shoulder. Wide eyes told him she understood.

Aranok picked his way through the detritus of limbs, torsos, helmets—some with heads still inside. It was like crossing the fields of Hell.

He was no swordsman, but the Dead were sluggish. He only needed to move faster than them. A swing from his right—blocked. Aranok stepped sideways. Something wet took his foot and he fell.

Instinctively, he tucked his shoulder and rolled, dropping the weapon. Bones crunched beneath his weight.

Up.

Up.

He had to get up!

A weight thumped onto him. And another. Another. Putrid hands clawed at his armour, searching for a gap, for skin to rend. Something sharp carved his cheek. Damn it all, he'd been here before! Did he have the energy left to use his armour again?

With a scream, the weight lessened. And again.

"Envoy!" Samily yanked him to his feet with enough momentum that he shoulder barged a pair of Dead from her back.

Crack.

Crunch.

They turned toward the sound.

The door had given.

Bodies poured through the open doorway. They'd never reach it in time.

Samily screamed and charged, battering bodies out of her way.

What else could he do?

"Gluais." If they were going to die down here, no point conserving what little he had left. Aranok threw corpse after shambling corpse to the side, trying to clear Samily a path, but the numbers were too great—there was nowhere left to throw them, except against one another, packed tight against the end wall and scrambling over themselves to reach her. A blade bounced off his back. Another caught his leg and his bad knee burned in response.

They weren't going to make it. After all they'd done to get here, all they'd achieved was to get themselves killed too.

A roar from ahead.

Too deep for Samily.

A demon, or some other beast down here too?

No.

He knew that cry.

Suddenly Dead were flying from the doorway like rag dolls.

Thank God.

Meristan.

But he wouldn't be able to keep that up. He'd lost too much blood.

"Samily! Heal him!" Aranok stumbled across the uneven ground, pushing the Dead away. They needed to regroup, to fight together. Did he have enough for another burst of *gaoth*?

Fuck it. He had to risk it.

"Gaoth."

The Dead flew back, shattering bones and crunching armour against the cavern ceiling. Now he had a straight line to the Thorns, but his head was spinning. Had Samily got to him?

Aranok reached out a hand to the slimy stone wall. Hells, just a minute of reprieve, just a chance to catch his breath. That was all he needed.

"Aranok!" Meristan's voice. "Cover!"

He didn't need to be told—he could barely stand. Aranok slumped down into a crouch and ducked inside one of the arches as bodies scattered beside him.

Bones crunching; meat carving; metal cracking.

Almost rhythmic, the beats.

Finally, the rain of gristle and gore stopped and a hand reached for his.

"Come, Envoy. It's time to go." Meristan grinned down at him. "There will be more. There are always more."

Aranok took the hand and let the White Thorn pull him upright. Meristan's ear had returned.

Aranok staggered along, watching as Samily dispatched the last of the Dead wave. But Meristan was right. More would be coming. Aranok imagined he could already hear them shuffling down the stairs.

When they were back inside the room, Samily used her skill to repair the door, replacing the bar. Aranok slumped into the chair he'd left Meristan in, and Samily leaned on the one opposite. She pulled off her helm to reveal florid cheeks and slick hair.

They wouldn't have made it without Meristan.

Aranok looked up to his friend and smiled.

"Welcome back."

Meristan put his hands on his head. His mind swam with memories—too many memories! But he was himself again. Heaven, it felt like breaking the surface of water he'd drowned in. But he didn't have time to reflect.

Aranok had dark circles under his eyes and his skin seemed to hang on his face. Samily wasn't much better, but her eyes smiled back at him. It was like seeing her after a long absence—but it hadn't been her who was gone, it was him. Still, they both looked shattered.

They may have been able to fight their way in here, but would they be able to fight their way out again?

"Where's Rasa?" Aranok asked.

"I don't know. She wouldn't tell me." He would make her tell him now. Meristan turned to the necromancer. "Where is she?"

"The metamorph? Gone."

Meristan held her gaze for a moment, then looked down at the Dead girl. "Fine. I'll take her head off."

Shayella stared at him defiantly. She didn't believe him. Meristan raised his axe.

"Stop! Don't!"

Now she did.

"Well?" he asked again.

"In a cocoon." She gave an indignant smile.

Samily gasped. "No."

"Where?" Aranok barked.

Meristan knew where. He'd seen it. He'd just assumed it was where the one he fought had... *Oh Heaven*. What if the Thakhati he'd fought...? Panic rose in him and his heart raced.

"Aranok. I... I fought one of those things. I fought... Could it be...? Could it have been?"

"When did you last see her?" his friend asked.

"Before bed. This evening. Last night."

Aranok grasped his arm. "It takes at least a day for them to change. That wasn't her. Wait, you fought one? Alone? Before...?"

"Aye." He'd fought with instinct. Physical memory. Only now could he see. Janaeus had not been able to take that from him.

"Heavens, what is this?" Samily had discovered the old man.

Aranok crossed to the bed. "He's alive?"

"He is." Meristan nodded to the blood-streaked board. "They had him on that. They've been torturing him."

"No. Not torture." Aranok stormed back to the woman and slapped her. "I knew you'd lost your mind, Shay, but what the fuck is wrong with you?" Rage seemed to overtake him as he punched her full in the face. Her head snapped back with the crunch of her nose breaking. She spat her own blood at the envoy.

"Why does she look so healthy?" He pointed to the girl. "Why?"

Meristan looked at the girl. What did she have to do with the poor soul on the bed?

Aranok moved to the girl and raised his fist. "Why?"

"Fresh meat!" Shayella shrieked. "Fresh meat keeps them whole. Leave her alone!"

Oh no.

It was even worse than Meristan had feared. She'd been feeding people to the girl. And Somal, presumably. Samily gasped as she too realised the meaning of the baroness's words. She took the old man's hand and knelt beside the bed. "Do not worry. It will be all right."

Scraping at the door. The Dead were back. And they needed to get out. They had to get to Rasa.

"If we kill her, the Dead will be at peace, yes?" Meristan asked.

"Yes," said Aranok. "But we can't do that yet."

"Why not?"

Aranok turned to Shayella. "Because you cursed the Blackened, didn't you?"

The necromancer smiled, blood dribbling from her burst lip.

"And if we kill her, maybe the Blackening ends too. And all those wretched people being kept alive by the curse will die a hideous, painful death. Alone." He looked up at Meristan. "Including Vastin."

Of course. If the boy's curse was lifted now, he'd die before his wound could heal. "But you said maybe?"

Aranok nodded. "Depends how the *mollachd* works. And she's not going to tell me, are you?"

Shayella licked at her bloody lip. That was the answer.

Fine. They needed the curse to stay. For now. Until they could arrange help for all the *damainte*.

Aranok stepped closer to the woman. "But she can release the Dead."

"No." Shayella raised her head defiantly.

"Then I'll kill the girl."

"Then you'll have no leverage, Ari. And what will make me behave, then?" Shayella's eyes glittered with what Meristan might have called glee. It was shallow, though. Forced.

"All right." Aranok walked away. "We're going to have to fight our way out of here again. Samily?"

"I will be fine, Envoy. I just need a moment." She hadn't taken her eyes off the old man.

"Me too." Aranok breathed deeply from his vial of oil. Another thing Meristan had forgotten before.

It was good to be himself again.

CHAPTER 9

Aranok buzzed with the hit of oil. His thoughts scattered, his mind doing too much and nothing. Keft had warned them. They needed to get to Rasa. When Allandria had been cocooned, he'd reached her quickly and she was already in distress. How long had Rasa been in the cocoon? How long could she survive? Her metamorph skill might help, but…

Something caught the edge of Aranok's attention. Shayella. Her lips moving—subtly, just a hiss of air escaping. The Dead girl watched her intently.

Damn it!

He stepped over and slapped the necromancer again. "No more! Keep your tongue still." As Aranok understood it, she needed gestures to raise the Dead, but once risen, she only needed incantations to control them. Perhaps they should gag her.

"Can she still command them? From in here?" Meristan asked.

Aranok looked to the door. Had the scraping intensified? "Yes."

"We need her alive, but silent?" Samily asked.

"We do." Aranok closed his eyes a moment as his head became too heavy. When he opened them, Samily stood before Shayella with a knife in her hand. She forced the necromancer's mouth open and rammed the blade inside.

"Samily!" Meristan cried.

Shayella screamed. Samily pulled something wet from her mouth and tossed it into the fire. She put down the knife and, still holding Shay's face, forced her fingers back inside.

"Air adhart."

Shayella stopped screaming to spit a mouthful of blood and saliva at the knight.

"Samily, what did you do?" Meristan asked quietly.

"She is alive, but silent," Samily replied.

Aranok had seen the Thorn behead Reivers as if chopping firewood, and yet this was more brutal.

"Samily, that was..." Meristan appeared to have no idea how to finish the sentence.

"After what she's done?" Samily looked to the old man, unconscious on the bed; to the meat roasting in the hearth. Aranok had been avoiding looking too closely at it for fear of seeing just exactly how much it resembled an arm. He fought down the bile that rose in the back of his throat.

Meristan put a hand on her arm. "I understand your anger, Samily, but in battling monsters, you must guard against becoming one. It is easy to let your anger take you, and I feel your anger, believe me. This cruelty is unforgivable. But we must not become cruel."

"She is silenced. Her pain was brief, and she would be dead if we did not need her alive," Samily said plainly. "She can't put us in more danger, nor anyone else. This was the most efficient way to save lives, not an act of anger or revenge, though she is deserving of both. Just not from me."

Meristan looked at her thoughtfully for some time before speaking.

"All right. All right. If that's all it was."

"God will deal with her soul. And I will happily send her on her way as soon as we are able. Shall I end the girl?" Samily lifted her blade. Shayella made a hideous, shrieking noise, straining at her ropes like a feral animal.

Aranok put up a hand. "Not yet." Shayella had been right about that. The girl was likely to be their only way of leveraging information. Not that he was going to trust her anyway. She'd always been devious, but whatever damage had tipped her over the edge had done a thorough job. There was painfully little left of the girl he'd once been infatuated with. Something had broken her. Anhel he'd always half suspected was capable of what he'd done. His anger, his self-righteous arrogance, were always bubbling under the surface. But Shay—for all her passion, she'd wanted a quiet life. A family.

He looked at the girl. The little blonde Dead girl who meant so much to her. Was that enough? Had losing a child been what tipped her into the abyss? The pain must be unbearable. Even Emelina...No, he couldn't think it.

Maybe it would be enough.

Even then—to curse the Blackened, raise an army of Dead and go to war against Eidyn, when Mynygogg had already taken the country from Hofnag and was making things better for *draoidhs*...for everyone...There was no excusing that. Still, a cold stone of pity lay at his core. For the girl he'd cared about. For the woman his best friend had loved. For all her horrors, she'd been important to him once.

The rabid, ragged thing tied to the board barely resembled her. The Shayella he knew was gone, and that was where he mourned.

Focus on the task at hand. "Meristan, you know where the cocoon is?"

"I know where *a* cocoon is."

"All right. If we have your back"—Aranok nodded to Samily—"do you think you can fight your way to her?"

A smile spread under the Great Bear's beard. "Oh, aye." He lifted Vastin's axe. "I've become quite fond of this thing, you know. Bit of a lucky charm. I'll be sad to give it back."

"You'll need a Green blade..." Samily's tone was insistent but unsure.

"Of course. And I'll be happy to see this back in its owner's hands." Meristan turned to Aranok. "Right, how are we doing this?"

A brief explanation later, Aranok stood with his hands against the stone wall. He'd never tried what he was about to do, but it should theoretically work. And it would give Meristan the space he needed.

"Ready?" he asked.

"Ready," both Thorns replied.

Aranok closed his eyes and focused on the wall. On the line where it met the original arch.

"Sgàineadh."

The stone groaned as a thick crack worked its way from the top of the arch down each side.

"Gluais." Aranok pushed with everything he had against the wall. Slowly, it began to shift. Stones crumbled away from the join as it creaked and strained until, finally, just when Aranok thought he might not make it, it tipped into the tunnel with a shattering crunch.

Limbs and armour jutted from the rubble, oozing with thick black blood. The knights stepped into the breach. Meristan was everything Aranok remembered. All Samily's precision, grace and efficiency, with his power. They moved as if linked by one mind—Meristan forging ahead and Samily protecting his flank anytime he turned.

The Dead fell away like melting butter. None of them even came close to landing a blow—they were simply too slow, too ponderous. Meristan swung the axe as if it were a toy, always knowing exactly where Samily was. He swung, she ducked and stabbed; she attacked, he defended. A violent dance to a silent choir.

A one-armed corpse lurched toward Aranok. He stepped over the rubble and lifted a broken sword. One clean swing took the head off as it staggered across the debris.

Back in the room, Shayella stared vacantly into the fire. She wasn't going anywhere. He turned and followed the Thorns along the tunnel, scrambling over the detritus in their wake. They were getting too far from the flames. Thankfully *solas* was a low-energy spell. He cast it and pushed the ball of light behind them, keeping himself a good five yards back—out of reach of those blades.

"Here!" Meristan called. "In there!"

The Thorns moved past the arch Meristan indicated, clearing the Dead from Aranok's path. He ducked into the space. There, at the back, was the cocoon. He stood with the sword limp.

What if this was the wrong cocoon? What if this wasn't Rasa? Hells, what if it was and she was already turned?

Fuck.

Aranok shook off the doubts like insects. He couldn't wait. If it was a Thakhati, he'd move quickly. His heart raced as he pressed the blade against the cocoon wall.

It didn't give at all.

He adjusted his stance to get better leverage, using his own weight. Still nothing. With a cautious hand, he pressed against the surface.

It was hard as rock. Shit, was that normal? Allandria's had cut easily enough, but then she'd only been inside for such a short time.

"Samily!" he called. "I need your blade!"

Samily appeared in the arch. "What?"

Aranok tossed his sword at her feet. "I can't cut it!"

Samily looked down and back to her left. A moment's hesitation, and she tossed her Green blade at him handle first. He fumbled the catch and it clattered to the stone floor. By the time he looked up, Samily was gone.

The blade was lighter, almost singing as it cut the air. Aranok brought it up to the cocoon and pressed again. This time, the edge dug in, but it was tough. He had to take care. Too deep and he risked cutting Rasa. Cautiously, he sawed at it, stopping when the resistance suddenly gave. Rank ooze leaked from the cut. He steadied his feet and sawed down the edge, like slicing old bread. Halfway along, the pressure gave and a stinking, slick body spilled out. Aranok only just dropped the blade in time to catch the head.

It was hard to see in the half light, but it looked like Rasa. Not right, though. Her skin was almost transparent. Was she breathing? He shook her gently. "Rasa? Rasa?"

She coughed up more of the stinking gunk that leaked from her nostrils. Aranok wiped it away, trying to get her eyes clean. He needed to get her out of there. He tossed Samily's blade back out of the archway, then got his hands under Rasa. Her skin was smooth and slippery. Aranok groaned as he stood, lifting her and stumbling back out into the tunnel.

"Here! I've got her!"

The Thorns were far along the tunnel. He could barely see them. They must be all but back to the stairs.

"Samily! Meristan!"

The sound of footsteps running toward him. Samily appeared in the glow of the orb.

"That's her?"

"Yes!" he answered over the crash of battle. "She's not all right! Your sword!" He nodded to the floor.

The knight scooped up her blade and dropped the other. "There are few left. Take her to the room!"

Aranok gestured at the globe to send it after Samily and stumbled his way back to the light. His ankle went over something—a rock or a body, it was hard to say—but he kept his balance, just. Once he was closer to the room, the firelight illuminated the ground, making it easier for him to pick his way through the mess on the floor. Carefully, he stepped over the rubble, bodies and scattered weapons. When he finally reached the chamber, Aranok sighed and looked up. Everything was as they'd left it.

Everything except the pair of empty ropes dangling from the bloody board.

Meristan scanned the ground for any remaining signs of life. It felt strange that part of him had enjoyed it. Fighting alongside Samily, of course, but the fight itself. He felt whole again. He felt like himself. It was good. A weight had lifted from his soul.

"Samily! Please!" Aranok's cry was almost frantic. Samily quickened her pace and Meristan moved to keep up.

She darted to one of the chairs. It took Meristan a moment to take in what he was seeing. It was humanoid, but its skin was an odd, shiny grey, and its features were smoothed, like a river-worn stone. But it was…changing. As Meristan watched, the head twisted and turned, shifted and pulsed first into a bear, then a dog, then a woman.

"What's happening?" he spluttered.

"I think it's her skill fighting the cocoon," said Aranok. "Samily, can you fix her?"

The girl shook off her gloves.

Aranok turned to Meristan, hands trembling. "Shayella—she's gone." He pointed to the corner, where several lines of bricks had been pulled open to reveal a hidden passage. Meristan glanced at the empty ropes. All that remained was the child's thumb leaking black ooze. S'grace, she must have bitten it off to escape her ropes. They should have thought of that.

"If she gets to Janaeus…" Aranok didn't need to finish. Meristan ran. The others had been exhausted before they cleared the Dead. It had to be him.

The passageway was small and cramped. And dark. Damn, he could have done with one of Aranok's glowing orbs. The axe was only getting in his way. He abandoned it against the wall, lest he trip and land on it in the dark. Hardly a fitting ending for a Thorn—split by his own axe. He shouldn't need a weapon to handle the woman. She couldn't summon help. And the girl was tiny, alive or Dead.

He carried on into the darkness, keeping his right hand on the stone wall. The ground was uneven and slippery. He doubted anyone had been down here in years. What had the old Lestalrics been up to? A tunnel into their cellar—smuggling, perhaps? Thievery of some sort? Perhaps consorting with criminals had led to the family's demise.

The passage opened up ahead of him. Meristan stopped and reached forward, exploring the space with his hands. A wall, dividing the path. Two choices—left or right. Which way had they gone? Everything may depend on this. His patchy memories were still firming in his mind, but he knew who the enemy was. If Shayella escaped and warned Janaeus…

Meristan stopped, closed his eyes and held his breath. He focused on his other senses. A gossamer breeze sighed across his hand. At least one of these paths led outside. He listened closely. Nothing but the sound of his own heart.

Then a breath: short, urgent, distant.

Left.

He hurried down the tunnel, which was definitely wider, and the walls felt less like stone—dirt, or clay. He sucked in a breath and retracted his hand as it hit something solid. Wood. A wooden pillar. Above him, a wooden beam across the ceiling. Was the floor sloping downwards?

The ground rumbled and the walls shook.

With a great bang, a cloud of dust burst toward him.

Meristan grabbed at the wooden pillars, hoping sheer force of will would keep them intact—keep the tunnel from collapsing in on him. He closed his eyes again and prayed. Prayed to see the light again. To see Samily and Baile Airneach. To get a chance to be himself again. It would be so cruel, so unfair to be restored only to be crushed here under the earth.

The trembling stopped and the dust settled. It took Meristan a moment to release his grip of the pillars, trusting that they weren't going to snap. Slowly, he drew his hands back.

God was with him.

An odd mewling from ahead. He'd heard it before. A wounded animal caught in trap. Shayella was alive.

Did he dare to follow? What if the tunnel collapsed again? What if he caused it to collapse?

No. Whatever she'd done, he couldn't leave a person down here to die alone in the dark. Besides, this was the only way to be sure she didn't escape. And they needed to be sure.

Meristan steeled himself and walked slowly, carefully, each step a chess move. The walls were still getting wider, but the air was thicker. The farther he went, the harder it was to breathe. He pulled his vest up to cover his nose and mouth. The cave began to lighten. Ahead, the source. A flame. A torch? Where had she gotten a torch?

"Shayella?" he called. The mewling became more frantic, more urgent. Meristan hastened toward the light.

Shayella wasn't trapped. She knelt on the ground, frantically pulling at her daughter's arms. All he could see of the girl was her head and shoulders. The rest of her was buried under the pile of rubble that ended the tunnel. The torch lay burning on the ground.

Shayella turned to look at him.

"Eeeeeeee," she howled. "Eeeeeeee!"

Was she saying "please"? Her eyes begged him to understand. To help. She turned back and began heaving at the girl again. Heaven, what could he possibly do for her? She was already dead and her body was trapped under a pile of dirt and rocks. But Shayella was a grieving mother. A mother who was not ready to let her daughter go. She was not going to leave her here. And Meristan needed her to come with him.

He stepped closer and crouched down to match the woman's height. "Shayella?"

She turned back to him. Tears carved sharp lines down her filthy face. He should hate this woman. She'd murdered thousands—tens of thousands. But all he saw in that moment was a mother trying to save her child.

God, give me grace.

"Shayella, listen. If I pull her out of there, it's going to tear her apart." She wailed as if he'd stuck a knife in her. "But listen. Listen." She quietened and fixed him with wide, red eyes. "Because of... what you've done." He decided against saying *Dead*. "She'll survive. We can take her back. You know what Samily did to you?"

Shayella lifted a hand defensively to her mouth.

"She may be able to restore your daughter's body. Do you understand?"

Her eyes widened further, and she nodded anxiously.

"All right. So if I get her out, will you come with me? Peacefully? You have my word, Samily will do what she can for her."

Shayella looked nervously down at the still girl and back to Meristan. She nodded.

"All right. Take the torch and stand back."

Shayella pulled herself slowly to her feet, lifted the torch and walked a few feet up the tunnel, giving Meristan the space he needed.

This was a huge risk. Pulling the girl out could cause another cave-in, and then they'd all be dead down here. He would be with God, and that would be fine. Though he would prefer more time. If this was to be his end, so be it. But if Shayella died now, they risked the Blackening ending. Many people would suffer.

Meristan crouched in front of the girl. If he yanked on her arms, there was every chance he'd just pull them out of their sockets. He needed a better grip. Reaching underneath her, he slid his hands down to her armpits.

The girl's head snapped to the side and Meristan jerked as teeth pressed against his leather vambrace.

"For Heaven's sake, girl, I'm trying to help you."

Placing his feet carefully and offering a quick prayer for success, he pulled. At first, nothing. It was like pulling on a chain fastened to stone. He tensed every muscle, pushing from the soles of his feet, up his legs and into his back, drawing the girl toward him. She moved. Just barely. Just an inch. The ground trembled ever so slightly, and small rocks poured down the side of the pile.

Hell.

He released his grip and sat back. This might not be possible. Could he get Shayella back without the girl? Could he even keep her alive without the girl? He'd heard of bereaved parents so overcome with grief they took their own lives. She was easily unstable enough.

"I don't know if I can do this without collapsing the tunnel, Shayella."

No answer. He turned to look back at the woman. She stood silently, staring at her daughter's dead body buried under a tonne of earth. Meristan was suddenly struck by the irony. This was where she belonged, in a way.

With a resigned sigh, Shayella reached into a pocket of her dress, fished something out and held it toward him. The torch flame danced on the blade of an elegant dagger. With the pair of them covered in filth, it shone like a beacon. The golden handle was studded with six emeralds and the blade curved like a crescent moon. Even in the circumstance, Meristan was taken for a moment by the beauty of it.

Had she planned to stab him in the back with it? Had she been waiting for him to pull out her daughter only to slit his throat?

Maybe.

Whatever she'd planned, she was giving him an answer. He just wasn't sure which one.

"You want me to . . . give her peace?"

She shook her head violently, anger flaring in her eyes.

"You want me to cut her free."

Shayella's lips pressed together firmly.

All right.

He could do that.

He could cut a Dead girl in half.

Meristan took the knife and moved next to the child. He placed his left hand between her shoulder blades and rested the curve of the blade against her side.

She wouldn't feel a thing.

She was already dead.

God give me strength.

Pulling the little dress taut, he sawed an opening. The knife tore through the fabric with a resonant rip that echoed off the rocks. Once he'd cut it all the way across her back, he lifted the fabric toward her head. The more he saw, the more he knew the girl's body was pulp beneath the earth and rocks. He'd never have pulled her out—only apart.

Meristan fought back the rising nausea.

Just like a rabbit, or a deer.

The blade slid carefully between two ribs as he sawed his way across, breathing slowly and deeply. Shayella whimpered to his left.

The knife clicked against bone. He'd reached her spine. This was the worst. This, he'd dreaded the most. He rested the curved edge in the slight hollow between two bones and leaned his weight on it. The tissue between the bones resisted and he sawed through. The sound—God, the sound—gristle tearing like a chicken leg ripped off. He leaned heavily, using all his weight to break through, until the knife finally loosened with a wet pop. A breath, a moment to compose himself, and he continued.

By the time he finished cutting, Shayella was sobbing uncontrollably, the torch visibly shaking.

"Turn around." He could spare her having to see this. But she shook her head, gesturing for him to give her the girl.

Maternal instinct.

Meristan put his hands under the girl's arms and pulled again. This time she came free with a wet slurp of organs hitting the ground. He lifted what remained of her torso, holding her face away from him.

So she could see her mother, he told himself.

Dark ooze dribbled as he placed the girl in her mother's arms, swapping her for the torch. Mother cradled her half daughter to her chest, wrapping the little arms around her neck, whispering quiet promises into filthy blonde hair.

It was the worst thing Meristan had ever seen.

He looked back at the cave-in and was reminded how perilous their position was.

"Come on." Taking a deep breath, he squeezed past the two into the dark passageway ahead, which led back to the light, and his friends, and sanity.

CHAPTER 10

Samily knelt before the chair, hands on Rasa's grey knees. Her skin was cold and slimy, like seaweed, and she stank like an infected wound. Her head jerked back and forth against the back of the chair, morphing every now and again into a new face. It looked nothing like a miracle.

"If she gets to Janaeus..." she heard Aranok say. Meristan tore from the room. A flutter of fear in her chest. He was whole again. He was Meristan. He would be fine. Rasa needed her. Aranok appeared over the back of the chair.

"Can you do it?"

"I will try. It depends"—she faltered, not wanting to speak her fear aloud and make it real—"if this is still her. If she's still there."

The envoy's face was almost as grey as Rasa's. In honesty, Samily was assuming it was Rasa. Physically, the figure looked nothing like her. But it had to be—the shifting and changing—it had to be.

Samily closed her eyes, focusing on where her palms touched her friend's juddering legs. After all her questions about how Rasa's power worked. About whether she was still a woman when she was a bear or a bird, here she was praying that whatever it was that was truly Rasa, her spark, her soul, was still here.

She pictured Rasa as she saw her: elegant, strong, majestic.

"Air ais."

Screaming.

Samily opened her eyes. The woman thrashed against the chair as her bones crunched against one another, pulled against tendons and sinews, forcing themselves into position. Her skin swelled and reddened. Samily gripped her legs tighter, trying to hold them in place while her power worked through Rasa. Aranok grasped the metamorph's shoulders. The woman shuddered and jerked, but her skin faded to a healthier colour.

And like that, she was still.

Samily was afraid to move. To breathe.

Had it worked? Was she alive? Her legs felt warmer, maybe. More human. Samily grasped them firmly to control her own trembling.

"Did it work?" Aranok asked.

"Is she breathing?"

The envoy jerked into life and placed a hand in front of Rasa's mouth. Samily fell back to sit on the rug. She may not have the energy to stand again. "Is she?"

"I don't know!" Aranok snapped. "I can't tell. Maybe?"

Samily raised a shaky hand to her throat. "Feel her neck. Here. For a heartbeat."

Please, God, let her have a heartbeat.

Aranok placed his fingers on Rasa's throat delicately, as if she were glass and might break under his touch. In the silence, the fire crackled. There was something familiar about it. Reassuring. A promise of comfort.

Aranok was still for a long, long time. Finally, he lifted his head, his bloodshot eyes rimmed with tears. "She's alive."

Samily dropped her head, every last ounce of energy gone from her like a wave.

Rasa was alive. Now that she knew, she could see her friend's chest rise and fall, ever so gently.

She was alive.

"Samily?" Aranok's voice was small. "Is it her?"

S'grace, that was a fair question. The fact she was alive didn't mean she was all right. They believed the cocoons were a combination of Shayella's and Anhel Weyr's powers—necromancy and demon summoning. Was it possible she'd only healed a demon?

"I hope so."

"Should I try to wake her?" Aranok weakly held out the vial of oil he carried everywhere.

"No. Let her rest." It would be best for Rasa. Of course it would. It would also delay an answer to their question. And Samily wasn't sure that was a bad thing.

"We should cover her." Aranok cast about the room for something. "Can you see anything we can use?"

Only then did it occur to Samily that Rasa was naked. But of all people, she'd never known anyone so comfortable with their natural state. Still, Aranok was right. This felt oddly like an intrusion while she slept, and they should find some way to preserve her privacy. They'd left their riding cloaks with the horses.

"I can't...I can't find anything," Aranok spluttered. "Can you see anything?"

Samily scanned the room. Repulsion came rushing back to her as she took in the board the old man had been nailed to, stained dark with his blood. What was left of him lay on the bare mattress against the wall and...in that moment, she realised what had happened.

S'grace, no.

Samily forced herself to her feet. She lifted the poker and battered the spit over the fire. Again, again, until it collapsed and the length of blackened meat dropped amidst the peat. Samily recoiled from the smell.

Damn that woman for her sins.

"Samily?" Aranok's hand on her shoulder. She spun to face him, angry tears on her face.

"Did you see?" she asked, her voice breaking. "Did you see what...?"

He nodded silently. Samily shook almost uncontrollably, her legs threatening to buckle beneath her. Aranok opened his arms and she stepped into them, welcoming the comfort.

"I couldn't find anything," he said after a while.

"No, there is nothing," Samily agreed, releasing him. "Just the rug."

Aranok looked down at it. "It's filthy." He looked as spent as she felt. Dark black bags hung like weights under his eyes.

"I know. It's no good," she said. "Let's turn her toward the fire. That will keep her warm, at least. She will need bathing." Samily shook the sheen of light green slime from her palms.

"No, we can't leave her like this." Aranok loosened the straps of his leathers. "Will you help me?"

Samily released a few straps and helped him remove the top half of his armour. Once the leathers were off, he lifted his dirty white shirt over his head and handed it to Samily. "Would you?"

Samily carefully slipped it over Rasa's head. Getting her arms into the sleeves was awkward, but she managed. Once that was done, it was easy to pull the rest down. Aranok's height meant the length was enough to cover her. When she was finished, Samily looked up to see that the envoy had all but replaced his leathers with his back turned.

"I'm finished. She's covered."

Aranok turned, and relief lit on his face. Rasa looked almost peaceful, as if she'd simply fallen asleep in front of the fire in her nightdress.

Footsteps.

Meristan emerged from the dark corner carrying a torch he had not left with. At first, she thought him alone and feared the worst, but Shayella stepped out after him, carrying the girl. Samily found her hand on the hilt of her sword.

There was something odd, though. The girl looked wrong.

"Samily." Meristan stepped forward, and as he revealed the two, she saw what was wrong. Where the girl's legs should have been, the woman's velvet dress was thick with gore. Samily gasped in spite of herself.

The girl was Dead. She was already gone. Samily had seen terrible things. But something about this made it more awful.

"Samily, we need your help," said Meristan.

"What happened?" Aranok lifted the ropes from the floor.

Shayella flinched from him, shielding the girl.

"It's all right." Meristan raised his hands. "She's not going to run. We have an agreement. Right?" He turned to look pointedly at Shayella. She nodded timidly.

Aranok moved toward her. "Forgive me, but—"

"No, Aranok," Meristan interrupted him firmly. "I gave her my word and she gave me hers."

"Meristan, you don't know her. What she's done..." said the envoy.

He was right. This woman should not be trusted. She was evil, and that was not something Samily took lightly.

"She could have killed me," said Meristan. "In the tunnel. She chose not to. So I could help her daughter. If you don't trust her, trust me."

Aranok stopped hesitantly.

"She still can't speak," Meristan argued. Why was he defending her? Samily did trust him, though. Whatever had happened in that tunnel, if it had given him reason to believe her... maybe.

"All right. What happens now?" Aranok asked, an uneasy edge in his voice.

Meristan turned back to Samily. "I gave her my word that Samily would heal her daughter."

"What?"

She'd misunderstood. Surely she'd misunderstood. Heal a Dead girl? This woman's daughter? "No. I will not."

Shayella moaned, grunted at Meristan. Samily snapped her head to look at her. "No."

"Samily..." Meristan's voice was gentle, but she ignored it, storming past him to face the woman. She flinched back, turning away what was left of the girl.

"I have nothing left to give," Samily seethed. "I am spent from fighting my way through your Dead. The men and women you killed and raised to serve you. I am spent from trying to save our friend, who you tried to turn into a monster. And if I have an ounce of strength left in me, it will be for the man you cut into pieces!"

Shayella whimpered, her eyes defiant and angry.

"How is Rasa?" Meristan asked. Samily did not turn.

"We don't know yet," said Aranok. "We'll know when she wakes."

Shayella shrunk from Samily. She had the sense to be ashamed, maybe afraid. *Good.*

"I will pray for her," said Meristan.

"As will I." Samily held Shayella's eye.

"Samily. Samily, can we speak?" Meristan placed a hand on her arm. She resisted the urge to shake it off.

"About what? There is nothing to discuss."

"Please, Samily."

Nobody else. She would not even consider it for anyone else.

"All right."

Outside the arch, ankle deep in human detritus, Meristan spoke in hushed tones.

"There was a cave-in. The girl was stuck. To get her out, Shayella agreed to come quietly. And she did. There was a point, a time when she could have slit my throat while my back was turned. She didn't. She gave me the knife."

"Why?" Samily asked.

"Because saving the girl was more important to her than saving herself. There was another route out. She could have killed me and run. She stayed for the girl."

That was interesting, but it had not been what she meant.

"I mean why did she give you the knife? What for?"

Meristan's face changed. Even in the half light, she saw blood drain from him. "The girl was stuck. I couldn't move her," he faltered. "I had to..." Samily placed a finger on his mouth. He did not want to finish the sentence, and she did not need him to. Were they all to be traumatised down here in the dark? Was this a taste of Hell? To remind them of what they fought? Why would God put them through this?

"I'm sorry," she said. "I'm sorry for you."

Meristan gave a weak smile. Samily looked past him, back into the room. Aranok sat in the chair opposite Rasa, silhouetted in the firelight. Shayella rocked the girl as if she were soothing a baby.

"I have nothing left for her," Samily said. "All I have I will need for the man, and then I will need to rest. I... *we* are exhausted."

"When did you last sleep?"

"I have lost count. A master, an energy *draoidh*, aided us."

Meristan grasped her hands. "S'grace, no wonder you're both dying on your feet!"

"It's fine. I am fine. I just need to rest. After I restore the man."

Meristan sighed. "Samily, I gave her my word..."

"And you had no right!" she snapped. "In this case, for this, my gift was not yours to offer. She does not deserve it. And you should have asked me."

The man's head bowed. "No, you're right. I didn't and I'm sorry. I would say I was not thinking clearly, but I suppose that would be an excuse. I should not have promised on your behalf."

"Good. Thank you. I accept your apology." She hadn't wanted to be angry at him. It felt wrong.

"But... Samily, whatever you may think, and I understand all of it—what she's done is unforgivable. Truly. She is a grieving mother. If we control the girl, maybe we control her. Maybe we save more lives that way, with kindness instead of wrath?"

"That's not fair." She'd made the same argument herself, but in very different circumstances. Not with a murderer, a necromancer who'd slaughtered tens of thousands and cursed more. Not like this.

But he could be right.

If Shayella truly cared more about the girl than herself, then perhaps this was the way.

"What about the man?"

"I saw poppy milk." Meristan gestured inside. "We can give him enough to keep him out for the night, while you rest, and you can restore him tomorrow. He will know nothing but rest."

Was that good enough? What of his dreams? Samily supposed they would never be the same, regardless. She doubted any of them would leave this cellar as they entered it.

"All right. I will do it. My way."

Meristan nodded. Samily brushed past him, hoping she conveyed the touch of disapproval she still felt. She crossed to Shayella. The woman stopped rocking and faced her, eyes wary but hopeful. Aranok did not move, watching them quietly.

"Your deal was with him, not me." Shayella nodded tentatively. "This is my deal. I can restore your daughter's body. I cannot bring her back to life." She nodded again, chin trembling. "I can also, if I choose, return her to this state." More nodding.

"First, I am going to give you your voice, and you are going to release the Dead. All of them." She took a moment this time, but eventually conceded. "Then you will end the Thakhati." Shayella's eyes widened. She looked to Aranok, then back again, shrugged her shoulders and shook her head.

"You will," said Samily, "or I will not help you."

She looked at Aranok again, her eyes pleading. Twice she made pathetic, pleading grunts.

"She can't," said Aranok. "She's saying she can't."

Shayella turned back to her and nodded vigorously. Samily breathed while she thought. That was a shame. She would have liked them gone.

"Fine. You will come with us willingly, you will not hinder us, you will end the Blackening when we say, and you will help us to defeat Janaeus. That is my deal. If you break it, at any stage, your daughter is returned to this."

Shayella looked away. Samily followed her gaze to Meristan. He cocked his head at the woman and raised his eyebrows. This was the best he could do. She looked then to Aranok. He merely unclasped his hands and opened them, offering her the same choice.

Good.

Shayella turned back to Samily and nodded.

"And finally, you will show us where your opium is kept so that we can give this man peace through the night."

She nodded quickly this time.

"Fine. Open your mouth."

She did. Samily found the stump she'd severed only a short while ago.

"Air ais."

Shayella's eyes widened as she closed her jaw and ran her tongue around, pressing out her cheeks. "Thank you."

"Do not thank me. Fulfil our bargain."

"I need my hands." She nodded to the girl. Samily instinctively recoiled.

"I'll take her." Meristan stepped between them and lifted the girl from her arms.

"Thank you. For everything." The necromancer cleared her throat, then made arcane gestures in the air. "Risen, *saor mi thu. Till gu fois.*"

Nothing happened.

"Is that it?" Samily asked Aranok.

He shrugged. "We'll find out."

"What about the servants? Upstairs?" Meristan asked.

"They are not Risen," said Shayella.

"What are they? Charmed? Did Janaeus wipe their minds for you?" The envoy's question dripped with derision.

"No." Shayella's tone was defensive, but she quickly shrank from it. "They are *damainte*."

"Cursed?" Aranok stood. "You cursed them to be your servants? For fuck's sake, Shay, did it not occur to you just to pay them?"

Her head bowed. "They are not good people."

A laugh burst from Samily. This woman, of all people, judging the character of others was one ridiculous step too far. A flicker of anger crossed Shayella's eyes, but again she quickly dampened it. "They're not."

The way she said it was pathetic, and Samily almost believed her. She wondered what they must have done to have such a woman consider them evil. It didn't matter.

"You will release them," Samily said. Resigned, Shayella nodded.

She looked past Samily to Meristan and the girl. "Now? Please?"

"Open your mouth first," said Samily.

"What? I agreed. I did what you asked."

"So far," said Samily. "I don't trust you."

Shayella's face stiffened and she pressed her mouth closed. Samily shrugged and made to walk away.

"All right!"

Samily turned back to see the woman's mouth open wide. She slipped her fingers back inside. "*Air adhart.*"

Shayella swallowed and composed herself, raising her chin.

Samily turned to Meristan. "We move upstairs and get settled. Find beds for Rasa and the man, and then for me. Once we do that, I will restore the girl, and we will rest. Aranok, do you have the strength left to move Rasa?"

"It's fine, I'll carry her," said Meristan. "Shayella?" She nodded and stretched her arms out for the girl. The pair of them were covered in dust, grime and gristle. The woman gave Meristan an odd look as he handed the little body back to her. Did she stroke his arm as she took the girl?

"Aranok, the man, then?" Samily asked. The grim fact nobody mentioned was that he'd be lighter than Rasa. At least they'd left him the merest scrap of dignity with a shirt and underclothes.

The *draoidh* cast his spell and the man lifted off the bed, grunting gently in his sleep.

Samily hoped he dreamt of happier times.

CHAPTER 11

Meristan shaded his eyes against the sun. A mass grave. That's what was left of the gardens behind Lestalric House. That was why they stank to Heaven.

Shayella had wanted an army at hand. So she'd buried it. Likely had them bury themselves.

The open pit gaped like a wound on the land. Meristan was moved with a desire to fill it, but he had neither the time nor the energy. He'd stayed up to let the others rest. But also, there was a tiny crack in his mind warning that maybe, if he slept, he'd wake as Brother Meristan.

"How does it feel?"

He turned from the window to see Aranok in the doorway. A wave of familiarity and happiness swept through him, seeing his friend now in less urgent, less desperate circumstances. The envoy looked more human now too. Anxious, hunted eyes replaced with the familiar spark of wit. It felt like years since he'd seen it.

"What do you mean?" Meristan answered.

"Being yourself again." Aranok stepped into the room, glancing at Rasa's still sleeping form and the Dead girl tied to the chair. "It must be nice."

Nice.

Nice was woefully inadequate.

"I feel like I can breathe. Like I have been suffocating under the weight of a burden I could not comprehend, and it is lifted. I owe you everything."

He offered a hand to Aranok, and when the *draoidh* took it, he pulled him into a bear hug.

"I can never repay you for what you have done, my friend. But I will forever be grateful."

Aranok stepped back, hands on Meristan's shoulders. "I'm afraid you will repay me. Several times over. We have a lot to do, and not enough of us to do it. We're going to need you. And the Thorns."

"Regardless of how you feel, Aranok, with every bone in my body I am certain you are doing God's work. There is nowhere else I would stand."

Aranok half smiled, as Meristan had known he would. They'd drunk away many evenings sparring over God, but whatever the man believed, he was good to his core.

"Any sign of Rasa waking?" Aranok turned to her, crouched by her side and gently took her hand.

"None. She's slept like the dead. Oh..." As the words left his mouth Meristan realised what he'd said. "I'm sorry..."

Aranok raised a hand dismissively. "I know what you meant. All right, I've searched the grounds. There's a cart at the side of the building and three horses in the stable. I picked up our horses too, so we have five. You, Shayella and the girl can ride on the cart with Rasa in the back. Samily, the old man and I will ride, assuming he's fit."

Meristan nodded. Aranok was doing what he did under pressure—taking control of what he could to avoid what he couldn't. Allandria would have known what to say to him, and Meristan wondered, now he thought about it, why she wasn't there. He'd joked once that the two must have matching scars where they came apart at the hips. It had been an oddity that they'd never got together romantically. Except they had—or at least Janaeus had made them believe they had—and in secret, though they'd been terrible at concealing it. Was that why she hadn't come? He hoped not. They were going to need every asset they had to take back the kingdom, and that meant Aranok and Allandria together.

"What about the servants?"

Aranok turned to him. "Fuck, I forgot about the servants. How many?"

"I've seen three. There may be more."

Aranok stood and looked out the window for a moment. "I suppose we get Shay to release them, and maybe we can take them to Lochen, or even Traverlyn if they want."

"That seems fair." But Meristan found himself unable to shake Shayella's comment. *They're not good people.* It was ridiculous, of course, to place value on her judgement. She was insane. But she'd been earnest. What had these people done to make her think them evil?

Half of him was curious.

Half didn't want to know.

Golden morning light cascaded onto the old man's face when Samily opened the shutters. He stirred, gently, his body shifting like a lazy cat. Tongue parted lips, mouth smacking in search of moisture. His right hand came up languidly to his face, rubbing at some itch. Samily watched him fondly—he was like a baby waking from a milk-addled doze.

Then his eyes opened, and he screamed.

The man bolted upright, staring at his right hand as if it were a foreign object he'd never before seen—some monstrous thing that had become attached to his body. He stared wide-eyed at Samily, took a breath and screamed again. His hands went to his thighs, throwing off the sheet that covered them, grasping and punching at them in disbelief. Confusion. Terror.

"It's all right!" Samily grasped his cheeks gently and held his face still before her as she would a frightened horse. "It's all right. You are safe. You are healed. God sent me for you."

The poor man was broken. He looked through her, around the room as if it were some cruel taunt, a dream of a past he would never visit again.

His right hand trembled implacably before him. Samily let go of his face and took the hand instead.

"I am a White Thorn. I have the ability to..." She stumbled as she realised that what she was about to say was not actually true. But for now, for this man, it was all he needed to hear. "... to heal. I have healed you. You are whole again. All of this is real."

His bloodshot eyes focused on her at last, and the manic, lost look receded like the tide. Samily was reminded of Morienne calming the Blackened.

"I'm... This is... real?" The man's voice was cracked and raw. Samily reached for the cup of water she'd prepared. He looked at it as if he had no idea what it was.

"Drink." Samily placed his hand around the cup. He stared at it, dumbfounded.

"How?"

Had he forgotten how to drink? Was his mind so broken?

"Lift it to your mouth." She gently ushered his hand upwards, but it jerked away from her, splashing water down the old man.

"How?" He held his hand out. "How?"

Ah. She might as well explain, if it would help put ground beneath his feet.

"As well as a White Thorn, I am also a *draoidh.* I have the ability to manipulate time. I used it to heal you."

That seemed to go in. The man settled more, releasing the iron grip on his left leg. Heaven, it must have been such a shock, so confusing to find himself with limbs he'd watched removed and...

"Real?" he croaked. "It's real?"

"It is. I swear by God's grace, you are healed."

He snorted then, shuddered, collapsed forward into her arms and wept great wracking sobs into her shoulder. He shook so hard Samily feared he may injure himself—he was so frail, his grey-white beard an unkempt, patchy mess.

When he had exhausted himself and Samily worried he may pass out again, the man finally lifted his head and looked at her, perhaps seeing her for the first time.

"Can you tell me your name?" she asked gently.

A breath as he cleared his throat, then sipped what little water was left in the cup, slowly, tentatively.

Finally, he set his shoulders and met her eyes.

"Darginn Argyll. King's messenger."

"It is a pleasure to meet you, Darginn Argyll. My name is Samily."

They sat in silence for a long, serene moment, and Samily found herself reflecting in God's love as she watched this man whose life she'd been allowed to save.

"I don't know how to thank you," he said in a tiny voice.

Samily placed a hand on Darginn's leg.

"You will never have to."

CHAPTER 12

Allandria shifted on the chair. It was not designed for comfort or for sitting on all day. She'd been extremely grateful when Mynygogg had come out that morning and offered her a cushion with a sympathetic smile. Samily hadn't had the time or energy to heal either of their aches the other night, so they'd both had to suffer through. The day of rest yesterday had been exceptionally welcome, but now she was back on duty—which currently consisted of sitting outside the monarchs' door.

The hospital was busier by day. Medics regularly passed, sometimes with patients in tow, sometimes with students scribbling on paper and following their tutor like an eager flock of ducklings. Allandria always caused a little stir. Since they hadn't had time to clear people's memories before Aranok left again with the charm, only a handful of people here knew the truth, but they were key people.

Opiassa had taken guard while Allandria slept the day before, and Keft had placed a charm on the door overnight, preventing it from opening to anyone but him from the outside. Both Mynygogg and Nirea had insisted all the fuss was unnecessary, and had they not been who they were, Allandria would have agreed. Neither really needed a bodyguard, but their stations demanded it. Particularly while they couldn't be sure who else was in Janaeus's pay.

It was time for a stretch. Allandria accidentally kicked the tray

Morienne had brought her lunch on as she stood. A pair of medics down the hall lifted their eyes to see what the noise was—a large woman with short grey hair and a younger, dark-skinned man. Allandria grimaced, raising her hands in apology, and the two looked down again. She was fairly sure the topic of conversation had changed to her, though, by the hushed tones and furtive glances. Presumably her identity was not a secret, considering how much time she had spent here recently, and how many different medics she'd encountered. So her guarding a room which did not contain the king's envoy was likely a topic of much speculation, especially amongst the younger medics and students.

The door opened behind her and the two medics looked up again, this time not even concealing their curiosity.

"Lady Allandria." Principal Keft nodded respectfully. She smiled and returned the gesture. Mynygogg followed him out.

"Are we moving?" Allandria had to consciously stifle the "sire" that should have followed the question. Mynygogg smiled and shook his head. She was still getting accustomed to his shaven look. His mane of dark hair and beard were so much of his identity that Allandria almost felt she was looking at a stranger.

"We are." Mynygogg gestured to Keft. "You can stay with Nirea."

"Oh. All right." Allandria tried to stifle her disappointment as Mynygogg and Keft disappeared along the corridor. She was quite keen on a change of scenery. Watching people all morning had exhausted its novelty some time ago. At that point, anywhere else would have been welcome.

"You should take up carving."

Nirea leaned against the doorframe, smiling broadly. Allandria nodded to her deferentially. "My lady," she said quietly.

"Oh, fuck that." Nirea gently lifted Allandria's chin until their eyes met. "After what we've been through... no, you don't defer to me. Not like that. It's bad enough you have to sit out here like some kingsguard."

"All right." Allandria had no real idea how to respond. The Nirea with whom she'd spent the previous weeks was not the queen who stood before her—and yet she was.

Nirea glanced up the hallway. The medics had moved on and there was nobody now within earshot. "Listen, I'm not always good with, you know, emotions, I suppose. I've never really had family. Other than Gogg."

Allandria had no idea where this conversation was going, but it seemed much more serious than she had been expecting. "Mm-hmm."

Nirea took hold of her forearm, nodding to Allandria to do the same. "Your official role may be bodyguard, but we both know you're more than that. After everything, you and I are sisters. In fact..." Nirea paused. "I'd like to ask you to be my envoy."

Allandria was stunned into absolute silence.

"Say something." Nirea smiled.

"I... I don't know what to say."

"I've seen firsthand how your voice of reason keeps Aranok in check. And I know exactly how much diplomacy that takes, believe me. You're intelligent, eloquent and most importantly, honest. You make good decisions and you have a cool head. I trust you."

"I... I'm honoured. Thank you." Allandria smiled back at her, suddenly aware she was still holding the queen's arm. She let it drop with a suddenness that surprised her.

"Listen, it's not always easy balancing me"—Nirea gestured to herself—"with, you know..." She drew a crown in the air above her head. "Pirate diplomacy isn't always..."

"Diplomatic?" Allandria smiled.

"It's an effort. I could do with someone to talk to. With a different perspective. Someone I'm not married to." Nirea slapped her on the shoulder. "Fancy a walk?"

"God, yes," she answered, immediately wondering if it was appropriate.

Nirea laughed. "I thought you might. Come on."

Queen's envoy.

Bloody Hell.

Traverlyn hummed with life in a way that had become unfamiliar to Allandria recently. She'd spent so much time travelling in daylight and only sleeping in towns that she'd become almost used to the echo of empty streets. Seeing the bustle of people going about their lives all around them was almost unsettling, particularly when she was responsible for keeping Nirea alive. A young girl carrying a basket brushed against her leg and she had to restrain herself from reaching for a knife. Instead, she checked that her purse was still in place. They were in more danger from cutpurses than assassins.

"Relax." Nirea nudged her playfully. "Nobody knows who we are." She leaned in close. "If anything, you're more famous than me."

The queen smiled broadly. She seemed so much more relaxed, more at peace than she had in the previous weeks. She'd spoken of wanting to get back to the sea then, but now she had Mynygogg back, and herself... Of course, the jagged pink scar on her face was a reminder of what they'd lost to get here. "Can I ask you something?"

"Why did I keep the scar?" Nirea preempted her question.

"I understand you don't want to forget him, but..."

Nirea stopped walking and turned to her. "I'll never forget him. But I was going up those stairs. I was first. He stopped me. Insisted on taking the lead. Not because I was his queen, because I was his friend. That's who he was. First into danger. First into a fight. The spike that did this"—she traced the scar—"came through him to get to me. Literally through him. So instead of dead, I got this.

"This scar is a gift. Glorbad gave his life for it. And every time I look in a mirror, it'll remind me of the worthless bastards I need to kill for him."

She might be queen again, but it was the pirate whose eyes burned with revenge.

"All right. I think he'd approve." Allandria smiled. In some ways, it seemed like the old goat's feisty spirit would live on with Nirea. But then, she'd always had her own fire. Maybe that was part of what made them such good friends—they understood each other.

Nirea turned and walked again. "Of course he would. He'd call me a silly bitch, but he'd love it."

Allandria felt a wave of heat as they passed a blacksmith with its doors wide. A boy of about ten sat outside, sweating and polishing something small that Allandria couldn't make out. He smiled shyly when she caught his eye. Vastin might once have been that boy. Would he find that easy smile again? She didn't envy whoever had to tell him Glorbad had died when he woke. They'd had a connection, those two. Could have been more, maybe. And the boy had already lost his parents.

"Can I ask *you* a question?" Nirea asked as they turned a corner, skirting the edge of a small market. The smell of fresh bread floated through the hum of barter.

"Of course."

"What's going on with you and Aranok?"

Oh.

That was not a question she was expecting. And the truth was, she didn't know.

"In what way?"

Nirea shrugged. "What are you doing here?"

Allandria looked around the busy market. There was no way to avoid someone overhearing her. "You know why I'm here."

"I know why you *said* you were staying. I'm not blind. I know what Janaeus did to you, and I can see it's bothering you both."

If it were bothering them both, she'd probably be more comfortable with it. Aranok seemed entirely unfazed by the whole thing. He'd first seemed to think it was funny and now he was behaving as if she was making things awkward for no reason.

"I'm not sure that's true."

They cleared the far end of the market and entered a quieter street. Mostly homes with a few shops. A heavy man swept the doorway into his tannery. Pots clanked together on a hook outside an ironmonger. A pair of gulls screeched overhead, fighting over a scrap of food stolen from the market.

"What's not true?" the queen asked.

"I don't think he's troubled by it."

Nirea stopped again. "You honestly can't see how much he's bothered by the wedge between you? Allandria, I only saw him briefly before he left, and it was practically screaming at me."

"Really?" That wasn't what she'd seen at all. She'd seen him in a huff because she wasn't just carrying on as if nothing had happened.

"Why do you think Janaeus did this to you?"

That was a question she'd been asking herself ever since Aranok had restored her memories. What purpose did it serve him? "I don't know."

"Has it occurred to you that maybe it was exactly this?" Nirea gestured the length of Allandria's body. "You know what they say: The best way to ruin a good friendship is a great fuck."

No. It hadn't. God damn it all. The crafty little bastard was manipulating her even now. Allandria felt her fist going numb as she squeezed it tight.

Nirea grabbed her arm and pulled her on. The tanner had stopped sweeping and was pretending not to watch them instead. How much had he overheard? Once they'd passed him and turned another corner, Nirea spoke again. "Don't let him win. We need you—both of you—to take the crown back. If he splits you, it only benefits him."

"I know, but..." She didn't really know where the sentence was going, just that it wasn't as easy as that.

"Oh." Nirea's face changed. "But you really are in love with him."

Allandria's hands trembled. Was she? That was the problem, wasn't it?

The truth spilled from her like a fountain. "I don't know. I don't know what's real. I don't know what I remember and what Janaeus put in my head. I... miss being with him. But did I always feel like this? Or is it just another lie?"

Nirea let out a long, slow breath. "All right. That's more complicated." They stopped at a footbridge and Nirea pulled her to sit on the wall. The gurgle of the stream running beneath would help mask their voices.

"Mynygogg explained to me why they think Janaeus changed so much for me. Why he wiped Gogg from my mind completely instead of inserting himself in my memory, like everyone else."

Allandria remembered the conversation from Dun Eidyn. "Yes, because he couldn't make you love him."

"Exactly," Nirea said. "He could make me remember him being my husband, but he couldn't make me feel like he was. Meaning whatever he did to your memory, your feelings were real, Allandria. Your feelings *are* real."

Hell. She was right. If that was how his power worked, if that was why then...

"Shit."

"You two need to talk."

They did. Or maybe they didn't. Maybe they didn't need this distraction in the middle of a coup. Especially if Aranok didn't feel the same way. What then? God, she was running round in circles like a bloody child with a crush! For now, it needed a lid on it. Regardless of how she felt, either way, this wasn't the time. That Nirea had been right about. She wasn't going to let Janaeus manipulate them into chaos when they needed to be united.

"You're right. I'll handle it."

Nirea put a hand on hers. "If you want to talk..."

"Thank you. And for this. I appreciate it." It was odd. Like she'd released a stone buried in her chest, but now her legs were water. She'd walked through a door; it was out.

Nirea stood. "Come on. We're nearly there."

"There?" Allandria followed her. "I thought we were just walking..."

The queen grinned mischievously. "If I'd told you where we were going, I thought you might try to stop me."

"Do you know who she is?"

The freckled guard looked blankly at Allandria and back to Nirea.

"No?" He was nervous. Uncertain. Good. That's where Nirea needed him. Wondering whether he should know who she was and whether he was going to get into trouble for not knowing. He was young, maybe twenty-five at most. Probably hadn't been in the guard long. Exactly the type she was hoping would be on duty.

Traverlyn had a modest gaol hidden behind a large warehouse so as to keep it discreetly out of people's minds. The town was supposed to be a place of cultural freedom, a celebration of art and knowledge. Crime was something they liked to pretend didn't happen here.

Nirea knew fine well human nature wouldn't allow that.

"This is Lady Allandria." Nirea gave a dramatic little flourish. "You know who that is?"

Of course he did. The whole country did, even under Janaeus's spell. He nodded and looked back to Allandria, giving a respectful nod. "M'lady."

Allandria looked slightly uncomfortable, which was part of the fun.

"Then you know she carries the authority of the king's envoy in his absence."

At that, Allandria furrowed her brow and gave her a sideways look. But the guard was looking at Nirea. "Does she?"

"She does," Nirea said firmly. "So if she wishes to see the prisoner, you are going to let her see the prisoner."

"I'm not... I'm not sure that's right," the guard stuttered. "I'm sorry, m'lady." He bowed again to Allandria. She raised an eyebrow. Of course it wasn't right. But he wasn't sure, and that was enough of an opening. "I'll need to confirm that."

"Son, what's your name?" Nirea asked.

"Brontid, m'lady."

"Brontid, how long have you been in the town guard?"

He stiffened up, pushing his shoulders back. "Eight months."

Perfect.

"So long enough to understand the hierarchy of authority, yes?" Nirea brushed an imaginary piece of dirt from the chest of his blue uniform.

"Of course," he answered.

"Then since the only people with more authority than Lady Allandria are the king's envoy and the king himself, who are you going to ask for confirmation of her command? I don't see either of them, do you?"

"I, well, no, but..." Brontid looked around for someone to save him from having to make a decision he clearly did not want to make.

Nirea leaned in close. "Brontid, I can personally assure you that letting us through that door is exactly what your regent wants you to do."

There was a snort behind her as her new envoy stifled a laugh.

Brontid swallowed hard. He looked pleadingly at Allandria.

"I assure you," she said, in a suitably authoritative tone, "I will make sure to mention you by name the next time I speak to the envoy."

Very nice. Appealing to Aranok's fame might be just the final push he needed.

"All right." His face changed to something approximating confidence. "If it's what Laird Aranok wants..." He pulled a set of iron keys from his belt and unlocked the heavy door behind him. "I'll have to lock it behind you, mind. He's locked in his own cell. There's nobody else back there."

"Understood," Nirea said gravely. "We'll knock when we want out."

The door swung shut behind them and the lock clanked back into place. There were only six cells along the corridor. Rotan sat against the wall in the middle-right one. Even the way he sat irritated Nirea. As if he owned the damn cell. As if he was being tragically inconvenienced by being held there. His stupid, floppy hair reeked of unearned privilege. At least the broken arm he cradled to his chest would be painful.

"Why are we here?" Allandria whispered. Nirea put a finger to her lips.

"Ah, hello." Rotan looked up with a cheerful smile, like they'd arrived to deliver his breakfast. "You're looking remarkably well."

Shit. Of course. He'd last seen her in a wheeled chair, wrapped in bandages. She had no right to be this healthy.

"Speak when you're spoken to," Allandria barked. She clearly felt as warmly about the shitbag as Nirea did.

"That's rather unfriendly." He shifted in his seat and brushed at his shirt with his good hand. "What can I do for you ladies?"

He spoke as though they were students who'd come knocking at his office door. Nirea was all but overcome with the desire to strangle him. It was probably for the best he was locked behind a door she had no key to.

"I want to know what you know. Now."

"About what?" Rotan smiled innocently.

"Who else is working for Janaeus?"

"Well, I'd assume everyone, aren't we? He is the king after all."

He was playing games. Fine. Nirea could play games. She stepped forward and leaned her face against the bars. Allandria placed a warning hand on her arm, but she shrugged it off. She was fast enough to move away if the one-armed idiot tried anything, and she doubted his ability to harm her anyway. He looked in need of a good feeding, despite his obvious wealth.

"Has nobody told you? We had a *draoidh* clear your memory in your sleep. Just in case you were a victim. If you were, you'd have woken up screaming about it. You didn't, did you?"

Rotan's face twitched as a satisfying wave of panic danced across his eyes. "I don't know what you mean."

"Yes, you do. You know what I mean, and you know who I am, which means you know what I can do to you. Don't you?"

"No, I do not."

"Rotan, please. If we'd restored your memory while you were awake, you could just have pretended you had no idea and claimed to be another of Janaeus's victims, couldn't you?"

Again his eyes betrayed him. "Oh, was that your plan?" Nirea's tone was now that of a concerned parent speaking to a disappointed child. "We rather ruined that, didn't we? You missed your chance."

Rotan looked to Allandria as if for solace and, finding none, at the floor.

"So, your choices are limited." Nirea casually tapped her dagger against the bar. "You can throw yourself on my mercy and tell me everything you know, or you can die."

Rotan's head shot up. "I... I didn't do anything! There's no evidence. The trial will..."

"Trial," Nirea scoffed. "You think you'll make it to a trial? You murdered one of the envoy's closest friends. Do you have any *idea* how much he wants to kill you? I wouldn't even have to ask him, just look the other way."

"But... you can't..."

"I'm the fucking queen," Nirea spat between the bars. "I can do whatever I like. You know what I'd do to you if we were at sea?"

Rotan stared at her, looking suddenly very grateful for the bars between them. Raised voices caught the edge of Nirea's attention. Muffled, but close. The door at the end of the corridor swung open.

"Who the fuck are you two?"

Damn it.

Nirea turned to see a large man with a thick head of grey hair and matching moustache, wearing the same uniform as young Brontid. He looked substantially less naïve. Nirea took a breath and replaced her calm demeanour. "This is Lady Allandria—"

"And can she no fucking speak for herself?" The man cut her off. This wasn't going to be as easy as getting in, apparently.

"I can." Allandria stepped forward, placing a hand on Nirea's arm as if she were subservient. Exactly what she should be doing. Nirea demurred and lowered her head. There was a sharp "Ha!" from the cell. Nirea glowered at him sideways.

"So you're the famous Allandria, are ye?" the guard asked.

Allandria offered a hand. "I am. And you are?"

"Wondering what the fuck you're doing in my gaol." The big man crossed his arms and looked down at them. He all but filled the door, but Nirea could just make out the twitchy form of Brontid hovering behind him like a midge.

"Laird Aranok asked me to speak to the prisoner," Allandria answered calmly.

"Did he now? That's funny, since Master Opiassa expressly told me that nobody except her, Principal Keft or Laird Aranok himself were to set foot in here. Never said anything about a famous bodyguard."

Oops. Nirea probably should have asked Opiassa about coming. Again, more forethought required. It was going to take a little adjusting to a world where nobody knew she was queen.

"Our apologies for the misunderstanding. We'll take our leave and get out of your way." Allandria made to step for the door, but the guard didn't move.

"Like Hell you will. You'll stay right bloody here until I establish who you are and whether you're meant to be here. And if you're not, you're going in a cell next to your friend." With a sharp nod, he turned and slammed the door shut behind him. Again, the lock clanked shut, sealing them in the dank corridor.

"Shit. Sorry," Nirea said to Allandria. "That didn't go quite as planned."

Allandria shrugged. "It's a change of scenery, I suppose."

Nirea laughed.

"Seems like you're the only one who thinks you're the queen."

Nirea turned to face the scrawny little git, who'd dared to step near the bars. She lunged at him, making a grab for his bad arm. He shrieked and stumbled back, tripping over the corner of the bed and landing on his arse against the back wall.

"For now. We're going to fix that. And when we do, you're a very dead man, 'Master' Rotan."

He pulled himself to his feet, smoothed the manky blanket on the bed and carefully sat again. "We'll see."

"I could kill him from here if you like." Allandria made a show of reaching for an arrow.

"Whoa, whoa, hang on!" he protested.

Nirea paused a long time before raising a hand to stay her. "No. It's fine. I want him alive."

"You sure?" Allandria asked.

Nirea looked Rotan dead in the eyes. "I am. Because I know what kind of man he is. I know he's going to do the calculations and work out that his best chance of staying alive is to tell me everything I want to know. Because he's a selfish, miserable coward who has no concept of loyalty or bravery. He's never endured real hardship in his privileged life, and he's a sleekit little bastard who'll turn on his master as soon he accepts he's got no other choice. Eventually, he's going to work out that his best chance of protection from Aranok is me."

Nirea lowered herself to sit cross-legged on the floor in front of Rotan's cell.

"And we're going to sit here with him until he does."

CHAPTER 13

Clouds of flies hummed below carrion birds circling and spinning in the afternoon light. Crows took flight as the horses approached, retreating to the low branches, waiting impatiently for the party to pass before returning to their macabre feast. Those on horseback were able to slowly pick their way through the blanket of rotting human flesh, but the cart could only rattle and jolt its way over the bodies. Aranok winced as something soft and wet collapsed beneath a wheel.

"S'grace, the stench." Samily raised a hand to her face. Aranok had already raised his scarf. It wasn't helping. Shayella must have called more reinforcements at some point during their confrontation, and they had dropped where they stood when she released them—a sea of human detritus awash on the Easter Road.

Aranok was grateful he hadn't had much appetite for lunch. If they had the time, or the people, he would stop and bury or at least burn these souls. But they had neither. Even Samily had not suggested it. Perhaps when they reached Lochen he'd see about raising a team of town guards to do the job.

How had Shayella become this? She'd always been a bit flighty, a bit wild, but she'd never wanted to use her skill for harm. She'd reanimated animals. For a time she'd spoken of working for the guard, bringing back murder victims to discover their killers. Her skill gave her some access to their memories when they were freshly dead. Before the brain tissue rotted.

Anhel going bad he'd understood—even cursed himself for not seeing it coming. Anhel was angry, and in retrospect, Aranok could see how he had manipulated the rest of the Hellfire Club to do things they would have rejected. Janaeus—maybe he should have seen that too. He'd been the butt of jokes—the smallest, the weakest. He shrank even from Shayella in an argument. But he'd always been clever. A lot went on behind those pale eyes.

But Shay—he barely even recognised this bitter, vicious woman who could feed a living man to the corpse of her daughter. The loss of humanity was incomprehensible.

Perhaps now was the time to ask.

Aranok dropped Midnight back alongside the cart once they were mostly clear of the corpses. Meristan held the reins, with the girl between him and Shayella. The necromancer had one protective arm around her restored daughter, despite her hands being bound together. In the back, Rasa lay still and silent, wrapped in blankets they'd taken from Lestalric. She seemed, for all they could tell, to simply be asleep. But nothing would wake her. Either side of her, the four servants sat like sentries. In order to lift their curses, Shayella needed certain equipment, and the most likely place they'd find it was Traverlyn—so they'd just had to take them with them for now in their disturbing sedated state. Along with the three Meristan had told them about, they also found a teenage girl in a room next to Shayella's. She seemed to have been using her as some kind of chamber or dressing maid. All four sat staring blankly, watching the world from behind a window.

Behind the cart, Samily rode alongside Darginn, who, despite his age and the trauma he'd been through, looked as sturdy as any king's messenger in the saddle.

"Meristan, would you like to ride for a while?"

The Great Bear looked up with a trace of surprise. He glanced at Shayella. "You sure?"

"She's not going anywhere. I could do with a change." Aranok arched his back and grunted as it crunched. Meristan glanced back to Samily and raised a hand.

Once they had dismounted, Aranok gestured Samily over.

"How is he?" he asked quietly.

Samily looked back at Darginn, who was scanning the countryside. "He seems fine. Nervous, understandably, I suppose. Not talking much yet. Do not worry, I will look after him."

"I know you will." He also knew that she wasn't going to like what he was about to ask her to do. "Samily, would you give Shayella her voice please?"

Her eyes flashed surprise, then distrust. "Why?"

"I need to speak to her."

"I would rather not."

To most people, that would have been her final word, Aranok suspected. But she still respected rank, and whatever disagreements they'd had, he liked to think there was at least mutual respect between them. Certainly, he regretted some of his early tone toward her in retrospect. He would restrict his philosophical banter to Meristan again, now, knowing that the big man was more welcoming of the debate than Samily seemed to be. Not that she was incapable, simply that she seemed to dislike the game. Interesting that he had had similar conversations with her to those he often had with Meristan over a bottle of whisky. However, for now, he just needed her to do as he asked, and he'd prefer it if he didn't have to order her.

"I understand. But it's important. Her hands are bound."

Samily looked over his shoulder to Shayella. "I will take the girl on my horse."

That was a good idea. Shay might be uncomfortable with it, but she wasn't in a negotiating position. "Fine."

The wooden cart seat was hard and would probably be even worse on his back, he realised. But it would give his thighs a rest from the horse, and that was something. Just using different muscles would be a relief.

"Shay?"

She looked at him defiantly.

"Samily's going to restore your tongue." Blinks of surprise. "Kiana is going to ride with her." Shay's mouth circled into a scowl and she pulled the girl tighter to her chest. "As long as you behave, Samily won't harm her." Shayella pursed her lips and stared hard at him. She shook her head firmly and nodded to Meristan.

"No." Aranok was equally firm. "I'm getting your voice back. She's our guarantee you don't try to escape. Or kill me."

She sighed and her scowl softened. She pulled the girl tight and kissed the top of her head. Slowly, she raised her arm over the girl's head. Aranok grabbed her under the arms and lifted her across to Samily. He was struck by how light she was in comparison with Emelina. The two were about the same age... Well, they would be if Kiana were alive. He wondered how much her body was still decaying, despite Shayella's effort to keep her whole.

Samily took the girl dispassionately, settled her at the front of the saddle and rode alongside Shayella.

"Open." She held her fingers down. Shay slowly obliged, but there was defiance in every move—the slow tilt of her head, the firm locking of her jaw.

"Air ais."

When it was done, Samily rode to the back of the caravan.

"Ready?" Meristan called from the front.

Aranok waved him on. "Aye."

They travelled for a while in silence. For all the questions Aranok had, he wasn't sure where to begin. Was the woman he had known still there, somewhere? Could he find that connection again? His heart was suddenly pounding in his chest as he worked up to saying something.

"What do you want?" She broke the silence for him. Her voice was softer than he might have expected. Curious, maybe. It was a relief. It was a way in.

"What happened?"

"When? To whom?"

Aranok gestured at her. "This. How did you become... this?"

She snorted. "I was always this."

No. That wasn't true. He'd known her.

"Was it Korvin?" He'd barely seen her since their friend's death. She might have been the only one to know him as well as Aranok did. Had they spoken at the funeral? He had an image of her in a midnight blue dress, dark eye paint smeared down her face. And a nagging memory of... something.

"Was it Korvin?" she sneered. "Did I lose my mind over the death of my first love?"

"All right." Aranok nodded behind them. "Kiana, then? What happened to her?"

"We are not talking about her," she spat.

"Then what are we talking about?" Aranok tightened his grip on the reins.

"You came to me, Laird Envoy. I was perfectly content with my daughter."

"Then maybe I should have Samily cut her in half again." As soon as he said it, he regretted it, but the words were out. The look of shock and pain in Shayella's eyes hit him like a winter wind. "I'm sorry. That was cruel."

He needed to get hold of his emotions. Which would be easier if he knew what they were. It was as if there were two women here: one the girl he'd grown up with, fantasised about and watched jealously as she became his best friend's lover; the second a cold-blooded mass murderer. He only needed to glance back at Darginn Argyll to remind himself what she was capable of. But part of him could still only see the Shay he knew. The one who loved to dance, and to drink, and to sing at the top of her voice. Who dragged them out in the middle of the night just to feel the rain on her face and smell the storm. Who threw off her shoes to walk through the river in spring. That wild, passionate woman was still there, right in front of him. But so was the other.

"Just. Tell me why, Shay."

She looked down. A tear threatened to fall, but she dabbed it away. "You're unbelievable."

"I want to understand. Help me." He glanced back at Samily and lowered his voice. "Shay, I might be the only chance you've got. I might be the only person alive who cares what happens to you. Once we get to Traverlyn, your options are going to disappear."

What did he mean by that? Was he really prepared to help her? After what she'd done? Or did he just want there to be some simple explanation? Something that would make it all make sense—that would absolve him of responsibility?

"Why *wasn't* it Korvin?" she asked quietly.

"What?"

"After everything you said. At the funeral. Why *wasn't* it Korvin? For *you*?"

Shit.

They had spoken. What had he said? The confusion must have been clear on his face.

"You don't remember." Shay's laugh teetered on the edge of a sob. "God, you don't even know what you did."

No, he didn't. But he had a sinking, sick feeling in his guts. The dreadful awakening of something he'd long buried. Aranok gripped the reins again, this time to stop his hands trembling.

"What *do* you remember?" Her tone now reminded Aranok of one of his early teachers. The one who could quiet the entire room with one raised finger. What was her name?

"Not... a lot. That was a bad time."

"For all of us. Not everybody drank like you, though. You were bladdered when we arrived."

"We?" Had she been with her husband, then? She must have been.

"Bloody Hells, Aranok. Me, Anhel and Janaeus. You honestly don't remember?"

He didn't. The dread was getting colder.

"What happened?"

"Oh, Laird Envoy. All this time, I thought you'd got cold feet after sleeping it off. But you honestly have no idea, do you?"

"Shay, just tell me."

He'd said it too loud. Meristan frowned over his shoulder at them. Aranok needed to get it together. "Please, Shay."

She shifted in her seat and turned her legs toward him; there was glee at the corners of her mouth. For whatever anger she was feeling, she was also enjoying this. Which only made Aranok angrier.

"You dragged us to one of the back tables in the Canny Man. Remember that?"

"No." He had lots of hazy memories of the Canny Man from that time. A jerk as the cartwheel caught a stone, and the judder pulled the reins from his left hand. He just caught them with his right, but the jerk made the right horse pull up.

"Whoa!" Samily called from behind.

"Sorry!" Aranok raised a hand and tried to smile apologetically. "Hand slipped."

Samily said nothing. Darginn was looking at him strangely. Suspiciously. He supposed if someone had tortured and mutilated him for days, he might be wary of the person holding a hushed conversation with them.

"Assume I remember nothing, Shay." Which he did not. Not a glimmer.

Shayella shook her head disapprovingly. "Fine. You were angry."

"I know." He'd been consumed with it for a long time after Korvin died.

"Angry like I've never seen you. The owner—the fat man…"

"Calador."

"He threatened to throw you out."

"For what?"

"Shouting. Banging on the table. Throwing your cup." Shay shrugged. "All of it."

That sounded familiar. Aranok felt a ball forming in his gut; a stone of shame and dread.

"What happened? What did I do?"

Shay leaned an elbow on the back of the seat and visibly relaxed. "I cannot believe you don't remember."

"Shay, for fuck's sake…!" He'd run out of patience and it felt like she was deliberately torturing him now.

"All right?" Meristan's deep voice. "You want to swap back?"

Aranok looked pointedly at Shayella. "Maybe."

She raised her bound hands in supplication. Aranok shook his head at Meristan, and the big man turned away. Aranok could feel Samily's eyes on his back. "Just tell me," he whispered.

"You said they'd never accept us," said Shay. "You said we would always be hated and mistreated and shunned. We'd always be 'less.' We'd be murdered without justice. And nobody cared."

That opened a raw wound Aranok had tried to forget. But it wasn't a surprise. That was exactly how he'd felt. He just didn't know he'd said it aloud. Not to anyone but Mynygogg.

"All right." Aranok gritted his teeth, the ball becoming a wave of nausea. "All right. So what?"

"Unless we did something, you said. Unless we stopped taking it. Unless we took over."

Shit.

Had he said that? Had he really felt that? Hells, he might have. Easily. But if he'd said that to *them*... The ball in his guts became an aching pit.

"Are you telling me...?"

"It was your idea, Ari."

His head spun and the nausea rolled up in a torrent. He threw the reins at Shay just in time to lean to the left and vomit down the side of the cart. The little lunch he'd had spattered off the turning wheel onto the ground. His stomach convulsed again, and again, until there was nothing left in him and he was just spasming repeatedly, a string of yellow bile hanging from his chin.

When it finally stopped and Aranok could breathe again, he realised they'd stopped moving. He looked up to see Meristan proffering his waterskin. "Hardly surprising after all you've been through these last days."

Aranok took a mouthful, swished it around, and spat it onto the ground. Then a few sips to soothe the back of his throat. He felt the cool liquid trail down into his now empty stomach, which gave a spasm of complaint. He didn't risk drinking more.

"Thank you." He handed it back to his friend.

"You all right, Envoy?" Samily was glaring at Shayella. The necromancer smiled serenely back at her.

"I'm fine, thank you, Samily."

"We all right to get going again?" Meristan asked.

Shayella held the reins out for him like a birth day present. "We are." Aranok took firm hold of the leather straps and urged the horses forward.

Holy Hell.

It was him. His anger, his resentment, his grief. He thought he'd handled it, killing Altric, Hammon and Kulan. He'd burned them with all the rage, all the pain, all the god damned injustice of life as a *draoidh*. And Mynygogg had pulled him back before he'd done more. But he was too late. Because in the raw grief of Korvin's loss, Aranok had revealed himself. He'd opened the dark, vengeful pit at his core and shared it with exactly the wrong people. The childhood friends with their own darkness. And he'd validated them. He'd given them permission. He'd *inspired* them. He'd told them that the dark was good, and right. And that they should act on it.

Even now, it was there, simmering at his heart. He didn't regret killing those bastards. He never had. He'd do it again. He was going to kill Rotan. But what had he started? Had he ever intended... this? Was he ever so angry that he would raze the country to dirt?

Fuck!

No. No, he wasn't. Not like this. Not like what Anhel had wanted. Aranok wanted justice, not vengeance. He wanted the new Eidyn. The better Eidyn. Anhel wanted chaos. Anhel wanted power.

He waited until the others had settled back to a comfortable distance again before speaking. That gave him time to work out what to say.

"Anhel was always angry. He wanted this long before Korvin."

Shayella laughed gently. "He did, yes. He agreed with you. The two of you were like kindling sparks, bouncing off each other. You set a fire."

"No. No, I'm not responsible for you and Janaeus. You made your own choices. Don't blame me."

"Oh, Laird Envoy, come. Janaeus always looked up to you and Korvin. He was so jealous of what you two had. Once you'd ranted for an hour about how everything had to change, he was sold. He'd seen the real you. The heart of the man he admired, railing against those who'd murdered the other. Whatever mask you put back on afterwards, he knew your true face that night."

Fuck.

Fuck, fuck, fuck.

Was Janaeus his fault? Maybe. Partially. Maybe. But Anhel wasn't. And neither was Shayella.

"What about you? You blaming me too?" He threw the words like knives. Shay didn't flinch.

"No. I knew you were just drunk. Full of piss and wind because you'd lost your friend. I knew you wouldn't do anything. You never had the stomach to avenge Korvin."

Somehow that hurt even more than the rest. The flame smouldered at his core again as the pain of Korvin's death reared up. The all-consuming rage he'd felt. It was still there. It always had been.

"I had plenty of stomach."

"Aranok, come on. You drank yourself empty until your old friend Mynygogg dried you out and filled you full of pretty lies. You honestly think that's what Korvin would have wanted? A bright new world where his murderers are still free to live their miserable lives? You abandoned him."

"I did not!" Aranok slammed his hand against the seat. It was all he could do not to backhand the woman for her bile. He no longer cared if he was drawing attention. "I found those bastards and I killed them."

For the first time, Shayella's face registered genuine surprise. It quickly melted into a smile. "Good. Good, that's exactly what they deserved. I suppose I owe you an apology, then, Ari. Maybe you are still one of us."

"What do you mean, 'one of you'?"

"A *draoidh*. A real *draoidh*, not the supine house pet you've been playing."

"Of course I'm fucking *draoidh*. That doesn't mean I have to declare war on everyone else."

Shayella looked back at the cart, at her cursed servants, then back to him. She rubbed her hands together as if washing them slowly. "We're not the ones who declared war."

Aranok looked them over again. Just normal, humble people. Two women, an older man and a girl. She'd called them "bad people." They looked entirely ordinary. He'd have struggled to pick any of them from a crowd.

"What did they do?" Shay stared silently ahead as if he hadn't spoken. "Shay?" Aranok put a gentle hand on her leg. "What happened?"

She mumbled something Aranok couldn't hear. He leaned in closer. "Sorry?"

"Drown the witch," she whispered.

The word stabbed at him. *Witch.* That was what they'd called the girl in Caer Amon. The child he'd watched destroy a village for killing her love.

"What does that mean?" Aranok asked, unsure if he really wanted the answer. But he needed it. He needed to understand.

"Kiana was late for supper." Shay's voice was small, her hands shaking. Aranok placed one of his on top, hoping it would be comforting. They were cold and delicate, like some precious artwork. Even then, he felt a spark as he touched her skin, reminding him of what he'd felt for her a lifetime ago. "I was looking for her. Her friends used to play in a field by the river. I told her to stay away from the water. I told her…" Her voice trailed off into nothing.

"Go on."

"There's a mill, on the river. Just downstream. I saw her dress first. I made it for her. Pale blue, with a white trim. She loved that dress. I struggled to get her to wear anything else. Said it made her feel like a princess." A hint of a smile. But it was broken. Hollow. "Her arm was caught in the wheel. It was just"—Shay gestured with her arms—"pulling her around and around, like a doll."

Her voice cracked completely then and tears dripped from her cheeks.

"I'm sorry," Aranok said. Losing a child, especially like that, must be awful, but it still didn't explain—

"I'm not finished," said Shay through gritted teeth. "None of the children would tell us what happened. They all said they didn't know. Hadn't been there. So I brought her back."

"And?"

"They were playing a game." She turned to look him in the eye. "Drown the witch."

Hell.

Aranok's head dropped.

"She was terrified. Held under the water. They sat on her, Aranok. Just at the edge, her face was inches below the water. But she couldn't move. She had no air in her. She thrashed and tried to get up but they laughed. They laughed. They thought it was funny. The last sound she heard, as she tried to call for me, to beg for her life, as her lungs filled with water, was laughter."

"I'm so sorry." They were the only words he could find. What else could he possibly say?

"She wasn't even *draoidh*. They drowned my daughter, my beautiful little girl, for being my daughter. They killed her because I was her mother."

It was unimaginable.

If Emelina had...And she wasn't even his daughter. Ikara would kill for her without a second thought, he knew. Was it so ridiculous that Shay had done the same? But still, that didn't explain her actions. Or excuse them. Grief was powerful, but to curse thousands? Murder tens of thousands? No, he couldn't defend that, no matter what had happened to her.

"And nobody cared." Shayella's tone was defiant again. The pain gone, replaced with steel. "I told the local guard. I told the town council. Nobody cared. They ruled it an accident. It was no accident. They *sat* on her, Aranok. And where did they get the idea? 'Drown the witch'? Children don't just make that up. They heard it. From their parents. They heard from them that I was a witch. That maybe Kiana was too. That witches are evil. Somebody taught those children to hate *draoidhs*, and when they acted on that poison, nobody wanted to take responsibility! My own husband..."

Her hands shook again.

"He wanted to let it go—to bury her and forget. To move on. My baby girl. My precious baby. He wanted to forget her..."

Aranok bit down on his lip to stop it from trembling. "I'm so sorry, Shay. I don't know what to say." His instinct was to tell her that still didn't justify what she'd done, but he couldn't bring himself to speak the words. They might be true, but they felt...disrespectful, somehow, to Kiana. To her memory. Whatever Shay had done, Kiana was innocent.

"He was first," she said. "I cursed him."

"Your husband? He was the first Blackened?"

Shayella nodded. "I intended to control it. Keep it to Lepertoun. Then Anhel came. Reminded me what you'd said. We'd all said. And then...I knew he was right. I knew you were right. If my baby could be killed in daylight and left to dangle from a damned mill wheel without anyone paying for it, I knew we'd never be equal. We'd never be free. So we'd rule. And fuck the consequences. Every single one of those bastards who looked away when my daughter was murdered deserved it."

She lifted her head, silently challenging him to rebuke her. To disagree. But in that moment, he couldn't think of a single thing to say that didn't sound pathetic. So he said nothing.

After a while, Meristan dropped back again. "You finished? Ready to ride again?"

No. He wasn't. But something did need to change. "Samily?" he called, pulling the cart to a halt. The knight rode up alongside him.

"Give me the girl." He held his arms out for her.

Samily cocked her head. "I'll take her tongue again?"

"No. I just want the girl."

"Envoy, I am not comfortable with—"

"Samily, I'm not asking," he interrupted. "Kiana is going to ride with us. Shayella's hands and feet are bound. She's not going anywhere."

"Aranok, are you certain?" Meristan's tone was becoming more concerned with each question.

Aranok sat up and looked at him firmly. "I am."

Meristan took a moment before nodding resignedly to Samily. She gave Shayella a last suspicious look before lifting Kiana from her saddle and handing her to Aranok. Carefully, he placed her next to him and smoothed her dress. Once she was settled, Shayella put her arms around her again and pulled her in with a smile that might have been the first genuine happiness Aranok had seen in a long time.

Without a word, he snapped the reins and urged the horses back into life. They couldn't be far from Lochen.

CHAPTER 14

My love," Mynygogg said, interlacing his fingers and smiling across the large round meeting table, "in future, perhaps it would be best if you took someone with you who has some authority, until we can remind everyone who you are?"

They hadn't been stuck in the gaol long, and it had been useful in the end. But Allandria was still glad to get back to the hospital. Its redbrick walls had become the closest thing she'd had to home recently. This makeshift council chamber seemed to be some kind of meeting room for the hospital's senior medics. A large chalkboard had been hastily wiped clean of an anatomical drawing that left a ghost of itself on the slate.

Nirea made a sweeping gesture toward her, and Allandria felt heat rise in her cheeks. "I took her. She's *famous*."

Mynygogg grinned. "Yes, but as you discovered, she doesn't actually have any authority without my envoy. Unlike, say, Master Opiassa, to whom I am extremely grateful for freeing you."

"It was my pleasure, my laird." Opiassa bowed and Allandria definitely saw a hint of a smile.

"Ah, but she does." Nirea took a seat opposite the king. "I've decided to make her my envoy. So she has *my* authority."

Mynygogg looked up to Allandria with genuine surprise and pleasure. "Have you?" He stood. To his right, Principal Keft made to join him. Mynygogg stayed him with a wave of his hand. "No, no, sit, Keft.

Please." The old man raised an eyebrow and did as asked. He seemed to be the only one in the room not amused by the royal banter. Allandria's impression of him as consistently sour was hardening. She didn't think she'd yet seen him smile.

Mynygogg, conversely, grinned as wide as his face would permit as he reached a hand across the table to Allandria. "There is no better or more deserving person for the position, Allandria. Congratulations."

"Thank you, sire."

Opiassa clapped her shoulder and echoed the congratulations. The woman's strength was ridiculous. She almost knocked Allandria off balance with a casual gesture. She was glad the physic *draoidh* turned out to be on their side. Keft, ironically, gave a simple smile and nod of his head when she caught his eye. Perhaps it was only power that ever brought a curl to his lips.

Mynygogg returned to his seat. "Of course, my love, that still doesn't solve your problem, since you can't imbue your envoy with authority nobody knows you have."

"That would certainly explain our embarrassing situation this evening, wouldn't it?" Nirea winked at her.

"Unfortunately, Allandria, your new position comes with very few advantages, I'm afraid. It does, however, give you a right to a seat at this table, and I would very much welcome your voice, especially in the absence of my own envoy." Mynygogg gestured to the seat next to Nirea's. She was so accustomed to taking a place on the edges, in the background, that the idea of a seat at the table with the rulers of Eidyn seemed ridiculous. She felt her left hand tremble slightly as she sat down, and gripped it tight. Nirea smiled at her, placed her own hand over Allandria's fist and gave it a gentle squeeze.

"Master Opiassa, would you also join us, please?" Opiassa took the seat between Keft and Nirea. There was a final empty seat between Allandria and Mynygogg.

"What about Master Balaban?" Nirea asked. "He's been a useful ally."

"So I understand..." Mynygogg gestured to Keft.

"Master Balaban has made some progress in his research and begs forgiveness to pursue it, my lady," the principal finished.

The king turned back to his queen. "So, what I'm interested to know is whether your adventure bore any fruit. Did Rotan tell you anything useful?"

It had. A lot more than Allandria had imagined. Nirea had picked away at the man's insecurities like a poorly-made quilt until he'd finally spilled his guts. He would have sold his own mother by the end for Nirea's protection. Rotan was exactly as spineless as the queen had imagined him.

"He did. He was first approached by Janaeus over two years ago."

"Two years?" Mynygogg sat back, wide-eyed. "My God, he's been planning this much longer than we thought."

"Indeed," Nirea agreed. "His task was to empty the library of any books relating to you or memory *draoidhs*, and to keep an eye on anyone nosing into them. He was to make copies of the books, substituting Janaeus's name for yours and removing all references to memory as a magical skill. He's been doing that in the *caibineat puinnsean*. He killed Conifax after he found the books, and Calavas to cut the string that led back to him."

Mynygogg nodded silently, his face giving away nothing. Rotan would be executed, no doubt, but probably less gruesomely than Nirea had suggested. "What else?"

"What we feared is true. He was under orders to send anyone especially difficult to Lestalric. Baroness de Lestalric is Shayella, and his letter asked her to kill Meristan and Rasa."

Mynygogg's cool demeanour cracked and he thumped the table with his fist. "God damn him. So if Aranok and Samily didn't catch them..."

Everyone in the room knew how that sentence ended and nobody wanted to give it voice.

"Right. Then we need an army," said Mynygogg. "Opiassa, how many guards can the town spare?"

"I'm not sure, sire. We'll need to leave enough behind to protect against the cocoon demons. Maybe a hundred?"

Mynygogg turned to Keft. "What about *draoidhs*?"

Keft jostled with surprise. "*Draoidhs*? Your Majesty, the *draoidhs* here are not warriors. We are scholars. Students."

Mynygogg's eyes turned dark. "Unfortunately, Principal, war sometimes robs us of the luxury of choice. Please ask any adult with a combative ability to volunteer for service. I won't press anyone against their will, but I will ask them to defend their country and their friends."

Keft nodded hesitantly.

"You have me, of course, Your Highness," said Opiassa. That was a blessing. Allandria reckoned the *draoidh* might be as useful as Samily in a fight. Maybe even Meristan. If she had any decent level of skill with weapons, her enhanced strength and speed would be formidable. Allandria also understood her physic ability allowed her to heal more quickly than normal, thanks to her direct control over her body. Definitely useful.

"Thank you, Opiassa." Mynygogg turned to Allandria. "Envoy, would you please arrange for a messenger to go to Lochen? Ask them to prepare every adult who can carry a bow to march with us. We'll arrive in two days' time. We'll need shelter for the night for maybe a hundred and fifty people, and we march at dawn the following day."

"Gogg, you're forgetting." Nirea reached across the table and took his hand. "You can't just raise an army in Lochen in *your* name."

She was right, he couldn't. But Allandria could. "I'll go myself. Lochen is my home. Enough people know me and my position. If I tell them the king needs them to march on Lestalric, they'll believe me. I just won't mention which king..."

Mynygogg smiled. "Thank you. But that raises another issue. They're going to see I'm not Janaeus when I arrive."

"Put Allandria in charge," said Nirea. "At least, of the Lochen troops. Opiassa can take charge of those from Traverlyn. Neither group will question their authority. You'll just have to issue orders through them."

Mynygogg considered a moment, then nodded. "All right. I suppose I'll have to take my own advice for now. Opiassa, you'll lead the Traverlyn contingent—Allandria, Lochen."

"Sire, if I might raise something else?" Keft shifted awkwardly in his seat. Whatever he was going to say, he wasn't keen to say it.

"Of course, Principal."

"If you're going to be seen in public, we should accustom ourselves to referring to you by another name. We can't risk mistakenly giving away your identity to another of Janaeus's spies."

Ouch. Aranok often chose a false identity to travel under, but that was his choice. The indignity of Eidyn's king forced not only to shave his head to disguise his appearance but to travel under a false identity must sting, Allandria imagined. But if it did, Mynygogg showed no sign of it, taking Keft's suggestion with his usual grace.

"Of course, yes. A fine point, Principal, thank you. My grandfather's name was Donal. He was a good man, a thoughtful man in a time of violence. I don't think he'd mind if I borrowed his name for a while."

That was definitely a less obvious effort than the "Gogg" that Aranok had come up with at a moment's notice when they arrived in Traverlyn. Allandria smiled and rolled her eyes at the memory. She'd have nudged him to remind him if he'd been there.

Nirea extended a hand across the table. "A pleasure to meet you, Laird Donal."

"And you, Councillor Nirea." Mynygogg stood, and this time the rest of the table joined him. "All right, we're adjourned. You all know your jobs. With luck, our friends will sleep soundly in Lochen tonight, return safely tomorrow, all this planning will be for nothing and we can focus on clearing memories and taking the throne back from Janaeus."

With luck.

"If not, we ride for Lestalric, either to save them or avenge them."

And that was the first time Allandria had had to face that possibility. She'd been skirting around it all afternoon, ever since Rotan confirmed their fears. Aranok had gone to face Shayella—and she had let him go alone. Well, not alone. He'd taken Samily, who in all honesty was probably a better bodyguard than her. And, in fact, he'd be needing a new one anyway, since her promotion. She doubted the Thorn would be quick to volunteer for the job. He wasn't easy to get on with for those with faith who didn't have the luxury of ignoring him when he challenged them for no reason other than his own entertainment. Though the pair did seem to have something of a connection, since she discovered her *draoidh* powers and he had been teaching her. Who knew—perhaps they would have bonded on their trip and she'd be the perfect candidate for the job after all?

The envoy was behaving strangely. And rudely, as far as Samily was concerned. Since he'd taken to riding the cart with the necromancer the day before, his mood had become sullen, and his communication with Samily had been little more than giving brief orders. The man she'd come to respect, and whose tutoring she appreciated, seemed to have been left in Lestalric. And she had no earthly idea why.

Not only that, but he seemed more interested in protecting the woman and the corpse than in the welfare of the man Shayella had tortured or the people she'd enslaved.

Samily had tried to speak to Meristan about it the night before, at the Loch Inn, but he'd had no solace to offer, other than to agree he was a little concerned about Aranok's behaviour. But Meristan hardly seemed himself either. Despite being...himself again, he retained the haunted look she'd become used to when he thought himself a monk. Was that also because of Lestalric? She wished none of them had ever set foot in that Hell.

Rasa still showed no sign of waking. She didn't know what else to do for her, except pray that someone at the hospital, or maybe the university, would be more able to help her.

Darginn Argyll looked healthier. A good night's sleep and some decent meals had done him good. Still, she'd heard cries during the night and strongly suspected they were his.

Darginn caught her looking at him and smiled. "M'lady."

Samily slowed Bear, dropping back from the cart. Darginn looked at her curiously but did the same.

"How are you today?" she asked quietly, when the cart was out of earshot.

"Well enough, thank you." Darginn arched his back. "Much as I like this old mare, I'm looking forward to some time on my own two feet."

"I'm sure you are. Darginn, may I ask, do you find this...uncomfortable?" Samily gestured ahead.

"How d'you mean?"

"I am not always good at...understanding people. Is it strange that we are travelling with your tormentor?"

Darginn looked ahead for a long time before speaking. "Can't say as I like it. I'd choose to see that girl back in the earth where she belongs, for a start. Two days ago, I was waiting to die—sooner the better. You and the lairds, I owe you my life. If you think she's worth something alive, I'd trade that for my own life every day. But I'll warn you—there's no a bone of sanity in her. Don't take your eyes off her a minute."

That, Samily was already certain of. No sane person fed another human being to their child. Of all the awful things she'd seen—the withered Blackened, the Dead in Auldun, the allies slaughtered by demons—of all of it, a fire spit in Lestalric's basement was what haunted her.

"Hold!" Meristan called from ahead. The group slowed. A rider was approaching. As the solitary figure came close, they sped up, racing to close the final gap. Samily recognised the dappled horse first—Dancer.

"Allandria!" Meristan called happily, dismounting to greet her.

"Allandria? The one's usually with...?" Darginn gestured to the envoy.

"Indeed." Samily climbed down from Bear and tied his reins to the back of the cart. "She is a fierce ally." Hopefully she could help speak some sense to her charge.

Meristan embraced her in a great hug and she beamed up at him. "What are you doing here?"

Allandria gestured to the cart, then to Samily and Darginn. "Raising an army to rescue you." She turned back to Meristan, placing a gentle hand on his face. "You're you again?"

Samily's mentor smiled and sighed. "I am."

For a moment, they silently smiled together.

They must have been friends before, Samily realised. It was odd that there was such a part of Meristan's life she hadn't been privy to. His time at Dun Eidyn, working directly with the king during the *draoidh* war, had made friendships she knew nothing about. And yet, she now considered them all friends, despite meeting them in what felt sometimes like a dream. Allandria moved to the cart and stopped, seemingly expecting Aranok to dismount. Her face changed slightly when he didn't, merely offering a hand, which she took. As Samily approached, she heard the edge of their conversation.

"How is she?" Allandria asked solemnly.

"Asleep. Has been since..." Aranok shook his head. "We don't know what else to do for her."

Allandria looked hard at Shayella. The necromancer looked away, pulling the girl tight to her. It seemed she had the sanity to know when to keep quiet.

"Can't *she* do something?"

Aranok looked down as if ashamed. "It was an experiment. She doesn't know either."

Allandria scowled. Her stare bled with suspicion. Good. That was what was needed. Shayella continued to hide from the archer's gaze.

"Hmmph." Allandria turned to Samily and smiled broadly.

"It's good to see you, Lady Knight." She wrapped her arms around Samily, whispering as she leaned in close. "I see you did my job. Thank you."

She made to break her grip, but Samily pulled her back, to her obvious surprise. "I have concerns about the envoy."

She released Allandria from the embrace and held her at arm's length. The archer looked confused for a moment. "Ride with me."

"First, may I introduce someone?" Samily led Allandria back to the horses, where Darginn had stayed mounted. His old bones were probably better off staying in one position than dismounting and remounting in such a short space of time. "This is Darginn Argyll, king's messenger. We rescued him from Lestalric."

Allandria reached a hand up to him. "Good to meet you, Darginn Argyll. You're amongst friends."

"Pleasure's mine, m'lady." Darginn tapped his temple. "I know who you are. And I'm grateful to be here."

"Darginn, would you mind riding up front with Meristan? I have some personal things to discuss with Lady Allandria." Samily had a feeling the old man wouldn't be happy with the idea of having Shayella behind him. She suspected having her in his sights was part of what kept him comfortable. That and having Samily alongside him. He'd seemed keen to stay near her since she'd healed him. Not dissimilar to how the boy had reacted after Mutton Hole, actually.

Indeed, Darginn looked nervously toward the cart. Samily placed a gentle hand on his leg. "She will never touch you again." His face stiffened and he nodded, nudging his horse forward. Allandria followed him to retrieve Dancer while Samily remounted Bear.

They were still maybe half a day from Traverlyn. Plenty of time to share her concerns with the person she hoped most able to allay them.

CHAPTER 15

We are not executing her!" Aranok slammed his fist against the brick wall so hard Allandria feared he might have broken a bone. If it hurt, he gave no sign.

The joy and relief of their return to Traverlyn in the night had quickly dissipated when the story of Lestalric was recounted. Even hearing it for the second time, Allandria had winced at the details. Samily described it as Hell. Allandria, selfishly, was glad she hadn't gone. It had been hard even to look at Darginn after hearing what Shayella had done to him.

They'd settled the servants into rooms at the hospital while Balaban arranged the required items for Shayella to remove their curse. Rasa got her own room, where Egretta did what she could for her, until they could figure out exactly what was wrong. She also insisted on having one of the other medics see to Darginn, after what he'd been through.

That left Shayella and the Dead girl. Having her as far away as the gaol had been agreed too risky, so they'd locked her in a room intended for the mentally disturbed. Allandria was still coming to terms with what Samily had done to the necromancer's tongue. Despite everything she'd seen her do, the knight was still a teenager—a girl—and to do something so brutal... She worried what effect Lestalric had had on her too.

Aranok had insisted on a private audience with Mynygogg, who had in turn insisted that Nirea and Allandria be there too. He'd registered surprise at Allandria's promotion, but she'd found it hard to read whether he was happy about it or not. In fact, he'd been unreadable since she'd met them on the Easter Road.

"Aranok, I don't understand." Mynygogg clasped his hands behind his neck. "This could end the Blackening. That's what you've been trying to do. It's why you went to Caer Amon. Shayella has murdered tens, maybe hundreds of thousands. By any measure, this is the right decision!"

"Aranok, she's insane," Nirea pleaded.

"Exactly." Aranok turned to her, wild-eyed. "Her mind's broken. It's been broken. She's not responsible for what she's done. No sane person could do what she's done."

This was exactly what Samily had warned Allandria about. During the war, he'd have killed Shayella given half a chance. Or Anhel. He was furious with them—maybe more so for the fact they'd been friends. His sense of betrayal had burned in him. But now, somehow, that had turned. It seemed like his connection to her had him... sympathising.

"Aranok, think about the good this can do." Allandria put a hand on his arm. "Cure the Blackened. Retake Auldun. All the lives we can save."

Aranok stepped away. "Except hers. Or her daughter's."

"Aranok, the girl's dead." Nirea spread her hands in obvious consternation. "There's nothing we can do for her."

"What about what she did to Rasa, Aranok? What if she dies?" Allandria asked. He had to see she was beyond redemption, surely. She'd put their friend, someone Aranok clearly cared about, in a Thakhati cocoon just to see what would happen. How could he forgive that? His eyes wavered as he looked at her.

"I know. Look, I... Please. We can't kill her."

"Why not?" Mynygogg's voice was as loud as she'd ever heard it. It was rare for him to lose his temper, even more so within this group.

The king's ire sparked a similar reaction in Aranok. "Because we did this to her!"

Mynygogg's mouth dropped open. "What?"

Aranok jabbed a finger at his friend. "You told me we'd outlaw anti-*draoidh* bigotry when we took the throne. You said we'd change Eidyn."

"Aranok..." Nirea began, but he continued as if she weren't there.

"You said we'd make it illegal. And you didn't! 'Patience,' you said. 'Give them time to adjust.' First a *draoidh* envoy, then, soon, enshrine it in law. 'Small steps,' you said, 'or we risk a backlash'!"

Allandria hadn't known that had been part of their plan. Or that it had been delayed. But it made sense of a few heated conversations she'd overheard before the war.

Mynygogg took a seat and a deep breath. "And that remains true, Aranok. You know how fragile this is. Building a new world takes care. It's a delicate thing. Use a hammer when a feather is called for and the whole thing breaks."

"Well, your feather drowned Shayella's daughter, Your Majesty. And nobody fucking cared." Aranok spat the words at his feet. Allandria'd never seen him this angry. It was frightening. She had a sudden and horrible wish that Samily were there in case they needed to take back something awful, and that unsettled her even more.

"What?" Nirea asked. "How?"

Aranok turned to Allandria, tears now evident in his red-rimmed eyes. "The girl. In Caer Amon. Remember?"

Of course she remembered. It was heartbreaking. Allandria nodded.

"Was she to blame? For what happened there?"

Allandria's instinct was horror. Of course she wasn't to blame. She was the victim. The victim of a backwards society that murdered her love and would have killed her just for being...who she was. But she saw the connection. How could she answer that question? She'd murdered hundreds, and Allandria thought her a victim. Was Shayella worse because she'd murdered thousands? Did the number make a difference? Where was the line? God, she didn't know.

"You see?" Aranok pointed to her. "She can't say! Because it's not that simple!"

"Aranok, please, I don't know what you're talking about." Mynygogg's voice was calm again. Good, that was needed.

"They drowned her daughter." Aranok's face was wet now, his voice breaking with every word. "Children. They drowned her in the river for being a witch. She wasn't even fucking *draoidh*. They drowned her because she was Shay's daughter."

Allandria's heart stuttered in her chest. Nirea gasped and took a seat beside Mynygogg, who remained stony silent.

"And nothing happened." Aranok spread his hands wide. "Lepertoun decided it was an accident. Nobody was punished. Nothing. No consequences for the bigoted parents who taught their children to hate. Nothing changed, Gogg." Aranok leaned to within inches of the king's face. "Nothing. Changed."

God, it was too much. The fire in Aranok seemed to have burned itself out, leaving a shallow grey husk in its place. He looked older than she'd ever seen him, and having no idea what she could possibly say, she did the only thing that came naturally. She stepped behind him, wrapped her arms around his chest and nestled her head on his shoulder. "I'm sorry," she whispered. He didn't answer but raised a hand to hold her forearm.

They stood like that a long time. What could anyone say that could ever make it better?

Nirea finally broke the awful silence. "Aranok, that's awful. I mean that with all my heart. I won't say I understand your pain, or hers, but I see it. But I have to ask you, does it justify what she's done? Hundreds of thousands dead or cursed—she all but set the country on fire."

"If Emelina went out to play and didn't come home, and *nothing* happened, I might just set the fucking country on fire too."

Of course. This was even more personal for him, having just discovered Emelina's abilities. She should have thought of that. And there was Korvin. There was always Korvin.

Mynygogg sat back in his chair, examining his envoy closely. "All right. I take your point. What about the greater good, Aranok? What about all the children who've died because of her? What about the ones who are going to die from the Blackening? What about their mothers? What about Rasa?" He gestured generally to the door. "She's *draoidh*. And Shayella tried to kill her."

"I know" was all he answered.

God. She'd never been concerned about a schism between these two, but this was... a chasm. They needed another option. They needed a compromise. Perhaps she had one. Allandria released her grip and moved to face Aranok.

"Will Shayella help us lift the Blackening?"

He shook his head mournfully. "She's not sure she can. When she cast it... she was already mad. Says she can't remember the words she used, or if there was a recantation. Could be it's like Morienne's *mollachd*."

"So killing her *might* end it." Nirea's words were pointed. Needles.

Aranok's face turned hard again. He stared back at the queen.

"I'll go to Haven. I'll get the heart. We'll use that to cure the Blackening, just like Conifax planned. Rasa's in the best place to be cured."

"If you can get it," Nirea said. "If."

Mynygogg stood. "We need it anyway. Keft and I have been planning while you were away, Aranok. There's no easy way to undo what Janaeus has done without the heart."

Aranok nodded. "I know."

"People will die from the delay, Aranok. From the Blackening. Are you going to be able to live with that?" Mynygogg asked.

Aranok didn't blink. "We need time anyway. To respond when they're cured. Egretta needs to make preparations. Someone will need to speak to Ikara about wagons for the cured. We had our own plan.

"Shayella lives. We use the heart to take back the kingdom. The day you're back on the throne, you outlaw anti-*draoidh* bigotry. We tried the feather; this time, it's the hammer."

The two men faced each other like statues of ancient heroes cast in flesh and blood.

"And if I say no?"

Aranok looked around. "At the moment, you're just about king of this hospital. You want my help putting you on the throne of Eidyn—again—those are my conditions."

"Aranok!" Nirea's shout was shock more than anger. "You would abandon your king over this? That's treason."

That wasn't fair. Nirea knew as well as she did that Mynygogg owed his throne to Aranok. It could just as easily have been him wearing the crown, but for the very fact he was *draoidh*. It might have been Mynygogg's leadership, his vision to change the country, but Aranok had made it possible.

Aranok opened his mouth, but Allandria beat him to it.

"With respect, no, it's not. Nobody in this room has any status. Your thrones have been deposed. Just like you took Hofnag's. He might have done it by deception, but Janaeus is king until we prove otherwise. If you want our help taking back the country, this is the deal."

Aranok turned to look at her, and for the first time since he'd returned she saw a spark of life in his eyes, and the hint of a smile.

"*Your* help?" Nirea asked. "You agree with him?"

She did, apparently. She'd been at Caer Amon. She'd seen Emelina's pure delight at creating her butterfly of light. If someone hurt that little girl... "I do. And with time, I think you will too. Your Highness. Killing Shayella now would just be... revenge. We should be better."

Mynygogg and Nirea looked at each other for a moment, before Mynygogg sighed deeply. "All right. As long as we get the heart, Shayella will not be executed."

Aranok turned for the door. "She should be treated, like any other patient."

Mynygogg threw open his hands. "Aranok, I don't even know where to start..."

"Ask Egretta," he called over his shoulder from the corridor. Allandria followed him, pulling the door closed behind her. He turned when he heard it thud shut, smiled weakly and came back. "Thank you. That meant... Thank you."

She put a hand against his chest and, for a moment, thought she could feel his heartbeat, even through his leathers. "You were right. What happened to her was awful. You always said she used to be a good person. Now you know what happened."

He smiled, and just for a moment, she thought he might lean in to kiss her. But it passed and he pulled away. "I need to see Master Ipharia about Rasa. Shay told me how the Thakhati magic works. I'll find you later?"

Allandria nodded.

"Are we all right?" he asked. "After... you know?"

She smiled. "We're fine. Go help Rasa."

This definitely wasn't the time.

CHAPTER 16

Nirea put her feet up on the table. "That went well."

Mynygogg smiled wryly. "That was your first experience of your envoy challenging you? It won't be the last."

"I thought it might have taken a little longer, I suppose. I haven't even officially given her the job yet." Nirea found herself wondering whether it had been a mistake already. Would Allandria's loyalties be split? If it came to a choice between following Nirea's order or siding with Aranok, could she be confident which way the archer would jump? Especially now that Nirea knew how she felt about her former charge? Usually their wills were aligned, she supposed.

"It's not necessarily a bad thing." Mynygogg leaned affectionately on her legs. Her skin tingled in response. It was good just to feel his casual touch again. "The worst leaders surround themselves with cowards. If nobody ever tells a king no, he loses his grasp on right and wrong. A strong envoy is a whetstone for a sharp king."

"Or queen," Nirea chided him.

"Or queen," Mynygogg agreed. "That said, I'm concerned about this. His protection of Shayella seems completely irrational. I think he's holding something back."

That was a worry. For all their butting of heads, the one thing Mynygogg had always said was that he and Aranok were completely honest with each other. It was the bedrock of their friendship. She was fairly sure there were things Aranok knew about her husband that she did not. If he were keeping something from Mynygogg, it didn't bode well. "What do you want to do?"

"For now, nothing. He should go after the heart. We need it anyway. But we need contingency plans. First, we need more of those jewels Aranok has. If Janaeus recasts his spell, we need to be protected."

"Wouldn't Shayella have had one? Aranok said all the Hellfire Club had them, didn't he?" If she did, that should be an easy one to get. Ideally, though, they needed to be able to produce more.

"Good thought." Mynygogg sat upright. "Let's find out. We also need to think about allies. The Reivers are a problem. We need to get them back on our side, or at least get them to stop raiding. If Janaeus keeps up the hostility we'll soon be at war with them again. The country won't survive another war."

No, it would not. Peace with the Reivers had been a monumental change in Eidyn's fortunes. The greatest period of prosperity in living memory. Shame it had only lasted a few years.

A bang on the door, so loud Nirea thought someone might have been trying to break it down. Mynygogg frowned and placed his hand on his sword hilt. Allandria should still be on watch outside. If she wasn't...

"Come!" Mynygogg called. The door swung open to reveal a hulking shape. Mynygogg's face broke into a wide grin and he hurried around the table to greet the man. "God's Own Blade!" He pulled Meristan into a great hug. "I hear you've been a monk!"

"Aye, well, not by choice, Your Majesty." Meristan stepped aside then, revealing Samily hovering behind him.

Nirea stepped in to hug the big man as Mynygogg shook the girl's hand in welcome. With a rush of guilt, she remembered how she had daydreamed about Meristan the last few weeks. It seemed both laughable and a little embarrassing now. A good thing she'd never said anything she couldn't take back. "I suppose I can stop feeling silly about you saving me from that demon."

Meristan grinned. "I suppose we both can." His face turned serious when he noticed her scar. "You kept it?"

She ran her finger down the tight, knotted skin twisting over her cheek. "I did."

"For Glorbad."

"For Glorbad."

"We'll drink to him when we can, my lady. In the great hall of Dun Eidyn, as he deserves."

Mynygogg put a hand on each of their shoulders. "Indeed, we will. His name will live as a great servant of Eidyn, and a good man."

Nirea caught Samily's eye. "Your Majesty." The girl nodded. Nirea pushed past Meristan to embrace her. "It's good to see you, Samily." The girl returned the embrace somewhat awkwardly, but Nirea didn't care. They had precious few allies just now, and fewer friends. It was good to see another one. "Do you know, it's funny..." She released the Thorn and stepped back. "I think there was always something familiar about watching you fight. Now I know why."

Samily glanced at her mentor and smiled. "Indeed, Your Highness."

"Come, come, sit." Mynygogg indicated the chairs. "It's not exactly a throne room, but it's what we have."

The seat the Great Bear settled onto seemed comically small, as if it were intended for a child. "You've seen Aranok?"

"We have," Mynygogg answered.

"He told you everything? About Lestalric?" Meristan asked.

He'd told them some, but with Mynygogg's concern about Aranok holding something back, Nirea wanted to hear it again. "Give us your version, if you will."

Meristan paused. "All right. But I have to forewarn you, it's not an easy story. In honesty, I'm keen to forget it."

Nirea had been kidnapped as a child and raised a pirate. She'd lived most of her adult life at sea and amongst some of the worst dregs of humanity. She'd seen them die of gangrene and she'd seen them hurl themselves over the side, sea drunk. Those bastards had told stories to make hardened soldiers look over their shoulders. Nirea had never heard one like the tale two White Thorns shared that day. It was worse than Aranok had recounted. When Meristan finished, the room lay thick with incredulous silence.

Mynygogg sat with his chin resting behind his hand, staring at the table as if it might provide some sanity. "God almighty," he muttered, then waved an apologetic hand across the table. "Forgive me. I just... struggle to understand how a person can do such things."

Nirea put a hand on his thigh. "No sane person could."

"Indeed." He nodded. "Meristan, you have seen this for yourself. If we execute Shayella, to release the Blackened, where would God stand?"

That was an interesting question. Not because Mynygogg cared one way or another for the opinion of God, but he would be interested in where Meristan—and Samily—saw the morals of the situation.

Meristan thought for a moment. "Our duty is first to God, then to God's children. Shayella is God's child, but when she has caused so much suffering…If there is no other way to cure the Blackening, then yes, I believe her execution is justified."

Nirea looked to the girl. "And you, Samily?"

The knight sat upright, as if steeling herself to answer. "God will judge her for her crimes. Our task is only to send her for judgement. If by her death we can end the Blackening, I see no need for debate."

Interesting. The girl's response was more certain than her master's. In fact, it was perhaps one of the first times she'd seen something akin to anger from Samily. The girl was usually the epitome of even-tempered, except when Meristan himself had been in danger. But this seemed to have raised something within her. Nirea found herself glad she hadn't been in Lestalric herself. She had more than enough of her own nightmares.

"All right, thank you both," said Mynygogg. "For now, we are going to try to recover the heart of devastation from Janaeus. If we can do that, we can cure the Blackening and retake the kingdom. But we can't presume success. We need another plan."

"How can we help?" Meristan asked.

"If we are unable to clear their memories, at least at first, do you think you could deliver the White Thorns to our side?" Mynygogg asked.

Meristan turned to look at Samily. After a moment, she shrugged and nodded somewhat halfheartedly. It was interesting to see how much these two could communicate without words.

"It's possible," said Meristan. "As you know, the Order does not prioritise any monarch. They will serve the one doing God's work. As head of the Thorns, my word carries weight. If I can convince the brothers too…yes, it is possible."

Where Janaeus had established that the monks were in control of the Thorns, the truth was more complex. As Nirea understood it, they had a more symbiotic relationship, whereby the monks both served and provided guidance for the Thorns, who also had their own leadership structure—with Meristan at the head. She wondered whether the memory *draoidh* had a reason for that or if it was just him forcing his own misunderstanding of the Order onto others as part of the memory spell. Of course, currently, that misunderstanding may play to their advantage, since the rest of the Order still believed Meristan both a monk and their leader. Could he command their loyalty so far as to have them dismiss their own memories? That would be quite the test of faith. And, now she thought of it that way, a little worrying. Should anyone have the power to command others to disregard the world as they know it? And yet, that was exactly what they needed him to do, for all the right reasons. The longer she was queen, the more she understood morality was less black and white than she'd once imagined—and she'd spent a lot of time knowingly on the dark side of that line.

"All right, good," said Mynygogg. "And perhaps you can reclaim a set of your rightful armour while you're there."

"Perhaps," Meristan agreed. "Is there anything else we can do before we go?"

"Not unless you know where we can find another memory *draoidh*." Nirea expected the laugh from Meristan, but something flashed across Samily's eyes that made her sit up. "Samily? Do you know something?"

"I might," she said hesitantly. "There was an innkeeper in Dail Ruigh—an awful man. But he said something confusing. I intended to ask the envoy about it, but it slipped my mind."

"Go on," Mynygogg prompted her.

"He said a *draoidh* had 'befuddled' his wife and stolen some coin. I wondered what kind of *draoidh* could do that. Now I wonder if it must have been a memory *draoidh*."

The four of them looked blankly at each other, hoping, Nirea assumed, that someone else would have an answer. Nobody did, so she took it upon herself to move them forward. "It seems like you'd still better ask Aranok that question, Samily."

"Indeed," Mynygogg agreed. "And if he concurs, would you be

prepared to follow that clue, Samily? You're free to take any companions you wish, with my blessing. If we can find our own memory *draoidh*..."

It would be invaluable. Their own innate ability would make them resistant to Janaeus's spell, meaning they would already know what he'd done, and that Mynygogg was the true king. If they were loyal, they could forge charms to protect many more against Janaeus using the heart again.

"I will ask the envoy what he thinks." There was something cold in Samily's voice, though. She certainly didn't seem to be the same girl who left. Then again, who would be, after what they'd seen?

"I... had thought Samily might travel with me," said Meristan. "To return to Baile Airneach."

Mynygogg slapped the table between them. "Well, I hope you'll settle for my company instead. We're going in the same direction, if not to the same place."

Nirea turned to face him. Where was *he* going? Her shock must have been evident, as Mynygogg's expression quickly became placating. "Under the circumstances, who else can petition the Reiver council to restore peace?"

"Me! I can go. You should stay here, where we can protect you." She could hear the strain in her voice. But she was not putting her husband in that kind of danger. If the Reivers decided against peace, they might just execute him on the spot.

Meristan cleared his throat and stood. "We'll take our leave, your majesties. Thank you for your time." Samily followed his lead.

Mynygogg stood and faced them. "Meristan, we'll speak in the morning. Get some rest. It's good to see you again."

"Sire." The Thorn nodded deferentially.

"And, Samily, please let me know what comes of your conversation with my envoy."

"Of course, sire."

As soon as the door closed, Nirea's mouth opened, but she didn't reach the first word before Mynygogg placed a hand across her mouth. An immediate sense of outrage nearly caused her to bite it.

"A moment please, my love. Please?"

She pursed her lips and fixed a promise of revenge in her eyes. But she waited.

"I need you to go to Haven, with Aranok. That's why you can't go to the Reivers. That's why I have to."

"What? Why?" There was no reason she needed to go to Greytoun. Allandria could go with him if he needed support.

"Because I can't go. If I'm recognised, Janaeus will have me killed immediately. You still have the cover of being on his council. Both you and Aranok can pretend to be under his spell. Tell him you survived Barrock, but Glorbad was lost. Just don't tell him what happened next."

"Allandria can do that just as well." *Without putting Mynygogg in danger.*

"After today, you're the only one I know I can *absolutely* trust. And I need that. Let me explain."

Nirea breathed out her anger. "Fine. But if you ever put a hand over my mouth again, be prepared to lose it."

Samily did not like the feeling in her stomach. Things were not well, and they were only becoming worse. She had been briefly happy at the thought of returning to Baile Airneach with Meristan. In fact, she almost wished she hadn't spoken up about her memory of the *draoidh* in Dail Ruigh. But it was the right thing to do. Now she had to speak with the envoy, whom she was not at all comfortable with at the moment. She was much more interested in helping Rasa, and the thought of leaving tomorrow without knowing she had survived was painful. The thought of never seeing her again opened a well of sadness in Samily that she had no idea what to do with.

When she had time, that evening, she would pray for solace. Solace for her and for Rasa.

For now, she needed to find Aranok. Allandria had said he was looking for Master Ipharia. Samily had traced the master's quarters, but there was no answer there, nor at her office within the university tower. That led her to her next stop—the library. She had only set a foot on the bottom step when the ornate oak doors burst open, and the very man she sought bustled out with a pile of books in hand, followed by a large woman with dark braided hair. She wore master's robes and carried a book of her own.

"Laird Envoy?" Samily's voice was higher pitched than she intended, practically a squeak.

Aranok almost dropped the books as he peered over them. "Samily! Perfect. Actually, yes, perfect. We might need you. Come with us." He tipped the top pair of books toward her and she instinctively caught them. "This is Master Ipharia. Ipharia, this is Lady Samily of the White Thorns. The one I told you about."

Ipharia's warm smile reflected in her kind, maternal eyes. "Pleasure to meet you, young lady. I very much hope you and I can spend some time together."

Samily's mouth hung open. She had no idea what was happening. However, a master had addressed her and it was only polite to return the greeting. "The pleasure is mine, Master. How can I help?"

Ipharia nodded toward Aranok, who was disappearing along the path Samily had just come. "Follow him."

Samily had to trot to catch up with Aranok, who strode with purpose between buildings and into the quadrangle that formed the heart of the university. Students scattered before him, a few stopping to stare, perhaps wondering if they recognised him and if he could be who they suspected. They continued on their way once Master Ipharia caught up.

"Where are we going?" Samily asked when she was close enough to avoid shouting.

Aranok stopped in front of the entrance to a building and placed his books on the ground. "Guard these. I'll be right back."

"Wait!"

Aranok paused halfway through the door to look back. "What?"

"What are we doing?"

"Saving Rasa. Can I go?"

"Oh!"

That was not any of the answers she might have expected. Not that she really had any idea what she expected. But it was a good answer. Aranok seemed to take her lack of response for assent and disappeared through the door.

"He's quite excitable, isn't he?"

Samily turned to see that Master Ipharia had arrived. She breathed heavily, clearly not used to chasing people around the university campus.

"Do you know why we're here?" Samily asked.

"I do, sweetheart. Because we think Master Conifax had something we need. And if he did, we can help Rasa."

"You know Rasa?"

"Very well. She was an outstanding student, and I expect her to become a colleague before long. Sharp mind, that girl, and exactly the right temperament to teach. Wise beyond her years, you might say."

There was something comforting in the master's voice and, Samily realised, in her words. She spoke of Rasa's future with hope, but also with presumption—a presumption Samily had not been able to make since Lestalric.

A distant sound of breaking glass came from somewhere above. A few students sharing lunch on the grass nearby looked up. Samily followed their gaze, but there was nothing to see from her angle.

"Hmph. I don't imagine Master Conifax would have been overly pleased at his display case being broken, but he's not here to complain about it." Ipharia smoothed her slightly dishevelled robes.

"I am sorry for your loss. Master Conifax was a good man."

Ipharia laughed. "He was a grumpy old pain in my arse! But yes, overall, he was a good man."

It felt wrong to speak ill of the dead, especially one so recently deceased. And yet, Ipharia did it with such enthusiasm and affection that it seemed somehow less offensive. Still, Samily did not know how to react, so she simply smiled.

"He'd have done just about anything for that boy, though. Aranok. Proudest damn day of his life when he was made king's envoy. I don't know how Conifax got his head in and out of rooms for a month after that!"

"I have seen students looking at him." Samily understood a little of why he kept himself so private if he could be so easily recognised in the right circles.

Ipharia leaned toward her conspiratorially. "That's only because they don't know who you are, darling."

Samily felt her cheeks flush. "Me?" She had changed out of her armour as soon as she'd had the chance. As usual, it needed cleaning, and she was glad of the chance to wear some lighter clothes for a while.

For its relative lack of weight, the White was still hot. "Surely they've seen a White Thorn before."

"Oh, honey!" Ipharia swatted her arm. "Not that. You're not a Thorn here, girl; you're the time *draoidh*."

Of course. It was not her prowess as a knight that gave her currency in Traverlyn, it was her magic. Curious, funny almost, that it was exactly the opposite in the rest of the country, where her status in the Order made her welcome and her magic drew suspicion. She understood why Aranok seemed so much more at peace here. It was where he belonged.

The door swung open behind her.

"Got it!" Aranok held a leather necklace from which dangled what appeared to be an oversized coin, carved with something that might have been a face, or perhaps the moon—Samily couldn't tell.

Ipharia seized it from him excitedly and turned it over in her hand. "Yes...yes. This is it. This is it!"

"We can do it?" Aranok's voice radiated excitement.

"I believe we can." Ipharia slapped the coin against the book she carried. "With these, if you're right, we can do it."

Samily still did not know what they were going to do. "Please. Envoy. Aranok. What are you doing?"

He turned to her, barely able to contain himself. "The Thakhati magic is a kind of possession. A demon's spirit takes hold of the body in the cocoon. We interrupted that."

"S'grace! What happens to the person?" Samily feared the answer, but with all the hope she saw from both Ipharia and Aranok, she had to assume there was reason for it.

Aranok's tone darkened. "They die, if they're not already dead. But Master Ipharia agrees with me that..."

"That if she's not waking up, it's likely because neither spirit is in control," Ipharia finished for him. "Rasa's spirit is still there, fighting the demon."

A demon? Inside her? Samily felt sick at the thought. And Rasa, alone, fighting for her life. "Heavens! Can we help her?"

"We can do better than help," said Ipharia. "We can kill that bloody demon for her."

CHAPTER 17

The spell had to work. Not just for Rasa, but for everything. If Aranok could save Rasa, it would be a lot easier to save Shay. But if she died...If Rasa died, he might not want to.

It was worse for being out of his control—in the hands of a novice.

Master Ipharia had insisted that Samily being a Thorn would be a benefit to her casting the spell. Ipharia was a renowned academic but also a woman of faith. As she saw it, the literature supported the idea that the Thorns had a God-given advantage over demons. Aranok had argued Samily's inexperience was too much of a risk, and Ipharia had read him several accounts where supposedly non-*draoidh* righteous men and women had banished demons. As far as Aranok was concerned, it was much more likely they just didn't know they were *draoidh*—like the boy at Caer Amon. Or the stories were exaggerated, or plain made-up. But Ipharia's final argument had convinced him to let Samily try—the heart of the spell was a battle of wills, and whatever else he might doubt, Samily had a will of iron.

"Like this?" Samily dangled the medallion over Rasa's chest. She and Ipharia had undressed the woman and lay her under a blanket just in case her powers were triggered again. No point destroying a perfectly good dress, Ipharia had said. Aranok smiled at the thought that his mother would have agreed.

"A little lower." Ipharia guided her hand down until the medallion was all but touching Rasa. She looked so peaceful, so beautiful. It was difficult to imagine there was a war raging inside her. He hoped so, anyway. Once they removed the demon, they'd know whether Rasa was still in there, or if they'd just freed her body. No, he wasn't considering that. He was weary of losing people.

"Aranok?" Ipharia's voice sounded urgent, as if something was wrong, but Aranok realised he'd just not answered her the first time she said his name.

"Sorry, yes."

"Move your fingers, man, you're covering the incantation."

"Oh, sorry." Aranok looked down and adjusted his grip such that Samily could read the words. "Are you comfortable with the pronunciation, Samily?"

"I believe so."

Ipharia wrapped her hands around the Thorn's fist, the one holding the necklace. "It's going to fight you, girl. It's going to do everything it can to make you scared. To make you question yourself. Just you hang on, all right?"

If doubting yourself was a weakness, Samily was definitely a better choice.

"Do you want me to go through it one more time?" Ipharia was like a nervous mother. Her mouth smiled reassuringly, but her eyes were wary.

"No, I have it. I am sure." Her voice was even. Stoic. Exactly Samily.

"You can do this. I believe in you." Aranok wasn't sure if he was telling her or himself, but either way her face softened for a moment.

"Thank you, Envoy."

"Right, then." Ipharia stood back against the wall. "Whenever you're ready, Samily."

The girl looked affectionately at Rasa, took a breath and began.

> *"Deamhain, cluinn mi.*
> *Tha mi gad ghairm.*
> *Ruasgail an t-anam so..."*

Aranok almost dropped the book as Rasa roared from the depths of the earth. Her head had become a bear's and snapped at Samily's fist.

Ipharia wrestled the book from his hands. "Give me that! You hold her!"

"Gluais." Aranok pushed the bear head down into the pillow. It roared and strained in resistance, but he held it fast.

Samily continued as if nothing had happened.

> *"Thigibh thugam.*
> *Faic mo bhuinn.*
> *Tha mi ag àithneadh dhuit."*

Another roar, louder even than the first, and Rasa's head became a dog's. Her hand spilled from under the blanket and it was a great bird's claw, mindlessly grasping for something to crush. The roar became a whine as her head became a horse, whinnying in distress.

"Hurry!" Ipharia bellowed. "Finish it!"

A muscle spasmed in Aranok's back and he realised how hard he was straining to hold her still. The pain caused him to lose concentration for a moment, and Rasa lurched forward, her equine mouth snapping again at the medallion.

Samily brought her free left hand round in an arc, punching the horse across its nose, snapping its head away from the medallion. The knight glowered briefly at Aranok.

"Sorry," he hissed through gritted teeth, regaining control and forcing Rasa's head down again.

> *"Is e am bhuinn seo do dhachaigh.*
> *Gabhaidh do spiorad fois an seo."*

Rasa made a noise Aranok had never heard a living being make; the buzz of a thousand bees and the crunch of iron on steel, from deep in her chest. Aranok blinked away the sweat that dripped from his eyebrow, desperately trying to ignore the pain spreading down his back.

> *"Is e seo do phrìosan maireannach.*
> *Tha mi ag àithneadh dhuit ann an ainm Dhè."*

The scream was agonising. Rasa's chest lurched upwards as her head arched back and her mouth gaped. A heat-like haze rose from her, hovered and coalesced around the medallion. It spun like a child's toy on the end of the necklace.

"Tha mi ag àithneadh dhuit ann an ainm Dhè!"

Samily was screaming now, all calm gone.

A popping noise, as if all the air were suddenly sucked from the room, and the medallion stopped spinning.

"Now! Destroy it!" Ipharia ordered.

Samily dropped the medallion, lifted her Green blade with both hands and drove the tip through it, into the wooden floor.

A great crack and a flash of light.

Then silence.

Aranok blinked away the spots dancing before his eyes. Rasa had stopped resisting. Her face was her own; her hand too. Like Aranok, she was slick with sweat, but she was human. He reached for the muscle in his back, kneading the knot beneath his shoulder blade.

"Did it work? Did I do it right?" Samily pleaded.

"Right?" Ipharia tossed the book on a sideboard and grabbed Samily's arms. "Pardon my language sweetheart, but you were bloody magnificent!"

Samily's eyes widened and her mouth opened but no words came out.

"You destroyed that demon like it was nothing. Did you see her, Aranok? Did you see her punch that horse in the face?" Ipharia was aglow with pride and enthusiasm.

"I did." It was just what he expected from the girl. Her heart was made of granite.

"She's a miracle." The voice was raspy and thin, but it was unmistakably…

"Rasa!" Samily scrambled to her bedside and seemed as though she might throw her arms around the woman, but stopped herself and instead took Rasa's hand between her own.

"Hi, miracle girl." Rasa's smile was as contagious as Aranok remembered, and he felt his own spread across his face.

"I didn't know if you... are you... was it awful?" Samily spluttered.

Rasa raised her hand to caress the knight's cheek. "I heard you. I heard you fighting for me. Calling me. I heard you." She looked for a moment at each Ipharia and Aranok before returning to meet Samily's eyes.

"Ah! My girl." Ipharia's hands were clasped before her mouth and tears streamed down her cheeks. "I knew you weren't done with us."

A banging on the door broke the daze threatening to overtake Aranok. He slipped the latch and opened it. Egretta stood flanked by three medics. "What in Hell is going on?"

Aranok pushed the door open and stepped back, allowing Egretta into the room. When she saw Rasa awake she sighed contentedly. "Well, that is a sight for sore eyes. Welcome back, dear."

"Thank you," Rasa answered. "I'm very happy to be back."

Egretta turned to Aranok and jabbed a finger in his face. "You need to tell me when you're going to do something stupid in my hospital."

Aranok nodded solemnly. "I'm sorry. We were in a hurry."

"Don't give me excuses. What if she'd needed a medic, eh? Then what?"

Aranok spread his hands wide, indicating the four of them.

"Don't cheek me, boy." Egretta's tone was hard, but there was a hint of amusement about the edges of her mouth. "Right, you lot, out. We need to check our patient. Do I need to be worried about that?" Egretta pointed to the shattered remains of the medallion and the newly carved scar in the floor.

"Not at all, except to throw it away. It's useless now." Ipharia leaned down to kiss Rasa on the forehead as she passed. "I'll see you soon."

"I'm... I'll come back and see you... later." Samily stood and made space for Egretta and one of the medics to get into Rasa's bedside.

"I'll look forward to it," she answered. "Laird Aranok?"

He turned back from the door. "Yes?"

"That's one less favour you owe me."

Once they'd collected the books and cleared out of the room, the three of them stood in the hall as if not quite sure what to do next. Unfortunately, Aranok knew exactly what he had to do, and he wasn't looking forward to it. Any of it.

"We should celebrate," said Ipharia. "Join me for a glass of wine?"

He'd have loved to. But he had far too much to do before he was going to get any sleep.

"Another time, Master. But thank you. I seem to be racking up debts all over the country, but I owe you for this. Both of you."

"Nonsense." Ipharia took his hand and gave him a look that seemed much more intense than necessary. "You know what a teacher will do for her students. Help me take these books back to the library?"

"Can I follow you? I need to ask Samily a favour."

"Another one? You *are* racking up debts." Ipharia turned to Samily and offered her hand. "Lady Samily, it has been an absolute honour to meet you. I very much hope to see you again soon."

"And you, Master Ipharia. Thank you."

Once she was out of sight, Samily spoke. "What can I do for you, Envoy?" Her tone was cautious. Not as warm as it had been before… He probably deserved that. He'd have to fix it later. For now, he was pretty sure he was going to make it worse.

"Samily, Shayella told me how the magic worked. That's how we knew what to do. To save Rasa."

Her face hardened. "She also did that to her."

"Yes. She did. I know that. And I understand how you feel." He thought he did, anyway. The Thorn was difficult to read. "What I mean is just… she couldn't have told me if she was dead."

Samily looked down at the floor, took a breath and answered. "No. I suppose not."

Hopefully that was enough, because he didn't really have time to argue with her if she said no to his next request. "I need to speak to Shayella. In private."

Samily's head snapped up. "Why in private?"

"Because it's my best chance of getting an honest answer from her." That might be true, but it wasn't the real reason. He hoped it was real enough for her.

The Thorn looked at the door to Rasa's room. The sound of the medics busying themselves was just audible through the heavy wood. "You need her to speak."

"I do."

“Fine. But I’ll be outside the room.”

“Agreed.” As he’d thought, another debt on his tally. With luck he’d make this one worth it.

Darginn waved his fingers before his face, watching the skin crease and stretch with each flex. He focused on his feet—the feel of them on the floor, the backs of his thighs against the bench. He shifted his arse slightly to relieve pressure and felt the tingle of blood returning to his soles.

It was incredible.

The shock was finally wearing off after a few days, but he wasn’t sure he’d ever lose his wonder at having his limbs restored. Was this truly his hand before him? It looked identical, down to the scar on his thumb when he’d managed to nearly slice it off chopping potatoes. It was, for all he could imagine, his hand. And yet he’d seen his hand removed. He felt its absence, like a phantom ache that scratched at his brain. As the Thorn had explained it, she’d turned back time—restored his hand before it was taken. And yet, his hand had still been removed, so was this truly his limb, the one he’d had since birth? Were these his feet, his legs?

Darginn flexed his toes, pushing his heels up off the floor. They felt like his. They felt real.

“May I join you?”

Darginn looked up to see Laird Meristan looming over him. He could see how men ran from such a beast, wearing the White or no, but so far all he’d seen from the knight was gentleness and consideration. “Of course, m’lord, please.” Darginn gestured to the seat across the table. “May I buy you an ale?”

Meristan took the offered seat. “I’d gratefully take a whisky, but… have you any coin?”

“I have enough.” In truth, he hadn’t a copper on him. He’d no idea what the baroness had done with his coin pouch, but it had been nowhere to be found when they recovered what they could of his possessions. He hadn’t been thinking awfully clearly, to be honest, so he hadn’t looked hard for it. He was too eager to get the Hell out of that place. But money wasn't an issue for a king's messenger. His credit was good in every tavern in Eidyn, bar maybe a few that he would never be keen to set foot in anyway. And the absolute least he could do for one of the people who'd pulled him out of that Hell was stand the man a whisky.

Darginn nipped to the bar and gestured to the serving boy. He made a note in the ledger under the bar after he handed over the drink and offered a respectful nod. Darginn was spending the night there too, before figuring out how to head home tomorrow. He hoped it would be an easier journey, but there was plenty about it still lay ill with him. Returning to Haven was the only thing in the world he wanted, but his family—his wife, children and granddaughter—were all still of the impression Janaeus was king. The king who had ordered him sent to his death at the hands of a lunatic. Was it even safe for him to return? What if his family were being watched?

"What's on your mind, my friend?" Meristan smiled at him as he retook his seat.

"Hard to say. I suppose I'm trying to figure everything out. Decide what to do next." He raised his beer in salute, and the knight returned the gesture with his drink. "*Slainte.*"

The big man sipped his whisky, rolled it around his mouth and sucked through his teeth. "Aye, I can understand that. Your position must be difficult. A king's messenger in a time where the king is a fraud." He said the words quietly, but even so, Darginn's eyes darted left and right, wondering if anyone had heard. As it stood, that talk was still tantamount to treason, he reckoned. Until enough knew the truth.

"Aye." He rolled the tankard in his hand. "That and other things."

"Like what?" Meristan's brow wrinkled. "You all right?"

All right? Darginn wasn't sure he'd ever be all right again. He was still jumping at shadows and his dreams were all the more terrifying for being memories. "Don't s'pose I am. But I'll be all the better for getting home. I think."

"Home is Haven?"

Darginn nodded.

Meristan leaned across the table. "Between you and me, I understand that's where the envoy is headed. If you're worried about the journey."

Indeed he was. Would he be safer for travelling with the king's envoy, though? Knowing what he knew? A stupid thought—how could he not be? One of the most powerful *draoidhs* in the country, who'd already been party to saving his life once? Of course he'd be safer with Aranok than alone—especially with the monsters they'd described coming out at night. The only real question was... "Would he be happy to have me travel with him?"

The Thorn's grin was as wide as his face. "You would be hard-pressed to find a better man in Eidyn." He took another sip of whisky and raised a finger as he swallowed. "A woman, perhaps, but not a man." The laugh that followed was infectious and Darginn felt himself smile for the first time in an age. He reflexively stopped. It felt wrong—sacrilegious almost—to smile after all he'd been through. After everything he knew.

Meristan's face straightened, and he reached a hand across to Darginn's arm. "Never be afraid to smile, my friend. Finding joy in the darkness is what makes the struggle bearable. If there was naught but misery, we'd never get out of bed."

Dargin allowed himself a smile then. But this one was not humour, nor maybe even joy, but appreciation. What Meristan had said about the envoy might be true, but if there was a better man to be found in Eidyn, Darginn suspected he might be drinking with him.

Aranok sat slumped against the wall, arms resting on his raised knees. It was an odd feeling, having what seemed to be something between a blanket and a pillow behind him, padding the walls. Egretta had explained this was to stop people from hurting themselves. Having watched Tilbark crack his own skull against the wall of his cell, he understood the need. The way he was feeling, he might need one of these rooms himself.

He needed another memory charm. At least one. And Shay had one. He kicked himself for not thinking of it before they left Lestalric, but that was a shitstorm.

"Well?" Shay looked down at him expectantly from the bed. Her hands twitched incessantly, likely anxious to be back around her daughter. Samily had insisted on taking her outside until he and Shay were finished. He'd offered token resistance, for Shay's benefit. The more she thought he was on her side, the more helpful she might be.

"How are you?" It was a stupid question. He knew how she was. Mad as a milliner and obsessed with her Dead daughter. And a prisoner. She was not well. The look she gave him agreed. "Sorry. I know. But is there anything I can do?"

Shay sighed and looked at him as though examining an item at market, deciding whether she wanted it and, if so, what to offer. He couldn't read her decision, but she eventually spoke.

"Kiana needs food."

Fuck.

"Shay, there's nothing I can do about that. You must know that." Her stony silence gave no quarter. "Shay, I'm sorry, no. I am devastated for your loss. I mean that with all my heart." He placed one hand on his chest. "It hurts me to even think of what happened to her—and to you." An eye twitched. Her face softened a little. "But, Shay, you know how your power works."

"No," she cut him off. "No."

"Shay, that's not your daughter. That's not Kiana. It's just her reanimated flesh following instincts and orders."

"No," she repeated even more forcefully. He wasn't sure if this was helping or not. He had little experience with madness—his own notwithstanding.

"You cannot expect to keep feeding her human flesh. You can't. It's intolerable."

Her head swayed a moment. She reset herself and stiffened her chin, stilling her hands from their idle fidgeting. "Recently deceased will suffice. We are in a hospital, aren't we?"

He closed his eyes as a wave of gooseflesh ran through him. Hells, she actually wanted to feed a dead patient to Kiana! Even for a man of no faith, that was sacrilege. His mind skimmed off the edges of Lestalric memories. The smell.

"No." This time it was his turn. "I'm sorry, Shay, but you just can't. It's too much to ask of anyone—" He almost said "sane" but caught himself. What he did know about madness was that few took well to being told they had lost their mind.

Shay sat abruptly back against the wall, a petulant child denied by an unjust parent. "You asked."

Aranok dropped his head. He had asked. But he couldn't lie to her. The girl was going to start decaying. Whether slower than normal because of her previous diet or not, it would happen, and Shay had to be prepared. He imagined it would be horrendous. He felt a spike of shame to be glad he wouldn't be there to see it.

"So what do you want? You came here for something." Mad, but perceptive.

"I need your charm. Your Hellfire charm."

A moment of silence, then a snort of laughter burst from her. Why was that funny?

"Shay, I'm serious. I need it."

She sat up and placed a hand delicately to her chest. "Oh, Ari, you don't think he thought of that? Really?"

What did that mean?

"Where is it, Shay?" He tried to keep an even, serious tone, but he was running out of patience. And he had more to do tonight.

She smiled sweetly and glanced down at her hand. "Right here. Where nobody's getting it." She leaned forward and whispered conspiratorially. "Necromancer magic."

"What does that mean?" Aranok sounded more desperate than impatient, he realised. That wouldn't help. He was in danger of giving her the power in this conversation. Or maybe he'd already surrendered it.

She leaned even further toward him and spoke slowly and clearly, as if he were the child. "It's embedded in my chest, my love. If you want it, you're going to have to kill me."

Aranok pushed himself upright. "Bloody Hell, Shay, seriously?"

She flashed that innocent smile again and nodded. God, she had no idea how precarious her situation was. What was he supposed to do now? If that got out, his fragile argument to keep her alive might just shatter.

His temper broke. He leaned down and jabbed a finger in her face. "I'm trying to help you! And you are not fucking making it easy!"

Shayella sat back, blinking, looking at him again like a predator, not a friend, not an ally. Maybe he couldn't keep her alive. Maybe she was beyond saving.

But he was still going to try, wasn't he? Because he needed to. Because it was the right thing to do. Because she was a victim too.

Because maybe he'd ignited the fire that devastated the country. And somehow, he was going to make that right.

"Shay, whatever you do, do not tell anyone else. Tell them you left it in Lestalric. Tell them it was destroyed. I don't care what you tell them, just do not tell them the truth. All right?"

The necromancer's look changed from wary to curious and finally to mischievous. "Well, Laird Envoy, it seems we are in cahoots."

CHAPTER 18

Aranok's eyes begged to close, the sting of exhaustion biting with every blink. Mynygogg had asked him to clear as many memories as possible before they left. In fact, he'd suggested giving the charm to Keft and letting him do it. The charm would work for any *draoidh* regardless of their skill. But knowing Janaeus had the relic, knowing he could recast his spell at any time, Aranok was reluctant to let it out of his hands. There was already a risk Janaeus knew something was wrong, between Rotan being taken and Shay's capture. If he had more agents in Traverlyn, or Lochen, he may already have been warned. And damned if Aranok was leaving it to anyone else to fix things if he recast his spell. He wasn't losing his mind again.

Mynygogg had agreed that this time Aranok was to keep the charm, since he was going into the heart of Greytoun. He had to be resistant to Janaeus's memory skill if he was to have a chance of getting the heart. So he sat in a university common room alongside Principal Keft, seeing one master after another. The swathe of empty chairs that would otherwise be filled with students chatting, laughing and studying seemed almost mournful. The absence of that life, that energy, felt unearthly—a sense that was only heightened by Aranok's lack of sleep. Keft must have recognised his slump, as he subtly placed a hand on Aranok's arm. The fire in the great hearth that dominated the north wall dwindled and Aranok felt a rush of energy up his arm and into his heart, from where it spread throughout his body. He took in a deep breath of cool air and felt his mind sharpen, the fuzzy edges of his sight crystallising.

He nodded his thanks to the energy *draoidh*.

"Principal. Laird Envoy." The woman who stood before them was perhaps thirty. She held herself with the easy confidence of nobility while showing the respect required by decorum. Not many nobles made master. As Conifax had often said, they tended to either be at the university through money alone and too stupid to be in any danger of academic success, or else be more interested in returning to their noble stations. Equally, the master had short black hair, not remotely the fashion in high circles, and her hands showed signs of actual work, unlike almost every noble he'd ever met.

"Laird Aranok, please meet Master Dialla." Keft introduced her as he had every master Aranok hadn't known. But that name rang a bell. Where had he heard it?

"Master Dialla, it's a pleasure." Had Conifax mentioned her? Or maybe Balaban?

"Laird Envoy, if I may, I share your grief over the loss of Master Conifax. He was a patron to me and a good friend." Her voice caught with what appeared genuine emotion. "I miss him, dearly."

That wound was nowhere near closed. He'd just buried it. For now. Until he had time for grief.

"Thank you."

"Master Dialla worked closely with Master Conifax," Keft explained. "Alongside Master Rotan."

That was where he'd heard the name.

Dialla stiffened. "I assure you I had no idea what he was doing. And I have no idea why on earth he would have killed Master Conifax, who was never anything but good to him—to both of us."

Of course, that's exactly what a spy would say, wasn't it? That she'd had no idea. Disavow any knowledge of her partner's betrayal. But it was also what she'd say if it were true, because she was smart enough to know she'd be suspect by association.

Which left him where?

Keft gestured for her to step forward. "Dialla, you are here for a matter of great urgency—"

Aranok cut him off. "Well, I don't know if *urgency* is the right word." He laughed a noble laugh, the kind that scoffed at any notion not his own. The kind she'd be familiar with and know exactly what it meant. Aranok was expressing his superiority over Keft. Belittling him, even. She needed to think his "urgency" was just deference to Aranok's station.

"There has been talk of some people being immune to the Blackening, you might have heard?"

She might have. Word of Morienne had surely escaped the hospital by now. Too many medics, too many students had come across her. Vastin was likely the subject of much interdormitory chatter.

"I may have heard a whisper, Laird. But I put little faith in gossip." She was guarded, though—beginning to wonder why she was here. If she was Janaeus's spy, it might be useful to let her think they were on the wrong track with the Blackening.

"We believe it comes from the blood—lineage, as it were." That was actually true, in a way. The best lies always were. "And I have devised a charm to test for that immunity."

Dialla's brow furrowed to match Keft's. Damn him, Aranok needed him to catch up and stop looking like he'd just found a frog in his pillow. He'd never met this woman before, so he could play up the foppish noble act and keep her attention. "Now I know it will seem somewhat dramatic, but I must insist that you neither see the totem nor hear the incantation. A matter of delicacy, you understand." He had no idea what delicacy it might mean. Hell, he was making up each sentence word by word. But he hoped her background would kick in. Any "delicate matter" in polite society was not to be questioned, at the risk of insulting the other's honour. Especially if they were a superior.

Her face turned serious. "Of course, Laird. What would you have me do?"

Good question. What the Hell would he have her do? He stood and lifted the scarf from around his own neck. "May I?"

"You may," she replied formally, but her look was reticent. As Aranok reached up to wrap the scarf around her eyes and over her ears, he glanced at Keft. The old man's face was awash with confusion. Conifax would have worked it out by now. Balaban too. In fact, Balaban would have warned him about Dialla before she came in, because he had the wit to have considered the same concerns Aranok had. He mouthed *shh* at the principal and nodded seriously. Keft sat back, a sceptical look on his long face. As long as he shut up and left Aranok to it, that would do for now.

Once he was happy he'd blocked Dialla's sight and at least muffled her hearing, he pulled the charm from his neck. If she was working for Janaeus, he may have warned her about this. He may have shown her the charm and told her the incantation to allow her to maintain her disguise. But if she didn't know what was being done to her, there was no way she would fake it. He stood behind her and gently rested the charm against her neck. She'd feel a slight presence, of course, but nothing she could identify. That contact was all that was needed.

"*Clìor*," he whispered in little more than a breath. But again, all that mattered was that he'd said it.

What happened next was crucial. If she did not react—if nothing happened—she was a spy and her memory was untouched. If she wasn't a spy...

Dialla screamed and collapsed to her knees. With a jerk, she fell forward onto her hands and vomited across the stone floor. "God help me!" she shrieked, heaving again. "What's happening?"

If she was acting, it was a fine performance.

Keft rose from his chair and crouched beside his colleague. "It's all right, Dialla." He put a hand under her arm, supporting her. "We should have prepared you." He said it to her, but it was pointedly aimed at Aranok. Fair enough. He'd explain in a minute. He had never known anyone who could vomit on demand. Aranok caught her other arm just as it gave way and Dialla surrendered consciousness.

"What the devil, man?" Keft asked accusatorially as they lifted her onto Aranok's seat. He pulled the scarf from her head and produced a cloth to clean the vomit from her lips. Aranok shrugged in a way he hoped was conciliatory.

"She might have been another spy."

Keft's face contorted as if Aranok had spat at him. "Dialla? Good lord, she was one of my finest students. I tutored her myself. Her control of her energy skill is almost unsurpassed! I would have happily spoken for her had you given me the chance before... this!"

She was an energy *draoidh*? Interesting. That explained the noble master.

She was probably considered an embarrassment to her family and had been sent to find another life. Aranok warmed to her, knowing exactly how that felt, and found the first sting of guilt for how he'd treated her.

Still, he'd been right. "If you had told me who she was before she stood in front of us, Principal, I likely would have given you that chance. As it was, I couldn't risk the possibility that Rotan was not working alone. You understand?"

He watched as Keft put the pieces together in his head and his demeanour softened. "I suppose I do see that, now that you say it."

It was about ten minutes, maybe less, before Dialla woke. She lifted her hand to her head, looking for all the world as though she had spent a night in the Sheep's Heid and had no recollection of the stumble home. "What happened?"

Aranok was about to speak when she bolted upright, eyes wide. "Oh my God! My God! That desperate, awful little bastard! I'll murder him!"

Those were words Aranok had not often heard from a noble lady.

"How could he?" she bellowed in a tone Aranok suspected was normally reserved for unruly students.

"Um, who?" Aranok asked, hoping her anger subsided before she turned it on him for not giving her fair warning.

"That little toad, Rotan! He twisted my mind in order to"—she paused, as if the words were more vomit in the back of her throat—"to court me."

Oof. So Rotan's rewards for working for Janaeus were more than just a position as master. He deserved every curse she put on him. At least Allandria had known Aranok was as much a victim as she, but for Dialla… He suspected he had no need to worry overly about her anger, and he was distinctly unworried about her being a spy. If anything, Rotan should perhaps be more afraid of Dialla than of Aranok. If she was as skilled as Keft said, her energy powers could literally draw the life out of him.

"Master Dialla, I am extremely sorry for what was done to you. And for not being able to warn you what I was going to do." He needed to get through this bit quickly, before she had the chance to get angry about it. "I hope you'll forgive my deception, but there is always a chance Rotan had accomplices, and as someone who worked closely with him, reason alone dictated I had to be wary. I assure you it was nothing personal and is absolutely no reflection on your reputation."

She raised her head and took the offered cloth from Keft to clean her face. "I understand, Laird Envoy—"

"Please, call me Aranok," he interrupted. More manipulation of the nobility's code, but an invitation from a superior to use an informal name was a sign of respect and he hoped she'd take it as such. And he hated being called "Laird." And that might be quite important if he got away with the idea that had been forming in the back of his brain. He was about to push his luck very, very hard.

Her eyes flickered. Yes, she knew what he'd meant. But there was suspicion there too. Justified, admittedly.

"Are you all right, my dear?" Keft asked. He seemed to have genuine affection for the woman. You spent a lot of time with a master of the same skill at university. Aranok knew that well.

"I will be, Master, thank you," she answered. "And please forgive me for… this." She waved her hand at the puddle of vomit between them.

Aranok laughed gently. "You should have seen me. I was up to my elbows in it. I think it was in my hair."

Dialla gasped, but her eyes lit with mirth. Good. Anything that warmed her to him was going to help.

"Master Dialla, I'm sorry to have to ask this now. I understand the anger you're feeling and it is wholly justified. What Janaeus has done to the country is unforgivable, and what he did to you, specifically, was awful. If it's any comfort, he did something similar to a close friend of mine." It wasn't the same, but it was close. And maybe, with this perspective, he was understanding a little more of Allandria's reaction. It was a violation, regardless of Aranok's innocence. Rotan had no such excuse. Perhaps allowing Dialla to finish him would be the greater punishment, and all the more cathartic for it. For both of them.

Dialla nodded warily. She was sharp. Everything more he learned about her made him more certain this was a good idea. But of course, there were no stupid masters—his reservations about Keft notwithstanding.

"I wonder if you might be interested in helping me to right these wrongs—not just your own, but all of them." Here came the push. He was stretching his luck unreasonably thin.

"Would you consider accompanying me to Greytoun?"

CHAPTER 19

Aranok stroked the neck of his new horse, a dappled grey with a dark mane and light tail. Tobin had all but begged them to let the Calladells rest, and the stable master, whose name Aranok had missed, had agreed. They weren't in the rush they'd been before, so normal horses would suffice. Especially with so many of them needed. Thus most of the stable's remaining complement were scattered around the paddock in various stages of readiness to depart.

Three groups. Five objectives.

Aranok was less than happy with some of the compositions, but he'd been firmly overruled by Mynygogg.

The king, Allandria and Meristan were going southwest. Meristan to Baile Airneach; Mynygogg and Allandria into the Reiver Lands, through the gate in the Malcanmore Wall near Gardille. Mynygogg had sent a messenger ahead, apparently, with a request for the Reiver council to meet in order to see him. That could easily go either way. They might welcome him with open arms or hang him for Eidyn's betrayal of the peace compact.

Aranok had been looking forward to having Allandria with him again, but Mynygogg had insisted Nirea accompany him to Greytoun instead, arguing that the king and queen should not be together in case their party were taken. It made sense, but Aranok didn't like it. He respected Nirea of course, and considered her a friend, but she was headstrong and reckless. She charged into fights he would approach more carefully. It might have worked for her so far, but how many good men and women had she gotten killed?

Then again, he was plenty guilty of that.

Nirea's presence also made him second-in-command, a position he'd become extremely unused to. He hoped they'd find common ground on any major decisions. Aranok had pointed out that Nirea's scar was too well-healed to play into the story of them being the only survivors of Barrock. She'd reluctantly allowed Samily to remove it temporarily. That hadn't been the result he intended.

Joining them were Darginn Argyll, who had requested their company on his own return to Haven, and Dialla, who despite Aranok's poor treatment had somewhat miraculously agreed to his request. Having an energy *draoidh* with them was a huge boon. He couldn't have asked Keft—the man was old and needed here to help maintain the sunspire and protect Traverlyn from the Thakhati. Aranok understood a student was performing the magic, under Keft's supervision, since Conifax's death. It was a more traditional, if larger-scale, usage of the sunstone magic.

Their mission was to pretend to remain under Janaeus's spell and retrieve the heart of devastation from the castle. Simple, but dangerous. Aranok was also minded to visit Madu, the head messenger, given the chance. Restoring her memory and getting her on their side could be an invaluable asset if they couldn't retrieve the heart.

Finally, Samily and Rasa. They would stay with Mynygogg's company as far as Mournside, where they would deliver a message to Ikara regarding the wagons and supplies in preparation for curing the Blackening. Then they were to go to Dail Ruigh in the hope of tracking down another memory *draoidh*. He hadn't realised they'd almost come across one at the Wheatsheaf. Even if Aranok had remembered they existed, Samily hadn't mentioned it. But from what she had heard, it sounded likely. He hadn't imagined for a moment Rasa would be fit or able to travel so soon, but she'd insisted she had been resting for days and that she felt more than well enough.

Every other mission, every objective, was a contingency in case they couldn't get the heart from Janaeus. Mynygogg was a wise leader—not relying on one solution. It was good planning. Strong leadership. He couldn't imagine them failing.

But if they didn't get the heart, they couldn't cure the Blackening without…

Aranok swung himself up onto the horse and looked around the paddock. In the early morning light, passersby would see a group gathering for a hunting party. Darginn was already mounted up. Dialla spoke with Opiassa, who was organising the town's defences in their absence. Already, Master Macwin and a number of nature *draoidh* students were fortifying the edges of the town—twisting and shaping the trees and bushes that bordered it into a natural barrier. Traverlyn had never been a walled city, but if it was to be the centre of a new rebellion, it was going to need better protection.

Mynygogg was mounted alongside Meristan. The two spoke in hushed but convivial tones. Allandria was attending to her pack, which was slung over her mount. Samily and Rasa were in deep conversation while their own animals were saddled by a stable hand Aranok had not seen before. They waited only for Nirea.

Aranok caught Tobin's eye as he crossed the yard, and gestured for the boy to come over. He hastened to Aranok's side, looking concerned. "Everything all right, Laird? Is your saddle well-fitted?"

"Fine, Tobin, everything's fine, thank you. I just wanted to ask a question."

"Of course, sire."

Aranok stroked the horse's neck and she cocked her head in appreciation. "What's her name?"

Tobin's face broke into a wide grin. "This here's Moonlight, sire. Might be the gentlest horse in the stable, her." He held his hand to Moonlight's mouth and the horse eagerly nibbled at whatever treat he'd offered.

Gentle. He'd never considered "gentle" a trait he'd want in a mount before, but he found it comforting all the same. "And Allandria's horse? What's his name?" The horse was a solid, dark grey, with even darker mane and tail.

"That's Sky, sire. Fine horse. Good and strong."

Sky. Aranok looked up at the thick, rolling cover of grey cloud and smiled. That was about right. He pulled a coin from his purse and handed it to the boy. "Thank you, Tobin. You do excellent work. Your horses are a credit to you. We owe them our lives."

Tobin took the coin without even looking at it, smiling brightly up at Aranok. The compliment was probably worth more to him than the coin, but a gold coin would be worth more in time. "Thank you, sire. Very kind."

At a nod from Aranok, the boy hobbled away. It occurred to him that, if the boy's limp was an injury, Samily could perhaps fix it for him. But if he'd had it from birth, there was nothing she could do. He'd try to find out, subtly. Wouldn't be fair to give the boy false hope, nor to embarrass him.

"You? Kind? Surely not."

Aranok turned to see Allandria walking toward him, eyes sparkling with mischief. He returned her smile. "Some people think so."

Her face turned serious as she put a gentle hand on his knee. "You all right?"

"No. Not really." He hadn't admitted that even to himself. Not until she asked. Until Allandria asked.

"I didn't think so."

She met his eyes and, it seemed, understood everything he couldn't say in that moment. Her support against killing Shay had been invaluable, and she didn't even know the full reason for it. If she did, she might be the only person who would forgive what he'd done. He ached to tell her, to spill every poisonous ounce of guilt and beg for absolution. But he couldn't. There was no time left. "I'd rather you were coming with me."

"So would I." The vehemence with which she said it was slightly surprising. But it felt good to know she would have been with him if she could. He'd have to get used to surviving without her, though, now that she was Nirea's envoy. She'd have her own work to do. And she'd be brilliant. "Aranok..." Her voice faltered, as if she wasn't even sure what was coming next herself. She sighed and squeezed his knee lightly. "Don't die, all right? When we get back, let's talk."

His first reaction was that she knew him so well she could see he needed to talk, but a moment of thought and he realised that she did too. The emotion in her eyes was complex and he couldn't have said if it were happy or sad. At a guess, he'd have called it bittersweet. "Yes, I'd like that. I'd like that a lot."

With that, her smile returned. She slapped his thigh, winked and turned back toward her horse.

"Sky!" he called after her.

She turned back, confused. "What?"

"Your horse is called Sky."

She smiled warmly and looked up. "Sounds about right. Yours?"

"Moonlight."

"Nice name."

"And you've met Tobin, right?"

This time she laughed openly. "I have. We're on friendly terms." She shook her head playfully, turned and walked away, her shoulders trembling slightly as she giggled.

Across from him, Nirea had arrived. She hugged Samily tight. Those two had become close too. Samily's animosity toward Shay could be a problem, though. He'd have to watch that.

"Everything all right?" he asked as Nirea approached.

She looked up at him mournfully. "Aye. Just went to see the boy before we go."

Vastin. Aranok had considered seeing him, but since both he and Morienne were reminders of other failings, he'd taken the cowardly way out and pretended he didn't have time. The boy would still be healing, and Morienne at least seemed happier for having her curse contained, if not removed. "How was he?"

Nirea's mouth crumpled. "Hard to tell, it's early, but they're not sure he's healing as he should. The wound still looks… angry."

Fuck.

If the boy died, Glorbad might drag himself back from the grave just to boot Aranok in the balls. But once they had the heart, who knew what they might be capable of? He said nothing in reply. He didn't need to.

When the queen had saddled up, Mynygogg raised a hand and gestured for them all to come close.

Aranok nudged Moonlight forward. They gathered in silence, waiting for their king to speak. Mynygogg sat up high in his saddle and took a deep, thoughtful breath. As he spoke, he looked around the circle, meeting each person's eyes.

"Thank you all for being here. I hope you know how much I appreciate what you're doing and how much I value your support. There's no easy way to dress this: We lost a war. We lost a war we thought we were fighting on two fronts, and neglected the third, which was the most dangerous. We allowed the country to be turned against us. We made mistakes. I made mistakes. I will try not to make them again.

"This war we fight now is not a war for land, for titles or power. It is a war for something we should demand as the very basis of our society. It is a war for truth. It is a war against manipulation and lies. It is a war for the very soul of Eidyn. It is a war we dare not lose, for our children and for our grandchildren. We dare not lose, else the men and women who died fighting were all lost in vain. They will not forgive us easily if we do not fix our mistakes and restore the country to the hands of those who have the welfare of Eidyn's people at our core.

"We have one ideal chance at getting it right, but we have to be ready if that fails. It's not going to be easy fighting a lie the whole country believes. It's going to be almost impossible. We have to do it anyway. Even if we fail, even if we die fighting, it is our responsibility to do everything we can to restore the minds of our countrymen and women.

"I am the rightful King of Eidyn and I take ultimate responsibility for the mistakes that led us here. And that is why I am so grateful to all of you, for the chance to put them right and return Eidyn to its people again.

"We say goodbye now, but we will meet again in the great hall of Dun Eidyn, and it will be in celebration. And I will share a drink with each of you as the architects of Eidyn's salvation. Good luck, my friends. And for those who believe, may God be with you."

He gave a good speech, Aranok had to give him that. Hopefully everyone else was feeling uplifted and inspired by their king's words. The part about it being hard—that was the truth. Mynygogg was terrified they would never restore him to the throne. Not for himself, but for the country he dreamed of creating. He'd held it in his grasp after a lifetime and had it taken from him in an instant. He presented a confident, regal front, but he would be a mess inside. Much like Aranok.

The king turned his horse, rode out of the paddock and turned south. Allandria, Meristan, Samily and Rasa followed. Nirea led the rest out and turned north. As he passed out of the gate, Aranok gave a last look down the lane. Allandria half turned back and raised a hand.

He did the same, and she was gone from sight.

CHAPTER 20

Darginn held his scarf close to his face. The stench was awful. Somehow already so much worse than it had been just a few days ago. The clouds of insects were so thick it was like riding through a light fog, and he was doing all he could to ignore the wet clattering from his horse's hooves. Hells, someone was going to have to come and clear the Easter Road of Dead eventually. Surely? They couldn't just leave them here to rot. They wouldn't need to worry about the Blackening if half the country were diseased.

When they finally got past the gruesome scene and the air was clear enough to lower his scarf, Darginn turned to the horse beside him. "Pardon me, Envoy?"

Aranok looked across as though he'd all but forgotten Darginn was there. "Yes?"

"I was just thinking—will someone sort that out? I mean, pardon me saying so, but is it no a danger to have them all lying there rotting in the road?"

Aranok looked over his shoulder and back to Darginn. "Yes, it is. I spoke to some men in Lochen last night. We'll need that road clear when we get the country back. You messengers more than most." He gave a weak smile.

"Ah, I'm no sure about that." After all that had happened, Darginn felt like perhaps it was time his messenger days were over. If they could manage without the wage, of course. Maybe they could, now his children were grown and moved out. “I'm not sure how much more these old bones will take.”

“Of course, I understand.” The envoy was quiet for a while before speaking again. “Darginn, are you all right? It occurs to me this might be hard for you—going back down this road again, so soon.”

“Aye,” Darginn mused, as though it were some other poor sod he was discussing and not himself. “I suppose it's not the easiest. But I'm thinking on my family, more than anything, if I'm honest.”

“I know how that is.” For a moment, Aranok was miles away, and Darginn wondered where his family was and when he'd last seen them. The war must have made that damn difficult for a man in his position. A man of his power. “Darginn, if you choose to retire—and you would be more than justified—I'd like to set you up with a stipend from the crown. A regular payment to keep you in good stead.”

Darginn's face must have registered some objection because the envoy raised his hand to stop him responding. “You've more than earned it through your service and your sacrifice. And if there's anything else the king can do—that I can do—please ask. It would be my genuine pleasure.”

Darginn was stunned into silence. The king would pay him not to work? That seemed... unlikely. But here was the king's envoy himself assuring him it was so.

I'll be buggered.

He could easily stop messengering, then. And still live a comfortable life, between a regular income and his savings. But there was one thing he had been thinking of, and wondering whether he could work up the courage to ask for. If he was going to ask, this seemed like the time. Darginn sucked down the butterflies of fear and tried to put the right words together.

“As it happens, sire, there is one thing I would appreciate.”

“If it's within my power, it's yours,” Aranok answered.

“Well, it's just, I've been thinking that maybe, what with all that's happening and all, maybe Haven's no the safest place for my family to be. You know? And I was thinking maybe I'd like to get 'em out and maybe over to Traverlyn, which seems a damn sight safer just at the moment.”

Aranok nodded understanding and his expression remained positive, so Darginn continued.

"But I reckon I'll have some difficulty convincing 'em all to come with me, what with them all still believing Janaeus is king and so on. So I wondered if, maybe, while we're in Haven, if you had time, if maybe you could restore their memories like you did mine? That would make it a whole lot easier to explain why they should come. I mean, my wife, Isadona, she'd likely come if I asked her, said it was important, I s'pose. She's accustomed to me not being able to tell her king's business and all that. But my children—especially my daughter. Her husband's a good man. Stonemason. Building houses in Haven as we speak, but he's a stubborn man. Wouldn't consider leaving his duty to the king without good reason. And they've a daughter—my granddaughter, Liana—most beautiful thing I ever saw. I just..."

Aranok smiled and interrupted, which was probably best since even Darginn could tell he was rambling. "Darginn, I would be happy to. First thing when we get to Haven, you take me home and we'll sort out your family."

The butterflies became a wave of joy. "Oh, thank you, sire, thank you. I would be forever in your debt, Laird."

The envoy's face turned serious, all of a sudden like. "Darginn Argyll, you could live another hundred years and never be in my debt. And please, call me Aranok."

That was a bit of a mad answer, Darginn thought. For all he was delighted to have it and excited about getting his family to safety, he wondered what exactly he'd done to earn such devotion from the most powerful *draoidh* in the country. Not that he was going to look a gift horse in the mouth, no sir. Darginn Argyll was no fool—it's how he'd lived this long to begin with. And the envoy was a fine friend to have, assuming Eidyn eventually got back to normal. So aye, he'd do whatever was asked of him to keep himself in those good graces, whether he knew why he'd earned them or not.

"Thank you, Aranok," he said enthusiastically. "It means the world to me."

Aranok smiled, and maybe he saw a flicker of happiness in his eyes. The envoy was a sombre man, in his experience—though they'd hardly met under ideal circumstances. He wondered what Aranok was like in peace—whether he found pleasure in the same things Darginn did. The way he spoke about family, he suspected at least they had that in common. He hoped so. For the kindness he'd shown Darginn, if nothing else, he wished him nothing but well.

The East Ferry Road was more of a path. It was much narrower than the Easter Road and wound through the trees, bending with nature. They could only ride two abreast here at most, but that was fine. Dialla had opted to ride alongside Nirea for most of the journey, while Aranok seemed protectively adherent to the messenger. Nirea supposed, if she'd seen what had been done to him, she might have felt the same way. She'd happily have slit Shayella's throat herself. Still might.

They hadn't spoken much. Dialla never instigated a conversation, only responding when Nirea spoke. Presumably that was some noble etiquette. Either that or the woman was painfully shy. Either way, she hadn't minded the peace. But being left to her own thoughts for too long had left her delving into every possible way things could go wrong. Imagining how easily Mynygogg could get himself killed before he made it to the Reivers council—assuming they agreed to call one for him. He had no authority for now.

She needed to talk to someone, think about something else. "Master Dialla, I hear you're from a noble line?"

"Indeed, Your Majesty. My father is a laird. My family have lands in Glabertoun."

Of course they did. Some of the wealthiest people in the country had vast, elegant homes in Glabertoun. It was known as the royal hunting grounds, but in truth, few royals ever ventured there just for hunting. Instead, the entitled wealthy built on the lands and used it for their own sport—presumably the honour of living in the royal hunting grounds was part of the appeal.

"What's your father's name?"

"Laird Clavel, Your Majesty. I don't know if you might have met him at some point?"

Had she? Honestly, she had no idea. Nirea wasn't good at remembering lairds. They were usually either petitioning for something, fawning in order to gain favour or just there so they could say they'd been in Mynygogg's court. Truthfully, neither of them had any real time for them, but it was useful to the kingdom to keep them happy and to keep their taxes flowing into the coffers for investment in the country. And the Lairds' Council still held a measure of power. They couldn't overrule the king, but they had enough sway to at least influence his thinking. Their income tended to be almost all from tenants and those allowed to farm on their land. They did no real work, and their lives had probably changed little from Hofnag to Mynygogg, or even now to Janaeus. Their wealth and status tended to protect them from societal upheavals that devastated the lives of commoners.

The new lairds—the merchants who made their own fortune and styled themselves lairds because they could afford servants—were generally shunned amongst the nobility. These people could trace their heritage back hundreds of years, in some cases back to the foundations of Eidyn. They seemed to feel this made them some kind of minor royalty and put them above those who had to work for their money and their title. Their very blood came with expectations.

"I'm afraid I don't remember, if I have."

Dialla nodded and smiled respectfully. Deferentially. Oh fuck this, she wanted a conversation. "Dialla, can I ask you a favour?"

"Of course, Your Majesty."

"Stop that, for a start." Dialla's eyes opened wide with a mixture of shock and slight terror—the look of someone who wasn't sure what they'd done wrong, but knew it must be something. "Please, just call me Nirea, and just speak to me like any other human being. I'm not one for all the graces of court and I honestly never will be. I'm a pirate, and Hell, I'm not even really queen at the moment. So could we start over and just…talk? Please?"

Dialla looked as though she'd swallowed her tongue as her throat pulsed and chin wavered. "Yes…of course…" she finally stammered, and Nirea felt a flash of amusement as she swore she saw the words *Your Majesty* die on her lips.

"Tell me about yourself, would you? How did you come to be a master? It's not many nobles choose an academic life over society."

The woman was blinking furiously but finally seemed to regain control of her expression and answer the question. "Well, my brother will inherit Father's title and the lands to go with it. My best hope, really, was to marry well, but I suppose I was always more interested in books than in choosing a husband. My mother tried desperately to get me to accept the attention of one of the many boys Father lined up to court me, but truthfully, once my *draoidh* skill developed, the idea of going to the university seemed so much more... interesting. All that knowledge and art and... I wanted to see it. I was schooled by my governess as a child and I wanted to know more than one woman could teach me. Knowing my skill would guarantee me admission made it an easy choice."

"How did your parents feel about your skill?" Nirea had wondered about exactly this point with Aranok in the past. She remembered now, with chagrin, how she'd instinctively not trusted him while her memory was changed, at least a little because of his *draoidh* abilities. That was poor. She knew better. If she was going to distrust him, there were better reasons.

"They were... not delighted, I suppose. It was not seen as a desirable thing amidst their society. They didn't argue awfully hard when I chose to leave." Dialla looked stoically ahead.

"So that's what took you to Traverlyn. What made you stay?" Nirea changed to a hopefully more pleasant subject.

"Oh, everything. Principal Keft is a wonderful tutor. I would never have honed my abilities as well had I not had him to instruct me, I'm sure. He's an incredibly wise man. But also, the life, the town, it's all so... enriching! Don't you find it so?"

On reflection, she supposed she did. Traverlyn, or the university, at least, asked no more of people than that they work to better themselves. They were not required to till the earth or chop wood to earn a coin, simply to "be" and to pursue more knowledge. Nirea could see how that would appeal to the right people. It was a place where merit, not wealth, earned you respect.

"I do, I think." Nirea liked the master, now that she was actually speaking to her. She had a mind to make her own way in the world—to follow her own path—not blindly accept the gilded carpet laid out for her. Nirea respected that.

"Could I ask...you a question?"

"Of course!" Nirea replied, pleased not to have to drive the conversation on at last.

"How did you meet the king? I know you joined his rebellion and that the two of you fell in love during the war against Hofnag. But how did you meet?"

Ah. That first time.

She treasured the memory all the more for having had it taken from her. "He came to Seafelde looking to raise a crew—a fleet—to take on Eidyn's navy. He knew he'd need control of the ports and shipping lanes if he was going to make his rebellion work. Sauntered into the Shepherd's Ha' like he owned the place, despite the fact it was full of some of the nastiest bastards you'd ever set eyes on. Even I wouldn't drink there single-handed. Always took at least two with me. But not Gogg. He strolled in like he'd walked into a pub on the High Street! That kind of confidence in a man is...appealing."

Nirea smiled at the memory. She could still see his face, clear as day, scanning the bar, deciding whom to approach and whom to avoid. He'd met her eye and she'd made the decision for him, tipping him a nod that welcomed him to join her.

"As he walked in the door, I swear a boy tried to have his purse off his belt within three steps. Gogg just shifted his hip and ran his hand down his side, protecting his purse as if he didn't even know the old cutpurse was there. You have to be a confident man to wear a purse in Seafelde, I'll tell you. Most keep their coin hidden in their boots, not announcing it to those who would have it at the end of a blade."

Dialla nodded intently. She was drinking in every word, by the look of her. For all Nirea knew, she was simply feeding the nobility's gossip, but she suspected better of the master.

"As he reached the table, my men stood to bar his way. I wanted to see how he handled himself, so I let them. Damndest thing. Both of them went for him when he refused to leave without speaking to me. Both ended up on their arses. He moved so quickly, like water, they were on the floor before they'd even got started. Gogg just seemed to...get out of the way. Their own momentum put them down. I'm not sure he even touched them—not much anyway. And there he was, just stood there grinning at me like a cat with a dead bird. He tossed the boys a coin each for their embarrassment and they quickly forgot it in their drink.

"Gogg sat down, and by the time we were done, I'd agreed to raise him a fleet and take down Hofnag with him. Truthfully, I never thought we'd win, but Hofnag was a cunt and his navy needed taking down a few pegs. Plus we could have done with them being weakened—would have allowed us to get in and out of Seafelde more easily to get about our business. Bugger me if I wasn't defending the shores of Eidyn by the time we were done!"

"What a wonderful story!" Dialla sat high in her saddle, her face a picture of genuine delight. "He seems like a powerful man."

That he was, but that was only what had piqued Nirea's interest. Hearing him talk about the future, about the Eidyn he wanted to build, that was where his heart lay, and that was when she fell in love with him. "He's a very good man. The best I know."

Powerful.

The word put an idea in Nirea's head. They rode in silence for a bit while she decided if it was a good idea or a very, very bad idea. A little too often recently she'd reached for a flower and grasped a nettle. But this seemed...wise. An effective fallback.

"Dialla, you said your energy skills are well-honed, yes?" She hoped the woman wasn't a braggart, but nothing she'd seen so far suggested that to be the case.

"I believe so," she answered. "I only know of Master Keft that I would consider more adept."

Excellent. She was a master after all, and they didn't allow any old idiot to teach, surely? Conifax certainly did not suffer fools gladly, and she'd worked closely with him, from what Nirea understood. Maybe it was a good idea. Maybe it solved a problem.

"Dialla, I wonder if I could ask something of you? Something I would need you to keep between us."

CHAPTER 21

Meristan had too much time to think.

The stench from the girl when he cut her—he kept imagining he'd caught a whiff of it, as if the reek had embedded itself in him. Of course, he'd smelled the Dead before, but there was something so much worse about the girl. She'd looked alive, from the outside. She'd looked like an innocent young girl. But on the inside, she was rotten. Her blood flowed like tree sap, black and sticky.

He could still feel the gristle as he severed her spine. S'grace, would that ever leave him? He had to hope so. He'd been praying for it.

Ahead Samily and Rasa chatted happily, as if two old friends reunited after a long absence. It was hard to believe they barely knew each other. Sometimes, he supposed, a connection just happened between like-minded people. But with Rasa being faithless, he wondered just how like-minded they were.

Truth be told, he was worried about Samily. Her brutal reaction to Shayella had been almost staggering. Cutting her tongue out the way she did, in anyone else he'd have called it an act of vengeance. But Samily was the most level, godly person he'd ever known. She did not become angry and she certainly never lost control. She struggled to understand people who did.

And yet, when she'd scolded him for offering Shayella her help, he'd seen a flicker of fire in her eyes, and everything she'd done since then had only compounded his suspicion. Samily was furious with Shayella being allowed to live. And that was not the Samily he knew.

Even when he'd found her, begging on the street as a child, she'd been even-tempered. Her big, soulful eyes were curious and hopeful. And tired, but there was no hate in them, no resentment for her suffering. Samily's even temper was something of a joke amongst the other Thorns, who would occasionally try to raise her ire with tricks and jokes. Usually she simply failed to understand what had happened, or why. But she didn't mind, if it amused her friends. She was such a beacon of light in a dark world that seeing darkness get into her at all felt like watching something precious corrupted.

He hoped she would find a way to come to terms with her feelings. It had been an extreme and hideous experience, and he understood why Samily had called it evil. It was hard to see it as anything else. But equally, in that tunnel, all Meristan had seen was a terrified and adoring mother, desperate to save the child she couldn't accept was already lost. It was hard to equate that woman, with all the love and pain in her eyes, with the horrendous things she'd done.

Aranok certainly saw it. His compassion would only be heightened by their old friendship and their shared *draoidh* history. That too was a worry, though. He hoped his friend would be able to see clearly what needed to be done, and when.

Their ride through the Black Meadows had been largely uneventful. They'd gone somewhat east of the junction with the Auld Road to minimise their chance of encountering Blackened and, indeed, had come across very few. There had been discussion of asking Morienne to travel with them for this very reason, but Egretta had insisted that she was crucial to Vastin's health and that taking her was likely to either kill him or cause an outbreak of the Blackening in the hospital. Without Aranok there to reverse it, that could wipe out Traverlyn the same way it had Lepertoun. That had been enough to convince Mynygogg to leave her behind.

Instead, they were all covered head to toe with gloves, hoods and scarves or a helm. They had learned from Morienne, though, and each had a supply of rags for blindfolding any stray Blackened they came across. Samily had handled one elderly man who stumbled into their path. Once he was calm, Mynygogg stood for an age, sadly regarding the poor soul. Even when the Blackening was lifted, there was little hope for him out here, alone, barely skin and bones. They likely left him to his grave.

"Copper for your thoughts?"

Meristan had been so engrossed that he hadn't noticed Allandria draw alongside him. "Ah, hello."

Allandria looked at him quizzically. "What's on your mind? You look…conflicted."

Conflicted? Was that what he was?

"I don't know that I'd say conflicted. Merely contemplating our situation. There's plenty of time for thinking out here." He gestured to the wide-open spaces littered with husks of wheat and barley, buzzing with life. "And plenty to think on."

"How do you see our situation?" Allandria asked.

Bleak was the honest answer. They had hope, of course, and he looked forward to seeing Baile Airneach again, but even if the queen's company were able to get the heart and undo Janaeus's memory spell, they would be straight back into a war with Anhel Weyr's demons. Taking Shayella was a huge advantage, but if Weyr could command the Thakhati, which they suspected he might, and still summon more demons, thousands more could yet die before this was done. But none of that would be at all helpful to say out loud.

"I think perhaps only in retrospect will we be able to see God's hand in this. Like my own Blackening served a greater purpose, I trust and hope that all of this will too. That in the end, we will be able to form a better Eidyn from these ashes."

Allandria "hmmed" and said nothing for a while. His answer had not been as comforting as he had intended, he suspected. It was the most positive thing he could say. Ahead, the foothills of the Black Hills rose on the horizon.

"We've killed no Blackened today. We haven't had to." Allandria's voice was flat and quiet. "That's something. Maybe God's hand is here, protecting them from us."

Protecting the Blackened from *them*? That was an odd way to put it. "Perhaps I should offer you a copper?"

She looked across at him, but her eyes wavered and she looked away again. Samily laughed at something and playfully slapped Rasa's arm. Farther ahead, Mynygogg rode silently, a dark figure, like a priest leading a funeral procession.

"I killed the baby. The one that Blackened Vastin and you. Someone had to...It was me. I did it." Allandria's voice broke on the last sentence. Meristan was not the only one carrying the trauma of things past.

"Allandria, someone would have done it. There, at that time, you believed that child already gone. If someone was going to finish them, I know you would have done it with kindness and love. That child is with God now, and the last thing they saw was someone who cared greatly for them. We can all only hope for so much."

With her head forward and her hood up, Meristan couldn't see Allandria's face, but a tear dripped onto her saddle. What a world it was, where those who tried to do a kindness were crushed with the weight of it.

He was certain they would only see God in hindsight.

"Identify yourselves!"

It was dark by the time they reached Mournside's east gate. The recent times they'd come here, Aranok's authority had been enough to have them open up, despite the Blackened threat. This time, unless there was someone Allandria knew on watch, Meristan held the most authority. Besides, now they knew what they knew, it might be best for Allandria to keep a low profile. She lowered her head, keeping her face in the shadow of her hood.

"My name is Brother Meristan of the White Thorns. I request entry for myself and my companions."

"What is your business in Mournside?" the guard's voice came back. He was a silhouette against the torch behind him, so Allandria had no idea if he was familiar or not.

"Simply passing through, seeking sanctuary for the night," Meristan replied. His tone was relaxed and easy, exactly what they needed. But still, the gate didn't open. There was a murmur of conversation from above as the guard turned away from them. A woman's voice came next.

"Forgive me, Brother, but you don't look like a monk."

Meristan broke into his easy smile, looked down and patted his leather-clad chest. "Sadly, the roads are not safe for a monk's robes. As you can see, I'm travelling with my Thorn companion. Did you know the Blackened have blocked the Auld Road?"

Good. That explained both his clothing and why they were arriving from this direction.

More murmurs from above. Why were they being so cautious? Samily's armour alone should have opened the gates.

A few minutes of hushed conversation from above, and Mynygogg drew near Allandria.

"Something's wrong," he whispered.

"It's fine, they're just being cautious," Allandria whispered back. She wasn't as sure as she hoped she sounded.

"Wait there, please!" The woman's voice again. Her silhouette disappeared, and several new ones replaced her, spread along the top of the wall. Allandria clearly made out the shadows of crossbows. They were very twitchy for some reason. Mynygogg made a low grumbling sound.

Allandria nudged her horse toward Samily's and drew alongside her, with her back to the gate. "Be prepared," she whispered. "Something's not right."

It was not comfortable, being out in the open, in the dark. There was a line of trees behind them, and if Thakhati came out of them . . . at least they had Samily and Meristan. Still, she'd much rather be inside those walls.

It must have been half an hour they waited there, worrying amongst themselves if they'd ever be allowed in, when a door opened in the gate.

"Hands on your reins! First person who raises an arm gets a crossbow bolt!" The woman's voice again. But it was not a woman who stepped out of the door, it was a man with a dark moustache. Bak! Thank goodness. She just needed to get his attention.

Bak approached Meristan and stood before his horse. "Brother Meristan, is it?"

Meristan smiled down at him. "Indeed, Captain. Is there a problem? Your guards seem awfully... careful?"

"We've had word of Reivers masquerading as others. Attacking groups on the road and stealing their clothing—their horses. You understand, we *have* to be careful."

"Have you now?" Meristan looked to Mynygogg. The king gave nothing away.

"Captain, may I?" Allandria asked.

Bak looked over his shoulder, confirming the crossbows were still trained on them. He raised a hand and beckoned her forward. Allandria nudged Sky toward him, making sure to keep her face down. As she closed, Bak's face softened into recognition. He opened his mouth but stopped when she shook her head. His look turned curious. He was a sharp man, though. Aranok had respect for him, and the little Allandria had encountered of him showed nothing to differ.

"Captain, I can assure you of our good intentions. The envoy sends his regards." She spoke quietly, deliberately. "He asks that you allow us to pass. Quietly."

Bak scanned her companions, taking in each one, perhaps for show, perhaps trying to ascertain who the rest of the party were, and why Allandria was travelling without her charge. Either way, after a moment's pause, he turned and raised a hand high. "Arms down! Open the gate!"

Gears clacked as the crossbows were relaxed and the great doors swung open.

"Brother Meristan, you and your companions are most welcome to Mournside." Bak spoke loud enough for his guards to hear, but no more. He wasn't announcing their arrival to the town. The gates swung shut behind them. "Allow me to escort you to an inn. Stable these horses!" Bak waved a man over and he went about collecting the reins as Allandria and the others dismounted.

Once they were out of sight of the gate, Bak moved close to Allandria and walked in step. "Lady Allandria, is all well?" His voice was barely loud enough for her to hear, never mind anyone else. How much should she tell him? How much could she tell him? It wasn't impossible he was Janaeus's man, though the way he dealt with Evenna's murder suggested not—assuming of course Janaeus had been behind that. He already knew the messengers were suspect, so perhaps she could simply play into that understanding.

"I'm afraid things are more complicated than they appeared, Captain. You've had another messenger?"

Bak nodded. "Indeed. With news of the Reivers, as you heard."

She needed him to know not to trust the messengers, but also not to challenge them and risk giving everything away. "We believe the messengers have been infiltrated and are being fed false information. They do not know this, and it is important we do not tip our hand. Be wary of what news they bring, but please say nothing."

"The Reivers news is false." It was a statement, not a question, and it sounded as though he'd already suspected as such. Allandria shrugged.

"It could be true, but we've heard nothing. If anything, there are fewer Reivers on the road than usual."

"I understand. Is Laird Aranok well?" A dangerous question. If he was Janaeus's man, he needed to know as little as possible.

"The last I saw him, he was. But he had urgent business elsewhere."

That seemed to be enough for the captain's curiosity. They reached a corner and Bak stopped. "I believe you know your way from here, my lady."

"I do, thank you, Captain." She shook the man's hand, and with a slight bow, he carried on up the road. They needed to go left to reach Mourning Square and the inns. They would stay at the Merchant's Arms tonight. Calador would recognise Allandria and probably Samily too. The inn would be entirely less pleasant and the bar much rowdier, but it would do for their privacy tonight. Besides, it was the etiquette of the Thorns to spread their business around, so as not to place too much of a burden on any one business.

"All well?" Mynygogg casually stepped close to her. You never knew who might be watching.

"I believe so. Bak is a good man. Aranok trusts him."

"All right," Mynygogg replied. "Good to know. The captain of the city guard would be an awkward enemy."

Indeed he would.

CHAPTER 22

Mournside stretched and awakened to the new day as shop-fronts opened and market stalls were set up. The streets hummed with activity as people went about their daily business, completely unaware of the secret war for their country. A young messenger scurried from one building with a basket of goods for delivery to some wealthy patron. He nearly ran straight into Samily, looking down at his cargo, but caught sight of her just in time to swerve, almost spilling the bread and fruit across the cobblestones. It took him a second glance to recognise her armour, his eyes lingering on the light symbol carved into her pauldron. He slowed long enough for her to catch his eye and smile. The boy blushed and looked away, as if he'd been caught doing something he shouldn't, and hastened off up the street.

The previous evening had been uneventful, if not quiet. The Merchant's Arms was not as refined a place as the Canny Man, and the patrons were accordingly rougher. They had chosen to eat and retire to their rooms, hoping to avoid too much scrutiny, but even so, a drunk had tried to pick a fight with the king. Mynygogg had easily avoided the man's sluggish swing and skilfully removed him from the bar without great effort. The innkeeper had barely raised an eyebrow.

Later, the bar became so raucous as to keep Samily from sleep until the small hours, something she was feeling this morning in her heavy eyelids.

"Are you sure this will be all right?"

Rasa had explained the situation with the envoy's sister, or rather with his niece, over breakfast. The fact that they had to hide her *draoidh* ability from the girl's own father was incomprehensible to Samily. It simply did not make sense to her that a father could love his own child less.

She knew absolutely that Meristan would always love her. The idea that her being a *draoidh* would affect how he felt about her was ridiculous. What parent's love is conditional? How must the girl feel knowing she had to hide something of herself from her father? She had a dark opinion of Pol before she'd even met him, and that sat uneasy with her. Samily did not judge people—that was God's right alone. But she found herself disliking this man she'd never met more intensely than she would have imagined possible.

Equally, she wondered why Aranok's sister had married such an odious person in the first place. There must have been something good about him, but it was hard to reconcile a decent person with such bigotry. She was reminded of the innkeeper they would have to visit in Dail Ruigh—the ignorant man who'd refused Aranok a room—and felt her nose crinkle in response. The man who had respected her for her armour but rejected the envoy for his.

As if to illustrate her thoughts, a well-dressed couple walking toward them smiled at Samily and gave a polite nod of their heads as they passed. She smiled back, but wondered whether they'd pay her the same courtesy if they knew she was *draoidh*.

Rasa placed a gentle hand on Samily's arm. "It'll be fine. Pol will be at work. If Lady Ikara is home, she'll be delighted to meet you. She's lovely, you'll like her."

"And she won't mind that I know...?" Samily didn't even want to risk saying it aloud.

Rasa shook her head. "I don't believe so. You and Emelina have a lot in common."

Samily found that a little odd. Beyond both being *draoidh*, she didn't see much similarity between herself and the grandchild of a wealthy laird. But Rasa knew them both and Samily trusted her judgement. Perhaps it would be clear when they met.

Ikara's house was a pleasant building in one of the nicer streets in Mournside—not that she had seen any unpleasant streets. Even those residential areas on the edges, inhabited by the workers and servants who made the town run, were more well kept than some of the nicest areas of other towns. It was not ostentatious, but it was welcoming, with flowers blooming in a window box and a basket hanging by the door. One scent caught her off guard, transporting her to her childhood, weeding the garden at Baile Airneach. It was a happy memory, but it reminded her how she missed her home and friends. She had no idea when she'd see them again. When they'd be themselves again.

"All right?" Rasa asked. She'd gotten lost in her thoughts.

"Yes, fine." Samily straightened up and pushed her shoulders back.

Rasa knocked at the door and stepped back beside her. There was no immediate answer, and Rasa's frown seemed to wonder if anyone was at home after all. But eventually there was the sound of footsteps on stairs and the door cracked open.

A woman's face, framed in chestnut hair, appeared in the gap. She eyed Samily sternly, but her expression melted when she saw her companion.

"Rasa!" Ikara opened the door wide. "Come in, come in. I'm so glad it's you." There was a fractured edge to her voice that gave Samily pause. Perhaps she was not as welcoming of a stranger as Rasa had anticipated.

The door was closed again and bolted before Rasa spoke. "Are we alone?"

Ikara glanced at Samily. "Emelina is upstairs, but otherwise..."

"Pol is not here," Rasa said plainly.

"No."

The metamorph's entire frame seemed to relax. "This is Lady Samily, knight of the White Thorns and a trusted companion of your brother. Samily, this is Lady Ikara."

Samily wasn't sure how trusted a companion she was at the moment, but she didn't argue.

"Oh!" Ikara smiled flatly. "It's an honour. Please, sit." She gestured to chairs by the fireplace. "Is Aranok with you?" Again, that slight edge in her tone.

"No, he has urgent business elsewhere," Rasa answered. "But he sent us with an important message."

"It must be, to have a Thorn deliver it!" Ikara pulled over a stool to join them, gathering her green skirt as she settled. "What can I do for my king?"

Rasa raised her eyebrows and rolled her neck. "Well, actually, that's quite the question."

"Oh?"

"Rasa!" A young girl came barrelling down the stairs, a fluster of light hair in a pale red dress. She barely noticed either Samily or her mother, throwing herself into Rasa's outstretched arms.

"Good morning, pupil," she said, releasing the girl. "Have you been practising?"

Emelina nodded enthusiastically.

"What can you show me?"

The girl's eyes opened wide as she turned to look at Samily for the first time.

"Um..." Ikara pulled her daughter protectively backwards.

Rasa raised her hands. "I'm sorry, I should have explained. Emelina, this is Samily. She's like us."

"Oh!" Ikara's surprise was much greater this time. "Really?"

"I am a *draoidh*, yes," Samily answered. That might have been the first time she'd said it out loud, it occurred to her. It felt unexpectedly liberating. Especially when she saw the delight on the girl's face.

"What can you do?" Emelina asked. "Can you turn into animals?"

"Samily's skill is time," Rasa answered for her. "Would you like to see what she can do?"

"Time?" Ikara all but stood up. "I've never heard of that."

"I have only learned of it recently," Samily explained. "I am still learning."

Emelina stepped toward her, eyes full of wonder and delight. "Is Rasa your teacher too?"

Samily felt herself blushing slightly, though she couldn't have said why. "Well, no. But your uncle has been teaching me." How much that might continue she couldn't say. She found herself more inclined, when she had the time, to return to Traverlyn and find out whether Master Ipharia would help her learn more about her powers.

"Uncle Aranok makes me fly." The girl spread her arms like wings and, as she did, something dropped from her hand, clattering onto the floor. She stared at it in horror, hands over her mouth. "My bird!"

Rasa picked up the toy and examined it. "It's not too bad, just a little crack in the beak."

Emelina's face crumpled and tears welled. In that moment, Samily would have done anything to make her happy again. And, of course, she could. "May I?" She held out a hand and Rasa gave her the little wooden sculpture. It reminded her of the things she had seen Nirea whittling at during her watches. She'd never seen anything the queen had finished and wondered if this was one of hers. If it was, she had a skill for it.

As Rasa had said, the beak was cracked, but she could also see where the edge of a wing had been damaged. She enjoyed the feeling of knowing she could make this better.

"Air ais."

Samily held out her palms, a nest for the newly restored bird.

Emelina gasped audibly. "You fixed her!" She plucked the toy from Samily and held it to her mother's face so excitedly Ikara had to sit back to avoid being struck on the nose. "Look, Mummy! She's fixed!"

Ikara took the bird and examined it. "So it is. How fabulous."

Emelina chirped, turned on her heel and threw herself at Samily, who barely managed to catch the girl in what it took her a moment to realise was a hug. She smiled as she felt her armour tighten slightly against the girl's arms. It was wonderful.

"Thank you!"

"It was my honour." Samily carefully wrapped her arms around the girl, conscious of not hurting her.

Emelina released her squeeze and brought her head round to the side, as though examining something. "Is that the sun?"

Samily ran her fingers over the engraving. "It is the symbol of God, child. But I suppose it does look like the sun." She knew Aranok was not a man of faith, but it still surprised her that his niece had never even seen the symbol of God's light. Her mother must never have taken her to kirk. That was a shame.

"Emelina, do you want to show Samily what you've been learning?" The girl turned at Rasa's voice and nodded enthusiastically. "All right then."

With no more warning, Rasa shrank from sight and disappeared into her dress. There was a chirrup and a flutter before a bright red and green hummingbird burst from the clothes into the space between them. Emelina clapped, then took a dramatic breath and held out her hands. Ikara glanced uncomfortably at the door, making Samily do the same. It was bolted shut, but Ikara was obviously still worried. Samily turned back to see a ball of light hovering before the hummingbird, matching its movements, like a mirror. Slowly, it stretched and moulded itself into a replica, until there were two hummingbirds dancing together before the fireplace.

Emelina giggled as Rasa darted away and the light bird followed, chasing it about the room. Ikara eventually eased into a smile, watching the game unfold. After a few minutes, Rasa landed behind her chair and returned to her usual form. It was still miraculous to Samily, and she felt God's presence ever closer each time she watched the woman transform. Emelina allowed her light bird to dissipate. Ikara clapped and Samily joined her.

"Well done, pupil." Rasa pulled her dress back on in front of the fire. "Next we'll try something bigger. Perhaps a cat?"

Emelina nodded excitedly.

"For now, though, I'd like you to go and practise your letters in your room, please."

Emelina's face fell. "Awww."

Rasa crouched down before her, still only half-dressed. "A *draoidh* cannot learn new magic if they cannot read."

Emelina rolled her eyes like a much older child, making Samily snort a laugh involuntarily. The girl looked at her out of the side of her eyes with a devilish glint. "Yes, teacher."

"Go on, angel." Ikara shooed Emelina away up the stairs. She got halfway there, and darted back to collect her bird, giving Samily another surreptitious smile as she did. The girl was a delight.

Once they heard Emelina's bedroom door close, the atmosphere turned serious again.

"I'm sorry to ask, but... Samily understands the situation? With her father?" Ikara was back to being uncomfortable.

"She does," Rasa answered. "I'm sorry, I intended to explain everything before, but Emelina..." She raised her hand in the direction of the stairs.

"Of course. Children have no sense of timing." Ikara softened.

"Lady Ikara, may I ask, is everything all right? You seem... on edge." So Rasa had noticed it too.

Ikara took a breath and leaned in toward them. Rasa did the same and Samily followed. "I think Pol might know," she whispered.

"How?" Rasa asked, equally hushed.

"The other night, we were sat down to dinner and..." Ikara glanced at the stairs and lowered her voice even further. "I mean, Em looks like me, of course she does. She's... But this wasn't that. I'm sure. I looked across at her and she was smiling and I swear... Rasa, I swear it was my own face looking back at me." Ikara's hands came up over her mouth as if to stuff the words back in.

"A *masg*?" said Rasa. "That would be precocious. But she has talent. It's not impossible. She likely wouldn't even know she'd done it. At her age, skills often manifest unbidden. And Pol saw?"

Ikara lowered her hands to her lap. "I don't know. I think Em must have seen the shock on my face because suddenly she was herself again and I don't know if Pol saw before, but... Rasa, what if that wasn't the first time?"

Rasa crouched and placed her hands over Ikara's. "Has he said something?"

"No, but... he's been distant. Cold. More than usual."

More than usual? Why would anyone stay with a man who was usually distant and cold? Samily did not understand this relationship at all.

"How can we help?" Rasa asked.

Ikara looked away. "I don't know. I thought maybe... if Aranok was here, he might... I don't know. I wanted to ask him. I think Pol's afraid of him. Maybe he could do something."

If the man hated *draoidh*, it didn't make sense that he'd listen to a *draoidh* about anything.

But maybe a White Thorn? "Would you like me to speak to him?"

Ikara jerked her head round, looking at Samily almost as if she'd forgotten she was there. "Oh. I..." She breathed out and her shoulders slumped. "No. Thank you, but no. I don't know what you could say."

"I could make him afraid of me." Samily wasn't sure how that would help, but she was happy to try.

Ikara smiled. "You certainly could. I'm just not certain it would help. It'll be fine." Ikara sat back and pulled her hands away from Rasa's. "I'll handle it. It might be nothing."

"Are you sure?" Rasa moved back to her chair.

"Yes. Thank you. Maybe I just needed to say it out loud to someone." Ikara straightened up in her seat. "You have a message for me, though, don't you?"

Rasa glanced at Samily. "We do. There's a lot we can't tell you, I'm afraid, but there is some good news. We think we'll be able to cure the Blackening."

Ikara's eyes lit up. "Oh! Oh, that's wonderful! I know Ari thought... but, he did it?"

"He did," Rasa said. "There is still some work to do, but he hopes to be able to cure everyone soon."

"How soon?" Ikara stood and began to fuss around the room. "You'll need wagons, of course. How long do I have?"

"Perhaps a week?" Rasa answered.

"A week? As little as that? Goodness, that's... No, it's fine. I can do that. I'll speak to Hayton, he has several, and I'm sure Corlas has a few he'll be able to spare." Ikara stopped pottering and stood firmly before them. "Yes. We'll be ready. You have my word. One week."

Rasa smiled warmly again, so genuine and infectious. It made Samily feel a little calmer, a little happier just for being near her when she smiled like that.

"What else?" Ikara sat down again, having, as far as Samily could tell, not actually done anything in her flurry of activity.

Again, Rasa looked to Samily, this time with more concern. Aranok had explained that they couldn't just tell people their memories were wrong; they'd struggle to understand it, and their minds would rebel against the notion. Some people had severe, violent reactions to the idea their understanding of the world was a lie. But they should tell Ikara something. They'd discussed this over breakfast too. Allandria had thought of coming with them, but they needed to set off early on their journey and it was better if she wasn't seen. Visiting Ikara would have increased the chance of that, if Janaeus had someone watching Aranok's family.

So they'd decided what Rasa could safely say. "This is sensitive, but we believe the king is being undermined. You should be sceptical about any information from king's messengers until you see your brother. In fact, you should assume it is untrue."

Ikara gasped and raised a hand to her mouth. "No. Someone in the castle?"

"We believe so." Factually, everything Rasa had said was true, just not quite in the way Ikara would have understood it. And that would hopefully do for now, until the envoy could restore her mind, along with the rest of Eidyn's.

Again, Ikara straightened herself. "All right. I understand. I'll do everything I can to be ready for next week. You'll come to me when the time is right?"

"I will." Rasa nodded.

"Fine. Fine." Ikara stood and looked about the room again, as if searching for something that wasn't there. She seemed to be having difficulty staying still. "Do you have time for tea?"

"We do, I think." Rasa said it almost as a question, looking to Samily for confirmation.

It was a full day's ride to the Digger's Arms, the inn they would next stay in on the way to Dail Ruigh, so they had opted to spend a day in Mournside and set off early the next morning. Part of Samily felt like it was a waste of precious time, but Meristan had pointed out they would only end up travelling in the dark otherwise and there was no need to take unnecessary risks. At the earliest, Aranok and Queen Nirea would only arrive in Haven that evening, and who knew how long it might take them to locate the relic?

And she liked the idea of spending a day with Rasa, without any urgent business to address. She hoped they'd have time to talk about her ability, and maybe Samily could ask her some of the questions she'd been harbouring. Perhaps she could even offer some tuition on Samily's own skills.

"Tea would be lovely, thank you."

CHAPTER 23

Lightning cracked the sky, illuminating the great wooden gates of Haven momentarily. The rain battering Aranok's riding cloak was like a constant rumble of thunder on his skull, and a throbbing headache pounded back against it. It had been a miserable ride from the ferry. The road was less travelled than the country's major arteries, but the sheer volume of rain had softened the ground such that the horses had struggled to move at anything above a walk.

Conversation had been minimal. Nirea's mood seemed to mirror his own, despite the fact she had turned her face to the sky with delight at the first spots of rain. Darginn had kept to himself as they plodded along, with only Dialla making the effort to smile anytime he caught her eye. He didn't know whether to feel grateful for her attempted cheeriness or strangle her for it.

Finally, hours later than expected, they'd arrived at the western gate. The most important mission of Aranok's life lay before him, and he wanted nothing more than a dry, quiet bed.

"Identify yourselves!"

Aranok winced as the voice spiked through his pain. Taking a slow, measured breath, he replied as loudly as the dull thud allowed. "King's envoy!"

A long pause.

"My laird, we need to see your face!"

In this weather he'd be lucky to see the horse from up there, never mind identify Aranok. Regardless, he lowered his hood and looked up. The rain quickly saturated his hair and ran inside his collar. It would take even longer to get dry and warm now. He shivered involuntarily as his body fought to retain some heat.

He could barely make out the shape of the guard on the rampart—were there two? Maybe. There were other ways he could identify himself.

"Teine." Aranok held his lit palm beneath his face. He could see even less of the guards now, but the sounds of commotion told him they'd seen enough. He raised the hood again, though now it was mostly just keeping the wet in.

The giant gates swung open before them, dragging in the mud. Aranok nudged Moonlight forward and the others followed. Nirea played the subservient role, allowing him to organise the stabling of the horses and deal with the guard's questions. There weren't many. It seemed he was still the envoy, at least in the eyes of these soldiers. That was a good sign. Janaeus hadn't disavowed him.

Once they'd rid themselves of the guard's attentions, the four huddled under the stable's canopy.

"Right," Aranok began. "I need to see Darginn safely home." The old man nodded his appreciation. "And then we head for the castle. Word'll quickly reach Janaeus that we're here, and he'll expect us to report to him immediately, so we need to move fast."

Nirea gave him an odd look. He hadn't explained about Darginn's request that Aranok clear his family's memories, but he wasn't going to argue about it. Queen or not, he was going. He owed the man that, at least. "All right. Dialla and I will find a tavern to dry out and eat something. Find us when you're done."

Good. That was easier than he'd thought it might be. "I recommend the Chain Pier." He looked up at the storm-black sky. "It has a lovely balcony."

They'd been walking about twenty minutes when Darginn nudged him surreptitiously. Aranok looked back the next time they turned a corner. Someone was there—a sleek, dark shape, tracking them through the streets. Hardly anyone was out in this—why would they be? And yet, someone was stalking them. Was Janaeus having them watched? Perhaps. Perhaps he suspected this might happen and had set men to keep an eye on the gates for his return. To find out if Aranok's memory was still as he wanted it.

Nothing he'd done so far would have given anything away, but if the man followed them all the way to Darginn's house and worked out who he was, that report would be a problem. How would a man sent to his death at Shayella's hands have come to be in Aranok's company?

They'd have to deal with this. Darginn had referred to himself as "sneaky" in passing. He hoped that meant the old man would be aware of how to lose a spy too. Aranok pretended to slip in the rain and caught Darginn's arm. "Catch him," he whispered, leaning close. The messenger nodded almost imperceptibly. He knew Haven better than Aranok.

They took two corners sharply one after another and quickened their pace down what was little more than an alley between buildings. When they came out the other end into an open square, Darginn ducked left and gestured for Aranok to go the other way. There was little need for them to be quiet—the rain was covering everything but wet footsteps following them up the alley.

A shadowy head poked out from the edge of the wall. Darginn cleared his throat, and the man turned toward him with a start.

"*Gluais.*"

The man grunted as his back was pressed against the stone wall. As soon as he was close enough to see the face, Aranok recognised him.

"Hello again."

"You know him?" Darginn asked, joining him back in the alley.

"I do. We're old friends, aren't we, Thül?"

The rat's face was as thunderous as the sky. Maybe he wasn't tracking them for Janaeus after all. Maybe he just wanted a bit of revenge for his humiliation at Vastin's forge. Still, bit of a coincidence, him happening upon Aranok within an hour of returning to the city. Too much of a coincidence. He needed to play this straight.

"What can we do for a servant of the king this evening?"

"I ain't done nothing to you, Envoy. Sire." The last word was so begrudged Aranok was surprised it made it out of the thief's mouth at all.

"You just happened to be going the same way as us? For the last half hour?"

"Aye," Thül hissed. His breath was as bad as Aranok remembered.

Aranok turned to Darginn. "That sound right to you?"

"Unlikely, sire, seen as we've just walked in a circle."

Clever. Argyll was a shrewd man.

"You out for a walk in a big circle, Thül?"

The thief's scrawny face withered, his eyes seeming to retreat further into his face. "I got lost, is all."

Pain stabbed behind Aranok's left eye, reminding him he wanted to get out of this downpour, quickly. His sense of humour washed away with the rain. Keeping Thül against the wall with *gluais*, he grabbed the man's throat with his left hand and squeezed. "Truth. Now." He kept hold long enough for the thief's lips to take on a hint of blue—partly from the cold, maybe—then released. He sucked in air like a drowning man.

"Fuck sake! You can't murder me for following orders!"

Orders. "Whose orders?"

Terror in the eyes again. "Can't say."

"Teine." Aranok placed his burning hand under Thül's face, much as he'd just done under his own. Thül wasn't immune to the heat. He scrambled aimlessly, trying to claw his way back into the wall, to escape the heat. "King's orders!"

"What orders?" Aranok needed answers. He was tired, and maintaining two spells was especially draining. He lifted his hand half an inch, enough to singe a few hairs. Thül shrieked.

"Follow you! Follow you if you showed up! See who you was with! What you did! That's all, I swear, please!"

Damn it. He'd hoped there was another answer. Aranok extinguished the flame and lowered his hand. At first, Thül looked relieved, but when he took in the look on Aranok's face, the fear returned.

Thül hadn't seen anything that would betray that Aranok's memory was back, but he'd tell Janaeus what had just happened. Aranok knowing he'd had a man follow him would be enough to raise suspicion, and Aranok would have to address it. He needed to avoid that confrontation.

If he could trust this idiot, he might try to pay him off. Buy his silence. But Thül wasn't that man. He'd take Aranok's money and report to the king anyway. Take the pay from both sides and loyal to neither. Too much depended on this.

He had no choice.

"Do you live near?" he asked Darginn.

The old man shook his head gravely. "Back the way we came."

He'd led them away from home. Good instincts. But that was more bad news for Thül. Aranok looked down at the thief's belt. The hilt of his dagger, the one he'd been so keen to show Aranok the last time they'd met, stared back at him. Before the man could open his mouth, Aranok drew the dagger from its sheath and buried it in Thül's neck. He jerked and gurgled in surprise, choking on his own blood. Darginn stepped away.

Aranok released his *gluais* grip and allowed the thief to slump onto the alley floor. He convulsed, the blood pulsing from his neck mixing with the rain, seeping into his clothes, turning the dirty brown black. Then he stopped.

Aranok turned his hand over in the rain, brushing away the splatter of red that led up his wrist. Darginn looked like he'd seen a demon. Maybe he had.

"We couldn't risk Janaeus knowing anything. Looks like he got himself killed in a street fight."

Darginn's wide eyes narrowed as he understood and nodded. "Aye, I see." He swallowed hard. "Best we move then, sire, afore the guard pass, eh?"

They took a different route back to Darginn's house, making use of several alleys and closes. Darginn was making sure they were alone.

When they reached his house, the rain was finally starting to ease. The drumming had become tapping. Darginn knocked three times before turning the key. When the door swung open, the warm smell of beef greeted them like old friends. Aranok's stomach growled in appreciation.

Darginn ushered him inside. "Isadona!"

"Ah!" A portly woman bundled in from the kitchen wrapped in a stained apron and brandishing a wooden spoon. "You're back! Thank God, I've been worried!" She paused when she saw her husband wasn't alone. "Oh."

"It's all right." Darginn removed his riding cloak and offered to take Aranok's. He was glad to be rid of the extra weight. Now it was just a barrier to the fire's heat. "This is Laird Aranok."

"Oh!" Isadona repeated. She quickly made an awkward curtsey. "It's an honour, sire." The woman turned and chased a large calico cat from a chair by the fire, brushing it clean. "Please, have a seat!"

A seat was exactly what he needed, but he had little time for it. "Darginn, we'll need to hurry. We've already lost time."

"Aye," he agreed. "Dona, you'll need to take the seat, ma love."

"Why?" She followed his suggestion regardless. "Is something wrong?"

"No, it's just... you need to know something."

Aranok pulled the memory charm from its place beneath his leathers. "Darginn, your children—how far are they?"

"No far. A few streets away each."

"Fetch them. I'll explain to Isadona."

An hour later, Darginn Argyll's home was filled with his entire extended family, all of whom had now learned the truth of their situation. The granddaughter, Liana, had taken it best, somehow. Aranok wondered if that was a fluke, or whether children were more open to having their minds changed than adults. Perhaps. Perhaps she'd had so little of her memory changed that she barely noticed.

Darginn's son-in-law, Yavick, a hulking stonemason, had the worst of it, throwing up and almost choking himself as he tried to catch his breath. His wife, Jena, had slapped him so hard on the back he'd nearly fallen over, but it cleared his throat. The man was still a little green about the cheeks.

"Right," said Darginn, holding court like a little king, "you all know the truth. There's more to tell you, but it'll keep. For now, I need you all to pack up and be ready to leave tomorrow. We're going to Traverlyn."

"Traverlyn?" Darginn's son, Ismar, asked. "Why?"

"Because we have allies there," Aranok answered. "Allies who will keep you all safe until this is over."

"It's only temporary," Darginn added. Aranok hoped he was right. He smiled and nodded in a way he intended as comforting. After a short silence, Isadona stood, smoothing her apron.

"All right. You all heard your father. Away and pack. We leave tomorrow."

Samily fidgeted with her goblet of wine. She felt awkward without really knowing why. As if there was something expected of her by some unknown person who would not tell her what it was but would silently pass judgement on her for failing. She glanced at the bar, accidentally caught the eye of the man behind it and looked away.

She'd spent a lovely day with Rasa. They'd had tea with Ikara in the morning, bought some freshly baked bread and had lunch outside. And now, to shelter from the hideous storm, they'd found another inn for dinner—the Hermitage. It was smaller and quieter than the Canny Man or the Merchant's Arms, but its huge bay windows allowed them to watch the rain as it battered the street outside.

Each table had its own candle, and the walls danced with customers' shadows. Rasa had insisted that Samily did not need to wear her armour for dinner, so she wore the outfit she'd bought with Nirea and Allandria. Perhaps that was why she felt so uncomfortable. This was not her natural home. This was how other people lived, in opulent clothes, eating fine food by candlelight. She looked down at her callused hands. Rasa's were smooth and soft. She hid one under the other, hoping their food would arrive soon.

"Are you all right?" Rasa smiled warmly across the table. "You look...I don't know. Not all right, I suppose."

Samily shrugged. "I haven't really done this before."

"Done what?"

Samily gestured to the room. "This. Eaten in a place like"—she gestured to her own clothing—"like this."

Rasa laughed and Samily felt her face flush. Had she said something stupid? Rasa put a hand on Samily's. "Well, it's my honour to be with you, then."

Samily felt a tingle of excitement where their hands met. No. Rasa was not cruel. She would not laugh at her. In fact, perhaps this was the time for everything she'd been bursting to ask.

"May I ask you a question?"

"Of course." Rasa sat back in her chair, so completely at ease with herself that it actually made Samily relax too.

"When you transform..." Rasa raised her eyebrows and Samily remembered that her being a *draoidh* was not common knowledge in Mournside, and was best kept that way. Samily lowered her voice and leaned in. "When you transform, do you become the new creature? Are you then a bird or a wolf? What happens to food and drink in your stomach? Where does it go? Can you still think like you, like a human, or do you have a dog's instincts? Do you get a wolf's sense of smell? Can you communicate with other animals? How does it work?"

An enigmatic smile spread across Rasa's face. "That's more than one question."

Samily's face reddened again. "Sorry."

Rasa leaned in close to meet her on the table and whispered, "Magic."

That was not really the answer Samily had hoped for. She pursed her mouth in consternation.

"I am always me," Rasa continued. "Whatever form I take, my essence, my soul, I suppose you would say, is constant. Rasa. This." She gestured to her own body. "When I change, I take on a different physical form, but I am still me, at my core. I think like me. Physically, I can do what the form I take can do. So I can sing as a bird, but I cannot understand birdsong. I have a stronger sense of smell as a wolf, but my mind does not process it as a wolf's does, allowing them to track prey."

That made sense. A soul is what it is, regardless of the body it inhabits. "So whatever your physical form, you are always you?" Being so close together at the table, talking in hushed tones, felt conspiratorial. It was thrilling.

Rasa looked at her thoughtfully for a moment. "Samily, this is not the body I was born into, or the face I was born with. It is the body I choose, because it's who I am. This body reflects my soul."

"But it is. It is your body. God gave you the ability to shape it as you choose."

Rasa sat back, crinkling her brow. Samily feared she'd offended her. If she had, she wasn't sure how. But eventually, Rasa leaned forward again, resting her chin on her folded hands. "That's an interesting way of looking at it. Either way, it's not a blessing most people receive."

"So you are blessed? With a miracle?"

Rasa laughed again, this time with an almost nervous edge. "Maybe I am. You're a fascinating young woman, Samily. You have a unique perspective."

Samily felt a rush of warmth at the compliment. Maybe it was the wine. "I really like you."

Rasa's face dropped. "Oh. Oh, Samily, no, I..." She was suddenly awkward, looking around the inn as if for an answer to an unasked question.

"What's wrong?" For all the ways Samily had worried she'd said something wrong, she couldn't imagine how she'd insulted Rasa now.

The metamorph leaned across the table again, her face now earnest, her eyes sad. "Samily, I'm so sorry... I didn't realise. I'm... not attracted to women."

Oh no.

Samily felt the heat rush to her face and she defensively covered her mouth with both hands. She wanted to get up and leave. To run away into the rain and never look back. To pretend she'd never seen this ridiculous place with its ridiculous people. But she couldn't move. She had to say something.

"I don't want to have sex with you."

Rasa sat back as though Samily had set the table on fire. S'grace, had she made it worse?

"You... what?" Rasa asked, as if Samily had spoken a foreign language.

"I just... I just meant that I like you. I like spending time with you. I want to be your friend. That's all. I'm not... I don't have sex."

She could feel tears welling in her eyes. Why was this so hard?

"Oh. Oh!" Rasa again leaned forward and tried to take Samily's hand, but she pulled it away defensively. "Samily, I'm so sorry. I completely misunderstood. It's entirely my fault. And I've embarrassed you. I'm so sorry. Please forgive me. I was careless."

Samily very much wanted to forgive her, but she was back to feeling like the awkward outsider she'd been when they arrived. She glanced at a few other tables. Had she spoken too loudly? Was everyone in the inn now secretly laughing at her? What had she done?

She had to get out. She had to go. She stood, knocking over her chair, pushed her way to the door and ran out into the storm. The rain felt good. Cleansing. She could hide in the rain. She ran for a time, following the streets until she came to a small square with a large platform in the middle. She reached it and stopped, leaning against the edge. Raising her face to the heavens, her tears were lost in the rain. How had she broken such a precious thing? Why was she so awkward with people? What was wrong with her?

"Samily?" Rasa moved slowly across the square toward her, her ruby red dress painted on her in the rain. Thunder rolled in the distance. Samily wanted to run again, but she also desperately wanted not to. To stay.

Clear your mind, trust in God and stand your ground.

"Samily, I really am sorry. It's my fault. Completely my fault. Please forgive me."

"Why did you...think that was what I meant?"

"Because I was stupid. I suppose because I get a lot of attention from men. And when a man speaks to me and looks at me the way you did, it usually means...he does want to sleep with me. And...I assumed. And I was wrong."

"I don't understand sex. Is that strange?" She had always felt different. This was a large part of why.

"Not at all, sweetheart. It's not...common. But it's you. You are unique in many ways, Samily."

"Really?" The rain was beginning to ease, making it easier to be heard without shouting.

"Really." Rasa stepped forward and took Samily's hands. This time, she let her. "You are a goddamned warrior—pardon my blasphemy. You are kind and brilliant and intelligent and brave and one of the most interesting people I've ever met. You don't have to fit anyone's expectations. And if you can forgive my idiocy, I'd very much like to be your friend."

Samily shivered and smiled. Yes. She would like that.

CHAPTER 24

Amollari, the serving girl, greeted Aranok with a cheerful smile as he crossed the main bar in the Chain Pier. He nodded back but avoided engaging. She would almost certainly have asked about her friend Vastin, and he wasn't ready for that discussion.

The women had long finished their meals, but Isadona had insisted on Aranok eating some roast beef before she would let him go. He preferred it a little pinker than it had been served, but it would have been churlish to refuse.

One of the guards would have reported Aranok's arrival by now, and someone may have found Thül's body. Hopefully it would be a while before word of his demise reached the castle.

If Janaeus were Mynygogg, Aranok would storm into the throne room and question him about Barrock. So that was exactly what he was going to do.

They spent a few minutes going over the story. They'd recount everything as it happened, up until they had to change it. Janaeus may have had reports of some elements—God alone knew where he might have spies. Anyone they'd encountered, even people they'd never noticed, might have reported back to him at some point.

Everything could be as it happened, right up until Aranok went to Dun Eidyn.

Instead, he, Allandria and Samily had ridden back to Traverlyn expecting to meet their friends with Taneitheia, only to discover what had happened. They'd leave out details: Nirea's injury, Samily's ability. Make out Nirea had killed the demon with Glorbad's help, but he'd died of his injuries. No point hinting Meristan might know who he was. Rasa they'd leave out completely. Aranok needed daggers up his sleeve.

Once they'd established what had happened at Barrock, Aranok and Nirea rode for Greytoun to update Janaeus. Dialla had come to keep them awake, so they could make the journey quicker, and to support Aranok in case of trouble. Allandria not being with him was a problem. So Meristan was wounded and Aranok had assigned her to guard him. She'd only agreed if Dialla came in her place.

It was plausible enough, if they left out Conifax's murder. He had to hope Rotan hadn't managed to get word of that here before he was arrested. Janaeus would expect Aranok not to leave Traverlyn without finding Conifax's killer—unless there was something more important.

It was risky, but feasible.

Nirea remained stony-faced through the conversation. He could rely on her to handle herself if everything went wrong. The only concern was whether she might be too quick to violence. Dialla, on the other hand, nervously picked at her nails and played with the hem of her sleeve.

The rain was back to its worst for their walk up to the castle. The steps that wound round Grey Rock were completely exposed. The wind drove mercilessly in off the sea, and Aranok was soaked all over again by the time his aching legs reached the top step and the castle gate.

"Identify yourselves!" The voice was familiar, but wrong. It didn't belong here. He looked to Nirea to see if she showed any sign of recognition, but her hood was pulled down against the storm.

"King's envoy!" Aranok held his hands wide. Best not accidentally start a fight at the gate.

"Step forward." Definitely familiar. A deep, sonorous voice. The huge shape of Leondar, captain of the kingsguard, materialised in the gloom. Of course he knew the voice. But from the court of Dun Eidyn, not standing in the rain outside Greytoun. What was he doing out here?

"Leondar!" Aranok stepped forward, offering a hand and a broad smile. He knew the man well. He'd fought beside him and they'd often shared a late whisky. He was quiet, intelligent and funny, and a welcome sight at that moment.

Leondar, however, did not return the gesture with his usual warmth. In fact, his face registered surprise and... confusion? Eventually, he did extend his hand, but more out of respect than friendship. "Laird Aranok. Welcome to Greytoun. May I ask who your companions are?"

It was formal and distant. He didn't know Aranok. He didn't know he was a kingsguard. Now Aranok thought about it, he didn't remember seeing any of the kingsguards he knew the last time he was here. Had Janaeus pushed them away? Brought in his own trusted soldiers and let the others believe they were normal guards? It reduced the risk of any of those who knew Mynygogg well seeing changes to his behaviour or routine. Similar to why he'd pushed Nirea away. She would quickly have realised something was wrong.

Leondar would be a useful ally to have, though. Was there a way to subtly restore the big man's memory?

"Captain Nirea, king's councillor, and Master Dialla, of the university."

Both women stepped forward and nodded politely. Nirea, of course, knew him, and raised an eyebrow.

Leondar returned the nods. "Captain. Master. You're welcome in Greytoun. Please follow me." He turned and gestured for the other soldier to open the gate. When they got close, Aranok could see the woman had dark hair, a strong jaw and a scar splitting her lower lip. He didn't recognise her. There were plenty of soldiers he didn't know, of course, but not knowing her meant she could be one of Janaeus's, and he couldn't risk her seeing him restore Leondar. How to do this?

They were going to pass through the warded tunnel to reach the courtyard. Apart from the murder holes in the ceiling, which were unlikely to be manned at the moment, he hoped, they'd be alone for the eighty yards or so of that walk. Maybe that could work. "Soldier, I haven't been here for a while. How is the tunnel warded?"

Leondar's brow crinkled. It was an odd question to ask—Aranok was likely to know more than he was. The other guard either didn't hear or didn't care. She was watching the women. "Multiple runes, sire. I can't claim to know what they all do, but I know where they are."

"Would you show me, please?" Again, an odd request. But he had the authority to make odd requests. Leondar seemed to remember that last fact, and his quizzical look melted into respect.

"Of course, sire, please follow me." Leondar strode up the tunnel. Aranok had to move sharply to keep up. He caught Nirea's attention behind the soldier's back and gestured for her to take a position on his left, tapping his chest to indicate the memory charm. She gave a faint nod and moved.

"First is this one, Laird." Leondar stopped in front of a large rune carved into the rock.

"Ah, interesting." Dialla's interest was genuine. That would help. "A revelation ward, isn't it?"

"It is," Aranok confirmed. "Designed to penetrate a *masg*, to prevent a *draoidh* entering in disguise." He glanced up at the murder hole over their heads. It was there for a reason. If an illusionist entered here and was discovered, they could be killed from above with boiling water or rocks. Or an arrow. There was no sign of movement, just a deep shadow. Still, he'd wait until they were farther from the gate. "What's next?"

Leondar moved on, his purposeful stride and long legs again making the others shift to keep up. Dialla was all but trotting while trying to maintain a semblance of decorum.

"Next one's here." This rune was only painted onto the wall, and with good reason.

"A firewall?" Dialla's voice went up a pitch. It was a dangerous enchantment, and not used often. Aranok had painted this one himself. Greytoun was a retreat, expected to be attacked in a time of war. The firewall enchantment would turn half the tunnel into an inferno if the corresponding rune was activated by a competent *draoidh*. But it could also be deactivated by breaking the pattern. Hence it was not carved into the rock. No murder hole above this rune, where the fire would only spread. And nothing would live to be murdered anyway, except a well-warded earth *draoidh* like Aranok. Or certain demons. And boiling water would be no more use against one of those.

Aranok glanced back down the tunnel. The guard had closed the gate, as she should. Ahead, the exit portcullis was down and he could see no sign of a guard inside or beyond.

Now.

He lifted the charm from his neck, closed it in his fist and held it out to Leondar. "Could you hold this a moment, please, soldier?"

Leondar instinctively offered a hand, his training overruling any question he might have as to what he was being asked to hold. Aranok loosened his grip and the charm fell into the big man's palm.

"Clìor."

Leondar's eyes opened wide and he stumbled backwards, reaching for support. He found it in Nirea, who caught his huge arm with both hands and eased him to lean against the tunnel wall. "Easy, big man." Even with her support, Leondar's sheer mass nearly pulled them both to the ground. Aranok darted forward and caught his other arm.

"Is he all right?" Dialla had had no forewarning of this, of course, and so was as surprised by the whole thing as Leondar himself. Aranok managed to flash the memory charm at her and then placed his finger to his lips, staring hard at the gate. They needed to be quick and quiet.

"Leondar, can you hear me?" The man's eyes were glazed. They needed him not to pass out. And preferably not to vomit.

"Hnnnggg."

Damn it, he'd taken a hard hit from the memory restoration. Much of his own life must have been rewritten. He might drop if they didn't act quickly. "Dialla, give him a rush of energy!"

Eyes wide, the master stepped forward, placed a hand on Leondar's massive chest and said, "*Thoir.*"

She stumbled back as Leondar lurched upright, eyes roaming wildly. He shook off Aranok and Nirea like bothersome children and grunted loudly, staggering away. "Leondar! It's me. Aranok."

The soldier turned to the sound of his voice, a flicker of recognition, but he was still at sea.

"Kingsguard, protect your queen." Nirea's voice boomed with authority.

And like that, a light sparked. Leondar's hand moved to the hilt of his sword and he took a protective stance in front of Nirea, his free arm across her defensively. Kingsguard training ran deep. Even disorientated, he would protect his monarch.

"It's all right, Leondar, stand down." Nirea placed a gentle hand on his arm. "It's only Aranok. We're safe."

"Aranok?" Recognition, finally. This was a harsh way to do this to him, giving him no time to recover, but this tunnel was all the time they had.

"It's me, Leondar. You're all right. Trust me."

"Have I... have we been drinking?"

Aranok couldn't help but laugh. "No. Do you think you can walk? We need to move." If they took too long to walk the tunnel, the soldiers on the inner ramparts might send someone to investigate.

"I think so. What's happening?" Leondar swayed gently toward Aranok, and he caught the solider with a hand on his shoulder.

"I've just restored your memory. Janaeus changed it. You're going to be a little confused for a moment, but your head will clear. In fact, here..." Aranok grabbed his vial of oil and shoved it under Leondar's nose. He sniffed, blinked and shook his head like he'd had a bucket of ice poured on him.

"My God. My God!" He was all but roaring. Aranok and Nirea both hushed him and he covered his mouth with a hand. "What did that bastard do?"

"We'll explain everything," said Nirea, "but we need to walk and talk."

By the time they reached the end of the tunnel, they'd given Leondar a quick and quiet update on the situation and what they needed him to do. As the portcullis raised, he returned to his stoic character, but Aranok was comforted now to see the flame of loyalty and friendship he knew in the kingsguard's eyes.

Aranok nodded and smiled politely at the interior guards. One looked familiar; one not. He wondered now if that was deliberate. The courtyard was otherwise empty—no surprise considering the weather.

"Oh, Laird Aranok!" He turned back toward the tunnel, shielding his eyes from the rain. Leondar nodded up toward the main castle. "You'll find King Janaeus in the great hall entertaining a party of nobles."

Fuck.

That made things more complicated.

CHAPTER 25

Laird Aranok, king's envoy, and guests!" the reedy boy bellowed in a voice much larger than his frame.

Aranok had expected to barge through these doors, not see them politely opened by elegantly dressed footmen and have his arrival announced to a crowded room full of half-cut fops and phoneys. This was not his crowd. At all.

To either side were two great tables laden with food and drink. Fires burned at each side of the banquet hall, with a group of musicians raised on a wooden stage at the far end. They played something familiar—"The Merry Fey of Curidell," maybe? Aranok wasn't good with song names. Servants bustled in and out of a door to the left of the stage, which he knew led to a hallway and then to the kitchen. The other door, to the right of the stage, led to an anteroom, if he remembered rightly. That seemed to be where drink reserves were stored.

Chattering, gossiping and guffawing were about a hundred of Eidyn's unworthy wealthy—the gentry whose ancient family roots bestowed upon them the kind of money and lands that allowed them to look on a king's envoy as a passing game whose existence would affect their dynasty not a crumb.

Women in dresses his father might well have sold them. Men in the kind of elegant finery that would fall apart after a day on the road. Their looks were a broad mixture of curiosity, disdain, excitement and opportunity. Some studiously did not turn—clearly more important than to be impressed by a *draoidh*. But someone was certain to try to ingratiate themselves within a short time. The irony, of course, was that one of his guests was the bloody queen, and yet nobody looked at her twice. In her red weather-beaten leathers with her fiery hair plastered down by the rain, she looked more like a lost interloper than their rightful monarch.

Only Dialla actually looked like she belonged in this room. With her riding cloak swept aside, revealing a pale blue dress and gold trim, she might have been invited herself. Though she was also looking somewhat worse for the weather. Still, next to unshaven Aranok in full leathers, she was a princess.

But ironically, she looked the most uncomfortable. This was her crowd—well, had been her crowd, once. But she'd chosen to leave it behind for the university. And she hadn't been expecting to walk into a room full of her past. Perhaps it would have been kinder to give her some time to prepare herself. To put on her "armour." But they didn't have that luxury. He had to confront Janaeus and it had to be now.

"You all right?" He leaned slightly toward Dialla without looking directly at her.

"Mm-hmm," she replied, distracted. So probably not all right. He'd just have to do what he could to buttress the master's confidence.

Slowly, the nobles returned to conversation, some unsubtly watching him sideways while pretending to drink or talk. As if he might juggle fire for them at a moment's notice.

Idiots.

But their money helped keep the country going. Interesting that Janaeus had called this gathering already. Mynygogg only held audiences like this when it was politically prudent. Janaeus was trying to consolidate his new power.

Speaking of which, where was the little bastard?

Aranok scanned the room. The false king was not too tall to be lost in this crowd.

Aranok touched Dialla's arm and gestured to the fireplace on the left. He needed a boost of energy, just in case. They strode toward the hearth, Aranok grabbing a chicken leg on the way past. He wasn't hungry, but it added to the impression he was supposed to be here.

When they reached the edge of the hearth, he stopped and turned back to Dialla. "I need energy. But subtly. Janaeus will see if the fire dips too much."

The master nodded, her eyes round and white.

"Dialla?" The voice was raspy and high, but male.

Dialla gasped audibly. "Father? Uh... Laird Clavel."

The man was thin and grey, with blue eyes so pale Aranok imagined he might struggle to see through them at all. He wore the unnecessary splendour of an entitled laird like air.

"Why are you here? What happened to your hair? Has your mother seen you?"

Dialla spluttered like a child.

Aranok knew what it was to have a difficult father. "Master Dialla is here at my personal invitation, Laird Clavel. You'll have to excuse our attire, we've been riding for several days. Dialla asked permission to change into something more befitting of the festivities, but I insisted we come straight here. You'll forgive me, I'm sure." Buggered if he was going to have this old fart shaming his daughter.

Dialla's face burned rouge, but a grateful smile played at her lips.

"Well... of course, Laird Envoy." Clavel raised his cup as if to toast.

Aranok grabbed a full one from the table and raised it in return. "To your continued good health, sir."

"And yours."

"Laird Clavel, is it?" Nirea's voice was hard. He'd heard that tone before and it rarely ended well for the other person.

Clavel's performative respect disappeared at the sight of a bedraggled sailor. "It is. And you are?"

Nirea stuck out a hand like a weapon. "Captain Nirea. King's councillor on behalf of the navy."

"Oh." The laird looked her up and down like a prize sow. Nirea waited for him to meet her eyes again and did exactly the same to him, hand still extended. Dialla's eyes opened even wider. She was likely concerned about the offence her father might unwittingly cause the queen.

Clavel finally swapped his drink into his off hand and shook Nirea's. "An honour, of course." The way he said it was ambiguous enough that it could have meant his honour or hers. The slippery nature of nobility.

"What are your thoughts on *draoidhs*?" Nirea asked pointedly. Dialla spun to look at her like a startled hare. Suddenly this was an interesting conversation.

"Well, I, uh..." Clavel turned to Aranok. Stuttering ran in the family. Aranok smiled innocently back at him, as if Nirea had asked his opinion of carrots. Dialla must have said something about him for the queen to take this line of questioning. It would be no surprise for a noble to disown his *draoidh* daughter. Aranok was always happy to watch a bigot squirm. It was a momentary distraction. And standing here, near the fire, was getting some heat back into his wet, tired bones.

"I have great respect for Laird Aranok's accomplishments of course," Clavel fumbled.

"And your daughter's," Nirea added for him. Dialla was still blushing furiously.

For all Clavel's discomfort was enjoyable, he didn't like what it was putting the master through. He put a hand on her arm and gently pulled her toward him. "Please excuse us, Laird Clavel. I need to borrow your daughter."

"Um, ah, of course, Laird Envoy. Daughter." Clavel performed an awkward sort of half bow to them both.

Aranok barely lowered his head, turned and drew Dialla away with him to the other end of the hearth. He was careful to position the woman with her back to the conversation they'd just left, and far away enough not to hear it. "All right?"

She still looked like that hare. "What is she doing, Laird?"

"I suppose she's standing up for you, she thinks." In the way she would have liked someone to stand up for her, once, perhaps. Whatever his reservations about Nirea's headfirst approach to everything, she had a good heart, and she tolerated no bollocks.

"But my father will..."

"Your father will pay due respect to a king's councillor and soon recognise that it was his queen torturing him. In fact, if we could get him outside, I could..." Aranok tapped his chest, where the charm lay hidden.

Panic returned to Dialla's eyes. "Oh no. Father is... not good with secrets. Well, not from Mother. And she..." Dialla raised her hands and grimaced. Her mother was a gossip. Fine. Best to keep them away if they would only be liabilities.

"All right." Aranok nodded to the fire behind them. It was telling that Janaeus hadn't come looking for Aranok the minute he was announced. What was he doing? Under normal circumstances, he supposed, Janaeus might consider milking the nobles of their riches a priority over seeing his returned envoy, but when there was supposed to be a foreign queen with him?

Dialla subtly placed her right hand at her hip, palm open toward the flames. With her left, she took Aranok's right, down low where nobody who wasn't studying them would notice.

"Sruth." Aranok felt his hand tingle and warm as the energy flowed into him. And the fire didn't even flicker unusually. Her control was exceptional.

Aranok surveyed the room again. A few familiar faces. Lady Halla seemed to have had a few more wines than agreed with her and was attempting to dance Laird Goulter away from the food table, but the man's turgid belly was inclined toward the buffet.

Ah, there was Janaeus. With his back to them, in conversation with two unfamiliar men. Both wore the expected finery, but at least one of them looked like his life had been somewhat rougher than noble. His skin was weather-beaten, his eyes jaded. The way he fidgeted, shifting his shoulders unconsciously—he wasn't used to the frills.

Aranok hadn't noticed how large the crown looked on Janaeus's head the last time he was here—a perfect metaphor for just how unsuited the fair, gaunt man was for the role. Mynygogg was a lion in comparison, taller, darker, broader and, apparently, with a larger head.

Seeing Janaeus in person stirred things Aranok wasn't prepared for, though. Regret. Sadness. Pain.

They'd been friends. A long time ago. He'd always been a little odd—the smallest, the weakest, the youngest—but they were friends. Not in the way he and Korvin were, but... What had Shay said? He looked up to them. Wanted to be like them. How had it ended here? Why? Could he have done something differently? Had Aranok's grief really pushed Janaeus to this? To murder half of Eidyn and steal the throne? From a good man too. Not Hofnag. Not the bastard who oppressed *draoidhs*. From a man who valued every life equally. Who wanted to build a country for everyone. How had he been poisoned like this? Shay at least he could understand. She'd been driven mad by a mother's grief. That was... something.

Justification? No. But it was getting harder to see the black and white for all the grey. If Mynygogg hadn't found him, if Anhel had got to him instead, could Aranok have been on their side? Maybe. In a different life.

Aranok felt his senses sharpen as energy flowed into him. Muscles stretched and breathed with new life. All right. He could do this. He could play the part of Janaeus's dupe. All he needed was to get them all time in the castle to find the heart. Just let him think they were still under his spell.

Dialla released his hand and it twitched slightly, eager to move.

"You all right?" Nirea had disentangled herself from Laird Clavel. Or perhaps it was the other way around.

"Fine," Aranok lied.

"Should I...?" Dialla glanced hesitantly at Nirea.

"Yes," said Aranok. "And yourself." They all needed to be ready. Just in case. Dialla reached for Nirea's hand, silently asking permission. But there was hesitancy too. Something between them that he'd missed? They'd talked a lot the previous day while Aranok rode with Darginn. Nirea nodded and moved her hand toward the master. Whatever it was, it would wait.

He couldn't leave it much longer if he was to maintain the angry facade. Aranok slipped between the backs of two lairds and navigated his way around a pair of couples engaged in deep conversation about curtains to find his way to the usurper's back. He stood there for a moment, still. Unsure of what exactly was going to come out of his mouth. Until it did.

"We need to talk. Now." It was even, hushed, but with all the insistence he'd have given Mynygogg. Quiet enough not to cause a scene. Janaeus stepped away from him and turned.

His eyes flared bright and quickly darkened. "Aranok. You're back." Janaeus stared at him a long moment, as if reading Aranok's face. He kept it stoically flat, giving away nothing. A glance to the anteroom.

That was where he needed to have this conversation. "You're... all back?"

The leather-skinned man over his shoulder shifted again. For a concealed weapon? The other was calm, as if this was nothing more than a social gathering. Maybe it was, for him. He looked like the kind of dunce who lived for these things: vacant smile and soft skin. But Aranok wasn't making assumptions. He didn't know either man, so he had to assume they were both dangerous. Guards were spaced about the edges of the room, of course, but these were the two Janaeus kept close. Probably a reason for that.

He fixed the memory *draoidh* with a cold stare. "Taneitheia was gone. Glorbad's dead."

Janaeus sighed and looked down. "Damn." He lifted his head and scanned the room. "All right. Come on." He walked for the anteroom, placing a hand on the rough one's shoulder as he passed. Aranok waited a moment, then swept between the two.

As he'd guessed, the anteroom was filled with drink. Vats of wine, barrels of beer and crates of whisky stacked haphazardly. A round wooden table in the middle of the room was laden with cups and glasses. There was something obscene about it. What little the farmers of Mutton Hole were living with, while their wheat and barley went to ply the nobility with enough drink to throw coin at the crown. He couldn't fix that now. They had to get Mynygogg back on the throne first.

Janaeus stood at the window behind the table. Rain still battered against it. Aranok closed the door behind him. This was the moment. His performance had to be perfect. He would rant about the poor information. Ask where the Hell Taneitheia was. Demand an explanation. He had to keep down the true rage he was feeling. Replace it with something controlled. Something he could keep hold of.

When Janaeus turned back, his face had changed. It was... resigned? He was fiddling with something at his chest. Janaeus sat at the table and Aranok felt his stomach lurch.

The "king" released the charm from his fingers and let it dangle freely. Aranok's first reaction was horror, but no, it couldn't be that one—the one he'd made for Allandria and given to Mynygogg. That was miles away. Even if something had happened to him, the chances of it being here already…No. This was another. Which meant he had an earth *draoidh*. How should he react? He had to get this right. Had to convince Janaeus he was still his man. How would he have reacted if it was Mynygogg?

He'd have gone in headfirst.

Aranok pointed directly to the protective earth charm. "Where the fuck did you get that?"

Janaeus looked down slowly at the little ball as though he'd already forgotten it was there. When he raised his head, his eyes were tired.

"You know, don't you?"

CHAPTER 26

Aranok felt his right leg tremble beneath him. He dragged a chair over and tried to sit casually, but his heart was pounding so hard he could barely hear.

"Know what?" Could he bluff this? Pretend he had no idea? Fuck, if Janaeus already knew before they even walked in here, were Nirea and Dialla in danger?

Janaeus lifted the crown from his head and placed it on the table between them. He ran his hand through his hair, and Aranok realised he looked even more tired, more grey. He looked ill.

"Let's not. I don't want to do this dance with you, Ari. We both know you know. I knew when Anhel told me about your visit to Wrychtishousis. Did you even consider doing what I told you?"

Anhel had come here. Aranok had suspected as much. If he was there, his demons could be too. Hells, everything he'd been trying to avoid, everything he'd been hoping would go right—everything was fucked.

Still. He had to try.

"Anhel Weyr? Came here? The man's a fraud! He tried to kill us. We only stopped there on the way to—"

"Aranok!" Janaeus slammed his palm on the table. "I won't be treated like a fool. I can see it in your eyes. We both know if I tried to manipulate your memory right now, it wouldn't work. You wouldn't have walked in here without the charm I made you."

He'd said too much now. There was no way for Aranok to pretend he hadn't heard that. Or understood it. Now what? They were protected from each other's magic. He could probably take the smaller man physically, but then what? A roomful of nobles, guards—demons? Where was Anhel? He had to focus. They needed the heart. That was the target.

"Fine. I know." It was actually a relief to admit. Like a burden falling away. Into an abyss.

Janaeus nodded. "I knew if I ever saw you again, it would be like this. I told them. I knew you'd be the problem we had to solve."

"Told who?"

"Anhel and Shay. They wanted to convert you. Make you an ally. Well, Shay did. Anhel was less sure. You know how he is."

Unhinged. Angry. Ruthless.

"And you wanted to kill me?"

Janaeus's head jerked up and met Aranok's gaze. This time, there was hurt. "No! Of course not. But I knew we wouldn't be able to keep you in the dark. I knew if we were to convince you, it would have to be in your right mind. Your own choice."

"But you still sent me to my death. You expected me to die. Right?"

Janaeus took an age to answer as the rain rattled against the windowpane and the muffled sounds of music permeated the door. "Actually, I hoped you'd be… Blackened. But honestly, I suppose, yes. I did. I hoped, but… I expected you to die. I knew you'd never believe I was Mynygogg. You'd never respect me the way you did him. I knew you'd start to wonder what was happening. We couldn't risk that. I hoped that keeping you all close—you, Glorbad and Nirea—I thought maybe I could keep you under control. But I could see it that day in the chambers. You would never have spoken to Mynygogg the way you did to me. It was only a matter of time."

It started in his gut, but there was no way to hold it in, no matter how ludicrous, how wrong it was in that moment. A laugh burst from Aranok like a wave and became a guffaw. It was insane. Ridiculous. Tears welled and broke down his face.

That was it? That was why Glorbad had died? And Conifax?

"What?" Janaeus sounded confused for the first time. Agitated. Of course he didn't understand. He never had.

Aranok breathed deep, but the bittersweet release stayed with him. "For fuck's sake. You sent us away to die because of the way I spoke to you?"

He looked unsure now, the tiredness replaced with a hint of fear. "Yes. You knew something was wrong. Even if you didn't know what, yet. You would have worked it out."

"Fucking Hells, Jan! I regularly tear Mynygogg a new arsehole! I was being nice because we were in company!"

Janaeus's face fell.

He'd done it for nothing. For his own insecurity. The timid little boy who'd wanted to be like him and Korvin had assumed Aranok knew he was a fraud—because he knew he was a fraud. It was fucking tragic.

"Your plan might have worked if you hadn't tried to murder us."

He sat back in his chair, eyes wide, as the full weight of his mistake sank in. Still, somehow, Aranok found it hilarious and had to stifle another giggle. "You fucking idiot."

"Stop it!" Janaeus stood, but there was nothing threatening about him. Nothing regal. Nothing to be afraid of. He was a child in a man's body, demanding attention. Stamping his feet for respect he would never earn. "I saved this country! I saved everyone."

That stopped the laughter. "How do you make that out?"

Janaeus jabbed a finger at him as he spat his reply. "I stopped Anhel and Shay. They would've killed you all. Everyone. Wiped out the whole country until they were in charge. I stopped them when you couldn't! With all your strength, and your army and your powers—it was me who ended the war. Me who found a way to satisfy them and end the killing. You should be fucking thanking me!"

Aranok stood without thinking. He was bigger than Janaeus, but from across the table he couldn't do much with that. "Thanking you? For wiping the entire country's minds? For stealing the throne Mynygogg earned?"

"Earned? He stole it! He took it from Hofnag! How many died for your rebellion? How many? I did it bloodless. Ended the war and took the throne without more death. How is that not better?"

Shit. That made a warped kind of sense. It didn't really, but... Aranok could see how Janaeus's ego had made that work. "Mynygogg isn't Hofnag. Mynygogg was building a better country..."

"For who? For *draoidhs*? What laws did he pass to protect us? What did he actually do? Remove the laws limiting us using our abilities? All that did was make people afraid, so they hated us even more! Was that supposed to help? We might have been legal, but we were still being spat at in the street!"

He was right. And Aranok knew it.

"I'm sure nobody spat at you, though, Laird Envoy..." Janaeus's words were a knife sliding between Aranok's ribs.

"Fuck you!" The anger burst from him, burning hot. "You think I got special treatment? I couldn't even get a bed in a fucking inn last week! A girl had to stand for me. Don't make me out to be a fucking traitor, Jan. I've always been on the right side!"

Janaeus softened. "Fine. Then why are you standing against us? Isn't this better?" He raised his arms as if to indicate the entire kingdom within the little room.

Was it better? Maybe for Janaeus. For Anhel. For Shay? Was this really what she needed? No. What Shay needed was help. A medic. Compassion. Justice? Maybe. But the Blackening had long taken care of that. It was no justice at all, and she'd have to answer for it, but Kiana's death had hardly gone unpunished. How did this help her?

"Better for whom? Hundreds of thousands are dead. Glorbad's dead. Conifax is dead. I should be dead. Because of you."

Janaeus paled and sank back into his seat. "Conifax is dead?"

He didn't know. Which meant he didn't know they had Rotan. It also likely meant he didn't know about Shayella or Meristan. That was all good. The less information Janaeus had, the more Aranok had to work with.

"Murdered. I assume for getting too close to the truth of your coup."

Janaeus had been a student at the university too. He'd known Conifax—every *draoidh* student knew him. He was a huge personality, overshadowing many of the other masters, even those technically his seniors. Maybe only Master Ipharia had been better respected.

"Hells." Janaeus looked genuinely pained, which somehow infuriated Aranok. How dare he be upset at the death of a man he was responsible for? "I'm sorry, Ari, I never wanted that."

"Sorry doesn't fucking bring him back to life, does it? Sorry does absolutely fucking nothing. You might as well have stuck the fucking knife in him yourself!"

Janaeus's face hardened. He glanced down toward Aranok's hand. "What good's that going to do?"

Aranok looked down.

Flame rolled around his clenched fist.

Had he said *teine*? Made the gestures? Without even realising? Fuck. He was losing control. He needed to be calm. To think. He still had to get them out of this. Somehow. Nirea's and Dialla's lives were in his hands. And a lot of other lives, for that matter.

The flame died as he relaxed his fist and stretched out his fingers. "No, you're right. We need peace, Jan. This has to end. For everyone."

"Peace? What do you think this is?" Janaeus spread his hands on the table. "Why do you think I did this? You think Anhel would have stopped? If not for me, the country would be overrun with demons! You'd still be out there in the fields. If not dead. Why do you think I did this, Aranok?" He stood again, staring across the table with eyes that were now almost begging for understanding. "I did it to save you. To save all of us. I did it so we wouldn't lose anyone else. Do you think this is what Korvin would want? Us at each other's throats? Trying to kill each other over a country that hates us? I found a peaceful solution to end the war."

Aranok could see it clear as water: Janaeus believed it. Fervently, absolutely believed it.

"What about me? All of us? You sent us to die, Jan. The Blackened on the Auld Road; the demon at Barrock. You knew what you were doing."

Were those tears welling in Janaeus's eyes now? "I hated it. It was Anhel's idea. He said we had to deal with you. And the others. I tried not to. I tried! I said I could keep you close, in the council. I made Meristan think he was a monk, for God's sake, so he'd stay out of the way! Because I know he's your friend. Anhel wanted him dead. Head of the Order? All the demons he's killed?"

It was Aranok's turn to slump in his chair. Fucking hellfire, he really thought he was helping. The naïve bloody idiot. That explained Meristan, though: no great conspiracy, no plan, just an idiotic attempt to keep him safe. "All right. All right. What about everything else? The demon at Mutton Hole, lying to Mournside, killing a messenger?"

Janaeus flinched. "I told you to stay away from Mournside. I told you!"

"You knew I wouldn't listen."

"I hoped you might." Janaeus sat again. "I knew you might not. The rest... it's temporary. While we transition. We need people focused on other things—not looking too hard at us."

Aranok leaned forward, resting his chin on his folded hands. He saw the man across from him. No king. No leader. A scared child trying desperately to please his elders. To stop them from fighting. To make it all go away.

Fuck it all.

"All right, Jan. You and I are going to fix this. All of it. And we're going to do it right this time, all right? No more deaths. No more war. Peace."

"For *draoidhs*?"

"For everyone. I've already spoken to Mynygogg. I've told him we didn't do enough. This time will be different."

"What if it's not? What if he doesn't agree? Again?"

It wasn't an unfair question. Mynygogg and his feathers. Surely he couldn't disagree this time. If Aranok delivered the kingdom again, bloodlessly, surely...

"If he doesn't, then I'll take the throne and do it myself."

Janaeus's eyes widened, first with shock, then with... happiness? Maybe even excitement? That wasn't what Aranok had expected. He'd never wanted the throne. Genuinely never wanted it. It wasn't an idle protestation against his brother-in-law's insinuations. But here he was, threatening to take it. From his best friend.

It wouldn't come to that. He knew Mynygogg well enough. This time, they'd do it right. Bigotry against *draoidhs* would be outlawed. No more hate. Sometimes, the only way to change people's minds is by law. By making it clear their views will not be tolerated. It would take a generation, maybe more, but they'd finally rid Eidyn of the curse of ignorance. And Emelina would grow up safe. Safer.

"You would do that?" There was eagerness in Janaeus's voice. If what

Shay said was true, if he admired Aranok so much... Yes, he could see that. Maybe he'd always seen it, and maybe he'd taken it for granted. Maybe he'd taken Janaeus for granted.

And he was going to have to betray him. But later. Not now.

"I will. You have my word."

Janaeus stretched a tentative hand across the table. Aranok took a moment to decide, swallowed the anger and grief still rumbling in his chest and took it.

"Where do we begin?" Janaeus sat up straighter, a weight lifted from him. He didn't want the crown that rested like an anvil between them any more than Aranok. He'd be glad to be rid of it, Aranok guessed. "How do we deal with Shay and Anhel?"

"I have Shay," said Aranok. "She's under control."

"You... Is she all right?"

"No. She's a fucking mess. She's dragging her Dead daughter around as if it were perfectly fucking normal."

Janaeus stood, turned to a crate and lifted a bottle of wine, proffering it at Aranok.

Why the Hell not? It might steady his nerves.

"You know what happened to Kiana?" Janaeus grabbed a pair of goblets from the corner and filled them both.

"I do. It's awful." Aranok accepted the cup and sipped from it. It was good. And it did help.

Janaeus returned to his seat. "And the Blackened?"

"I know about that too. That's why I'm here, Jan. We need the relic. The heart of devastation. To cure the Blackened."

A half-snorted laugh escaped Janaeus. Not a response Aranok was prepared for.

"What?"

Janaeus looked almost confused.

"The thing you could have used to undo my spell? Why would I keep that?"

Aranok's stomach flipped.

"Where is it?"

It had to be safe, somewhere.

They needed it for the Blackening.

They needed it to restore the kingdom.

"Gone. We smashed it and scattered the dust at sea."

No. Surely not. *Surely* not.

Aranok stood urgently. "You did not."

"Of course," Jan replied, a tone of genuine surprise in his voice.

No. It made no sense. For all Jan might have thought it wise, there was no way Anhel would surrender that kind of power. To increase his own skill like that? "I don't believe you."

But did he, really? Was he just flailing in the dark, because losing the heart meant so much was fucked? Not just the country, not just people's memories, but the Blackened—and Shayella.

"Aranok, it was always the plan. If you rewrite history the way we did, you can't leave traces. You don't leave a means for the truth to be discovered. This plan only worked if there was no way to undo the spell. Nothing else could clear everyone's memories. If a few people recover, I can handle them individually. If the whole country recovers... we're back to war. We always intended to destroy it. To make this final. Permanent."

He said it as though it were the most obvious thing in the world. And of course, it was, now Aranok thought about it. Janaeus was smart. Logically, dispassionately, it was the clever thing to do.

And now they were screwed.

"Fuck, Jan! Fuck! Now what? How do we fix this without the heart?"

Janaeus was weirdly calm. "It's fine. I'll work with you to restore people's memories. And Mynygogg. With a united front, there's no reason for anyone to refuse. It won't be a problem." His smile was wide and benevolent. But he'd missed the point.

"What about the Blackening?" Aranok could feel the anger, the agitation rising again. He clenched and unclenched his trembling fists.

"Shay can fix that, can't she?"

The innocence again. The trust.

"How, Jan? How can she fix it?"

The confidence wavered with his voice. "She said she could. She said there was a way, without the heart."

Of course she did.

"Jan, it's a contagious curse. The only way to lift it, for everyone, without the heart, might be for Shay to die. *If* that works."

Janaeus's face turned ashen. "No. No, she said she could control them. She summoned them to the Auld Road, right?"

True. She clearly had some control over them. But that didn't give her the power to lift the curse across the entire country. Maybe she could limit the spread, though. Bring them together somewhere they could contain them, and remove the curse piecemeal. Fuck, this was going to be a lot harder than he'd hoped. They were going to have to get Shay onside for a start, something that was unlikely since Samily cut her bloody tongue out and threatened Kiana. Then again, if they brought them together in Lepertoun, or even Lestalric... maybe it would make it easier to treat them, once they were cured. Maybe that could work.

"No, Jan. She can't lift the curse alone any more than I can." He didn't finish with "surely you know that," but only through force of will. Janaeus should have known that before he destroyed the relic.

"But she said..."

"She lied to you. She doesn't want the curse lifted." And that was the root of the problem. Hell, was he going to have to use her daughter to manipulate her? Again? Maybe he could get through to her. Find another way.

"Oh, fuck, Aranok, I didn't know. She swore, and Anhel said—"

"Anhel is a manipulative cunt."

Janaeus recoiled like he'd been slapped. "You... you really think that?"

"He lied to you." That was far from the worst of Anhel Weyr's crimes, but it was the most salient right then.

Janaeus looked down sadly. "So did Shay."

That looked like it hurt. Maybe Aranok hadn't been the only one with an unrequited flame for Shay when they were younger. Maybe the embers still glowed in Janaeus. "Shay's mad, Jan. I mean, actually mad. Sane people don't do what she's done."

"No, she—"

Aranok cut him off. "Kiana broke her. Her mind's cracked. I don't think she'll ever be the same." It was harsh, but he needed to understand. And Aranok needed him not wallowing in self-pity. He'd do what he could for Shay, but he'd already accepted she wasn't coming back. Not really.

Janaeus nodded sadly. "Aye. Aye, all right. So, what do we do?"

What did they do? Weyr was the problem now. He wouldn't be turned, and he'd never repent. Aranok was going to have to kill him. "Where's Anhel?"

Janaeus pursed his lips as though deciding whether to free the words. This was the moment, of sorts, where he chose. He couldn't play both sides. Either he betrayed Anhel or he betrayed Aranok.

"He's in the guest quarters. Northwest tower."

"All right." Aranok stood. "Stay here. Carry on with the party. Say nothing. We'll handle Weyr."

"Wait." Janaeus rose and circled the table to join him. "Every guard in that room is a changeling. Anhel's demons. Assume he knows you're here."

Fuck. Fuck, fuck, fuck.

"What is this, anyway? Why are the nobles here?" In a room surrounded by demons...

"To get them onside. We're passing the *draoidh* laws. They're going out with the messengers this week. I just have to sign and seal the papers." Janaeus's chest opened out a little and his shoulders moved back.

"Stop that. You can't do that now. When the truth comes out, it'll work against us. You have to let Mynygogg do it."

The shoulders slumped. The reason he'd done all of it, and he wasn't going to finish it. He'd never be credited with it. Well, tough. A lot of people weren't remembered for their achievements. It didn't make them any less real. Aranok put a hand on his arm.

"It'll still happen, Jan. And this way, it'll last."

"And what if you have to do it? What if you have to take the throne, like you said?"

"We'll kill that boar when it charges. Let's hope it doesn't. Anything else I need to know? Who were the men you were speaking to? Before."

"*Draoidhs*. Anhel recruited them."

Damn it. That made things even worse. "What skills?"

"Physic. And earth."

Aranok looked down at the earth charm on Janaeus's chest. The man took it in his hand and nodded, answering Aranok's unspoken question.

"Anhel has one?"

Another nod.

"All right. Any other *draoidhs*?"

"Not here. But there are others. Aranok, did I…Is this my fault?" His voice broke on the last words. Was it? Aranok could hardly tell anymore. Korvin's murder; his own drunken ranting; the rebellion; their failures in governing; Shay's madness; Anhel's bile…Who was really at fault? Maybe there was no one cause, no single spark that set this blaze. Maybe it smouldered up from the ground unbidden, overtaking them before they knew they were burning.

"It doesn't matter. Nobody can change what they've done, only what they do next."

Janaeus nodded silently. Aranok had no idea if that placated him, but he needed him to keep playing this role for a little while longer. To pretend to be the king and act as though Aranok was still under his control. If he could do that, and Aranok could get to Anhel tonight—the nightmare could be over in a matter of months.

"Right, listen. We're going back out there together. You're going to carry on with this party exactly as before. If you're asked, everything is fine, and we're still under the spell. Right?"

"Right."

"We'll get Anhel. When we're done, I'll find you, and we'll make plans. All right?"

"All right. Aranok?" A wealth of sorrow and regret trembled in his old friend's eyes. "I'm sorry. I really am."

"So am I."

Janaeus moved to open the door, but Aranok stopped him. "You're going to need that." He pointed to the crown, abandoned on the table. Janaeus slowly picked it up and placed it back on his head.

It was far too big.

CHAPTER 27

They'd been in the room a long time. Nirea was itchy, desperate to do... something. Maybe it was the energy Dialla had given her—maybe it was too much. They'd stood there fending off drunk men who appeared to think Dialla was artwork for their admiration, and ludicrously bejewelled women who found Nirea a source of incredulity.

She'd never enjoyed the company of nobility, and they were doing a fine job of reminding her why. Their phoney admiration when she wore the robes of a monarch melted away when presented with her true self. Barely a decent human being amongst them. She'd take a Leet tavern full of drunk sailors over this any day.

And she missed Glorbad, who should have been standing beside her thinking the exact same thing.

"Are you all right, m... my... Nirea?"

Bless the girl for her concern and for the frankly adorable way she stumbled over not using Nirea's title. It reminded her that everyone in the room was going to remember who she was eventually, and remember everything they'd done and said tonight. There were going to be some very distressed conversations amongst the gentry.

"I'm fine, thank you."

Dialla smiled, looking a little confused that her question had caused such a reaction. She was a sweet girl and had bowed and deferred appropriately to every old goat who'd tried to engage her in conversation.

Her father had kept his distance, though, since Nirea scared him off. The man deserved every bit of discomfort that was coming to him.

And maybe it had been a little cathartic too. Nirea was still bothered by how easily she'd slipped into prejudice against *draoidhs* before, no matter how slight. She wanted to blame Janaeus for that, but the truth was it had come from her, and that grumbled like an infected wound. She wasn't that person. She was better than that.

Out of the corner of her eye, Nirea noticed that the odd, grubby-looking man had moved up toward the doors and was hovering awkwardly. Not speaking to anyone, not drinking, just...watching. Regularly looking to the door Aranok and Janaeus had disappeared through. He was no noble. He belonged in that Leet tavern. If things went wrong, she'd need to deal with him first. Him and all the guards. She counted nine, that she could see. The nobles might get in the way. She should try to keep them alive.

The thug's head snapped to attention and Nirea followed his gaze. The antechamber door stood open. First Janaeus, looking serious, and then Aranok, smiling.

Smiling?

The charade had worked, and the "king" still believed them his subjects. Hopefully Aranok had also managed to get a clue as to where they might look for the relic.

Nirea turned to Dialla. The woman had stiffened and her expression turned dark. She had no love for the man who'd twisted her mind.

"Daughter?"

Dialla shook herself from her stupor, instantly putting on a cheerful mask to greet the newcomer. She looked in her sixties, red hair faded to grey bundled on her head and wrapped in blue lace that matched the trim of her over-tailored cream dress.

"Mother. How are you?" Much more composed this time. She'd had a chance to prepare. And maybe her mother was easier to deal with.

"I am well, my dear. And who is your companion?"

Straight to the point, then. No dance; just the dagger.

"This is Lady Nirea," Dialla faltered. "She is a crucial member of the king's council, Mother." She stressed *crucial.* Bless her, she was trying to prevent her mother from making the social missteps that would embarrass her later.

"I'm sure she must be, to be allowed to dress so at a banquet." A small, guttural giggle, as if to minimise the cut. Instantly, Nirea knew the type. She'd stab you in the face and smile as if it were a playful slap. Hells, how she hated these people. Speak your mind and stand by it, but never hide behind the pretence of humour. This was a coward's attack; a knife in the dark.

"Lady Nirea, this is my mother, Lady Finnia."

Nirea brushed her hands down her battered red leathers. "Hides the blood." She smiled back, and then, quite markedly, returned the giggle. The woman's face remained cheerful, but her eyes turned black. That was where Dialla learned it. For all Nirea's lack of family, perhaps she'd only missed a life of scented barbs and fatuous giggling.

"Will we see you for the Midwinter Feast, my dear?" Dialla's mother pivoted back to her, finding the sport she'd looked for less fulfilling than she'd hoped.

"I... I haven't thought about it," the master answered. "Perhaps?"

"Excuse me, Lady." Finnia stepped sideways and turned to see who had dared touch her arm without permission. She softened when she saw him.

"Laird Envoy, it is an honour." She curtseyed stiffly.

"Is it?" Aranok's reply was absent-minded, as though he'd never heard the phrase before and wasn't overly interested in hearing it again.

Lady Finnia's mouth puckered as she gave another little laugh. "Of course, Laird. We are all grateful for your protection from that awful Mynygogg."

Aranok closed his eyes for a moment, tilting his head as if besieged by an unseen pain. "My lady, you'll excuse us a moment? I have things to discuss with my friends."

A little eyebrow raise. Whatever else she thought, her daughter described as a "friend" to the king's envoy was inherently pleasing, apparently.

"Of course. Do come and speak to us, daughter, when you have a moment." Finnia withdrew with the same dead smile she'd arrived wearing, only turning to cross the room when Aranok had turned his back on her.

"What news?" Nirea hissed at Aranok when the woman was out of sight.

"We're leaving. Now." Aranok looked uneasily about the room, seeming to scan the guards in particular, but also noticing the man Nirea had been watching.

"The relic?"

"It's gone. Destroyed."

Fucking Hell!

That was it, they were done. They couldn't undo the memory magic without the heart. Why was he so calm? What happened in that room?

"How do you know?"

Aranok grabbed Nirea's forearm and drew her toward the door. "Because he told me. We need to go."

She yanked her arm free and took a step back. "No. Explain. Now."

Several heads turned their way. Aranok lowered his head along with his voice. "*Not. Here.*"

She stepped toward him, putting herself between him and the doors. Close enough to keep her voice down and to be absolutely clear about her intent. "We are not leaving this room until you tell me what happened."

Aranok's mouth puckered like a cat's arsehole before spreading into a terse smile. "Fine. Follow me." The three of them weaved through flamboyant waves of half-full glasses, florid guffaws and hostile glances until they found a relatively quiet corner near a candelabra.

Aranok leaned faux-casually against the wall. "For fuck's sake, smile; we've got enough people looking at us as it is."

Nirea threw back her shoulders, ran her fingers through her still-wet hair and plastered on her "duty" smile. Dialla gave a sort of shrill giggle that turned both their heads. Nerves were taking her. Nirea put a hand on her forearm and took a deep, slow breath in and out. Dialla did the same and nodded sheepishly. Nirea turned back to Aranok.

"Now. Tell me."

"Jan will help us. If we kill Anhel."

"What?" That made no sense. Why would Janaeus help them? Why would he want them to kill Anhel Weyr? Why would they have destroyed the relic? None of it added up.

A horrible, dark thought crept up in Nirea. "Aranok, show me your charm."

His face crumpled into confusion. "Why?"

"You know why."

He'd been alone in a room with a memory *draoidh.*

Aranok put a protective hand to his chest. "Nirea, it was never off my neck. I know what I'm doing."

Nirea concentrated on keeping the smile on her face. "Maybe. But why would they destroy such a powerful weapon? Why would Janaeus want to help us? Why would he want his ally dead? Aranok, you have to see this all seems like... nonsense. So maybe he affected your memory or maybe..."

As she was speaking, Aranok drew the yellow ball from his chest, clenched his fist tightly and quietly said, "*Clìor.*" He stared directly into Nirea's eyes. Nothing happened.

"Or maybe he just lied to you," Nirea finished. "And this is a trap." She'd already walked into one of those. Fucked if she was doing it again.

Aranok opened his mouth, closed it again, licked his lips and sighed. "He wasn't lying. They destroyed the relic to prevent us from doing exactly what we wanted to do. Anhel's in charge. Jan thought he was stopping the war. He was... trying to help."

At least he had the sense to look embarrassed as the words came out of his mouth. *Help?* It took Nirea a few moments to find words.

Dialla cleared her throat. "I'm sorry, Laird Envoy, but if his plan was to end the war, would it not have been simpler to change his allies' minds?"

Aranok shook his head and tapped his chest. "They both have these. We all did."

The master clasped her hands nervously before her. "No, sorry, I simply meant... *change their minds.*"

Aranok looked wistfully across the room to where "King" Janaeus had returned to entertaining sycophants. "It's not minds we need to change—it's hearts."

It was an odd, wishy-washy answer, and regardless, it got them no further forward. They might never get this close to Janaeus again, now he knew. And if the relic wasn't destroyed... "Aranok, how do we know he's telling you the truth?" *And that your judgement isn't compromised?*

He put a hand on her arm, pulling her toward the doors. "You need to trust me. Please."

And that was the problem.

"I'm sorry. I can't."

What the fuck was Nirea doing? Why now of all times had she decided to fight him? The longer they waited here, the more chance there was of this going wrong. They needed to leave and go after Anhel now, before he was ready. Before his demons warned him they were here.

Nirea turned and gestured to Dialla, and the master nodded hesitantly. What was that about? What had he missed while he was talking to Jan? He stepped back toward the queen. "What are you doing?" It was barely more than a whisper. The chatter was loud enough to cover them from anyone who wasn't trying to listen, but if anyone nearby decided to pay attention...

"What we came to do." Her jaw was set, her eyes solidly set against his. *Fuck!* What did that even mean? They came for the relic, and it was gone.

"Nirea, please. I have a plan. We can fix this. But it has to be now."

Her shoulders went back as her head tilted slightly. "We already had a plan. Be ready."

Be ready? For what?

"Nirea, please. Just wait." Panic rose in his chest. Aranok did not enjoy not knowing what was happening—but the bigger, the much more dangerous question was, *why* didn't he know?

They needed to get Anhel. Whatever Nirea thought she was doing, it was wrong. He reached for her arm, but she whipped it from his reach again and stepped away, moving back into the throng of the crowd. He followed, trying to keep up. Where was she going? Why was she doing this? She made for the centre of the room, purposefully striding—like the queen. Aranok followed, simultaneously trying to get her attention while not drawing any more to himself.

Wait, where had Dialla gone? He turned and scanned the room. It took a moment to find her—curtseying to Janaeus. He offered a hand, glancing up to Aranok with a look of some confusion, but trust.

He assumed Aranok was behind this.

Oh, fuck.

Suddenly, he knew what was happening. He knew what the plan was and he knew why she'd kept it from him. Because he might have stopped it.

And, as it turned out, he was right to.

Aranok burst into life, shoving his way past overstuffed bellies and overtaut corsets. Nobles staggered away, gasping with appalled shock. It didn't matter. He had to get to them before...

Dialla took Janaeus's hand. Her head was bowed, but as far away as he still was, Aranok saw her mouth move.

Fuck!

Janaeus went grey. He looked up at Aranok, his eyes filled with confusion and hurt. He thought Aranok had done this. That he'd betrayed him as soon as he'd walked away. And he didn't understand why. Because there was no why.

It was a pointless, stupid waste.

Pale eyes rolled back and Janaeus crumpled like a discarded puppet. With a sickening crunch, his head hit stone. The crown clanked and rolled away.

The room held its breath. And screamed.

"To the king!" came a cry from his left as the nobles bustled and shoved—some to get away, some to get a better look. Aranok was knocked sideways, caught himself against a thin, older man with a walking stick who nearly buckled under him. When he finally made it clear of the crowd, Janaeus's dull-looking *draoidh* held Dialla by the throat. His outfit was too small now, too tight, too short.

The physic *draoidh*.

Dialla couldn't defend herself. She had no air to speak. Aranok needed to break that grip.

"Balla na talamh!" The stone floor cracked as a spike drove itself up, snapping the physic *draoidh*'s elbow. His arm popped backwards, releasing the master and throwing him away, howling in pain. His forearm dangled uselessly from the joint.

From behind Aranok, a raspy voice: "*Teine.*"

He dived for Dialla, who was crouched on one knee, holding her throat. She was lucky it wasn't crushed. Aranok spread himself over her like a blanket, taking the brunt of the fire blast against his armour and natural defence. Intense screams told him nobles had been caught in the spread. He threw back a hand and returned a wave of water, hoping to put out as much flame as he could.

"Get up!" He pulled Dialla to her feet. The woman's eyes were black moons. She was terrified. No fucking wonder. She was a teacher, and her queen had just ordered her to commit regicide.

Aranok pulled Dialla away as demon guards lunged toward them. The chance to take Anhel was gone along with Janaeus and their hopes of fixing this unholy mess. Now they just needed to get out with their lives.

"Treason!" shouted a voice. "The envoy has murdered the king!"

Brilliant. That was exactly the story they didn't need spreading.

Where the fuck was Nirea? Metal on metal somewhere to his right. Probably her. She could look after herself. This was her fault.

A large woman fell across their path and Aranok all but landed on top of her, just catching his balance. The demon guard that barged over her lunged with its spear. Reflexively, Aranok threw an arm down and pushed it away with *gluais*. The prone woman gave a wet, surprised "hurk" as it skewered her through the back.

Dialla screamed, threw out an arm, and the guard flew back against the wall. The force of the impact cracked stone as the thing practically disintegrated with the sheer force of the blow. Dialla could barely keep still, her head darting back and forth. She must be bursting with energy from draining Janaeus. Hopefully not too much. The danger for energy *draoidhs* was either in giving away too much energy or taking on too much. They risked either passing out or their body failing. He'd heard of energy *draoidhs* whose hearts simply gave out from beating too fast. But Dialla was young and she'd expended a lot on that demon. Much more than required. That should help.

The crowd of nobles parted, leaving them a route to the door. And the earth *draoidh*.

The man faced them with two burning fists. Aranok could handle most of his attacks. Dialla, on the other hand…

The flames poured toward them. Aranok turned, trying to put himself between them and Dialla again, but she wasn't the terrified victim she'd been a moment ago.

"Sùghadh." The flames disappeared into her open palms. The other *draoidh* looked as stunned as Aranok. Clearly, he hadn't seen that before either. Dialla almost vibrated with energy. She looked as though Aranok was viewing her through rain, never quite able to focus directly on her. The master turned her hands over and said, *"Spreadhadh."* The earth *draoidh* flew backwards. The wooden doors exploded into splinters as the man kept going, until a stone wall finally stopped him with a crunch. He slid down into a heap. He wasn't getting up soon. If ever.

A roar from behind them. Aranok pushed Dialla out of the way and took the full force of the push in his left side. Even with his armour on, the wind was knocked from him and he fell to his knees. The physic *draoidh* had only one working arm, but it was strong enough to break a horse. Aranok looked up at the man, eyes blazing with fury, as he drew back for another blow. If it landed, it would take Aranok's head off.

Instead, he screamed and collapsed, grasping at the backs of his own knees.

Nirea's blade dripped blood. She was spattered with it—most of it black. Demon blood. How many guards were left? It didn't matter. They had to go. Aranok forced himself back to his feet and stumbled over the dead woman toward the door. Nobles screamed, some in pain, the rest in fear.

The guards who had been outside the doors were face down on the floor covered in a shower of wooden shards. At least one of them was human. The one who'd announced them. He hoped the man was alive. Nirea followed him out, dragging Dialla behind her.

Fuck fuck fuck!

He didn't know Greytoun as well as Dun Eidyn. His mind raced back to when they arrived. Which corners had they turned, which stairs had they taken?

As they rounded a corner, half a dozen guards came rushing at them. Nirea stopped, poised. That wasn't the answer. They didn't know what had happened. Aranok put a hand across her and stood proud.

"Get to the banquet room. We're under attack!"

"Aye, Laird," the lead woman answered, and the group shuffled past them back the way they'd come.

"Well done." Nirea breathed heavily. Aranok's instinct was to tell her to fuck herself, but he held it for the moment. Again they ran, round one corner, along another corridor, down more stairs. Finally, a window, and Aranok got his bearings. Left at the next turn and down the steps would get them to the courtyard, and from there to the gatehouse.

They burst out into the dark night, rain still thundering against the cobblestones. Guards were alert, but confused. They knew something was happening, but not what. Not yet.

"To arms! To arms!" A cry from a window above them, clear even through the rain's drumbeat. "Treachery! The envoy has murdered the king!"

Fuck.

A confusion of soldiers gathered around them—maybe ten or twelve. Some appearing from buildings around the courtyard, still getting their helms on. Most hesitant. A few, Aranok guessed, were changelings. They looked more feral; more eager. Somewhere behind them, Anhel Weyr knew what had happened. He could be summoning a major demon at that moment. Bringing it to crush them. They had to get out. But these soldiers... some of them, at least, were good people. Nirea put a hand on his shoulder as water streamed down his head and into his collar. Fire wouldn't last long and he didn't want to kill. He needed something nonlethal.

Dialla.

"Dialla! Can you do that thing again? Around us?"

The master looked at him as though he'd appeared before her from the void. "What?"

"That thing!" Aranok mimed shoving his hands out, hoping she would understand. The soldiers were closing the circle. While many were still cautious, a few were getting very close.

Dialla nodded timidly. "Get down."

Aranok grabbed Nirea and pulled her with him to their knees. Dialla extended her hands, said, "*Spreadhadh*" and turned. Rain broke like glass and the guards fell backwards as if swiped with a tree. He'd never known energy *draoidhs* were this powerful. Or maybe he'd just never known an energy *draoidh* this powerful.

"Run!" Aranok pushed himself back to his feet and rushed toward the tunnel, glancing back to ensure the women were following. Dialla was a mess, and Aranok suspected her face was wet with more than rain, but still they ran. Into the tunnel and no guards, except the ones at the end. The murder holes would be empty. They were nearly free.

"Leondar!" Aranok called. The gate ahead creaked open as they charged toward it, but behind them, footfall. They were still being chased. Every guard in the castle likely wanted them now.

Aranok's lungs were burning. He couldn't keep up this pace. At last, they reached the gate, and Leondar, as he'd promised. The huge man beckoned them forward. As Aranok breached the gate back out into the rain, he saw the second guard slumped against the wall. Unconscious, he assumed. Leondar wouldn't have wanted to kill her.

"Hurry!" the big man bellowed to the women, who were only ten yards back. Dialla's dress was hampering her running—Nirea was all but dragging her. At least it gave Aranok a second to catch his breath. And think.

As soon as they were through, he acted.

"Balla na talamh." Stone rose from the ground, sealing the end of the tunnel. An arrow clattered somewhere nearby.

"Run!" Aranok bellowed again. Leondar lifted his huge shield over Nirea's head and ran. In the rain and the wind, arrows were unlikely to hit, but a few did catch the edges of the shield as they ran down the wet steps, back into Greytoun.

Now Aranok was grateful for the godawful weather covering their escape.

When they finally reached the bottom, out of sight of the archer windows, they slumped against the rock.

"Now what?" Nirea barked.

"Now what?" Aranok repeated. "Now what? Are you fucking kidding?"

Leondar scowled at Aranok's tone, but he was far too full of venom to be dissuaded.

"I beg your pardon?" Nirea's tone was equally acidic.

"Now you want my counsel, do you? Now you've fucked us?"

"Mind who you're speaking to, please, Laird." Leondar spoke evenly, but the implied threat was clear. Not that he could hurt Aranok. Not really. But he didn't want to fight the big man. He'd had more than enough violence.

"I am not interested in debating you, Aranok. We need somewhere to go. Now."

"Can't we just get the horses and leave?" Dialla's voice was high, thin, pleading.

"By the time we get there and saddle up, they'll be on us," Aranok answered. His wall would only hold them so long, and they'd be after them again. Especially if their earth *draoidh* woke up. Assuming he was going to wake up. And once word got out, they'd be suspicious of anyone coming for those animals. No, the horses were lost to them. For now, at least.

How the fuck had it come to this? He had a plan. He'd got Janaeus onside. Everything was about to be fixed, and now…

But in this, Nirea was right. What they needed was somewhere to regroup and make a new plan. Somewhere nobody was going to look for them.

He knew exactly where they were going.

CHAPTER 28

Do you have any fucking idea what you've done?" The envoy's face was almost as red as his scarf. Darginn and Isadona had been packing when Laird Aranok, the queen and their companions arrived back at his door, wet, bedraggled and desperate. They'd all but bowled him over getting in the door, pulled the curtains and waited some time before saying much of anything to each other. The envoy had paced like a caged animal.

Now they'd begun, it seemed the floodgates were open.

"I've done what you should have done!" the queen barked back at him. "I finished our enemy. I ended this phony war."

Aranok got even louder. "He was on our side, you fucking idiot! He was going to help us!"

The huge guard stepped between them, a hand raised to Aranok's chest.

"It's fine, Leondar. Take a seat." Nirea waved him away like an insect. The man slowly stepped aside but didn't actually sit.

"What do you mean he was on our side? Against who?"

"Anhel Weyr!"

Darginn winced, both at the name and the poison with which the envoy spat it at the queen. It was hard to choose the more disturbing thought: the demon summoner's return or Eidyn's rulers at each other's throats.

"How is Weyr the concern?" Queen Nirea was losing her ire. She sounded almost as confused as Darginn. Isadona stood in the kitchen, supposedly brewing tea, but wringing a cloth, watching the spectacle.

"Because he fucking is!" Aranok smacked a hand on the mantelpiece. "He's the only problem left. I had Jan onside. I turned him."

"How do you know he wasn't lying? That's what he does."

The envoy turned back to face her, running his hands through his soaking hair. "Because I do! Because I've known him since we were children. Because I looked him in the eye."

The queen paused for a moment, taking in the answer. She didn't seem angry, or even emotional. It was as if a wave had drained from her. "No. No, it's too easy. He was playing you, Aranok. What was in it for him? Why give up the throne? Especially with the relic gone—if it is—why would he do that?"

Aranok waved his hands as though trying to contain some explosion within him. "It's... it's more complex than that! He was going to help us."

"Aranok, I cannot believe that..."

"Well, we'll never fucking know now, will we? Because you murdered him! You got her to murder him!" He pointed to Master Dialla, who had sat quietly on the floor since they arrived. Her pretty dress and shoes were coated with mud, and maybe some of it wasn't mud, now Darginn looked closer. She'd been soaked through and shivering, but the fire hadn't seemed to still her trembling hands. She stared at the wall as if she could see right through it. Darginn had seen that look before, but on soldiers, not young women. Now he knew why. Killing changed people.

This was more than he should have been hearing, he was sure. With a grunt of effort, Darginn pushed himself to his feet. "You'll excuse me, Majesty, Laird."

Aranok snapped his head round. His eyes widened and he shook a half-extended finger at Darginn.

"No. Actually, no, Darginn. We're going to need you. Tonight. Now."

They needed him? What use was an old man in matters like this? But he would do his duty if he could. "Of course, Laird. How can I serve?"

Aranok returned to pacing, as if the movement somehow fed his mind. "Two things. You know a way out of Haven without going through the gates, don't you?"

He did. The old kirk had a tunnel in the crypt that led out into the forest. Designed to allow for escape in a siege. That's what Haven had been built for. Backed into a corner by an enemy, they could escape to the sea or get behind them by stealth. The location was a closely guarded secret. But the messengers knew. They knew all the secret passages and hidden paths in Eidyn. They had to.

Darginn nodded.

"Good. That's how we're getting out. Secondly... the head messenger. Where will she be?"

"Now?" Where would she be? For now, she lived in the apartment built into the tower at the harbour, from where the messengers operated since Auldun fell. "I know where she might be. I mean, where she's likely to be, I suppose."

Aranok nodded emphatically. "All right. Good. That'll do. That's where we're going."

"What? Why?" Nirea demanded.

The envoy was already crossing to the door. "Because the truth is all we've got now. And thanks to you, this could be our only chance to get to her." He turned to the soldier. "Leondar, stay here. Protect Dialla. Drink tea." He gestured to Isadona, who was arriving with cups. Her mouth twitched as she caught Darginn's eye. "And you, do whatever the fuck you like," he spat at the queen, turning his back on her. Most men would be hung for the way he'd spoken here. Darginn wasn't certain he wouldn't be, by the look on Nirea's face.

"Aranok!" Her tone was hard. Regal. Commanding. *"Enough."*

The silence was thick. Every eye in the room, bar Dialla's, was on the envoy. He paused, straightened his shoulders and lifted his chin.

"Darginn, you better go first. Make sure it's clear."

Havenport was an unusual combination of structures: Huge warehouses loomed over rows of white cottages, reflecting the evolution from fishing village to the country's second port. Behind them, rows of some of the poorest housing in Eidyn—built cheap, rented to dock-workers and other labourers. Aranok had come here with his father as a child, collecting materials for the business or delivering clothes for shipping abroad. The silks and exotic fabrics from faraway countries had fascinated him, as had the smell of imported spices from barrels rolled down gangplanks. In his memory, seagulls whirled overhead and waves lapped lazily against the harbour walls.

Not tonight.

As the rain hammered down and water returned to the sea in torrents, the harbour was a dark, unwelcoming place. Waves crashed against the breakwater and lightning flashed offshore, thunder rolling through only seconds later. Fishing boats bobbed violently, straining against their moorings as the sea swelled and relaxed, as if the storm had enraged its beating heart. The great ships, anchored farther out, shifted and danced in the moonlight, dark leviathans roused from sleep.

The journey here had been slow, but safe. Darginn knew his way around the town's underbelly and kept them away from the roaming groups of guards. The rain cut both ways: There was nobody else on the streets, heightening their chances of being discovered, but the sheer murk and noise helped hide them.

At some point, though, someone was going to think that if they weren't trying to escape through the gates, they might try to take a boat, which meant they couldn't hang around the harbour.

"There, look. Light." Darginn pointed to the tower halfway along the promontory that formed the southern border of the harbour. As Aranok understood, it was the original home of the import tax officers, but when Haven's traffic became too large, their offices were moved to one of the nearby warehouses. It had instead been used as a local messenger office in recent years, and was now, apparently, the office of the head messenger. For the moment—until Auldun was restored. And Darginn was right, there was light from a third-floor window.

There would be nowhere to hide once they broke cover from their current nest between two rows of cottages. Many now operated as brothel rooms, servicing a new wave of sailors with every tide. Aranok had a notion he might be able to hear exactly that from his left and was grateful again for the rain's drumbeat.

"I see it. How do we get there?"

"We run." It was the first Nirea had spoken since they'd left Darginn's. Aranok could have done with her staying behind. She always thought she knew better than anyone else what was needed. Attacked every problem like it was an enemy. No appreciation for complexity. And no regrets, apparently. That might be the thing that irked him the most. She was so bloody adamant she'd been right.

"If we just run, we could be spotted. And then we're done."

Nirea opened her hands wide. "In this? What other option have we got?"

This time she was right. There were no other choices.

They would run.

The slick cobbles made for unstable footing, and Aranok was reminded of the damage he'd done himself in Auldun. The phantom of that pain stabbed back at him. He slowed a little, making sure of his steps, carefully placing each foot. The splashes of their boots were louder than the thundercracks in Aranok's head as he prayed to nobody for them to make it along the path unseen. When he finally reached the outer wall of the building, Aranok slapped himself against it and looked back, beyond the two figures following him, for any sign of guards. His panting breath echoed inside his skull. Was that movement beside that warehouse? A flicker of a torch? No. Just a trick of the light—or his imagination.

Nirea and finally Darginn reached the wall.

"I think we're clear," Aranok whispered.

Nirea looked back, made the same assessment and nodded. "How do we get in?"

"There's a gate at the side, leads into a sort of courtyard," said Darginn. "Back door's been knackered for doggie's years."

It was good to get in out of the storm, but once the door shut out the moonlight, they were pitched into blackness.

"*Solas.*" Aranok threw a ball of light ahead. Despite the day, the running and the panic, he still felt fairly fresh. Must be the energy Dialla had given him. He'd probably drop like a stone later, when the lack of rest caught up with him.

Darginn put a finger to his lips and gestured through a doorway, which led into a short hall ending at a coil of steps. They passed a room with shelves bowing under the weight of parchment and ink drops spattered across the dark wooden floor. The dispatch office, where notices were written up for delivery.

When they reached the steps, Nirea pushed her way forward. "I'll go first."

Darginn deferred and Aranok just couldn't be arsed to argue. There was no sign of life on the first or second floors, just deep black silence disturbed by the echo of padding feet. When they reached the third, Nirea slowed, carefully checking the corridor before stepping out. That was unlike her. Once she was happy the way was clear, she allowed Darginn to retake the front, leading them to the door of the apartment where they hoped to find the head messenger.

Darginn knocked and Aranok extinguished the light. A little darkness may be useful if someone else answered.

Something clattered to the floor inside. "Who the hell's still here? Vadine? Is that you?"

Darginn cleared his throat. "Uh, Darginn Argyll, actually. Sorry to interrupt, head messenger."

The footsteps that had been stamping toward them slowed. The door opened carefully. Despite knowing whom to expect, Aranok noticed a hint of surprise in the woman's face. Madu's pale blonde hair was piled in a bun, and she wore a relatively simple purple dress with gold trim. The stitching was intricate and would have cost a talented seamstress many weeks. It had clearly been made to measure, hanging on her like a shadow. It was expensive, but not extravagant. His father would have called it a sign of class.

"Darginn Argyll. Forgive me…It's late. I wasn't expecting anyone. What can I do for you?" She looked the man up and down. "You're… dripping."

"Beg your pardon, m'lady, but it's a matter of urgency. I believe you know the laird envoy." Aranok stepped forward into the light beaming from her chambers. The surprise returned to her face.

"Of course! Laird Envoy, it is an honour to see you." She raised a hand to her chest. "I'm sorry I'm not more prepared for your visit. If you'd sent word…"

"We weren't able to, I'm afraid. Matters overtook us. May we come in?" Aranok didn't wait for an answer, moving forward even as the head messenger stepped back to give him room.

The apartment was as exquisite as the dress. Tasteful, but the expense was in the details. It seemed the crown was paying even more than Aranok had thought for her services. The messengers were always well paid, of course. Their job was both dangerous and essential to the smooth running of a country. Without their communication lines, the kingdom could quickly fall apart. The job was attractive to those prepared to do it and the punishment for interference was severe. Communication mattered. And that was exactly why they were here.

The main room was dominated by a long sofa covered in one of those exotic fabrics Aranok had seen in the harbour. In fact, the curtains were also made from expensive, unusual material. A natural result, he supposed, of the offices being on the harbour and Madu being one of the best-paid people in the kingdom. Aranok couldn't afford such luxury. Or at least, he wouldn't have wasted money on it. A great deal of coin had been poured into this lifestyle.

Madu closed the door and folded her hands. "Um, tea?"

"No. I'm sorry, we don't have time." Aranok pulled the memory charm from his neck. "I need to ask you to sit down. And take this."

Madu's eyebrows raised. "You want me to do what?"

Aranok glanced toward the window, even though the curtains were closed. They could run out of time at any moment, and they needed Madu onside. "I don't have time to explain, please trust me."

The head messenger looked slowly from Aranok to the others. When she met his eyes again, it was with a slow smile. "I'm afraid I'm not in the business of 'just trusting' anyone, Laird Envoy." She moved to the sofa. "I will certainly sit, but you're going to have to tell me what that is before I touch it."

God damn the woman and her suspicious mind. Though it was why she had the job. Truth was her livelihood. Ironic, considering the lies she'd unwittingly spread. All right. Her help now was going to be invaluable. They needed her.

Aranok spent as little time as possible explaining the situation, skipping over the night's murder and chaos until after she'd had her memory returned. Madu's eyes widened, particularly at the knowledge that she was in the presence of the true queen. When Aranok finished, she examined him like a curiosity.

"That's quite a story. And this charm will restore my memory?"

"It will. But please, we need to hurry."

"Why?"

Madu's lack of urgency was beginning to grate. He was half-tempted to shove the thing in her hand and just get on with it. "Because things have become complicated. We need your help."

Madu turned to Darginn. "And you, messenger. You know all of this to be true?"

"Aye. I do, m'lady."

Then, to Nirea: "And you are our usurped queen?"

"I am."

"Where, may I ask, is the true king, then?"

"He's on his way to meet with the Reiver council. To restore peace until we can retake the throne."

The woman rubbed a finger across her lips as though they might provide her with some insight.

Aranok was struck by how little Madu was affected. Some people handled it better. It made sense that a woman whose job was to be open-minded had little to fear from new information. It was the stock she traded.

"All right. Give me the charm." She extended a hand at last, and Aranok all but threw the yellow ball into her palm.

"Beware, it may make you sick, or dizzy." Or it could make her pass out entirely, but he hoped not. The fact she'd taken the news so well suggested she hadn't had too much of her memory changed—that was a good sign.

Aranok wrapped his hands around hers. *"Clìor."*

Madu sat back with a start and blinked, shaking her head as though it were filled with bees. She let out an odd yelp and started to her feet. Aranok caught her elbow. "Are you all right?"

"I think...I think I just need some air." Madu staggered to the window, pulled aside one curtain and opened out a pane. The rain was finally easing to a drizzle, and out this side of the building Aranok could see nothing but dark sea stretching to the horizon. The closed curtain billowed in the stiff breeze, hiding and revealing the head messenger as she sucked in the sea air.

"My God," she said. "My God. It's all true."

"It is, and I'm sorry, but we need you to hear more," said Aranok. "Something happened tonight that changes everything."

Madu continued as if she hadn't heard him. "And this…this little ball. This is all we need to restore everyone's memory?"

It hadn't occurred to Aranok she was still holding the memory charm, and he felt a sudden stab of panic as he realised it was out of his reach. "Yes. Could I have it, please?"

Madu turned to face them, her face sharp, her eyes hard.

"You can try to recover it from the sea if you like."

No.

Aranok's stomach lurched into his throat. "You…you dropped it?"

The head messenger clasped her hands together and gave a sickening smile. "Oh, dear boy. I threw it."

"What?"

Nirea reacted first, dancing forward, shoving past Madu and hanging out the window. "Fuck! Aranok! There's no land! It's a straight drop into the water."

Aranok felt a chill take him. His hands trembled. "What…what have you done?"

Madu walked casually to the large oak desk at the end of the chamber. The chair legs scraped the stone floor as she drew it out and sat. Aranok stood limp. He couldn't move.

"All that privilege. All that entitlement. And neither of you truly understand how *power* works."

Nirea drew a dagger and stalked toward the desk. Madu raised a hand, almost casually, as if the knife were a child's toy. "Touch me with that thing and people will die. People you care about."

"Not if you're fucking dead, they won't," Nirea spat back.

Madu fixed her with a cold stare. "*Only* if I'm dead."

That stopped Nirea. "What the Hell does that mean?"

Madu sat back in her plump, red leather chair. "It means, my little naïf, that I have arrangements in place with all manner of people across

Eidyn. If anything should befall me which prevents my sending them instructions not to, they will kill someone precious to you. You, Queen Nirea. You, Laird Aranok. King Mynygogg. General Glorbad. Laird Meristan. Even your bodyguard, Allandria. All of you have people you care about. Kill me, kill them." She raised her hands as if presenting a magic trick.

"Your choice."

CHAPTER 29

Nirea's fist closed tight on the dagger's handle. How dare she? How dare the bitch threaten innocent lives?

It didn't matter. She'd cost them their memory charm. The only way they had to restore the kingdom. The only way back to the throne. And she knew everything. They'd told her everything.

Nirea stepped forward.

"No!" Aranok shot out his arm toward her. "Please, Nirea."

She turned to face him. The envoy who argued with every decision she made. Who was angry she'd killed their enemy. Who wanted to keep the necromancer alive. Whose side was he on? Mynygogg loved him like a brother. But his *draoidh* nature was pulling hard on him. Would he be loyal to his "brother" if it came to a real conflict?

"What choice do we have, Aranok? If we let her live—what then?"

His voice faltered as he answered. "My family, Nirea. Who are you prepared to lose?"

Madu sat like a contented cat, contemptuously daring Nirea to challenge her. It only enraged her more. "I have nobody, except Mynygogg. He can take care of himself. Glorbad is dead, so he won't care much either way."

That registered on Madu's face. She didn't know about Glorbad. Good. The thought of her harming someone he cared about was even more infuriating than what she'd already done.

"You really think there's nobody, do you?" Madu's tone was cream smooth. No hint of agitation. No hint of fear. She absolutely believed she held the power in this room. And that was like needles in Nirea's brain. "What about Leet? You have no friends there? Not the innkeeper who took you in? Not the merchant sailor you bedded on and off for years?"

The floor tilted beneath Nirea. During the rebellion, she'd got herself cut off from her crew, fighting on the streets of Leet. Injured, exhausted and desperate, she'd stumbled in the back door of the King's Wark, hoping it would be empty. Most Leet businesses had been boarded up during the war—the running street battles made it too dangerous to go out. She found the owner, Ailen, cooking. He'd hidden her. Treated her wounds and lied to the guard. He was a good man, and she owed him her life.

And Joliander—gods alive, that was something else completely. He was patient, kind, gentle and everything she'd never had before. He'd saved her from an abyss she never thought she'd climb out of. Started her on the way out, anyway. She'd climbed out herself, but he'd shone a light—shown her there was a way.

She would die for either man without hesitation. And somehow Madu knew that.

"How?" Her voice was tiny, cracked.

"Information is my life, Your Majesty," said Madu. "Secrets are useful information. I make it my business to know the secrets of anyone I serve. It is a policy that has yet to disappoint."

Nirea felt sick. But she couldn't show it. *Never let them see your wounds.* And even if she knew Nirea's secrets, that didn't mean she really had an elaborate network of assassins on her payroll. She stood straight and looked Madu in the eye. "I don't believe you. And if I did, it wouldn't matter. I am the fucking queen of Eidyn and I won't be held to ransom."

Madu smirked, and Nirea felt her fist clench again. "I think you're going to have to discuss that with the laird envoy, m'lady."

Nirea looked again and Aranok was coming toward her, his eyes shot through with scarlet. "Nirea, we can't. Please. My sister. My niece. I can't..."

"Aranok, stand down. Now. Step outside if you haven't the stomach for this. I'll deal with her."

Madu breathed an insult of a laugh. "Again, dear, you're failing to understand where the power lies. Janaeus took my advice and hosted a party for the nobles this evening. As long as he keeps them onside, he'll be fine. The peasants are too busy trying to scrape together food to rebel against him, the farmers have enough on their hands and the merchants . . . they'll just be delighted to be able to get back to normal trading when the crisis has passed. And all of them will be grateful to great King Janaeus for restoring the country to its former glory. And Janaeus will be grateful to me.

"Information controls power. In this room, the power is there"—she flicked a hand toward Aranok—"and I control him."

Fuck.

She was right. If it came to it, she'd never beat Aranok in a fight. Even at these close quarters, if she could catch him unawares, his bloody armour would protect him from her swords. Her only chance, her only option, would be a blow to the head. For a fleeting second, she questioned whether she was willing to kill him to get this done—to save Eidyn. But it went as quickly as it arrived. Of course not. There had to be another way.

"Urk!"

Nirea snapped her head round. It took her a moment to understand what she was seeing.

Madu's head hung oddly to one side. Her eyes bulged with surprise, blood seeping around the dagger Darginn had rammed in her neck.

"No!" Aranok lurched toward the messenger, but he was already too late. Darginn lifted his hand and hammered it down again, again, as if he might hack the woman's head from her shoulders. Blood sprayed up at him, spattering his face, drenching his clothes.

"You knew! You knew!" he cried, like a child woke screaming in the night. "You knew!"

Aranok tackled him, blade spilling from the old man's hand. They clattered onto the floor, rattling the room. An inkwell overturned on the desk, dark black knives stabbing into red pools of blood.

Aranok pulled Darginn up to face him, kneeling behind the chair. "Why? Why did you do that? Why?"

"She knew!" Darginn's voice was broken glass. "She sent me to that woman! She knew what she'd do to me! She knew!"

Aranok's face crumpled from confusion and anger to pity. He closed his eyes, releasing the tears, and put a comforting hand on the back of the old messenger's head. The two of them sat in silence on the floor, covered in blood.

Madu had been wrong about the power. It had been in the hands of the one person she'd forgotten. The person she'd sacrificed. The ordinary man who'd suffered more than anyone should have to bear and would not be beaten down again. Whose pain and rage and damage overtook them all.

Nirea doubted she'd learned any of that in the moment of her death, but she enjoyed the poetic justice all the same.

Was there a spark of life left in Madu's eyes? Maybe. Nirea leaned to within inches of the former head messenger's face and smiled.

"Janaeus is dead, bitch. And so are you."

Aranok stumbled in the door of Darginn's house all but carrying the old man behind him. It had taken them too long to get back, avoiding the guards swarming the town, two of them covered in blood and the rain no longer offering cover. The noise of their footsteps slapping in puddles was a beacon. Thank God for the dark—it was the only reason they'd made it. And it was why they were going to have to leave again.

Isadona balked at the sight of her bloody husband, running to take him in her arms. But Darginn held out his hands to warn her away. "Don't! Don't touch me."

Isadona looked to Aranok and Nirea as if to find the source of the massacre.

"It's not his blood," Nirea reassured her.

"But... what happened?" the woman asked.

"Madu was a traitor," Aranok said flatly. "We executed her." No point in telling her what actually happened—that her husband was a broken man who took vengeance on someone he could, because he couldn't get it from the person responsible. Because Aranok was protecting her.

"The head messenger?" Isadona looked no less confused.

"She was conspiring with Janaeus." Nirea unbuckled her sword belt, hung it near the door and collapsed into a chair. "Her memory was unaffected."

"Oh Heaven," said Isadona. "Janaeus has allies in the kingdom?"

Nirea turned to look at Aranok. "Janaeus has allies in the kingdom."

It was even more complex than they'd imagined. God knew who would step in to take the throne now, but if Janaeus had allies, it could be any one of them. One of the nobles, maybe?

Leondar's heavy feet thumped down the stairs. "Majesty. Envoy. Are you injured?"

Nirea waved him off. "Fine. Madu is dead."

Before the big guard could ask anything more, it occurred to Aranok he might be able to give them some insight into who else might take control. "Leondar. Who would you think next in line, with Janaeus dead?" Saying the words out loud again was painful. He'd let him down.

Leondar thought for a moment. "I would have said you, under normal circumstances, what with there being no queen or heir. As it is, with you a 'traitor' and the king's council scattered, it's difficult. I don't suppose there's a clear line of succession."

No. There wasn't. Which could mean civil war, if the nobility fought for it. How had it fallen apart like this?

Because Nirea killed Janaeus.

He couldn't focus on that now. They had no time.

"Where's Dialla?"

Leondar glanced to the stairs. "Resting. She's not well."

"Rouse her. We're leaving. Now." Leondar turned to Nirea for confirmation. She nodded.

"Aye, Majesty." The kingsguard plodded back up the stairs.

"Now?" Isadona asked. "But the children..."

"Go and fetch them," said Darginn. "While I wash."

Isadona almost stepped back from her husband's tone, almost raised a hand to reach for him, but in the end did neither. She lifted a cloak from its hook and went silently into the night.

Wordlessly, Darginn walked into a back room and closed the door behind him, leaving Nirea with Aranok. Just the thing he'd been hoping to avoid. He crossed the room and took a seat by the fire. No point trying to clean up. This blood wasn't going to wash out easy.

What did he do from here? The country was on the verge of falling into chaos, the true king on his way to negotiate peace with the Reivers and his family under threat from some unknown assassin.

But he knew where he was going, of course. He'd known all the way back here. There was no other choice.

"I'm going to Mournside." He said it to the ceiling, but she knew it was for her.

"We're going to Traverlyn." Nirea rubbed at her face. She was tired. They both were. The energy Dialla had given them was wearing off. The master may have burned herself out too. That would explain…No. He was looking for comfort. Dialla was a mess because she'd killed a man. She was a master, a noble, and she'd just murdered a man in cold blood. That was the truth of this hideous mess of an evening. They'd come for a solution, a way to end the Blackening and restore the country, and all they'd done was make a fucking mess.

"I'm going to Mournside," he repeated. "And then to Lochen. After that…we'll see."

His family and Allandria's parents needed to know they were in danger. He had no idea how long he had to warn them; how soon these contracts—if they existed—would be triggered. But he would not allow them to die for lack of trying.

Nirea stared blankly at him for a moment. "Fine."

"You're not going to Leet?" Whoever the people were that Madu had threatened, they meant something to her. He had seen it.

Her eyes wavered and she rubbed a hand across her mouth. "Aranok, I am the queen of Eidyn. Every life in this country is my responsibility."

And his. That was what she meant. That he should be prepared to sacrifice his family for the good of Eidyn.

Fuck her.

"If you had family, you'd understand."

Nirea sat forward in her chair. "If you had the crown, maybe you'd understand."

Something broke, and the floodwaters came rushing. "Maybe I

should have the fucking thing! Anhel would be dead, Janaeus would be helping us clear memories and a lot of innocent people would be alive!"

Nirea burst to her feet. "Or we'd all be dead! Did that even cross your mind, Aranok? Did it?" She jabbed a finger up at his face. "Did it occur to you that Janaeus could have been walking us straight into another trap? Like Barrock? Why are you so fucking certain he wasn't lying?"

"Because I was there! That's why. You should've fucking trusted me. Hell, you shouldn't even fucking be here!"

"There's a bloody good reason I am!"

What the Hell did that mean? Aranok's chest heaved and his fists were aching knots. The two stood only a few feet apart. He swallowed and stepped away. "What reason?"

Nirea turned and paced away from him. "For fuck's sake, Aranok, there was always a fallback plan. If we couldn't get the relic, we kill Janaeus. The risk of him casting the spell again once he knew that our memories were restored was too high. That was not a gamble we could afford."

There was a fallback plan. A plan he hadn't been told. She was keeping things from him.

"So you *don't* trust me."

Nirea spun back to face him. "I'll remind you that you've just told me you should be king. Fairly sure that's treason, Laird Envoy."

"Oh, fuck off." He'd told Mynygogg he should be in charge more times than he could count. They both knew what he meant. "You should have listened to me. You should *still* be listening to me! The whole point of having a counsellor is that you fucking *listen* to them!"

"And then I make decisions!" Nirea beat her palm against her chest. "Because *I* am queen! You think I made a choice because I didn't listen to you, Aranok, but I heard everything you said, and I *disagreed* with you!"

Aranok threw his arms wide. "Well, here we are, then. Running for our fucking lives! Everyone thinks I murdered the king—me, not you, mind—God knows how many nobles died back there, God knows how many more people are going to die. Oh, and Dialla's a fucking ghost because you had her murder a king—in front of her parents." He leaned toward her, an acrid smile cutting across his face. "Good choices."

"They were the right choices!" Nirea's voice cracked with fury. "This isn't about one person or a few people, Aranok, it's about the whole country! We underestimated Janaeus once and look where it got us. Look! Because that's really why we're here, isn't it? That's why we're here screaming at each other in a stranger's home! Because last time, we decided the memory *draoidh* wasn't a threat. Right?" They stared at each other, seething. "Right?"

He'd had enough. Aranok turned for the door and reached for a cloak.

"That's it, is it?" said Nirea. "You're abandoning us?"

"I'm not fucking abandoning anyone, Nirea! I'll come to Traverlyn. I'll do my duty. But first, I'm going to warn the people whose lives you put in danger tonight!"

"Me? I didn't fucking kill Madu!"

"You might as well have! You were going to! And you fucking killed Janaeus!"

Nirea stormed toward him again. "He stole the fucking throne! He tried to get us killed! *He killed Glorbad!*"

Aranok lost all pretence at control. "Fuck you! Don't you dare put that at my feet! Anhel killed Glorbad. Anhel manipulated Shay and Jan into all of this. I told you, Jan thought he was stopping a war, not starting one!"

Nirea stepped back, her brow furrowed.

Aranok was in full flow. "He did it to end the war! He did it to stop the killing. Anhel wanted to lay waste to the whole damn country and watch it burn, and Shay was mad as fucking God and would have done whatever Anhel told her to! Jan stopped them. All right, it was a fucking mess of a plan, but it was a plan!"

"He stole the throne!" Nirea threw her arms wide in frustration.

"*We* stole the bloody throne! Mynygogg isn't Hofnag's son! We took the throne. And I'll tell you this—we didn't do enough! If we had, Shay's daughter might be alive and this war might never have happened."

Nirea's wide eyes stared back at him in disbelief. "You... agree with them?"

Did he?

"No... but they're right that we didn't do enough. I couldn't get a fucking room in Dail Ruigh because the innkeeper was a bigoted cunt. The most high-ranking *draoidh* in the history of Eidyn, and I can't rent a fucking room because it's still acceptable to hate *draoidhs*."

"Aranok..."

"No! Don't patronise me. You don't understand. You don't know what it's like to have strangers look at you with suspicion just for who you are. To fear you. To hate you. To spit at you. To murder your child. You do not know!"

Nirea put her hands up. "Aranok, stop. I wasn't going to disagree with you."

The fires were still burning hot, but Aranok could feel them dimming.

"Listen." Nirea's voice was calming. Quieter. "Neither of us is thinking clearly. We're tired and running on magical energy. Right?"

That was true, he knew that.

"We need to calm down. Both of us. This isn't the time. We need rest and we need time to deal with"—she waved her hands at the walls—"all of this. We're on the same side, Aranok. I want what you want. Mynygogg wants what you want. The better Eidyn, right?"

The better Eidyn.

Would he see it in his lifetime? Once, he'd believed it. Now... He'd seen the worst of humanity. He'd seen those they stepped on and abused. And he'd seen how they would eventually, inevitably, fight back.

Emelina was going to grow up in this world. She was going to be abused and ignored and spat on. And the fury, the sheer rage he felt at that idea, was almost enough to consume him.

But there was Vastin. Vastin, who'd lost both parents fighting a war against *draoidhs* and swore his allegiance to a *draoidh* without hesitation. Vastin, who'd been prepared to defy the king to ride into Hell with a *draoidh*. Vastin, who would protect Emelina with his own life. Aranok wouldn't even have to ask. And maybe that was enough. Maybe the future of Eidyn could be better than their parents. Maybe.

Leondar cleared his throat. He'd appeared at the bottom of the stairs without either of them noticing.

"Beg your pardon, Majesty, Laird, but the doors are not thick and, well..." He shrugged.

"And everyone in the house can hear us," Nirea finished for him. Leondar nodded sheepishly. "It's fine, we're finished, aren't we, Aranok?"

He had no words then. Nothing he could say would make her understand any of it. He didn't want to appease her, and he didn't want to fight. He just wanted it to stop. So he turned away.

Nirea grabbed his arm, forcing him to look back at her. "Aranok?"

"It's fine. I'm still with you."

For now.

A wolf moaned into the forest sky as Aranok walked out of the cave. The tunnel was long—it had to be, to bypass an invading army. He turned to see the ragged group following him.

Nirea's face was still dark, her eyes hooded. She was trying to maintain a demeanour of leadership, but she was as scattered as he felt. Dialla was a mess. Darginn's daughter, Jena, had given her a clean dress to replace her own muddy and blood-spattered one. Jena had offered to pack it for her so she could have it cleaned. Dialla put it in the fire. She'd barely spoken since the castle. In fact, the only person he'd seen her say anything to was Leondar, who hovered protectively behind her.

Darginn was a pale, hollow shell—back to the man they'd found in Lestalric. He'd lost control in Màdu's chambers, and that was something else he'd have to live with. Aranok suspected it would only add to his nightmares. Isadona fussed around him, trying to break his melancholy, but he barely seemed to notice. The only time he reacted to anyone was when little Liana giggled or spoke directly to him. She was scared and tired, though. Her father, Yavick, carried her along with his family's packs.

Ismar, the last one out of the tunnel, was sullen. He seemed resentful and angry. He'd argued against leaving, again, but conceded at his father's flat insistence.

None of them were fit for what was ahead. No horses. Half of them without cloaks. At least the rain had finally stopped.

"Right, then. Where now?" Isadona forced a cheery tone, winking at her granddaughter as if this were a great adventure.

"I have an errand to address," Aranok answered. "I'll meet you in Traverlyn." He probably wouldn't—there was no real reason he needed to see them again—or them him, for that matter, but it felt the right thing to say in the moment. The comradely thing.

"You're... not travelling with us?" Darginn's voice was raspy, and his left hand shook.

"He is not. But we are." Nirea gestured to Dialla and Leondar. "We will see you safely to Traverlyn."

Darginn twitched and turned his head toward her but seemed to look right through her.

"That's good, isn't it?" Isadona brushed affectionately at his chest.

"Aye," Darginn muttered. "That's good."

Aranok caught Nirea's eye and gestured for her to join him away from the group. He'd been thinking on their underground walk.

"You can't take the ferry."

Nirea nodded. "It's the first place they'll look for us. If they send horses..." They would reach the crossing before them and likely arrest the whole group for treason.

"Go north. Pick up horses on the way. There'll be farms... inns. But move quickly." Aranok poured gold coins from his purse and dumped them into Nirea's hand. "Go through Leet. Maybe... take care of things."

Nirea looked up from pouring the coins into her own purse. "I already said..."

"I know what you said. Mynygogg won't be back for days—maybe weeks. We're the most wanted people in Eidyn. We're going to have to live quiet until we see what happens."

Nirea chewed the inside of her lip as she looked off into the trees. "We'll see. Listen, if we go the long way round, we'll pass Lochen. We'll get there before you."

Yes. She probably would. Aranok couldn't risk trying to pick up a horse en route to Mournside. God knew where word might have got out about him by the time he reached the nearest farm or village. He was going to have to walk cross-country. It was at least three days to Mournside from here. And that was pushing it. Without Dialla, he was going to crash hard soon. He may not make it through the day. Yes, she'd get to Lochen before him. "Their names are Vanack and Mori.

They have a cabin on the eastern edge of town with a woodworking business. Tell them…" What should she tell Allandria's elderly parents? To protect themselves? To get out? To go back to their nomadic life and run?

Nirea put a hand on his forearm. "I'll make them understand."

What else could they do?

Liana sneezed and giggled as her father overreacted.

"We need another memory charm," said Nirea. "If Samily and Rasa can…" Her eyebrows rose.

"If." Aranok didn't hold out much hope for that. Tracking a *draoidh* who can erase memories of themself was hardly a simple task. But there might be another way. He'd been avoiding it, because it was too much. Too much to think about. Too much to feel.

There was one other person he knew had a charm.

CHAPTER 30

Five straight days on a horse.

Allandria had all but given up hope of ever sitting comfortably again. Adding salt to the wound, they'd had to camp last night. She thought wistfully back to her warm bath in the Digger's Arms the night before, listening to the storm battering down on the roof.

"You all right?" Meristan looked at her sympathetically, and she realised she'd been squirming in the saddle.

"I wasn't planning a family anyway." She gave him a weary smile.

The knight laughed gently. "Me neither."

Was he even allowed a family, as a Thorn? She knew they weren't held to the monks' vow of chastity, but considering their lives...

What was she thinking? Meristan had a daughter. A phenomenal, exceptional daughter. She may not be his blood, but she was his kin.

Allandria's life was no more suitable for children than a Thorn's. She was hardly in one place for long enough and wouldn't be any more so for becoming Nirea's envoy. Besides, she was past the time for it. She had her family—her mother and father. She hoped they were well. It had been too long since she'd been to Lochen. Once this was all settled, once Mynygogg was back on the throne, she needed to get back there. She missed walking in the forest behind their house, listening to the breeze shushing through the grass.

Mynygogg raised a hand and drew up his horse. Raised voices ahead.

They were nearing Gardille. Running into a patrol of Eidyn's soldiers was almost inevitable. Mynygogg dismounted and put a finger to his lips. Allandria was eager to do the same, and swung down off Sky.

They led the horses slowly up the road. At the crest of a bend, a group of soldiers faced off against a small group of Reivers. But they weren't engaging. Just shouting.

"We need to stop this," Mynygogg said firmly.

How were they supposed to do that? The king had no authority. Allandria was queen's envoy in name only. That only left...

"My friends! Surely on such a beautiful afternoon there is no need for harsh words." Meristan strode forward as if greeting a group of squabbling friends in a pub. "Can we not come to some agreement?"

There were maybe ten soldiers, she reckoned. Four Reivers. Now they were closer, she could see their leathers painted with bright, artful colours. That must be the mark of a clan, but she didn't know enough to name which one. Maybe Jethart or Galche. Or Hamhaig?

One of the Reivers, an older man with a white-streaked beard, turned and threw out an arm toward Meristan. "Aye, see? We're only wanting home. We're nae here for a fight."

As they got closer, Allandria saw the rest of the group. A dark-skinned woman with golden hair leaned casually against a tree as if there were no danger there at all. A boy of about thirteen, maybe, carried a bow, which was currently nocked and pointed at the ground. Another woman, lighter-skinned with a completely bald head, which made it difficult to age her. Didn't look much like a raiding party. More like scouts—set to move quickly and quietly. And not get caught. Their leathers were hardly useful camouflage, if that was the case.

"You will submit to arrest or you will be taken by force." The guard captain was a wiry, pale man, but he had that spark of intellect in his eyes. He was no fool. He was calm because he had the advantage. Ten mounted guards against four Reivers on foot was no contest at all.

The bald woman rolled her head, cracking her neck loudly. "No, we'll no."

"Please!" Meristan was practically standing between them. He was going to get himself in trouble unless he had an actual plan. Allandria resisted the urge to draw an arrow. It would make her more comfortable, but it was just as likely to start a battle they couldn't win. Mynygogg's face was stony, but he must be in turmoil. He needed peace with the Reivers, and if he could stop this, it might earn some goodwill.

But he had no power.

The captain was unmoved by Meristan's plea. "I don't know who you are, old man. Move on with your day."

"Brother Meristan?" The voice was that of a young woman, but Allandria couldn't see where it came from until several of the guards' horses bustled aside to reveal an olive-skinned woman in gleaming white armour. A Thorn! Thank God. Now they had a chance of ending this peacefully. The woman dismounted and walked to Meristan. "It is you. I apologise, I didn't recognise you in your... clothing."

"Asha!" Meristan threw his arms wide and embraced the woman, who seemed a little surprised and confused.

"You are Brother Meristan of the Order of the White Thorns?" the captain asked. There was murmuring from the guards.

"I have that honour," Meristan replied boldly. "And I would see no conflict here today. I can say with surety it is not God's will, nor in anyone's interest."

Badger-beard looked back to his Reiver companions. Something unspoken passed between them. Recognition?

"With respect, Brother, you understand these are Reivers, illegally on Eidyn soil. Their presence here is an act of war." The captain's calm was a little reduced.

"Is it?" Meristan's tone was thoughtful, as if he were leading a seminar back in Traverlyn. "Have you witnessed them performing any crime or act of aggression?"

"Specifically? No," the captain answered tersely. "But I have standing orders to—"

Meristan cut him off as if he'd finished speaking. "Can a person be illegal by their existence? Have we closed Eidyn's borders?"

"Well, no, but..."

"Then perhaps they are simply here for"—Meristan turned dramatically and looked over the Reivers before continuing—"an artistic pilgrimage to Traverlyn."

The bald woman snorted a laugh. The captain shifted in his saddle.

A young soldier three horses down twitched his crossbow. Meristan needed to be careful. There was a fine line between levity and the kind of disrespect that would enrage a soldier.

"Reivers are not artists, Brother. They are raiders. They raid. And pillage. That's why there is a wall between us. The roads are teeming with them, and it is our duty to put a stop to that." The captain's tone was terse. He wasn't happy.

"Teeming, you say?" Meristan waved toward Allandria and Mynygogg. "My friends and I have been on the road for five days, and these are the first Reivers we've laid eyes on."

That was true. The Reivers who'd been in the country when Janaeus cast his spell seemed to either have retreated home or been killed. Not least by Allandria, a fact that stung even more for her remembrance of how angry she'd been at them. Here were four of them, standing before her, every bit as human and as innocent as she was. She was not going to see them killed. Not one more Reiver would die needlessly while she could help it.

The captain sat up straight in his saddle. "Brother, with the greatest respect, I am not going to debate this with you. I have standing orders from the king that all Reivers are to be captured or killed. Please step aside."

Meristan looked to Mynygogg before answering solemnly. "I'm sorry. I can't do that." He understood what was at stake.

"Brother?" Asha's brow furrowed. "You would defend the Reivers against Eidyn's army?"

Again, furtive looks amongst the Reivers. The golden-haired woman stood up now, more alert, scanning the ranks of the soldiers lined down the road. The bald woman gripped the sword at her side.

"I would, Asha," Meristan answered. "And I have good reason."

"I understand." The younger Thorn turned and stood shoulder to shoulder with Meristan.

The captain's face was first confused, then incredulous. "Asha? You stand against us? What of your duty to Eidyn?"

"My duty is to God and God's children. If Brother Meristan believes this to be God's will, my duty is clear."

The captain swallowed hard and looked back at his men. Eight of them. Mounted. But the road was narrow. Not good ground to make best use of the horses. The Reivers only needed to retreat into the trees and their advantage was all but nullified. And they had a Thorn—two Thorns, not that the captain would recognise that. He fingered the horn at his side, betraying his thoughts—but Gardille was too far for reinforcements to arrive in time. Perhaps he'd be lucky and another patrol would be nearby. Perhaps not.

The Reivers seemed to have decided their best route out of this was to stay quiet. But they were ready for a fight. Badger-beard had a longsword strapped to his back, and his right hand now sat casually at the back of his neck. He rubbed at a tight muscle inches from his blade's hilt.

Things were about to get ugly.

"Please, everyone, wait a moment." Mynygogg strode forward, every inch of him the king. Even in simple leathers and riding cloak, he demanded respect. "Let's not have this deteriorate into battle for lack of patience."

The crack of a crossbow releasing and the thud of metal hitting meat. A bowstring released and an arrow clattering to earth.

The Reiver boy slumped to the ground, crossbow bolt through his neck.

Chaos.

"No!" The bald woman drew her sword. Allandria bolted forward to Mynygogg. When she reached him, he was frozen in horror, eyes wide. Allandria followed his gaze. Tree branches grasped the crossbow soldier from his horse, lifted him into the air and, with a jerk, tore him clean in half. Blood and entrails spattered the nearby soldiers.

"*Draoidh!*" bellowed the captain, lifting his horn. Allandria released an arrow, spearing the horn from the man's lips. Reinforcements would only mean more deaths. The soldiers needed to retreat.

Golden hair stood proud, making *draoidh* gestures. Roots and branches grew around her like a suit of armour, protecting her from the crossbow bolts that followed the first. Soldiers were swatted from their horses like insects. Others dismounted before they were unseated, drew weapons and charged.

A bolt tipped past Allandria's shoulder. She dived to the right, taking Mynygogg down with her and rolling them both into the ditch. "Stay down!" she barked. Mynygogg was a fierce warrior, but she wasn't having him killed here for a stupid skirmish that should never have happened, damn it all.

"Asha! Defence only!" Meristan's voice boomed over the clang of metal. The Thorns, the bald woman and male Reiver formed a semicircle, holding off the advance of five soldiers. The captain remained on his horse, barking directions and firing crossbow bolts. One pinged off Asha's armour and embedded itself in a tree.

"Stay here," Allandria hissed at Mynygogg. He would or he wouldn't. Allandria rolled farther into the long grass until she could slink into the treeline. As quickly as she could without sounding like a wild boar crashing through the undergrowth, she got herself around the back of the captain's horse. A scream of pain from somewhere made her glance back at the king, but he had done as he was told, keeping his head down. Someone else. She didn't know whom to hope it was.

Allandria scrambled onto a half-fallen tree and, with a grunt, leapt onto the back of the horse. She pulled the surprised captain's arm away and the crossbow tumbled onto the dirt.

"Tell them to stand down," she said. "Now."

The arrow at the captain's throat was persuasive.

"Hold!" he cried, and the soldiers stepped back into defensive positions. One was down, holding a bleeding leg wound. The other four looked quickly between their captain and the enemies, who had also paused.

"Now. If your guards drop their weapons and remount their horses, we will let you all ride away unharmed."

"Unharmed?" The captain's voice went up a pitch. "I've a man cut in half!"

"And they've got a boy with a bolt in his throat." Allandria really, really didn't want to kill him. In a matter of days—weeks, maybe—they should be allies again.

The silence lasted forever. Eight warriors waiting for the word that would end this or set them back to murdering each other. Finally, when Allandria had begun to wonder if he would ever speak, the captain cleared his throat. "Stand down. Relinquish your weapons."

Reluctantly and slowly, they did. Swords were placed on the road and the men and women of Eidyn stepped back.

The bald Reiver made to lunge, but Meristan held her back with his own weapon and a cold look. She growled but calmed.

"You will hold your bargain?" the captain asked.

"I will. When you drop that dagger." Allandria poked the arrowhead a little harder into his throat. With a sigh, he tossed the little dagger from his left hand. He'd slipped it from his sleeve, exactly as Allandria might have done.

"Meristan, check them all for weapons!" She wasn't about to let the captain go until she knew the soldiers were unarmed. The big man carefully put down his own weapon and moved to the soldiers, arms open.

Mynygogg approached then. He must have hated everything about this—his own soldiers battling his allies. And him powerless to stop it, lying in the dirt. Were there tears in his eyes? Maybe. The frustration he must have felt, knowing once he'd ruled over a kingdom of peace, and now he couldn't control anything. As Aranok had said, he was just about king of Traverlyn hospital. He stood, watching, as if in a nightmare from which he could not wake.

When Meristan had confirmed the soldiers were unarmed, Allandria dismounted and released the captain. "I trust I don't need to threaten you with consequences. We have a *draoidh*. There is no shame here." She didn't want to embarrass the man, but she did need him to understand this battle was over.

He nodded quietly. "We can take our wounded?"

As well as the soldier with the injured leg, another who had been thrown from her horse was struggling to stand. A back injury, likely. She was luckier than the other, whose neck looked to have snapped when he hit the ground. Three dead, all for a twitchy trigger finger. The stupid arse. Well, he'd paid for his idiocy. "Of course. And your horses. Leave the two without riders." They could use the extra horses for the Reivers. They were going to need to make haste. As soon as this party made it back to Gardille, there would be floods of soldiers hunting them—especially with a Reiver *draoidh* inside Eidyn.

"Agreed" was all the captain said.

Meristan and Asha kept watch as they prepared to leave, standing between them and their weapons. At some point, the younger Thorn was surely going to ask where in Hells "Brother" Meristan learned to fight.

Mynygogg approached the soldiers, arms spread wide. "Captain, I hope we can agree this was misfortune. Nobody committed any crime today. There's no need for retribution—on either side."

The captain looked down at him darkly. "I've two dead men who see it different."

"And they've a dead boy who'll never see adulthood. This is done. Please."

The horse whinnied as its rider kicked it into motion. "Shouldn't have been here then."

Allandria crossed to the Reivers. The bald woman cradled the young boy on her knee, his blood mingling with the beautiful art on her leathers. "I'm sorry."

"You did what you could." The bearded man offered a hand. "We'll no forget. We're maybe alive cause of you. Teyjan."

"Allandria. This is..." She turned to indicate Mynygogg, but her mind went blank on his false name. What the Hell was it? They'd been using it for days. She realised her hand was trembling and stuck it in her belt. *Fuck, come on, Allandria, get it together*!

...

Donal!

"Mynygogg, rightful king of Eidyn," said the king.

Allandria's first thought was to check the soldiers were out of earshot, but the last horse was disappearing up the road and its rider did not turn back.

Teyjan took Mynygogg's offered hand cautiously, as if he expected it to burn. "Your Majesty."

"But you know that, don't you?" Mynygogg asked. "You're scouts, not raiders, and you're trying to get out of the country quietly. You were sent by your chieftain to find out what the Hell is happening in Eidyn and why the country that called on our alliance for aid is attacking your people."

Teyjan nodded. "And why those who made it home have gone mad."

"What have you learned?" Mynygogg asked.

The bald woman stood suddenly, only slowing to lay the boy's head down carefully. "Some cunt called Janaeus is king, and apparently's always been king and we're still at war. Want to fucking explain that?" She poked Mynygogg in the chest with her final words.

Allandria lifted a hand to force her back, but Mynygogg waved her off. "We lost. We didn't allow for a memory *draoidh*, and we didn't know there was a relic that could massively enhance his power. So much that he could change the memories of the entire kingdom."

Teyjan put his hand behind his neck again. "Well, that'd surely explain..."

"Fuck off!" The woman sneered. "A memory *draoidh* couldnae do that in a hundred years. The whole country?"

"Cuda!" Teyjan snapped. "Whatever you think, that's a king you're talking at."

"Apparently fucking not," Cuda snapped back. But she stepped away from Mynygogg.

"My deepest condolences for your loss." Meristan slid his sword away. "May I offer a prayer for the boy?"

"You're a monk?" Cuda asked.

Meristan paused. "I am a man of God."

Cuda's lips trembled as she nodded. Meristan and Asha sat cross-legged beside the boy and closed their eyes. Teyjan put a hand on Cuda's shoulder as she joined them. Allandria bowed her head. She hoped his soul would find peace.

When they'd finished, Meristan took the woman's hands between his own. "Your kin?"

"We're all kin," she answered, her voice breaking.

"What's his name?" Allandria asked.

Cuda's face crumpled as the answer caught in her gullet.

"Tecatt," said Teyjan. "His name was Tecatt."

Allandria had heard of the Reivers' fierce loyalty to their clan. They fought for each other like demons and mourned like family. No wonder the *draoidh* had ripped that soldier apart.

But he was also someone's kin. And he wasn't going home either. Two pointless deaths. Two more pointless deaths. Because of Janaeus.

Mynygogg was right. They needed peace with the Reivers. Allandria had been sceptical about his decision to do this now, instead of focusing on the relic and restoring memories, but people were dying every day. They had to stop this before it was too late and they really were back at war.

"May we help you to bury him?" Meristan asked.

Cuda shook her head as tears ran down her face. "You'll no need to." She stood and waved the Thorns away from the body. "Jazere?"

The *draoidh*, who had been sitting quietly since the fighting ended, gestured toward the boy. The earth shifted and fell around him as roots crawled out of the earth, wrapped around his limbs, covered his face in a death shroud and pulled his little body into the earth. A green sprout emerged from the dirt, twisting and dancing, reaching for the sun. It thickened, turning brown. Leaf buds sprouted as it grew, reaching its arms wider, stretching, yawning into the sky.

It was over in less than a minute. The boy was gone into the ground as if he'd never been there, and in his place a mighty tree stood sentinel at the edge of the road, marking his grave and his life.

Cuda kissed her fingers and placed her hand against the trunk, then took a knife from her belt and carved a *T* into the bark. When she was done, she turned away from the group. "Right. Let's move before they cunts come back."

"Would you allow us a moment, please, Cuda?" Meristan's tone was still gentle. For all the woman's steel, she was in pain.

"Do what you like, it's no matter to us, is it?"

"Actually, I think it may be, if you're willing," said Meristan.

Cuda looked to Teyjan and shrugged. "Be quick."

Meristan pulled Mynygogg and Allandria away from the rest and spoke in hushed tones. "I fear this may have to be where we part ways. I have likely caused a schism between Eidyn's army and the Order. Asha and I must make directly for Baile Airneach. You won't be able to leave through the Western Gate. Your best chance is almost surely to travel with these Reivers."

He was right. The roads were no longer safe, especially not going toward Gardille. But going with the Reivers? "Are you sure? Can we trust them?"

"We don't have much choice." Mynygogg watched the three of them having their own huddled conversation. "I don't know where we'll find a gap in the wall. Do you?"

Allandria did not. And if it were just the *draoidh* and the man, she might not be too worried about it. He was reasonable and she was... well, quiet. But Cuda was another twitchy trigger finger and she worried about her loosing unexpectedly.

"All right. It's settled. Good luck, my friend. I hope God travels with you." Mynygogg put a hand on Meristan's shoulder.

The Thorn smiled. "God is always with me. And you." He clapped the king on the shoulder and turned to Allandria.

It probably wasn't appropriate, but in that moment she felt the need to hug him. Whether for her or for him, she couldn't say, but she did. "Look after yourself. I feel like we just got you back."

"I'm going to the home of the greatest warriors in the country." His voice was light, almost mocking, but on the kind side.

Allandria held him at arm's length. "You are the greatest warrior in the country."

Meristan smiled widely. "I wouldn't like to have to test that against you." He looked over his shoulder to where Asha stood patiently. "And I'm going to have to explain that to her." He crumpled his mouth in mock consternation and Allandria smiled. The thought of their timid monk explaining that he could beat every one of the Thorns in single combat was amusing. In this time, any small light was worth clutching tight to her breast.

"All right. Let's get on. Cuda is right. We don't have time to dawdle." Mynygogg slapped Meristan's shoulder once more and moved to the group of Reivers.

The Thorn gave Allandria a final nod and smile. "See you in Traverlyn."

She nodded and he turned away to the younger Thorn.

Allandria followed Mynygogg and came into negotiations already underway.

"Why should we?" Cuda was asking. "We've lost hundreds—thousands for you."

Again, that stab of guilt. How many had Allandria killed? Best never to reveal that fact. Not in Cuda's hearing, anyway.

Mynygogg remained calm. "We're on a peace mission. I want this as much to save Reiver lives as Eidyn's. If we can stop this wound from bleeding, it will have time to heal. And we'll reach Calcheugh quicker for your assistance—especially once we're through the wall."

That was a good point. The Reiver Lands had not been welcoming to Eidyn before the peace. They likely weren't now. A Reiver escort sounded like a very good idea.

"There's sense in that." Teyjan rubbed his beard.

Cuda's mouth puckered. "Nut. I don't like it."

The *draoidh* had still said nothing, observing from a few feet away as if watching a play put on just for her. "What about you? You haven't said anything." Allandria asked.

"Jazere disnae speak," said Teyjan.

A mute *draoidh*? That was interesting. Allandria wondered how she invoked her spells without speaking any words. Maybe nature *draoidhs* didn't need them? "But surely she still has an opinion?"

Jazere looked them over casually for a moment, shrugged her shoulders and nodded.

"See? Jazere agrees it's a good idea." Teyjan's tone was coercive but careful. He was obviously used to handling Cuda's hot temper.

The woman gave Jazere a look of disappointment, finally settling her eyes on Mynygogg. "Seems to me a king with no kingdom's no fucking use to anyone." She turned to Teyjan and stuck a finger in his face. "If one of these cunts murders me in my sleep, I swear I will fucking haunt you."

Cuda stomped into the trees.

"Wait," Allandria called. "The horses!"

"Better without 'em," Cuda barked over her shoulder.

Maybe here, as they tried to travel stealthily, but they'd need them on the other side of the wall to get to Calcheugh. "We can't just leave them!"

"Then bring 'em!" Cuda disappeared into the forest. "I'm not fucking bothered!"

CHAPTER 31

All Meristan seemed to do at the moment was worry.

He worried about the king going into Reiver territory—especially after seeing Cuda's reaction to him. The Reivers were angry about lost lives, understandably. If they held him responsible, it was an even more dangerous mission than he had imagined it. Mynygogg was a persuasive man, though. And Allandria was the best companion he could have. More even-tempered than the queen, in fact. He'd still rather have been going with them.

He worried about Aranok and Nirea going into the heart of the enemy. He worried what they might have to do to get the relic. He worried how it might affect Aranok if they could not. His friend was unravelling since Lestalric. No doubt it had changed all of them. But he'd seemed especially damaged by it, and preoccupied by Shayella.

And he worried about Samily. Something had changed in her. Whether it was directly in Lestalric or over the course of learning the truth—both about her abilities and the kingdom—he couldn't say. She'd killed many Blackened, so he was told. Her brutal reaction to Shayella was out of character. Or maybe it was just out of his vision of her. She was a Thorn after all, and while they were trained to be merciful, that mercy was often expressed as clinical. Kill swiftly; act decisively. She was still adjusting to her new understanding of her abilities.

Was it so unusual what she'd done to Shayella, knowing she could heal her? Knowing her silence would save lives? Maybe not.

Maybe.

"Brother, forgive me, may I ask a question?" Asha had been silent as they rode away from the others, and for a long time since. She must have been bursting to understand how a monk fought like a Thorn. But Janaeus had her believing Thorns were subservient to the brothers of the Order. It had been unfair of him to rely on that, to delay providing her an answer. He had not allowed for encountering a Thorn on the way to Baile Airneach and certainly not that he may have to fight alongside them. In truth, he had not yet worked out how to explain the situation. He knew from Aranok's warning that he couldn't simply tell them their memories had been altered. Some would cope fine, but others would react badly—vomiting, fainting—and he had no way of repairing that once it began. So he had to tread lightly. Tell Asha as little as possible while still giving her some satisfaction.

"You may, of course, Asha, but as I expect I know what it is, will you allow me to speak first? If you have any further questions, then I will be happy to try to answer them as best I can."

Asha nodded respectfully, of course. But her mind must have been racing beneath her demure exterior. Asha's strength had always been speed—speed of thought, speed of action. She'd taken down Thorns larger and stronger than her in training because they couldn't lay a hand on her.

"I will tell you all that I can, and ask you to trust me for all that I cannot."

Asha nodded again, this time more enthusiastically.

"Asha, I am not a monk. I have been disguised as a monk for reasons I cannot explain. The truth is that I am, and always have been, a White Thorn. I trained at another monastery before I ever arrived at Baile Airneach."

Asha frowned thoughtfully. It was an unsatisfactory lie. But it was safe. It would not ask Asha to re-evaluate her own mind.

"If you are a Thorn, where is your White armour? Where is your Green blade?"

"Fine questions, not easily explained. The truth is I lost them. To a *draoidh*." What had happened to his sword? Aranok said they'd found his armour on the Wester Road, and he just about remembered his confrontation with Janaeus, but actually leaving there was still blurry—in fact, his whole journey back to Baile Airneach was hazy. Was there still more of his memory to come back? Would it ever come back?

"I'm sorry, Brother..." Asha caught herself and stopped mid-sentence, her look one of consternation and frustration.

"I know. It is all difficult to explain. Just let me reassure you, who you know me to be, here"—Meristan thumped his chest—"is true and real. I am the man you know me to be. I am your friend. And your leader. Please trust me."

For a moment, Asha's breathing seemed to quicken, and Meristan worried that he'd pushed too far, said too much. But with a sigh, she seemed to calm.

"All right...Meristan. I believe you. And yes, I trust you." She smiled, and a glint of devilment shone in her eyes. "Does this mean I can speak to you as I would any Thorn?"

Meristan's shoulders fell with relief. "I'm still the head of the Order, child. But actually, yes. I'd like that."

A balance—give Asha enough truth to accept the situation without forcing her to question her own mind, her own sense of self. He seemed to have managed it. For now. For her. But could he do the same for the entire Order? Convince them all to accept him as a Thorn and to follow him against the man they believed to be the King of Eidyn, if it came to that?

Something else to worry about.

"There is only so much I can tell you."

Meristan rubbed his hand through his beard, as though it might somehow comfort him—give him guidance in explaining the mess to his mentor. He could almost certainly get the rest of the Thorns to follow him on faith alone, but to truly believe him, they would need more than just his word. And he needed them to believe with absolute certainty.

Severianos stared back at him, emerald green eyes sparkling in his leathery, brown face. The eyes, Meristan had always assumed, that inspired his title—the Green Laird.

"Is that so?" The old man turned away, hands clasped behind his back. It was a tactic the teacher had used for decades to unsettle students. Looking away at something "more interesting," asking them to wonder whether what they wanted was truly important, depriving them of being able to read his face for clues to his mind. The old fox had manipulation burned into his bones. "And why would that be, Brother?"

"Well, obviously, Laird, if I could tell you that, I could tell you more."

In the following silence, the Baile Airneach courtyard hummed with life. Bees bumbled over the hedges and crows welcomed the morning from the old oak in the middle of the great gardens. It was an unusually warm morning for the season, especially welcome after the days of rain and misery they'd endured. It felt like God was welcoming Meristan home, and he was grateful for it.

Severianos ambled slowly past the tree, contemplating the ground as though hunting for mislaid treasure. He paused a moment at a hawthorn bush—the symbol of the White Thorn Order. In late spring, flat white blooms flourished on its thorny branches. But now, in the dark brown days of autumn, the old man examined the bush's bright red berries as if to determine their ripeness. Despite his age, he moved like liquid, like a cat, flowing around the yard. Meristan wasn't going to play into the old man's hands. He was leaving the silence, trusting that Meristan would feel the need to fill it with words, saying more than he intended. But it had been a long time since he would fall for such a tactic. In words as with swords, he knew how the Green Laird fought. That in itself gave him an advantage, since the old man did not remember training Meristan.

When the Green Laird finally came full circle, Meristan smiled innocently back at him, waiting to be asked for more information.

"So what *can* you tell me?"

"Laird, you know me to be a good man, yes?"

"To the best of my knowledge." Severianos tilted his head. "But haven't you just told me I don't know you at all?"

Of course. No thrust without parry. No question unasked.

This was the crux.

"I am not a monk."

Severianos looked him up and down with an exaggerated frown. "You certainly don't look like a monk."

Meristan had retained the leathers. He wasn't going back to monastic robes, and while he ached to wear the White again, he had not yet sown the seeds to harvest that reward. This was the beginning of that path. "I am, in fact, a trained White Thorn. And I can prove it."

"Now, Brother, I know you're wasting my time. Surely if you were a Thorn here, I'd have trained you myself—and that did not happen."

It had, of course. But he couldn't challenge that memory without the magic to restore it. A White Thorn always stayed where they trained. It was up to each monastery to decide whom to train and to take responsibility for those they did.

"No, you did not. But a great man did. The greatest teacher I've ever known."

A green eye twitched at that. It was mischievous, but Severianos would soon enough know Meristan was describing him. "Is that so? And what monastery allowed you to leave?"

"That I can't tell you. But my teacher is a good and faithful man. Both his teaching and his character are beyond reproach."

A simple "hmph" was all that elicited. Severianos waved a bee away from his face and puckered his lips in thought. "All right. You're a Thorn. Why pretend to be a monk?"

That didn't mean he was convinced, Meristan knew. It meant he was ready to move on to the meat of the conversation—what Meristan wanted from him.

"I am on a secret mission from the king. He has been usurped. The man on the throne, a *draoidh*, has taken his name, his face and his title, but he is not the king. The real king is rallying support and requests the assistance of the Order. I need every Thorn available to follow me to Traverlyn." An illusionist could do that. Or a metamorph, perhaps. Severianos would have heard tales. They were oft used to spread fear about *draoidhs*.

The Green Laird looked hard at Meristan, stepping toward him and even reaching out to lift his chin, inspecting him like a horse. "And how would I know if a *draoidh* had done the same to you? Hmm? And was playing me at the very game of which you accuse the king?"

That wasn't a line of thought Meristan had prepared for. The old man was sharp. A little too sharp, sometimes. What was the answer? "I suppose that's a valid question. How could I prove to you that I am truly myself?"

Severianos stood back dramatically, as if from a fire. "You've already told me you are not. At least, not who I think you are. How would you propose to prove to me both that you are and are not who I believe you to be?"

Meristan sighed. Conversations with Severianos tended toward the philosophical. Usually he had whisky to quiet the frustration. And it had been days since he'd had any of that, having been too tired last night to do anything but sleep. What could he do to prove to the laird that he was telling the truth?

Of course.

He stood and took the old man's hands in his own. Severianos allowed it but eyed him suspiciously.

Meristan cleared his throat. "In what do you have faith, young man?"

The eyes lit with recognition. It was the question asked of every Thorn on their first day of training. In private. Never to be repeated. "God. My armour. My blade. The White Thorns."

Meristan grinned. "And where does your most vital faith lie?"

The correct answer was "in myself," but no student got it right on first asking. It was a sign of maturity when they finally understood the question. But that was not the answer the Green Laird gave.

Placing a hand on Meristan's chest, he said instead, "It seems it is here. What do you need from me?"

CHAPTER 32

The training area was still under repair. Meristan had clear memories now of why. Anhel Weyr had sent three demons against Baile Airneach. Perhaps to destroy their base; perhaps to murder the trainees; perhaps to kill the Green Laird himself. Each had a tactical advantage to the demon summoner. But there had been enough Thorns in residence, led by Severianos, to repel them—at substantial loss to the Order. Seven trainees died along with three Thorns. Meristan had not been there. He was at the king's side when his brothers and sisters were lost defending the monastery.

Severianos had told him the story—as much as he needed to know to understand what had happened—but he went no further. The night haunted the old man. Meristan had not seen such intense sadness before or since. To see his students slaughtered before him... Children, whose lives had barely begun, taken far too soon. His only comfort was knowing God had embraced them. How could he bear it otherwise?

Today, Meristan stood on the Green Laird's teaching platform—a wooden stage at one end of the yard that allowed him to see across the entire space, to watch his charges as they sparred. There was no clashing of wooden swords. The students had been given the day to enjoy, and instead, Meristan faced a gleaming white sun. He knew each of the fourteen knights here, of course. Some better than others. Quick, clever Asha. Wily, mischievous Merrick. Along with Tull, who wasn't there, Samily's closest friends. And there were those closer to his own age. Brontas, the giant Meristan had feared Aranok was describing when he talked of the empty armour—his own armour—abandoned on the Wester Road. Despite his size, the most humble man Meristan had ever met—and he lived amongst monks.

Greste, the quiet, thoughtful woman who told wonderful fairy stories around campfires. The woods of Curidell, nearby, was a renowned home for pixies and other mythical creatures, and the knight filled the students' heads with beautiful fancies and fabulous nonsense. The children adored her and would pester her for new stories each time she was home. He didn't know if she heard them on her travels or if they came from her own imagination. The beauty was in the telling, though. Greste would make any story seem wondrous, waving her arms around and putting on voices, slowing the story for tension and speeding it for terror.

They all looked up at him curiously. Monks did not generally enter the training yard, so to see him here, and in leathers, was a substantial oddity. For Meristan, it felt good simply to be amongst them again. To be where he belonged, with a sword in his hand. It would feel even better when they knew he was one of them. While he did not relish what needed to be done, part of him felt the thrill of it, reminded of the drills and competitions of his youth. The joy of combat amongst friends and rivals. Despite beginning his training late, he'd had a natural aptitude for it, which was, he'd always believed, why Severianos had agreed to take him on, against the monks' reservations.

Today, it was not the monks he needed to win over.

"My friends, it is wonderful to see you all again. It has been too long for many of us."

Respectful nods and smiles from the Thorns. They would not speak until he directly addressed them, of course. Instead of working with the Thorns, servicing their needs and providing guidance, Janaeus had the monks giving orders and controlling the Thorns. What purpose that served, Meristan could not fathom, any more than he could understand why the man would have made him believe himself a monk in the first place. But it did not matter. The truth awaited them all in Traverlyn, and he would lead them to it.

"I have something incredible to tell you all today. Something so unlikely, it may test your faith. But I know every one of you has the resilience and belief to understand and, eventually, accept."

Some wrinkled brows and raised eyebrows. Curiosity and a little suspicion? Exactly what he would feel, were he standing in the crowd looking up at himself. Meristan dusted himself down, as if there were some comfort to be had, some soothing of his own nerves. A gentle clearing of his throat as he looked back up.

"I am not a brother of the Order. In truth, I am one of you. I am a White Thorn." His entire body tingled as he said the words. Now, every face was a mix of confusion and disbelief. Except, he noticed, Asha's. She merely cocked her head and seemed to examine Meristan more closely.

"I understand this will sound incredible. But whatever else you think, please trust that I am fundamentally still the man you know. I am the same person, and you can, I hope, still share the same faith in me that I have in each of you."

Smiles of befuddlement and looks to one another asking unspoken questions. *Is he joking? Is he mad?*

Severianos stepped forward from the place he'd stood quietly behind Meristan, lending him his authority, his gravitas. "Let me assure you, this is no jest. You will take this as seriously as it merits."

The smiles were quickly hidden, and a few eyes swiftly lowered. The light hum of disbelief became absolute quiet.

"But of course, I will not ask you simply to take my word. Faith is vital, but where proof exists, we should always seek it. So I will prove my claim beyond doubt."

This was it—the moment of truth. It should be fine, he was confident. But it would have to be good.

"I will prove my skills in combat. I will show you that I am a match for any of you in battle."

More looks between them—this time in disbelief, searching one another for some explanation.

"Who is prepared to meet me in combat?"

Asha's hand was first up. She'd already seen him in battle. She knew what he could do. For her, this was validation, not curiosity. She had no fear of harming him. Merrick, stood next to her, looked down with some measure of surprise, then his hand went up too. Then others. Before long, all fourteen hands were in the air. Good. He had them this far. A lot of thought had gone into who should be his opponent. But if it was to be without question, he had to make it unquestionable. And that made the choice clear.

"Brontas, will you oblige me?"

The big man looked, if anything, more surprised than the others at his selection. There were others with more skill, more speed, quicker of thought than Brontas, but there were none stronger. The man's arms were like logs run through with steel. Even Meristan would be lost in his armour.

It had to be Brontas.

"All right, clear the circle!" Severianos gestured as if wafting away more bees. Everyone but Brontas retreated outside the combat circle. The Thorn himself walked for the weapons rack, already half unsheathing the Green blade at his side. "No. Brontas, hold your sword. You'll be sparring with it."

Audible gasps. Real blades were forbidden in the training arena. A Green blade was only for use when the fight was real. Severianos had all but insisted they use training swords, but for absolute proof, it was going to have to be real.

"Would someone be kind enough to loan me their blade?" A Thorn's weapon was a sacred gift from the Green Laird, to be parted with only in the most extreme circumstances.

And yet, Greste stepped forward and offered hers wordlessly. Meristan took it respectfully, smiling and nodding his thanks. Heaven, it felt good. It was lighter than his own blade, and a little shorter. The Green Laird made swords to measure for each Thorn, so no two were the same. But still, it was a Green blade, and it felt right. He swung it flamboyantly across himself. There was no need for it, except maybe to loosen up his shoulder and get the feel of the blade, but he mostly did it to show he knew how to handle it.

Brontas gave a shrug and a "huh," drawing his own blade. He moved it directly to the ready position, feeling no need to repeat Meristan's show.

Severianos moved between them, the small red cloth that began combat held high. "Knights of the Order. When this flag reaches the ground, begin."

Meristan inhaled deeply. He knew all of this, like waking. Like breathing.

Severianos stepped back as the flag puffed a cloud of dirt. Brontas immediately swiped across him, taking advantage of his longer reach. Meristan danced back, easily avoiding the blade. He'd swung short. A warning—or he was still concerned Meristan wasn't really able to defend himself. Meristan countered with his own swing. He also came up short, but a lot less so than Brontas. That truly was a warning. By his expression, the big man took it as such.

Another swing from Brontas. Meristan blocked and attempted a parry, but the other man's strength was enough to push him away, fending off his counterattack. But that was enough. He was taking it seriously now. The next attack was full-blooded, coming up from the left. Meristan deflected and danced right, turning and bringing his blade around to attack Brontas's back. He launched himself forward and rolled away, as Meristan knew he would, returning to his feet and facing him again. He could see it in his eyes. Brontas knew. He recognised a Thorn.

He came at Meristan hard next, feinting a high swing, then pirouetted, cutting low instead. Meristan hurdled the blade and countercut. Sparks squealed as Green blade scraped White armour. A smile crept across Brontas's face as he looked down at his pauldron. He opened his stance, empty hand forward, sword back. A standard starting pose for a training exercise every Thorn knew—the exchange of blows. Meristan mirrored the stance and gave him a nod.

They moved together, like shadow and flame, first meeting swords high, then low. Both turned and brought their blades around one side, then the other. Each time they met, sparks burst. The familiarity was pleasing, comfortable, and Meristan's muscles seemed to move almost without his will, flowing from one move into another. He dipped his shoulder and rolled to the right, returning to one knee and lifting his blade to meet Brontas's exactly where he knew it would be. Back to their feet and a high left swing, then right, each time meeting exactly in the middle. A step back and a wider swing this time...

"Brother Meristan!"

The panicked call was enough to shake his attention and leave him off balance. His blade was too low and missed Brontas's coming to meet it. Instinctively, Meristan relaxed his body and allowed himself to fall backwards. Still he felt the blade cut across him, catching enough to tear through his leathers. He felt the dull sting of pain across his chest as he landed hard on the dirt of the training arena and felt the air burst from his lungs.

His vision went red, then black, and the world spun.

"Brother Caparth!" Severianos's tone was incensed. "You must not interrupt training exercises!"

Meristan's vision returned to see the concerned face of Brontas looming over him. "You all right?"

Was he? His chest was burning like Hell itself, but it didn't feel serious. Asha fell to her knees at his side, pawing at the rip in his leathers. After a moment, she sighed and leaned back. "It's not deep. Only flesh!"

Suddenly the yard was alive with chatter as Brontas helped him back to his feet. He hoped it had been enough, because he now wanted nothing less than to spar with Brontas. He wanted a monk to tend his new wound, and then to drink a large whisky.

"Brother Meristan?" Brother Caparth bustled his way through the chattering Thorns. He stopped dead when he reached them, looking Meristan up and down as if he were a goat in a dress. "Are you...? What are you...?" The monk looked around anxiously for some answer that would explain the head of his Order wearing leathers and engaging in combat.

"It's fine, Caparth, I'll explain later. What's so urgent?" Meristan leaned a little on Asha, who'd offered herself as a steadying support.

Caparth lost all colour from his face, which was something, since the man was already deathly pale. "Brother, there is a company here from Gardille. They demand to see you. You are accused of treason!"

"You're Brother Meristan?"

Stripped to the waist, his chest freshly bandaged, Meristan imagined he must look very little like a brother to the general. He decided to answer as truthfully as he could. "I am Meristan, head of the Order of the White Thorns. What can I do for you?"

He already knew exactly what. The captain from the Reiver fight sat mounted right alongside him, and fifty soldiers, at least, ranked behind them. For himself, Severianos stood beside Meristan in the forecourt, and each of the fourteen fully armed Thorns stood behind.

So much for Mynygogg's plea to let it go.

The general turned to the captain. "This is him?" A nod of agreement.

"Brother Meristan, it is charged that you attacked a party of my soldiers near Gardille and aided a group of Reivers to escape, along with the Thorn named Asha, who has been stationed with us. Do you dispute this?"

"I do."

The general's raised eyebrows betrayed this hadn't been the answer he expected. "Sir, you are a man of God. There were witnesses. It does not become you to lie."

"Indeed it would not, were I to lie," Meristan answered calmly. "But I maintain that is not an accurate account of events as they occurred."

"You would play politics with my words?" A scowl of disapproval from the general. "Answer faithfully, Brother: Did you attack my soldiers in defence of a group of Reivers?"

Meristan cocked his head. "That is certainly closer to the truth. We acted in defence of a small group of Reivers." He felt Severianos's head whip toward him but did not turn to meet the laird's gaze. There could be no sign of weakness or disunity here. Nothing less than absolute confidence. "But we attacked no one."

The general frowned even deeper, glancing again at his captain. "Damn it all, man, what point is it you're trying to make? I have two dead and one injured, and I'm told you were responsible. Is that true or not?"

"It is not." Meristan kept his voice quiet and even. "You lost one man in retaliation for the murder of a young boy, and one who was unfortunate when he fell from his horse. Thereafter, your soldiers attacked a group including a White Thorn and suffered no fatalities. Do you understand how rare that is?"

The general's face turned scarlet and Meristan worried for a moment that his skin may burst under the pressure. "You admit you attacked my soldiers. That is all I require. You and Asha will surrender yourselves to our custody, to be tried for treason against the throne of Eidyn."

"No, they most certainly will not." Severianos stepped forward. "A knight of the Order of the White Thorn cannot be tried for treason. They swear no allegiance to king or country. Their duty is to God alone, and only God will judge whether they have kept that pact."

The general all but threw himself down from his horse and stomped toward them. Meristan knew without need to look that every Thorn hand would be on its sword. He gestured for calm without looking away from the man in front of him. He was, in many ways, reminiscent of Glorbad, a detail that stabbed Meristan with loss. He was taller, a little less rounded, and his beard was ginger rather than black. But he had all the same bluster and bombast of Meristan's lost friend.

"I don't give a toss about your religious laws." The man just about poked Meristan in the face. "You are citizens of Eidyn and you are subject to the laws of Eidyn. You attacked soldiers in Eidyn's royal army and you will be tried for treason."

Well now. How was he going to calm this fire? Perhaps a little sprinkling of truth was needed. Again.

Meristan put his arm around the general's shoulders and pulled him conspiratorially to the side. "General, I am going to have to trust you with some extremely sensitive information. Can I trust you?"

The bombast changed to bluster. "I...what...well, of course you can. Do you know who I am?"

"I don't, actually. May I ask your name?"

"Bielsed." A name Meristan had heard, but they'd never met.

"General Bielsed, I am part of a secret peace mission to the Reivers on behalf of the king. That skirmish we fell across was a vital part of that mission. I assure you, neither I nor Asha harmed your soldiers. In fact, if you ask them, some may remember my distinct command to her that we fight defensively."

The general's chin raised at that. He'd already heard it. Good.

"Can you offer another explanation for all of them surviving an encounter with a Thorn relatively unscathed?"

His mouth puckered, but he didn't answer. There was pride to be hurt, and he didn't seem to want to acknowledge that his soldiers, as fine as they might be, were no match for a Thorn. It also reminded him that even fifty of them could not be confident of defeating a substantially smaller number of Thorns.

"All right. If you're on some secret mission for Janaeus, I'll send a runner to Greytoun. If they confirm your story, we'll let this go and call it misfortune. If not, you're coming to Greytoun."

Blast. He'd backed himself into a corner. A corner likely to expose him to Janaeus. And maybe expose all of them. If Aranok and Nirea were still in Greytoun when the runner arrived...

"Of course." What other answer could he give? Better to postpone the problem than fight a battle here. The Thorns would win, but at what cost?

After a brief and animated discussion between Bielsed and his captain, the soldiers rode out of Baile Airneach. He'd half expected them to set up camp nearby, but it seemed Bielsed considered there were more important issues requiring the attention of his soldiers. As soon as they were out of sight, Meristan huddled the Thorns around him.

"All right. We're now on a time limit. We have no more than twelve days before the runner Bielsed sends to Greytoun is missed."

"Missed?" Severianos asked.

"Missed." Meristan found Merrick with his eyes. "Pack. Quickly. You're going to track them back to Gardille. When a runner leaves for Greytoun, let them get well away before you take them. Alive. Bring them back here. They are to be treated well, yes?" He asked the question to Severianos, who shrugged, as if the answer were obvious. "The rest of you—how many of our brothers and sisters can be reached and returned here within a week?"

Asha piped up. "I can bring Tull back from Crostorfyn in four days."

"Good, good. Who else?"

Other names were quickly added, bringing the total to six. The rest were either too far north or east to be back in time.

Six Thorns were assigned to ride out the next morning and retrieve their siblings, along with a warning against sleeping wild at night. Some of them had encountered the Thakhati. They all needed to know about them.

Meristan took a deep breath and clasped his hands behind his neck. The new stitches across his chest made themselves known. "All right. Twenty. Twenty Thorns will be a vital asset."

Brontas cleared his throat. "Twenty-one."

Meristan grinned. He hadn't counted himself.

"Of course. Twenty-one."

Severianos turned and walked for the monastery. "A week to forge a new set of White and a blade? You don't ask for much, do you?"

Meristan hastened after him. He would have questions, and it would be better if Meristan volunteered the information. "Laird. Severianos?"

The old man slowed and allowed him to catch up. "Something else you need?"

He was playing coy, giving Meristan the rope he might hang from.

As much truth as possible.

"There is more I cannot tell you. It's true, I am on a secret mission from the king. I cannot yet share the details, even with you. But it is vital that the runner does not reach Greytoun. Everything will become clear, but I swear to you, on my honour, on my faith, that we act for God's children. And for Eidyn."

The Green Laird frowned thoughtfully, clasped his hands behind his back and regarded the ground before him. "You ask a lot, my friend. But I believe you have earned the right to ask it. I will extend you my faith. But tell me this: What happens in a week? Are we really to battle Eidyn's army?"

Meristan smiled. "Oh, no. We won't be here when they return."

Surprise then from Severianos. Perhaps the first he'd seen, despite all he'd presented his mentor. "We won't? Where will we be?"

"In a week, we ride for Traverlyn."

CHAPTER 33

Aranok had never been able to come here. He knew it would be too painful. The reality of it was crippling.

He crouched before Korvin's grave.

In the faint glow of a light orb, his fingers traced over engraved letters. He wasn't really in the kirkyard; it was a dream. Someone else's nightmare. Not his. He'd wake soon, in his own bed, ready to meet Korvin for beers after his performance, and everything that had happened since would be a faded memory of an imagined Hell.

The chill wind bit his fingers, reminding him just how real it was.

Four days of walking to get there, eking out rations, sleeping under mounds of rock. He'd slunk around Mournside's walls like a shadow and used *gaoth* to sneak over in the black of night. He'd skulked through the backstreets of his hometown, avoiding guard patrols. Climbed the fence behind the kirk; crept through tombstones in the pitch black.

And this was the worst part. It would always be the worst part. Aranok's heart pounded, his chest wracked with sobs. He missed his friend every day; missed his humour, his comfort, his counsel. But here, sitting in front of a stone monument to his death, the hole in Aranok's life felt like a gaping chasm. Everything he'd lost, every happiness Korvin had taken with him, opened like a black void, pulling him down into the dark.

And even now, when Aranok could not imagine ever feeling more pain, he knew he had to do more. He had to twist the dagger further, to bleed for his sins. And he had to hurry. Eventually another guard patrol would come past. He had to be gone by then.

He breathed deep, slowly taking control. Trembling hands were shoved in his armpits to warm them. Finally, after an age, they were still enough to perform the gestures.

"Fosgail."

The grave dirt cracked and writhed, climbing and pouring sideways, carving a hole in itself. Dank air blossomed into the night, bearing the stench of decay. Aranok stood at the edge of the grave, peering down at his friend's casket. Fusty old planks of wood swathed in mould and rot.

He looked up at the kirk spire looming over the graveyard; the "light of God" carved in stone, beckoning believers to worship.

There was no God here.

"Gluais."

A cloud of dust followed the casket lid out of its hole. Aranok raised a defensive hand, covering his mouth and closing his eyes against the stour. Once the dust settled, he wiped his face clean and opened his eyes.

It was worse than he imagined. An involuntary gulp of air had him coughing like an old pipe smoker.

The red-and-gold doublet Korvin's parents had picked for him was blood and piss now, faded and grimy. The leathery remains of his skin stretched tight over bone. Empty eyes stared accusingly back.

Where were you?

"I'm sorry." The only words he had, and they were woefully inadequate.

Carefully, Aranok clambered down into the hole, sliding first one foot, then the next, onto the edge of the casket. The wood creaked and groaned in complaint. He straddled his friend's legs.

It was too much.

It was far too much.

Aranok took a deep breath and crouched down, pulling the light orb with him.

He'd hoped the charm would be over his clothes, easy to reach, but no. The faint glint from the chain around Korvin's neck at least confirmed it was here. He hadn't desecrated his friend's grave for nothing.

"I'm sorry." Barely more than a whisper. The crack of brittle remains as he carefully lifted the tattered collar and gently pulled at the chain. A tug, a light crack, a small bone breaking under the slightest strain, and the little yellow ball came free.

He stopped for a moment, staring at its grimy surface. This tiny orb was their hope for reclaiming the country. Such a small thing.

Allandria would tell him it was a final gift from Korvin. That would be a nice way to see it. But Aranok knew exactly what he was. A grave robber, vandalising his friend even in death, to fix yet another of his mistakes.

Footsteps. Boots on wet cobbles.

He'd been too slow. Lingered too long. The alley alongside the graveyard was walled on the opposite side, but the iron fence around the kirk would offer him no secrecy from whoever was passing. At this time, there was a good chance it was guards—and a decent chance they were looking for him by now.

Aranok slipped the charm into his pouch, extinguished the light and clambered out of the hole. Quietly and quickly, he crossed to the back of the kirk and pressed himself into the shadows. Voices. At least two. Both male. He couldn't make out the words, just the lilt and fall of their speech. When he was sure they were far enough along, he slipped around the opposite side of the kirk and jumped the gate again.

He hadn't even been able to refill Korvin's grave, to restore his dignity in death. Maybe they wouldn't tell his parents—spare them the horror of their son's grave being violated. He'd not seen them in years, for exactly the same reason he hadn't been here.

Because he was a coward.

A coward and a traitor.

"Aranok? Aranok, wake up."

His mother's voice, soft and pleading. As he rose from the darkness, the pain bit. Everything hurt. His right knee pulsed with his heart. His neck was stiff as stone, brittle as glass. Eyes opening defensively against the early-morning sun, he looked down at himself slumped in his father's armchair beside the cold hearth.

He was filthy. Hands covered in dried and flaking mud. His leathers streaked with that and Madu's blood. By the stretch and crack as he loosened his jaw, his face was spattered too. He must look like he'd crawled from his own grave. The look on his mother's face certainly suggested so.

"Here." She handed him a warm cup of tea and despite everything, he smiled.

Home.

Sumara then scuttled back into the kitchen. Likely giving him a chance to wake up before the inevitable barrage of questions: Why was he here? Why was he filthy? Why had he arrived in the dead of night?

The tea was sweet and comforting, soothing his dry throat. He felt it trickle all the way to his stomach, which growled at the rich smell of sausages. He'd had nowhere near enough sleep, and his body would complain about the chair he had it in for the rest of the day. But he'd made it here, and they were safe. That was everything.

When Aranok had almost finished the tea, Sumara laid a plate of sausages and eggs on the table. "Go and wash those hands before you even think about touching this."

"Yes, Mum."

Once he'd cleaned up, she let him scarf down half the plate before deciding he'd had enough chance to collect his senses. "So, tell me everything."

Where to begin?

The first priority had to be restoring her memory. Nothing else would make sense until he did that. "Mum, I have to tell you something that's going to sound mad, and I just need you to trust me. All right?"

"You know I do."

"First, just hold this…" Aranok reached for the charm around his neck and had a brief moment of panic when it wasn't there. He'd lost that one to the sea. He needed Korvin's. In his pouch.

Sumara's hands felt fragile as he placed the orb in them. They still bore the calluses of decades of sewing, and many of the joints were bigger than they should be. She'd worked hard for the life she had now. For Aranok's life. They both had. For all the ways he clashed with his father, Dorann had always provided for them.

Aranok held his mother's hands between his own, as she'd done with his so many times. "Mum, a spell has been cast over the country. Over everyone. It's made us all believe lies. It's made us forget the truth. I can fix it, but it might be unpleasant. All right?"

"What kind of lies?"

He didn't want to say much more. The more he challenged her memories, the more likely she was to have a violent reaction. Better if he could just restore them and explain afterwards.

"Trust me?"

Her mouth opened, but melted into that warm smile that felt like spring sun. She nodded.

"Clìor."

"Oh!" Sumara blinked and shook her head but made hardly any more reaction. Aranok stayed quiet, allowing his mother to set the pace of conversation. He chewed on a sausage while she recovered.

"My God. Ari, my God! How did this happen?"

Slowly, gently, Aranok took his mother through everything. Right up to Janaeus's death. He'd decided it would be best to let it all sink in before he landed the real news—that her life might be in danger.

"It... it doesn't feel real," she said when he'd finished. "It's like something you'd hear in a story. Like the ramblings of a madman!"

It did, of course. Who would believe such a conspiracy had taken in the entire kingdom, without proof? Without a way to learn the truth of it. Few. If any.

Sumara leaned in close. "So, what now? What will you do now?"

"About what?" Dorann's question was delivered through a yawn halfway down the stairs. He'd hoped to explain everything to his mother before having to deal with his father, but maybe it would be easier to explain to them both.

"Dorann, goodness, come and sit down, I'll get you tea. You're never going to believe this." Sumara bustled back into the kitchen.

Dorann stretched as he reached his chair, stopped and examined it for a moment before brushing some flakes of mud off. When he finally sat, he looked his son up and down. "You been wrestling pigs, boy?"

It wasn't an entirely inaccurate metaphor. Aranok gave his father a functional smile and finished his breakfast. The men sat in silence until Sumara returned with more tea.

"Have you told him?" she asked eagerly.

"He's been busy stuffing his face with my sausages!" Dorann's tone was humorous, but Aranok felt the knife all the same. *His* sausages.

Sumara batted her husband across the shoulder. "Quiet and listen." She turned to Aranok and nodded encouragingly.

Aranok wiped the grease from his mouth. "All right, Dad. You're going to find this hard to believe."

Dorann raised his eyebrows and settled back in his chair, holding his tea to his stomach.

"Your mind has been twisted. By a spell. A spell more powerful than anything we've ever seen." *Not since the fall of Caer Amon.* "Your memory has been altered. Janaeus is not the king of Eidyn. Mynygogg is."

A moment of stunned silence collapsed into a guffaw so strenuous Dorann only narrowly avoided pouring tea down himself. "Are you mad, boy? Don't be bloody ridiculous. Everybody knows Janaeus is king."

"No, I know that's what you believe, but it's not true." Aranok reached out placating hands. "It's a lie."

Dorann looked incredulously at Sumara. She nodded and put her hands on his arm. "It's true. He can prove it."

"My God, not you too. What the Hell is wrong with you?"

Aranok took a breath, as he often had to with his father, and relaxed his shoulders. "Dad, you don't have to believe me. I can show you. Look." He opened his hand to reveal the grubby memory charm. "Just hold this and..."

Dorann batted his hand away, and the charm tumbled to the floor. Aranok was on his knees instantly, scrambling after it like a starving animal chasing prey. When he'd recovered the orb, frustration overcame him. "What did you do that for?"

"What is that thing?" Dorann looked accusingly at Aranok's hand. There was fire in his eyes. Aranok could feel his own embers flaring.

He stood and held out his closed fist. "It's a charm. A charm that protects you from memory magic. A charm that will allow me to restore your memory."

"Memory magic?" Dorann's face crumpled as if he'd bitten an underripe pear. "What the Hell is that? I've never heard of memory magic."

Aranok gripped his fists tighter, tamping down the ever-growing frustration. "Dad, please just listen for a minute. It's a *draoidh* skill. It affects—"

"You think I don't know my own mind, is that it?"

"No, I—"

"No *draoidh* skill can affect a person's mind, Aranok. That's a nonsense!"

Deep. Breath.

"That's exactly how illusions work. You understand that, right?"

"Illusions? Lights in the air? How is that affecting my mind? You're talking nonsense, son."

"Dorann, please..." Sumara tried to pull the man back to his seat, but he shrugged her off and stepped toward his son.

"Hang on. Where did you come by this notion? That Mynygogg is king?" The words dripped with contempt. "Did Mynygogg do this to you? If anyone can manipulate a mind, I'd believe it of that bastard!"

"Dorann, would you please just listen?" Sumara's tone was as insistent, as angry as Aranok had ever heard from her. Dorann dismissed her with a scowl.

"That's not what happened. Please just let me explain—"

"How do you know? You think my memory's been changed, but I've had no contact with a *draoidh*. I've seen no yellow ball. The only one whose mind we know has been affected by magic is yours—and by the look of it, your mother's too. For God's sake, boy, you've played right into his hands!"

The dam burst. Forty years of rage and frustration rushed free.

"For fuck's sake, will you sit down and shut your mouth?"

For all the catharsis, Aranok regretted it as soon as he saw his mother's face.

Dorann settled into his stance and raised his head defiantly. "Who do you think you're speaking to, boy? Whose roof is it you think you're under?"

Aranok ran his hand through his hair and closed his eyes, releasing an exasperated sigh. "You're not listening..."

"I'm hearing you fine. You think my mind's been toyed with. But we know yours has. Think about it logically, Aranok. Who's more likely to know the truth?"

It was infuriatingly logical, if completely flawed, making it actually quite difficult to argue with. He needed to be calm. To dull the fire and handle his father as he'd always done. "Dad, listen, I need you to trust me. I know what was done to you. I know how it was done. I could sit and talk you through every detail, but when I do that with people, some of them . . . react badly. I reacted badly."

"When Mynygogg did this to you."

"No, listen, please." He waved at his father as if trying to quell his own flames by wafting them away. "Mynygogg has no magic." A derisory grunt from his father. "I had to do this. To myself. I did the magic. I know what the spell does. It simply clears the memory. It restores the truth."

"That's what you believe. After Mynygogg cast a spell to make you think so."

"God damn it, why can't you just trust me? All I'm offering you is the truth!" Aranok thrust out his hand, fist gripping the orb tight. "Why would you not want the truth?"

Dorann walked for the stairs. "Get that damned thing away from me, boy. I know the truth. How could I not? You think you know more than me because you're a *draoidh*? You went to university? Because you're the king's envoy? You're the one that's been played, son."

Fuck it all to Hell. He was never going to listen to reason. Aranok would have to ask forgiveness in lieu of permission. Dorann had one foot on the bottom step when Aranok reached him, tugging him round by the shoulder. Learning his lesson from earlier, he did not risk trying to place the orb in his father's hand. Instead, he simply opened his palm and held it to the exposed skin where Dorann's shoulder and neck met.

"Clìor."

Dorann's face turned scarlet. "No! No! What have you done?" The old man stumbled away from the steps before tumbling backwards. Aranok half caught one arm, cushioning the blow as his father landed hard against the wooden stairs.

"Dorann!" Sumara rushed to his side, cradling his head like an infant's. "Dorann. Are you all right?"

Fuck. Could this have gone any worse? Maybe he should have got more sleep. Planned it better. At least his father's memory was restored.

Sumara sat him up. His face was pale as snow, with a sickly green edge. He looked about to...

Dorann dropped his head between his legs and vomited violently. Aranok hoped it was from the spell and not from the blow to the head. The former would pass. He wiped his mouth on the back of his sleeve and limply lifted his head. Aranok wasn't sure what he had expected. A smile of recognition. A conciliatory look.

That was not what he saw. Dorann's eyes blazed with hatred. "What have you done?" Aranok's father staggered back to his feet, shaking like a young deer on unstable legs, supported by his wife. "What have you done?"

What?

"Father, I..." Aranok had no idea what words should come next. What words possibly could? Nobody had ever reacted this way.

"Don't 'father' me. Tell me. What have you done? Because I've got two sets of memories now and no way of telling between them! You might think you know which one's true, but do you? Do you really? With absolute certainty?"

"I do." Aranok's tone was solemn. Calm, despite the twitching in his arm. "Because Janaeus himself admitted it to me. All of it."

"Or you think he did. Because now you'll never know, will you? If you can manipulate people's minds, how will anyone ever know what's true? You've crippled me. You've violated me!"

"Father..."

This time, Dorann's voice was pure rage. "Do not 'father' me! I told you I didn't want your magic, and you forced it on me. Who gave you that right? Who?"

"Dorann, please. Surely you remember now?" Sumara's voice was pleading again. Soothing. Desperately asking her husband to calm, and to settle and to listen. He couldn't hear her.

"I will not have it! Not in my house! Get out!"

Aranok blinked rapidly. He'd misunderstood, surely. How could his father still be angry with him, now he'd restored his memory? Now he'd cleared it of Janaeus's lies? Why would he be upset with Aranok?

"What?"

"Dorann, no..." Sumara put a placatory hand on his shoulder. "No, you go too far."

"Too far!" Dorann snarled. "The boy's bewitched my brain! Twisted my mind! I remember things that didn't happen! How can I go too far?" He turned and stomped ungracefully up the steps. "I want you out by the time I'm dressed. Or I'll call the guard and have you thrown out!"

Aranok stood open-mouthed, silently begging his mother to make sense of it. The floor had dropped from his world, and he had absolutely no idea how.

Sumara shook her head, looking as surprised and confused as Aranok felt.

"What... happened?" Aranok followed his mother to sit back at the table.

She folded her hands on the tabletop before answering. "You know your father. He's... not an easy man. He likes to feel in control. I think maybe you took that from him."

"But I just... I just gave him the truth."

"And he wasn't ready to hear it."

Hells. That was the heart of it. That was why he hadn't reacted when Aranok first told him. He simply didn't believe it. It hadn't occurred to Aranok until this moment that that might even be a problem. That people might suspect he was the one casting a spell on them. Mistrust of *draoidhs* was already high. What of all the people who were more inclined to believe Janaeus than him? Who absolutely believed Mynygogg to be an evil *draoidh*, capable of incredible things?

And with Janaeus dead...

Hells. Nirea had done even more damage than he'd thought. Without Janaeus to admit his own crime, he'd be a martyr to those who chose not to believe the truth. Most likely the ones who felt strongly against the *draoidhs* already. The bigots, for whom Mynygogg was a beast, to be hated and despised for his magic. If his father was indicative of how others might react...

They were in trouble.

"Mum, I..."

"Give him time, Ari. I believe you. I believe all of it. I'll work on him. For now, you should go."

How he wished he could. But there was more. And it was worse. It was the real reason he'd come here.

"I can't. Not yet. Mum, you're in danger. Both of you. And Ikara, and Emelina."

Sumara sat back, one hand raised to her neck. "How? Why?"

As quickly as he could, Aranok explained Madu's threat and her death.

"Mum, you have to hire protection. A bodyguard. Dad can afford it. Please."

"I don't... Aranok, I don't know if he'll—"

"You have to make him, Mum. Please. I don't know if it's real, but I cannot leave here until I know you're safe. All of you. Please."

Sumara nodded slowly. "All right. Leave me to speak to him. I'll find the right moment."

Aranok felt his pulse quicken. "It has to be soon, Mum. I don't know how long we've got."

"I understand, Ari. I'll find a way. Trust me."

He did. He knew she'd do everything to make his father understand. He just didn't know if Laird Dorann would ever hear the truth from his son again.

She reached across the table and stroked his hand reassuringly. "For now, you better go."

Yes. His father was going to need time to calm down. If he ever calmed down. Damn it all. Aranok stood and stretched. His muscles still ached and his brain was still foggy. But he had another stop to make. Ikara would be easier, and Em, he hoped, would be fine, based on how well little Liana had handled the orb.

Children have so much trust in adults. They're so adaptable, soaking in new information. He wished adults retained that ability. He wished they could.

"One other thing, Mum, before I go." He'd hoped to stay here, for a bath and a change of clothes. And maybe a haircut. He needed to be inconspicuous until he knew what news had reached Mournside.

Sumara paused her hustle toward the door. "What?"

"Can I borrow a cloak?"

CHAPTER 34

Aranok had intended to go quickly and quietly to Ikara's house, but within minutes of being out in the street, it was apparent something was happening. There was an unspoken energy in the air as people walked a little faster than normal, chattering and speculating about what news the messenger had brought—all going in the direction of Mourning Square.

It would be about him. And Janaeus. What would the lairds have done?

The sun was not long up. It was rare for a messenger to make an announcement this early, but it was rare for a king to be murdered. They would have arrived in the night and most likely shared the guts of the news with folk in the inn—probably the Canny Man. Which meant that Calador likely thought Aranok a traitor.

He ducked into a side alley to think. On the one hand, he needed to warn Ikara. On the other, he needed to know what had been decided about the throne and what the official story was going to be. It was risky. There would be guards around the square. But the cloak he'd borrowed would keep his identity hidden as long as he didn't get too close to anyone. All the same, he'd stay off the main thoroughfares. No need to add risk. He'd stay at the edge of the crowd, easy to slip away quickly if needed. Once he knew what he was dealing with, he could go straight to Ikara from the square.

Mourning Square was packed to the edges. The bakery was doing a roaring trade feeding the crowd. After breakfast the baker would likely close for the day. Other businesses weren't even bothering to try to open. The blacksmith leaned lazily against his doorframe. A candlemaker sat in a chair she'd pulled outside her door. Everyone wanted to hear the news. The chatter was exactly what Aranok expected from a crowd like this. The sniff of disaster somehow got everyone excited. Even when they expected the news to be bad, the very notion of something momentous happening made it somehow thrilling. Hearts beat a little faster, eyes opened a little wider, as the throng of lairds and ladies, servants and working folk struggled to see the platform from which the messenger would make their announcement.

It reminded Aranok, nauseatingly, of the crowd in Caer Amon, clamouring to see the boy's execution. Why were people drawn to misery?

"I heard Mynygogg's free," an older woman whispered loudly as she brushed past Aranok.

"Back to war, then," her companion answered, nearly knocking Aranok off his feet as she blustered her way through. He grasped his hood, making sure it hung close enough to keep his face in shadow.

The women were both right, but completely wrong. It brought home to him just how twisted the situation was. This crowd, this whole town, believed Janaeus had been their liberating hero. That Mynygogg was the villain—the source of all woes. And somehow, he, with one little charm, was supposed to rectify that for an entire country, when he couldn't even convince his own father of the truth.

Fuck.

He needed not to go down that hole. Allandria would have something positive to say. Something hopeful and uplifting.

He wished he could imagine what the Hell it would be. He missed her. More than he was prepared for. His mind flitted back to the inn, the first time they'd slept together. Despite his worries, it had been good. Really good. He remembered the weight lifting from him. The sense of peace.

It seemed like another life. A stranger's life.

A clatter of excitement through the crowd and Aranok looked up to see a figure take to the platform. From this distance, he could barely tell it was a man, never mind whether he recognised the face. No matter, as long as he could hear. The chatter became a hush as the man raised a hand for quiet.

"Lairds and ladies, I beg your indulgence. I bear grave news from Greytoun. I ask you all to please keep calm, keep quiet and allow me to read the entire statement before asking any questions. I will do my best to provide you with what answers I can."

His voice was deep and resonant. Aranok could all but feel the words in his chest.

"I have been tasked with reading the following letter."

A ceremonious and very serious opening of a scroll.

"It pains me deeply, my friends, to bring you this news. It is the worst news any good subject of Eidyn could think to bear. King Janaeus is dead."

Gasps from the crowd. Chatter and a tangible sense of panic.

"Please! Please! Try to stay quiet! There is more!" The messenger was wading against the tide, but the voices did abate at the notion there was more to hear.

"I am comforted, and I hope you will be too, with the thought that a good man such as Janaeus will certainly be with God. But that comfort cannot outweigh the grief, pain and anger I feel at his loss. I do not believe any salve will ever truly heal that wound upon our country's soul. He was a great man, and we will miss him."

Many heads bowed in solemn reflection. Others looked hungrily at the platform, eager for the further details that were promised. Aranok found a moment for his friend. Not a bad man. Just flawed, mistreated and too easily manipulated.

"The means of Janaeus's death, though, make it particularly hard to bear. For the truth is, he did not die of any natural cause. He was murdered—assassinated—by the one person he trusted most. By his closest ally, Laird Aranok, the king's envoy."

The simmering crowd erupted.

"Bloody *draoidh*!"

"Bastard!"

"Traitor!"

A man not two feet from Aranok spat on the ground and muttered, "Cunt."

How quickly the "good *draoidh*" fell from grace. He pulled his hood a little tighter. It suddenly felt very stupid to have come here.

"Please! Please!" The messenger again waved for calm. "There is more! Please!"

It was harder to calm the voices this time. Even when they quieted, there were constant murmurs of discontent and anger. When it was quiet enough, the man continued.

"To our great horror, this was not the envoy's only crime. In fact, the list is so heinous, it is difficult to repeat, but I must, so that you can all truly understand the depth of his betrayal."

The letter writer was laying it on thick. What else was he going to hang Aranok for?

"Firstly, it seems apparent that he murdered at least one of the king's council, and co-opted another to his treachery."

Fuck. Glorbad? They were laying Glorbad on him? How did they even know about him?

"Secondly, for reasons best known to himself, it seems an inescapable conclusion that he and his allies were also responsible for the murder of the head messenger, Madu."

Shite.

Shite!

With that news out, whatever assassins might have been paid to take revenge in the event of Madu's demise could decide it was time to fulfil their contract. Fuck it all, he should have gone straight to Ikara. Whatever else was going to happen here, he needed to get to her. Now.

"But finally, and in some ways most hideous of all..."

Most hideous? Worse then regicide? Now what? Aranok paused with his back to the crowd. A moment to hear this... no more.

"...for reasons unknown, after assassinating the king, the envoy took it upon himself to murder a roomful of senior lairds—blockading them in Greytoun's ballroom to burn to death."

What?

That never happened! Aranok's head spun. Who would have done that? And why? And if the lairds were all dead... who the Hell was in charge? Who had written this letter? His stomach sank even further at the realisation that Dialla's parents were dead in that room, along with Eidyn's hopes for some stability during this crisis.

Fuck.

He had to stay now. Just to hear the end. To understand.

"It is also our belief, though we have not been able to confirm this, that the envoy may have freed Mynygogg from Dun Eidyn and is even now working with him to overthrow the country. It is possible they have been working together from the beginning."

Howls from the crowd. Fear and anger and confusion poured from people like spilt wine. Aranok crept a little farther away. This was not a wise place for him to be. It felt dangerous. He needed to go.

Soon.

"Please! Please!" the messenger begged. "I have almost finished!" He was going to have to bellow to be heard. Some people were already leaving—fear driving them to turn for home—for family and comfort. Others were infuriated, looking for something on which to vent their rage. The messenger tried to carry on.

The next sentence or two was lost to the wind, but the crowd did indeed quiet as they strained to hear his words.

"For now, in the absence of both the king's council and the Lairds' Council, and with no heir to the throne, we are forced to accept the king's wishes on his successor. It is therefore with great sadness and honour that I tell you I have accepted the throne, as my good friend had committed to writing, should anything happen to him."

Oh, fuck.

"In these difficult circumstances, we must come together, for the sake of Eidyn, to battle this evil that has hidden amongst us. I know I can count on you all to do your duty, to serve Eidyn and to help us all see the brighter day that beckons when we finally rid this land of the shadow of Mynygogg, and his ally, Aranok, who is hereby stripped of all titles, authority and possessions."

How had he not seen this coming?

"As the roads are not safe to travel, the coronation was carried out in private, in Greytoun, overseen by the most senior lairds available. I will do my best to serve you, and to serve God as your new regent.

"Your faithful servant, King Anhel Weyr."

Aranok ran.

No point being subtle. The town was in chaos. People hurried home, carrying the news of the coup. This was bad. Very bad. Anhel had outplayed them. Janaeus would only have left written instructions at Anhel's instigation.

Aranok's feet pounded on the cobbles, his blood thumping as loudly in his ears.

Was this Anhel's plan from the beginning—kill Jan and take the throne for himself? When he'd discovered Janaeus dead, he'd realised the Lairds' Council was his only remaining obstacle to the throne, so he'd killed them and pinned it on Aranok. They'd actually made it easier for him.

Fucking Nirea! If she'd just listened to him, if she had trusted him, they wouldn't be in this bloody disaster.

Aranok turned a corner and barrelled into a girl coming the other way. She stumbled back against the wall, shock mixing with instinctive anger. Her face changed when she looked up at him.

Something was wrong.

His hood had come down in the collision.

Aranok raised his hand before his face and grunted, "Sorry," turning and lifting the hood again. He didn't recognise her. But that didn't mean anything. He was better known here than anywhere else in Eidyn, except Traverlyn. She might have recognised him. If she went to the guard, he'd have even less time.

Heart pounding and air wheezing from his lungs, Aranok arrived at the back of Ikara's house. A quick glance to see he was alone, and he clambered over the garden wall. No sign of life in the cottage from there, but that didn't mean anything. He crept to the back door and pressed his ear to it. Still no sound he could make out. He needed to get inside. A neighbour overlooking the garden might spot him at any moment and wonder why a cloaked man was skulking around. If they connected who lived there... He had to risk it and hope.

The door opened into the kitchen. Nobody there. But there were at least sounds of activity from upstairs. He hoped Pol was out. He needed to not have to deal with that arse right now. Though clearing his memory might at least help.

A giggle. Em was there. Em was happy. Regardless of everything, that made him smile. He found his niece and sister in the girl's bedroom. She had made a small bird of light, and it flitted about the room, changing from red to blue to yellow. Rasa's training had been effective. How he wished he could just stand there and watch.

"Uncle Aranok!" Emelina dropped her spell and ran to him, arms raised. He picked her up and drew her into a tight hug. God, it was good to feel those fragile little arms gripping his neck, her head nestling against his shoulder.

His face must have betrayed his emotions because Ikara's expression moved quickly from surprise to worry. "Ari, what's wrong?"

"I don't have time to tell you. You need to go to Mum. Now. Take Emelina and stay there."

His sister paused for only a moment. "All right. I'll pack a bag."

"Wait. Can I put you down, sweetheart?" Emelina nodded and released her grip. "I need to do something first. Just trust me, all right?"

"Of course."

Aranok sat them both on the bed before using the orb to clear their memories. Ikara swayed like a drunk but quickly recovered. Emelina just said, "Oh! How funny," and hugged her mother until Ikara's head cleared.

"Oh my God, Ari. Oh my God!"

"I know, kid. It's a lot. But..." How could he tell her the rest in front of Emelina? "Em, would you give Mummy and me a minute to have a grown-up talk, please?" The girl looked at her mother, then back to him and nodded cheerily before dancing off down the stairs.

Ikara only waited for her daughter to get halfway down them. "What is it?"

"Your lives are in danger. Mum will explain, but an assassin might be after you. And I need you to tell Mum and Dad—it's even more urgent now. The thing that was supposed to trigger the contract, if it's real—well, it's out. The news is out. I saw it announced this morning. You're going to hear a lot of lies about me—Mum knows the real story. Get safe. Convince Dad to hire bodyguards. Don't let him say no. Whatever you have to do, insist. All right?"

Ikara nodded, leaned forward and took his hands in hers. "Are you all right? You look like Hell."

No, he definitely was not all right. He was exhausted and angry and terrified, but he didn't have the luxury of feeling any of that. Just by being here, he was putting his family at risk. He had to get out of Mournside—back to Traverlyn. His every instinct was to stay here and protect them, but if he did that, he'd just get himself arrested—and then he'd have to fight his way out. Bak was a good man, but he couldn't just break the law for Aranok. Wouldn't.

"I'm fine. I'm just worried about you. Please go straight to Mum and Dad's, all right?"

She nodded again. Shortly, the two of them were heading out the front door with a bag. Emelina smiled and waved at him as though nothing in the world was amiss.

It was heartbreaking.

Aranok went out the garden door and began the long creep through backstreets to find a place to hide until dark, when he could sneak back over the wall and head for the Black Meadows.

CHAPTER 35

The Reiver Lands were as unforgiving as Allandria remembered. What wasn't rocks was chalky, infertile soil. It was why all of the Reiver towns—Calcheugh, Hamhaig, Selecirice, Jethart, Galche and Pebyl—had grown at river junctions, where the soil was at its most fertile. Or least infertile.

It was why so many lived a nomadic life, regularly moving with their herds to find pastures that would sustain their animals, only really returning to town for markets.

As a result, Reiver culture had historically been warlike. Initially, they'd raided each other, scrapping over resources and killing each other for food. When they finally agreed a fragile peace, the Reivers began raiding their neighbours instead.

Eidyn's soil was immensely more generous and their crop yields more bountiful. Only when Mynygogg came to power and realised that the way to end the cycle of violence was to barter with the Reivers—to give them what they needed to stay out of Eidyn—did peace finally come. And with peace, an alliance. A partnership that saw them come to Eidyn's aid when she called. A partnership Janaeus had skewered with magic and lies.

The ride had been simple, if long. They'd encountered a few Reiver parties past the Malcanmore Wall, but a wave from Teyjan or a nod from Cuda and they were left undisturbed. Teyjan and Mynygogg had spent much of the journey chatting—Mynygogg keen to understand the politics of the Reiver council and Teyjan seemingly happy enough to talk. That left Allandria with Cuda, who stopped frowning only to complain, and the mute Jazere, who smiled flatly if their eyes met. They were mourning Tecatt, and grief is a fickle monster.

Allandria had thought often of her parents. How difficult it would have been to raise a child in that nomadic life, in an inhospitable country like this. No wonder they'd settled when she was young in Lochen, where the land was bountiful and the people welcoming. How different her life might have been, had they kept to their ancestors' life. She'd often wondered if they might return to it in her adulthood, but they had found their home in Lochen, and she couldn't see them leaving now.

The silence was a distant drumming in the back of Allandria's mind by the time they reached the foot of the great white hill where the Crioch River met the Tain.

Calcheugh. The effective capital of the Reiver Lands. Where the market was the hub of the country's economy and the Reiver council sat in rule over their shared lands.

Cuda spat dramatically. "Fucking white hill."

It was an accurate description, but Allandria had a hard time understanding why even Cuda would dislike a hill—aside from the obvious. She was delighted to see it, herself. The guts of another three days' travelling to get here and she'd had more than enough of horseback, walking, rain, rations... everything. A seat that was neither saddle nor stone was about all she wanted from the world—preferably cushioned.

When they reached the town gate, Teyjan exchanged a few words with the guards. The looks they gave Mynygogg and Allandria could have been anywhere from suspicion to hatred. They were certainly not welcoming. Allandria found herself gladder than she'd imagined that they had fallen across their little escort group, because it seemed far from certain now that they'd have been welcomed here at all without them. She hoped Meristan had avoided any consequences of that misfortune. She hoped the captain had listened.

Allandria's hopes for a rest and a decent feed were quickly scuppered as the party were hastened toward the large wooden structure at the peak of the hill.

"What is that?" she asked Cuda. "Where are we going?"

Cuda's forehead wrinkled. "Council chambers." She said it as if Allandria had asked her the colour of the grass, or of the sky. Cuda was not, apparently, going to give an inch in her hostility. Ah well. She'd got them here. Under protest, but still.

"Right. Afraid this is where we leave you." Teyjan had stopped at the entrance to the great hall. The doors stood open, revealing two large braziers burning inside. That was all Allandria could see from her angle.

Mynygogg took the Reiver's hand. "Thank you, Teyjan. I owe you a debt I hope I will have the chance to repay."

"No debt far as I see it." The man frowned emphatically. "We'd be in the ground with Tecatt, not for you."

A guttural sound rumbled from Cuda at the mention of the boy's name. She tilted her head at Allandria. "Good luck." Before she could even open her mouth to reply, Cuda had turned and walked into the building. Jazere gave the same enigmatic smile Allandria had seen for days, and followed her.

"Lady Allandria." Teyjan gave a respectful nod.

"Thank you, Teyjan." For the escort, the kindness and the respect. The man also disappeared through the great doors. Allandria stepped close to Mynygogg, allowing them to speak without being overheard by the guards or the slow but steady stream of Reivers flowing through the doors.

"What happens now? Is this a welcoming of some sort?"

Mynygogg's eyes were wide when he turned to her. "Apparently, this is our trial."

"What? We just arrived!" She was far from prepared for an audience with the council, pleading their case, having just stepped off a horse. "Surely we can be allowed some time..."

"It seems not. The council have been called, expecting our arrival, thanks to the message I sent ahead. It's Reiver tradition that a trial happen as soon as all parties are available."

"Which is now?"

"Teyjan said they'll keep us out here until everyone's seated, then call us in."

"Wait. Did you say a *trial*?" That was not a word she'd expected to hear. It was not a word she was glad to hear. It seemed like a very, very bad word. A disastrous word.

Mynygogg's look was almost piteous, as if delivering bad news to a child. "It seems, if I understand it correctly, that Eidyn's attacks on the Reivers has been taken as an act of betrayal. An act of war. And if I am the rightful ruler of Eidyn, I am responsible for those acts."

"What?" They were here specifically to argue that Mynygogg was still the rightful king of Eidyn. That, as such, the treaty still held and perhaps even that the Reivers might be allies to remove Janaeus. But if arguing that Mynygogg was the rightful ruler meant him being responsible for an act of war... "How long have you known?"

A joyless smile curled below hollow eyes. "Teyjan explained it to me on the first day. Their scouting party was one of several sent in advance of an attack."

And she thought Aranok was bad for keeping things from her. The bloody king himself had just allowed them to be walked into a trap, in a country preparing for war with Eidyn. She scanned the surrounds, looking for escape routes. An alley to their left. They could disappear down there and...then what? She didn't know this place at all. Their weapons had been taken at the gates. She could hardly defend the king by hand.

The slow stream of people continued to drift into the hall. Only now, Allandria looked closer at the river of faces passing them by. Nobody looked directly at them. Several spat as they passed.

Fucking Hells!

If Aranok had got them into this, at least she could have relied on his magic to get them out. All they had now was...hope. Mynygogg's words. That was it. Mynygogg's words to convince the Reiver council he was their ally. That he was worth keeping alive.

They'd better be pretty fucking words.

After an age, they were finally shown in by the guards. The room was a great circle with six raised, decorative chairs at one end and four rows of tiered wooden benches curving round each side. The chairs were empty, the benches all but full.

Allandria and Mynygogg were ushered to a pair of seats at the edge, on ground level. As far from the raised chairs as it was possible to sit. It seemed like a slight. A deliberate one. This was not how a visiting king was treated. Allandria felt a knot growing in her guts.

Each of the raised chairs had a different symbol carved into its head—one for each clan, she assumed. Above them all, a flag displaying the Reiver standard. The closed fist. It felt more like a symbol of violence than she'd ever considered. She needed a plan to get them out of here alive. She could have had a plan.

In truth, if Mynygogg had told her what he knew, she would have demanded they turn around and go home. She might well have forced him, given her new authority as queen's envoy.

Which he knew.

Which was why he didn't tell her.

Because he was certain he could talk his way through this.

Damn it!

She missed Aranok in that moment, more for a desperate need to speak to him, to have his confidence and his counsel, than for his power. She missed the man, not the *draoidh.* But she would get them out of this.

Somehow.

"Be upstanding for the liber!" a voice called, and the benches stood as one. Allandria and Mynygogg awkwardly rose to join them, late enough to be noticed, but hopefully not to be considered yet another slight to their hosts.

"What's a liber?" she whispered.

"Record keeper," the king answered. An elderly man in white robes shuffled from the dark and took a seat to the side of the empty chairs—the raised desk before him presumably equipped with parchment and ink.

"Lot of respect for a record keeper."

Mynygogg shrugged. "They consider it a noble calling. He's seen as the keeper of truth. Avoids any disagreement after the matter of what was said by whom, what was agreed."

That made sense. In a culture so easily fractured, a trusted arbiter of truth would be invaluable. A key to peace. Assuming everyone accepted their arbitration. She imagined some might not, when the liber's truth conflicted with their beliefs.

"Chieftain Lavole!"

A tall, leather-clad woman strode across the platform to what appeared to be a bowl on a plinth. She stopped before it, gave a slight bow and dug her hands into it, raising them to splash water across her face. She rubbed her hands as though washing them, gave another barely noticeable bow and took a seat.

"Who's she?" Allandria asked.

"Chieftain of Hamhaig. Teyjan says she's a great warrior. Doesn't give much away. Keeps her own counsel."

That didn't tell her much.

"What's the water about?"

"Reiver tradition. The host provides water for the visiting chieftains to wash in. It's a form of welcome and humbling of the host, who washes last. It also symbolises a washing away of the past, and of old grievances."

"Teyjan told you all that?"

Mynygogg smiled. "I already knew that."

Allandria knew little of the Reiver culture, beyond what her parents had told her. They had only passed through the land themselves, but they'd spent enough time here to understand the people. Part of Allandria felt like she was learning more about her history as she understood more about the Reivers.

"Chieftain Hombuck!"

A tall man, this time, wearing painted leathers and a sword that almost scraped the ground. His face hidden behind a bush of ruddy brown beard, it was difficult to read any expression from him as he too went through the bowl custom and took his seat.

"Chieftain of Galche," Mynygogg explained. "Says he's a good man, more soldier than politician. According to Teyjan, the best swordsman in the country."

"According to Teyjan," Allandria echoed. She assumed the man would be biased in favour of his own chieftain. Again, though, not a lot to work with. Would Hombuck be an ally?

"Chieftain Dacred!"

A round-faced, bald man wearing a red tunic trimmed with gold stalked out. His face was almost as florid as his clothing. The very air around him seemed irritated to be disturbed. He made cursory gestures at the bowl, barely even wetting his hands, and took his seat.

Allandria was not hopeful. "He seems cheerful."

Mynygogg's stoic expression fell into a frown. "He's a concern. Jethart."

Jethart. She'd heard of Jethart justice. Hang first; try later. And their chieftain did not seem in a convivial mood. "What do we know about him?"

"Not to be indelicate"—Mynygogg leaned in close—"but Teyjan described him as a malicious bastard. Never wanted peace with Eidyn in the first place."

Bollocks. Three chieftains out, and the most they knew was that one of them was a lost cause.

"Chieftain Stamary!"

An older, darker woman in a flowing white robe entered. She glided across the platform and carefully performed the bowl ritual, lifting her face and muttering something quietly as she finished. She took her seat, folded her hands in her lap and smiled serenely. She was the first Allandria had any positive feelings about. "She seems pleasant."

"Selecirice. Deeply religious. Teyjan speaks well of her. Says she is guided largely by her faith."

Hmm. That might be useful, or it might not. Mynygogg was known not to be a man of faith. But surely her faith would lean toward peace and preserving life?

"Chieftain Burrox!"

"What?" Mynygogg looked around, confused, as a middle-aged man with mahogany skin and long, black hair strode across the platform. The man looked every bit as regal as Mynygogg himself, carrying an ornate wooden staff carved with black sigils.

"What's wrong?" Allandria asked, following his gaze, but with no idea what she was looking for.

"Burrox is Calcheugh. He should come out last. One's missing."

What did that mean? Only five of the six chieftains? Mynygogg looked worried. "Is that bad?" Allandria asked as the man completed the bowl and took one of the central seats.

"The cornet of Pebyl is supposed to be a wise man. Likely to side with us, Teyjan says. Thoughtful. Peaceful. They worship the old gods." Mynygogg swallowed hard. "I was counting on him."

"You've met him?"

"No. Pebyl's different. They elect their cornet every Beltane. He wasn't cornet last time I was here. I'd never heard of him."

Fuck. Of all the people to be missing, the one they probably had in the bag to balance the one they knew would be against them.

Burrox looked directly at Allandria, then to Mynygogg, giving a small nod. Was that a good sign? Hells, she had no idea! She didn't know these people, didn't know their ways. She had absolutely no fucking idea how this was going to go, and no way to get out of it. Now she missed the *draoidh* a little more than the man.

Burrox stood and held his hands out like a priest on kirkday. "My friends. As you can see, we are one member short. Risimfar has not yet arrived from Pebyl, but we expect him soon, and will begin without him, under the rule of *cuòram*."

"Shite," Mynygogg hissed. His confidence had been the only thing keeping Allandria from the edge of panic. As she watched it seep away, her heart stuttered.

They were in trouble.

CHAPTER 36

"I'm not sure how to address you, my friend. Are you King Mynygogg, or Laird Mynygogg? Were you a laird...before?" Chieftain Burrox's tone was friendly, but there was something not quite true about it. He called Mynygogg "friend," but there was an edge to the word, as if he intended it to cut. Mynygogg had hoped the leader of the Reiver council would be an ally—he had been the one to strike a deal with Mynygogg years ago—but Allandria saw no camaraderie. Perhaps he was required to be detached, to give the appearance of impartiality, at least. Perhaps he saw what way the wind was blowing, or imagined he did, and it was not in Eidyn's favour.

"I suppose that's what we're here to establish, isn't it?" Mynygogg smiled up at the chieftains as if he were strutting a stage, not standing in the dirt between two armed guards, pleading for his country. The confidence had returned, or at least the bravado. He was a compelling man—but if the politics here were against him, it might not matter how beautifully he spoke. Allandria scanned the faces raised above her king. Dacred's small mouth puckered at the heart of his turgid red face. He looked at Mynygogg with barely concealed disdain. In fact, it wasn't concealed at all. Of the others, Lavole and Hombuck remained unreadable. The woman leaned forward with her chin nestled in her raised hand; the man seemed more interested in his fingernails than the proceedings. Only Stamary continued to give

Allandria hope. She sat stiffly, hands upturned in her lap, watching attentively.

"I suppose it is," Burrox answered. "But it seems you're in a quandary. If you're not the king of Eidyn, then you have no standing before this council. If you are king, then your people have betrayed our alliance, and we are at war. Making you our legitimate prisoner."

Those were not good choices. Allandria shifted uncomfortably in her seat. She needed a plan. But there was no plan that would get them out of here easily. Or at all.

"I hope, Chieftain, that we can find a third option beneficial to both our countries."

Burrox broke into a wide smile. "I'm sure you do." He banged the twisted staff on the ground. "Liber! Please read the charges!"

The old man stood and shuffled to his podium. The room fell into absolute silence, such that Allandria only then realised it had not been so before. Hushed conversations and minor chatter ceased, leaving only the sound of creaking wood burning in the braziers. When the liber spoke, it was quietly and evenly.

"It is recorded that, during the *draoidh* war, Eidyn's people did turn on Reiver soldiers sent to their aid, and murder them in an act of treachery, breaking our alliance and effectively declaring war. There are multiple reports of this, and none to the contrary."

The liber sat down again as if there were no one else in the room. Only when his backside hit the chair did the low chatter resume. Allandria felt a gentle nudge in her side and turned to find a pair of dark eyes looking intently at her from under a black hood.

"S'he a good man?" the boy asked. He looked about Vastin's age. Maybe a year or two older, but no more than that. His face was thin and his elegant cheekbones would have been the envy of Eidyn's noble society. Not least the women.

"He is. One of the best I know."

The boy raised an eyebrow. "Only one of them? Ye ken better?"

"I know good people."

The boy gave an appreciative frown and turned away.

"Is that true?" Burrox seemed to loom even heavier over Mynygogg as he leaned forward onto his staff.

The king cleared his throat and raised his head. "That is true, but it is only part of the truth. Reivers also attacked the people of Eidyn."

"Lie!" Dacred sprung from his chair with an agility Allandria wouldn't have given him. "He insults our warriors! We will not stand for this! Silence him!" The murmur of the crowd grew louder.

Burrox raised a hand to stay the guards, who shuffled uncertainly, seemingly unsure whether they were supposed to react to Dacred's outburst.

"Burrox! You will not defend our people?" Somehow the man's porcine face was getting redder.

"Calm down, Dacred. This is Calcheugh, not Jethart. We will hear him speak." Burrox barely even looked toward the man as he slowly retook his seat, simmering with indignation. Next to him, Lavole rolled her eyes.

"Is he always so angry?" Allandria asked the boy.

He turned and looked thoughtfully past her for a moment. "Aye."

Burrox waited for the chatter to quieten. "Mynygogg, please continue."

"It is true, but it is only true because all of the people within Eidyn, Reivers included, were deceived. Deceived by a memory *draoidh* who convinced them not only that he was the king of Eidyn, but that I was the true enemy of the *draoidh* war and that Eidyn and the Reivers were still in conflict."

The council erupted.

A sea of faces crested opposite Allandria's position; a wave of sound washed from behind her. People stood and bellowed at Mynygogg. Something landed in the dirt at his feet. Dacred screamed something about "nonsense." Burrox seemed to be calling for calm, but his voice was lost in the maelstrom. This wasn't good. Mynygogg was too vulnerable. Too exposed. If this turned into a riot, she'd never be able to protect him. Her hand closed on her belt, where her sword should be. She flinched at the feel of another hand on her own.

The boy looked calmly at her. "The guards'll no allow him to be harmed. Anyone tries'll be executed. Council's sacred."

His tone was soothing, but he was a boy and looked like he'd never been close to a battle. His porcelain skin and smooth hands had never held a sword. His reassurance felt…hollow. But she wanted to believe him.

A resonant thud and finally the noise began to settle. Burrox stood now, fist clenched around the staff he'd just battered against the platform. A signal of some sort, it seemed.

Dacred was still bellowing. "This is an outrage. We cannot sit here and tolerate these lies, we will not—"

Burrox cut across him. "Dacred. Sit down."

"I will not!" he spat. "I will not be silenced! I will not..." Whatever he intended to say caught in his throat. Beside Burrox, Hombuck had risen to his feet. The man was a giant, towering over everyone else. He rested one hand, almost casually, on his sword hilt. He said nothing. He didn't need to.

Dacred sat.

Hombuck nodded in mock respect and did the same. Looked like Teyjan wasn't the only one who saw his chieftain as the greatest Reiver warrior. Clearly, tensions between the Reiver clans had not evaporated with the establishment of truce. They'd just been stifled.

The quiet now was even more fractured than it had been, but it was enough for Burrox to retake the conversation. "We've had memory *draoidhs*. None of them have that kind of power. How do you explain that?"

Aye, that was the root of it. If it weren't for the heart, if she hadn't seen its power herself, Allandria might not have believed it either.

Despite the setting, despite everything, Mynygogg still managed to look regal standing there, looking up at the chieftains. He still had that gravitas. That credibility. It meant something. It had to.

"He had possession of an item—a relic—which massively amplified his power. It allowed him to cast it over the entire country."

More chaos from the crowd. Dacred all but spat on the floor. Stamary frowned, her serene expression changing for the first time. Allandria felt her stomach turn.

This wasn't going their way.

"Madness." The boy was shaking his head. "No such power has ever been given to *draoidhs*."

"It has," Allandria hissed.

"Never heard of it. We'd surely seen something..."

There was an edge in the boy's tone that finally pushed Allandria past restraint. "How would you know? You're about twelve!"

The corner of the boy's mouth curled. "I'm no. And I've studied *draoidhs*. There's no record of such a weapon."

"Your teachers might not know of it, but I do. You know of Caer Amon?"

"The ghost ruins?"

Allandria nodded curtly. "Caused by the relic. And a time *draoidh*. I was there. It's no ghost ruin—it's..." What was it? A time hole? A tear in time? How the Hell did one even describe what Caer Amon was now?

"A time *draoidh*? That's a rare skill." The boy was chatting as if they were alone in the room, not surrounded by howling Reivers calling for her king's head.

More banging from the platform.

"There will be silence!" Burrox bellowed, "or I will clear the chamber and we will sit in judgement before the liber alone!"

It took another moment, but that did the trick. As the crowd sat again, Allandria caught sight of Cuda. It was the first time she'd seen her in the crowd. The woman sat calmly between Jazere and Teyjan halfway along the third row. Despite her personality, there was something comforting about seeing her. Even an unfriendly friend was welcome. She longed to be back on the road—it still felt unreal that they'd got off their horses and walked straight into this.

"What evidence do you offer for this assertion?" Burrox had retaken his seat. Even Lavole was leaning forward in her chair.

The king coughed gently. "There is none I can give, beyond my solemn word. Eidyn is under the spell of a *draoidh* who has convinced the country of his intricate lie. That, I swear, is the truth. I can speculate as to why. I believe that in order to better control the people of Eidyn, he has chosen to instil them with fear. Fear of an enemy that can be easily identified and used as a weapon to chasten them should they question his rule. As an excuse for raising taxes, in order to spend it on the military. As a distraction from his own failings, should they become restless at the injustices of their own lives. I believe the Reivers have been vilified, our peace sacrificed and your people murdered all in the cause of serving one man's vanity. And I beg you not to be part of it."

Burrox hmmphed but barely moved.

"That would make some sense, Chief Burrox." Stamary's voice

was slow and easy, like rich honey. "It would explain those who have returned."

Good. Some Reivers had made it home with the same story of Janaeus and the war. Would have sounded like mad ravings until they knew the truth of it.

Burrox nodded silently, gazing down at—through—Mynygogg. Dacred looked fit to burst when the chieftain finally spoke.

"What would you have us do?"

"I ask you no more than to pull your people out of Eidyn until we can retake it. We have worked hard to make peace between our people. We ended generations of bloodshed. I would not see that ruined for nothing. You came to our aid when we called. I will not see another Reiver die for Eidyn's ails. Please. Give me time. Let me protect our people."

"Fine words," the boy said.

"Fine man." He was. And those were pretty words.

"Bollocks!" Dacred again. Of course. "Power makes a king! He's either king and responsible for his people's betrayal, or he's not, and we're at war with the new king of Eidyn. The miraculous *draoidh*! It's a simple choice."

"It is a complicated choice," Stamary said. "The question before us is what is best for our people. If what Mynygogg says is true, if he can retake the kingdom and reinstate our treaty, then that would be a clear best option. Avoiding war is a noble aim."

"You'd see our people go unavenged?" Lavole's tone was dismissive. Disdaining.

Hombuck grunted in apparent agreement.

The words weren't enough. They were going to lose.

Burrox sat with his chin resting on his folded hands, his silence as worrying as the others' words.

"I call for a canvass!" Dacred's grating voice again. Allandria disliked the man intensely, and she'd barely been in his presence. He was poison. And by the look of him, quick to start a war he'd send others to fight.

Burrox raised an arm toward the empty chair. "Risimfar is not here."

"We have *cuòram*." The first words from Hombuck's mouth. And not helpful.

"Should they wait for him?" Allandria asked the boy, whom she seemed to have adopted as her companion in the absence of another.

"They should, but they might no," he answered, never taking his eyes from the platform. The liber scribbled silently, documenting their demise. She needed to do something. To say something. Anything!

"May I address council?"

Allandria jerked her head round. Teyjan stood, alone in the crowd opposite.

"Control your man, Hombuck," Lavole drawled.

Hombuck glowered across at her a moment and raised an eyebrow to Burrox. The leader nodded gently.

Hombuck stood. "Teyjan. You arrived with them? You got something to say?"

"I do, Chief, if you'll grant me leave."

"I will."

Teyjan inched his way along to a set of steps and made his way to the floor. Mynygogg gave him a half-hearted smile as the man arrived beside him. Allandria tried to catch his eye, but he either didn't think to look at her or chose not to. They were in it now. There was nothing she could do but pray.

"Chief, we was on the way out of Eidyn, run into a troop of soldiers. Near Barrock. Lost Tecatt."

Hombuck closed his eyes and gently pressed his fist against his heart.

"That's where we met the king. Him and his people."

"That right?" Hombuck's face darkened as he switched his gaze to Mynygogg.

"Aye, Chief. But he stood with us. Took our side against his own men. And they didnae know him. I swear to you, they'd no idea who he was. But he stood with us. Him and two White Thorns. And Lady Allandria."

As Teyjan pointed, it felt like every eye in the room turned to look at Allandria. She felt heat rise in her cheeks.

"They killed their own people?" Hombuck asked. His voice softer now. Confused.

"Well, no. But they did protect us. Lady Allandria, she took their captain, had 'im surrender. Ride off. That's how we're here."

Allandria scanned the chieftains' faces, searching for hints as to what they were thinking. Maybe Teyjan was helping? They only needed three, and they had Stamary, surely? Maybe Burrox too? If Hombuck listened to his man, Dacred's hatred and Lavole's sour mood were meaningless.

"But you lost Tecatt?" Hombuck's voice was still low and dark.

Come on.

"Aye, Chief, we lost Tecatt. But I wouldnae be standing here telling you we lost Tecatt if no for them."

That got his attention. "You'd stand by this man, Teyjan? You would speak for him?"

Teyjan nodded slowly. "Aye, Chief. I would. I do."

Mynygogg put a hand on the man's shoulder and they exchanged a smile.

Surely that was enough? *Surely.*

"Cuda? What you saying?" Hombuck looked to the crowd, where the two women still sat.

Cuda slowly took her feet. "Chief?"

Fuck. This could go badly.

"That true?" the big man asked.

The old woman crumpled her face, as if considering whether to spit out the wasp she'd been chewing. "Aye. S'pose it is."

"And what do you say to King Mynygogg?"

Cuda again took her time, staring at the king, who looked stoically back at her. "Bit of a cunt, doesnae listen when he should, but he's decent."

"Would you fight for him?"

Cuda snorted. "For him? Fuck no. Beside him? Aye, maybe."

Allandria hadn't expected that. Coming from Cuda, it was glowing praise.

"And Jazere? What you saying?"

Cuda sat as the *draoidh* rose to her feet. How was she going to "say" anything? She looked to her chieftain, then to Mynygogg, frowned and raised a thumb.

Presumably that was good, as she caught Allandria's eye and smiled widely before sitting.

"All right. Teyjan, you can sit."

Hombuck took his own advice as Teyjan made his way back to the benches.

"Choice is still the same." Dacred broke the silence. "He's king or he's not. Makes no difference what he's done."

"Makes a difference to me," Hombuck growled.

Dacred shook his head dismissively. All right. Maybe they had Hombuck. Maybe this would work after all.

"What'll he do? If you lose?" the boy whispered to her.

She didn't know. She didn't know what she'd do. But in any situation, there was one thing she could predict about the king's choices. "Protect who he can."

"Huh." The boy looked back to the stage. "Good answer."

"I called a canvass!" Dacred sat on the edge of his chair. "Let's have it, unless there are any more stories to hear?" He waved his arms toward the crowd mockingly.

Burrox looked across his fellow chieftains, each nodding in response. "All right, Dacred. How do you vote?"

The poisonous toad stood again. "He's a deposed king. His throne was taken from him, same as he took it from Hofnag. I say we take him prisoner, might be worth something to the new king someday. For now, we return to raiding. Those northern bastards aren't going to be shipping us any goods soon, and we're going to need them for the winter. We take what's ours, we look after our own."

He nodded seriously, as if he'd delivered some great work of oratory, and sat. Allandria imagined she'd never tire of punching that ripe tomato face.

Burrox turned to his left. "Stamary?"

Selecirice's chieftain stood. She moved smoothly, like liquid, like a cat. A woman of her age had no right to such elegance, Allandria thought. She was reminded of just how much she ached and how badly she needed to rest. Stamary's flowing white dress made her look even more angelic.

"I do not see how war helps us. I do not see how sending our people to die for supplies we can have in peace helps us. We can manage, for a time. All King Mynygogg asks for is our patience. He asks for no warriors. He asks for no help. He asks only that we retreat from Eidyn and allow him time to reclaim his kingdom. I say we give him that time, and pray God is with him."

Allandria felt a weight lift from her. God, but she needed to hear that. A voice of reason. At last.

Burrox nodded in acknowledgement. "Hombuck?"

The chieftain of Galche took his time getting up. He looked... indecisive. Come on, after everything he'd heard... surely he would listen to his own people.

Hombuck licked his teeth, looked to Mynygogg and then to his clansfolk. The silence stretched directly into Hell.

Finally, he spoke.

"Aye. Give him time."

Allandria's hands were shaking as he sat. This time it was good. It was relief and... hope.

"Lavole?"

The woman stood. Her bored expression had gone, replaced with steel. Her hair was tied back tight, giving her face a severe look. "Dacred's right. He's no king. He has no power. No benefit in us allying with him. We deal with what's in front of us. We raid."

Damn it.

But still, Burrox had the casting vote. He sat for a long time, chin still resting in his hands, looking down on Mynygogg. The king returned the look, unflinching.

Fuck. He wasn't decided either. He had to side with them! He negotiated the peace with Mynygogg. The king spoke highly of him.

When he stood, his voice was tired. Mournful. "What I can see is this, my friend. You no longer have the throne. If we do as you ask, if we accept the acts of aggression by Eidyn as a trick, we don't know what the usurper will do next. Maybe he chooses to attack us. We lost a lot of people fighting your war. We can't afford to be on the wrong side of another one.

"If you can't guarantee peace, we have to assume war."

Oh, God, no.

Spattered cheers from the crowd. The chatter of excitement and alarm spread like wildfire through the benches. Allandria looked to her left. To the exit. Could she get to Mynygogg? Fight her way out the doors, at least? If they moved quickly, they could maybe get to the horses before word reached the gate...

"But!" Burrox raised the staff high until it all settled. "But I will not imprison a man I believe has acted in good faith. You and Lady Allandria are free to return home. I wish you luck. If you retake your throne, we can talk again."

"What'll you do?" the boy asked, leaning in.

Allandria's heart thumped in her chest. It could have been worse. It should have been better. "Go home. Try to retake the kingdom. Try to save lives. Same as we would have done." Except now they had to take the Reiver threat seriously. Janaeus had succeeded in restoring the Reiver war, and he'd likely use it to whip up the kingdom to his rule. Nothing brought a country together like war.

"S'what I thought." The boy stood, lowered his hood and walked to the middle of the chamber. "I vote we give them time!"

What the fuck?

"Risimfar?" Burrox's surprise was carved across his face. "What in Hells are you doing down there?"

"There's a saying in Pebyl," the boy answered as the crowd settled. "If you want to ken a person, meet their friends." He turned and smiled at Allandria, whose jaw might have lost contact with her skull. "Mynygogg's a good man. One of the best, I'm told. And Hombuck's people clearly agree. He didnae have to come here. But he did. So I say he's earned the chance to take his throne back. Maybe he lost the war, but we were allies. So we lost too. We lose together and look to a future where we win, together, again. In peace."

Allandria wondered whether she was hallucinating through exhaustion. The delicate, curious young man she'd been confiding in was the cornet of Pebyl? He was twelve! Well, clearly not, but not an adult. And yet, he spoke with the wisdom of a much older man. Of an actual man! She could see why the people of Pebyl might have elected him, though. He was almost as compelling as Mynygogg.

The cornet gave Mynygogg a respectful nod, which the king returned, before mounting the steps to take his proper place on the platform.

But what did this mean? It was tied, now, at least. Three for; three against. Now what?

"It's combat, then," Dacred grumbled.

Combat? That did not sound good. It sounded a lot worse than them being allowed to peacefully return home.

"Indeed." Burrox's voice was low. Deep. Sad. "As per our traditions, a conflict unresolved in council will be settled the old way. It's combat."

Mynygogg's head bowed. Allandria willed him to say something, anything, to make this go away.

Burrox turned to his left. "Hombuck, will you stand for the council?"

Oh God, no. The greatest Reiver warrior? Mynygogg was quick—maybe unmatched in hand-to-hand combat, but with a sword? He was competent, better than that, but he was a long way short of legendary. Glorbad had been a better swordsman, even allowing for his age and belly.

Hombuck frowned and delivered his answer directly to Dacred. "I'll no fight for a cause I don't support. You want combat? You fight him."

Thank God. Maybe he had a chance.

Dacred snorted. "Lavole, then."

Hamhaig's chieftain rose. "Aye. I'll stand."

Was she any good? She certainly looked the part. Allandria scanned the crowd, looking for some sort of hope. Unexpectedly, she met Cuda's eyes, looking straight back at her. Allandria raised her eyebrows, looking for comfort, hope. Cuda glanced to Lavole and slowly shook her head, her eyes dark.

Lavole was as good as she looked.

All right, then. This was it. Finally, Allandria could do something with certainty. She stood and strode to her king.

"I stand for Eidyn."

Mynygogg's head whipped round. Lavole was descending the steps.

"Lady Allandria. I'm afraid you have no standing here." Burrox fidgeted with his staff. He hadn't wanted this either. "Our customs dictate combat is between leaders, not champions. It must be the king."

Fuck!

Wait.

She wasn't just a bodyguard.

"With respect, Chieftain Burrox, I do have standing. I am Allandria, envoy to Nirea, queen of Eidyn. In the queen's absence, I carry her authority. I claim that authority before this council."

Risimfar's eyebrows arched. She'd given him a little surprise too. Burrox sat up straight. "Is that true?"

Mynygogg looked at her, his expression impossible to read. What was he thinking? Maybe whether Aranok would forgive him if he got her killed? "Yes. It's true. Allandria is envoy to the queen."

"Then she may stand for Eidyn," said Burrox.

Allandria rolled her shoulders. She was sore and tired, but it wouldn't matter. Once it started, she'd forget all that. Lavole was younger than her. Taller too. But she had experience. She'd never been killed yet. She wasn't going to start now. Not with everything at stake. They were going home. She was going home. To Aranok.

A guard handed her a sword as Lavole drew hers. The woman stared impassibly down at her, cold eyes as hard as her blade. Once Mynygogg and the guards moved out of the space, she'd probably come at her fast. Looking to end it quickly. It's a myth spread by children's stories that sword fights are long, epic, exciting encounters. Most are over in the first minutes. The first misstep, the first overreach, and you could be done. Allandria won by avoiding mistakes. By being clear-headed.

She felt calm settle on her. Her hands were steady. She could do this. For Mynygogg. For Eidyn.

"No."

It was Mynygogg. He remained between the two women, refusing to allow the guard to move him away.

"What?" Burrox asked. "What is your objection?"

"All of it." The king shook off the guard's hand and stepped even more centrally between them, directly blocking the two fighters' paths. "I will not allow this. I will not see another life taken to spare mine. Neither Reiver nor Eidyn. I will not."

"Your Majesty, please," Allandria begged. "Think what the queen would say." What would she say? "She'd tell you that you are too important. That you are the figurehead. That without you, Eidyn is already lost. Please. Let me do this."

A glint, a hint of a smile. "But she would be wrong. You and I both know there are others who can take my place. But not here." He turned to face Lavole. "If blood has to be spilled here, then it will be mine. I mean what I say. No more lives for my failure."

Mynygogg raised his arms wide. Lavole looked to the council and, when no signal came, raised her blade level with the king's heart.

She was going to execute him, right in front of Allandria. She had seconds to act—or not. Should she intervene? Save the king's life whatever he said? Oh God, what should she do? Could she really stand there and watch Mynygogg be executed?

She'd been sent to be a bodyguard to the king. But she was also Nirea's envoy. Empowered to act on her authority in her absence. Once she thought of that, there was only one answer. She had to do what Nirea would do.

She had to save him.

Allandria lurched forward, wrapped her free arm over the king's shoulder and spun him away, putting her back between him and Lavole's blade. It was a gamble. She was defenceless if the chieftain decided to strike.

No blow came.

She pushed Mynygogg away, and taken by surprise, he stumbled to his knees, bellowing, "No!" even as he hit the ground.

Allandria spun to face Lavole. The Reiver stood defensively. She'd chosen not to stab her in the back—so she had honour. Or maybe she just knew it would do her reputation no good.

"Come on, then." She nodded to Lavole. The woman nodded back and stepped toward her.

"Stop!"

Every head in the room turned to Burrox. He swallowed hard, pressed his lips firmly together.

"I recant my vote." He raised his arms high. "King Mynygogg has shown his character. I am persuaded. He deserves the chance to retake Eidyn." The final words he directed straight at Dacred.

"We'll give him time."

CHAPTER 37

Nirea could barely keep her head up as the Traverlyn stables finally came into sight. When she was scrubbing decks and cleaning shirts from wake till sleep, she'd had the benefit of youth's boundless energy. Dialla could have boosted her, she supposed, but she was loathe to ask the master for anything after what she'd put her through.

It hadn't even occurred to her that taking a life—a necessary life—would be damaging, and yet she'd seen two people shattered by it in quick succession. What did that make her, that she found murder so mundane, so ordinary that she didn't see consequences?

How many people do you have to kill to forget how it's supposed to affect you?

Darginn was not her responsibility. She'd have killed Madu for him, but Aranok's protestations had stayed her hand long enough for Darginn's…What would she call it? Madness? Grief? Whatever, he was not in control of his senses when he gouged the woman's throat.

She'd hoped time—the time on the road—might help them recover. It hadn't. And guilt kept her from trying to do anything for Dialla, not least because she had no idea what to do. She didn't imagine explaining that it got easier the more people you killed would benefit the master.

Leondar had continued to tend Dialla like she was the queen, and Nirea had happily allowed it. It slightly assuaged her own guilt. For such a big man, he had a gentle nature and a kind heart. That, his strength and his skill made him an ideal kingsguard. He had the soul and the steel. And the loyalty.

Darginn—God, what could she possibly do for Darginn? The man had been to the depths of Hell and likely expected he'd never see light or his family again. That he'd initially seemed fine had been a naïve assumption—a convenient one, if she was honest. He should have been in the hospital, not leading them into Haven.

But he wanted to get his family out, and they'd done that, at least. That was something.

They'd skirted the edges of Leet in the end. She'd decided it was too dangerous to try to reach the King's Wark and warn Ailen. Maybe if she'd been alone. But if a messenger had made it there before them, she could be risking their whole party, and for all she desperately wanted to warn her friend, she also knew he'd tell her to stay the Hell away if it meant putting Darginn's family at risk. She'd get back there when she could, she'd promised herself. It felt like an empty promise. A lie to salve her conscience. But those were the choices she had to weigh—one life against many. Joliander she had no idea how to reach anyway. He'd be at sea, most likely. Best she could have done was leave word for him in every Leet inn he might frequent. And if anything, that could just put him in more danger.

Goddamn, what a mess. When they'd arrived in Lochen under dark, she'd actually hoped there might have been a messenger—to give them a glimpse of what was happening in Greytoun after their escape. But no. Nothing.

Without Aranok to clear their memories, and without a memory charm to do it, she'd had to lie to Allandria's parents about everything. Who she was, why they were in danger, all of it. But as soon as they heard she was a friend of their daughter's, they'd taken the whole caravan into their cottage and insisted they stay the night—even though it meant bedrolls on the floor. Allandria's family home truly was one. Mori's broth had warmed their bones and Nirea had quickly drifted to sleep, feeling something close to safe for the first time since they'd left Traverlyn.

And it was better than taking an inn. She might well be wanted by the Lairds' Council now. They all might. That was another gift she'd given Dialla.

And yet, despite all of it, would she have done anything differently? As queen, her responsibility was to the whole kingdom, not just her companions—her friends.

Janaeus had to die. They couldn't risk him using the relic again. Especially now, when none of them were protected from his influence. If all their memories were rewritten again, they were lost. And whatever Aranok thought, they couldn't risk trusting the memory *draoidh*. He'd shown, by his actions, who he was. A man willing to send them all to their death to preserve his stolen power. Maybe if Aranok had been there, had seen Glorbad's limp body impaled on that black spike, maybe then he'd have been less willing to swallow the idea that the bastard was on their side. Maybe if his head hadn't been stuck so far up his own arse, he'd have done the job in private and prevented the carnage that came after.

But they were where they were and now was the time to be decisive. There wasn't much she could do before Mynygogg returned from the Reiver Lands. She hoped he'd managed what he'd gone to do. A return to war with the Reivers was a distraction they could not afford.

Samily and Rasa's mission mattered more than ever. What had been a wistful prayer was now an urgent need. They had to get a friendly memory *draoidh* onboard, or at least one who was prepared to make charms for them. One charm. Something.

The truth was only a weapon if they could prove it.

"Welcome, m'lady." The stable boy hobbled across the yard to greet them. "Hope yer journey was fine."

How to answer that? It was anything but fine. And she didn't have the energy, the willingness to lie, even knowing the boy's question was just polite conversation. She did her best to force a smile onto her face. Reminded herself she was the damn queen and she needed to set an example. A standard. Keep people's hopes up.

"Thank you. Can you tell me, has there been a messenger in our absence?"

"No that I know of." The boy took her reins and stroked the horse's nose affectionately. "You look tired," he whispered.

She absolutely bloody was.

Behind her, Leondar helped Dialla from her saddle as Darginn's family dismounted.

All right, Nirea. Stop feeling sorry for yourself and do your job.

She threw back her shoulders, shook off the fatigue and strode over to Darginn. "What will you do, now we're here?"

The man's grey face was as expressionless as it had been since Madu's office. "Not rightly sure, Majesty. We can get rooms for a while. Few weeks at least. Maybe a month. Don't suppose you've any idea how long it might take to sort... everything?"

Isadona took Darginn's arm and caressed it like a child's.

How long would it take? Hell alone knew. It was confident of him to assume they would succeed, after everything he'd seen. Maybe he had to cling to that hope. That the world would eventually return to normal. For the rest of them, at least. She wasn't sure Darginn Argyll would ever see "normal" again.

A wave of anger rose in Nirea. Frustration at their situation and anger at Shayella for what she'd done. What Janaeus and Anhel had done. The lives they'd taken. The lives they'd ruined.

She breathed deep. She was queen. She had a job to do.

"I imagine you'll be fine in that time." She smiled. "But if things get difficult, come to the hospital. Ask for Egretta. Tell her I sent you. They'll find a way to accommodate you all, if necessary."

"That's very kind, Your Majesty." Isadona gave a little curtsey.

"Aye. Thank you," Darginn agreed.

"You've shown yourself to be a loyal servant, Darginn. That won't be forgotten."

A hint of a smile, but it looked as false as the one Nirea gave back. She turned to her kingsguard and the woman she'd been avoiding for days. "How are you both?"

"Well, Your Majesty," Leondar answered, stiffening his stance. "Where to?"

Dialla managed a tiny "mm-hmm" and another false smile to join the collection. Her eyes barely lifted from the ground.

"I'm going to the hospital, Leondar. I'd be grateful if you would see Master Dialla back to her quarters at the university. Feel free to stay as long as necessary to make sure she is"—what the Hell was the right word?—"secure." *Secure?* Oh fuck it, he was a clever man, he'd know what she meant. *Make sure the woman doesn't slit her wrists the minute she's left alone.*

"Aye, Majesty."

But that wasn't enough. She needed to do more. Stepping forward, she drew Dialla into an embrace. "I cannot thank you enough for what you have done for Eidyn. You have saved lives and hastened the king's return to the throne. You served your queen. Followed orders without hesitation. You are a hero of Eidyn, Master Dialla."

It was slightly cruel, an appeal to the woman's societal culture. Her ego, in a way. But perhaps if she could help Dialla see the positive side to what she'd done, and give her a way to absolve herself of responsibility... maybe.

The master's arms came up, feebly, not quite returning the embrace, but making a show of it. Nirea could ask no more of her.

As she knew well, each person's trauma is a unique demon.

Samily blinked furiously, willing her eyes to focus. She raised a hand against the sunlight through the window.

Where was she?

Was someone screaming?

As her eyes struggled, she became aware of the weight in her hand. The Green blade hung limp at her side. Why had she drawn her weapon?

There was a bed. Samily nudged her leg against it and settled dizzily onto it. The room formed around her. It appeared to be a room in an inn—but not her room. None of her things were here. Nothing was familiar. It smelled as if someone had slept here, and the sweet, musky funk was not her own.

It was someone else's room.

Her blade was bloody. Heaven, what had bloodied it?

She lifted it, turning it over in her hand as if it were someone else's. Whom had she fought? Whom had she wounded?

A brown-and-white lump of fur on the floor provided the answer. A dog, bleeding from a pair of wounds where a blade had skewered it. Her blade.

Had she hit her head? Had there been someone else here?

The door was open—raised voices. Someone screamed, "Mad woman!" and another called for the guard.

What did she remember?

Rasa.

She and Rasa had come to Dail Ruigh. They were looking for... something. Someone?

Why couldn't she remember?

Something had happened. Something she couldn't remember.

Memory. That was important. Wasn't it?

Last thing she could remember was...what? Breakfast. Breakfast with Rasa and...They had a clue. Clothing. Clothing left behind by the person they were looking for. Yes. It was a person. Yes. Clothing. And Rasa had an idea.

Oh God. Oh, please, God, no.

Samily fell to the floor beside the dog's corpse.

"Rasa! Please, Rasa, no! What happened? What happened?"

She could fix this. Whatever had happened, she could fix this. And she'd be ready. Ready for whatever she found in the past. This would not happen again.

"Air ais!"

Samily shuddered as power burst from her, encompassing the widest area her will would reach. She pictured the inn, its grounds, the stables—she needed it all.

A strange woman stood beside the window. She had short black hair and crystal blue eyes.

Rasa!

The dog stood at her side. It barked and the woman recoiled. Whatever was going to happen next, Samily needed to stop it.

"Say nothing!" She raised her blade level with the woman's chest. "Speak or move at all and I will run you through before you finish a breath!"

The woman's eyes widened as quickly as her mouth closed.

"Samily? What's wrong?"

She turned to find Rasa had retaken her human form. Samily had done enough to change things. Thank Heaven, she'd done enough! "Rasa!" She battled back tears of joy, of confusion and frustration. "I don't know what happened! You were dead. Why are we here?"

Rasa's face hardened as she turned to the stranger. "What did you do?"

The woman opened her hands in what appeared to be genuine confusion. "You just walked in!"

"Don't speak!" Rasa raised a warning finger. "Not another word until..." She cast about the room, hunting for something. Samily felt the sword tremble in her hand. She was not fearful. She just did not understand why they were here. Or who the woman was. It was disorientating. But Rasa was all right. And Rasa seemed to understand.

With a leather belt, her friend bound the hands of the stranger whose room they seemed to have invaded. The woman pouted dramatically.

"All right. Now speak. What did you do?" Rasa asked.

The woman gestured to Rasa with her bound hands. "Are you really just going to stand there... with your tits out... shouting at me?"

"I'm sorry. Do you find it distracting?"

"A little." The woman seemed more unnerved by Rasa's nakedness than by the fact she'd just transformed from a dog, which was interesting. She must be a *draoidh*—that would explain why Rasa had bound her hands—to prevent her from making gestures.

"I am sorry that it unsettles you." Rasa moved to within a foot of the woman. "Samily's not distracted, are you, Samily?"

"No."

"Well, she doesn't necessarily seem to be right in the head, so..." the woman replied.

"She's holding the sword to your chest. I would not be so quick to insult her." Rasa stepped back. "Samily, this is the memory *draoidh* we've been searching for. She must have erased your memory."

Samily's head felt light as the room tipped a little sideways. Rasa grabbed her elbow. "Whoa! All right, let's get you sat down." The metamorph lowered Samily back onto the bed. It felt good to have something solid beneath her. The weight in her hand lifted as Rasa took the sword from her. It was forbidden for a Thorn to surrender their Green blade, but in the circumstances, she wasn't worried about it.

"Now," Rasa said firmly. "Fix her."

"I didn't do anything to her!" the woman protested. "You two barged in here and she went odd! I'd barely drawn breath to ask what the Hell you wanted."

"Your name is Quellaria. You're a memory *draoidh*. We've been looking for you to ask for your help. Clearly, when we asked, you did not respond well."

Quellaria was silent for a long time. "What?"

Samily's head spun even worse than before. She lay back on the bed, resting her head against the wall. The cool stone was a helpful focus, a grounding. She closed her eyes against unstable reality.

"I'll explain, but first, fix her, or I'll stab you myself. Touch her. Say '*clìor*.' That's it. No other word leaves your mouth."

There was a shuffling of bodies and Samily felt a clammy finger against her forehead.

"Clìor."

A wave of memory rushed back. They'd entered the room. Samily explained who they were. Quellaria had refused—told them she had no interest in helping. Samily insisted, and then... it was blurry. The woman had said some *draoidh* words and... the dog. She was afraid of the dog. It was dangerous. Rabid. It had to be put down. S'grace, she'd murdered it. Murdered her. Rasa. More *draoidh* words and... nothing. Next thing, she was standing in the room alone with Rasa's body and no idea why.

The room began to settle as Samily sat up.

Rasa confirmed the door was locked and waved Quellaria onto a chair.

"How you feeling, miracle girl? Ready to take this back?" Rasa proffered the blade. Samily took it firmly, the familiar weight now a comfort in her hand. She stood and stretched, cracking her neck.

"Can I speak now?" Quellaria asked Rasa.

"You may."

"What the fuck?"

Rasa turned to Samily. "May I explain?"

Could she reveal Samily's skill? It had come in extremely useful just now. Mostly because Quellaria did not know about it. Aranok was always saying how he kept his abilities from others because it gave him an advantage. It seemed to Samily that this was exactly such a case. Since she'd been a child, she'd kept her healing talent hidden because Meristan told her it had to be so. She'd resented that. She wanted to help people. But she did as she was told, because Meristan was her guardian and, later, the head of the Order. And she trusted him.

And maybe he'd been right. To an extent. But it had never been her choice. As soon as it was her choice, it had felt like a relief to finally tell people what she could do. To be able to use her gift, to be depended upon. But here, now, in this moment, it was her choice, and her choice could be different.

"Actually, I would rather you didn't."

Rasa's first reaction was surprise, which gradually became understanding, Samily felt. And maybe respect. They'd gotten to know each other well these last days, sometimes staying up later than they should have just…talking. And now, Samily felt she understood her friend's intent without need for words. It was intimate and comforting. It felt good.

"Would one of you please tell me what the Hell is going on? And considering I'm sitting, I'd really appreciate it if you'd put those things away." Quellaria nodded at Rasa's chest.

"Here's what you need to know." Rasa turned back to the memory *draoidh*. "My friend is a White Thorn and I am a graduate of the university. I know how your skill works. And you're not going to use it on us. Are you?"

"No?" The woman's tone was condescending. Samily did not like it.

"Good. Now, as a memory *draoidh*, you are immune to the effects of your own skill. Meaning you are one of the few people who know that Janaeus is not the king. Mynygogg is. Correct?"

Quellaria's eyebrows rose. It was the first time she'd seemed genuinely unnerved.

"Your king requires your help," Rasa continued. "We will take you to him, and he will explain how. Agreed?"

"If you're giving me a choice, then no. Not agreed. At all."

"Why not?" Samily asked. "Why would you refuse your country's needs? Your people's needs?"

"These people?" Quellaria looked to the floor and, Samily assumed, the people in the bar below. "These people are idiots and arseholes. I don't rightly give a solitary fuck about them."

That was not an answer Samily had expected. Or was prepared for. The idea that someone could ignore people in need was...incomprehensible. "Why not?"

"Why not?" That tone again. "Because they don't give a fuck about me, or any other *draoidh*, for that matter." That last part was directed at Rasa. "They treat us like monsters. Like we're something to be scared of. Ought to be locked up."

Rasa leaned in toward her. "They're scared you would do exactly what you've done."

Quellaria straightened in the chair. "They were scared before I did anything."

"That's how fear works. You don't dispel it by feeding it."

The woman tightened her mouth and stared defiantly back at Rasa before noticeably relaxing into her chair. "I'm not interested who's king. Makes no difference to my life. I reckon maybe a *draoidh* on the throne's a good thing."

"Even a memory *draoidh* who might see you as a threat to his throne? Someone who could undo his magic?"

A glint flickered across the woman's eyes. A spark of excitement, or devilment, perhaps? "Oh, you've not heard. There's been a messenger this morning. Good King Janaeus is dead. Long live King Anhel Weyr."

"What?" Samily almost struck the woman for saying something so vile. Anhel Weyr on the throne? The man who'd poisoned her? The man who'd worn the garments of God like child's play? *Never.*

"Explain" was all Rasa said.

Quellaria looked pleased with herself, relaxing even more. As if she'd drawn some secret weapon. "Apparently the laird envoy assassinated the king, along with the entire Lairds' Council. Anhel Weyr has been *forced* to take the throne in the absence of any clear heir." Between her anger at the words and the infuriatingly smug way the woman spoke, Samily felt her open hand ball into a fist.

"Hell, Samily, if that's true…I mean, it can't be true. Aranok wouldn't kill the Lairds' Council. Would he?" Rasa's voice wavered as she asked. Could it be true? Samily wasn't as sure as she'd once been. Everything she had known of the man would have said no. He was a good man. But since Lestalric…something had taken possession of him. He made poor decisions. Shayella seemed to have some hold over him, and she was no longer as sure of him as she had once been. He was erratic. Emotional. Dangerous?

"I do not think so." But she wasn't certain.

"We need to move even quicker, then. Get her back to Traverlyn. Let the king decide what happens next."

"Agreed."

"Hang on," Quellaria interjected. "Who said I was coming with you, Tits?"

Rasa had clearly lost any sense of amusement in this encounter. She turned with a face like thunder. "You can come with us, or we can hand you over to the guard as the *draoidh* thief who's been robbing inns in the town."

"Thief? I beg your pardon. I'm an artist. Not a bloody cutpurse."

"The result is the same." Samily sheathed her blade, grabbed Quellaria's bound hands and pulled her to standing.

Rasa morphed back into the hound she'd arrived as. Nobody would question or particularly notice a Thorn making an arrest, but they might wonder why she was accompanied by a naked woman. And they'd remember it. And they might talk about it. Discretion was of use to them now. Especially if Anhel Weyr really had taken the throne. He'd tried to kill Samily once already.

She pulled on the belt and the memory *draoidh* stumbled to the door. "Is Quellaria your real name?"

"It's the only one you're getting," she sneered. "You can call me Quell."

CHAPTER 38

Calcheugh dawn had an edge. The air crackled with—not excitement, more exhilaration. No, that wasn't it either. It was the hum of anxiety—the buzz of people living through an event that had changed their lives. Allandria covered her mouth with her hand. "Is this about us?"

Mynygogg pursed his lips, his eyes scanning the Reivers bustling about them as they walked up the hill toward the council chambers. Most talked in hushed, urgent tones. "I don't know. But it doesn't feel like it."

She wasn't sure if that made it better. Or worse. Had something happened overnight? Burrox had offered them rooms for as long as they wanted to stay and suggested a formal meal with the council that evening. But the king had demurred, begging forgiveness for the urgency of their departure. In other circumstances, it would have been a diplomatic slight, but as things stood, Burrox had agreed. In fact, she wondered whether the offer had been no more than a show, an expected mark of respect for a foreign dignitary—the kind of reception she'd been expecting.

It still felt unreal that they'd stepped off their horses straight into that trial. And how close they'd come to losing everything. God, it was...it was unthinkable. She wondered whether Mynygogg would sugar the story for Nirea—omit how he'd all but offered up his own life. She'd be furious and terrified. Allandria hated to think how she'd have reacted if she'd had to go back and tell the story herself. Thank God Burrox had changed his vote.

When they'd discussed it the previous evening, before they both collapsed into a long-needed sleep, she'd expressed her surprise that Burrox hadn't voted with them from the beginning. But Teyjan's insight had made sense of it for Mynygogg. Apparently the Reiver peace was not as strong as it might be, and the breakdown of the alliance with Eidyn had prised open cracks thought healed.

It was fascinating to learn just how interconnected societies could be, and how seemingly isolated events in one country could directly affect another. The kinds of things rulers had to consider—the kinds of things she was going to have to start considering as Nirea's envoy. Politics and economics. God, the thought dulled her mind. She was not a diplomat. But then, neither was Nirea—not by nature. Maybe that was why she saw the potential in Allandria.

Still ten yards from the council doors, they heard raised voices inside. Mynygogg caught her eye and grimaced. That didn't seem good. Burrox had asked for the opportunity to see them off this morning, despite their early start. But something had started even earlier.

"Tread carefully." Mynygogg opened the giant door with a creak. "This could be a bonfire in search of a spark."

"You ordered this. Admit it!" Standing in the dirt beside the still-smouldering brazier, Hombuck towered over the portly form of Dacred, who stared defiantly back up at him.

"I absolutely did not!" Dacred's ripe face was verging on purple. His eyes threatened to bulge entirely from his skull.

Burrox was equally vehement—the careful statesman of the council chambers jammed a finger in his counterpart's face. "You might as well have! Your words inspired them! Your hate and vitriol, your paranoia and nonsense! You infuse your people with the passions that drive them to violence!"

"How dare you?" Dacred repeated, his faux offence given in almost pristine performance. But the edge was there, the blunt, unbreakable edge of derision, daring Burrox to prove him wrong. "I tell my people the truth. Always. If Risimfar's actions drew ire from the common people, then it is him who should be held to account, not me!"

"Looks pretty fucking accountable to me," Hombuck grumbled, looking to Pebyl's cornet. The boy held his arm across his chest in a sling. "Funny they went for the boy and no me or Burrox, eh, Dacred? Wonder why?"

"How should I know?" Dacred's hands went up in mock confusion.

Lavole stood as quiet as ever, impassive, giving nothing away. Stamary, though, looked distressed. Her serenity had also been left in the chamber.

"You fucking know!" Burrox had lost none of his fire. "You spew this rubbish about 'northern bastards' and how they don't understand our culture. They've been feeding us for years to keep the peace, you bloody idiot! And asked for nothing but peace in return! Are you so fucking stupid you'd see our people return to starving just to satiate your own fucking pride?"

Dacred's face turned at that. But before he could respond, Stamary caught sight of Allandria and Mynygogg lingering just inside the door. "King Mynygogg. Lady Allandria. Please, join us."

Dacred turned, sweeping an open hand in their direction. "There's your problem! There's your aggressor! If anyone, he's the one you should be accusing! He's the enemy!"

"*Quiet*, Dacred." Lavole's words were sharp, if gently spoken. The Jethart chieftain cut her a vengeful look where she leaned against a wooden pillar, but his mouth stayed closed.

Mynygogg ignored the rant and responded as if he'd been offered a heartfelt welcome. "Chief Stamary, Chief Dacred, fellow councillors."

Allandria caught Lavole's eye, and the Hamhaig chieftain gave her the slightest of nods. They'd almost tried to murder each other a matter of hours ago. Had that bought her the respect of the quiet warrior? She hoped her willingness to defend her king and kingdom would be enough to maintain that respect. She would rather not have to earn it with steel.

"I am sorry to interrupt, we merely came to say our goodbyes," said Mynygogg.

Allandria admired the king's diplomacy. She was dying to ask what in Hell was going on and, knowing her, that curiosity was probably writ large across her face.

"But have we inadvertently caused some distress?" Ah. He was curious too.

"You've done nothing." Burrox was calming, but the anger remained.

"It's a Reiver matter. Thank you for your visit, Your Majesty. The Reiver council's best wishes go with you."

Dacred looked as if to speak again, but a dark look from Hombuck stilled his tongue. All that came out was an indignant huff.

"Maybe the council should adjourn for a bit. I'll escort our visitors to the gate." It was the first thing Risimfar had said, and it somehow took the pressure out of the room. Whatever had happened, he was obviously at the heart of it, and his calm seemed to settle the choppy waters.

Dacred threw his arms up and slapped his hands against his thighs in a show of dramatic exasperation, turned and walked away.

Burrox gave a resigned sigh. "Aye, fine." The chief extended a hand and leaned in close when Mynygogg took it. What he said to the king was too quiet for Allandria to make out, but the king's reaction told her it wasn't good. He looked to Risimfar and back, giving only a considered nod in reply. "An honour to meet you, Lady Allandria." Burrox made a small bow.

"It was my pleasure, Chief." She smiled in return.

"God be with you both," Stamary offered in that smooth, rich voice.

"Aye, safe home," grunted Hombuck, giving her a look and a nod that suggested something more, but she had no idea what so simply nodded in reply.

Lavole nodded but said nothing.

As Risimfar walked them down the hill shadowed by three Pebyl guards, he explained what had happened. He and the Pebyl delegation had been taking part in a traditional evening ceremony when a group from Jethart had attacked their accommodation. The resulting fight had left three injured—and one dead. One of the Jethart raiders. Risimfar's arm was broken in the melee, and one of his own people was still unconscious.

The Reiver union was even less stable than they'd imagined. The country was living on the permanent edge of a bloody civil war, and the breakdown of peace with Eidyn had nearly tipped it over. Ironically, there was more unity when the council had decided to return to raiding Eidyn. Perhaps that explained Burrox's first instinct.

Well, they couldn't heal the Reivers' divisions for them. For now, it would have to be enough that they'd fended off one war.

"What will Pebyl do?" Mynygogg asked as they approached the stables.

"For now, nothing. This is temporary." Risimfar indicated his injured arm. "It'll heal. The Jetharts who attacked us'll be punished, as they should."

"And Dacred?"

Risimfar gave a half grimace. "Dacred is a politician. There'll be no tying this to him. Not so's it'll hold up in council before the liber. Burrox was right. He just leaks poison on his folk and they do as they think he wants—which he does, he just doesnae want the responsibility. So here we are."

"You could take it as an act of war. But you won't." Allandria was confident, despite how little she really knew the boy.

"What end would that serve? War's nowt but a necessary evil, and I deem it unnecessary."

"Will your people accept that?" Mynygogg asked.

"They will. It's my choice, and they chose me to lead. If enough disagree, they'll replace me at Beltane and maybe things'll be different."

"I hope they don't. Replace you," said Allandria.

"Thank you, Lady. And I hope you'll forgive my wee deception yesterday."

"Forgive? I'll forever be grateful. And I'll pay more attention who I'm sitting next to from now on."

Risimfar smiled with a wisdom his youth had no claim to. "I look forward to seeing you both again, maybe in Dun Eidyn."

"At the first available opportunity, Cornet." Mynygogg shook his hand.

"I'll leave you with your escort." Risimfar gestured to the stables.

"Escort?" Mynygogg asked. They hadn't requested an escort.

"After last night, we were concerned about you making it safely back to Eidyn. Hombuck agreed to provide you with companions."

"One fucking night. That was our lot, was it?" Cuda led a horse toward them, followed by Teyjan and Jazere. Risimfar smiled with a little more mirth than was probably appropriate, gave a half bow and walked back up the hill.

"You're our escort?" Mynygogg asked.

"Apparently so. Chief said. Reckoned you'd prefer us to strangers." Cuda left a silence, perhaps hoping Mynygogg might disagree, giving her the option to go back to bed.

The king gave a respectful bow. "It is our absolute honour to have you as our escort, thank you, Cuda."

The woman hmmed and gestured to the stables. "Best get your animals, then, Your Majesty."

Mynygogg took her direction and stepped inside. Allandria paused before following. "Thank you. Thank you all, for speaking for us yesterday."

"No thanks needed," said Teyjan. "Just told the truth."

"Still. Thank you."

"Aye, all right, let's no make a fucking ballad oot it, eh?" Cuda turned and fussed with her pack.

Jazere smiled—this time all the way to her eyes—and made a series of gestures. Allandria looked around to see what spell she'd cast, but saw nothing. "I... Should I be looking for something?"

"She just said, 'You're welcome,'" Cuda answered.

"She... she can communicate? With gestures?"

Cuda looked aghast. "Of course she can. You think we'd just leave her with no way to speak to us? Fuck's sake, you northerners really are cunts, aren't you?"

Allandria was appalled. How had she spent so many days travelling with the *draoidh* and never known she could communicate on more than a basic level? "I'm so sorry. I just... I don't think I saw you communicating and it just never..."

Jazere waved away her apology with a shrug.

Cuda hoisted herself onto her mount with a grunt.

"Right enough, I suppose she doesnae say much."

"We've made a total fucking mess of it."

Aranok had brushed past Leondar, barging the meeting room door open. He was exhausted, and hungry, and a little light-headed, to be honest. But he needed to see her.

"Excuse me?" Nirea said through a mouthful of bread.

"We're fucked. Has there been a messenger?"

Nirea lifted a goblet and slugged back enough wine to clear her mouth. "Not yet." Her tone implied she knew there should have been, and that it was strange there hadn't. Why not send a messenger to Traverlyn, but to Mournside? Because he knew—or at least suspected—where they were and didn't want to tip his hand? They'd caught Rotan, but there could easily be another spy here. More than one.

"Weyr's taken the throne. Murdered all the lairds at the party, blamed it on us—on me. I'm the most sought-after criminal in the history of Eidyn for assassinating the king and the Lairds' Council!"

Aranok slumped into the chair opposite Nirea and helped himself to a chunk of the bread on her plate. "So well done."

"Well done?" Nirea had found her voice, and it was angry.

Aranok didn't care. He'd had three days of skulking on foot across the Black Meadows. He'd run out of rations the day before. He'd left his family behind to face God knew what and all of it might have been avoided if Nirea had just fucking listened to him. And he'd had three days to stew on that, so it was coming out hot.

"Yes. Well done. Murdering Janaeus gave Anhel exactly the opening and the excuse he needed. Now he's king, the people think he's a hero and I'm a traitor. Oh and the news is out about Madu too, so everyone we care about is in danger. Of course, I couldn't stay in Mournside to do anything about it, because I'm a fucking traitor!"

Leondar stuck his head around the doorframe. Nirea raised a hand to him. "It's fine. Close the door." Once it was shut, her demeanour changed. "Who do you think you're fucking talking to?"

"The woman who didn't listen to me and threw away her kingdom." He was angry. And he wanted to hurt her. She deserved it. This was her fault.

Nirea rose and leaned on the table. "You are the problem here, Aranok. You're unstable. You defended Shayella, despite everything she's done. Hells, you should see the mess Darginn's in! She did that. She fed the man to her Dead child. How can you defend her?"

"It's not about Shay!" But he felt the fire of that argument rise in him too. Maybe it was about Shay. Some of it. Maybe it was his frustration that without the relic, they had no way to cure the Blackening without killing her. And maybe he knew he was going to have to face that soon. He felt the sting of guilt over Darginn. She was right. About him. And she knew it. She knew how Aranok felt about what had happened to him, and she was using it against him. Hitting back at him the same way he had lashed out at her.

Well, fuck her.

"What about Dialla? How's she doing?" Nirea's face paled. Not good, then. He guessed the master might not be recovered. She'd been a damaged mess last he'd seen her.

"I wouldn't have had to ask her to do the job if you'd done yours." Nirea's voice was low. Like an animal bracing to attack. "Your task was to get the relic or—"

"Or what?" he demanded. There had been no "or." They'd never discussed what to do if the heart had been destroyed. Aranok had never even imagined Janaeus would do it. But he was clever. He'd *been* clever. But also stupid. Naïve and weak and stupid. A boy masquerading as a man. And Anhel had twisted him like toffee, moulded him into the illusion he could hide behind.

"Or do what was necessary to restore Eidyn to Mynygogg."

What was necessary. That phrase hid a wealthy history of sin. "You want to justify your actions with your successes, you might want to take a look around, *Your Majesty.* You've only made things worse."

"You could have killed Janaeus in private, in that bloody room, and spared us the entire chaos. Spared Dialla from having to do it for you!"

Aranok swept the plate from the table between them, scattering bread and meat across the floor. "I would have returned Mynygogg to the throne peacefully if you hadn't bloody interfered! If you'd listened to me and helped me kill Anhel, we'd be halfway back to Dun Eidyn by now! But you can't do that, can you? You can't do subtlety or complexity. You treat every problem like a beast to slay—cut off its head and call it victory! Your bloody stubbornness is the problem!"

Nirea's face was turning red, and Aranok could feel heat spreading up the back of his neck. The anger, the frustration, the pain, the guilt, the fear—everything he'd been drowning in for days threatened to overwhelm him.

"For God's sake, we've had this argument!" the queen bellowed. "You trusted Janaeus! He was lying to you. About everything. Maybe he still had the relic. Maybe he was sending us into *another* trap with Weyr. Like the one that killed Glorbad. Or the one that killed Conifax."

Aranok felt that like a hammer. "Don't. Don't use him to bait me. Do not."

Nirea brought her tone down, glancing to the door as if she were worried who might overhear. Or who might enter. "Aranok, you are compromised. You are compromised by your attachment to Shayella and you were compromised by your connection to Janaeus. You have made poor judgements. Reckless decisions. Choices that have put your real friends at risk, as well as thousands of innocent lives. Your loyalty is divided. Until you recognise that fact, you are a child with a blade—as likely to cut your friends as your enemies."

"So I'm not loyal enough because I'm a *draoidh*? Is that it?"

Her eyes darkened. "You know that's not what I said."

The fire burned down as Aranok's energy dwindled. He needed a real meal. The hunger was so strong he felt sick, and the mouthful of bread he'd scarfed down in anger had only made it worse. "Fine. We'll see what Mynygogg thinks when he gets back."

Nirea sighed through her nose and crashed back into her chair. "Bloody Hell, Aranok, whose idea do you think it was for me to come with you?"

What?

"You didn't think it odd that he insisted I come with you, and he took Allandria? You think I wanted to be away from him? I just got him back!"

Aranok fumbled for words, but none came easily. "I don't... I..."

"He suspected you wouldn't kill Janaeus after the way you reacted to Shayella. And Hell, we couldn't ask Allandria to do it, she's..." Nirea paused, as if she'd been on the verge of saying more than she should. "She's more loyal to you than to Eidyn. She'd have done what you asked."

Exactly. Allandria would have followed him. Trusted him. Believed in him. God, he felt her absence like a chasm in that moment. If she'd been there, or here, everything would have been better. More bearable. He'd be able to breathe, to think, to... live. If she were there, everything would be better. They would have done it the right way.

But she wasn't. And it had all gone to shit. Because Mynygogg hadn't trusted him.

Aranok threw the door open and stormed into the hospital corridor. "Fuck you. And fuck your king."

CHAPTER 39

Nirea took a moment to calm herself before leaving the meeting room.

Whatever else Aranok had given her to deal with, and it was a lot, there was one thing she had to do right now. If she waited, if she delayed at all, she might talk herself out of it, and that would be unforgivable.

"Leondar?" The giant guard turned rigidly as she stepped into the hall. "Oh, please, I need you to be less... formal. This is not Dun Eidyn."

"Majesty." He nodded but made no sign of actually relaxing. Allandria would have been slumped in a chair, feet up on another, most likely. Yet still completely alert. Leondar made her feel safer in the castle, but here, in their makeshift home, his stuffiness was just a reminder of everything they didn't have. Like a solid gold spoon in a pauper's kitchen. She would have to work on him.

"Leondar, we have to make a visit." Indeed, it was "we." She wasn't taking him as a guard, though he'd hardly have allowed her to wander off alone anyway. But that wasn't why she needed him.

The crisp evening air helped clear her head on the walk to the university quarter. She'd all but gotten used to the constant daylight. There were long shadows on the way, but no route into town for the Thakhati, even if they got past the wall of vegetation the nature *draoidhs* had built. She wondered how long it would take Aranok to create a stone wall around Traverlyn. The hospital and the university buildings had been constructed with the assistance of magic, but also with the work of stonemasons, blacksmiths and joiners. While there were plenty of those in Traverlyn, it would take them an age to produce the materials for a wall around the entire town. Perhaps a decade. But could an earth *draoidh* simply grow one from the earth that would be as safe and substantial as the ones around Auldun, Haven and Mournside?

She didn't know, but they might yet have to find out. If Traverlyn were to become the home of the rebellion, it would need fortifying. The idea of it as open to all was laudable, but not when the "all" included demons and Thakhati. And Eidyn's army under Anhel Weyr's control. Hell, how would they ever fight a war against their own people?

They wouldn't. Mynygogg wouldn't allow it. In truth, he might let Weyr win before he'd harm the people of Eidyn again. But that wouldn't help them in the long term.

Hard choices were coming. And she'd have to help Gogg navigate them, steering him toward some unpalatable decisions. Just like she'd had to make.

Leondar didn't say anything when they arrived at the door. Should she have forewarned him? Had he already heard? Aranok was hardly quiet. Maybe. Either way, he would know in a moment.

Dialla answered the door in what appeared to be a silk dressing gown. She retained some trappings of her family's station, then. And why not? Why dispose of all home comforts just because home itself is not comfortable? If anything, Nirea thought she was more entitled to some luxuries.

Especially now.

The master still looked drained. But there was more life in her eyes than Nirea had seen the last time they parted. Time heals all, they say, but only because they don't know what else to say to pain. It never heals, you just learn not to think about it. Nirea was about to inflict another undeserved wound on this woman.

"Your Majesty." Dialla manufactured a smile. "Leondar." The smile solidified as she saw the big man. Whose comfort had Nirea brought him for, really? Dialla's or her own? Maybe both.

"May we come in, Master?" She gave her her title, hoping she took the power that came with it. The respect.

"Of course. I'm sorry, I am not dressed for company. I wasn't expecting visitors."

"And I'm not dressed for visiting." Nirea gestured to her own shirt and trousers. Not the ceremonial garb of a queen of Eidyn.

The room was not messy, but it was untidy in a way Nirea imagined it would not usually be. Cleaners surely came regularly to the masters' chambers, but Dialla's bed was unmade, and the room had the musky smell of recent sleep. An open bottle of wine sat beside a single glass on a table at the fireside. The runner on the table was unbalanced, one side all but dragging on the floor. Unkempt was the word. Dishevelled. Disturbed.

"May I pour you some wine?" Dialla asked, moving to a large wooden sideboard.

"Please." She turned to her guard. "Leondar. Have some wine with us."

"Majesty?" His scowl was disapproving. Drinking on duty was an offence for which he'd have beaten the guards under his command. Rightly so, in normal times. This was not those.

"Sit with us." Nirea patted the seat next to her as Dialla poured for them all. "Consider it an order. You are off duty."

He inched toward the seat as if he suspected it may bite. "Majesty, is that... safe?"

Nirea waved dramatically at Dialla. "We are in the home of one of the most powerful *draoidhs* in Eidyn. I feel extremely safe."

Build her up again. Remind her how strong she is.

Leondar nodded and finally sat, bowing slightly to Dialla. "Master."

They surely hadn't been this formal in Nirea's absence. These two had made a connection, she was certain of it. It was the reason she'd brought him. Dialla would need him in a moment.

Nirea raised her glass high. "To Eidyn. To retaking the kingdom and releasing her people."

"Eidyn," the others answered.

Nirea drank a little longer than she might have. Slowly. Savouring the wine. Savouring the time before she said what she had to say. But there was no more time. She had another visit to make, and it would be no easier than this one.

"Dialla, there is something I have to tell you. I wanted you to hear it from me, because you deserve that. That and more. What you have done for Eidyn, for me, is an unrepayable debt. When the kingdom is ours again, I intend to try, regardless."

Dialla demurred, lowering her eyes.

Come on, Nirea. Stop dancing.

"After we left Greytoun, I have been told that Anhel Weyr committed an atrocity." Dialla looked up, eyes wide. Nirea leaned forward, reached for her hands, and drew back. Did she have the right to touch her? Instead, Dialla reached for Leondar and found his huge paw waiting for her, engulfing her own hand.

Good. That was right.

"I'm told he murdered all of the lairds at the castle. Everyone. Including, I assume, your parents. I am so sorry."

Silence. A deep, hollow, echoing silence that spoke of shock and unimaginable pain. Slowly, Dialla reached one hand out for the fire, stretching her fingers wide. Her hand seemed almost to flatten the heat for a moment, until she drew her fingers in and the light dimmed. As it grew darker, Dialla sat taller. Straighter. She ran the hand through her uncombed hair and turned to look at Leondar.

Only in that moment did it occur to Nirea that she had the power to murder them both right there if she chose.

And Nirea would hardly blame her.

But that wasn't who she was. Her stare was met by kindness from Leondar. Kindness and pity and empathy. Dialla was gripping the guard's hand so tight, she dug white halos in his skin.

Nirea needed to finish what she'd come to say and then get out of the way.

"Dialla, I want you to know, firstly, this was not your responsibility. It was mine. Mine and mine alone. I made the decision that led to this, and the weight is mine to bear. If you should ever doubt that, ever wake in the night angry and guilty, please, I ask you, as your queen, to remember that everything you did was under my command, and it was done for the right reasons. We had no way of knowing what Anhel would do. Aranok was as shocked as I am, and the blame has been put on him by Weyr, now that he's usurped the throne."

Hells. She had meant to leave that bit out for now. But her mouth was running away with her.

Dialla turned back to face her. "I understand, Your Majesty. Will there be anything else?" Her glass trembled only slightly as she raised it to her mouth and slowly drained it. The life Nirea had seen when they first arrived was gone again.

She stood, emptied her own glass and moved for the door. "Nothing. I apologise for interrupting your evening." Leondar began to rise, but Nirea waved him back down. "Leondar, I have reason to be concerned for Master Dialla's safety. I am assigning you to guard her until further notice." She stared hard at her loyal servant. He needed to understand her meaning. Not to argue.

"It will be my honour, Your Majesty."

Good man.

Leondar placed his free hand over Dialla's protectively. Nirea needed to get out. The woman would be caught by the expectations of Nirea's station until she did, and she needed to fall apart, to collapse and grieve her loss.

"I'm sorry for disturbing you, Master, but I wanted you to hear this from me." She nodded, but it was clearly taking every ounce of strength she had just to hold herself together. As soon as Nirea closed the door, she thought she could hear sobbing. Whether it was real or her imagination didn't matter, and it was not her place to intrude on Dialla's grief.

For now, she needed to be somewhere else. Anywhere else.

Samily turned the dead leaf over in her hand and felt a cloud of memory close in around her. The outcrop they sat huddled on might have been the same one she'd shared with Aranok and Allandria the night he'd begun teaching her how to control her skill. It likely was not, but by all she could see of it in the firelight, it felt the same.

Oddly, she felt a pang of sadness for that time. For the lost innocence, perhaps, for a time when she'd believed the war over and their mission was one of hope, to end the Blackening. That had been their only concern. Now there was so much more to fret about.

That night, she'd had concerns about Meristan. She'd worried about his state of mind. Now while she was delighted to have him back—really back—she had many other reasons to worry.

"What are you so miserable about, Mad Girl?" Quellaria took a bite of rabbit and grease spurted into the fire, hissing and spitting as it landed. She shook her bound hands and wiped the back of one on her dress. It was not made for travel, but they hadn't allowed her to pack anything else. They weren't prepared to let her out of their sight. So her elegant rose gold dress was now a dirty, dusty, greasy wreck. Samily would hardly have noticed but that the memory *draoidh* complained about how much it had cost her a dozen times a day.

It seemed odd, since she was certain it was stolen. Even if Quellaria had paid for it from the dressmaker, it would have been with stolen money. She had not earned it with service.

A stone hit Quellaria on the shoulder and she winced dramatically.

"Leave her alone." Rasa's voice was firm. "Or I'll put your gag back in."

Instinctively, Samily almost protested. She did not need protection from the barbs of this crass woman. But equally, she appreciated Rasa's instinct to defend her and did not want to appear ungrateful. So she chose to leave it be and simply address the question.

"I have greater concerns than where I might next steal myself a pretty dress."

Quellaria arched her back. "Oh, you think it's pretty? Thank you."

"That's... that's not what I... I meant..."

"She knows what you meant, Samily. She's trying to aggravate you." Rasa may have addressed her, but she was glowering at Quellaria as she spoke.

Why was this woman so intent on being an annoyance? And considering how uncooperative she had been so far, what were the chances they'd convince her to help even once they got her to Traverlyn? Samily could only hope that Mynygogg's persuasive powers would be more effective than their own so far. Though, in fairness, perhaps they had not truly made an effort to appeal to her. Samily did not really understand the woman, but Rasa seemed to have a better comprehension of her motivations. Perhaps if Samily understood them too, she could help persuade Quellaria to do the right thing?

"Why do you take pleasure from being unpleasant?"

The memory *draoidh*'s eyes widened in mock surprise. "Me? Unpleasant? I'm an absolute delight."

Rasa sighed deeply.

"What's wrong, Tits? Not amused?"

"You see?" Samily pressed. "That's what I mean. Why do you refer to her by a crass reminder that you've seen her undressed? You refer to her as if she were no more than her breasts. As if that one part of her defines her. You have seen her perform a miracle of transformation and yet you reduce her to... what? A joke? Is it intended as an insult? What is the point?"

Samily had said more than she intended, but once she'd begun, it had simply spilled out.

Quellaria took another mouthful of rabbit and spoke through her chewing. "Miracle, huh? I suppose a God knight would see it that way. So is your time skill a miracle too? Are we all God's little miracles?"

"My...?" She had not revealed her power. In fact, she'd carefully neither used it nor discussed it in Quellaria's presence. Had Rasa told her? She turned to her friend, mouth open.

"You worked it out," Rasa said flatly.

"Wasn't hard," Quellaria answered. "Once I had time to think about it. Only way all that gibberish made sense was if she'd turned back time after I wiped her."

S'grace, she'd given herself away before she even realised she had a choice in the matter. Perhaps she needed to be more circumspect with her abilities. Use them only when necessary. Be more careful what she revealed. If she was to have control of her skill, she might need to keep control of knowledge of it too. Master Ipharia's excitement came back to her, along with her words.

Only because they don't know you're a time draoidh.

Meristan's worry had always been that people would want to use her.

She had no intention of being someone else's tool. Only God's.

"If you know about time *draoidhs*, you've studied. At the university," said Rasa.

"And?" Quellaria's tone was defiant, but defensive.

"Skipped moral philosophy, did you?"

"Old Conifax's class? Hell, wish I had. Think I slept through a few. He was a mad old bast—" Quellaria stopped cold at the sight of the knife in Rasa's hand. "What's that for?"

Rasa spoke with a voice Samily had not heard before. "Master Conifax is dead. Murdered. You will not disrespect him."

Quellaria raised her bound hands defensively. "All right. I didn't know. No disrespect intended."

"You were about to call him mad bastard," said Samily. "What did you intend, if not disrespect?"

The *draoidh* turned to her. "Well, aren't you full of the piercing questions, Mad Girl?"

"Questions which you do not answer because, I assume, you have no answer. You have no substance, Quellaria. You are a jester and your every word is tipped with poison. Your thoughts are meaningless except as a means to manipulate others. You are selfish beyond redemption and unnecessarily cruel."

The calm veneer slipped then, and Quellaria's eyes flashed anger. "You don't know anything about me, girl. You don't get to judge me."

"Of course not. Only God will judge you." Samily leaned toward her and lowered her voice. "I will merely send you to God, should you give me reason."

Samily stared up at the cloudy mass of dark grey above her. Her prayers usually settled her, but they had not come easy tonight. She'd prayed for clarity. For peace. She trusted God in everything, but people had free will, and their choices had consequences.

Was there something more she could be doing? Should be doing? The Blackening needed to end. That had to be their first priority. Once that was done, they could restore Mynygogg to the throne. He seemed a good man and Meristan believed in him. Surely it would be God's will that he should rule Eidyn over a scoundrel like Anhel Weyr.

But she also worried over the envoy. Aranok was crucial to so much, and he was unpredictable. Unstable? He had no faith to guide him, which bothered her for the first time. She had previously believed he would do the right thing; now she feared he may not be able to see what the right thing was. A misguided righteous man was a dangerous thing.

What should she do?

Sleep was not going to come, so she might as well take over the watch and let Rasa rest. She'd barely sat up when the metamorph spoke.

"You've been awake the whole time, haven't you?"

"How did you know?"

"You breathe differently when you sleep."

Samily pulled her legs up and leaned on her knees, feeling the warmth of the low fire on her face and hands. Rasa was a ghost of flame across from her, and Quellaria a dark, rumbling shadow.

"What's troubling you, miracle girl?"

How much should she say? Rasa was in many ways loyal to the envoy. And yet, she was Samily's friend. She was certain of that. Perhaps a question to tease out Rasa's thoughts? To see if she had the same concerns?

"Do you think the envoy is all right?"

Rasa cocked her head and rubbed her hands together. "I have to confess, that's not what I was expecting. In what way do you mean?"

"I am not sure he has been the same since Lepertoun. Since..." She was loath to remind Rasa of her ordeal, but it was difficult to even broach the topic without doing so. "Since we encountered Shayella."

"I suppose I've seen less of him than you since then. Since I was... indisposed." She smiled as she said it, and Samily's discomfort dissipated like smoke. "In what way do you think him affected?"

That was the crucial question. What did she mean?

"He insists on keeping Shayella alive, when executing her could free the Blackened. He protects her when she has done such... evil."

"So you want to execute Shayella? Is that it?"

Was that the root? It seemed... simplistic. But if Aranok were prepared to do that, would she have the same reservations about him?

"I suppose. That is the meat of it."

"Do you believe that is what God wants?"

Saving the most people? Protecting more from being harmed? She could not see how it was not God's will.

"I do."

"And Shayella? She deserves to die?"

"For what she's done?"

"What about what was done to her? What about her mind? If it is broken? Is it still just, still right to murder her?"

Murder? That was an ugly word for it. If anything, she saw it as putting the necromancer out of her misery.

"I believe it is. Think how many Blackened will die because we delay in saving them."

"Think how many *draoidhs* have died because the country has not acted to protect them."

That gave Samily pause. "But the Blackened are innocent."

"Not all of them. Some of them likely deserve punishment. Some of them likely deserve worse, for crimes they've committed. Is it your place to say which is which?"

"Only God judges, I merely—"

"But you have judged Shayella, haven't you?" Had she? Perhaps. But if she had, it was because it was so easy. So obvious. "Is that because of the Blackening? Or is it because of what she did to Darginn Argyll?"

"Both!" The answer was out before she intended to speak.

Rasa's eyes narrowed. "Is it? Are you certain? I understand your desire to cure the Blackening, Samily. I do. After what you and Meristan went through... and Vastin. I understand. But you were close to Darginn. You were close to what was done to him. Do you think, perhaps, it affected you?"

The smell of the roasting meat. The spit of the fire. The heat. The blood. The dark.

Samily turned her head to the side and retched rabbit meat onto the dirt.

"Oh! I'm sorry." Rasa was at her feet in seconds, one hand supporting Samily's arm, the other holding back her hair. The knight spat bitter globules after the stomachful she'd just emptied.

What had caused that?

"The rabbit must have been undercooked," Rasa said softly. "Here."

Samily took the offered waterskin gratefully and washed out her mouth. The acrid taste of bile lingered at the back of her throat. She drank heavily until its sting abated. Neither of them spoke. It took Samily some time to find an answer.

"I believe it does the most good to end the Blackening. And I believe Shayella's actions justify her execution, in service to God's children." There was a snort from her side, and Samily turned to see Quellaria watching her in the firelight. "What?"

"God's children?" the memory *draoidh* sneered. "Is that what we are?"

"It is what I believe, yes."

"So what about the pricks who treat *draoidhs* like animals? Are they still God's children?"

"Of course. We all are."

"You grew up in the monastery, right?"

Samily nodded.

"Did they know you were a *draoidh*?"

Rasa reached out a hand. "You don't have to answer her questions."

"I know." Samily could hear the fatigue in her own voice. "It's fine." She turned back to the memory *draoidh*. "No. I did not know. Until recently."

"Ah, I see." Quellaria flopped onto her back.

"I beg your pardon?"

Quellaria closed her eyes as she continued speaking. "You didn't grow up *draoidh*. You haven't lived through what me and Tits have."

Samily rankled at the repeated nickname but recognised that she'd used it as a deliberate prod. She chose to ignore it. "I lived a life in God's hands. I still do. *Draoidh* or not."

"Aye, very good. My point is you might not be so keen to off another *draoidh* if you'd had to grow up being spat at and abused. Might make you more sympathetic." She sat up, stretching her hands toward Rasa. "Am I wrong?"

Rasa threw something into the fire, kicking up sparks. "I understand what you're saying. But I'm not sure Shayella being *draoidh* justifies what she's done. She cursed an entire town. A contagious curse. In theory, it could kill the whole country. The whole world. Samily does have a point."

"Aye, and what was done to her? To us? Ask yourself, honestly, does this country deserve to survive?"

Samily was appalled. Surely nobody could really think that way. "You would kill the entire population of Eidyn for the flaws of some? You cannot mean that."

She flopped down again. "I assure you, I can. As long as I get out first."

"You would see me dead? I have done nothing to you."

Quellaria turned so quickly Samily actually recoiled slightly. "You defend a country that has done nothing to protect me from being treated like a monster. If I am God's child, where were you when I needed you? Where were the Thorns when I was spitting my teeth into the gutter? Where was God when I was beaten by a girl two years older than me while her friends laughed?" Quellaria's face melted into a grin. "Did I just not pray hard enough?"

"You're not being fair," said Rasa. "Samily wasn't even born when you were a child."

Quellaria stared at her a moment. "Aye. Because that's the point I was making. You know what, Tits? You might be worse than her. Because you've been through it, haven't you? I can see it. You've had the same shite as me, and still you'll kidnap a *draoidh*, execute a *draoidh*, for the country, for the people that shat on you? For what? So one day they might treat you like a human being?"

Rasa cleared her throat. "Not everyone is as bad as you think. King Mynygogg—"

"King Mynygogg? My life was no different under him than it was under Hofnag. You know what changed? It was a bit harder for the guard to arrest me."

She was so full of anger. Of hatred. Her corrosive behaviour made sense now that Samily saw the pain beneath the veneer. "Perhaps it is you who needs to change, Quellaria. To be open to change. If you are only prepared to see darkness, you will never find light."

The *draoidh* looked at Samily in apparent consternation, then to Rasa and back again. "You think I'm the problem? Tits? You agree with her? Am I just too cynical, is that it?"

Rasa slowly rose to her feet, crossed the short distance to Quellaria and crouched before her.

"My name is Rasa. I am a graduate of the university. In a few years,

I will be Master Rasa. While I am sympathetic to your pain, I'm tired of your insolence. So you may either keep a civil tongue in your mouth or try to sleep with a gag in it." She dangled the strip of cloth from her hand. "It is entirely your choice."

Quellaria shaped her mouth into a dramatic frown. "All right, master. I'll be a good girl. Please don't punish me."

They stared at each other for a time before Rasa returned to her seat.

How would they ever get this woman to cooperate with them? They needed her to create memory charms, so that, in case Aranok did not retrieve the heart of devastation, they had a way to clear the memories of the people of Eidyn and remove Anhel Weyr from the throne.

Perhaps that was the best hope. She would pray that Aranok and Nirea had been successful and that the events as they'd heard them were a result of that.

Though why, if he had the relic, had he not already reversed Janaeus's spell? She hoped there was a good reason.

If they had to rely on this bitter memory *draoidh*, they were in trouble.

CHAPTER 40

In the early-morning light, Traverlyn hummed with life, as if the town existed outwith the hellfire in which Eidyn burned. Birds fluttered between trees; people hurried past, argued, flirted and laboured as if nothing in the world were awry.

Aranok was pleased just to get out in fresh air, after three days of clearing memories. He considered for a moment how nice it would be simply to stay here and live in this fantasy. With time, he could clear the memories of everyone in town, and Traverlyn could be an enclave of sanity and peace. It was already a model for the country—if only the rest of the country saw it that way.

But today, finally, he needed to take on a burden that was rightfully his.

The girl answered the door still in her nightgown. Students had a proclivity for sleeping late, he well remembered, but he assumed this one would be up with the sun. Though, with the demands placed on her, he could easily forgive her taking all the rest she could find.

"Hello?" The girl stepped back and crossed her arms. She likely hadn't expected an adult in the dorms at this time, never mind a man.

Aranok closed his eyes and turned his head away. "I'm looking for Girette."

"Who are you?" Her voice was as defensive as her stance.

"I am Aranok, envoy to the king."

"Oh! Oh. I... She's not here." A rustle of fabric. "You can open your eyes."

The girl had put on a thick robe. Aranok tried to smile comfortingly. "Where is she?"

"She'll be at the kirk. She's there every day. You know, for the..." The girl raised her hand and wiggled her fingers to suggest, he assumed, sunlight. The light from the kirk's orb. Girette was up even earlier than him. Good girl.

"Thank you. I'll find her there."

As he left the dorm, it occurred to Aranok that if he did not recognise the girl, nor she him, then she had not been to have her memory restored and did not yet know the truth. He rolled Korvin's charm between his fingers. Keft had wrinkled his nose at the state of it and suggested having it cleaned, but Aranok had resisted. He couldn't really identify why, except that it felt like another insult to his friend. Or perhaps it was because he deserved a little discomfort. A little inconvenience.

But maybe Keft was right. It did seem to give people pause in taking the charm, and they didn't need more reasons for people to be sceptical.

They'd already had one refuse.

The cook.

He'd really hoped to be wrong. That nobody in Traverlyn would reject the truth. That his father was an exception. But he'd known in his gut.

When she asked agitatedly why she was there.

When her eyes widened as he explained.

When she said almost the exact words his father had used.

"How d'you know it's not you's been bamboozled? How do I know you're not manipulating me?"

Keft had almost coughed up a lung trying to find a way to convince the woman just to take the charm, but she screamed bloody murder and would likely have assaulted him if he'd tried to force it on her.

She was certain she knew the truth already. She would not countenance an alternative.

She wasn't going to be the only one.

Aranok wondered if she was prejudiced against *draoidhs* already. If her bias affected what she was willing to believe. But it hardly mattered. If it was the case, half the country had the same bias.

How bad would it be outside of Traverlyn? How many would refuse having their memories restored? If they forced them, how many would still reject the truth? Had his father come round with time? Half of him wanted to go home and find out. The other half was terrified to. If they couldn't even get people to agree on truth, where would that end?

Civil war?

The steps up to Traverlyn kirk sparkled with dew as he climbed toward the massive oak doors. Inside, the sheer size of the space was imposing. The air seemed to hum with possibility, as if some presence slumbered there. If ever there was a place he'd be inclined to believe in a higher power, it was probably this kirk. Sound was deadened and his skin almost tingled as he worked his way around the edge of the room, down the sides of the pews. Light streamed through the great round window above the pulpit, its yellow tinge giving the room an even more otherworldly feel.

Maybe it would be nice to believe in something that felt like this.

Maybe he was just tired.

Footsteps on the iron stairs ahead, winding their way down toward him. At this time, he assumed it would be Girette and Keft. Bells did not ring this early, so there was no obvious reason for anyone else to be up there.

Indeed, a student led the way; white socks flashed below black gown. Her light brown hair was tied back in an almost severe braid that looked as if it might pull her hair from its roots above her high forehead. As soon as she turned down the last twist to face him, he recognised her. She'd been one of the first students he'd cleared. Had he known then who she was? That she was an earth *draoidh*? Hells, he couldn't remember. It was a blur of faces.

The girl startled slightly, then smiled nervously and continued toward him.

But the person behind her stopped Aranok in his stride. Not Keft.

"Laird Aranok. What can we do for you this morning?"

He hadn't seen her since he got back. He should have. He had been to see Vastin—and the boy wouldn't even know. He'd spoken to him quietly anyway. Told him about Glorbad. About how sorry he was. For both of them.

"Master Dialla. How... how are you?"

"I am well, thank you. Have you met Girette?" She was formal. Cold and hard as granite. Maybe he deserved that. Or maybe this was how she coped—playing her role, a master to her student. Perhaps the kindest thing he could do was play along.

"I believe I have, but it is a pleasure to see you again, young lady." He offered a hand, which the girl took. She was, what, thirteen, maybe fourteen? Maybe younger. He wasn't good with children's ages. He'd have asked Allandria if she were there.

"Laird Envoy." Girette made a light curtsey and Aranok almost laughed, but stifled it before he insulted her. The formality of it just seemed so absurd in the circumstances. Technically, it might have been appropriate. He'd never been good with protocol. But he hated people bowing to him.

"Please, call me Aranok. I've come to thank you. And to relieve you."

"Laird?"

Dialla raised an eyebrow but didn't speak.

"What you've done, Girette—taking over from Master Conifax, maintaining the sunspire—you're a hero of Eidyn." The girl blushed pink around a shy smile. "But this is too much to continue asking of you. You need rest, and to focus on your studies. You must be exhausted. I will take over. For now, at least."

"Oh, I... I don't mind, Laird. Really. I'm happy to help. And Master Dialla will keep my energy up." She was like a young child insisting she wasn't tired enough for bed. Perhaps there was some fun in this for her? Or maybe a bit of fame amongst her peers?

Then again, if he'd been asked to do this at her age, to perform magic well beyond his years and training, would he have given it up easily? Perhaps it was that simple. But still, it wasn't in her interest. "I have to insist, Girette. Besides, aren't you feeling a little... scattered? Jittery? Finding it hard to concentrate?"

She turned her head to Dialla questioningly. The master shook her head slightly and Girette turned back to him. "No, sire. Not at all."

How could that be? When he'd had Dialla propping him up with energy reserves, he'd been fractious and unfocused.

"If I may, Laird," Dialla said softly, "Girette is able to sleep each night. I think, perhaps, your experience is different from hers."

"I sleep very well." The girl nodded enthusiastically.

It hadn't occurred to him that Girette could be doing this without harm. And if she could, why was he still spread so thin?

Footsteps on stone drew his eye across the vast chamber. Just the priest, pottering. Making preparations for... whatever priests did during the day. The old man nodded at Aranok warily. Almost as if he could read his disrespectful thoughts. Or perhaps he just knew Aranok was not one of his herd. It didn't matter, he had no business with priests today.

"Still, Girette, I cannot let you carry this burden. I will be spending the day with Master Keft anyway, and he will keep me in good health."

Her mouth flattened and her shoulders fell. And now he recognised it. It was the disappointment of not being part of something bigger than herself. For all the awfulness of the situation, for a child like Girette, perhaps there was some excitement to be had from living through interesting times. Maybe he would have found it a grand adventure himself at her age.

But he'd actually seen the monsters her magic was keeping at bay. He'd seen what they could do to a girl like her. Would do, if her magic failed.

"Laird Aranok, would I not be right in saying that you will be spending the day with Principal Keft because you will be using magic throughout the day?" Dialla was still rigid, but he felt some familiarity in her voice this time.

"Yes, that's right."

"Then, with respect, why take on more burdens unnecessarily? Girette and I can certainly handle the sunspire and, as you can see, it is having no lasting effect on her, except to cause her deep and restful sleep. You do not have to carry all of these burdens alone, Laird Envoy. You will be needed for things only you can do. You will be called away from here. Why not allow those of us who can to help with the weight?"

She was halfway through the speech when he suspected she might not just be talking about the sunspire. Was it also an offer of understanding? Of absolution? Or was he reaching for something he wanted? The hint of a smile, perhaps? Though her eyes remained sad and cold.

For pity's sake, Aranok, the woman just lost her parents. Why would she be anything but sad?

But she might be right, either way. If Girette could handle the stone, it would help him conserve his own energy for clearing more memories.

Keft, of course, had suggested allowing another *draoidh* to carry on while Aranok slept. But he'd let go of his own charm for only a moment, and Madu had stolen it. Until they had more, he could not risk losing Korvin's. No matter how much he believed Keft was on their side. He'd been sure about Madu. Now he was only sure that they had enemies in high places.

Aranok put a hand on the girl's shoulder. "Girette, you are an exceptionally brave young woman. With Master Dialla's grace, I will allow you to continue serving Eidyn. The country owes you a debt. If you ever want anything, you only ever need ask." His eyes flicked to Dialla. He hoped she understood too. "I'm sorry this burden was ever placed on you. I'm sorry you have to grow up in this... mess. You will forever have my respect and gratitude."

He was racking up debts like a drunken gambler—Girette, Dialla, Darginn. But maybe that was the way of forging a rebellion: You inevitably end up in more debt than you can pay.

Girette nibbled at her bottom lip, looking up at him from beneath her eyebrows. "There actually is something..." Again, she nervously turned to Dialla. The master smiled reassuringly at her with all the warmth he'd seen before... before he'd taken it from her.

"I had mentioned to Girette that perhaps you might be able to spend some time with her. Since Master Conifax is gone, we have no resident earth *draoidh* on staff. It would be invaluable to her education."

Girette looked up at him hopefully.

Him? Replace Conifax? He wouldn't know where to begin. And the very thought stabbed at his chest with renewed pain. Conifax was only gone because he'd been helping Aranok.

And that, of course, made this girl his responsibility. Conifax would expect him to help her.

He would demand it.

"Girette, once we have returned the country to Mynygogg, it would be my pleasure to spend time with you whenever I can. I don't know that I'll be much of a teacher, but I'll do my best."

The girl smiled, her eyes lit with excitement. Even Dialla had a spark of happiness about her as she spoke.

"That is all any of us can do, Laird Aranok."

"Laird Aranok!"

Aranok nearly stumbled as he helped the student to a seat. The boy's eyes were glass and his legs had all but crumpled beneath a wave of restored memories. When he was settled, Aranok turned to the new arrival.

"What can I do for you, Tobin?"

The stable boy's chest heaved and his face was bright pink. "It's the king, sire. He's back. Says come quick—and bring Lady Samily."

Bring Samily.

Hells, that meant one thing. Someone was injured.

Allandria.

Aranok brushed past the boy and raced along the corridor, bounding down the stairs and out into the university quadrangle. He vaguely heard Keft's voice out a window, but whatever he said was lost.

Aranok barrelled through Traverlyn's streets, barely noticing the sharp pain in his bad knee begging him to stop. His body pulsed with fear, and the fear burned.

Allandria was hurt, and Samily wasn't here.

He couldn't lose her. She couldn't die. His arms trembled even as they pumped at his sides.

Faster, damn it, run faster!

A pair of men practically dived from his path as he rounded a corner and careened into them. Shouts of protest were lost to the wind.

Had to get to the stable. Had to get to Allandria. She had to be all right. She had to.

By the time he saw the stable's fencing in the distance, his lungs were on fire and pain coursed up his leg into his back.

It didn't matter.

Nothing mattered.

Aranok vaulted the fence and stumbled as his knee exploded in pain on impact. A small crowd was gathered around a pair of horses in the paddock. The animals had some kind of cot hung between them.

Oh God, how bad was she that she had to be carried?

A woman turned to face him as he crossed the yard. Older. Hair shaved to a grey stubble. Hard-faced. She nudged the figure beside her and she also turned.

The moment he saw her eyes, a shiver ran through his body and his legs crumpled beneath him. He landed in the dirt on hands and knees, breathing so hard he feared his stomach would empty itself.

She was fine. She was alive. It wasn't her.

"Aranok?"

He lifted his head to see her standing over him, utterly confused. His grin was so wide it ached.

"Hi."

"What…? Are you all right?"

"I thought…I thought…Tobin said you needed Samily. I thought…"

Allandria crouched in front of him. Goddamn, his knee ached.

"Did you run here?"

He nodded, still trying to get hold of his breath.

"From where?"

"University."

"The university? That's…" She stood and looked back the way he'd come. "That's, what, a mile away?"

"Is it?" It felt like farther. Aranok rolled over his hip onto his arse and brought his knees up. He was just about breathing normally again. Allandria was fine. Allandria was back.

She reached across and gently placed a hand on his cheek. "I missed you too."

God, he really had missed her. It felt like home had come back to him.

Wait.

"Who's in the cot?"

Allandria stood and offered him a hand to get up. He needed it.

"Teyjan. Reiver. Long story."

"What?"

She walked toward the horses, and he followed. "We had an escort from Calcheugh and—Thakhati. Just inside the wall."

Fuck. "It's bad?"

"It's bad. Took a hit to the head. Big one."

That was never good.

They reached the horses and the small crowd parted to reveal Mynygogg fussing over a man with a distinctive black-and-white beard and a florid red gash through his hair, matted with dry blood. He was lucky to be alive.

"Aranok." Mynygogg looked up. "Where's Samily?"

His face must have fallen, because the king's hopeful look faded. "She's not here. She's not back."

"Damn." His head dropped.

"Is that your fucking miracle shagged, is it?"

Aranok turned to confirm the words had come from the old woman to his left. First, he hadn't expected the tone from her, and second, people did not usually address a king so.

"You are?"

The woman nodded to the man in the cot. "I'm with him."

"Aranok, this is Cuda, one of our escorts from Calcheugh. This is Jazere." Allandria indicated a dark-skinned woman with radiant golden hair. She gave Aranok a solemn nod.

Allandria pointed to the prone man. "And that's Teyjan." He was an awful colour. The green-grey of rotting chicken. Barely a hint of life in him.

"All right, if Samily isn't back, we need to get Teyjan to the hospital," said Mynygogg. "Aranok, could you move the cot with him on it?"

Could he? He was shattered after the run. In fact, he was feeling lightheaded. Only then did the words Keft had shouted out the window after him come into focus.

You're low on energy!

The haze of fear was all that had got him there. He couldn't risk trying to transport a sick man even the relatively short distance to the hospital. "We'd better use the horses."

Mynygogg nodded. He understood. "Right, we'll have to avoid any narrow alleys, then. Let's get moving."

Tobin appeared across the yard. The boy must have followed as quickly as he was able. He moved nimbly, despite his limp. Aranok had a limp of his own now, as pain stabbed his knee with every step. He could do with Samily coming back too.

As they led the horses through the streets, Allandria pulled at his arm and they dropped back from the others.

"How are you?"

"Oh, I'm all right. My knee is just—"

"Not that, you idiot. How are you?"

"Oh, right. Not good. Things are... bad."

God it was good to see her again. To speak to her. To tell someone the truth and just... share it.

"Did you get the heart?"

"Janaeus destroyed it. To stop anyone undoing his spell."

"Fuck."

"I know."

"But that means... the Blackened?"

"I know. We'll find another way."

"Aranok, *is* there another way?"

He didn't know. He'd been trying to find one. Asked Balaban to scour the books in the *caibineat puinnsean* for some way to clear the curse without the heart. But he had nothing. "I don't know."

"Have you asked Shayella? If she'll cooperate?"

Of course, that was the most obvious option. It was the one most likely to work. Shay could summon them, the way she'd summoned them to the Auld Road, and try to release the curse herself. The problem would be those who were too weak to come and remained out of range for her retraction to work. Once they found one.

But those would be weak. Likely already dying. Unlikely to spread the curse further.

But the truth was, he hadn't asked her because it was his last hope. His fallback plan. If nothing else worked, then he'd ask her. He couldn't risk it until there was no other option, because...

"She might say no."

Allandria blinked slowly and nodded. She understood. "If she does..."

Then there would be no saving her. No justification for keeping her alive beyond the fact it was the right thing to do.

"Aranok, we're going to have to make that decision. Soon. The Blackened..."

He couldn't.

"I know. I'm working on it. Please..." He didn't even know what he was asking for, beyond a respite from this line of argument.

"What else? Does Janaeus know? That we know?"

Hells, they mustn't have come through any towns on the way back. Of course not. They travelled with Reivers. They'd have avoided everyone they could.

"Al, it's bad. Janaeus was...a puppet. For Anhel. But...God, he thought he was helping. By ending the war. He thought—"

"What? How did that help?"

"It didn't. It was a fucking mess, obviously, but...he was going to help us fix it. Help me."

Allandria shook her head as if trying to clear mist. "I don't understand. What do you mean he was going to?"

"Nirea killed him. Had him killed."

"Oh." They walked in silence for a while. Aranok didn't know what to say. To tell her how furious he was at Nirea's idiocy? A part of him instinctively held that back. That questioned whether it was justified. She would tell him if it wasn't. So he just waited for her to speak instead.

"Well...doesn't that make things easier?"

The casual way she accepted Jan's death was jarring, and it took Aranok a moment to let that go.

"No. Anhel took the throne. Framed me for murdering the entire Lairds' Council."

Allandria's eyes widened and she stopped still. "Anhel Weyr is king? The Lairds' Council are dead?"

"I did say everything was shit."

"Fuck."

"There's more."

"There's more?"

On one hand, saying it out loud was unburdening. On the other, he couldn't lie to himself about how truly awful their situation was. They walked again, keeping the horses in sight.

"We went to Madu, the head messenger. She was working for Anhel. Janaeus. She stole the memory charm. She destroyed it."

"We have no charm now? No way to clear memories?"

"No. We do. Got another one."

"From where?"

Aranok swallowed hard. "Korvin."

Allandria stopped, grabbed his arm and pulled him to face her. "You went to his parents?"

He couldn't even look her in the eye. Just shook his head pitifully.

"You got it... from Korvin?"

He nodded. She knew what it meant. A tear dripped off his nose onto his vest and she pulled him to her, enfolding him in her arms. God, if seeing her had felt like home, this was... everything. The smell of her neck, the feel of her body against his. It was so right. Was it wrong that he was thinking like this? She'd been angry at him when she'd left. Though she said she wanted to talk. Was this...? Fuck it, he was taking the comfort while he could. He wrapped his arms around her and sank into the embrace.

"I'm sorry," she whispered.

"For what?"

"I'm sorry I wasn't there."

He lifted his head. "We should keep up with them." The horses were out of sight now.

"We know where they're going. But yes, let's walk." She released him but took his hand and pulled him forward. He had no idea what that meant—if it meant anything—but it was nice. She didn't seem to be angry anymore.

He still had to tell her about Madu.

"Al, there is something—something bad. We've handled it... sort of. Nirea did. So... don't panic. All right?"

She stopped again and turned to face him. "Telling me not to panic is a really good way to make me panic."

Aranok's tongue felt like it might choke him.

"Madu claimed she had assassins on contract—if anything happened to her."

She waited, as if he'd stopped halfway through a joke. Perhaps he had. "And?"

"Darginn killed her."

"Darginn? The old man? How?"

Nearly cut her fucking head off, that's how. For a moment, Aranok was back in that room, seeing the animal ferocity with which he hacked at her neck. The frenzy in his eyes, the wet sound of the blade striking bone. "Cut her throat."

"Fuck. So...we have assassins after us? That's...I suppose that's complicating, but—"

"Not us. Our families."

Allandria's face drained of colour. "What?"

"Nirea went to Lochen. She warned your parents."

"What did they say?"

Hells, what did they say? He had no idea. Nirea had warned them. He didn't know what else. Had she said? God, had he asked? He should have asked. Did he ask?

"Aranok, what did they say?"

"I don't know. I...Nirea and I haven't spoken much."

Allandria looked at him as if he'd suggested they dance the rest of the way to the hospital. "What? Why not? Haven't you been making plans? Working together?"

Because he was still fucking angry with her, that's why not. But in the cold breath of Allandria's question, that didn't seem like enough. It seemed petty and like he'd neglected his duties to the country. And the king.

But the king had ordered Janaeus killed, apparently. And hadn't trusted him. So maybe the loyalty he owed was a little less than it once was.

"It's a long story. It doesn't matter. We'll find her. She can tell you."

Allandria nodded nervously. "All right."

They walked on in silence for some time after that. Aranok afraid to speak until Allandria had time to come to terms with all he'd said. The hospital was in sight by the time she spoke.

"They'll be fine. They'll just go."

"Go where?"

"Go. They're nomads. They know how to survive on the move. They'll go. Leave no trace. Live on the land. They'll be fine."

How would that work? How would they know to come back? How would they contact Allandria?

"How—" He'd barely formed the first word when she cut him off.

"I may not see them again. But they'll be safe. That's what matters." Her jaw was tight, as if she were clenching her teeth. Her eyes glistened slightly in the sunlight.

"Do you…do you want to go to Lochen?"

Allandria shook her head adamantly, but her voice was fragile. "No. I might just lead an assassin to them. Or they might stay, to see me, and leave too late. They're probably gone already. And I'm needed here, right?" The smile was frail, but it was there. God, she was wonderful. He was lucky to have her on his side. In his life. "Is that everything?"

No. It wasn't. Somehow, there was still worse.

"My father. He—"

"Is he all right? Oh God, Aranok, I didn't ask, I'm sorry. Are your family all right?"

"Yes. Well, they were. I warned them. Told them to take on guards." He hoped they had. Ikara would make their father listen. With her and Mum on the same side, he would give in.

Surely.

"Oh, good." The relief was palpable, and Aranok felt shame that her instinct was to fear for them when he'd been so…careless in asking about her parents.

"But he didn't believe me. Al, he still thought Mynygogg was the *draoidh*."

Her brows crumpled. "But you just…"

"Even after I restored his memory. He rejected it. Thinks I'm the one under a spell. Thinks I put him under a spell. He's adamant Janaeus is the rightful king and we're the ones believing a lie."

Aranok had rarely seen someone's mouth actually hang open, but there was no other description for Allandria's expression. It was a perfect reflection of how he'd felt about it himself.

"I know. And he's not the only one. A cook here refused the charm.

Believed the same. Janaeus is king and we're attempting a coup. Well, *was* king."

Allandria stared back at him in silence, and the meaning of that passed between them, the way things do between friends.

"Holy Hell. What do we do with that?"

He shrugged. They had all but arrived at the hospital doors. The Reiver women were carrying the cot up the steps, where a pair of medics waited. "Nirea put her in gaol."

"Gaol? For what crime?"

Exactly what he'd asked. "I know. She argued we can't have people who believe in Janaeus leaving here and spreading news of what we're doing. If the country thinks we're attempting a *draoidh* coup before we can get the truth out to enough people..."

She sighed, closed her eyes and nodded.

If that happened, there would be another civil war. Maybe bloodier than the last one.

With both sides absolutely convinced of two completely different realities.

Allandria smiled and released his hand as they climbed the steps. He didn't know what that meant either. It would wait. For now, they needed to get a council together.

They needed a new plan. Offering the truth wasn't going to be enough.

Somehow, they were going to have to force it.

CHAPTER 41

"You should have fucking trusted me!" Aranok roared across the table. Allandria didn't know where the energy had come from. His skin was nearly grey and his eyes glassy. They shouldn't be having this conversation now. But the conversation needed to be had.

She'd understood things were bad when she heard the story from Aranok. When Nirea explained it to Mynygogg, it got worse. She saw the gulf between Aranok's and her versions of the story. Both adamantly believed in their choices, as Aranok was proving, bellowing his indignation at the king.

Even Mynygogg's usually calm demeanour was looking fragile as flawed glass. Inevitably, it would shatter. "Aranok, you did exactly what I was worried you would do. You can't say I should have trusted you when I was right. And I did trust you. I have always trusted you. But you were in an impossible situation, where the right choice was to kill someone you clearly still felt a kinship with. Nirea could make that assessment without being blinded by her emotions. It was the right decision."

Aranok slumped back in his chair. His eyes were even darker. "If we'd done it my way, Anhel would be dead and Jan would be helping us restore memories."

"Or we'd be dead." Nirea's voice was ice. "Janaeus would have had us killed the minute he could."

Aranok's head snapped to face the queen. "He wouldn't. I know him."

He seemed to realise he'd spoken of the memory *draoidh* as if he were still alive, pressed his lips together in grim determination and scowled at Nirea.

She stared daggers right back.

Hells. It was worse than Allandria feared.

"All right, we are where we are." Mynygogg held out placating hands. "You both made choices you believed in. I have no doubt in either of you. But we need to work together now and decide what to do next."

He was right. Allandria was glad she hadn't been there. Hadn't been forced to make a choice. She genuinely didn't know who'd made the right one. She might have trusted Aranok, but his perspective on the Hellfire Club was definitely skewed. It was clear from the way he was avoiding dealing with Shay. And the passion—the pain he was feeling about Janaeus. And having to raid Korvin's grave—God, how could anyone bear being asked for so much? His childhood friends dead or broken—the only one left revealed as a monster. And each of them, in a way, fighting for the same things he wanted.

Respect. Justice. Peace.

"Well, that's a fucking mess too." Aranok put his boots on the table, his aggressively casual posture obviously intended to provoke Mynygogg further.

"In what way?" the king asked, keeping his tone measured.

Aranok explained about his father and the cook who'd rejected the memory charm. When he'd finished, Mynygogg looked to Nirea for confirmation. She nodded gravely. The king sat back in his chair, running his hands down his face.

"Well. That's not good." Mynygogg stared up at the ceiling for some time, as if divine intervention might provide him with some hope. Nobody spoke. There was nothing to say. Nothing would soften that wound. If people refused to hear the truth, what could they do?

"What did you do with the cook?" the king finally asked.

Aranok's look to Nirea would have spoiled fresh meat. The queen sat up higher as she replied. "She's in gaol."

"Hmm." Mynygogg's face was hard to read.

Aranok's was not. He was looking for a reaction from his friend. The lack of a clear one seemed only to agitate him further. "You have no opinion on that?"

Mynygogg turned to him, hands open. "I'm considering my opinion. Why are you so intent on needling me? What am I missing?"

It was a fair question. Aranok was being an arse. But Allandria didn't know what she could say that would stem that flood. Telling him he was being an arse was likely only to fan the flames.

"I'm waiting for a response! For some passion! To see that you actually give a damn about this bloody shit pile we're drowning in. You're the king!"

Mynygogg burst to his feet. "Of course I bloody care! You know I do. You know what this means to me! To all of us! Don't sit there pretending you're the only one who cares. Hell, I could walk away now. Leave the whole damned kingdom and go back to the Reivers. Live in Calcheugh or Pebyl. Is that what you want? Shall we just bugger the whole thing and ride south?"

The king breathed heavily, staring down at his envoy. She'd seen arguments between these two, but she couldn't remember seeing Mynygogg this angry. Hopefully Aranok would recognise that and rein in his own venom.

"Why the fuck would I want that?"

Or not.

Mynygogg sat again, visibly calming himself. "What do you want, Aranok? Why don't we start there?"

Aranok finally brought his feet from the table and leaned forward. "We have one memory charm and no *draoidh*. People are going to refuse it. A bastard has staged a coup and made me a criminal. What I want is to hear what your plan is, Your Majesty."

"For fuck's sake," Nirea muttered. That wasn't helpful.

Mynygogg leaned back in the huge wooden chair and breathed deep. "You're angry. You're angry that Nirea made a decision against your advice. You're angry I asked her to do it. And it strikes me that what you want is an apology."

Aranok bristled but said nothing.

"You're not going to get one, so get over it. I'm king. Nirea is queen. We have to make hard decisions, and ultimate responsibility for them lies with us. If you wanted that burden, you should have taken the crown yourself."

Again, he paused, allowing space for Aranok to speak. Again, the *draoidh* stayed silent. It was a battle of wills.

"So if you want to do what we've all been trying to do for years, if you want to take back this country and make it the better country we want, put your bloody ego away and—"

"You think you can do this without me?" Aranok interrupted.

"I will do it without you. You think there are no other *draoidhs* in the country? We're in Traverlyn, Aranok! I'm not limited in access to power." The king raised his arms wide.

That would have hurt, Allandria knew. And it wasn't fair, reducing him to his skills. He was so much more than that. It took her a moment to realise she could say so.

"That's unfair."

Her voice came out quieter than she intended. But perhaps a bit of quiet would help take some of the temperature out of the room. All three turned to look at her.

"Pardon?" Mynygogg asked.

"That's unfair. Aranok is worth much more than his magic."

Mynygogg's face softened. He looked to Aranok and back to her, retaking his seat. "You're right. It was unfair. I apologise." The last sentence was delivered directly to Aranok. He gave no sign of hearing it. "Allandria, you've said little. What are your thoughts?"

Oh Hell. She hadn't intended to interject quite that far. But he'd asked, so she'd better come up with something. Honestly, the idea of running away to Pebyl had been appealing. But she needed better than that.

"I don't know what I would have done in Greytoun. But I know both of you did what you believed was right. And you both know it too." Nirea had shown no real rancour toward Aranok. It was him who needed to hear this. In truth, she didn't believe he was angry with Nirea, but at the situation. At the world that had put him here, torn between two increasingly hostile pillars. At God, for all that. "But I don't think it matters now. We are where we are. We have to move forward."

Mynygogg nodded thoughtfully. "How do we do that?"

Hells, she didn't know. Her heart was a bodyguard, not an envoy. She didn't have the experience to make these kinds of decisions. But she was being asked to speak, and for the moment, she seemed to be the only one who could make everyone else in the room listen.

"I have serious doubts about gaoling people for what they think.

But..." Was she really going to say this? "I don't see another solution. If anyone were to spread the idea that we're the ones staging the coup against an apparently popular and decent monarch, we're likely finished. I don't like it—at all—but it makes sense, short of a better idea. So I think we should carry on restoring memories and gaol anyone who refuses. And hope Samily brings us a memory *draoidh*."

Allandria would never have believed she'd say these words, but on the cold facts of it, there was no better option she could think of. The people were under a spell. They were a danger to themselves and the country until the spell was lifted. They had to do it. But she hated it.

Nirea smiled approvingly, which Allandria appreciated, but she feared Aranok would see it as a betrayal. Was this where she was to be too? Torn between her new duty to the Queen and the man she loved? If so, it was only him putting her there. She'd said what she did because it was what she honestly believed, unpalatable as it was. If he took the huff with her too, then...

"You're probably right." Aranok stared intently at the table, his voice a lifeless dirge.

"You agree?" There was hope in Mynygogg's voice as he leaned toward his envoy.

Aranok ran his hands through his long hair, locking his fingers behind his head and puffing air through his lips. "I honestly don't know what else to do. If they're too bigoted to see the truth of their own memories—"

"That's not necessarily the case," the king interrupted. "For some, perhaps, but for others, it may simply be the difficulty of accepting their minds have been compromised. Every person believes they understand the world. They have a vision of how it works and their place in it. To have that threatened could undermine a person's entire concept of themself. It could be terrifying. It may just take time to adjust."

Aranok looked up at him weakly. "I hope you're right." He was exhausted. He needed either sleep or Principal Keft. There was little point in taking this conversation further. It could end very badly. She should ask for an adjournment—at least a short one.

"What about the Blackened?" Nirea asked.

Aranok's hackles went straight back up. "What about them?"

The queen stood and walked to a sideboard, spearing an apple with her knife. "I know what we discussed about Shayella, but we need another plan. If we're not going to execute her, we need to know she'll work with us, at least. Have you spoken to her?"

"She's slightly encumbered with a missing tongue at the moment."

"Hells, Aranok, she can nod her fucking head!" Nirea plunged the knife into the sideboard this time, the resonant thud rattling the room. "Or write!"

"Fine," Aranok answered flatly. "I'll speak to her. But until we can get to Mournside and get the wagons we need, and have the medics here ready to go..."

Nirea shrugged. "I'll speak to Egretta. Arrange the medics. When Rasa returns, she can go to Mournside, see if they're ready, yes?"

Nirea was pushing him to commit to a plan he wasn't ready for. But he had no excuse for rejecting it. He couldn't admit the potential fatal flaw—that Shayella might refuse. Even if she did, Nirea was making the right preparations. Whether Shayella cooperated or not, they could end the Blackened, and they needed to be ready.

Aranok nodded silently.

"Good." Mynygogg sat back in his chair, relief palpable across his entire being.

She felt for the king in that moment. The empty crown might never have weighed more. He'd already risked everything to secure peace with the Reivers. Now, while trying to retake his own throne, he also had to save the country from a plague its new king had all but inflicted on them. He'd just used a grieving, broken woman to do it.

Aranok was right. Shayella was a victim. But she was also a murderer. And the former did not outweigh the latter. Eventually, she believed Aranok would see that. But it would be easier for everyone if the necromancer just cooperated.

Hope was not a bud that flowered easily, but with every ounce of her heart, Allandria hoped she would.

Aranok closed the door softly behind him. He winced even at the slight click. Keft might have restored his energy, but he felt like an open wound. There was lightning in his skin and it was a battle to focus on what was in front of him. He needed to sleep. But he had to do this first.

Shayella sat with her legs curled under her, holding Kiana to her chest like a child's toy. The girl's eyes stared lifelessly back at him. Through him. She was no more aware of her mother's love than the stones in the walls. She wasn't there. Whatever it was that made her herself was long gone. Still, Shay smiled serenely, eyes closed as she hummed a gentle lullaby to the corpse.

A dank, musty fug permeated the room, making Aranok gag a moment until he became accustomed to it.

The girl was rotting.

If they were going to blackmail Shayella, it would have to be soon, before her daughter became unrecognisable. Hells knew what she would do then.

"Shay?" His own voice rattled in his head.

Quieter.

The necromancer sighed and opened her eyes. There seemed to be genuine peace there, in the world where it was just her and her daughter. Aranok almost envied her madness, that she could blind herself with a happy lie. He pulled a chair over and sat, meeting her level.

"Shay, we need to talk."

She gestured to her mouth, as though he had forgotten.

"I know, sorry. *I* need to talk. About the Blackened."

Shay's mouth puckered and the peace faded.

"Shay, I understand why you did it. I swear I do. But it's killing innocent people."

She hugged the child a little tighter, and the girl's lack of reaction left her looking awkward—more obviously lifeless. Her point was clear. Kiana was innocent.

"We need to end it. And we need your help." How much should he tell her? Did she already know the heart had been destroyed? It didn't matter. She needed to understand the options were limited and included her death. "The heart of devastation is gone. Janaeus destroyed it." What about Jan? Should he tell her that?

No. He had no idea how she would react. Better leave her in ignorance for now. No point introducing information that might sway her against them. Against him.

"I need you to understand the situation. People want you executed. I won't let that happen, but I need your help. Do you understand? We have to end the Blackening. Together. If you do that, I can protect you. I will protect you. Both."

Shay's head tilted as one eyebrow rose. She gestured to Kiana. For all her self-deception, she knew the girl was fading. She couldn't fail to smell it, even allowing for the familiarity that comes from living within a stench. And he had no answer to that.

No honest answer.

"We'll work something out for Kiana. Perhaps executed criminals." He was flailing for ideas. There were rarely executions in Traverlyn. "I'll talk to Mynygogg. We will come up with something. He'll agree. I promise."

An absolute lie. Mynygogg would be morally set against the idea. Aranok almost wanted to believe it himself. But he didn't need to believe it. As long as Shay did.

"Will you help me? To help you? Please?"

Something turned in her. The cynicism she wore like armour faded, replaced with—what? Sympathy? Pity?

God, how pathetic must he look that the mad, grieving mother pitied him? Aranok ran his hand across his unshaven face. The skin was like leather—clammy and lifeless. Yes, maybe he deserved her pity. Maybe that was all he had left.

Finally, after a decade of silence, she nodded. But before the smile could crack his face, she held up a finger. He nodded, confirming she had his attention, and she pointed forcefully to the girl.

And he knew everything that meant.

If he wanted to cure the Blackened, save Shayella and avoid a cataclysmic fight with Nirea, he was going to have to feed the Dead girl.

"What difference does it really make?"

It had not taken long for Quellaria to begin needling Samily again.

Rasa had flown ahead to scout the Auld Road to see if they should cross in the dark or wait for morning. They couldn't risk a fire here, out in the open of the Black Meadows, so it was a blessing the cloudless sky allowed them moonlight. It did, however, also make it colder—Quellaria was wrapped in a blanket. Even in the dark, the buzz of insect life was incessant.

They'd seen a few Blackened as they rode, including a small group that had somehow become tangled in the remains of a crop field near Lepertoun. Samily's armour allowed her to touch the man who'd limped toward them that morning, and a strip from Quellaria's dress had done the job of blinding him. She'd felt bad about leaving him wandering aimlessly without his sight, but he'd be less likely to infect anyone else. And they would be cured soon, she hoped. She had faith.

Which was where the conversation had turned, and Quellaria had begun her interminable interrogation.

"What do you mean?"

"What difference would it make to your life if there was no God?"

Part of Samily knew that the woman's intent was only to aggravate her, and that part could dismiss her as an irritant. But she was also heartily tired of this, and some part of the holy warrior in her burned with a passion for defence.

"You think you ask a clever question, but in truth it is a simplistic and ignorant one. You would as well ask a fish 'what if there were no water?' The fish would not exist to answer the question."

The memory *draoidh* smirked and rolled her head back. "That's no answer. You're assuming God exists! I want you to consider, what if there is no God?"

Samily turned to her horse, mostly because she did not want to show Quellaria that she was succeeding in irritating her. She began rubbing the animal down, which gave her something else to do than think about the infuriating woman. Perhaps if she just ignored her, she would stop talking.

"You don't have an answer, do you? Because there isn't one."

S'grace, even in silence she couldn't win. Fine.

"Perhaps you could clarify the terms of your question, since you do not appear to understand what you are asking."

"Huh." The woman let out a burst of air. "All right. Say everything is as it is right now, and I give you incontestable proof there's no God. How is your life different?"

She would be bereft. The loss of that love, that warmth and sense of purpose, would be hideous. But even the thought of it was empty, because she had no doubt in God's existence. She never had. "Honestly, I do not know."

"See?" Quellaria crowed. "That's what I mean! You're just a good person, Samily. You would do this shit"—she waved her bound hands in her direction—"regardless of God."

It was disarming that she'd called Samily good, and used her name instead of the derogatory "Mad Girl," while also arguing with her. She didn't know how to feel about that. "But I would not be who I am without God in my life. I was raised a Thorn because of God. Had I not been, I could have been a completely different person."

Quellaria waved again as if batting away one of the insects that buzzed around her. "Rubbish. People are who they are."

That made no sense.

"You think a person's upbringing has no bearing on their morals? What if you had been found by a Thorn, as I was? And you were raised in God and the Order? You could just as easily have been my sister, had life turned for you."

The horse whinnied a complaint and Samily realised she'd been rubbing the same muscle repeatedly. "Sorry," she whispered, stroking her mane and moving on.

Quellaria awkwardly fumbled her way to her feet, hampered by her bindings. "You really think so? You think I might have been a Thorn?"

Samily couldn't tell if it was a serious question or sarcasm. It could be either. So she would answer seriously.

"I do. Any child brought to the Order can become a Thorn with the right training."

"But God didn't choose me, right? So I mustn't be good enough."

Samily took a deep breath. Words from her youth came back to her. One of the Green Laird's earliest combat lessons:

Some battles can only be won by ending them.

"Fine. I concede your point. Perhaps you are simply unworthy."

Samily continued busying herself with the horse as a moment of silence passed in the dark.

"Hells, Mad Girl, that was brutal."

"What?" How was it brutal? She'd agreed with the woman.

"I mean, it's one thing for me to think I'm unworthy, but..."

Samily felt the air move at the back of her neck.

Instinctively she ducked forward, away from the *draoidh*'s hands, crouched and kicked out with her right leg. She felt Quellaria's knee buckle and heard the crunch of bones breaking. Her scream cracked the peaceful dark as she crumpled to the ground. Samily's horse startled and might have bolted but for its reins secured to the tree.

Samily turned to see the woman rolling on the ground like an injured child, howling like an animal. She needed to be quiet. It was too dark for Blackened to see them, but dark enough for Thakhati.

She dropped to her knees beside Quellaria and slapped a hand over her mouth. "You are going to get us killed. Be quiet and I will fix your leg."

Quellaria's huge eyes reflected the moonlight up at her. She did not understand. Of course, knowing she was a time *draoidh* did not give her the insight into her ability to heal. She stopped howling but continued with a stunted groan, whether out of pain or rebellion, Samily could not be sure.

"Will you be quiet?"

Quellaria nodded defiantly. Samily moved her hand from the woman's mouth and adjusted herself to kneel above the broken leg. She gently lifted the end of the dress to reveal her shattered knee. It was a mess. Even in the dark, Samily could see the immediate swelling, and her shin jutted backwards at an inhuman angle. It must have been extremely painful.

Samily placed her hands delicately on the knee, closed her eyes and spoke. *"Air ais."*

Quellaria grunted as, with a crack, her knee reset itself, pulling her leg back into place. "Fuuuuuuuuuuuck." The woman rolled onto her side and back. "Agghhhhh. What did you do to me?"

Samily opened her mouth to answer and froze.

A sound behind her from the dark.

She leapt up, drawing her sword from her back. Had Quellaria's screams brought the Thakhati?

A figure, walking toward them. Too upright to be Thakhati.

"Samily? Are you all right? I heard the scream a mile away."

Rasa.

Samily resheathed her sword. "It was not my scream." She stepped aside to allow Rasa a view of Quellaria, still prone in the dirt.

"Welcome back, Tits."

"What happened?" Rasa asked, ignoring the memory *draoidh* entirely.

"She tried to attack me while I attended the horse."

Rasa snorted derisively and looked down at Quellaria. "You tried to sneak up on a White Thorn? Are you an idiot?"

Quellaria pulled herself to a seated position. "Apparently."

"Well, I'm pleased to see your idiocy received its entirely predictable reward. Perhaps you might choose your victims more wisely in the future?"

Quellaria frowned. "Seems unlikely."

"Anyway, we have problems." Rasa lifted her clothes and began dressing. She must have been freezing, Samily realised belatedly. "We cannot travel tonight. But we should be entirely safe tomorrow."

"Thakhati?" Samily asked.

Rasa nodded. "Much worse than we feared. You said you destroyed many of them, yes? With Laird Aranok?"

They had. His sunstone spell had turned dozens of them to ash. "That's right."

"There are many more. Hundreds of cocoons in the trees. And I suspect I know why." Rasa pulled her dress on over her head and stopped to look directly at Samily. "There are hardly any Blackened left on the Auld Road."

Why would that...? *No.*

No, it couldn't be. They'd left them there in safety. They'd left them unharmed so that they could be cured. Healed. Saved.

"You think...?" Samily's voice caught in her throat. She couldn't even say the words out loud.

Rasa spoke them for her.

"I think the Thakhati have been harvesting the Blackened."

CHAPTER 42

Did you talk to Shayella?" Allandria asked, sinking into the armchair opposite Aranok. He lay, exhausted, across the bed, his head against the red stone wall. It was a basic hospital room, designed for a patient who needed isolating—who couldn't be kept on one of the massive wards at the heart of the building. Just a bed, a bedside cabinet, a small fireplace and a chair. But since all he did in it was sleep, it was more than he needed.

Another evening of clearing memories. Another refusal. This time, a member of the city guard. One of the last people they needed against them. If Traverlyn was producing people who refused the charm, how bad would it be in Mournside? Or Dail Ruigh? Or Haven? Getting the army onside would be a priority, but if they were not inclined to listen?

It was a bloody mess. All of it.

"I spoke to her." At least with Allandria he could tell the whole truth. "She agreed." The archer's face lit with surprise. "But only if we feed her daughter."

"Oh, shit. How do we do that?"

He'd had a thought about that. It wasn't a good thought. And he knew what she would say.

"Rotan. What if we just…?"

He watched Allandria's face fall as she realised what he was asking. "Aranok, are you insane?"

"I know, I know, but... hear me out. He's going to be executed anyway. This way, we use his death to do something. To cure the Blackened!"

Allandria blinked at him. A lot. "What?"

It was a horrible idea. But on his understanding that the flesh had to be fresh, and not from an old corpse, he didn't have a better one. Not one he could live with, anyway. He could barely stomach this one, and he'd been sitting with it for hours. "Why wouldn't that work?"

Allandria stood, placed a hand against her forehead as if to keep her brain from exploding and paced the space between them. "For a start, it's hideous! But even if we get past that, which I definitely am not, you can't just execute him, Aranok. He has to go to trial. How are we going to organise that when you're the most wanted man in Eidyn? And I imagine I'm not far off, what with..." She waved her hand back and forth between them.

"Al..." Aranok had no idea what to say next. He needed a justification, a reason why it was acceptable. And the truth was, he really wanted the little fucker dead. He wanted to do it himself. "It's that or dead hospital patients!"

Allandria stopped pacing and looked at him with something close to the pity he'd seen from Shay. It hurt even more from her. "Aranok, what are you doing? You're talking about feeding the deceased to a Dead child. Are you... all right?"

Was he? He didn't know, to be honest. The words to answer wouldn't come. All he could do was drop his shoulders and look at his feet.

After a moment, Allandria sat beside him and wrapped an arm around his shoulders. "You're not. Are you?"

Where to begin?

"I don't... It's just... I don't know what else to do."

"About what?" Her voice was calm. Soothing.

"All of it. It's all a fucking mess. And it's my fault."

"How is it your fault?"

And there was the question. The one that scratched at the sickening truth. That all of this was avoidable. If only he'd acted differently. If only he'd been different. Could he even say the words out loud?

"I was late."

"Late? For what?"

He'd opened the door now. Might as well step through. His heart raced, pounding against his ribs.

"For Korvin," he whispered. "I was late."

"I don't understand." She sat back from him, so as to see his face. "When?"

He was going to have to spell it out. All of it. The shameful truth he'd been hiding from for seven years. The black hole he'd fought a rebellion to climb out of. The stain he hadn't even been able to tell Mynygogg.

"I was supposed to be at his performance... that day. Help him pass the hat for coin. But I was late. I was"—he pounded his fist into the mattress, hunting for the strength to finish his confession—"I was fucking a girl from the tavern. And I didn't want to leave. So I was late. I was late, and Korvin died."

With the weight of his guilt released came a huge, racking sob and tears streamed down his face. It was difficult even to catch his breath as he gasped out the years of pain.

It was all his fault. Without Korvin's death, without him drunkenly swearing revenge on the whole country, they'd never be here. Jan and Shay wouldn't have succumbed to Anhel's manipulation, maybe Kiana would be alive. Emelina would know her real father. The world of possibilities was endless, if only he hadn't been such a selfish, stupid prick.

The bed shifted as Allandria stood. He looked up, blinking away tears, to see her look of horror and surprise. Exactly what he deserved.

"My God, Aranok."

"I know."

"What? No, no, you don't know." She knelt at his feet and took his hands in her own. "You don't know anything."

Was she crying too? It was difficult to see.

"You think Korvin's death was your fault because you weren't there to save him? You've been living with this?" She released his hand and cupped hers to her face. "Why didn't you tell me?"

"I didn't know how. I can't... I can't bear it."

"Aranok, you cannot save everyone. You can't. It's not your responsibility."

He could hear the words, and a small part of him knew this was what she'd say—hoped, maybe—but it didn't matter. "If I'd been there—"

"So what?" Allandria exploded to her feet. "So you made a selfish choice? Fuck me, Ari, I've made thousands! We make a hundred decisions a day that affect other people. You can't be responsible for consequences you had no knowledge of—no control over!"

"No, you don't understand. It's worse," he plead. "Korvin's death is why the Hellfires started the war, but it was my idea. I suggested it!"

Allandria's face paled. Now she was beginning to understand. "What?"

"At the funeral. I said we should take the country. Run it for *draoidhs*. It was my idea."

Silence.

Yes, this was what he'd really expected. He'd revealed himself, the truth of himself to his closest friend, and she hated him for it. Exactly what he deserved.

It was a straight line from his selfishness to Korvin's death, to his suggestion of insurrection, to Anhel manipulating Jan and Shay to war. All those lives lost. Every one of them on Aranok's conscience. He had no right to wear the pretence of leadership. The title of envoy was sullied with his name.

Allandria sat in the chair again, distancing herself from him. "All right. Tell me about it. What exactly did you say?"

"When?"

"At the funeral. You were drunk? And grieving. I know what you're like. What exactly did you say?"

He had no idea. He didn't remember. "Just that, I suppose."

"You suppose? You don't remember?"

"No, I—"

"So how do you know you said anything at all?"

"Shay told me."

"Shayella?"

Aranok nodded. Allandria paced again, fingertips pressed against her forehead.

"Bloody hellfire, Aranok, how are you... how are you this stupid?"

"What?" For all the criticism he deserved, that seemed unfair.

"When? When did she tell you?" She was all but yelling now, and Aranok couldn't tell what, specifically, she was angry about. It was unnerving. Enough to stem the tears for the moment.

"On the road. From Lestalric."

"Are you fucking serious?" His face must have shown the shock and confusion, because Allandria softened and knelt before him again. "Has it not occurred to you that it could be her that's manipulating you? Look at you! You're killing yourself trying to protect her. You're talking about executing a man to protect her. Aranok, what if she's lying?"

She wasn't. He knew she wasn't. He knew her well enough to know. And he remembered how he felt after Korvin. "She isn't."

"All right, what if she doesn't know she's lying, then? What if Anhel told her you said that, and she believed him? Isn't that feasible?"

Aranok stopped.

Suddenly aware of his own breathing, the absolute silence in the room felt huge. Because she was right. Not only was that feasible, it fit exactly with Anhel's behaviour. The number of times there had been arguments amongst the Hellfire Club, stoked by Anhel. It was years afterwards that Aranok could see it, but Weyr would recount something said by another in a way that seemed innocent but ended in resentment. He played them against each other. Used his position as the eldest to keep them from bonding too strongly with each other.

It was Anhel who'd brought them together. He already had Janaeus by the time Aranok and Korvin met him, and Shayella came a matter of months later. It was Anhel's club, and he liked it that way. He'd even been jealous of Aranok and Korvin's relationship. When Korvin was with Shay, he'd dropped poisonous little barbs about Aranok being jealous. They were true, but they hadn't needed to be said.

Of course, their relationship was stronger than that. They left Anhel behind long before he might have damaged their friendship. But he'd tried.

Allandria was right. That was possible.

"Maybe," he finally answered. "I suppose."

"Right. So can we let that one go?"

Even so, it didn't matter. He knew he'd felt that way. He just didn't know if he'd said it out loud. "It's still my fault, Al. If Korvin had lived—"

"I never met Korvin," Allandria said, cutting him off. "But from everything I've heard about him, do you know what I think? I think, given the choice, he'd have told you to stay and screw that girl, and he'd have laughed about it with you in the pub later. The only people responsible for Korvin's death are the bastards who killed him, and if you blame yourself for it you're letting them win."

Aranok's heart raced as he gasped breath in and out. Was she right? Could he? The pain in his chest became a stab as his heart raced faster and his hands trembled. What was happening?

"Aranok? Are you all right?"

He could hardly hold his hands still. God, what was this? A side effect of the energy process? He could hardly catch his breath. And fear, a crippling fear grabbed him. He was dying. Was he? His heart felt about to burst. "I don't know…"

Allandria grabbed his shoulders and pushed him gently down onto the bed. "All right, lie back, close your eyes. Take a deep breath and listen to my voice."

Aranok did as he was told. His heart hammered against his ribs. Whatever was happening, it was no more than he deserved.

"Concentrate on your breathing. Breathe in, deep, slow, and out again. Breathe into your gut, and out from there." She placed a hand on his stomach. "As slow as you can, all right?"

Aranok focused on the breathing. Trying to catch it, slow and control it. He didn't know how long had passed by the time he could breathe normally again. He felt Allandria's hand still on his stomach, the other on his chest. Gentle. Reassuring. His heart slowed and the trembling in his hands abated.

When he finally felt in control, he opened his eyes.

"What happened?"

Allandria smiled down at him. "The medic called it a panic. Mum had them when I was young. Dad used to sit with her like this until they passed."

"A panic? What the Hell is it?" Awful was what it was. Bloody terrifying.

"I don't know, but I would guess the weight you've been carrying, the work you've been doing, the exhaustion, the energy charges without enough sleep… They're all bad for you, Aranok. You need rest."

That made sense, he supposed. Keft had warned him about side effects of the energy magic. And he'd been taking a lot of it.

Allandria nudged his hip with hers. "Budge over."

He did, and she lay on her side next to him, draping an arm over his chest. They lay there for an age, saying nothing. He'd almost fallen asleep when Allandria spoke.

"You can't live your life hanging on to old regrets, Ari. You're not a bad person, you're just... human. For God's sake, let yourself be human."

If only it were that simple. Sometimes he felt like he was nothing but pain. A hollow corpse shambling through the world, chains of regret gouging great scars in the earth behind him. How did he let them go? They were part of him.

Something poked at him then. A little thing. An oddity.

"Did you call me Ari?" It was a nickname from his family. Some of his childhood friends had picked it up, but nobody else had ever really used it.

"I suppose I did. It just fell out. Is that all right?"

It was. In fact, it seemed ridiculous she'd never used it before.

"Yes. I like it."

Mynygogg leaned against the mantelpiece, a silhouette against the flames. The image reflected his mood perfectly, Nirea thought. She finished lacing her boot and crossed to him, running a hand down his back.

"What are you thinking, my love?"

A sigh puffed out his cheeks, and he didn't raise his head. "I can't even decide which problem is the most pressing, never mind what to do about them."

She knew. Teyjan would die unless Samily returned soon, and Mynygogg seemed fond of the man. People rejecting the memory charm was a critical blow to them retaking the kingdom. They needed to cure the Blackened without forever alienating Aranok. And he was already cracking below the waterline.

But Mynygogg needed to be focused on what they could do. She pulled her husband to a chair and sat opposite him. They now had what she understood was the best room in the hospital, reserved specifically for royalty, should they ever need care. It was one of the few she'd seen with a hearth rug, and it easily had the largest fire. They didn't need it, but it was a symbol of who they were. A reminder that they still had weight.

"There are things we can do and things we cannot. If Samily isn't already on her way here, she will arrive too late to save Teyjan. There is nothing more you can do for him or the Reivers. They will tell their chieftain you did all you could, I'm sure."

"I know." His voice was low and dark.

"There's nothing to be done, so fretting about it is only costing you focus. We can do no more about those who reject the charm. We will do what we can to convince them, and we have a plan for those who refuse. That is in hand."

"Aye." The voice was smaller, raspy. She needed him bigger. Larger than life. The man who could inspire a nation to find itself again.

"As for the Blackened, we can cure it anytime we choose. As soon as we know preparations are in place, we either use Shayella or execute her." There was no point dancing around words. Gogg knew what might have to be done.

"That might not work, Aranok said. It's only a possibility."

That was true. Well, it was true that Aranok had said it. "I know. But we have options. If neither works, we find another."

He nodded wordlessly.

"So the remaining problem is Aranok."

Another sigh. Another tired, resigned nod. "What do you do with a broken soldier?" He sang the words of the lullaby ironically, almost as a challenge. Nirea did not rise to it.

"You need to talk to him. Remind him what's at stake. Why Glorbad and Conifax are dead. Why Vastin lies mindless in a hospital bed. Remind him that if we want to take the kingdom back, first we have to ensure there will be a kingdom left to save. We have to end the Blackening. Whatever that takes."

"Hmm." Mynygogg laughed hollowly. "Whatever it takes. Easy thing to say. Harder to live with. Sometimes the apple you fight for is too bruised to eat."

"What does that mean?"

"Aranok's right. We were too slow with the *draoidh* laws. We didn't do enough."

This wasn't the time for self-doubt. She needed him clear-headed. "You did what you thought would work. What you said, about hammers and feathers, that's all true. It just hadn't worked *yet.*"

"That's of no comfort to Shayella. Or her daughter. Or the Blackened. The feather didn't take root and we reaped the consequences. We should have treated the bigotry like an invasive plant. Burned it out and salted the earth."

Nirea put a hand on his thigh. "Always easier to see the path once you've walked it."

"Aye," he answered glumly. "But kings don't get the luxury of being wrong."

"Kings are only men. And men are often wrong."

Mynygogg's face turned back to the fire. "I know. I just... needed to acknowledge that, I suppose. I should tell him. That he was right."

They sat in silence for a little while, appreciating the heat. The weather was turning. It would soon be harbour season, when the boats came in out of the sleet for winter, and sailors found inns with warm fires to drink away long nights. Memories of the Shepherd's Ha' drifted back to her. Singing shanties till dawn, knee deep in rum. Good days. Free days. Days when the only things she had to worry about were her purse and her bed. And who she shared them with.

But she couldn't keep putting off the conversation they really needed to have. And the one she was sure Mynygogg had been avoiding too.

"Gogg, we need to consider what we do if it comes to a confrontation. To a war."

"It won't."

Nirea had expected that, she supposed. "It might. If Anhel gets word of what we're doing too soon, before we can clear enough of the guard, and the army—we may have to fight."

He turned from the fire and looked directly at her. "They are not our enemies. We cannot kill our own people because we failed them."

"We're not. But we can't leave them in Anhel's control either, can we? Love, this is still a war, whether you want to see it as one or not. Anhel is going to do all he can to keep the throne. That includes using our own people against us. He'll rely on you not being prepared to fight. He'll use that against you."

Mynygogg shot upright and swiped a candlestick off the mantelpiece. It crashed loudly to the floor and would have set the rug ablaze had it been lit. "No! No more deaths! None! Not for me!"

"It's not for you, it's—"

"No." Mynygogg cut her off. "We will find another way or we will fail. But I will not see another innocent person die for my throne."

Nirea felt the fire rise within her. Her instinct was to snap back, to attack his naivety with the harsh truth of it—that if they were not prepared to fight, they would fail. But it wouldn't help. She was a queen now, not a pirate, and sometimes, she had learned, diplomacy wins more wars than violence.

"Fine," she said calmly through clenched teeth. "We will find another way."

And that other way would likely be preventing Mynygogg from "seeing" what had to be done until it was done. She would take no pleasure in it, but neither would she see the country lost for her husband's idealism.

The knock at the door was, as it happened, a welcome relief from having to continue the conversation.

Mynygogg straightened himself and brushed down the front of his clothes. "Enter."

Nirea could not have prayed for a better sight.

"Samily!" Mynygogg's face lit with a joy she'd not seen in an age. "You're back!"

The knight stepped grimly into the room, followed by Rasa, who led another woman on rope. She seemed to have begun well-dressed but had been ravaged by their journey. Her dress was torn in several places at the hem and wore a layer of dirt even more than Nirea usually accumulated.

"And Rasa. And is this...?" Nirea gestured to the strange woman.

"Majesties." Rasa made a curt bow to each of them. "This is Quellaria, the memory *draoidh* Samily spoke of."

Nirea's face broke into a huge grin. Hells and heavens, they'd done it!

Not only was Samily back in time to save Teyjan, they'd brought a memory *draoidh*! It was all they could have hoped for! She felt a chill run up her back and across her scalp. A laugh of genuine delight followed.

Mynygogg wrapped Samily into an embrace as if she were his own child, but the Thorn did not reciprocate. And her face never softened from the dark scowl she entered with. Nirea looked to Rasa and found her face equally serious. Nirea's joyful feeling was quickly turning to dread.

Mynygogg released Samily and made a sort of odd bowing gesture to Rasa. He appeared to have lost control of his senses with giddiness. "Ladies, I cannot tell you how welcome you are. But, Samily, before anything else, I must ask something of you." He turned to the memory *draoidh*. "I hope you will forgive my rudeness, Lady Quellaria"—the woman gave an amused snort—"but I have an urgent matter only Lady Samily can deal with."

He was half out the door already when Samily spoke and halted him. "Your Majesty. First, I am afraid we bring dire news."

Mynygogg's shoulders fell. Watching the joy leave his eyes was almost physically painful. "Dire? What news? About what?"

Rasa and Samily exchanged a glance before the elder woman spoke.

"It's about the Blackened, sire. And the Thakhati."

CHAPTER 43

"So you're the miracle girl, are ye?" The woman looked at Samily with what she would almost call scorn.

"Cuda, this is Samily. She's the person I told you about. And she's happy to help," said the king.

"A White Thorn. We're honoured."

Samily could not say if the woman was sincere. It didn't matter. She was here to complete a request from the king, and then she had more important business.

In the corner, lying on a bed, was a bearded man she assumed was Teyjan, the man Mynygogg had asked her to heal.

A noise from her right startled Samily and she almost reached for her sword. She found a dark-skinned woman with incredible golden hair smiling at her. At the other side of the window was possibly the most unusual thing in the room, though. A bush, in a large pot. What in Heaven was a bush doing in a hospital room? Was it some odd Reiver tradition? She had heard some of them had a religious connection with nature. Perhaps this was that? Samily decided not to ask, rather than risk causing offence, and instead offered the woman a hand. "Hello. I am Samily."

The stranger did not answer, but stood and made some unfamiliar gestures before taking Samily's hand.

"She's Jazere. She doesnae speak." The woman's voice from behind her. Cuda?

"Does not or cannot?" Samily asked. She directed the question to Jazere, though she knew the answer would come from the other woman. Jazere's forehead wrinkled.

"What fucking difference does that make?" Cuda's tone had turned aggressive.

Samily turned to her. "I meant no offence. I ask only as I wondered whether it was something I could help with." She turned back to Jazere. "If it were an injury, perhaps, I may be able to repair the damage."

Jazere's eyes widened in wonder, but she shook her head. Again, the gestures.

"You're kind, but it wasnae an injury. Born wi' it, she was. Or without, I suppose," Cuda translated. "Can ye fix that? That's me asking, no her."

Samily remained focused on Jazere to answer. "Sadly, no. I am afraid my ability does not work like that." Jazere closed her eyes, shook her head serenely and replied.

"She says it's no bother. But it's kind of ye to offer." Cuda's tone had wavered abruptly between sceptical, aggressive and now, Samily would say, gentle. This was a volatile woman. She would tread carefully.

"Samily, we need you to help Teyjan." The king bustled his way to the bedside. "Would you be so kind, please?"

Mynygogg looked haggard and anxious. He must have had a difficult time since they'd seen each other last. She felt a twinge of guilt at having brought him more bad news. But it had to be done. Hiding from a threat did not make it disappear. Ignoring the Blackened had allowed many of them to be taken by the Thakhati. If they'd dealt with the problem before, they would not have this problem now. It was leaving the Blackened alone and unprotected that had given the Thakhati the opportunity to pick them off and add to their hideous ranks.

They should have done something sooner. They should be doing something now.

"Of course, Your Majesty." Samily stepped to the side of the bed and all but had her hands on the man when she realised there was a roomful of spectators. And as she'd recently come to realise, privacy was a shield. "Would you all mind waiting outside, please?"

Mynygogg cocked his head at her curiously.

"I prefer to work in private, Your Majesty." She hoped not to have to argue or explain any further.

After a moment's hesitation, Mynygogg waved the others toward the door. "Of course. Please, everyone. Outside."

Jazere went willingly, but Samily noticed Cuda gave a lingering stare as she passed out into the hallway. A complicated woman.

When the door was closed, Samily placed her hands on the man's head. She wasn't sure how far back she needed to take him, but it couldn't be more than a week.

She took a deep breath, focused on her energy and pictured it flowing through her fingers into the Reiver's head. Just enough, and no more. Her fingers began to feel warm. She'd noticed this recently, when she used her skill. It was difficult to tell whether it was real or imagined.

"Air ais."

She breathed out as the power ran from her, pulling his head back through time, searching for the moment it was damaged and going just beyond it—no further. Colour returned to the man's face like the blush of a spring flower. His eyes sharpened and the glassy veneer lifted. He blinked repeatedly, as if he had accidentally stared at the sun.

"Hello?" His voice was hesitant, weak and confused.

Samily put on a comforting smile. "Do not worry. You were wounded, but you are healed. You are in a hospital."

"In Galche?" The man tried to lift his head, winced and lowered it again.

"No. You are in Eidyn. I believe there is a story to share with you. By your leave, I will allow your kinfolk to explain."

"I... Aye, of course." A weak hand reached for hers. "I expect I owe you thanks—in case I dinnae see you again. You a White Thorn?"

"I am. My name is Samily."

"Then thank you, Lady Samily. It's an honour."

"The honour is mine." She placed his hand gently back on his chest. "I am sorry, but I must go. I have urgent business."

Teyjan nodded and closed his eyes. The pale corpse had become a vibrant man again, albeit a tired one. Samily offered a quick thanks to God for her skill and crossed to the door.

Eager faces waited on the other side. "He is well but will need to rest."

"Seriously?" said Cuda. "Fuck me."

Samily scowled at the obscenity. There was no need, especially here.

Jazere gestured inquisitively to the room.

"Of course." Samily stepped out of the way and Cuda strode past her. As she followed, Jazere grasped Samily's arm, smiled and made a simple gesture, as if offering her hand to Samily. It seemed, somehow, an obvious "thank you." Hoping she was not misunderstanding, Samily replied, "It was my pleasure."

Jazere's smile widened as she nodded and turned into the room.

"Bloody Hell," she heard Cuda say. Being honest, she took a little delight in their surprise, but nowhere near what she took from what she'd been able to do.

"Samily, you've not only just saved a life, you've strengthened an alliance that Eidyn needs. You should be proud." Mynygogg clapped her on the shoulder.

Proud?

"Thank you, Your Majesty. But I have only done my duty to God's children, using God's power. There is nothing here to be proud of."

Mynygogg gave her an odd smile. "You did a good thing, Samily."

"Why would I not?" Samily worried she was being difficult, but she genuinely could not understand the king's reasoning.

He looked at her for a moment, as if she were a puzzle to be solved, then took a deep breath and pronounced, "Exactly." As if that made sense of it.

She did not understand, but it did not matter. There were more pressing issues. "What of the Blackened, Your Majesty? We must cure them. Now."

Mynygogg's shoulders slumped. She almost felt guilty for taking the joy from him. The king looked into the room wistfully, turned and walked back the way they'd come. "Walk with me."

When they were far enough from the room not to be heard, Mynygogg spoke again. "Aranok was not able to get the heart. We think it has been destroyed. He believes we can use Shayella to lift the curse, when we are ready. But, if not, we may only have one resort left to us."

S'grace.

"I believe I know." Executing Shayella. What they should have done at Lestalric. What they could have done at any time since Aranok returned without the relic. And yet, somehow, they had not. They had allowed the Blackened to continue suffering, and that had allowed the Thakhati to take them.

"Then you understand how complex the situation is," Mynygogg said quietly.

She did not. It seemed perfectly simple, in fact. She did not understand why the king had allowed it to become so complicated. Perhaps his loyalty to the envoy clouded his judgement. Perhaps he could not do what was needed without causing a rift between himself and Aranok, risking their alliance. But none of that applied to Samily. She had one priority, and the road was clear.

"I believe I do, Your Majesty. Please excuse me."

With a curt bow, Samily turned for the stairwell.

It was not enough.

Samily had explained how the Thakhati were murdering the Blackened. Their response was insufficient. They were "addressing" it. The envoy was negotiating with the necromancer. Preparations were being made. It was all taking too long. They should have freed them after Lestalric. She should have freed them. How many had been murdered, defiled by the Thakhati because she had not acted?

God's children were suffering.

Samily closed the door behind her. It had not been difficult to convince the guard to let her in. White Thorns were considered all but above reproach within the Eidyn military.

The basic little room in the hospital basement was no dungeon, and yet it bore the reek of a prison cell. That had more to do with its inhabitants, she surmised, than the room.

Shayella sat draped off the side of her bed, her daughter's corpse working at something in her mother's hand. S'grace, had they fed the monster? Bile rose in Samily's gullet at the thought. Even a corpse deserved more respect than to be fed to this Dead thing. The girl's body deserved more respect than shambling about as her mother's puppet, long after the girl herself was with God. It should have been in the ground, returned to the earth.

Samily could not comprehend why the necromancer tortured herself like this. What benefit was there in having her daughter's body performing as if she were still here, when her soul was gone? Surely she only deferred her grief, prolonged her suffering? When Meristan was Blackened and Samily had thought him gone, seeing him still there but unreachable was torture. She would never have wished for that to continue.

Though, she recognised, had she had her wits about her then and chosen to put him out of his misery, it would have been she who unknowingly killed him—like all the other Blackened she'd killed, believing them already gone to God.

And that, because of the woman before her.

Anger rose again. Samily took a breath, deep and cleansing, released it slowly and focused on her duty. Anger was as much her enemy as the necromancer. She was in the right of this. God was with her.

"Shayella, we need to speak."

The necromancer cocked her head and opened her mouth wide, defiantly displaying the stump of her severed tongue.

Samily moved toward her only long enough to restore it, stepped back and drew her sword. "Speak one word of *draoidh* and you will be dead before the second."

"Charming," Shayella drawled.

Samily ignored the barb, a skill she found herself calling on all too frequently in recent days. "Are you going to cure the Blackened?"

Shayella sat upright, careful not to disturb the girl. Samily made herself ignore the bestial chewing noises. "You should be asking the king's envoy that question. We've already discussed my terms."

"I am asking you." She was not going to the envoy. He was compromised and, she now suspected, maybe even under some charm to this woman that robbed him of his good sense. He was part of the problem that she would solve.

The woman was unflustered by her answer, and something about that irritated Samily further.

"We have an agreement. If he fulfils his end, I will fulfil mine."

"What agreement?"

Shayella paused before responding. "Why are you asking me? Why not ask him? I thought you were allies."

Samily took a step toward the woman, and Shayella shifted, almost raising her free hand in defence. "I will not ask again."

The necromancer's face hardened. "He feeds Kiana, I help him."

Bile rose again. That was as bad as she'd feared. The image of Darginn Argyll's dismembered body came rushing back unbidden and Samily felt her hands trembling at the memory. The smell of the flesh burning on the spit. The crackle as fat dripped into the hissing fire.

"No. This is your offer. Cure the Blackened or die."

It was as if a mask fell from Shayella. Her expression became manic. Taut. Twisted into a sneering, skeletal grin, her eyes somehow straining at their sockets, flesh stretched over bone. "You think I'm afraid of dying? I am a necromancer. With what I've done? With what I've lived? You think you can frighten me with death, girl? I live in it."

Samily stepped back. As quickly as the woman had changed, she returned to the placid, caring mother, like a door briefly thrown open by the wind and slammed violently shut. It took her a moment to consider a response.

"Fine." Samily waved at the Dead girl. "She has been fed. Uphold your bargain."

Shayella looked down at her daughter with a smirk. "Oh, sweetheart. You don't understand a mother's love."

The necromancer lifted her hand from behind her daughter. At first, Samily could not understand what she was seeing. Whatever meat they had fed the girl was almost picked clean; rivulets of blood trickled down Shayella's arm. All that remained was gristle, tendon and bone. Only when the remains moved—waved—did she understand what she was seeing.

Shayella had fed the girl her own hand.

Samily's legs weakened beneath her as the horror enveloped her.

"Necromancy. We can do wonderful things with our bodies. And you can restore it for me anyway, can't you, dear?"

Samily's stomach convulsed. S'grace, what monster was this woman? This mad, this lost, how could they allow her to live? It was cruel. It was a mockery of life.

It could not stand.

Samily raised her sword.

Shayella stood abruptly. With her ruined hand, she was every inch the dark *draoidh*.

She spoke a *draoidh* word and a noxious vapour caught the back of Samily's throat. Her eyes immediately stung and began to water, blurring her vision. What had the woman done? S'grace, she should not have given her back her tongue. She'd been too lenient again. Given too much faith.

This had to end.

Samily stepped forward and stabbed with her blade, aiming square for the necromancer's chest. But with her eyes twitching, struggling even to stay open, she missed—or the woman dodged—and the blade jammed through padding into the brick wall, painfully jarring Samily's wrists. She pulled the blade back, levelled it at shoulder height, turned and swung in a clean arc where the woman was, or where she seemed to be. Samily tried to focus her eyes. Where had she gone?

Tears streamed down her cheeks as she blinked furiously, trying to find her vision. A deep breath and the acrid fumes caught the back of her throat. Heavens, it burned! She needed this to end quickly, before she choked.

Keeping her sword in guard position, Samily calmed herself. She stifled the coughing, closed her eyes and listened. The room was not big enough for the necromancer to hide. She was here, somewhere. Close.

A step behind her. The scrape of a shoe on stone. Samily twisted to her right and stabbed back, under her left arm. The Green blade found its target, punching through flesh and bone.

A scream. An inhuman lament like nothing she'd ever heard. An animal caught in a trap, raging against its hunter, disbelief at its capture, wailing in unbearable agony. The cry of a dagger, cursing God for its edge.

And it came from across the room. Samily's sword had not found the necromancer. She withdrew the blade and heard the wet slop of a body crumpling to the ground. She must have skewered the girl's head. It was good. She should be at rest. Her body shambling around, a mockery of life, was wrong. It was blasphemous.

The scream told Samily where the attack would come from. Abandoning caution and reason, Shayella came at her. But Samily had set her ground and swept the woman aside as she lunged into her. Skeletal fingers clawed at her face as the woman fell and Samily felt the sting of broken skin. She could just about see where Shayella was now—a blur of red, a flurry of anger. She seemed to pause, something distracting her. The girl. The girl's body on the floor.

This was her moment to strike. To put an end to the madness. Save the Blackened and send this broken, tortured soul to God's loving hands.

A gust of wind buffeted Samily and her blade missed, crashing into the stone floor. Where had that come from? But it helped. The poisonous mist cleared and Samily's blinking began to work, her tears washing away the irritant and returning her vision. When it finally cleared, she saw the necromancer on her knees, cradling the husk of her child. But at the door, the worst person to be there in that moment.

"Samily." The envoy's voice was low. "What have you done?"

CHAPTER 44

The wailing cut Aranok like a shard of ice. Shayella's loss, seeing her daughter murdered—again—was too much. Too much to bear. Too much to inflict.

He'd never imagined Samily cruel, but this... this was inhuman.

Shock held him for a moment as he waited for the Thorn to say something, anything, that would explain what she'd done.

"Envoy, this was an accident. It was not my intention to end the girl."

"An... What were you trying to do?" How could a holy knight accidentally stab a child in the face? She was Dead, fine. But not to Shayella. Not to her mother.

"Save the Blackened." Samily said it as though it were obvious. As if there could be no other thought.

"I was doing that." Aranok tried to keep his voice calm, but it was coming from somewhere else. Not from his mouth. Far away. An echo.

"We have waited too long. I have waited too long. No more." Samily raised her blade and turned to Shay. "This ends."

"Samily! Stand down!" Aranok's fists trembled with fear and rage. He could not let her murder Shay. He would not fail her again.

"Let her."

What?

He hadn't noticed Shay's wailing had stopped—become a pitiful sobbing. Quiet, almost... resigned.

"Shay?"

His old friend's eyes had lost their colour. All was gone but the pale lilac of a setting sun.

"I don't want to be here. Not alone."

"You're not alone." Each word came out of him like stone. He meant it as comforting. As solace for this broken woman who had seen everything she cared about taken from her. But it was also anger. Fury at the people who had made her this. At the woman—no, the girl—who stood before him, defiant in her ignorance. Proud in her certainty. "Samily. Stand. Down."

The knight looked at him a moment, as if assessing him. As if she'd never seen him before. He had to make her stop. To see the humanity in Shayella. "You were never alone, Shay. I'm sorry I ever let you think you were."

A faint smile. Weak, not quite reaching her damp, mournful eyes. But it was there. And in it he found understanding. And gratitude. Maybe even forgiveness. She held his gaze for a long time. When she broke, it was decisive. A sharp turn of her head.

"Do it."

The Green blade sang in an arc, severing Shayella's neck.

The world stopped.

Shay's head toppled to the floor as her body collapsed onto her long-dead daughter.

Aranok slumped against the doorframe. A distant scream echoed the one in Aranok's head.

Shayella was dead.

He'd failed her.

Again.

Grief swallowed him in a black pit.

Korvin. Janaeus. Shayella.

Dead because he wasn't enough to protect them. To save them. To change the country. To do anything.

Dead because of him.

Because he followed Mynygogg's path. Because he agreed to a plan for all of Eidyn instead of demanding protection for *draoidhs*.

He'd failed Kiana, drowned for being born to a *draoidh* mother.

He'd failed Emelina.

He'd failed the girl in Caer Amon and her murdered love. Their pain, their suffering, lost to history. Sacrificed to a God whose devotees slaughtered *draoidhs* in their ignorance and fear. And arrogance—to assume they knew the will of their imagined deity—to commit murder in its name.

These people who dressed their barbarity in a mask of righteousness, who proclaimed themselves glorious atop a mountain of corpses.

These people whose ignorance persisted. In Korvin's murder. In Kiana's. In Shayella's.

He'd been on the wrong side from the beginning.

Still, the distant screaming.

Aranok looked up at the knight standing in a pool of blood. The Thorn who was also a *draoidh*. The girl of two worlds. "Why?"

"Because it was the right thing to do, Envoy. You know this now, surely. The Blackening had to be ended. And her mind was lost. It was kindness."

It was kindness.

Fury lit like oil in Aranok and pushed him back to his feet. Samily stepped back defensively.

"Kindness?" he hissed. "You murdered her, Samily. Have the courage to speak the truth, at least."

"I executed her, Envoy. She murdered thousands. Hundreds, maybe thousands more still suffer at her hands. Now, God willing, they are free. How can you not support this?"

"We had a deal!" Aranok spat, jerking a finger toward the room. "I handled it!"

Samily's face darkened. "She told me about your deal. It was unholy. You should not have made it."

The fire exploded.

"*Unholy?* You think I care about your fucking God? You think God has any place in this? Fuck your God!"

"You need not speak so of God, Laird Envoy."

"Really? Tell me, *Thorn*, where was your God when *draoidhs* were murdered? Where was God in Caer Amon? Where was God when a girl was drowning, her friends kneeling on her chest, giggling together as her last air escaped her lungs, begging for her mother? Where was God then?"

She actually smiled. "Waiting, with love, to take her home."

"Oh, fuck you." Aranok's hands balled into tight fists.

Samily raised a hand before her, eyes wide. "Envoy, calm down. I suspect you have been under the influence of a charm. I had hoped it would go with the necromancer's death, but perhaps it lingers."

What the Hell was she on about? "I'm not under a fucking charm!"

"You are!" she insisted. "I saw her cast it. On the road from Lestalric. I wasn't sure then, but—"

"For fuck's sake!" Aranok ran his hands over his head, grabbing fistfuls of hair in frustration. "Samily, I am not under a charm. Do you know how I know that? Because *I* was *raised* a *draoidh*. I was taught all we know about *draoidh* magic by some of the greatest minds in Eidyn. And do you know what they taught me?"

The knight looked back at him blankly. Was that a tremble in her eyes?

"They taught me that there is only one magical skill that can confuse the mind." Aranok reached into his shirt and drew out the memory charm. "And this protects me from it!"

For the first time, he saw absolute surprise in the girl's face. Surprise and maybe even fear. Or was it disgust? He couldn't tell the difference anymore. He didn't care.

"The only 'charm' I've been under is empathy, Samily. Empathy for a woman driven to madness by a cruel society. By people who thought themselves better than her because they were born 'normal.'"

Samily stared at him, wide-eyed. Aranok wanted to hurt her. To punish her for what she'd done. She was a hypocrite and a murderer.

"Envoy, if you—"

"Stop fucking calling me that! My name is Aranok." He pounded a fist against his chest. "Aranok!"

Samily swallowed hard. "Aranok. If that is true, we have much to discuss. With cooler heads."

Aranok wasn't cooling any time soon. "How could you, Samily? How could you? You're a *draoidh*! You were there in Caer Amon! You saw what those bigots did to children!"

"I saw what they did to a child, Aranok. And I saw what a child did to them. Do you believe the entire settlement—the seeds of a civilisation—they all deserved to die for that boy's execution?"

"Yes!" he roared, spittle raining before him. "You saw them! They cheered! Fucking animals!"

"That is not what I saw. I saw innocent people, misled by their priest, doing what they believed was right by God. You would execute them for that? For being wrong? For believing a lie?"

"When they murder children in their god's name, I absolutely fucking would."

For a long moment, the only sound was distant screaming. The Thorn said nothing.

"Turn time back. Now." She could do that. He could still save them.

Samily sighed and dropped her shoulders. "I will not."

"You fucking will! That's an order." The rage was boiling through him now.

"Aranok, I do not take orders from you. I serve God and—"

"You said you wanted to save the Blackened. If it worked, you've done that. Saving Shay won't change that. So what is it, Samily? Are you a saviour, or was this revenge? Do you presume to know God's will?" He was grasping blindly, trying to find the argument that would reach her. Force her to act before it was too late.

"Of course not. But I know her will." She pointed to Shay's fallen body. "She asked me to give her peace."

"Because you killed her fucking daughter!"

"Her daughter was already dead. I only showed her that. She was living a lie. A lie that had to end. Innocent people suffered while she deceived herself. Please, Aranok, can we move beyond this? We are allies."

Were they? He wasn't sure anymore. Wasn't sure they ever had been.

"Fucking bring her back or this alliance is over!"

Samily sighed sadly. "Then perhaps we have nothing to discuss. Shayella was a murderer. Her execution has saved lives, whether it cured the Blackening or not. I make no apology for it, except for your pain. God alone will judge me."

The fire burned bright. The fucking self-righteousness. The arrogance. The hubris to murder a sick woman and call it godly.

The screaming was so loud.

The Thorn was right. There was nothing left to say.

Allandria bounded up the stairs. Whatever Mynygogg wanted her for would have to wait. Nobody screaming that loudly, that incessantly, was all right. And considering where she was, there was a horrible likelihood who it might be.

Medics rushed along the redbrick corridor toward her, stopping at the door—the door she'd feared. She knew who was in that room, and she knew what that screaming meant.

Allandria barged past the medics into the chamber, pushing in to see what had happened, what had caused such piercing agony.

Vastin writhed against the bonds holding him to the table, eyes wild and terrified.

Three medics stood hesitantly. Why were they…? Of course. They'd been trained not to touch him. Because he was Blackened. Morienne must not be near. Not near enough.

Allandria stepped forward, took the boy's good left hand and placed her other hand gently against his face. If he was screaming, he wasn't Blackened. He'd grown a respectable stubble since she had last seen him. It seemed an odd thing to notice, in the moment, but there it was.

"Vastin," she said, as gently as she could, still making herself heard over the boy's screams. "Vastin, it's me. It's Allandria. Can you hear me? You're safe."

"It hurts? Oh God it hurts!" the boy wailed.

Of course. They'd have given him no poppy. The Blackened was its own dampener. "Opium! Now!" she barked. One of the medics jolted into life and ran from the room. The remaining two, an older man and a sturdy woman, finally roused themselves. The man moved to hold the boy's wounded arm still while the woman shifted up to his head, supporting his neck.

"Vastin?" she asked. "Can you hear me? My name is Inalla. You are in hospital. You were wounded. I need you to lie still so we can assess the damage. Can you do that?"

Still the boy strained against the bonds. He felt trapped. He was scared. They needed to free him. It was against the logic of keeping him still, but the boy seemed intent on freeing himself even if it meant ripping his wound open.

"Release the straps!" Allandria ordered.

Inalla looked at him as if she had ordered her to murder the boy herself. "But he'll—"

"Do it." A familiar voice behind her. Egretta. Thank God. "Do it and step away."

Inalla nodded, and the pair quickly and carefully loosed the boy's bindings.

"Vastin, I'm here. You're safe. We're going to help you," said the elderly medic.

"Lady…Lady Allandria?" He looked half his years in that moment. Maybe younger. A tiny boy wailing for his mother. "What happened?"

"You were injured. In battle."

"Battle? I don't…I don't…" He was utter confusion, but it was working. As the last strap was freed, the boy settled. "Where…?"

The young medic returned with a glass of white liquid. A large one. Good. For the best if he wasn't awake for this.

Allandria grabbed the boy's face with both hands. "Vastin, just listen." He nodded, clearly still terrified. "You were injured battling demons. You were injured, but you survived. You will be fine, I promise. But first you have to rest, all right?"

The boy shook like a wet dog, but he was listening. A nod. Just enough.

"I need you to drink this." Allandria reached out and the glass was placed in her hand. She raised it to Vastin's lips and tipped.

"Slowly," Egretta warned. "Or he'll bring it back up."

Allandria steadied her right hand with her left, supporting it to tilt the cup back. Inalla gently raised his head and shoulders to help him swallow, and the boy winced away from the angry, swollen right one, spilling some of the milk down his chin.

"Sorry." Allandria wiped it with her sleeve. "Inalla, sit him up?"

She looked to the other medic and he moved beside her, helping her to lift Vastin to a seated position without putting pressure on his wound. When he was upright, tears streamed down his cheeks, or perhaps his eyes simply watered with the pain.

Allandria returned the cup to his lips.

"Do you want me to...?" Egretta offered, but Allandria waved her away. This was her responsibility.

When Vastin had all but emptied the cup, the medics carefully lowered him onto a stack of pillows, supporting his back and head. Already his eyes were glassy. Between the pain, the drug and the stupor of the Blackening, it was hardly surprising, Allandria supposed. She hoped the pain was less.

"I fought... demons?" The words were weak—watery. He was fading.

"You did. You were outstanding." Why not give the boy a little lie to ease his rest? He'd more than earned it. The truth would out later. For now, let him be a hero. Let him rest. His eyes fluttered closed.

Allandria's heart pounded. It likely had been since the beginning, but she was only now aware of it. She turned to Egretta. "Will he recover? Can you heal him?"

Egretta's lips pursed. She waved her out into the corridor, closing the door behind them.

"His wound was catastrophic. It has healed—somewhat. But not as much as it should have in this time. Then again, I've never seen a wound that severe heal. Truthfully, I can't say. But we will do everything we can for him. You have my word."

Allandria put out a hand and leaned against the wall. Her legs trembled beneath her. Hells, this was worse than after a battle.

"What happened?" Egretta asked after a moment. "Why isn't he Blackened?"

That was exactly the question now nagging at her.

She was going to find the answer.

CHAPTER 45

Samily struggled to believe what she was seeing. But it was there, plain before her.

The envoy's fists coursed with fire.

"Go back, Samily."

"I will not."

Plumes of flame burst toward her. Disbelief and confusion might have cost her her life, but her body reacted before her mind even understood what was happening.

Even rolling away and with her armour's protection, the heat was agony. Her hair caught flame, the heat braising her flesh. In a moment, it would be too painful, too agonising to focus. And she had to focus.

She had to do it now, or she might never have a chance again.

"Air ais."

The relief. Like cool summer air tingling across her skin.

Samily looked up. She'd been careful. Only going back to before he attacked. A short burst of her power. Enough to save her. Not enough to bring back the necromancer. Not using too much of her energy.

The envoy's hands lit with flame again. Samily had believed him a fundamentally good man. Could she have been so wrong?

Aranok's eyes were almost black, his face contorted into a demonic grimace.

She had nowhere to retreat. She could not evade.

Instead, she drew her sword from her back. "Aranok, please. I am not your enemy."

Again, the flames poured from his hands.

Samily threw herself to the floor, curled into a ball, her back to the fire. The agony bit hard again, and its sting forced her hand more quickly this time.

"Air ais!"

The absence of that searing pain was again a rush of pleasure. But she did not have time to appreciate it. Again, she stood, facing the envoy. His hands coursed with rolling flame, his eyes dark.

Her sword was in its place on her back. This time, she would leave it there. For now. Instead, she raised both hands before her in a gesture of peace.

"Aranok, I do not wish to fight you. Whatever our disagreements, we want the same things. Peace. For all. You must see that. We *are* still allies."

A waver then? A glimpse of sanity? Heaven, she hoped so. Others must be coming. The guard would go for help. She only needed to delay. To allow them time to arrive.

Time was her tool. Perhaps she should go back a little further, to before the envoy lost all reason. Perhaps she could find better words this time. Words that would make him see clearly. But that would take more energy and if she failed again...From her brief experience, the increase was greater the further she went. Turning back hours at Anhel Weyr's home had cost her everything. She'd managed numerous short bursts with a controlled energy release at Dun Eidyn but she'd only gone back a few minutes. She was already low on energy—what if she went back too far and left herself defenceless, alone before a revived Shayella?

But she needed to change something. She had to stop this.

She would not burn again.

"Listen to me, Aranok!" Samily leaned against the wall, air heaving from her lungs. "Twice you have tried to kill me. I am begging you to stop."

The man's rage still burned; madness had him. She likely had the energy for one more spell without risking falling unconscious.

But her knees threatened to buckle, and the world was in danger of fading.

She could not risk it.

Aranok gave no answer.

His face still contorted in hatred, fire wrapping hungrily around his fists.

Perhaps she had the answer. The only answer.

Her instinct had been to defend.

But she was a White Thorn.

If there was to be another death, it would not be hers.

One last effort. Samily pushed herself upright with a deep breath.

"Please, Aranok. I am not your enemy."

...

"Please."

Nothing.

No flicker of recognition.

Just fury.

Hate.

So be it.

Samily dived forward into a roll, blade tucked across her. Heat coursed above her. She pushed up from her crouch, bringing her blade up sharply.

The flames extinguished.

The wet slap of meat hitting stone.

Aranok staggered back into the hallway.

He slumped against the wall opposite, staring mutely as blood poured from him.

The enchanted armour might have protected him from her blow, even from a Green blade.

But his hands were vulnerable.

She'd ended the fight and left them both alive, thank God.

"Aranok!" The shriek came from the corridor. Allandria arrived in a flurry, crouching at Aranok's side. He sat motionless, transfixed by his bloody stumps. Samily had thought he might pass out from the injuries, but his rage must have been enough to keep him awake. It would have been better had he slept.

Allandria would be able to reason with him. Samily slumped against the doorframe, her energy drained. "He went...mad. Tried to... kill me."

"Why?" Allandria's tone was almost as aggressive as Aranok's as she whipped her head around. "What did you do?"

Samily opened her mouth but had no words. Was Allandria upset with her? Surely she knew Samily would not have acted without reason. Aranok was the aggressor—she had ended the fight. What more did the archer want?

"I executed the necromancer."

Allandria closed her eyes and grimaced. "You bloody idiot."

What?

How could she not see it was the only thing to do? Why could nobody else see this clearly?

"Give him his hands! Now!" Allandria demanded. The envoy's eyes rolled in his head. His arms were bleeding heavily. He would not remain conscious for long.

Still, Samily was not inclined to heal him until she could be sure he would not attack again. It would use more of the precious little energy she retained. "Will you control him?"

"Yes," Allandria grunted.

"Are you certain? Because—"

"I said yes!" the woman snapped. Allandria's hands trembled noticeably. Heaven, was she going to attack too? Samily prayed not.

Fine. She would heal the envoy and take her leave. Her body was screaming for rest, anyway. Samily crouched before the envoy. His eyes roved as if watching magical beasts flutter about him. He was suffering for the blood loss. Samily had seen this before.

She avoided making eye contact with Allandria, reaching across to take both trembling arms in her hands.

"Air ais." The tiniest amount of energy. The absolute minimum.

The bleeding stopped as Aranok's hands reappeared. He sucked in a great breath and juddered violently.

Allandria took his face in her hands. "Aranok? It's me. Can you hear me?"

The envoy groaned, but his eyes closed. "It will take a little time for his body to adjust," said Samily. "He will be fine." She heard the bitter tone in her voice. It was unbecoming of a Thorn, but she resented that Allandria's concern was for the envoy when he had attacked her.

Allandria gently caressed his forehead. Samily carefully moved past the pair. It would be best for her not to be here when he woke.

"You might have done the right thing, but that doesn't mean you were right to do it."

Samily turned to face Allandria. "Pardon?"

The archer pointed to the necromancer's cell. "Maybe Shayella had to die. Maybe it had to end this way. But that wasn't your choice to make."

She was wrong. Emotion was clouding her thought. Her care for the envoy overriding her good sense. "It was the only choice. The Blackened are being turned by the Thakhati on the Auld Road. It had to end. Now. Lives are at stake."

Allandria's eyes widened at that. She hadn't known. Perhaps now she would see.

"All right." She ran her hands across her face. "And what about all the Blackened who are now going to die in agony or freeze to death because you turned them before we were ready? Before the medics Egretta is arranging could be out there to save them? Before the wagons Ikara is organising were there to collect them and bring them here? What about them, Samily? Are you going to save them?"

Samily's certainty melted like snow.

She had not thought it through. She'd been certain this had to happen, but Allandria was right—people would suffer for her actions too. Suffer and die. Between the exhaustion and that horrifying realisation, tears welled in her eyes.

"And Vastin. He might die now. The wound that was healing under the Blackening might kill him. Did you think of him?"

The tears came thick. She'd forgotten Vastin. In her drive to rescue the Blackened, to protect them from the Thakhati, she'd not remembered that he relied on the curse for his life. Still, would that have stopped her? It would have been selfish to protect a friend and let strangers die. But she should have remembered him.

Allandria appeared to soften then and stepped toward her. She reached out and gently took Samily's hand. "You may look like and act like a woman in many ways, Samily, but you're barely more than a girl. Sometimes I forget that. There were no simple answers here. No black and white. Every decision was a compromise. You made a child's choice in an adult situation. I know you believed it was right, but there is more to decisions than you might see. When you make choices like this, you take on the consequences too. Sometimes they're more than you understand."

Samily nodded, covering her mouth with her free hand. Had she made a terrible mistake after all? It had been such an obvious choice that it had felt like no choice at all.

A groan from Aranok. Samily glanced down at him, rousing gently on the floor. "He did try to kill me," she said defensively.

"I know." Allandria looked mournfully back at the envoy. "I'm not excusing that. There will be consequences. But there is more here you don't understand. He's still a good man, Samily. But everything cracks if you apply enough pressure."

Samily did not entirely understand, but she nodded. She needed to leave before Aranok awakened.

"I take it you can't go back in that room and undo what you've done?" Allandria asked.

Would that be the right thing to do? It would not re-curse the Blackened—the effect would be limited to the room. And if she understood the power correctly, it was like a bubble around her. Once she'd left the room, could she return and undo what she'd done? It would do no good anyway. The necromancer would be alive and the returned Blackened would still be suffering. For nothing.

And she had no energy left for it anyway. Samily shook her head. "She wanted to die. She asked me to do it."

Allandria sighed. "Why don't you see if there's anything you can do for Vastin?"

Yes. That was a good plan. Go to Vastin. Help him. If he lived. Then rest, and find a way to help the returned Blackened.

How, she did not know.

But she would find a way.

Allandria watched Samily until she turned the corner out of sight. The girl had been reckless, dangerously so. But she meant well. And she was young. For all her prowess in battle, emotionally, she was as fragile and complex as any girl her age.

But she'd keep. Allandria had more to deal with.

"Aranok?" She gently caressed his hand, kneeling before him as his eyes fluttered open. He looked at her as though he'd never seen her before. Then down, to his free hand, which he raised and turned in the air before him. In the room, the bloody remains of his other hands lay still.

"She killed her."

"I know."

"God, Al, she killed her. And I... What do I do?"

It was gut-wrenching to see him so small and broken. A shadow. "Nothing. There's nothing to be done. You're going to rest. Then we'll make plans."

A burial. Two burials. The Blackened. The kingdom. A lot of plans.

"Al..." He raised his head to look her in the eye. "I think... I lost control."

He *thought* he'd lost control? God in Heaven, what would he need to be certain? "Yes. You did." She meant the words to be comforting, but they came with a sharp edge. She might have defended him to Samily, but what he'd done was attack a young woman—albeit one of the most powerful people in Eidyn.

"No... I didn't... The invocation. I didn't... make the gestures." Aranok looked up at her piteously.

Holy Hell.

Was he saying...?

"You lost control... of your magic?"

Aranok nodded, his lips quivering. "Is that...? Is that possible?" *Draoidh* magic first appeared naturally in children. Wild. But...

"It shouldn't be."

Fuck. What did that mean? If he couldn't control his powers, if he could be lost to anger or despair and lash out without control—was that better or worse?

"I could have killed her," he whimpered.

"I know. You didn't."

His restored hand trembled in hers.

"I don't think that matters." Tears streamed down his face.

"It matters."

"I don't think I can do this."

He meant it, with every ounce of him. He was exhausted. Broken. "Then we won't. We'll walk away. Leave Eidyn. This doesn't have to be your fight, Aranok. You can let it go." And maybe Eidyn would be safer without him. At least until they understood what had happened.

His eyes seemed to focus on her then. Some clarity returning to him. "You would do that? For me?"

Allandria nodded. She could feel her own tears building. "I would."

"Why?"

Her heart was racing, the enormous weight of the moment pressing down on her. It was nothing like perfect. But it was right. It had to be.

"Because I love you."

As she said the words, the weight released, replaced with a sickening fear. Was it fair to tell him now? What if his reaction was coloured by his grief?

Aranok looked up at her, his eyes searching for some answer—something familiar he could grasp. But in the end, all he did was repeat his question.

"Why?"

A nervous laugh burst from Allandria—of surprise and relief. There was something utterly ridiculous about the question, the situation, him, her, all of it. And in that moment, all she could do was laugh. "Because I know you, Aranok." She stroked his cheek gently. "And I love you."

His face crumpled and the tears became sobs. Allandria turned and sat beside him on the hallway floor. Someone would come soon. A medic, a guard, someone would come looking for them.

But for that moment, she sat beside him, took his head to her chest and wrapped her arms around him. They sat there together, crying bitter-sweet tears.

And nothing else mattered.

CHAPTER 46

Nirea plastered a smile on her face. Mynygogg's was more genuine. Across the round meeting room table sat Rasa and a woman in a tattered dress that had once been elegant—a fitting metaphor for Nirea's situation.

They needed this memory *draoidh*, and the woman did not look likely to join them willingly.

She'd try the queen first and keep the pirate in reserve. "Rasa, perhaps you could give us a proper introduction?" Nirea smiled ever more sweetly.

"Well, that would be marvellous," the woman replied, raising her chin and sitting back as if Nirea had invited her to tea.

"Of course, Your Majesty." Rasa sat up rigidly. "We found Quellaria in Dail Ruigh, where she had been using her power to steal from locals. She wouldn't agree to come voluntarily, so we brought her." She gestured to the ropes around the *draoidh*'s wrists.

Quellaria pursed her lips and gave Rasa a sideways glance that said everything about the relationship that had grown between them.

"May I call you Quellaria?" Mynygogg asked, standing and moving around the table.

"You're a king, call me what you like."

"What would you like to be called?"

She stared at him a moment. Taking his measure.

"Friends call me Quell."

"I'd like to be your friend, Quell. Let's make you more comfortable." Mynygogg reached for her bound hands.

"I wouldn't do that... sire," said Rasa. "She already used her skill to try to escape once. She had Samily... stab me."

That explained the ropes, right enough. Presumably Samily had used her time power to heal Rasa, but that must have been unpleasant. Enough to justify Rasa's caution.

Mynygogg paused. "Quell, may I have your word that you will not use your skill, if I give you mine that I will not harm you?"

The woman looked him up and down. "Depends. What's your word worth?"

"Good question." Mynygogg smiled appreciatively. "A great deal, to me. My wife would vouch for that, but then she would, wouldn't she? Can we agree to give each other a little good faith?"

Quellaria glanced at Rasa. They needed to get rid of her. Even with the danger of the memory *draoidh* using her ability. They'd have to rely on their wits. "Rasa, there's no need for us to keep you here any longer. I'm sure there are things you'd like to attend to?" Nirea hoped Rasa would take the easy exit. For a moment she looked confused, conflicted, as if torn between desire and duty. But desire won.

"If Your Majesties wouldn't mind?"

"Of course not, Rasa, please, don't let us keep you." Mynygogg understood. "And thank you. There are not enough words for what you've done for us."

Rasa smiled broadly. "Then I will take my leave, thank you." She moved quickly to the door, turning as she left to bow gently and give Quellaria a look that said *I will hunt you down again.* For all her grace, Rasa was not a woman Nirea wished to upset.

Once she was gone, it was Quellaria who spoke first.

"So you're the king, are you? Every picture I've ever seen of you is all hair and beard. D'you have an accident?"

Mynygogg smiled and ran his hand over the stubble darkening his head. "Yes, well, there were sacrifices to be made. I hope to be able to return to my usual good looks soon. So... are we agreed on good faith?"

"Suppose it would be in my interest to agree, eh?" The *draoidh* extended her bound hands.

As Mynygogg knelt and loosened the ropes, Nirea's hand went to her knife. She wasn't certain how memory magic worked, but she did know Aranok required contact with his charm to reverse it, and Mynygogg was putting his hand in a bear's mouth.

Nirea was so intently watching their hands that she missed the *draoidh* watching her in return. "Your woman looks tense. You sure we're all friends?"

Nirea looked up, met her gaze and forced her face to relax. "Forgive me. I'm protective of my husband. We were only recently reunited." She almost stopped there but realised it might be an ideal opening to play to the *draoidh*'s sympathy. "I didn't even remember him until a few weeks ago."

"So you're not keen on memory *draoidhs*, right?" Quellaria shook her hands out, now they were free. Angry red marks around her wrists looked painful. Nirea wondered whether they would be able to convince Samily to heal them. Either way, best not to offer it without the Thorn's agreement. She could do something more mundane about it.

"Not at all." Nirea crossed to the door. "I only hold responsible the person who was." The big guard turned at attention when she opened the door. "Leondar, would you please ask the next medic that passes if they could bring some salve? Our guest has injuries."

"Yes, Majesty." He nodded respectfully, casting a little side glance into the room. It did no harm to remind Quellaria he was there. Leondar was not only a beast of a man, he was sharp as a Green blade. Exactly why they'd made him captain of the kingsguard.

"Thank you," said Quellaria as Nirea retook her seat.

Mynygogg placed his hand over hers. "As I said. Good faith. We don't want to be your enemies. Nor your gaolers."

The *draoidh* crossed her arms and legs and leaned back in the chair. "I'm here because you need my help. Your kingdom's been taken by Janaeus and you want it back. You need my help restoring people's memories. That about it?"

"You cut to the heart of it." Mynygogg gripped Nirea's hand a little tighter.

Quellaria's face turned hard. "Why would I do that?"

Damn it. It would have been too much to hope she might just want to do the right thing.

"All right. I understand that perspective." Mynygogg's voice stayed calm, which was not how Nirea was feeling at all. Her instinct was to remind the woman she was a thief and belonged in a gaol, despite the king's gentle words. Perhaps that was not the right way to go. Yet. "I assume you consider the idea of a *draoidh* on the throne to be a good thing for you. Maybe things will be better for *draoidhs*?"

Quellaria gave nothing away. The woman had the stare of a statue.

"Fine," Mynygogg continued. "I will tell you what I told my envoy when I asked him to join my rebellion. I may not be a *draoidh*, but I care. I care about the prejudice you have to live with. I care about how difficult your life has been. The same as I care about every person in Eidyn. The country is a mess. People are starving. Dying. The Blackening has taken thousands. The war took hundreds of thousands, including many *draoidhs*. Demons still ravage the land. Eidyn is suffering. We can stop that. All of it. We can make everyone's life better. Safer. But to do that, we have to be in control. People need to know the truth. Please, help us."

Even now, after she'd heard such speeches for years, including the one that sold her on joining the rebellion against Hofnag, hairs raised on Nirea's arms. The passion with which her husband spoke of making the country better was intoxicating. He was an ideal monarch. A genuinely good man.

"Sorry, I don't see it." Quellaria's words broke Nirea's trance. "You've been king for years, and my life hasn't improved a single ounce. Spat at. Thrown out. Turned away. Only way I get by is making sure nobody remembers my face when I'm gone. If you were really going to make things better for *draoidhs*, you should have done it by now."

Nirea's hand reached again for her blade.

Mynygogg released one hand to grasp the other, preventing Nirea from drawing. "You're right. We haven't moved quickly enough. And that is my responsibility. My fault. I thought promoting a *draoidh* to be my envoy would be enough of a signal to the people of Eidyn that the kind of intolerance you have faced was unacceptable. That Aranok's example, fighting for all of Eidyn, would change minds. Unfortunately, he became an exception instead of an example."

The *draoidh*'s head jerked back. "You think *draoidhs* are at fault? Because not enough of us rallied to your cause?"

Mynygogg raised his hand to cover a cough, freeing Nirea's to grasp the hilt of her dagger. The woman was verging on hostile, and she did not like it.

Mynygogg raised both hands in defence. "No, please forgive me, I wasn't clear. I meant that he was seen as an exception by the people. That his example was treated as unusual, rather than proving that being a *draoidh* was no measure of a person's character. I have always been committed to ending bigotry."

The *draoidh* banged her hand on the table and Nirea's blade was free but remained in her lap. "How is my life better?"

That was enough. She would not tolerate this woman attacking her husband any further. "Quell, if I may, there are things you do not see." She needed to keep a calm tone. Still the queen. "For example, the king ended all of Hofnag's laws limiting the practice of magic. He also secured funding support for the university, allowing it to expand, guaranteeing that all *draoidhs* would be able to study there without charge, and that many more students could be accommodated."

"So?" the woman snapped. "*Draoidhs* have always been free to study here."

"Indeed," Mynygogg answered. "But expanding the number of masters widens their education. And increasing the number of students better educates the next generation. And their exposure to *draoidhs* here will counter any bigotry their parents have raised in them. The university is the future of Eidyn, Quell. It's how we weed out ignorance. With education. Enlightenment. Experience. Truth."

"That's your plan? Teach children to be better? I'm not planning on having children, big man, so how does that help me?"

It wasn't working. Appealing to her better nature was getting them nowhere. They needed leverage. What did she want? What did she care about? Where was her weakness? Nirea didn't know enough about her. She didn't want to resort to brute force, but it might become their only option.

Mynygogg was still valiantly trying, though. "Quell, culture takes time to change. I can make it illegal for a man to abuse you for being a *draoidh*—and I will—but that won't change what he thinks. Not immediately, anyway. And he'll pass that on to his children. Prejudice is not born, it's taught. We can limit its expression now, but we can only kill it for future generations."

The knock at the door broke a moment of awkward silence. Quellaria at least appeared to be listening, but Nirea didn't think they were really getting through to her. "Enter!" she called.

A medic entered carrying a wicker tub—a maternal woman with kind eyes. Nirea vaguely recognised her from the hallways. But she'd seen so many she hadn't even attempted to remember names. The curse of leadership was having too much to remember.

"Your Majesties." The woman bowed. "I was asked to bring salve?"

"Indeed." Was this a chance for Nirea to make things better? Perhaps. She slipped her dagger away and crossed to the medic. "May I?"

"Of course, m'lady." The woman handed over the tub with another unnecessary bow.

"I take it I simply apply it liberally to the wounds?"

"Um." The medic hesitated. "It depends... on the wounds?"

Nirea turned to Quellaria, and the woman made a show of reluctantly holding out her wrists. The medic took a step toward her, examined them for a moment, humming and making other little ponderous noises. "Yes, a generous application should be fine. Not too much. Don't want it dripping all over that pretty dress." The dress was a torn, dusty state, and everyone in the room could see it. "Ideally they ought to be bandaged too. I think I have some..."

She rustled in the pockets of her apron, finally producing a small roll of white cloth. "Yes! Here we are. Are you... practised in applying bandages, Majesty?"

Nirea laughed involuntarily. "I'm sorry," she said when she saw the surprise on the medic's round face. "It's just... Yes, I know how to put on a bandage."

"Of course, Majesty." Another bow.

Nirea needed to undo the damage she'd accidentally done with that laugh. It seemed cruel now, in immediate retrospect. The woman thought she'd been laughing at her. Her slightly flustered demeanour remained. Nirea took one of her hands. "Thank you so much for bringing this to us. You've been extremely kind. Please, don't let me keep you from your patients."

That brightened her up. Odd how just being touched by a queen was enough to make some people happy. As if she were a deity bestowing a gift upon them. In truth, she pissed and snored like everyone else. There was an absurdity about it that Nirea had never become accustomed to.

When the medic was gone, Nirea kneeled before the *draoidh*, just as Mynygogg had done, scooped out a few fingers full of salve and raised her eyebrows. After a moment, Quellaria offered first her right wrist, then, when it was done, the other. She winced as the salve was applied but seemed to relax as the pain-dampening effect took hold. Nirea carefully bandaged them too, taking care not to spill any salve onto the dress.

"Better?" she asked, getting to her feet.

"Yes. Thank you." It wasn't a grudging response, more a guarded one. Was it a step in the right direction? Still difficult to say.

Quellaria waited for her to sit again. The break had proven useful. The tension had dissipated. The medic had delivered more salve than she realised. "What is it you want from me?"

Mynygogg sighed. It was an opening, at least. "We'd like your help. We don't have the means to clear memories on a large scale, so we're going to have to do it one at a time."

"Mm-hmm," she said, nodding. "But your memories are clear. So either you have a memory *draoidh* already, or...?"

Nirea looked to her husband. How much should they reveal? If this woman turned traitor, if she chose to go against them, could they risk revealing what assets they did have?

Mynygogg paused a long time before answering, and she knew he was having the same debate. "We have a charm. We hoped, in fact, that you might be prepared to make some more of those as well."

Quellaria's face changed. "You did, did you? And do you know how they're made?"

The monarchs exchanged bewildered looks. Neither of them had any idea. Aranok had never said.

"Thought not." Her voice was cold as ice. "That charming yellow ball is made from a very specific fluid. It comes from my spine. It's extremely painful to extract."

Nirea gasped. Mynygogg's face looked as shocked as she felt. Neither spoke. She had no words. Hadn't Aranok said something about Janaeus making a number of these charms?

"Do you know why we're taught to make them?" Quellaria sat with her arms crossed, head cocked like an angry schoolteacher. "Because even other *draoidhs* are afraid of us. Because the only way for us to have friends is to give them one of those damned things so they can be sure we haven't twisted their minds." She leaned forward onto the table. "So you tell me, King Mynygogg, how does your education help me, when even other *draoidhs* hate me? Where's my role in your fabulous society?"

There it was. Her weak spot. And holy Hells, but Nirea might just have the perfect way to make use of it. If it worked, it would solve another problem too. She was almost giddy at the thought as she worked through the idea. Could it work?

Mynygogg remained respectfully silent. He had nothing helpful to say and would not insult the woman by spitting empty platitudes.

But Nirea had an answer.

"Quellaria, firstly, I am deeply sorry. We didn't know how the charms are made. We would never have asked if we did." She meant every word. Unless there was no other option, they could not ask that. "But I think I might be able to answer your question. Not here and not now. Would you consider being our guest—such as that means"—she gestured to the hospital's austere walls—"for the night? Bathe, eat, rest and allow us to have your dress repaired? Tomorrow, I hope I will be able to show you exactly what your role can be, and how we—how Eidyn—needs you. Not just to help restore us to the throne."

Curiosity. She had the woman's interest. Quellaria had spat her question considering it a dagger in the heart of their argument. She'd not expected an answer. And Nirea had a brilliant one. Maybe.

The *draoidh*'s armour went back up, her anger replaced with the cocky disinterest she'd worn when she arrived. "All right, Red. You think you've got an answer for me, I'll hang around. And I could live with a bath."

Mynygogg smiled broadly at her, but there was an obvious question in his eyes. As soon as they had Quellaria installed in a room, she'd explain it to him. If she was right, it might just be the most brilliant idea she'd ever had.

Today was a good day to be the queen.

CHAPTER 47

Samily! Hello." Morienne moved as if to embrace her, hesitated and stopped. "Are you all right?"

Samily's fatigue must have been evident on her face. She needed to see Vastin—to help him—but it was challenging. She was partly responsible for his situation. Not as much as Shayella, but the fact remained, her actions led to his current pain.

Thankfully, he seemed to be unconscious as Egretta examined his wounds. That was likely for the best. And helpful that the medic was here so Samily could ask her advice.

"I am... well enough," she answered Morienne's question. "How is the boy?"

The woman grimaced. "Not well. The Blackening just ended! Which is wonderful, of course, but for Vastin..."

"It was too soon."

Egretta turned from her patient. "I don't know what more we can do. We can keep him asleep, mostly, but if I'm honest..." She pursed her lips and shook her head.

The boy was going to die.

"Is there nothing you can do?" Morienne asked. "I mean, you could take him back, right? Make him Blackened again? Just temporarily, until he could heal..."

"No." Samily would not consider the risk of bringing back the curse she had just ended. The price had already been paid. It would not be for nothing. "But I have another idea. Egretta, if I were to take the wound forward in time, speed the healing—might that work?"

Egretta pursed her mouth and examined Samily like a curiosity. "Honestly, dear, I have no idea. If the wound were to become infected, if it healed wrongly... I just don't know how your ability will work. Do you?"

The question was valid. She did not. She had seen it grow plants. In theory, it should speed up the healing, like Nirea's face—assuming it was going to heal. But what if the boy was going to die? Would she only bring the rot of death closer? Would she kill him quicker? That was the crux. "I am unsure. But I am willing to try."

"Are you sure that's wise? You look shattered," said Morienne. "Do you even have the energy?"

Another valid point. She'd worn herself down fighting the envoy. Resting now would be sensible. But if she slept and the boy died waiting... "I will be fine."

Egretta crossed her arms. "Come, girl, you're clearly exhausted. I can see the half-moons under your eyes from here. I'm not having you pass out halfway through and making this worse. You need to rest first."

"I will be fine," Samily insisted again.

"Um, I have a thought." Morienne raised her hand like a schoolgirl. "I could fetch Master Dialla? She could replenish your energy now, and..."

It was a good idea. "Yes, all right. If you don't mind?" She had other things to do. Plans to make. Not having to sleep away the afternoon would be a blessing.

"Of course I don't mind!" Morienne looked excitedly around at Egretta. The old woman nodded after a moment's consideration, and she tore from the room. The transformation in her was all but miraculous. The sullen, resigned woman they'd met in Lepertoun was a memory replaced with such happiness and enthusiasm. It was pleasing to see, and Samily offered a quick thanks to God for her.

"Right." Egretta lifted Samily's hand. "There's absolutely no chance you're touching him with these filthy hands. Get out of that armour and I'll fetch a bowl of water. We're scrubbing these clean before you go near that wound."

"Yes, ma'am." Samily nodded and began working at her straps.

"Good." Egretta gave a stern nod of approval and bustled out.

When she had finished removing her vambraces, pauldrons, cuirass and the rest, Samily sat in the chair beside the bed, closed her eyes and listened to the boy breathe. She'd seen him as odd. But she'd since learned that it was more likely her who was odd, and that Vastin's behaviour was entirely normal for a boy his age. Well, she was as God had made her and would make no apologies for it. But it did, perhaps, give her a more sympathetic bent toward the boy. He seemed a good person. A companion. Someone who did not deserve the misery that had been heaped upon him.

He would be saddened to learn of Glorbad's death. She would not choose to be the person who had to share that news with him. But she would try, at least, to ensure he woke.

By the time Egretta returned with soap and water, and by the time she was satisfied that Samily's hands were clean, Morienne had returned with Master Dialla.

Once the master had given her a small boost of energy, she pulled the chair close to the bed, placed her hands gingerly on Vastin's shoulder and focused on her breath.

"Air adhart."

The wound knitted itself together, the angry purple bruising disappearing like snow in spring. The shoulder tightened, pulling itself into a more natural position. When it looked normal, healthy, Samily raised her hands away and stepped back, allowing space for Egretta to examine her work.

"It looks good. To me," Morienne whispered.

"It is a marvellous talent," said Dialla. "I would very much appreciate the opportunity to see more of it sometime, Lady Samily."

Ipharia's words came back to her again. Everyone would want to know her once they knew she was a time *draoidh*. Samily did not relish the notion of fame. Still, it would be impolite to flatly demur, so she simply smiled at the master.

After a great deal of humming and poking, Egretta delivered her verdict. Her face broke into an uncharacteristic grin. "I think it worked, you know. I think you might just have saved his life—and his arm!"

Samily's heart sped a little and a tingle ran up her neck. She hadn't killed him. Perhaps it hadn't been the mistake she feared. God was still with her. Of course. God was always with her. "When will we know? For sure?"

Egretta dug in her apron and produced a small pack of herbs. "Shortly. These should wake him. Then we'll be able to ascertain if there's any residual damage."

The old woman held the herbs under Vastin's nose, and after a moment, he jerked forward, eyes wide. "What's...? Whoa." The boy put a hand to his head and slumped back against the pillow.

"How are you, young man?" Egretta put a hand on his forehead.

"I'm...everything's...am I drunk?" Vastin's eyes roamed the room, seemingly unable to focus on anything.

"No, son, that's the opium. You've been in a lot of pain. But you're healed now, all right?"

"All right," he said, and broke into a wide grin. "I feel wonderful, actually. Floating on a warm sea. Oh!" His head jerked up. "I've not peed myself, have I?"

The women laughed. "Not that I can see, no," Egretta answered. It was pleasing to see him in good spirits, even if the poppy milk had a lot to say for it. "Now listen, I just need you to do something for me, all right?" The boy nodded feebly. "Can you raise your right arm, please?"

"Of course!" Vastin answered, his expression suggesting confusion as to why that might be an issue.

It turned to consternation and then confusion as his upper shoulder moved forward but his arm did not. He repeated the action, jerking his shoulder, causing the arm to shake and tremble, but it did not move.

Vastin's eyes searched for comfort. "What's...? Is that...? Why can't I...?"

Egretta grasped the wounded shoulder. "It's fine, lad, it's fine. Don't fret. Just the effects of the opium. No need to worry. Tell you what, you rest again now, and we'll leave you alone to sleep. I'll come back later to see how you're getting on, all right?"

Vastin nodded, but the look of confusion did not leave him. He knew something was wrong.

"Ladies..." Egretta hustled them out into the corridor.

"Is it the opium?" Samily asked when the door was closed.

"No. Likely the shoulder was too badly damaged. We'll do more tests, but I suspect his mind can no longer communicate with his arm. He'll live, but that arm's going to be useless."

Heavens, the boy's bad luck had no end. Samily felt a hand on her back.

"He lives, Lady. He lives because of you. Do not allow that miracle to be lost in the disappointment." Dialla's words were soft and kind, but Samily did not feel them. It didn't feel... good enough.

"Thank you, Master. You are kind. I wish there were a way for me to heal him properly without the Blackening returning."

"Well. Actually, there might be." Everyone turned to Morienne. She looked like that shy girl again. "I... Maybe I shouldn't say. I don't want you to think me selfish and... well, it is selfish, I suppose. And it might be too much to ask, but... there might be a way. I think."

If there were a way, there was no "too much to ask." Vastin was a child of God. "Tell me."

Morienne grimaced.

"It would be better if Master Balaban explained."

"He's not good." Allandria was sugaring the tea—Aranok was a mess. He was sleeping, full of poppy milk. A little coercion and she'd convinced him to let her take the charm. She would go to Keft and stay with him while he cleared memories. It was the only way Aranok would let it go. He barely spoke. Stared blankly at her, at the wall. He wasn't entirely... there.

Regardless, she would protect him—even if just from the judgement of their allies. So she played it down. Best not to reveal he might not have been in control of his powers. If Mynygogg knew that, it would raise dangerous questions. Allandria had already seen more than she liked of the regents considering him an asset, and not a man. She had no intention of stoking that fire.

Mynygogg frowned back across the table at her. "And Samily? She's fine?"

Not fine, but better than Aranok. "I believe so. I think she went to see if she could help Vastin."

Mynygogg nodded thoughtfully. He looked around as if surveying the room for the first time. It was relatively simple. The red brick of the hospital, one large window. A round table with eight seats dominated the space. Spare seats were stacked next to a chalkboard and two large chairs bookended a tattered rug before the hearth. It was not a king's chambers.

"I didn't see this coming, Allandria. I never imagined the challenge in taking back the kingdom would be holding our allies together. He really attacked her?"

"So she said."

"And she cut off his hands?"

The image came back to her: Aranok slumped against the wall, bloody stumps trembling before her, and she felt her own hands twitch. As always, she'd been calm in the moment, but...

"Yes."

"Fucking Hells." The king sighed deeply. "Drink?"

God, yes.

"Please." Mynygogg poured wine from a decanter on the sideboard. "How did it go? With the memory *draoidh*?"

The king gave a cynical, breathy laugh and a took long slug of wine. "It could have been better. She's not interested in helping us. Not for the cause, anyway."

"But?"

"Nirea has a plan. Thinks she can convince her—coerce her—I don't know. It might work. But we have to assume it won't. We can't rely on her."

"Shit." That wasn't good. One memory charm was going to make it difficult to clear people quickly enough.

"So we ended the Blackening, then." His tone was cautious. He was trying to gauge Allandria's feelings on what Samily had done. Truthfully, she wasn't sure herself how she felt about that part of it. Except that she knew it was not the right time.

"Has Nirea spoken to Egretta? About getting medics out?"

"I don't think so. She took Quell to find a room, and then she was going to see about her plan. I doubt she'll have had time to see her."

Someone needed to deal with that. To get people out to the Blackened. Especially if it was true and the Thakhati were turning them. They could become a worse plague than the Blackening.

And they were going to have to deal with that too. At some point. She was starting to wish she hadn't accepted Nirea's offer. Usually she just had to follow orders. Now she had to help decide them. "I'll speak to her about it. We should get something moving as soon as possible. People are already dying, I'd think."

A lot of them would have died instantly—those who were so far gone the Blackening was the only thing keeping them alive. Allandria hoped it had been quick for them. For others, it was surely agony. Perhaps some who were healthier would help them. She hoped so.

But that was not for her to do. Egretta, and maybe Ikara, if Rasa could get word to her, would have to deal with that. As queen's envoy, and with the king's envoy indisposed, she needed to help with the larger scale. "Your Majesty, what's our next move? If we only have one charm. What's our plan?"

Mynygogg licked his teeth thoughtfully. "I've been considering that. It occurs to me that, if Anhel Weyr knows we're here—and I think we can assume that—it's only a matter of time before he attacks. Perhaps knowing we had Shayella—if he did—was staying his hand. Perhaps not. Perhaps he doesn't want to murder all the *draoidhs* here. I don't know. But staying here and digging in is not an option—not least because there's an army of Thakhati at our gates—such as they are.

"The sunspire keeps us safe. But only from them. If Weyr comes with other demons—real demons—we'll be in trouble. And the longer we wait, the more he can summon."

"So we need to move?" At some point it was inevitable. But the idea of it being soon was... disturbing. They were in no state for it.

"I think so. We need to hit Weyr somewhere that actually hurts—that weakens his hold on Eidyn. I see three options." He counted them off on fingers. "The military, the messengers and the money.

"The military are farthest away, and considering our recent encounter with them, not inclined to trust us. I had thought to send Aranok, until..."

Indeed. Now that he was the most wanted man in Eidyn, he was the last man they should send. And Meristan was burned there too—possibly all of the Thorns.

"As for the messengers, after Madu's death, I can't imagine Weyr will let us near them again. That leaves the money. Mournside is the largest individual source of taxes in Eidyn. Cut them off and the new king will struggle to pay the army he relies on. I can tell you, hungry soldiers are less inclined to war."

"So we go to Mournside? Clear the memories of the merchants?"

"I think so. I would have suggested the old lairds, but after Anhel murdered them, God knows who's left there. They'll likely be scattered too—heirs squabbling over their parents' corpses."

"They'll be looking for Aranok in Mournside." But he'd be glad to be near his family. Even if he couldn't possibly stay with them. The guard would be watching them like a pack of starving dogs. Still—Bak was captain of Mournside. Perhaps there was room for manoeuvre there. Perhaps if they got to him...

"I know. He'll need to change his look. And keep his head down. We'll sneak in at night. Maybe find a warehouse or something to hole up in until we can get enough allies on board. If we can turn enough of the merchants..."

Assuming she could get Aranok on his feet again. That was far from certain. And only she knew it.

If so, maybe they still had a chance of taking back the kingdom. It made sense. This was why Mynygogg was king. He had the tactical mind and he understood the complexities of governance. Allandria's best thought had been to get to Anhel himself—but that would mean a fight—against their own people. And that was something Mynygogg would not relish. In Calcheugh, he'd been determined nobody else would die for him. He wanted a bloodless insurgence. It was a noble aim. She wasn't sure it was possible.

Allandria knocked back the last of her wine. "Right. I'll speak to Egretta about the Blackened and then take this"—she indicated the charm around her neck—"to Keft."

Mynygogg considered the little yellow ball for a moment. "It's bad, isn't it?"

Of course Mynygogg knew. The fact Aranok had let the charm go was enough, now she'd pointed it out. His friend had seen him lose himself before. If she lied now, Mynygogg would know.

"Yes. It's bad."

CHAPTER 48

A*ir ais.*"

The little terra-cotta pot re-formed itself in Samily's open hand, the fractured pieces knitting back together seamlessly. The eight students stared open-mouthed. Their eyes were lit with wonder; Samily warmed in their reflection.

When she and Morienne had arrived at Balaban's office to find him in the midst of a tutorial, Samily had assumed they'd be asked to wait. When the master had, after a moment's pause, enthusiastically invited them in, she'd been confused and wary. Justifiably, as his next request was for her to demonstrate her ability for his students.

She'd been irritated at first, thinking he'd revealed her power without permission, but after a moment's thought, she realised that while he'd asked for a demonstration, he had not specified of what—leaving Samily the option to demur if she so chose. That being the case, and seeing the mostly enthusiastic faces before her, she had chosen to do so—though only something small and quick. Her energy was still waning and she was feeling rather raw after everything. She looked forward to a quiet evening of reflective prayer and a good night's rest.

Balaban was smiling broadly at her under his full-moon spectacles. He turned to the students. "Questions?"

All eight hands reached for the ceiling. Balaban pointed to a young boy—the smallest in the class, if not the youngest. "Brath?"

The boy sat up proudly, as if he had won a prize. The other hands slumped down. "What would have happened if you only had one piece of the pot? Would it have regrown the entire rest of the pot? And what would have happened to the remaining pieces? Would they still exist? Could you grow another pot from each piece? Does that mean—"

"Brath." Balaban cut him off. "When I asked for questions, my intention was not that you should ask all of them at once."

The other students chortled and Brath reddened a little about the cheeks, shrinking back into his chair. "Sorry."

It took Samily a moment to comprehend everything the boy had asked, and when she did, she realised she had no answers herself yet. She did not understand this ability beyond the one use she'd always made of it. Perhaps spending some time here, studying with Master Ipharia, would be a good thing. "No need to apologise—those are good questions. Unfortunately, I cannot yet answer them myself. But you have made me want to learn the answers."

Brath smiled shyly, looking up at her from under his eyebrows.

"Excellent!" Balaban seemed especially pleased at that response. Odd, since she'd had no satisfactory answer for the boy. "Any other questions?"

After each student had asked something of her—mostly around how she learned she had the power to control time and what she had been able to do with it so far, Balaban cheerfully dismissed the class, leaving the three of them alone in his office.

"Thank you greatly, Lady Samily. I am indebted to you for making my students' day and likely increasing my reputation with them at the same time!" Balaban dropped back into the rich leather chair behind his impressive dark wood desk. The walls were lined with shelves, books scattered somewhat haphazardly across them, on top of them, on surfaces and on the floor—many with ribbons or snatches of torn paper protruding from their edges. It was as if knowledge itself had exploded here.

"It was my pleasure, Master." She meant it. It had been a pleasure to see the students' enthusiasm for her ability—similar to seeing the Thorn trainees when she demonstrated martial manoeuvres. "I'm only sorry that I did not have better answers."

"Ah, my dear," Balaban said as he steepled his fingers before him. "A teacher's job is not simply to provide their pupils with answers, but to encourage them to ask the right questions. In that regard, you were an excellent teacher."

Samily felt her cheeks warm. "Thank you." It was pleasing to feel appreciated for something other than being a Thorn. Perhaps she took that for granted. And perhaps she should not.

"Anyway..." Balaban looked to Morienne. "I trust you've come for a reason other than enthralling my students with rare magic. What can I do for you both?"

Morienne shifted uncomfortably in her seat. Why was she so nervous?

"Well, Master Balaban, um, I wondered if... You see, there's a thing, well... the Blackening—it's gone, and—"

Balaban burst to his feet. "Gone? It's gone? Heaven's gates, girl, that's fabulous! How? Did Aranok retrieve the relic?"

"No, um..." Morienne looked hesitantly at Samily.

No point dancing around the subject. He would know soon enough what had happened and she was still not sure she should be hiding it. Allandria may have planted doubts, but she had not yet decided how valid they were.

"I executed the necromancer."

Balaban's face slowly melted from delight to confusion and, finally, understanding. "I see. Well, however it was done, it is good that it is over."

There was something particularly melancholy about his reaction, and Samily realised that, if Shayella had been a student here, she may have been known to the master. Closely, perhaps, given his penchant for darker magic. She hoped she hadn't made an enemy of Balaban too.

"But Vastin... he's... Well, his arm is healed—Samily healed it—took it forward," said Morienne. "It's healed, and he'll live, but... the arm is useless."

"Ah. I am sorry to hear that. But I suppose we must be grateful that he will live. Fortune favours him at last." The master returned to his seat, fiddling with a pencil on the desk. "It is odd, perhaps, that I am so invested in the fortune of a boy I have never actually met, as such."

"I've never really 'met' him either. I mean, I've been tending to him and he has no idea who I am. I think it just means... you care." The change in Morienne really was stark. The quiet, resigned, dark woman had become excitable, enthusiastic and outspoken. In a matter of weeks. Samily supposed her own curse being suppressed—unexpectedly, no less—must have had a profound effect.

But they had business here, and she had things to do. Most importantly, form a plan to help the former Blackened. "Morienne, I am sorry to insist, but you said there might be a way to help Vastin?"

The woman flushed again. Why was she so reticent to simply explain? Rather than answer, she turned toward Balaban.

"Master, Samily mentioned she wished there were a way for her to heal Vastin without succumbing to the Blackening. And it occurred to me that... maybe... there is? But... I didn't know if it was my place to... or if I should..."

Balaban's face lit with understanding and a wry smile. "Of course. No, you were right to come to me, Morienne. It is something we can discuss, of course. And the decision will rest with Lady Samily."

"Of course." Morienne nodded enthusiastically.

The master turned to Samily, took a deep breath and straightened his mouth in contemplation, as if he were unsure where to begin. "The reason Morienne is unsure about suggesting this to you, Samily, is because it benefits her. And it would require a great sacrifice on your part. A sacrifice I would not assume you, even as a Thorn, or anyone else would choose to make."

What was he talking about? What sacrifice would they consider too far? And how would it benefit Morienne? "I do not understand."

"It's relatively simple, actually. I have not yet discovered a way to lift Morienne's blood curse. But I have found a way to transfer it to another person. If it were transferred to you..."

She'd be immune to the Blackening, as Morienne was, and could use her ability to take Vastin's body back to before he was cursed. "Of course! Yes, do it."

"Hold on..." Balaban waved her down. "There is more to consider before you jump at this. Morienne's charm should work for you as it does for her. As long as you wear it, the effects will be suppressed. However, this is a bloodline curse. You will pass it on to your children and grandchildren. Your descendants will also bear this curse. You see? This is a larger sacrifice than just your own. It is not a decision to make hastily."

Samily smiled. It was always a pleasure to be in a moment where she saw God's plan clearly laid before her. When she finally understood a mystery. When everything made sense. Not only could she help Vastin, she could help all of the Blackened. Every one of them.

"Master, that will not be a problem. I have no intention of bearing children. If I choose to become a parent, it will be to a child of God, like me."

"Are you certain, Samily? You are a young woman. What might seem certain to you now may become more complicated as you age. I speak from experience."

She was absolutely certain. This was where she was meant to be and what she was meant to do. "I am certain. When can we perform the transfer?"

"Well," Balaban said. He sat back in his chair, pushing his glasses up his nose. "I will need to prepare some items, and we will require a *draoidh* to perform the incantations. Perhaps Aranok would—"

"No. Can I do it myself?" Balaban's eyebrows raised and Samily realised her tone had been too harsh. "Sorry. I would like to keep this to ourselves. Until it is done?"

"Hmm." Balaban stroked his chin, but it was not clear whether he was considering her question or the reason for her request. Either way, this was what she wanted. "Theoretically, I suppose. If you're confident. My only concern is that it may be a little tricky for a relatively untrained *draoidh*—no offence intended. If you were to make an error, well—I don't know what the consequences might be."

Samily wasn't worried for herself. After her experience removing the demon from Rasa, she felt entirely confident. But confidence can be a weakness when misplaced. A fundamental lesson of combat. And it was not only she who was at risk of the consequences. Morienne looked across at her, wide-eyed and chewing her lips. "I understand. Is there someone else? I could ask Rasa."

"I'm sure we'll be able to find someone," Balaban answered. "Shall we say a few days' time?"

No. Not a few days. The Blackened did not have that luxury. "Master, if I may, once I heal Vastin, it is my intention to travel to the Auld Road and help as many Blackened as possible. I would like to leave in the morning."

"Ah. Of course. Those returned from the curse will be in need of assistance. I understand. Then we shall waste no time. And, perhaps, your plans suggest the very *draoidh* we need." Balaban stood, looking around purposefully at his piles of books. "Morienne, would you do me the favour of fetching Master Dialla?"

Aranok awoke in the dark. It was pleasant.

Warm.

Cool.

Comfortable.

Where was he? It didn't matter. Everything felt good. His back didn't ache. His knee had stopped throbbing. Everything was... fuzzy. No need to wake up, really. Just close his eyes and go back into the quiet dark.

"Laird?"

Oh. Someone was there. A woman. Allandria? She was here, wasn't she? She'd given him the cup. Of milk. He'd drunk it all. Had he? Maybe there was some left. He should drink the rest.

His left hand banged against the bedside table, searching clumsily for the cup. It was there somewhere. With more peace.

"Aranok?"

Oh. Yes. There was someone there, wasn't there?

"Yes?"

"Laird, it's Rasa. Can you... hear me?"

His eyes were tired. Stinging. Eyelids heavy. He blinked, trying to peer through the gloom. A glimpse of moonlight. A pretty face. A sad smile.

Why was Allandria sad?

No. Not Allandria. Rasa.

Who was Rasa? Why was she sad?

"I hear you."

"I spoke to Allandria. I heard what happened."

"Mm-hmm." What was she sorry for? Was Allandria sad too? Was Aranok sad? He didn't feel sad. He felt... nothing.

"I just... Samily is a good girl. To her core, she is good. She would not hurt you, nor anyone, by choice."

Of course Samily was good. She was a Thorn. Sworn to do good. Why would she hurt him?

"Can you see my cup?" His hand clipped the edge of the table again, fumbling. Did his fingers work? Could he feel fingers? Did he still have fingers? He rubbed the tips of his fingers against his palm. Yes, still there.

"It's here, Laird. It's empty."

"Oh." That was a shame. He must have spilled it. There was definitely some left. He was sure. "Could I have more?"

"I... Maybe. I will ask Lady Allandria."

"Thank you." Aranok closed his eyes and sank back into the pillow. It still felt nice. Soft. Comfortable.

"I wanted you to know. I'm going to Mournside. To Emelina. I'll protect them. I promise."

That was good. He hadn't seen them for an age. It would be nice to go home. "Give them m'love."

"Of course. I will."

Silence. Peace. Heavy eyes.

A creaking—a flood of light. Aranok raised his hand against it.

"Goodbye, Aranok. I wish you... well."

Allandria was leaving. Was there something he wanted to tell her? Something important? It was there, in the dark, slipping away, hiding in fleeting corners.

What had she said? It meant something. Something to hold on to. Something that mattered.

She loved him.

That was real, wasn't it? It felt real. It felt... wonderful. It felt like the only thing that mattered.

"Al?"

"Pardon?" The door stopped creaking.

"I love you."

She didn't answer. There was no need. She already had. He smiled and relaxed again. The dark sang a gentle lullaby.

A sigh in the distance. "Goodbye, Aranok."

And then nothing.

The bliss of absolute peace.

It was odd that it never got dark anymore. Nirea looked out the window, down at the town of Traverlyn, lit now in the haze of dusk by the giant sunstone. It made it difficult to know when to sleep—to sleep at all. She'd hung a hammock in their room so she could go to it when she found herself awake in the small hours, so as not to disturb Mynygogg. He slept soundly, if fitfully. The hammock helped her rest. She could close her eyes and imagine herself at sea. Rum helped too.

She closed the shutters, barring most of the unnatural daylight, leaving the room lit by the fire. Mynygogg was off somewhere, speaking to someone. She wasn't sure who. The guards, she thought. They'd largely been restored now, and the king had felt it right to address them personally. There's little grabs a person's loyalty more than a handshake from their king. With pirates, it's dominance. Strength to keep them in place. But most folk wanted to see the strength to protect them, to lead. That was where Gogg's easy confidence made allies.

A knock, and a guard entered at her command. Not Leondar. He was resting. Perhaps, she wondered, with Master Dialla. This was a city guard whose name she did not know. "Lady Rasa to see you, Your Majesty."

"Of course."

The *draoidh*'s face was pale. Haunted. It had been a good day for Eidyn, but not everyone had escaped unscathed. "What can I do for you, Rasa?"

"Your Majesty. I just came to inform you I am leaving tonight. I make for Mournside."

What? That wasn't a good idea. Ignoring everything else about her—what a formidable ally she was in battle—Rasa was their best means of communication over distance. If they were to split up, to move some of them to Mournside soon, they'd need her to keep them in contact. "May I ask why?"

"To protect Laird Aranok's family. From the assassin."

Of course. She was the girl's tutor. But they needed Rasa now more than Aranok's family did. And even if the family was in imminent danger, Hells, even if it did cost them their lives, they needed Rasa here.

She would not like that. And Nirea wasn't keen to test her authority right then, when the crown was a matter of debate. It would simply be down to Rasa to decide how much weight the deposed queen carried. If any. She didn't like that lack of leverage. But perhaps there was another way.

"Of course, I understand. But I wonder if there might be a better use for your abilities?"

"Majesty?"

Nirea turned away as if considering her thoughts. "Well, the Blackened require assistance. I understand Ikara was arranging for carts to be ready to move at our signal. Now is the time of need. Now is when we require those carts to help bring the sick to Traverlyn, where they can be treated. You could carry that message to her?"

"Of course, Majesty. That was also my intention. If you like, you could ink a short letter for me to convey."

There. Good. She was on the hook.

"Then, of course, we'd need you back here, to help coordinate. You're essential to our communications—helping to ensure the victims get here safely."

Hesitant this time. Did she grow even more pale? "With respect, Majesty, I have given Laird Aranok my word I would protect his family. I would like to keep that promise."

"I understand. But, between you and me, we'll soon be moving to Mournside. And Aranok's family have the wealth to hire other protection—from people who are not needed by their country for crucial communication."

"We will?"

Good, she was talking as "we." That's what Nirea needed. "Indeed.

Though it is a closely guarded secret for now. I must ask you to keep it to yourself."

"Of course." The woman nodded seriously and was quiet for a long time. Nirea recognised the silence. It was reticence and hesitation. It was doubt.

"I'm worried about them."

There was more Rasa wasn't saying. Or more she wanted to say but could not. Whether for fear of breaking a confidence or perhaps fear of offending her queen. Nirea wanted to reassure her to speak freely, but in doing so she would surrender some of the little authority she had—and might need.

Things were simpler as a pirate. Violent, but simpler.

"Of course you are. I am too. As I am for my friends who may be targeted. And Allandria's family." Mynygogg had no living family, and neither had Glorbad. She was almost relieved at the thought that as one's wife and the other's closest friend, she was the only likely target for an assassin who wanted to hurt them. And Glorbad was beyond pain. "But I have to ask you to do what is best for the greater number of people, Rasa. Your service here could be crucial in winning this war."

Rasa's brow furrowed. "Is it a war? Is that where we've come to? Again?"

God, the optimism, the naivety to think it was anything else. "It always has been, Rasa. We didn't know it for a while. But the war was always there. It never ended. It just changed."

Rasa's shoulders sank and her gaze fell. "I suppose that's true. I just... We saw so little of the war here. I'd hoped we'd been fortunate."

Traverlyn had been almost unscathed by the war with the Hellfire Club. They'd left it largely alone—whether out of respect for the *draoidhs* there or for fear of inspiring them into action, she didn't know. Tactically it made sense, but ethically too. She wondered if the reasoning had been different even amongst the three of them. From what she'd learned, it was likely Shayella, at least, acted on principles—as warped as they'd been.

"I know. But that is the way of war. It creeps into every corner."

Rasa's chest rose and fell as she sighed deeply. Her beauty was not much diminished by her obvious malaise. Nirea understood why men—and women—were drawn to her. She was flawless. But physical perfection could not mask emotional torment.

"We need you here, Rasa."

Her sad eyes rose. "Is that an order, Majesty?"

There it was. The moment she'd wanted to avoid. "It can be, if that would make it easier for you. But I would prefer it not be."

Rasa met her eyes directly. Did she see how fragile Nirea's position was? Did she see that, in truth, she needed Rasa more than Rasa needed her? Was she sympathetic to Aranok? Did she know what had happened at Greytoun? Or with Shayella? She was a *draoidh* after all. Were her own loyalties as divided as the envoy's? All these questions and more Nirea prayed the metamorph could not read in her.

"I understand," she finally said. "I will take your message to Mournside and return, if that is your will."

If that is your will.

It wasn't enthusiastic, but it was agreement. Hopefully it would be enough to hold them together. They couldn't afford to be shedding *draoidh* allies—especially not one as powerful as Rasa—when they were already in danger of losing Aranok.

To lose them both, or worse, have them as enemies, would be a disaster.

Thank God they could rely on Samily.

CHAPTER 49

"Aye, it feels grand. Like new!" Vastin stretched his arm for the ceiling and swung it back down with a carelessness that made Samily wince. Even knowing she had repaired it completely this time, she had expected the boy to feel pain.

Master Dialla had been happy to perform the transfer spell. Samily now carried Morienne's curse, along with her protective charm. She had taken Vastin back to before he was Blackened, fighting a panicked instinct to lift her hands when the Blackening returned, a desperate fear that she might release the plague again. But the black handprint faded as quickly as it rose, Morienne's curse protecting her from its touch.

They'd saved him, thank God. And now she had proved she could save them all. She just had to get some rest first. Dialla had given her a boost of energy, but Samily knew from experience how her mind would fracture without sleep. That would be dangerous.

"Well, I'll be a mouse's twitch." Egretta poked at the boy's shoulder.

Vastin laughed and flinched away from her touch. "That tickles!"

Everyone else laughed with him. Balaban, Morienne and Dialla had all been interested to see the fruit of their labours. It also seemed like half the medics in Traverlyn were waiting in the hall to see the miracle of the boy grasped from death's maw.

Egretta took Samily's hands. "My girl. My bonny girl. I knew you were a gift the day I met you."

Samily felt her cheeks blush. "It is only God's will."

Her smile turned wry. "That may be what you believe. But I see a fearless young woman who makes sacrifices for others as if it were nothing. And I'd rather thank her than God."

Samily did not know how to answer that, so she smiled as naturally as she could and lowered her eyes. Egretta released her hands and clapped dramatically. "Right! Everybody who isn't a medic, out! I have a patient to tend and students who need to learn."

"Of course." Balaban opened the door and waved them all out. As Samily was about to cross the threshold, Vastin's voice stopped her.

"Samily?" She turned back to the boy. "I owe you my life. Again." He shrugged, grinning sheepishly. "Thank you."

"It was my honour, Vastin. I have confidence you will repay me one day."

The boy grinned wider.

The cluster of medics bustled to get into the room.

Samily moved toward the others, getting out of the way as they crowded in. Several openly stared at her. It was odd.

"Well, that went beautifully." Balaban clapped Samily's shoulder. "I think, perhaps, this merits a proper write-up for the records. Would you agree, Master?"

"Absolutely," Dialla answered. "Thank you for allowing me to be a part of it, Master Balaban. It was an incredible, unique experience."

"I'll... be in a book?" Morienne's voice cracked.

"You will, young lady! We all will!" Balaban seemed barely able to contain himself. Samily saw the miracle in what they'd done, but it was pleasing to see it reflected so strongly in the others. "And you must be delighted. You are free!"

Morienne chewed her lips as her eyes filled with tears. She nodded frantically before falling against Samily and wrapping her in her arms, sobbing.

"I... Are you... all right?" Samily returned the hug, not entirely sure what was happening.

"I believe our Morienne is grateful, Lady Samily," said Balaban. As quickly as she'd thrown herself on Samily, Morienne released her and nearly bowled the old man into the wall with an equally aggressive hug.

"Oh! Yes, of course, you're welcome, my dear." The master patted her back.

"Well, it's been an honour, but I should return to my charge." Dialla made a slight bow to Balaban.

Before she could move, he raised a hand. "Actually, there is more I planned to discuss, if we may?"

"Of course. What can I do for you?"

"Well, it's not for me, as such. It's for Samily. Though, really, I suppose, it's for the Blackened. The... We need a new phrase for them, don't we? Seeing as they're not Blackened anymore. The Returned, perhaps?"

A shiver crossed Samily's shoulders. *Returned* was too similar to *Risen*, the name the necromancer had used for the Dead.

Dialla looked confused. "I suppose we can decide that out at our leisure, Master, but I understand who you mean."

"Of course, yes. Anyway, it is Lady Samily's intention to use her new immunity to the Blackening curse to heal those who have been cured." Balaban's face lit up. "The Cured! That seems a natural result, doesn't it?"

Morienne smiled as she dabbed her eyes dry. "You're thinking of your writing, aren't you?"

"You see through me." Balaban was like a giddy child. Under normal circumstances, it would be a pleasing sight, but Samily was as keen as Dialla to get on. "But yes, Dialla, Samily intends to heal the Cured."

"Forgive me, but isn't that dangerous?" Dialla addressed the question at Samily. "If you turn one of them Blackened and lose control, if they infect one other... you could rebirth the plague."

"That is true." Balaban turned serious. "And I believe that Samily could do with assistance in preventing that from happening. Not least, in helping her not to make errors of judgement due to being overly tired."

"Of course. I see your intent," said Dialla. "You think I should go with her to help her do more. Quicker."

"Quicker and safer. I believe not only your skill but also your care would benefit Lady Samily."

"You flatter me, Master Balaban." Dialla turned to her. "I would be happy to accompany you, Samily, but I have a responsibility here, supporting the student who maintains the sunspire."

Samily was on the edge of offering her understanding, but Balaban spoke again before she could do more than part her lips.

"I am certain that Principal Keft would take on that role again. And I would be happy to check in on the girl throughout the day while he is otherwise detained."

The master seemed intent on his idea.

"I could come!" Morienne excitedly announced. "I'm not needed here anymore, and I'd quite like to see the Cured. To help. I've learned some healing. Here and Lepertoun. Not much, I suppose, but I can clean a wound and wrap a bandage..."

It would be pleasant to have the company, Samily supposed. And Master Dialla would be a true asset. As long as they could build fires, she could keep Samily energised to heal the Cured much more quickly. In fact, it would be largely ideal—as if it were part of a plan.

"I would be delighted to have you both, if you are willing. But I do intend to leave early tomorrow."

"Tomorrow?" Dialla almost took a step backwards.

"Indeed. People will already be dying. Some will have died as they were cured. Others may be taken by the Thakhati tonight. We cannot leave them any longer than necessary. If nothing else, they will need food and drink."

"You see, Master Dialla, time is not our ally," said Balaban.

The younger master clasped her hands and rubbed them together, as if she would wash them clean. "All right. Of course, I will accompany you, Lady Samily. It would be my honour. Please excuse me. I will need to prepare."

Dialla turned and hurried away down the corridor. Samily was unsure, but the master did not seem enthusiastic to be going. She hoped there was not something underlying Dialla's reaction that she did not understand.

"Samily!"

Rasa brushed past Dialla, coming toward them. Samily warmed. She'd missed her friend after spending so many days in her almost constant company. She had wanted to go to her after Aranok—but there had been more pressing needs. In fact, she'd barely stopped since. It would be nice to speak to her, to have her listen. And things were better now than they had been this afternoon. Rasa would understand.

Balaban and Morienne took their leave, Morienne promising to meet her at the stables in the morning. It took Samily the walk from the hospital to the Sheep's Heid to explain everything that had happened. The fight, the curse, healing Vastin and her plans. Rasa listened almost silently and said very little of consequence until they were sat with drinks in front of them.

"Samily, do you think perhaps you acted too hastily?"

She nearly choked on her whisky.

"What?"

The last thing she'd been prepared for was her friend not to understand. To disagree. Samily hadn't realised until that moment how much she needed her support.

"I'm not blaming you, don't misunderstand. I'm not. I know why you executed Shayella. After everything we've seen—after everything you've seen. After what she did to that poor man. I understand. But—"

"But what?" Samily's voice had a harder edge than she'd intended.

"Sometimes our actions have unintended consequences."

Samily placed the glass down on the table. Her hands trembled ever so slightly. Her heart raced. It was difficult even to meet Rasa's eyes, so it was a blessing when a pair of drunks rolled into the bar, singing something about battle or a woman—it was hard to tell. They were happy, laughing despite the lyrics of the song seeming melancholy. A song about loss, delivered with glee. The barman shushed them with a good-natured smile and greeted them as old friends. Just people being people. Unafraid. Part of Samily wanted to shake them, to scream about the danger they were in and the losses Eidyn had suffered, but what would be the point? One of the most uplifting things about people is their ability to find solace in horror and hope in ruin.

Rasa had also turned to watch the men. When she turned back, it was with a conciliatory smile. But Samily was not consoled. "I cured the Blackened. I saved Vastin. I will save the rest of the Cured. I do not see a problem, I see God's path."

"Samily, please." Rasa reached across the table but stopped short of touching Samily's hand. "I'm not angry. I'm not criticising you. It's just... There may have been a better way."

That was the problem. Everyone else thought it was complicated, but in fact it was entirely simple. "I don't see how."

Rasa frowned sadly. "Samily, some of the Blackened will have died already. Because nobody was there to help them when they were cured."

She knew that. It had been eating at her since Allandria made the same point. "And how many died because we took no action? How many are Thakhati now because we waited?"

Rasa sat back and pursed her lips thoughtfully. "Yes, that's a fair question. And I agree. Someone should have considered that risk. Someone should have taken responsibility. But that person is not you, Samily. That is what kings and queens are for. And envoys."

Envoys. It was the envoy who allowed the Blackened to be harvested. Trying to protect the necromancer. "When God's children are suffering, kings and queens have no meaning."

Perhaps this was the line where their connection would break. Rasa's lack of faith. Perhaps it was not possible to maintain such a friendship. She had hoped it would be.

"I didn't mean you had no right, Samily, I meant it was not your responsibility."

Another eruption of song. The men had moved to a table now and swung their mugs of ale along with the new tune, which, Samily gathered, was about a boat lost in a storm. A few others, from a table she could not see, joined the chorus. Her heart pounded a faster rhythm, consumed in its own maelstrom.

"As a servant of God, it is always my responsibility. It is when responsibility is refused that suffering flourishes."

Rasa sighed and closed her eyes, running her hands through her hair. "I'm not saying it well. I'm sorry."

There was silence between them. Samily drank and looked away to the fire, where a group of muddied men warmed their hands. Farmers, maybe? Some other labourers? They also laughed and nudged one another with the easy manner of close friends.

Rasa finally leaned forward and spoke quietly. "I'm leaving tonight. To Mournside. I'll be back soon, but—"

"I will be gone," Samily finished.

"I don't want to leave on a sour note, Samily. These weeks we've spent together have been, for all they were difficult, very pleasant. You really are a miracle—whatever that means." Rasa paused with more words on her lips. Samily struggled to feel the compliment—there was clearly something else coming.

"There is still something you want to say."

She dipped her head. "Laird Aranok is not well."

That felt like an excuse. "He tried to kill me."

"I know. Well..." Rasa seemed to consider finishing the thought but changed her mind. "He has suffered a great deal. He has lost a lot. I shared that pain with him. Conifax was, to him—to me—much like Meristan to you. Remember how scared you were when you thought you'd lost him? How much it hurt? And then Lestalric. I think maybe that changed him. I think maybe it changed you, Samily. In honesty, I don't see how it could not have."

Samily gripped her hands together beneath the table to keep them from shaking. She had not changed. She was who she had always been. God's servant. "He tried to kill me."

"Did he?" Rasa looked more surprised than Samily felt—as if the words had come from someone else's mouth. After a moment of apparent consideration, however, she continued. "From what you said, he was trying to force you to use your power. If that was what he wanted, there was no benefit in killing you. It seems like he was trying to save Shayella, not kill you."

Samily remembered the heat. The searing pain as her skin blistered. Did it matter if he was trying to kill her? He might have, had Samily refused to use her skill. And she had the right to defend herself. "I might have killed him."

"I know. And I think he did too. Maybe not consciously, but I wonder how much he expected you to defend yourself. Completely."

Samily didn't know how to answer. If she understood what Rasa was saying, Aranok could have attacked knowing she might kill him. It made no sense. "Why?"

Rasa leaned toward her. "I think the envoy is unwell. I've seen this sickness. My mother had it. A darkness. A crippling shadow that weighed her down. I didn't understand it then. There was an emptiness to her, some days. Too many days. As if she weren't really there. Just passing through. A sickness of the mind. Of the soul.

"From what I have seen, from what Allandria has told me, I suspect Aranok has the same sickness. And I fear it is consuming him."

Was that possible? Was a sickness responsible for the envoy's erratic, illogical behaviour? If so, it would colour everything. If he was suffering… Whatever his belief, he was also God's child. But did that truly excuse or forgive what he'd done? Could anything?

Perhaps. Perhaps not. It was not for her to decide either way.

"What happened? With your mother?"

Rasa took a long, slow drink from her wine. When she put her cup down, her eyes were wet.

"She hanged herself."

Samily gasped involuntarily. Taking a life is a heavy burden. How heavy the burden of life must be to take your own, she could not imagine.

"I am so sorry. That must have been very painful." In all the time the two of them had spent together, talking into the night, Rasa never said much about her childhood. She happily recounted tales of her time in Traverlyn, but almost nothing before. In fact, the story of how she discovered her ability was the only instance Samily could recall of hearing anything about that time. She knew Rasa had painful memories, but she had not imagined this.

"Thank you. But that isn't why I told you. I wanted you to understand. You are an unusual… maybe unique person, Samily. You see things clearly. But not everything in life is clear. Does that make sense?"

It sounded like something Meristan would say, deep in his cups. In fact, it was similar to something he had said. And not a little like what Allandria had said to her after the fight. Part of Samily wanted to rebel—to reject this idea that things were not as simple as they appeared—but it would make her a poor student to ignore the same message from so many sources. But neither would she lie about it. "No. Not entirely. Because it seems to me that there is good and bad to be done. There is making the right choice or the selfish choice. My choices, my life, have led me to a place where I ended the Blackening and will now be able to heal the Cured. I understand your perspective, and I will not reject it, but I see God's path clearly before me."

Rasa took a deep breath and another drink. A new song from the drinkers. This time a sea shanty. A happier tune, about salt air and sun in the sky. A young man with a significant scar through one eyebrow drummed along on his own table.

It was some time before Rasa answered. "Samily, let me put another idea to you. If, instead of taking action yourself, you had waited for the opportunity to discuss options with the king and queen, with Aranok—what if the idea of taking the curse from Morienne had been suggested then? What if Aranok really had struck a deal to have Shayella end the Blackening, but under control, at a time of our choosing? What if the two of you could have worked together to save all of them? Or, at least, most of them?"

Samily's skin rose in gooseflesh. How could she have worked with the necromancer? Who had killed all those people. Who had helped murder half of Eidyn. And what price would that deal have demanded—for her and for Eidyn? "I do not believe she would have cooperated. She had no reason to."

"She loved her daughter, Samily. Love makes people do unimaginable things."

"Her daughter was Dead."

"Not to her. And that is what mattered. Do you see? It wasn't so simple. Not to her."

"No. I still do not believe she would have cooperated."

"Samily." Rasa's face hardened. "Is it possible that you are choosing—even unconsciously—to believe that, because it justifies your actions?"

Samily recoiled from the table. The words were like a knife to her. She trusted Rasa. Why would she accuse her of something so... awful? "Why...? I thought we were friends."

The metamorph softened and reached across the table. This time, it was Samily who pulled her hand away. "Oh, sweetheart, we are. Please, don't mistake this for an attack. I'm not trying to hurt you. I'm not trying to blame you, even. I only want to help you see there is a larger picture."

"But why? Why would you say something so hurtful? Why would you think me capable of something so base?" Samily felt tears rising. But she would not have them. Not now.

"Samily...for all your wonders, you're human. None of us are flawless. None are completely innocent—though you might be the closest I've seen. We are all the product of our lives—for good or ill. The best we can do is try to understand why and resolve to be better, when we can."

A stab in her gut—a twinge of pain, of nausea. "I am sorry that you think so badly of me."

"Oh, oh, Samily, no." Rasa stood and moved around the table, dragging a chair next to Samily's own. This time, she let the woman take her hands. Rasa's were warm and soft. Only through the contrast did she realise her own were cold. They tingled at her touch, warmth running up her arms. "Conifax was closer to me than anyone else in my life. And nobody...nobody tested me harder. I resented him for it for some time. Until, finally, I broke. In a tutorial, I screamed at him, God"—she raised one hand to her cheek—"in front of half a dozen other students. I accused him of picking on me. Of being cruel."

Samily swallowed hard. She didn't understand how this story related. Was she saying that we have to accept cruelty from people we care about? "What happened?"

"After the class, he had me stay behind. I thought he would expel me. I thought I was going to have to leave the university. I was terrified. Instead, he gave me tea. He talked me through the problem I was having. And he told me something that forever changed our relationship."

"What?"

"He said, 'Rasa, only the people who care the most about you will tell you the difficult truths you need to hear.' Do you understand? I'm saying this because I care."

Samily felt unmoored. As if the chair beneath her were suddenly made of wool. Maybe she had made a mistake. She'd always had difficulty with people, but this was...something entirely new. The notion that what felt like cruelty, like criticism, could be born from affection. This was not how Meristan taught.

She would pray on it later. For now, she needed to change the subject. At least the focus.

"All right. I accept your intention. And perhaps I could have acted differently. I still do not believe the envoy's actions were excusable."

Rasa released her hands and folded her own together decisively in her lap, sitting upright. "That's fair. You may be right. Perhaps I'm being too generous. I've seen him as a good man since we met, but I have reservations. Maybe I lean too heavily on our shared connection to Conifax. Maybe my experience with my mother leads me to see dark clouds in a clear sky. I don't know. But whatever the truth, I'm sorry it happened. I'm sorry it happened to you."

The tears finally broke. "Thank you."

Rasa offered a handkerchief from her sleeve. Samily wiped her eyes.

"I have to leave soon, but..." Rasa lifted her cup and emptied it. "One more?"

Samily gave a weak smile. "Yes, please." One more.

With a complex smile, Rasa crossed to the bar.

The singers had moved on again, to a lament for a friend long gone. This one was mournful.

CHAPTER 50

The hammering from the blacksmith's forge as Vastin scarpered past was pleasantly familiar. Funny how just a sound, something so common and normal, could have such a strong effect on him. He smiled despite his heaving lungs.

He'd hoped to catch Samily at the stable, but by the time he'd got there, the women were already gone. He hadn't missed them by much. Which was why he was now racing through the streets of Traverlyn.

When he was all but out of breath, the rear of a horse finally came into view. Vastin almost stumbled straight into a freshly steaming pile of straw-filled dung. That would have been particularly unpleasant in bare feet.

He'd had many odd looks from the locals as he careered through the town.

Egretta hadn't wanted to let him go, but he had no idea when he'd get this chance again. And he'd spent more than enough time in bed. His legs all but walked him out of the hospital of their own accord, desperate to move.

"Samily! Samily!"

He could just make out the lead figure turning in her saddle. Pure white armour glistened in the morning sun. That also made him smile.

All three horses stopped their trot, allowing him to catch up at last. But all he could do was lean on his knees, waiting for his lungs to settle.

"Vastin? What are you . . . what are you wearing?"

From his current position, he could see very clearly the hospital nightgown he'd run out in. He would have stopped to dress, but as he'd just proved, he'd have missed them. And he wasn't prepared to do that. Not after everything Egretta had told him.

"I'm sorry . . . I . . . didn't have . . . time . . ." he panted.

The woman on the horse nearest him dropped down and leaned a hand on his shoulder. He'd seen her yesterday, when Samily repaired his shoulder. She had sharp features and dark hair with a streak of bright red that looked almost unnatural. "Are you all right? Should you be out of bed?"

The woman had kind eyes, and her voice felt almost as familiar as the blacksmith's hammer.

"I'm fine. Just need a minute. You're . . . Morienne, right?"

She was not much older than Samily, he reckoned. Maybe not at all.

"I am."

"Hello. I'm Vastin." He went to offer a hand but instead, as he lifted his head, felt a wave of kinship and gratitude that wouldn't be contained in a handshake. Before he knew what he was doing, Vastin had thrown his arms around the woman and held her as if clinging for his life. "Thank you. Thank you."

It took her a moment, but she returned the embrace. "It's wonderful to meet you."

"I had to reach you before you left. I had to thank you. And say goodbye. To all of you." He turned to see the Thorn and the woman he assumed was Master . . . Dialla? That was the name Egretta had said, wasn't it? "Especially you, Samily." He still felt slightly awkward in the knight's presence, but knowing everything she'd done for him, for all of the Blackened—frankly, he was too full of the sheer joy of life to worry about much else.

Samily dismounted and crossed to him. "I did only what God would have wanted of me, Vastin. But I am honestly glad to see you up and well. I thank you for providing me with such a kindness."

Him? Providing her with a kindness? When Egretta told him they were leaving this morning, he knew he had to find them. He could imagine his mother telling him how rude it would be not to give thanks for such a miraculous gift; his father telling him it was only honourable. Both of them were right. Making this effort was the very least he could do.

The relief at knowing what could have been—what was! And how so many people had come together to help him. To keep him alive. It felt incredible.

It felt like family.

"Do you know where everyone else is? Laird Aranok? Allandria? Glorbad and Nirea? Meristan?"

Samily's face turned pale, and Vastin felt his stomach drop. What had he asked? What was wrong?

"Vastin, I am sorry. Did nobody tell you?"

"Tell me what?"

Samily turned to Morienne with a look of confusion and loss. "I do not know how to…I am not good at…?"

Morienne, wide-eyed, gave a shrug in response. What were they not telling him?

"Please, what is it?"

The master, who had until then remained quietly watching from her horse, was the one who finally spoke.

"I'm sorry to have to be the one to give you bad news, Vastin, but we have lost a number of people—good people—since your accident. Amongst them was your friend Glorbad. I'm sorry to say he died in battle. I understand he was valiant to the end."

Every ounce of joy bled from Vastin. The glow of relief that he had survived, now drained by the knowledge his friend had not. He felt sick, and the ground lurched beneath him. Morienne caught his arm, and he grasped back at hers.

"What…what happened?"

"You should ask Nirea," said Samily. "She was with him. But it was a demon. A trap laid in Barrock by Janaeus."

"King Janaeus? He…he laid a trap? For who? Why?" The world upended again. The king had sent them into a trap? How could that be?

Morienne gasped. "Oh. Oh. He doesn't even know—"

"Know what?"

Again, Samily looked as if she were somewhat lost. Dialla came down from her horse and took Vastin's hand. "There are things you need to know, young man. But first, you need medical attention. I suggest you go back to the hospital, return to your room and find yourself some appropriate clothes. Then perhaps Egretta can help you find Lady Allandria. She should be at the university with Principal Keft. They will explain everything for you. I promise, once you have seen them, everything will make sense. All right?"

It didn't feel all right. But Vastin knew better than to question an elder, especially a master of the university, so he didn't. But seeing the three concerned faces looking back at him, he felt the first sting of regret at making this trip.

He could have lived a little longer not knowing Glorbad was dead.

It felt wrong to Samily, leaving the boy in the street like that, his nightgown fluttering around his legs. He'd been so happy to see them, so enthusiastic to thank them, and they'd left him devastated and alone. Should they have stayed longer? Seen him back to the university, at least, until his memory was restored?

No. He would live. And that was not necessarily true of those they went to help. They could not afford any more delay. Egretta would send out a group of medics that day who would pass them on the road, she hoped, and tend to those farther ahead, keeping them alive until Samily could reach them. And Rasa was going to arrange the same from Mournside, through the envoy's sister. Between them all, with Dialla's help, they would keep many alive—and get them away from the vile nest of Thakhati they were about to ride through.

Perhaps they should have dealt with them first. Killed as many as possible. They could burn the trees during the day. Though that, she supposed, would risk a larger fire—one that could burn down the verdant wall around Traverlyn. They needed a better solution. For now, the sunspire worked. Samily wondered if killing Anhel Weyr would destroy the Thakhati in the same way Shayella's death had ended the Blackening. It might be too much to hope for, but she did not know how demon-summoning magic worked.

Either way, the priority was to save as many people as she could. The Thakhati were the next problem. And Anhel Weyr the next. She would end the demon summoner for what he'd done to God's children, or die in the effort.

"Hold!" An elderly, round man with a ginger ring of hair around a bald pate held up an arm as they approached the edge of town and the great living wall. "Who are you and...? Master Dialla! What can I do for you this fine day? You're surely not leaving again?"

"Good morning, Master Macwin. I'm afraid to say that I am. We are on a mercy mission."

"Are you now?" the man asked, grinning widely. He seemed oddly chirpy considering the circumstances. Considering his wall was holding horrors at bay. "And is this the White Thorn I've been hearing about, by any chance? The one who's also a *draoidh*?"

Samily leaned down to him and offered a hand. "Samily. Pleased to meet you, Master."

The man had not been at the gate when they had arrived just the day before. But she had heard his name. The wall was his concept and his responsibility.

"My pleasure entirely, young lady." Macwin shook the hand a little more vigorously than was comfortable. "And who is this young woman?

Dialla made a very formal gesture of introduction. "This is Morienne. Recently of the hospital and accompanying us on our mission."

"Hello." Morienne nodded agreeably.

"A pleasure, my dear. An absolute pleasure. Well, I suppose I should be letting you all out, should I?"

Dialla again gestured rather more formally than seemed necessary. "If you would, Master. We would be grateful."

"Allow me." Macwin spoke some *draoidh* words Samily did not catch, performed an incantation and waved his hands at the wall of bark and leaves. The boughs and branches contorted themselves into a perfect, beautiful arch. The wall was much thicker than it seemed from the inside. She hadn't paid much attention when they arrived, as her mind had been fiercely focused on getting Quellaria to the king and reporting on the Thakhati.

Now, with a clearer head, she saw it was at least fifteen feet thick with huge trunks, branches, ivy, leaves and bushes. Anything with a blade would be able to hack through it eventually, but could they do it while the wall repaired itself? It was, in some senses, as good as a brick wall—with one exception.

Flame was the fatal weakness of a nature *draoidh*. Everything they worked with would burn. As they rode under the arch, Samily looked back at Traverlyn. The people went about their days as if nothing were amiss. A woman collected eggs from her hens. A boy ran from an alley, a bundle in his hands—intended for someone's urgent attention, she assumed. Some bookkeeper, perhaps? Whatever, she felt they were leaving a small slice of normality behind. A place where many people knew the truth. Where their minds were their own and their king was a good man. Where they bore no burden of manipulation and lies.

Samily would miss this place. It felt safe in the way only Baile Airneach really had before. Well, it had done, before the envoy attacked her.

She'd drunk a lot more whisky last night than intended, carrying on for several more after Rasa had to go. She hadn't wanted to leave. Not straightaway. Perhaps because she hadn't been sure where to go. In the end, the tavern offered her a room on charity, and she gratefully accepted. It was good to have a bed under her own terms again. To be under her own control.

For everything that had happened, this still felt right. Ending the Blackening, healing the Cured, this was her path. This was where she belonged. It felt like a final puzzle piece falling into place. She was going to do this because she was uniquely placed to do it. Her skill gave her the ability. Morienne offered a solution and her own choices; her own life had allowed her to take it without reservation. And Master Dialla would allow them to do as much as was needed without Samily's human limitations holding her back.

It could not have been designed better.

Still, she looked back at Traverlyn with sadness.

It was a good place.

She hoped to see it again.

CHAPTER 51

It felt like a huge gamble. Yesterday it had seemed like a stroke of genius, but today, standing outside the memory *draoidh*'s room, Nirea's plan seemed an awful lot more fragile.

Could she be sure this was what he would want? No. If she convinced Quellaria and he refused, the whole plan would be holed below the waterline. She had no other way to convince the woman to work with them.

Well, maybe one. But was she prepared to take that route? Her own reticence only served to bolster the growing cracks in her confidence.

No point standing out there fearing what might be. The only way to know was to do.

Quellaria took her time answering the door, as if to show her indifference. Nirea almost smiled at the trick. It was a display of power. She knew she had some here. She knew she was needed. Nirea disliked being in the weaker position, but they were up to their necks in it. So she let it go.

"Quellaria. I trust you slept well?"

"I mean, it's not the four-poster I'm accustomed to, but it sufficed." She smiled and looked over Nirea's shoulder. "Who's this? Your grandfather?"

Nirea stepped back and opened her body. "This is Darginn Argyll, king's messenger. I wanted you two to meet."

Darginn dipped his head respectfully. "M'lady. A pleasure."

The *draoidh*'s eyes sparkled with curiosity. She was trying to work out what Nirea was doing. Why she'd brought this old man to visit her. Her eyes darted back and forth.

"All right. And?"

"May we come in?" Nirea asked innocently.

A moment's pause, and Quell stepped back into the room. It was small—a single bed, bedside table and chair the only furnishings. It was barely bigger than a store cupboard. But they were fortunate to have the hospital as a base. The building had been designed for a population twice what it now was. Even with the long-term injured patients from the war, there were empty rooms to be had. Without access to the royal treasury, they were trading entirely on loyalty and goodwill. Egretta, as senior medic, had simply brought them in. In many ways, she was queen here.

It made sense. They had prioritised funding the hospital and the university as part of the vision to transform Eidyn. Mynygogg believed in their research and in teaching more medics. Of course Egretta would support them.

Quellaria threw herself casually onto the bed, crossing her legs and leaning back on the pillows. Another power display. She was taking up more space than necessary, leaving only the chair between Nirea and Darginn. The man looked sheepishly at Nirea, hands folded before him.

"Please, Darginn, take a seat." She may not be in a position of power, but she could show leadership.

"Oh, no, Majesty, it should be yours," Darginn protested.

"I insist. Please."

Hesitantly, he shifted sideways and took the chair. "Thank you, m'lady."

He was worse than she'd last seen him. Fidgeting. Agitated. Hollow. Nirea doubted he was sleeping much. She'd hoped getting him and his family here would be good for him. Help him recover. But what he likely really needed was home. And home was no longer safe. So maybe she could do something else for him.

But she was going to have to hurt him first.

"So, why are we here?" Quellaria broke the silence. That was good.

"You asked me what your role is in Eidyn. What your place is."

The *draoidh*'s eyes narrowed. "Right."

She was expecting an answer. Nirea wasn't going to give her one. Instead, she turned back to the old man. "Darginn was held captive by Shayella, the necromancer we've been at war with."

"I know who she is. So?"

"Darginn, could you tell Quellaria what was done to you?" It took all her strength to force the words out, to make them sound firm and strong, despite her every instinct screaming that she was being cruel. She was. But for good reason.

Darginn held his right arm across himself defensively, rubbing the other as if to confirm it was still there. His eyes dropped to the floor. "Majesty…I'd…I'd rather no, if—"

"I'm sorry, Darginn. It's important." She had to be steel—this was for his benefit.

Eventually.

His eyes came up, pleading with her.

"It's all right," she reassured him. "You're safe." That likely meant nothing to him. He'd probably never feel truly safe again. After what she'd seen him do to Madu—God knew where that ended.

Darginn nodded feebly. Quellaria made a show of being unmoved, but Nirea could see cracks forming. A little twitch of the hand. The man was obviously in pain and only a monster could feel nothing for him.

"I was…she…she tied me to a board." He shuffled his feet on the floor in little circles, still rubbing at one arm. "I…" The small voice faded entirely.

Quellaria raised her eyebrows at Nirea. *So what?* they asked. Darginn had to finish the story.

"Please, Darginn. Continue." It would help him in the end. It was for his own good.

"She…" He was rubbing his thighs now, probably more firmly than was comfortable. "She cut off my limbs, and…"

Confusion on Quellaria's face. The inexplicable mismatch of a man with all four limbs telling her they'd been hacked off. But she was interested.

Darginn was visibly shaking. She wanted to kneel before him, take his hands and comfort him. But Quell needed to see this pain. The damage. "Go on."

Darginn's trembling hands came up to cover his mouth, as if hiding it would stop the words coming out—being real. "She roasted them and... fed them to her... daughter."

There it was. The look she needed from the *draoidh*. Incredulity, confusion and horror. "I don't understand. How...?"

"You've seen Lady Samily's ability?" Nirea explained. "This is what she can do. Restoring a man's lost limbs." She turned back to Quellaria then and met her eyes directly. "But not his soul."

"Fuck... that's brutal. Is he...? Are you all right?" Quell asked.

Darginn looked up at her but didn't answer. He was lost somewhere in his memories. Reliving the terror.

Good. She needed the *draoidh* to see this too. The absolute worst of it. The devastation.

Nirea left them there for a moment, Darginn staring blankly at Quell; the *draoidh* becoming more uncomfortable with each passing second.

Finally, when the tension was all but too much, Nirea spoke. "Darginn, thank you for sharing that. Could I please ask you to wait outside for a moment?"

With a jerk, his head turned toward her. "Majesty?" It seemed as much a question of her identity as for clarification.

"Could you wait outside, please? Just for a moment?"

Darginn looked to the door as if it had appeared from mist. "Outside? Aye."

Slowly, he raised himself and shuffled out the door. Nirea closed it behind him. As soon as the latch clicked, Quellaria started.

"What the fucking Hells was that? Why the fuck would you bring that broken old man here? Are you trying to manipulate me into helping you because the necromancer is awful? Fuck me, Red, big hint—she's a necromancer!"

Interesting. So even within *draoidh* circles, and with her own experience, Quellaria had a prejudice against necromancy.

They were all human. All flawed. All guilty, in their ways.

"I told you my intention when we walked in, Quell. To show you your place in Eidyn. This is it."

She didn't see it yet. Funny that someone with her skill hadn't thought of it immediately. Nirea supposed it was how she considered her own skills. What she considered them for.

"What is?"

"This. Right here. This hospital. Him."

"What?"

"Quell, come on. It's right in front of you." Nirea pointed to the door. "That man is haunted by hideous memories of torture and mutilation. He thought he would die in that room. He can't get over it. So help him.

"Take the memories."

Silence as the *draoidh* took in what she had asked. It was a gamble, putting Darginn through this. Making him relive his horrors in stark daylight. But if it convinced Quellaria that she had a role, that she could help people, that she could be accepted—appreciated. It was a calculated risk.

"Do you have any fucking idea how complicated that would be? How long it would take?"

Good. She was thinking about it. "No. But I know it's possible, after what Janaeus did."

"Demon's bloody ring piece, woman, Janaeus had some magic relic to amplify his power! D'you not understand the difference that makes? It would take hours—at least!—to do something as complex as you're asking. Total concentration. Exhausting. One slip and I could make him forget his own name. His own family. Everything."

All right. She could work with that. "Firstly, I can arrange for an energy *draoidh* to support you." She wasn't sure about asking Dialla. If Darginn said no to this, the master was her backup plan. Well, the first one. Plan B. But her damage was less obvious than the old messenger's. And less awful. Still, she might be another that Quellaria could help, given time. But Keft would do it because his queen asked him to. It would mean a break from clearing memories, but perhaps another *draoidh* could be found to do that, under Allandria's supervision. Assuming Aranok was still unfit to serve. Maybe this could be the thing to motivate him from his sick bed.

Or maybe they were better off with him staying there.

"Secondly, if that happens, if you make a mistake—you can reverse it, can't you? You can use the same spell we've been using to clear people's memories?"

Quell pursed her lips. She probably wasn't used to dealing with people who understood how her magic worked. As Nirea understood it, nothing would be taken from him, just covered with new memories. "All right. Yes. I could do that. But still. Hours. Maybe all day, depending on how long he was there for."

"Fine," said Nirea. "I can arrange for food to be brought to the room for you both. What else would you need?"

"Wine! Actually, fuck, no. Wine later. Wine tonight. Lots of bloody wine. Right?"

"Done." She had no idea where wine was coming from, but she'd find some. "So you'll do it?"

"I didn't say that."

She would do it.

"Quellaria, this is it. This is your place. Do you have any idea how many people came through here during the war?" The few lucky to make it off the battlefields and survive the journey to Traverlyn. Still, it was a lot. "Can you even guess how many of them suffer like Darginn?"

Like Glorbad.

"This is your chance to be a healer, Quell. This could be your calling. Right here. Healing people's minds."

The woman stood bolt upright. Her eyes flitted around the room as if chasing her own thoughts.

Come on. Come on.

"If I do it...no promises. All right? I'm not promising anything. And it might not work."

Got you.

"I understand."

"Are you going to tell him? What I'm going to do?"

Tell him? No. She was going to ask him. "Of course. We need his permission. But you'll need to take today from him too. So he doesn't remember what happened. If he suspects his memories have been taken, even if he knows they're awful, he might itch to have them back. But we'll ask him first."

Nirea had thought about this a lot. Because there was a plan C. If she couldn't convince Darginn or Dialla.

Herself.

She had more than enough traumatic memories she would happily live without. But there was more to it than that. Her memories were old. Childhood memories. Early adulthood. Dreams she still had, twenty years later. Thoughts she still had about herself, at night, in the dark. In the quiet hours when her mind became loud. The ones she drowned in rum.

But they'd made her who she was. When she'd been under Janaeus's spell, she'd been a different person. More free. Less cautious. Less considered. In some ways, she remembered that woman fondly. She was more pirate and less queen. It had been liberating.

But did she want to be that person again? Who would she be without her trauma? Would she have become the woman she was? How much did memory make her personality? How much of who she was came from her experiences? Meristan had been a different person with his life rewritten. Would she be the same?

She'd prefer not to find out. Unless she had to. She'd reconciled herself with her ghosts—mostly. Most days.

Quellaria paced the room liked a caged animal. "All right. All right. If he agrees, and fuck me I can't believe I'm saying this, I'll try."

Yes!

But there was more Quell needed to know. "There's something else. Something else you'll have to take from him."

Madu.

The *draoidh* raised a suspicious eyebrow. "Aye?"

"He killed a woman. The..." Should she tell her? Fuck it, they needed to trust her if this had any chance of working. "The head messenger. You'll see for yourself, I suppose."

"All right." Quell moved back slightly—hardly at all, but enough for Nirea to notice. She needed to keep her on side.

"Madu sent him to Shayella. And Darginn learned that."

"Hmm." A nod. Noncommital. "And what should I do with that?"

Nirea had thought about this a great deal, and there was only one option that made sense. "Make him remember *me* killing Madu. I was going to anyway."

After a moment's thought, Quellaria frowned and nodded. "All right. I can do that."

Right. All they had to do now was convince Darginn. Nirea reached for the door handle.

"I'm fucking holding you to wine, Red. No kidding."

In the hall, Darginn leaned against the opposite wall like a lost child, trembling and staring into the middle distance. Nirea's heart broke for him again. But now, she was halfway to helping him.

He just had to let her.

"It's wonderful to see you up and about, Vastin. Honestly, it's a tonic." The queen, as Vastin now recognised her after Principal Keft restored his memory, stood proudly in the centre of his room. She'd always been somewhat intimidating—the whole party had, to be honest—but now there was something even more imposing about her.

She stood a little taller, maybe. A little prouder. It was hard to say exactly where the difference was. She still wore her red naval leathers and swords at her side, but she just seemed more... confident. More regal.

"Thank you, Your Majesty." Vastin bowed. He'd leapt to his feet when she'd arrived, of course, though it took him a second to realise he should.

Nirea laughed gently. "You don't have to bow to me, son. We're still who we were. We're still companions." She offered a hand and Vastin hesitantly took it. Imagine his folks could see him then, shaking hands with a queen like an equal. Madness.

It was odd, though, how happy Nirea seemed. How light. Allandria hadn't told him much, but it was all bad. Laird Aranok was sick. They'd missed the chance to get the magic item that would have fixed the country's memories. People had died.

Now they were down to one memory charm, hoping it would be enough to show the entire country what had been done to them by Janaeus.

And Glorbad was dead.

Why was she so happy?

"I'm sorry, but... can I ask...? I saw Samily this morning as she was leaving—"

Nirea cut him off before he could find his way to asking the question. "What? Samily left? Where to?"

Oh. Had he dropped Samily in a bucket of swill? It seemed like something Nirea would have known... "Um, I think she's gone to tend the Blackened? That she cured?"

That took the smile off her face. Something about that bothered her. Probably something beyond Vastin's understanding. Queenly things. He didn't want to get himself between the queen and the Thorn, so he clumsily ploughed back into his question.

"I know. About Glorbad. And Samily said you might... tell me what happened?"

With a deep sigh, the pain he'd expected rose in Nirea. There was something reassuring about it. Something that connected Vastin to their time together. She should be sad. He was sad, and he'd known the man a lot less time than she had. Sadness was right. Respectful.

The chair creaked and groaned as Nirea slumped into it, and Vastin sat back on the bed. The bed Egretta was determined to keep him in. The bed he was already sick of the sight of.

"It was a trap." She waved her hand as if to paint a picture for him. "Barrock was a trap. We should have died there. All of us." Nirea ran her hand down the left side of her face and seemed surprised, as if she'd suddenly remembered a thing forgotten.

"And?"

"And we walked into it. Glorbad, Meristan and me."

"Not Laird Aranok and Allandria? Not Samily?"

Nirea seemed to tighten at the question. Glorbad and Aranok had argued constantly about going to Barrock at all. What had happened while he was Blackened?

"No. They had another mission by then. A chance to end the Blackening—so we thought. It didn't go as we hoped."

Vastin wondered how that had played out. Glorbad had been insistent they had to go to Barrock. He imagined some fire was exchanged between him and Aranok. "So... what was it? The trap?"

"A demon." Nirea's eyes moved to the floor. "A bloody awful, slick, black"—she shuddered—"beast of a thing. It was all"—she raised her hands and waved her fingers—"limbs. Spindly, sharp limbs. And spikes. The spike on the tail, that was the bastard. That's what got him."

A demon. Hells, a demon. Waiting for them in Barrock. Vastin was supposed to have been there. They all were.

"He insisted on going first. Glorbad. We heard a noise and he insisted." Nirea's voice cracked. "Beat his fist on his bloody metal chest and he insisted." Tears then. She wiped them away. "It went right through his armour. Right through his shield. Right through him. Nearly took my damn head off too." She rubbed at her cheek again and Vastin wondered if she'd taken wounds that Samily had healed. He guessed it likely.

The shield.

Glorbad's shield.

He'd made it. He'd told him it was the strongest, lightest shield he'd ever carry. And the demon went right through it.

Hells.

"How did you escape?"

Nirea wiped her face dry and raised her eyes to meet him, with a renewed hint of light. "I wouldn't have. I'd be dead. It would have had me too. But Meristan..." She stood abruptly and opened the door, fumbled with something outside and turned back in.

It was his axe.

"Meristan had this. Meristan, who thought he was a bloody monk, had this axe." She banged the handle on the floor and Vastin winced. That wasn't good for the wood. "Meristan the monk cut the bastard thing's head in half with this axe. Bloody thing's skin was like stone. Meristan waited for the mouth to open and took its jaw off." She was beaming again, though her face was red and her eyes puffy. "Your axe has tasted demon blood at the hands of a White Thorn. I don't imagine there are many blacksmiths can say that."

No, not many. Him and the Green Laird, maybe. There was a little comfort in that. Some revenge in it. His shield might not have saved Glorbad, but his axe avenged him. That was something.

There was an old blacksmith tradition of naming a special weapon.

One wielded by a hero or used in a famous battle. As Nirea passed the weapon across to him and he felt the weight of the blade against his palms, Vastin considered whether it had earned that right.

He decided it had.

Demon's Blood.

It was a fine name. He would make sure it lived up to it.

"I'm sorry, Vastin. I can't stay long. I just wanted to... Are you well? You look well."

"I am. Thank you. I just have to decide what to do now, I suppose."

Nirea grabbed him by the shoulders. "I told you. We're comrades. You stay here as long as you like. For now, the hospital—Traverlyn—this is the extent of our kingdom. But we're going to take it back. We're going to take it all back. We're going to take you home, Vastin. And you'll be able to do whatever you want with your life."

That sounded good. And the queen clearly meant every word.

Vastin wished he shared her conviction. From what he'd heard, taking back the kingdom was a long way off. If ever.

"I'm sorry. I really do have to go. There's a lot happening today and... I'm the queen."

Vastin found a smile for her. "You are. Thank you for coming. And thank you for this." He raised the axe slightly. "Means a lot to have it back."

When she was gone, Vastin examined the blade's edge. It had dulled a little. Not much. There were some new scars. He closed his eyes and ran his hand across the metal, feeling the curve. He needed a whetstone. The hammering from the forge came back to him.

Whatever came next, Vastin intended to have a sharp axe.

CHAPTER 52

She is extremely..." Principal Keft's entire face seemed to pucker as he searched for the precise word. "Crude."

Nirea stifled the smile. It wouldn't help her relationship with the energy *draoidh* if she was amused by his complaints about Quellaria. "She is, Principal, but hopefully she can also be an asset to us. How did the session go?"

Nirea had come to check on Quell's progress with Darginn only to find Keft bustling out of the room like an elderly lady batting an indignant fan. He'd been "asked to leave" he said. Told to fuck off, more likely. So the two stood there in the hallway waiting for the door to open again.

"It was difficult," the principal answered. "What she is attempting is...complex. But she is skilled. Such a shame she left us without finishing her education. What we could have done for her..."

Quellaria came to the university? Did Nirea know that? And left early. She wondered where the woman might have honed her talent. To a level that impressed Keft, no less. Where else would a *draoidh* learn? She had no idea. Then again, she knew Anhel Weyr had been rejected from the university. Some were obviously self-taught.

"But successful? Do you think?"

Keft sighed and raised an eyebrow. "It is hard to say, Majesty. She has been highly focused for hours now. Even with my help, that level of concentration is difficult to maintain. It asked a lot of her to..."

The door creaked open and they both swung toward it. Darginn Argyll's silver pate appeared, looking first one way, then the other, and he gave a little judder of surprise to see them. "Ah, Your Majesty. Principal. Lovely to see you. How are we?"

Nirea had no words. The grey, insipid pallor of the man she'd brought to the room was replaced with a spark of light in his eyes she'd never seen before. He looked... whole.

"Is everything all right?" Darginn asked.

Keft was apparently as stunned as her, because neither of them spoke. She should say something. "Yes, sorry, hello, Darginn. How are you?"

The old man smiled and weight lifted from him. "Better, I think. Aye. Better. Miss Quellaria's been fine helpful."

"Well, I'm delighted to hear that." What else to say? For all her joy that this seemed to have worked, and her genuine happiness for Darginn, Nirea was desperate to get past him into that room and find out if she'd really succeeded. So she smiled politely.

Keft seemed to take the hint. "Master Argyll, I am going back to the university. Shall we walk together?"

Darginn looked slightly bemused at being offered an escort by the principal but was too polite to do anything but accept. "Aye, sir, that'd be grand." He glanced up and down the corridor before giving a deft little bow. "Your Majesty."

Keft also gave her a subtle nod—one which she took to mean he looked forward to hearing the full story. Nirea barely managed to let the pair get around a corner before rushing into the room. But she still needed to show restraint. Desperation is a treacherous offering. So she fixed a beatific smile and walked in as calmly as she could manage.

She wasn't ready. Quellaria sat, almost as grey as Darginn had been, hair bunched in sweaty clumps, staring at the wall. The woman looked drained. Ill. Nirea crouched and reached for her hand. "Quellaria?" She flinched away, seeming only then to recognise that Nirea had entered. The *draoidh* swallowed and looked at her—through her.

"What she did to him..." A shake of the head; her lips curled in. "That's... not right. You can't... you can't just *do* that to a person. It's... *fuck*."

Good. She was sympathetic. Getting Quell to see what they were fighting against hadn't really been part of the plan, but it was welcome. All peat for the fire. But she didn't like the look of the woman. "It worked, though, yes? You healed Darginn. So you see what you could do here, Quellaria. You see *how much* good you could do? You've changed a man's life."

"Aye, maybe." She looked at the floor. "We'll see if it holds. There was a lot. I can't promise there won't be holes—gaps in his memories. If he goes poking at them..."

"I know. You said. I've dealt with that."

Quell looked up at her, brow crumpled. "How?"

She'd spoken to his wife. Quell had been clear there were risks. Isadona had waved them away with a story of how forgetful Darginn was. That didn't chime with the man she'd met, who seemed to know every inch of Haven like his own home, but if his wife said so, she wasn't going to argue. "I managed it. Don't worry. How about you, how are you?" *What do you think?* was what she was dying to ask, but it would be rash. This needed delicate fingers.

Quellaria took a deep breath. "I'm fine. Wasn't me had to live through it. I just got to watch."

Nirea didn't know enough about memory magic to know how the *draoidh* would have experienced Darginn's memories. Would she have felt his fear? The pain? Or just seen it, like a dream? None of it would have been easy. And Keft had said she'd put Quellaria through a lot. "I'm sorry. That must have been difficult."

"Didn't factor that in, did you, Red? In your big plan. Didn't consider that if I take a memory, I'm the only one left with it."

No, she hadn't. The optimism drained from Nirea. It wasn't so simple. What she was asking of Quellaria was hard. She'd offered her a place in society, yes, but it was a harsh place. The kind of place only some people would choose. People like Samily or Egretta. People who would dedicate their lives to the service of others. Not everyone had that in them. That strength.

"Thank you. Whatever happens next, thank you for doing that. For him."

"Aye." Quell stood on uncertain legs and moved to sit on her bed. "Next it is, isn't it?"

She had to tread carefully here. "If you're ready to talk about it."

Quell leaned back and closed her eyes. "Maybe."

Maybe what? "You're ready to talk?"

"Maybe I'll help you."

Maybe. "What can I do to persuade you?"

A faint smile appeared on the memory *draoidh*'s lips. "We discussed wine."

Nirea felt like she was losing her mind. She needed an answer. "Of course, of course I will get wine." The madness of the queen of Eidyn running out to find wine flickered across her mind. "But whether you decide this is the right life for you, or if it's too hard, or if there's some other compromise, some way to use your gift to help people, to truly be part of Eidyn... will you help us build the country that would give you that choice? Please?"

Quell sat up and crossed her legs. "Honestly, Red, you know what the problem is with you? I can't read you. Your husband's easy. That man's all moral fortitude and sacrifice. I believe him. But you... I can't tell if you actually mean anything you say, or if you'll just say anything to get me to help you. Do you even care about that old man?" She pointed out the door. "Or me?"

Fuck.

Now what?

Honesty. That was all she had left. Nirea sat on the end of the bed and faced Quell.

"I have no fucking idea what I'm doing."

The *draoidh*'s face changed but she said nothing.

"Before I was queen... Before, I would have asked the same questions you are. Truthfully? My instinct was to force you to help us. Stick a knife at your throat and tell you to serve your country or die. Because that's who I am."

A glint of recognition in Quell. A hint of a smile. Still, she said nothing. Waiting.

"I was crushed for Darginn. Genuinely. It probably didn't look like it when I dragged him in here to relive that Hell for you, but I was... I..." She felt tears welling and beat back the instinct to suppress them. "It was necessary, but I hated it. And I am sorry for the shit you've been through. And I'm sorry that you had to see what he suffered. And I'm sorry you have to remember it. But I'm delighted for him. And I really do think this could be a life for you." She stood and spread an arm to the door. "But you're free to go. You did what I asked. This doesn't have to be your fight. We need you. Badly. And you'll be treated with respect and consideration, or I will know why. But if you choose to go, nobody will stop you."

Quellaria smiled widely and leaned back. "Well, fuck, Red, nice to meet you."

It was nice to be herself. But it also left her hideously vulnerable. She returned the smile, as best she could. "What do you think?"

The woman blew out her cheeks and looked up. "I suppose I think you better find us some bloody wine so we can talk about your plans."

Had the birds always sung so? Darginn was sure the cacophony of song on the streets of Traverlyn must be louder than before. More constant, maybe. Had something agitated the creatures into life? Were they songs of excitement or danger? Perhaps they sang for the joy of their own voices.

Or maybe it was him that was different. He felt slower. Lighter, perhaps. Whole.

He'd been struggling since his release from Lestalric. A cloud had hung over Darginn, threatening to drown him in its grey embrace. But the mists had cleared.

Not completely. He still felt a lingering malaise; a soulful sadness. But for the first time, it was bearable. The wound would heal with time. And that was new. That was hope.

Quellaria had been helpful in ways he'd have been unable to imagine just that morning. And all they'd done was talk. She'd asked him about his time in Lestalric, what disturbed him the most. And in talking, the burden had evaporated like a veil of frost in spring sun. He remembered the fear he'd felt, the certainty he would die there, held hostage by the baroness.

But no harm had come to him. His fears, his dreams of mutilation and brutality, had come to nothing. Laird Aranok and the Thorns had rescued him.

They'd got his family out of Haven and to safety in Traverlyn. Certainly, their life was less than ideal here, forced to take charity. It was... humbling. Darginn had fended for himself his whole life. A king's messenger made good coin and lived a good life. He'd grafted to earn their home and comforts. But all that meant nothing when they had to flee in the night, fearing for their lives.

Yet he'd seen no signs of resentment here. While most of Eidyn's population was devastated, leaving empty homes waiting to be filled, Traverlyn remained largely populated. Families had lost people to the war, but the town itself had survived mostly unscathed. Meaning there were few houses sitting empty.

Still, he hoped they might find one if they were to be there much longer. Living in one room, albeit a large one, was a lot to ask of a family of six. Liana was coping the best, of course. The girl was a delight—the warmth in Darginn's heart. She enjoyed the simple pleasure of playing with a ball in the grass outside the inn, or paddling in the pond on the edge of town. Jena and Yavick seemed to take solace in her. Ismar he worried about. The boy had come with nothing—left his entire life behind.

Isadona suspected Ismar was courting someone back in Haven, but he'd never said, and it seemed a pointless topic to bring up now he was separated from them. Ismar's mood had soured such that even Darginn in his dark days had been aware of it. He was reclusive and quiet, disappearing alone for the day and saying nothing of where he'd been.

Perhaps, now Darginn was thinking clearer, he could help his son adjust to their life here. Perhaps he could help him find something to bring him joy, in the way Liana did for Darginn.

But the real solution was in getting to go home again. To return safely to the lives they'd built—to the honour of self-sufficiency and work. Well, maybe not work for him. The envoy had promised him a regular payment from the treasury. He'd be happy to put his feet up and watch his family grow on the king's coin.

Perhaps he'd earned that.

But they couldn't stop their life in the hope of a new start later. For all his faith in the monarchs and the envoy, there was no way of knowing how long it might take to restore them to the throne. There were a lot of altered memories to repair. It could take years. They needed to have a life here—some sort of life. For Liana, at least.

Lost in thought, the streets had passed Darginn by and he was surprised to see the inn ahead. He stopped at the door, took a deep breath and braced himself. The past was done. That was it. No more brooding on what was or might have been. Today was the first day of the rest of their lives. It was time to make what they could of it.

Nirea all but danced back up the hospital steps carrying three bottles of wine.

It had actually worked. Darginn was a different man. A man she'd never truly met. The darkness was gone from him. The emptiness. God, she'd actually done something she'd not imagined possible. She'd changed history—for Darginn, anyway.

Even better, she'd given Quellaria a purpose. She'd shown her that she could have a place in Eidyn. A place where she could be herself and be appreciated. A place where she could be of service.

Ah! It was so damn perfect she was almost embarrassed to be so pleased with herself. This was the golden arrow. The perfect strike that killed the beast.

She'd played the queen and won the gambit. Things were finally flowing their way. Peace with the Reivers, the Blackening ended and their own memory *draoidh* to undo Janaeus's damage. And Janaeus gone. No longer a threat.

As was Shayella, for all the problems that had caused.

Only Anhel Weyr left. His days were numbered. Once they cleared enough memories, they would take him down, demons and all. They had the ability. They would have the numbers. It would be a quick, decisive war, if it came to war at all.

She was still not entirely convinced that the heart of devastation was lost to them, and the hope that they might yet retrieve it and solve the problem at one swipe was a further spark of light.

The dice were falling for them.

Nirea cleared the last landing onto the fourth floor and strode along the corridor to Quellaria's room. She swung the door wide with the pirate queen's grandeur, the grin on her face as wide as the sea.

Her stomach flipped.

Three bottles crashed to the floor.

The room was empty.

Nirea's eyes darted about, looking for something, anything to convince her that her instinctive fear was unfounded. That she was panicking for no reason. That Quell had only gone for food, or some other small errand.

But the room had been left bare. No clothes, none of the woman's jewellery, not a personal thing left behind. Just the faint waft of floral perfume.

She'd told Quellaria she would be free to go if she did this thing for Darginn, certain that the doing of it would change her. That she would see the good she could do. And she must have. Surely!

But still.

It wasn't enough.

Nirea felt the hope in her wither.

Quellaria was gone.

She wasn't coming back.

They were on their own.

The room stank of farts and feet. Allandria covered her nose, knowing it would be a temporary pain. After a wee while, she'd stop noticing it. For now, she cracked open the little window, letting some blessed fresh air in.

Opening the shutter brought a flood of light from the sunspire. Aranok groaned, raising an arm to cover his eyes. "Wha's…? Who's…?"

"It's me, Ari. It's Allandria."

"Oh…" He slumped back down into the pillow. "Hi."

She'd reduced the poppy milk he got today. Hopefully he might not take more tonight. It had seemed like a good idea, initially. Drug him into rest—give him time to heal—emotionally and physically. But she might have overdone it. After Korvin's death, he'd drunk himself unconscious for months. She wasn't going to let that happen again. He might not come back. And they couldn't afford the time.

They needed him.

She needed him.

It was time to get him back on his feet.

"Aranok, you need a bath."

"Nah." It was almost more grunt than word. "Can't be bothered. Gonna sleep."

She arranged it anyway. The wash would refresh him, sharpen his mind. Clear the dulling effects of the opium.

Maybe she shouldn't have gone this way. But where would he be if she hadn't?

Egretta had agreed with her. She had to hang on to that and stop questioning her own judgement. They had to stop the bleeding before they could operate. Now she just had to figure out the operation.

Aranok snored through the bathtub being delivered and the water being heated. She closed the window before rousing him. The room had become chilly, but the fire would warm it by the time he got out of the bath.

He took a little coercing, but not as much as she feared. In his sluggish state, he was biddable enough to do as he was told if she put it strongly. The half-hearted way he attempted to wash himself, though, was infuriating. Like watching a sulking child make a haphazard job of an unwanted chore. It wasn't out of spite, though. More apathy.

Finally, she tired of his weak-wristed attempts and did the job herself. There was something oddly detached about the task. She knew his body now, but under such conflicted circumstances. There was no thrill in his nakedness. Not like this. Somehow, he was both vulnerable child and broken old man. The glazed eyes were almost colourless—the spark of green, insipid ditch water.

God, it was almost too much. Allandria knew the man who was in there. Somewhere. Infuriating, funny, sharp, kind and brave. He lived still in the chest she scrubbed clean. But she had to find him.

"Shay?"

Startled by the sudden break in the silence, Allandria dropped the soap into the murky water. "Pardon?"

There was a little more focus in the eyes. An ember of life. "What's…? With Shay…Is she…?"

Hells.

Did he not remember? She'd heard of trauma being blacked out in people's minds. Had he erased his own memory of it? Or had the opium? "She's dead, Aranok. I'm sorry."

Irritation flashed across him. "No…I know…I…Buried. Body." He swallowed awkwardly. "What happened?"

"Her body? Is that what you're asking? About her burial?"

A vigorous nod.

"A pyre's been built for her and her daughter." Allandria had insisted on a proper funeral rite. When he came back, Aranok would want to know she'd been given respect, regardless of everything she'd done. "Do you…do you want to be there?"

A look of conflict, then confusion. Aranok slapped his breastbone. "No. Yes. There's…another." He pounded his chest so strongly Allandria grabbed his wrist, worried he might hurt himself.

"Another? Another what?" Another necromancer? God, surely not.

"No…another…Fuck. Words…" He pointed at Allandria, stabbing a finger at her. "Thing. Another thing."

Allandria rocked back on her haunches. "What thing, Aranok?"

"Thing!" He lurched forward, sloshing water over the bath's edge, grasping at Allandria. What the Hell was he doing?

"Aranok? I don't understand. What do you want?"

He pawed at her, pulling back her collar, finally grabbing the leather strap around her neck and drawing it from under her top. The yellow ball dangled beneath his fist. "Another thing."

Another memory charm? Shayella had a memory charm? How had they missed that? She'd looked at the body herself, though she hadn't examined it closely. But Aranok would have known before now. Why would he not have said something?

"Are you sure, Aranok? I didn't see—"

"No!" he interrupted. "Here!" He slapped his free hand against his chest again. "In here!"

"Are you saying it's... in her chest? There's a memory charm inside her chest?"

His face crumpled into a bittersweet half grin. "Yes. In her."

Bloody Hell.

Shayella was to be burned that night. Would fire destroy the charm? She didn't know. She didn't want to find out.

Allandria burst to her feet and rushed out the door. Aranok could soak or get himself out. He'd survive either way.

If there was a chance to retrieve a second memory charm, she had to go.

It could be the winning of the war.

CHAPTER 53

"Tell her what you told us."

Allandria looked from Mynygogg to the pair of city guards standing uncomfortably opposite Nirea and him. One looked familiar.

It had been a long but extremely productive day. Having retrieved the second memory charm wedged in Shayella's breastbone the night before—an experience she would happily have forgotten, given the opportunity—they'd doubled the number of people whose memories they could clear. Principal Keft had brought in Master Macwin, and the nature *draoidh* had quickly got up to speed with the principal. They'd burned through a great deal of firewood to keep both their energies raised, but that had been partly why Keft chose Macwin. He'd grown more wood to feed the fire. In fact, the two masters were the ideal pairing to keep clearing memories all day.

Still, even with a second charm now, Allandria had stayed with them.

More people, of course, meant more people refusing the charm. Three that day. An elderly husband and wife, and a young man who had the ruddy cheeks and hardened fingers of a farmer. They had a pair of guards on duty now, just to take people like them away.

It left a sour taste in Allandria's mouth, but they had few alternatives. Knowing the truth, it was exasperating to see people cling to the lie. But there it was. They felt their reality as strongly as she did her own and were not prepared to surrender it.

If someone came to her now and told her she was the one under a spell, and that her mind had been altered, would she easily accept it? She'd done so the first time because it was Aranok. And she trusted him completely. Plenty did not. Would not.

She'd been looking forward to seeing him, to tell him how much good they'd done with Shay's charm, when the runner had come for her.

"King Mynygogg requires your urgent attendance" was all she'd been given to say. So here Allandria was, standing in an awkwardly silent meeting room with the monarchs and a pair of city guards who looked like they'd very much rather be somewhere else.

"Aye, well..." The big one scratched at the back of his neck and looked intently at his feet.

The older, more regimented one with the grey moustache threw back his shoulders and spat out his message. "We come with grave news. One of our prisoners has been murdered."

Allandria gasped. "Which one?" Had they sent some poor ignorant soul to their death for refusing the charm?

"Rotan, m'lady."

"Oh!" That was not what she'd expected. In fact, in honesty, she'd forgotten the little bastard entirely.

"Had 'is neck broken. Proper snapped," the big guard added. "Near turned right the way round." He turned his own head, his thick neck straining to demonstrate.

"All right." Allandria looked to the king and queen. Nirea stood with her arms folded, stony-faced. Mynygogg looked grey. What was she missing?

"Tell her the rest," the queen said.

"Well, my lady," the old guard continued, "it was the envoy that did it. Laird Aranok."

Allandria felt time slow about her. She breathed deep, forcing her heart to keep a steady pace.

"What?"

The big man nodded. "S'true, Lady. M'lady. Walked right in, he did. Said he'd business with the prisoner. Next thing, I 'eard a squeal like a stuck pig. Went back to see if the laird was all right. Walked right past me like I wisnae there. But in the cell..." He grabbed his own jaw and made a twisting gesture, as if Allandria might not have understood the first time.

She looked to Nirea and saw her fears reflected back in stone. The queen was not happy. Mynygogg traced a finger across the table before him, staring down at the floor. "Thank you. You are dismissed."

The guards shuffled out as if they'd been spared a hanging, the older one apologising under his breath as he passed. When they'd gone, Hell broke free.

"What the fucking Hell, Allandria? I thought you had him under control!" Nirea's anger seemed greater than necessary—not least at her. Even if Aranok had executed the prick, was that so awful? He was a murderer. And a spy. Why was she so agitated?

"I do. I did. I...didn't think he was capable of leaving his room." It sounded feeble when she spoke it aloud, but it was the truth. She'd returned last night to find him still sat in a tub of dirty, lukewarm water. In retrospect, she'd considered herself lucky he hadn't slipped beneath the surface and drowned of lethargy. It made no sense he'd recovered so well to commit murder. She'd cut his opium to a minimal level this morning, just enough to keep him calm, really, but surely not so little as to lead to this. It didn't add up.

"Well, apparently you were wrong," said Mynygogg. "He's better than you imagined. Or perhaps worse."

"Are we sure...? Could they be mistaken?" Allandria was casting for hope where there seemed none to be had, but somehow, somewhere, there must be an answer.

"Allandria, he outright said he would murder the man!" Nirea was still shouting. "He's had a mental break. It makes perfect sense that he would take out his pain on a person who deserved it. For fuck's sake, he tried to kill Samily!"

She was right, for all her bluster. It did make sense. Sort of. But the thing with Samily was...complicated. Born in the heat of the flame. This was more considered. Planned. It didn't fit with the man she'd left behind that morning. He was tame as a kitten. That man did not have murder in him. Then again, he'd also suggested feeding Rotan to the Dead girl.

"I just...I'm not sure..."

"Allandria, we have to address this." Mynygogg was looking up at her. Emotionless. Pale. Drawn. Was there more here she didn't understand? "We can't have my envoy openly murdering people without trial. I honestly don't give a damn the shit is dead, but I do care that it happened in a way that makes us look like bandits—in a gaol full of people who already think we're traitors to the crown."

That was fair. It did not look good to have the king's closest advisor carrying out a summary execution. Not least one as brutal as the guard suggested. It would not win them any supporters.

"I understand. What would you have me do?"

Nirea breathed out heavily and turned away to the window. The king stepped toward Allandria like a condemned man. "You and I are going to see him. Now. I'm going to assess whether he's fit to be under his own control."

"What?" Allandria heard the horror in her voice. Did he intend to have him placed under the enforced care of the hospital? That was reserved for raving madmen and those likely to harm themselves. It was no situation for the third most powerful person in Eidyn. The most powerful, depending on how it was measured. "You'd admit him to the lunatic wing?" The thought of Aranok in one of those padded rooms they'd kept Shayella in was horrifying.

Mynygogg stepped back as if he'd been stung. "What? No. I wouldn't... No. But we need to make a decision, Allandria. We need to get him under control."

"Control?" For some reason, her calm was finally pierced. "He's not an animal."

"He's behaving like one," Nirea snapped. "It can't go on. He's not helping us."

"He is, actually." Allandria drew the charm from her chest. "We've got two now, thanks to him." It had been late last night, and she'd gone directly to Keft that morning, so she hadn't had a chance to tell Mynygogg or Nirea about the second charm. She'd left the other with Keft, as she'd wanted to do all along. But she would still hold one. Always one.

Nirea visibly softened. "What? How? When?"

"Shayella had it. Inside her." Allandria touched her chest. "Here. Buried in bone. Aranok told me about it last night."

Mynygogg reached for the charm, cradling it delicately between his fingers as though it might break under his touch. "We have two?" He turned to his wife. "We have two."

Nirea breathed deep and nodded in a way Allandria might have called reluctantly. "We have two. All right."

"That's something, right? That is something." Mynygogg seemed to be growing in confidence with each passing moment. "We have two."

"Yes. Yes, that's something."

What was Allandria missing? This was just positive news, surely? A splinter of resentment formed in her—considering what she'd had to do to get the bloody thing, she'd hoped for more excitement.

"We lost the memory *draoidh*." Nirea's words were flat and lifeless. "Quellaria. She's gone."

That was what was missing.

What Allandria had seen as an overreaction was not entirely about Aranok. She wanted to ask how, but it wasn't the time. Emotions were clearly raw. She'd wait, and they'd tell her what happened—or not. It didn't matter. The result was the same.

They had no memory *draoidh*. Which made the second charm all the more precious. Which meant Aranok pointing them at it was worth even more. And it had hurt him to do it.

Allandria stood a little taller. "I'm sorry. I didn't know."

"It's fine, it's fine." Mynygogg waved away her sympathy, focusing on Nirea. "We have two. We can make that work. We can do twice as much. Two towns, maybe."

Nirea swallowed hard. "We can... It'll work."

The king turned back to Allandria. "We still need to see Aranok. This has to be addressed. He can't be executing anyone he pleases."

Allandria's hackles raised again. "That's... not really fair. Rotan wasn't 'anyone.' I mean, if he'd murdered Nirea..." As soon as the words left her mouth, she regretted them. They were all living with the unspoken threat of Madu's assassins. Every time she awoke, it was usually with a start, checking the room for safety. "I'm sorry, you know what I mean."

"I do," Mynygogg answered quietly. "Still, we need to see him."

"Fine." Allandria would go, of course. She hoped this wasn't going to turn into the test of her loyalty she'd been fearing.

Though, if it did, it felt like she'd chosen her side.

His eyes were clearer. He was awake and eating what smelled like soup. That was positive. Or was it? If Aranok had been passed out, drugged into a stupor, would it have been more evidence in favour of the idea he couldn't have killed Rotan? Or that if he did, he wasn't in his own mind?

Allandria didn't know the answer. But then, Mynygogg hadn't seen him in days. He hadn't seen how bad he had been, so maybe he'd look at his weakened, dishevelled friend and see what she hoped for. Find compassion in place of anger.

Maybe she was being unfair. Maybe the king knew how this went. After all, it had been him who pulled Aranok out of the last hole he'd fallen in. Did he have the strength, or the capacity, to do it again? She would welcome the help.

"Aranok. How are you?" His voice was steady. Gentle.

Aranok looked up from his meal, swallowed and put the bowl down. The back of his hand wiped across his mouth. "Gogg."

"Ari, how have you been today? What have you done?" She hoped the open question would make it easy for him to answer without feeling attacked.

It took a moment for his gaze to shift from the king to her. "Not much." A faint smile. A flicker of light. A hint of the real man. "I have soup."

Allandria felt her face warm as she smiled back. He was in there. She pulled across a chair, sat beside him and took his hand. "Something's happened. There's been a murder. Rotan."

Aranok's eyebrows stitched together. "Rotan? Rotan killed Conifax." He said it as if he needed Allandria to confirm the truth of it. As if it were in question.

"That's right. He's dead." She left a space then. Silence, to see what would fill it.

After a moment's thought, Aranok snorted air and shrugged. "Good. Wish I'd been there."

"God in Hell," Mynygogg muttered, covering his mouth as he turned away.

There was an explanation.

There would be an explanation.

"Ari, this is what's confusing us. The guards... at the gaol? They say they saw who did it. They said it was you."

Again the eyebrows came together—even harder this time. "Me? When?"

"This afternoon, Aranok." Mynygogg was clearly exasperated. "They report that you visited him in his cell and broke his neck."

"What? I... No. I've been here." Aranok cast his hands out as if to display his bed. "I've been here."

"Have you? All day? You're certain?" The king's tone was more accusatory with every sentence. Allandria felt her hackles rising. She wasn't going to allow this to continue much longer.

"Yes." Aranok sat up straighter. "I'm sure."

Mynygogg sat on the end of the bed. "You murdered those men. The ones who killed Korvin. You understand... it makes sense."

"It wasn't me." Aranok was more adamant with each rebuttal. More forceful.

"Why not? He killed Conifax. You wanted him dead. You even said you would kill him, I understand."

"Yes. I would've. Was going to."

"And? Why should I believe you didn't?" Mynygogg was shouting now, and that was the end of her tether. She turned to rebuke him, but Aranok got there first.

"Because I wouldn't have left witnesses!" Whether the king was stunned into silence by the outburst itself or the fact that he realised it was true hardly mattered. "Can't just murder our enemies. Not in public."

His speech was sharper with every sentence. And his mind clearly was too. The reference to Shayella's execution was not lost on her. Nor Janaeus's. And she knew it would land with Mynygogg.

Cracking his knuckles, the king stood and paced. "All right. Then who did?"

Something changed on Aranok's face. "Fuck. When... when did it happen? How long?"

Allandria felt her stomach flip. He'd realised something. Something worrying.

"Three, four hours ago," Mynygogg answered. "Why?"

Aranok threw back his sheets and scrambled amongst the pile of clothes on the floor, pulling on trousers. "They're here. For fuck's sake, he's here!"

"Who's here?" Allandria wasn't sure whether to be worried for him or for what he was trying to say.

"Weyr!" He pulled his leathers over his head. "Assassins!"

"What?" Why would Weyr have his own spy assassinated?

"Oh Hells." Mynygogg seemed to have realised what Aranok was getting at.

"It's a *masg*! He's got a fucking illusionist!" Aranok pulled on one boot, then the other.

"Nirea." Mynygogg turned and bolted from the room.

Oh God.

An illusionist assassin? They could be anyone. The perfect killer.

Aranok thrust an arm at her, silently asking her to lace up his sleeves. "What time is it? When is it?"

"Early evening."

"Fuck."

"Why? What's wrong?"

As soon as she released his sleeve, Aranok stalked to the window and threw open the shutters.

"The sun's going down."

Aranok hammered on the door. He prayed she would answer; prayed she would be fine. She had to be fine. She had to be. He couldn't be too late.

Damn it all to fuck, why hadn't he known sooner?

Allandria fidgeted anxiously beside him. He was still woozy. Twice on the run here a flash of dizziness had almost sent him sprawling across the cobbles. But he needed to be clear. He had to be clear. They were in trouble.

No answer.

He tried to be quiet, to listen for sounds of life from beyond the door, but the pounding of his heart and the rasp of his breath were a maelstrom.

They couldn't wait.

He tried the door. Unlocked, it clicked open.

The dank iron smell of blood.

Fuck.

He recognised the body. They'd only met once, when she'd answered this door half-dressed, expecting someone else. Her wide eyes were cold and pale, her school robes sticky with her blood. She wasn't even the one. She was just in the wrong place. Had the wrong dorm mate.

The other girl, the one slumped in the corner, blood pooling around her from multiple wounds. She was the target. She was the reason both of them were dead.

Another *draoidh* sacrificed to Weyr's ego.

He'd promised to protect her. He'd said he would teach her.

But he didn't have time for guilt.

Without her to activate her spell, there would be no sunspire tonight.

"Fuck," Allandria breathed, crossing to the girl and pressing her fingers to her throat. There wouldn't be a heartbeat. Whoever the assassin had come as, the girls had let them in. Closed the door. Given them the privacy they needed to take their time. She shook her head ruefully as she confirmed both girls were gone. "What now?"

Aranok leaned on the windowsill, staring out at the great ball that had been absorbing sunlight all day—that should start glowing within hours. Girette could see it from her window. Every day, she saw that thing and knew she was responsible for keeping Traverlyn safe.

And she'd died for it.

"Now it gets dark."

The story continues in . . .

THE DAMNED KING

Book THREE of The Eidyn Saga

Keep reading for a sneak peek!

ACKNOWLEDGEMENTS

Well, here we are again. This book went through quite the gestation process. It started out over 200K words and went through some major surgery to get it down to nearer 160K, then grew again in edits to more like 175K. It's been quite a ride!

So, in order, I'm going to thank the people who helped with that process:

First, my alpha reader and constant support, my wife, Juliet. She was the first to tell me: "It's good. It needs work, but it's good." Thank you, my love.

My beta readers, Kathryn and Kelvin, who were both pleasingly excited to be back in Eidyn. Thanks for all your enthusiasm and feedback, guys.

My agent, Ian Drury, whose support and analytical eye were invaluable. Thank you.

My editor, Bradley Englert, whose collaborative style and enthusiasm for the work make the editing process a genuine pleasure. Thank you.

Then there are all the people at Orbit, both US and UK, whose work is so vital to making this series happen, and who are all a pleasure to work with. That includes, non-exhaustively, Tim, Lauren, Rachel, Angela, Natassja, Paola, Tiana, Ellen, Xian, Bryn, Caroline, Nadia and Nazia. Thank you all!

Jeremy Wilson, for a beautiful cover, and Tim Paul, for a gorgeous map: Thank you both for lending me your incredible talent.

With every Eidyn book, I'm always indebted to the friends who allowed me to take their roleplay characters and use them to do something else. Sean, Kirsten, Neith, Craig, Jan and Juliet (again), thank you, I love you all.

My friend and partner Nathan, who I keep telling he has changed my life and made these books possible at all. I hope you know how sincerely I mean that. Thank you.

One of my oldest friends, Liam, who expertly hosts my book launches and helps with promotion. Thank you.

My stepson, Nick, who is patiently trying to teach me to use TikTok—thank you!

To the incredibly supportive SFF community, whether it be SPFBO and Mark Lawrence, the many friends I've made at Fantasycon, BristolCon and Cymera, or the vast community of readers, authors and reviewers online. I wouldn't have believed, eight years ago when *Carpet Diem* was first published, that I would feel so at home and welcome amongst you all. There's no rivalry and no jealousy, just kind people cheering each other on. Thank you all.

And finally, to every reader who's ever talked about a book they love, left a review online or passed it on to a friend: You're why we can continue to tell stories. I hope you enjoyed this one. Thank you.

Slàinte!

J

extras

meet the author

Melody Joy Co.

Justin Lee Anderson was a professional writer and editor for fifteen years before his debut novel, *Carpet Diem*, was published and won the 2018 Audie Award for Humor. His second novel, *The Lost War*, won the 2020 SPFBO Award. Born in Scotland, he spent his childhood in the US thanks to his dad's football (soccer) career and also lived in the South of France for three years. He now lives with his family just outside his hometown of Edinburgh.

Find out more about Justin Lee Anderson and other Orbit authors by registering for the free monthly newsletter at orbitbooks.net.

if you enjoyed
THE BITTER CROWN
look out for
THE DAMNED KING
The Eidyn Saga: Book Three
by
Justin Lee Anderson

It began in silence.

The whisper of a crackling fire. The hush of the twilight breeze. The hammer of Aranok's heart.

They waited, in the vast, heavy quiet of inevitability.

No words of camaraderie. No encouraging smiles.

Just the coming dark.

Traverlyn was not made for a siege. Its people were academics, medics, artists and musicians. Many were elderly, or young. The bulk of the population were still hurriedly evacuating to inns, the hospital or the university. Anywhere they could huddle together against the horror.

But what they had were *draoidhs*.

Aranok, Keft, Opiassa, Macwin and a few other masters, as well as some senior students. Three more physic *draoidhs*. Six more nature.

Aranok's skin itched with the energy boost Keft had given him to burn the opium out of his system. He clenched and unclenched his fists, shuffled from foot to foot. Allandria put a hand on his arm. With an illusionist assassin in Traverlyn, he wasn't letting her out of his sight.

But there was no conversation. No easy banter. Nothing to say.

Hells, how they could have done with Dialla, Samily and Rasa. But there was every chance that was why Anhel's assassin had struck. Because they were gone. Because Aranok was crippled.

They'd discussed, in the bare twilight hours, mounting a major defence here at the southern road into town—of summoning the guard, digging a pit, setting shield walls. None of it would have worked. The Thakhati would not fight like an army. They were a swarm. They would come from every angle. Hunt like wolves. They could handle a few. Small numbers. But if what Rasa had told Mynygogg was right, that there were hundreds, maybe thousands waiting in the trees...

They'd harvested the Blackened. He didn't have time to think on that, now. How all those people he'd thought waiting to be saved were gone. How Shay's death had meant nothing for them. They were already lost.

The nature *draoidhs* could try to keep them out, using the natural wall that surrounded the town to hold and entrap them, but there weren't enough of them to defend the whole perimeter. That too was a doomed strategy. Instead, the guard were sent to organise the evacuation. Get everyone off the streets. Lamplighters were roused for the first time in weeks, asked to set not only torches but bonfires anywhere they could be made. They needed as much light, as much flame, as the town could muster. As much energy.

Their only hope was not to win, but to survive. Come morning, come sunrise, the Thakhati would be forced back into their cocoons. But standing there, watching the last of the purple sky fade to black, morning felt like another country.

When the last light dipped below the horizon, the chattering began. Like stone screaming in hunger. Like death.

"Are we really doing this?" Allandria whispered.

"We are." Aranok tried to sound reassuring. But the truth was, of the fourteen of them gathered on this little hillock, some were likely to be dead by sunup. Maybe more than likely. But this tactic, mad as it had sounded when he'd come up with it, was going to give them their best chance. "Everybody ready?"

Keft's face was ashen, but he nodded silently.

"As I'll ever be," said Macwin, with a smile that seemed a little too genuine. Others made noises of agreement. Opiassa slapped one of her giant pauldrons. The physic *draoidhs* stood at least seven foot tall and about as wide, each carrying a warhammer too large for any normal human to bear. They, at least, were prepared for battle. Opiassa took her role as head of security seriously. Apparently, she'd arranged for the outsized armour and weapons to be forged during the Hellfire War. The untested metal glinted in the firelight like virgin snow.

They were ready. They had to be.

Aranok turned to Macwin. "All right. Let them in."

The nature *draoidh* raised his arms and the enormous wall of trees, bushes and vines parted like a theatre curtain, exposing a pitch-black void. For a moment, the chattering slowed—curious. Wary. It burst to a crescendo as a wave of grey claws came shrieking through the gap.

My god.

"Draw them in, but keep them back!" Aranok already needed to shout over the havoc.

Allandria nocked an arrow. "That makes no sense."

"I know."

Two new walls of trees grew toward them, on either side of the Thakhati horde, funnelling it toward the *draoidhs*. It only served to heighten the demons' frenzy. Aranok felt his guts twist in horror as they came roaring across the grass toward them. Nobody could stand in the face of that carnage and not feel their certainty shudder beneath them. They had to slow but not stop the monsters.

"Sgàineadh!" Aranok raised his arms wide as a trench opened before them and Thakhati poured in.

Screeching, furious, they rolled into the pit, clambering over each other to reach their prey. One crawled up over the edge and was met with a blow from a warhammer that all but took its head off. It sank back into the morass, only increasing its frenzy as they ripped the wounded demon apart. Another breached the lip and got the same. Several were trying to climb the tree walls now, but vines twisted and contorted to hold them tight. Still they poured through the gate. Easily hundreds. Could already be a thousand. Rasa hadn't exaggerated.

The pit was filling. In moments, they'd start pouring out and into the town.

"Keft! Now!" Aranok called.

A burst of energy from the principal punched the Thakhati back, shattering into each other. They tussled amongst themselves briefly, paused and came again.

"Balla na talamh!" The near edge of the pit rose from the earth, trapping those trying to climb out. For now.

"Opiassa!" Aranok pointed to each side. The four physic *draoidhs* split, each pair taking a side to patrol against Thakhati making it out of the pit.

Allandria pointed to the gate in the natural wall. "Fucking Hell, they're still coming."

They were. And they needed all of them. But God in Hell, they weren't slowing.

The morass closed in again, pushed by the sheer pressure of numbers. They were in less of a hurry, but they came, grating, snarling.

A cry, from somewhere in the middle. High pitched. Painful enough it made Aranok lift his hands to his ears. And they all stopped. No more frenzy. Barely a sound at all, beyond the scrape of Thakhati skin against itself. They crouched, all down on their six limbs, except one.

One stood proud of the crowd, forelimbs raised. A leader? They'd seen behaviour like this before, but not on this scale.

"Does that look like...?" Allandria left the question hanging.

"A general," Aranok finished. *"Creag."* He tore a chunk of rock from the nearby wall and hurled it at the leader. The monster screamed again and a wave of Thakhati raised before him, taking the hit—crushed under it.

Fuck.

The general raised its arms wide. Another screech—and the horde parted like liquid. They made en masse for the side trees, clambering up the new walls that penned them in.

"Envoy!" Macwin called. "We can't hold them all!"

He was right. They were starting to break over the pit wall too. Opiassa's physics were in danger of being overrun. It had to be now.

"Right. Stand close." The others pulled in tight around him. *"Colbh talmhainn."* A pillar of earth rose beneath them, lifting them up just as a pair of Thakhati were scrambling close. Keft punched them back with a burst of energy. The pillar took them up twenty feet, well above the reach of the Thakhati. But they would just go on past, into the town. They were still pouring through the gap. It wasn't all of them. But they'd waited as long as they could.

Aranok lifted his hand high. "Cover your eyes!

"Spreadhadh!"

The sunstone exploded in light. Thakhati screamed.

"God almighty!" Allandria yelled over the noise of the dying things. It was the awful sound of rage and death, of creatures cursing their gods, whatever they might be.

In a moment, it was done. The field before them was a smoking mass of singed stone. But still, there was movement. Here and there, a wriggle, a slight shudder of limbs. Some had survived—probably shielded by the bodies of others. And in the distance, in the dark, the insistent chattering.

"Macwin, close it!" Aranok ordered.

The *draoidh* gestured and the gate he'd opened in the tree wall stitched itself together, shutting what was left of the monsters outside. For now.

He pointed to the field of corpses. "Opiassa! Finish them!" The physic master gave a gesture of salute. Aranok dropped the earth wall back into the pit, crushing anything left alive inside, he hoped. It didn't quite give the physic *draoidhs* a solid footing to cross, but they didn't need it. Each of them made the leap across with what seemed like relative ease and stalked the field, hammering the life out of anything that moved.

Aranok lowered the pillar back down. "That was it. That was our one shot." He held out the dead sunstone. "Now it's a street fight."

"Who the fuck are you!?"

Nirea pinned the woman to the redbrick wall, forearm across her neck, wary of her hands.

"For God's sake, put Brode down!" Egretta tugged at her arm. "She can't answer if you're choking her!"

Brode? The name wasn't familiar. The woman had smiled at her. Said, "Hello again, Majesty" and reached into her apron.

It was the *again* that did it. A pretence at familiarity. She did not know this woman.

Mynygogg had burst into their chamber what seemed like minutes ago but must have been an hour. Maybe two. Raving. Manic. He couldn't explain himself until, in what seemed more desperation than love, he'd kissed her passionately. She'd thought his mind lost until he explained what Aranok had claimed—that Rotan's murderer was an illusionist assassin. Mynygogg had to be sure she was herself and safe, which was sweet. The kiss had been enough. His first thought had been to find her. Even as king, his instincts were for Nirea.

That had been minor solace when the sunspire had not begun to shine as the light faded over Traverlyn. At first, it had seemed so normal. The sun sinking into the trees as dusk settled like a blanket of peace. It was when she reached for a candle that she'd realised.

It should not be dark.

The fretting over the assassin was lost to absolute panic over the Thakhati outside the town. Aranok had sent a runner with the news that the student maintaining the sunspire had also been murdered—and Nirea had no reason to suspect him of that. They had been formulating a plan to defend the hospital when this woman approached her.

Anyone could be an assassin, now. *Anyone.*

But that didn't mean everyone. Egretta was insistent the woman was innocent. Nirea relaxed her arm, allowing the medic to take a breath. "Please, Majesty," she panted, "I only brought this." A tear trickled down her nose. "I thought you might need more."

From the apron, Brode produced a small tub, and Nirea remembered. This was the woman who'd brought salve for Quellaria's wrists. She'd been so distracted, so focused on Quell, that she'd barely looked the woman in the eye. Gods, she'd handled this badly. She was jumpy. Paranoid.

Fuck!

"I'm sorry, I..." What could she say? They couldn't go around announcing that they knew about an illusionist assassin to every medic in the building—one of them could be the very person they were worried about. And then they would be more careful. "There is a lot happening." That would have to do. For now, they needed to secure the hospital. She released Brode completely, stroking her shoulder in passing, as if that would make a difference. The assassin was only looking for them, probably. They'd killed Rotan and the *draoidh* girl. She couldn't think who else would be a target, now. Just her, Gogg, Aranok and Allandria, likely. They might be after the history book too. The thing that would help prove the truth. Maybe.

She'd told Egretta, though. The senior medic needed to know there could be an assassin in her hospital. She knew her staff. Would know if one of them behaved oddly. Nirea had just had to make sure that the old matron was herself first. A brief conversation, quizzing her over their arrival and the events she'd been witness to since, was enough. The two of them were working together to organise the staff and patients while Gogg went with Leondar to help bring people in. It was a large building, but solid. It could, perhaps, keep out the monsters. More so than many of the houses in Traverlyn.

They had so little time.

Brode wiped her eye, bowed and backed away. Nirea had done nothing for her reputation as a benevolent queen. In fact, it was the second time she'd treated the woman badly, and neither was deserved. A problem for later. The more immediate problem was Egretta's fucking stupid plan.

"We can't put all the patients in the lecture hall."

The central lecture hall was where much of the hospital's teaching occurred. It was the biggest single room, constructed with decorative arches and intricate carvings to be the centrepiece of an inspiring building. They could fit many of the patients in there, given need.

Egretta frowned. "Not all, obviously. Some cannot be moved and—"

"No," Nirea cut her off. "They stay where they are. We lock their rooms."

The medic's eyes opened in a mix of ire and surprise. "I can't take care of them all if we can't move around the building!"

"If we put them all in one place, behind one set of doors, when those doors give—and they will, eventually—we're serving them up as a banquet. If the Thakhati get in here, the best hope we have is to fight them in small numbers. Let them spread out around the building. If they get through one door, they take one prize only. We have to make this difficult for them."

Egretta's face hardened. "Those people are sick. Injured. *Children.* They'll be alone and defenceless. Some will die without care!"

"Then leave a medic with them."

Egretta's hand went to her head.

"You would leave them to die too?"

"I'm trying to save as many of them as I can, and I don't have time to argue. We lock them in their rooms, Egretta. It's the best chance for the most people."

The medic's mouth crumpled into a sceptical pout and defiance danced at her lips, but she didn't argue further. "Fine."

Egretta had been calling her a stupid child not long ago, but now Nirea was queen again.

And the queen's word still had weight.

"Excellent. Let's get it done. We're running out of time."

if you enjoyed
THE BITTER CROWN
look out for
THE PHOENIX KING
The Ravence Trilogy: Book One
by
Aparna Verma

In a kingdom where flames hold magic and the desert hides secrets, an ancient prophecy comes for an assassin, a princess, and a king. But none are ready to face destiny—and the choices they make could burn the world.

For Elena Aadya Ravence, fire is yearning. She longs to feel worthy of her Phoenix god, of her ancestors who transformed the barren dunes of Sayon into a thriving kingdom. But though she knows the ways and wiles of the desert better than she knows her own skin, the secrets of the Eternal Fire elude her. And without them, she'll never be accepted as queen.

For Leo Malhari Ravence, fire is control. He is not ready to give up his crown—there's still too much work to be done to ensure his legacy remains untarnished, his family protected. But power comes with a price, and he'll wage war with the heavens themselves to keep from paying it.

For Yassen Knight, fire is redemption. He dreams of shedding his past as one of Sayon's most deadly assassins, of laying to rest the ghosts of those he has lost. If joining the court of flame and serving Ravence's royal family—the very people he once swore to eliminate—will earn him that, he'll do it no matter what they ask of him.

But the Phoenix watches over all and the fire has a will of its own. It will come for all three, will come for Sayon itself... and they must either find a way to withstand the blaze or burn to ash.

Chapter 1

Yassen

The king said to his people, "We are the chosen."
And the people responded, "Chosen by whom?"
—from chapter 37 of *The Great History of Sayon*

To be forgiven, one must be burned. That's what the Ravani said. They were fanatics and fire worshippers, but they were his people. And he would finally be returning home.

Yassen held on to the railing of the hoverboat as it skimmed over the waves. He held on with his left arm, his right limp by his side. Around him, the world was dark, but the horizon began to purple with the faint glimmers of dawn. Soon, the sun would rise, and the twin moons of Sayon would lie down to rest. Soon, he would arrive at Rysanti, the Brass City. And soon, he would find his way back to the desert that had forsaken him.

Yassen withdrew a holopod from his jacket and pressed it open with his thumb. A small holo materialized with a message:

Look for the bull.

He closed the holo, the smell of salt and brine filling his lungs.

The bull. It was nothing close to the Phoenix of Ravence, but then again, Samson liked to be subtle. Yassen wondered if he would be at the port to greet him.

A large wave tossed the boat, but Yassen did not lose his balance. Weeks at sea and suns of combat had taught him how to keep his ground. A cool wind licked his sleeve, and he felt a whisper of pain skitter down his right wrist. He grimaced. His skin was already beginning to redden.

After the Arohassin had pulled him half-conscious from the sea, Yassen had thought, in the delirium of pain, that he would be free. If not in this life, then in death. But the Arohassin had yanked him back from the brink. Treated his burns and saved his arm. Said that he was lucky to be alive while whispering among themselves when they thought he could not hear: "Yassen Knight is no longer of use."

Yassen pulled down his sleeve. It was no matter. He was used to running.

As the hoverboat neared the harbor, the fog along the coastline began to evaporate. Slowly, Yassen saw the tall spires of the Brass City cut through the grey heavens. Skyscrapers of slate and steel from the mines of Sona glimmered in the early dawn as hovertrains weaved through the air, carrying the day laborers. Neon lights flickered within the metal jungle, and a silver bridge snaked through the entire city, connecting the outer rings to the wealthy, affluent center. Yassen squinted as the sun crested the horizon. Suddenly, its light hit the harbor, and the Brass City shone with a blinding intensity.

Yassen quickly clipped on his visor, a fiber sheath that covered his entire face. He closed his eyes for a moment, allowing them to readjust before opening them again. The city stared back at him in subdued colors.

Queen Rydia, one of the first queens of Jantar, had wanted to ward off Enuu, the evil eye, so she had fashioned her port city out of unforgiving metal. If Yassen wasn't careful, the brass could blind him.

The other passengers came up on deck, pulling on half visors that covered their eyes. Yassen tightened his visor and wrapped a scarf around his neck. Most people could not recognize him—none of the passengers even knew of his name—but he could not take any chances. Samson had made it clear that he wanted no one to know of this meeting.

The hoverboat came to rest beside the platform, and Yassen disembarked with the rest of the passengers. Even in the early hours, the port was busy. On the other dock, soldiers barked out orders as fresh immigrants stumbled off a colony boat. Judging from the coiled silver bracelets on their wrists, Yassen guessed they were Sesharian refugees. They shuffled forward on the adjoining dock toward military buses. Some carried luggage; others had nothing save the clothes they wore. They all donned half visors and walked with the resigned grace of people weary of their fate.

Native Jantari, in their lightning suits and golden bracelets, kept a healthy distance from the immigrants. They stayed on the brass homeland and receiving docks where merchants stationed their carts. Unlike most of the city, the carts were made of pale driftwood, but the vendors still wore half visors as they handled their wares. Yassen could already hear a merchant hawking satchels of vermilion tea while another shouted about a new delivery of mirrors from Cyleon that had a 90 percent accuracy of predicting one's romantic future. Yassen shook his head. Only in Jantar.

Floating lanterns guided Yassen and the passengers to the glass-encased immigration office. Yassen slid his holopod into the port while a grim-faced attendant flicked something from his purple nails.

"Name?" he intoned.

"Cassian Newman," Yassen said.

"Country of residence?"

"Nbru."

The attendant waved his hand. "Take off your visor, please."

Yassen unclipped his visor and saw shock register across the attendant's face as he took in Yassen's white, colorless eyes.

"Are you Jantari?" the attendant asked, surprised.

"No," Yassen responded gruffly and clipped his visor back on. "My father was."

"Hmph." The attendant looked at his holopod and then back at him. "Purpose of your visit?"

Yassen paused. The attendant peered at him, and for one wild moment, Yassen wondered if he should turn away, jump back on the boat, and go wherever the sea pushed him. But then a coldness slithered down his right elbow, and he gripped his arm.

"To visit some old friends," Yassen said.

The attendant snorted, but when the holopod slid back out, Yassen saw the burning insignia of a mohanti, a winged ox, on its surface.

"Welcome to the Kingdom of Jantar," the attendant said and waved him through.

Yassen stepped through the glass immigration office and into Rysanti. He breathed in the sharp salt air, intermingled with spices both foreign and familiar. A storm had passed through recently, leaving puddles in its wake. A woman ahead of Yassen slipped on a wet plank and a merchant reached out to steady her. Yassen pushed past them, keeping his head down. Out of the corner of his eye, he saw the merchant swipe the woman's holopod and hide it in his jacket. Yassen smothered a laugh.

As he wandered toward the homeland dock, he scanned the faces in the crowd. The time was nearly two past the sun's breath. Samson and his men should have been here by now.

He came to the bridge connecting the receiving and homeland docks. At the other end of the bridge was a lonely tea stall, held together by worn planks—but the large holosign snagged his attention.

WARM YOUR TIRED BONES FROM YOUR PASSAGE AT SEA! FRESH HOT LEMON CAKES AND RAVANI TEA SERVED DAILY! it read.

It was the word *Ravani* that sent a jolt through Yassen. Home—the one he longed for but knew he was no longer welcome in.

Yassen drew up to the tea stall. Three large hourglasses hissed and steamed. Tea leaves floated along their bottoms, slowly steeping, as a heavyset Sesharian woman flipped them in timed intervals. On her hand, Yassen spotted a tattoo of a bull.

The same mark Samson had asked him to look for.

When the woman met Yassen's eyes, she twirled the hourglass once more before drying her hands on the towel around her wide waist.

"Whatcha want?" she asked in a river-hoarse voice.

"One tea and cake, please," Yassen said.

"You're lucky. I just got a fresh batch of leaves from my connect. Straight from the canyons of Ravence."

"Exactly why I want one," he said and placed his holopod in the counter insert. Yassen tapped it twice.

"Keep the change," he added.

She nodded and turned back to the giant hourglasses.

The brass beneath Yassen's feet grew warmer in the yawning day. Across the docks, more boats pulled in, carrying immigrant laborers and tourists. Yassen adjusted his visor, making sure it was fully in place, as the woman simultaneously flipped the hourglass and slid off its cap. In one fluid motion, the hot tea arced through the air and fell into the cup in her hand. She slid it across the counter.

"Mind the sleeve, the tea's hot," she said. "And here's your cake."

Yassen grabbed the cake box and lifted his cup in thanks. As he moved away from the stall, he scratched the plastic sleeve around the cup.

Slowly, a message burned through:

Look underneath the dock of fortunes.

He almost smiled. Clearly, Samson had not forgotten Yassen's love of tea.

Yassen looked within the box and saw that there was no cake but something sharp, metallic. He reached inside and held it up. Made of silver, the insignia was smaller than his palm and etched in what seemed to be the shape of a teardrop. Yassen held it closer. No, it was more feather than teardrop.

He threw the sleeve and box into a bin, slid the silver into his pocket, and continued down the dock. The commerce section stretched on, a mile of storefronts welcoming him into the great nation of Jantar. Yassen sipped his tea, watching. A few paces down was a stall marketing tales of ruin and fortune. Like the tea stall, it too was old and decrepit, with a painting of a woman reading palms painted across its front. He was beginning to recognize a pattern—and patterns were dangerous. Samson was getting lazy in his mansion.

Three guards stood along the edge of the platform beside the stall. One was dressed in a captain's royal blue, the other two in the plain black of officers. All three wore helmet visors, their pulse guns strapped to their sides. They were laughing at some joke when the captain looked up and frowned at Yassen.

"You there," he said imperiously.

Yassen slowly lowered his cup. The dock was full of carts and merchants. If he ran now, the guards could catch him.

"Yes, you, with the full face," the captain called out, tapping his visor. "Come here!"

"Is there a problem?" Yassen asked as he approached.

"No full visors allowed on the dock, except for the guard," the captain said.

"I didn't know it was a crime to wear a full visor," Yassen said. His voice was cool, perhaps a bit too nonchalant because the captain slapped the cup out of Yassen's hand. The spilled tea hissed against the metal planks.

"New rules," the captain said. "Only guards can wear full visors. Everybody else has to go half."

His subordinates snickered. "Looks like he's fresh off the boat, Cap. You got to cut it up for him," one said.

Behind his visor, Yassen frowned. He glanced at the merchant leaning against the fortunes stall. The man wore a bored expression, as if the interaction before him was nothing new. But then the merchant bent forward, pressing his hands to the counter, and Yassen saw the sign of the bull tattooed there.

Samson's men were watching.

"All right," Yassen said. He would give them a show. Prove that he wasn't as useless as the whispers told.

He unclipped his visor as the guards watched. "But you owe me another cup of tea."

And then Yassen flung his arm out and rammed the visor against the captain's face. The man stumbled back with a groan. The other two leapt forward, but Yassen was quicker; he swung around and gave four quick jabs, two each on the back, and the officers seized and sank to their knees in temporary paralysis.

"Blast him!" the captain cried, reaching for his gun. Yassen pivoted behind him, his hand flashing out to unclip the captain's helmet visor.

The captain whipped around, raising his gun... but then sunlight hit the planks before him, and the brass threw off its unforgiving light. Blinded, the captain fired.

The air screeched.

The pulse whizzed past Yassen's right ear, tearing through the upper beams of a storefront. Immediately, merchants took cover. Someone screamed as the crowd on both docks began to run. Yassen swiftly vanished into the chaotic fray, letting the crowd push him toward the dock's edge, and then he dove into the sea.

The cold water shocked him, and for a moment, Yassen floundered. His muscles clenched. And then he was coughing, swimming, and he surfaced beneath the dock. He willed himself to be still as footsteps thundered overhead and soldiers and guards barked out orders. Yassen caught glimpses of the captain in the spaces between the planks.

"All hells! Where did he go?" the captain yelled at the merchant manning the stall of wild tales.

The merchant shrugged. "He's long gone."

Yassen sank deeper into the water as the captain walked overhead, his subordinates wobbling behind. Something buzzed beneath him, and he could see the faint outlines of a dark shape in the depths. Slowly, Yassen began to swim away—but the dark shape remained stationary. He waited for the guards to pass and then sank beneath the surface.

A submersible, the size of one passenger.

Look underneath the dock of fortunes, indeed.

Samson, that bastard.

Yassen swam toward the sub. He placed his hand on the imprint panel of the hull, and then the sub buzzed again and rose to the surface.

The cockpit was small, with barely enough room for him to stretch his legs, but he sighed and sank back just the same. The glass slid smoothly closed and rudders whined to life. The panel board lit up before him and bathed him in a pale blue light.

A note was there. Handwritten. How rare, and so like Samson.

See you at the palace, it said, and before Yassen could question *which* palace, the sub was off.